A PILLAR OF IRON

A
PILLAR
OF
IRON

TAYLOR
CALDWELL

DOUBLEDAY & COMPANY, INC., GARDEN CITY, N.Y.

With the exception of actual historical personages, the characters are entirely the product of the author's imagination and have no relation to any person in real life.

Power and the law are not synonymous. In truth they are frequently in opposition and irreconcilable. There is God's Law from which all equitable laws of man emerge and by which men must live if they are not to die in oppression, chaos and despair. Divorced from God's eternal and immutable Law, established before the founding of the suns, man's power is evil no matter the noble words with which it is employed or the motives urged when enforcing it.

Men of good will, mindful therefore of the Law laid down by God, will oppose governments whose rule is by men, and, if they wish to survive as a nation they will destroy that government which attempts to adjudicate by the whim or power of venal judges.

—CICERO

In those days the word of the Lord came to me, saying, "Gird up your loins and arise, and speak to Juda all that I command you. Be not afraid in their presence, for I will make you not to fear their countenance. For behold! I have made you this day a fortified city, and a pillar of iron—to the people of the land. And they shall fight against you, and shall not prevail, for I am with you," says the Lord.

—JER. 1:17–19

Any resemblance between the Republics of Rome and the United States of America is purely historical, as is the similarity of ancient Rome to the modern world.

There were many personalities in the great Roman, Marcus Tullius Cicero: the poet; the orator; the lover; the patriot; the politician; the husband and father; the friend; the author; the lawyer; the brother; the son; the moralist; the philosopher. A book could be written about each of these personalities alone. His letters to his publisher and dearest friend, Atticus, fill many books in the Vatican Library, and in other great libraries all over the world. His life as a politician alone would fill a library, and he has been called the Greatest Lawyer of Them All. His own books are voluminous, concerning law, old age, duty, consolation, morals, etc. His family life deserves a novel in itself. Though a skeptical Roman he was also very devout, a mystic and philosopher, and was finally appointed to the Board of Augurs in Rome and was highly regarded by the wise College of Pontiffs. His life as Consul of Rome (similar to the office of President of the United States) would make a thick volume without reference to his office as Senator. His law cases are famous. His Orations constitute many volumes. Patriots for two thousand years have quoted his books concerning man's duty to his God and his country, notably *De Republica*. His letters to and from the historian Sallust could fill several books, without referring to anything else. (Vatican Library and other famous libraries.) A bibliography is included at the end of this book.

His letters to Julius Caesar reveal his conciliatory and affable nature, his humor and sometimes his irascibility, and his awareness of Julius Caesar's own antic, subtle, light-hearted, and powerful temperament, not to mention his deviousness. Though so different in natures they were, as Julius Caesar once said, "like the Gemini." Julius rarely deceived him—though he tried! "I trust only you in Rome," Julius once said. They loved each other in their own individual way—with caution, wariness, laughter, anger, and devotion. Their association is a fascinating subject.

The dearest and most devoted friend of Cicero was his editor and publisher, Atticus, and their correspondence, covering thousands of letters over a long lifetime, is touching, revealing, tender, despairing, and vexatious. Atticus frequently wrote that Cicero would not be appreciated in his lifetime, "but ages yet unborn will be the recipients of your wisdom, and all that you have said and written will be a warning to nations yet unknown." Cicero's visions, hundreds of them, of the terrible future—which we now face ourselves in the modern world—are related in his letters to Atticus. He was deeply involved in Judean theology and philosophy, and was well acquainted with the prophets and particularly with the prophecies of the Messias-to-come, and was a worshiper of the Unknown God. He longed to see the Incarnation, prophesied by King David and Isaias and other of the mighty Israelite prophets, and his vision of the end of the world, contained in the first and second chapters of Joel (King James Version) and Sophonias, (Douay-Challoner Version) is recorded in one of his letters to Atticus (Vatican Library) and certainly describes the world in a nuclear holocaust. His last letter, just before his death, to Atticus, is most moving, as he relates his dream of the vision of God's Hand.

Cicero was particularly struck by the fact that in all religions, including the Indu and the Greek and the Egyptian and the Israelite, there is the prophecy of the Messias and the Incarnation of God as man. He was so fascinated, and so hopeful, that many of his letters include speculation on the Event. He desired, above all things, to be alive when it occurred. His Jewish friend (whose name he does not mention, but to whom I have given the name of Noë ben Joel) is frequently spoken of in his letters to various friends, and he was much drawn to the famous Jewish-Roman actor, and father of the modern theatre, Roscius, about whom another book could be written.

He hated and feared militarism and was a man of peace in a world that did not contain peace and never will. His relations with the great soldier, Pompey, are very troubled, for he suspected Pompey's militarism but honored his conservatism—and brought about his own exile when Caesar marched on Rome. Caesar, though a patrician and a soldier, himself, belonged to the populares (popular) party, and claimed to be a great democrat and a lover of the masses, whereas he and Cicero well understood that he despised them. Cicero, as a middle-class ("new") man, was at odds with this prevaricating and hypocritical attitude of "my dear young friend, Julius," who thought his own hypocrisy very amusing. Cicero, himself, was never a hypocrite; at all times he was a "moderate," the man of the middle way, a believer in the intrinsic honor and decency of the common man, a man who loved freedom and justice and mercy and kindness. It was inevitable, then, that he should be assassinated. Never did he run to the extreme of deifying the average man, or denigrating him. He merely accepted him and was compassionate concerning him, and fought for his rights and freedom.

Cicero's strongest worldly devotion was to the Constitution of Rome and especially its Bill of Rights—both eerily similar to our own. For this he suffered calumny in a Roman world which had begun to respect neither— and this too is only too familiar in America to all of us. He suspected the capriciousness of judges, however, and was always fighting them in the courts when representing a client. To him rule by law was an Edict of God, based on the natural laws of God, and rule by men was most terribly to be feared in a nation. He lived to see the latter come to pass in the Roman Republic, and tyranny to result.

His orations against Lucius Sergius Catilina (sometimes called Catiline in English translations) could be used by freedom-loving politicians today, for they are extremely modern. Catilina's own addresses, and incitings of the people are not this author's inventions. Sallust records them, and if they appear contemporary it is not the author's doing! Cicero has often been referred to "as the first real American," and Catilina to various politicians sadly extant, and in the near past.

The histories of the Roman Republic and the United States of America are oddly parallel, such as Cincinnatus, "the father of his country," strangely like George Washington. Present politicians may find many of their private images in Catilina, and many of their secret desires. Were Cicero alive in the America of today he would be aghast and appalled. He would find it so familiar.

The Pax Romana, conceived in a spirit of peace and conciliation and world law, is mysteriously like the United Nations of today. The rest is mutual history, including foreign aid and recalcitrant nations, and disintegration due to the fact that so many nations disregarded the spirit of the Charter of the Pax Romana just as they disregard the spirit of the Charter of the United Nations now. I have drawn no overt resemblance between the Pax Romana and the United Nations. Where such an overpowering and sobering resemblance occurs it is a matter of recorded history. For, as Cicero said, and Aristotle first of all, "those nations who ignore history are doomed to repeat its tragedies."

The Romans were meticulous historians and recorded events to the very hour they occurred. Therefore, if readers are struck by the weird similarities of Rome and America they need only to study Roman history for themselves. I have spent nine years on the writing of this book and have been as objective as it is possible for a human being to be. I intrude none of my own opinions. I merely present Marcus Tullius Cicero and his world for the reader's own judgment and conclusions.

This book was dedicated to John F. Kennedy before his assassination—

so similar in many ways to Cicero's—and we had some correspondence on the matter, and the letters will eventually be given to the Kennedy Library. It is now dedicated to his memory in sorrow and in sadness.

Cicero was a human being, as well as a politician and a lawyer and an orator. It is in the nature of man to desire that his heroes be perfect, and that is laudable if unrealistic. So Cicero is shown in this book as a man, with his own peculiarities which he shares with all men, and not as a shining marble image. He suffered fearfully from the natural irresolution and confusions present in a temperate man of much moderation, who thought that other men should be reasonably civilized, and rational. He never recovered from being a rational man in a most irrational world, and this too is the fate of all moderates.

While hundreds of histories about Cicero, Caesar, Mark Antony, Crassus, Clodius, Catilina, et. al., are available in libraries in English and many other languages, and thousands of writers quote Cicero's letters, and thousands of politicians, I translated many hundreds of letters to-and-from Cicero and his editor and publisher, Atticus, myself in the Vatican Library in April 1947, and many more from Cicero to his brother, wife, son, daughter, Caesar, Pompey, and other people, in 1962 while again in Rome, and in Greece.

The work on this book by both myself and my husband was begun in 1947, and is contained in hundreds of typed notes and in thirty-eight notebooks. Long before a book is actually written—and the actual writing began in 1956—notes are made and put in order, translations done and comments prepared. Any book is like the one-seventh of an iceberg which appears above the surface of the sea. The other six-sevenths lie below the surface in the shape of preparation, notes, bibliography, constant study, translation, coordination, and endless thought, and, of course, perpetual checking of sources, and in the visiting of scenes pertaining to the background of any historical novel. We spent many days among the ruins of ancient Rome, consulted many authorities in Rome, in order to know the exact position of the various temples and other buildings mentioned in accounts of the Forum. We also studied, in Roman libraries, ancient Roman authorities as to the physical appearance of the great city at the time of Cicero. All this was in the interest of authenticity. The description of the Acropolis of Athens and in particular the description of the majestic Parthenon are authentic, for not only did we spend many days among the ruins but consulted archeologists in Greece when we were guests of the Greek government in 1962. (Particular thanks are due to the Minister of Culture in Athens for his kind assistance.)

As few footnotes as possible have been used, but in every place where it is written, "Cicero wrote—Atticus wrote—etc.," the letters are authentic and can be found in many histories in libraries almost everywhere. It is Cicero the patriot, the lover of Constitutional Law and the Bill of Rights, who should command our admiration and deep reflection today. He was attacked as a "reactionary" and also as a "radical," depending on who was attacking him or in whose path he stood. He was maligned as "living in the past in these modern, dynamic days" and he was equally maligned as "violating points of law and using abusive methods." He was "against progress" to some, and an extreme "conservative" to others. (If these terms seem depressively familiar to readers, it is the fault of history and man's nature, which never change.) But Cicero stood always on the middle way, which made for him violent and relentless enemies among ambitious men.

The statement that the Romans had a daily newspaper which was often used as a propaganda broadcast is not an anachronism. They actually had three competing newspapers at the time of Cicero, but the *Acta Diurna* was the favorite. They even had columnists, of whom Julius Caesar was a prime example. They had cartoonists—very witty fellows in their own estimation, and satirists, and carried news of the latest Stock Market dealings, and libelous gossip.

Cicero's speeches and letters are as freshly modern for today as they were pertinent to Romans two thousand years ago, and as momentous as our daily newspapers and carried similar events.

Sic transit Roma! Sic transit America? Let us pray not, or we shall drag down our world with us as Rome dragged down hers, and another long night of the Dark Ages will face us. But when, as Aristotle mourned, did men ever learn from history? *Ostende nobis, Domine, misericordiam tuam, et salutare tuum da nobis.*

TAYLOR CALDWELL

PART ONE

The Child and the Youth

Os justi meditabitur sapientiam, et lingua ejus loquetur judicium; lex Dei ejus in corde ipsius!

CHAPTER ONE

Marcus Tullius Cicero winced when the hot plaster was placed on his chest by his physician, and in the somewhat pettish voice of a semi-invalid he demanded, "What is that stink?"

"Vulture's grease," said the physician, proudly. "Two sesterces a pot and guaranteed to allay any inflammation." Slaves stirred up the coals in the brazier and M. Tullius shivered under his blankets. A fur rug had been placed over his feet but he was still cold.

"Two sesterces," he repeated with gloom. "What did the Lady Helvia say about that?"

"She does not as yet know," said the physician. M. Tullius smiled with anticipation. "The money will go on the household accounts," he said. "It is an excellent thing to have a thrifty wife in these profligate days, but not always, when such a thing as this vile unguent is added to the cost of beans and kitchen utensils. I thought we had a medical account."

"I bought the grease from another physician," said the physician with some small rebuke in his voice. "The Lady Helvia will not deal with merchants if she can avoid it. Had I bought this in the shops the price would have been five sesterces, not two."

"Nevertheless, the two sesterces will go on the household accounts," said M. Tullius. "The cost of the linen and wool for the expected child will also appear among the kettles and the fish and the flour. Yes, a frugal wife is excellent, but in some way, as a husband, I resent being numbered between new chamber pots and goat cheese. I saw it for myself." He coughed heavily and the physician was pleased. "Aha, the cough is much looser," he said.

"There are times," said M. Tullius, "when a patient, in order to save his life, must hasten to get well and escape his physician's ministrations and his stinks. It is a matter of self-preservation. What is the weather today?"

"Very bad, and most unusual," said the physician. "We had a snowstorm. The hills and pastures are deep in it, and the river is frozen. But the sky is blue and clear and fresh, and there is a brisk wind from the north. This will be helpful in your cure, Master. It is the east wind we fear, and especially the southeast wind."

M. Tullius was beginning to feel warmer, not with the heat of fever but with returning health. The woolen shift he wore began to prickle; he moved, and the stench of the vulture's grease became very powerful. He hastily pulled the blanket over his chest again. "It is a moot point," he said, "whether I shall be asphyxiated by the stink or by the congestion in my lungs. I think I prefer the latter." He coughed tentatively. The pain in his chest was subsiding somewhat. He looked about his bedroom, and saw the slaves industriously heaping the brazier with more wood. The thick glass of the window was dripping with moisture. "Enough," he said, irritably. "I am beginning to drown in my sweat."

By nature he was not an irritable man, but kindly and very gentle, and always somewhat abstracted. The physician was encouraged by this irritability; his patient would soon be well. He looked at the thin dark face on the white pillows, and at the large brown eyes which always failed, in spite of efforts, to appear stern. His features were mild and clear, his brow benevolent, his chin undetermined. He was a young man, and he seemed younger than his years, which annoyed him. He had the calm and somewhat passive hands of the scholar. His fine brown hair did not take to cropping amiably; it merely lay on his long skull as if painted there and could never be induced to stand upright in the manner of a very virile man.

He heard footsteps and winced again. His father was approaching the bedroom, and his father was an "old" Roman. He closed his eyes and pretended to fall asleep. He loved his father but found him overpowering, with all his tales of the grandeur of the family, a grandeur Tullius sometimes suspected did not exist. The footsteps were firm and heavy and the father, also named M. Tullius Cicero, entered. "Well, Marcus," said the loud and hectoring voice, "when are we arising?"

M. Tullius could see the sun-glare through his lashes. He did not answer. The white wooden walls of his bedroom reflected the glare, which, all at once, appeared too intense to him. "He is sleeping, Master," said the physician, apologetically.

"Eheu! What is that stench?" asked the old father. He was lean and tall and irascible and cultivated an old-fashioned beard which he believed gave him a resemblance to Cincinnatus.

"Vulture's grease," said the physician. "Very expensive but efficacious."

"It would arouse a man from the dead," said the old father in his dogmatic tones.

"It cost two sesterces," said the physician, winking at him. He was a freedman, and as a physician, then, he was also a citizen of Rome and could take advantages.

The old father smiled sourly. "Two sesterces," he repeated. "That should make the Lady Helvia count the coppers in her purse." He breathed deeply and loudly. "Frugality is a virtue, but the gods frown on greed. I thought I was master in the art of making three sesterces grow where two grew before, but by Pollux! the Lady Helvia should have been a banker! How is my son, eh?"

"Recovering, Master."

The old father leaned against the bed. "I have a theory," said the old father. "My son retreats to his bed when the Lady Helvia becomes too dominant—and she with child! What do you think of my theory, Phelon?"

The physician smiled discreetly. He glanced down at his presumably sleeping patient. "There are gentle natures," he offered. "And retreat is often a way of securing victory."

"I heard," said the old father, "that the Lady Helvia has suddenly taken to her bed. Is the child due?"

"At any day," said the physician, alerted. "I will go to see her at once."

He hurried from the room, his linen garments swirling about him. The old father bent over the bed. "Marcus," he said, "I know you are not sleeping, and your wife is about to give birth. Do not try to delude me with that affectation of sleep. You never snored in your life."

M. Tullius groaned faintly. He could do nothing but open his eyes. His father's eyes, small and black and vivid, were dancing on him. "Who says she is about to give birth?" he asked.

"There was a scurrying in the women's quarters, and pots of hot water, and the midwife in an apron," said the old father. He scratched his hairy cheek. "But as this is the first child no doubt it will be some time before it is born."

"Not with Helvia," said M. Tullius. "She does all things with dispatch."

"I find her a woman of many virtues," said the old father, who was a widower and thankful for it. "Still, she is subject to the laws of nature."

"Not Helvia," said M. Tullius. "The laws of nature are subservient to her."

The old father chuckled at the resignation in his son's voice. "So are we all, Marcus. Even I. Your mother was a sweet and bending soul. I did not appreciate her."

"So you are afraid of Helvia, also," said M. Tullius. He coughed loosely.

"Afraid of women! Nonsense. But they create difficulties, which a wise man avoids. You have excellent color. How long do you believe you can hide in your bed?"

"Unfortunately, not for long, and not after Helvia sends for me, Father."

The old father meditated. "There is virtue in taking to bed," he remarked. "I am considering it, myself. But Helvia will not be deceived. Two men in bed would arouse her suspicions. You will name the child after us, certainly, if it is a boy."

M. Tullius had had another name in mind, but he sighed. He opened his eyes widely now and saw the drift of snow against the window. The woolen drapery over the window blew in a short, sharp wind, and M. Tullius shivered.

"I am truly sick," he said, hopefully. "There is an inflammation of the lungs."

"The gods have said, and the Greeks also, that when a man wishes to evade his duties he can summon any illness to assist him," said the old father. He picked up his son's wrist and felt the pulse, and then threw the hand from him. "Vulture's grease!" he exclaimed. "It must be miraculous. You have a fine pulse. Ah, here is the midwife."

M. Tullius shrank under his coverlets and closed his eyes. The midwife bowed and said, "The Lady Helvia is about to give birth, Masters."

"So soon?" said the old father.

"Very soon, Master. She took to her bed an hour ago, by the water-clock which is not yet frozen, and has had one pain. The physician is with her. The birth is imminent."

"I told you," said M. Tullius, miserably. "Helvia defies the laws of nature. She should have been in labor at least eight hours."

"A sturdy wench," said the old father. He flung back the coverlets in spite of his son's cowering. "A woman," said the old father, "wishes the presence of her husband when she gives birth, and especially a lady of Helvia's ancestry, which is impeccable. Marcus, arise."

M. Tullius tried to rescue the blankets but his father threw them on the stone floor. "Your presence, Father," said the young man, "will be much more sustaining to Helvia than mine."

"Arise," said the old father. He looked at the slaves. "Bring a fur cloak at once."

A fur cloak was brought with unseemly alacrity and was wrapped over M. Tullius' narrow frame. His coughs, now violent, did not convince his father, who seized his arm sturdily and marched him from the room into a stone hall that blew with bright cold wind. The Nones of Janus! What a time to be born! M. Tullius thought with longing of warm islands in the Bay of Naples, where the sun was benign even now and flowers clambered over brick and wall and the people sang. But the old father believed there was virtue in being wretched, and in this he resembled his daughter-in-law.

It is not, thought M. Tullius, weakly trying to keep up with the strides of his father through the bitter bright halls, that I do not love Helvia, though she chose me and I had nothing to say concerning it. But she is a formidable girl. It may be that I am a poor Roman; it remains that I prefer sweet voices and music and books and tranquillity, though I admire the military. At a distance. A long distance. There must be Greek blood in me, from some far time.

They passed an open space between the halls and M. Tullius could see the snow-strewn gardens, the strong white sunlight, the distant Volscian Hills standing in white fire like Jupiter, himself. Even in Rome, northeast of Arpinum, it would be warmer than this; the multitude would heat the air, and the tall buildings would soften the winds or oppose them. There was also shelter every few steps in doorways, and heated litters. But here in the countryside there was no shelter from the winter, which had been unusually severe this year. The old father liked to dress himself in fur and leather and ride over the country, surrounded by grooms, and hunt deer, and come back abominably rosy and hearty and exuding frost, stamping his feet and thumping his chest. The very thought was enough to make M. Tullius cough again and cling to his fur cloak. Helvia was, unfortunately, very rugged also, and thought fresh air salubrious, whereas any physician with a modicum of wisdom knew that fresh air could be fatal under certain circumstances. Only yesterday she had snared two rabbits herself, in the snow, and she weighty with child. M. Tullius found himself heartily disliking healthy people who liked winters. The old father was not really old; he ought, thought M. Tullius, to have married Helvia, himself. Then they could not only plow through the snow together but compare genealogies and eat rabbit stewed in garlic sauce and drink the sour Roman wine in happy company.

M. Tullius thought of the years he had spent in the army; he had been proud of those years until today. Now he shivered. Hearty people irritated him; they usually expired, very suddenly, with a small ailment that lesser people would simply have dosed with a cup of hot herbs.—They had arrived at the door of the women's quarters. There was no attendant except for a very old woman with a mustache and with thick shawls over her shoulders. She was a favorite of the Lady Helvia's, for she had been the young wife's nurse in her childhood. She shuffled up from her stool in the piercing cold of the hall and glared at the masculine intruders, who were always intimidated by her, even the old father who had a bull's voice on most occasions.

"Were you waiting until the child was robed in the regilla?" she asked caustically. "Or, perchance, the toga?"

M. Tullius said, "Is the child born? No? How then is it possible, Lira, to know if the child will wear a puerile robe or a regilla?" He tried to smile at the old woman whom he privately called Hecate.

Lira muttered some obscenity under her breath while father and son tried not to glance at each other. The old woman then wheezed her way ahead of them to a farther door. "A time of travail," she said in a rusty, mourning voice. "But who is at hand but slaves when my child is suffering?"

M. Tullius and the old father could not conceive of Helvia needing any soothing or assistance at all, for she was a redoubtable girl, but M. Tullius said anxiously, "The physician is with her, and I hear no commotion!"

"The physician!" shouted Lira, with her hand on the door and turning to fix a direful eye on the two gentlemen. "Of what use is a man except to cause a lady agony? That physician and his smells and his big hands! In my day no man approached a lady in her travails; it is disgusting. Commotion! My lady is of great and gentle blood; she is not one to scream like a wench in the hay."

"Open the door, slave!" said the old father, recovering some of his courage.

"I am no slave!" Lira exclaimed, in as loud a voice. "My lady freed me on her marriage. Her marriage!" she repeated, in a spitting tone.

The old father became as purple as ripe grapes, and he raised his clenched fist, which his son caught deftly, shaking his head.

"Am I not master in my own house?" roared old M. Tullius Cicero. "Is this the new Rome that gutter filth dares lift its eyes to the Master?"

"Hah," said Lira, and pushed open the door to her lady's chamber. But she stood in the doorway for another baleful moment. She shook her finger at the old father. "It is a great and noble occasion for this family of the vetch—Cicero. The child will be a boy and there have been portents." She nodded her ancient head and her eyes glowed on them with triumphant malice. "I have seen them myself. When my lady's pain came there was a flash in the sky like lightning, and a cloud shaped like a mightly hand holding a scroll of wisdom.* The child will be known in history, and but for him the name of Cicero would die in dust."

She saw something in the old father's eye that made her shuffle aside hastily, and the two men entered a room hardly warmer than the hall, for there was but a brazier of small proportions in it and only an ember or two. The stone of the floor struck even through M. Tullius' thick leather shoes, and cold appeared to blast from the plastered white walls. Helvia was never chilly, being always in the most robust of health. Three young female slaves were standing near the window and aimlessly rearranging the blue wool curtains, and the midwife was dropping a handful of wood chips on the little brazier. The room was stark, modestly furnished, and dominated by a plain wooden bed. In the bed, with her account books all about her sat Helvia, a pillow at her back. Lira rushed to her side, murmurously, but Helvia saw her visitors and frowned. Her pen had stopped at an entry in a very large and very heavy book. The physician stood at the head of the bed and looked helpless.

* This phenomenon was actually recorded.

"Helvia," said M. Tullius. He understood, vaguely, that it was the part of the husband to leap to his wife's side on these momentous occasions, take her hand, reassure her, and offer up a prayer in her behalf. Helvia frowned. "There is a difference of three sesterces," she said, in her hearty young voice.

"Oh, gods," muttered the old father. He looked at the small statue of Juno before which three votive lights were burning.

"Your bookkeeper is either illiterate or a thief, Marcus," said Helvia to her husband. She suddenly yawned, showing a healthy pink cavern and a set of admirable white teeth, large and glistening. M. Tullius approached her timidly.

"I rose from my sick bed, my love," he said, "to be with you at this hour."

Helvia appeared puzzled. "I am not sick," she said. Her great belly swelled under her blankets. "But, do you not have a cough, Marcus?"

"I rose from my sick bed," M. Tullius repeated, feeling absurd. Helvia shrugged. "You are always in a sick bed," she said heartlessly. "I cannot understand this, for the air is very healthful here. If, Marcus, you would but ride daily or walk in the freshness of the winter, you would not resemble a shade. Even Phelon agrees with me."

The votive lights flickered in a strong and icy breeze and M. Tullius saw that one window stood open, and he coughed loudly. He approached the bed and sat on the plain wooden chair beside it. Helvia looked at him with a sudden fondness, reached out a capable hand, felt his brow, demanded to see his tongue, and dismissed his sickness at once. "It is nonsense," she said firmly. "But what is that vile odor?"

"Vulture's grease," said her young husband. "On a plaster, for my chest."

She wrinkled her nose. "Carrion," she said. "I thought I recognized the stench."

"Vulture's grease," said Phelon. "It is very efficacious, lady. It relieved the lung congestion almost immediately."

Helvia's gaze became intent. "And, without doubt, very expensive. How much?" she demanded of the physician.

"Two sesterces," Phelon admitted.

Helvia reached for an account book, and neatly inscribed the two sesterces therein. M. Tullius, the kindest of young men, was exasperated. "Is it true that you have come to labor, Helvia?" he asked.

"I had a pain an hour ago," said Helvia, abstractedly. She closed the book, shut her eyes and thought. "Those three sesterces! I shall never rest in peace until I discover the error—or the theft."

"My bookkeeper is a man of the highest integrity," said the old father. "If it matters so much to you, Helvia, I will give you the three sesterces myself."

"That would not satisfy my accounts," said the girl. She opened her eyes and frowned. She had beautiful eyes, large and changeful of color, so that in one light they appeared bluish and in another olive, and yet in clearer light they appeared a deep, golden-gray. They stood in thickets of thick black lashes which could sweep her cheek. She had a perfectly round face, faintly olive in tint, as smooth as silk and flushed like a ripe pear. Her brows appeared plucked, so sharply dark and straight they were. Her forehead was somewhat low, which the old father in moments of vexation against her would remark augured a poor intelligence. Her nose was just slightly aquiline, with good clear nostrils, and she had a large mouth as full and guileless as that of a child, and a dimpled plump chin and a short neck that went at once into dimpled shoulders. Her black hair was so thick and curly that it fell only to her shoulders and refused to grow longer, merely increasing in riotous profusion and shining like new coal. She came of the noble Helvius family, yet no one would have been startled to find her in the kicthen or in the barns, and often enough she was there indeed, watching her domestic thieves. Her big bosom pushed against her shift, and her short arms were dimpled yet muscular, and her hands were broad and strong. She was all health and vitality and vividness, and though she had patrician blood it was not evident.

When she did not annoy or bully him the old father considered her an excellent matron and his son very lucky. He was usually afraid of her, young though she was, and just come to womanhood, being only sixteen years old.

"Are you not cold, my love?" asked M. Tullius, hoping for a larger fire in the brazier. His wife opened her eyes wide at him. "I am not cold," she said, in her firm voice. "More illness is caused by too much heat than by freshness." She eyed him closely. "Are you cold in all that fur and leather?"

"Very cold," he said.

She sighed, caught up one of her blankets and threw it over his knees maternally. "We shall be warmer," she said, and ordered a slave to throw another handful of chips on the brazier.

"If we could but close the window," said M. Tullius, huddling gratefully under the warm blanket. "I have a cough."

"You also have a smell," said Helvia. Her young face was contorted for a moment, and the physician bent over her solicitously. "It is nothing; it is gone," she assured him, impatiently. Then she flushed deeply and looked embarrassed. "I fear the child is here," she said.

The old father hastily left the room. Old Lira began a crooning; the female slaves knelt before the statue of Juno. The physician thrust his hand under the blankets. M. Tullius fainted quietly. The physician was very excited. "The head!" he cried.

With no more effort than that, or confusion, the child was born, a boy, on the third day of January, in the Latin year of 648, to Marcus Tullius Cicero and his young wife, Helvia, and in his turn he was named Marcus Tullius Cicero also.

"The child is the mirror of you, my lady," said Lira to her mistress four days later. Helvia was at her table with her account books again, but the physician at least kept her to her room for the prescribed time.

Helvia looked critically at the babe in Lira's arms; he was swaddled in folds of white wool.

"Nonsense," she said, touching the thin little cheek with one finger, then chucking the child under his small and sensitive chin. "He is the mirror of my husband. He has a distinguished appearance, does he not? I will grant you, however, that he has my eyes." She opened her bodice and put the child to her breast, and over his head and her protecting arms she considered the books again. "Ten more linen sheets," she said, severely. "We shall be bankrupt."

"The child does not resemble his father in the least," said Lira, obstinately. "He has your noble father's expression, Lady. There is the aura of greatness about him. Am I ever mistaken? Did I not tell you the very day he would be born? And is there anyone like me who can read omens so exactly?"

"And two hecatombs sacrificed in his behalf when he was born," said Helvia. "One should have been sufficient."

"A lovely babe," said Lira. "Rome does not know this yet, but a Hero has been born." She stroked the delicate fine hair of the sucking child. "Do you know what the Jews say, Lady? They are expecting a Hero. They are all excitement. They say it is in the prophecies. And at Delphi, I have heard, the Oracle spoke of the Great One who is about to appear. There have been portents in the sky. The priests murmur of it in the temples. The Hero."

Helvia said, "He seems more like a lamb born before its time, or a little goatling without hair. I still cannot find those sesterces."

"He is a Hero," said Lira. "Ah, there will be magnificent events in Rome when this is a man!"

CHAPTER TWO

Many years later, the child, Marcus Tullius Cicero, the third of the name, wrote to a friend, "It was not that my mother, the Lady Helvia, of the illustrious Helvius family, was avaricious, as I have often heard it meanly remarked. She was simply thrifty, as were all the Helvii."

He often thought of the very modest household near Arpinum where he had been born on that very cold day in the month of Janus, for there, for many reasons, lay his sweetest memories. After his naming, to avoid confusion, his father was no longer addressed as Marcus Tullius, but simply as Tullius, which maddened the old father who roared that it appeared that he, himself, had lost his own name after the birth of his grandson. "It is that woman!" he would shout at his son. "I am the grandfather, to whom respect and all honor are due, yet I have heard the very slaves speak of me as 'the old father!' I am despised in my own household."

Helvia thought him unreasonable. Had not the old father insisted upon the name of his grandson? Life was indeed complicated enough without three males with the same name, in the same household. "I insist on your calling me 'grandfather,'" said the old father, "for it is due me now." As Helvia had always addressed him so from the moment of her first son's birth she thought him more captious than even before, and shrugged. Men were not to be understood. It was illogical for a woman to expect a man to be logical. "He is old, Helvia," her husband, Tullius, told her mildly, to which she replied: "My father is older than he, and of a better temper. That is due to my mother, who will permit no roaring in the household, not even at the basest slave. Once," said Helvia, with a look of pleasure on her agreeable young face, "my mother hurled a dish of sauced fish at my father's head when he became intemperate at the table."

Tullius, thinking of his own father, and smiling, asked, "What did your father do on that catastrophic occasion?"

"He wiped the sauce and fish from his head and face with his napkin," said Helvia, surprised at the question. "What else could he do?"

"He did not object?"

"My mother was larger and stronger," said Helvia. "Moreover, there was a dish of beans near at hand. My father contemplated the beans, then asked a slave for another napkin. There were few quarrels in our household. Your mother did not insist upon her authorities when she married your father. It must be done at once, as my mother told me before I married you, my love. Later, a man is less tractable."

"Am I tractable?" asked Tullius, still smiling but feeling some vexation. Helvia patted his cheek fondly. "I have a wise mother," she said.

So I am tractable, thought Tullius, without much happiness. Helvia did not bully him, as many matrons bullied their husbands in covert or overt ways. He knew that the household was placid, which was good for his delicate digestion, and that his father roared far less than he had done in years past, which was also good for the digestion. No one appeared afraid of the redoubtable Helvia, or at least not notably and obviously, yet no one dared to be very fractious in her presence, or complaining. She had only to stare with her beautiful eyes, stare as a child stares, and even the old father would subside though not without a grumble to show that he was still head of the household in spite of a daughter of the Helvii. In private, alone with his son, he would become sardonic on the subject of women. He preferred, he thought, a household where a woman knew her place.

"Helvia knows her place," said Tullius, gloomily. "And that is the trouble."

Helvia had her staff of authority, though it was tipped with strong serenity. Rarely was she disturbed or openly annoyed, and never was she completely angry.

"She has no emotions, no fire, no passions. Therefore, she is stupid," said the old father to his son.

Tullius knew that Helvia had passions in bed, somewhat unnerving to a young man of his retiring nature. But Helvia, in passion, was as honest as she was when inspecting household accounts. Nothing was subtle to her, nothing immeasurable, nothing wonderful or inexplicable. She had no doubts about anything. She performed all her duties to perfection, and was greatly admired. If she never truly saw a star or a flower, and never felt a rapture at the spring, was never seized by nameless sorrows or awed by immense vistas, did that argue that she was stupid? Tullius sometimes had the thought that Helvia saw as a calm animal saw, accepting everything with simplicity and without marveling, having forthright appetites and expecting good and sound behavior from man and beast at all times. Once, when they were newly married, Tullius had read one of Homer's poems to her. She had listened politely, then had asked, "But does it mean anything? All those words are a confusion."

She was not talkative, which was a virtue in a woman, Tullius would remind his father when the old man began to stamp like a bull with exasperation.

"She has nothing to say!" shouted the old man, stamping harder.

"That is wisdom, when one does not speak when one has nothing to

say," said Tullius, who thought words in themselves were beautiful and
capable of infinite meanings beyond the mere seeming. Tullius had always
lived in himself, in silent recesses. But he was lonely. He turned hopefully
to his little son, who had his face and introspective expression.

The family did not live in Arpinum, itself, but with Arpinum they enjoyed the Roman franchise, and so were Roman citizens. They could see
the town on one of the Volscian Hills, a small city of some consequence,
looking down upon its steep-banked poplars and oaks at the edge of the
blackly glittering mountain stream of Liris; they had a view of the small
river of Fibrenus where it joined the Liris and the island on which they
lived, and which the grandfather owned and cultivated. The island was
curiously shaped, like a great ship whose prow divided the waters; seen
at a distance one thought of sails furled and a vessel caught in the furious
stream. The water broke on the earthy prow with a noisy vehemence and
the sound of plunging. The air was serene and very cool and bright, and
untouched by the gold of Umbria except on some resplendent sunsets. It
had a northern rather than a southernly atmosphere, heightened by the
enormous majesty of crowding trees, especially the sacred oak, the fresh
green meadows of the interior, the lush vistas, the springing earth which
on occasion broke forth in mossy stones. The area had none of the wild
color of southern Italy and none of its gay exuberance. The people were
calmer and colder and spoke of Rome disdainfully as a welter of polyglots.
Here the spirit of Cincinnatus and the Republic still lived. The inhabitants
spoke of the Constitution, which the Roman Senators and the courts were
continually violating without challenge from a supine urban populace. The
people of Arpinum remembered the old days when a Roman was truly
fearless and free and revered her gods and practiced the virtues of piety,
charity, courage, patriotism, and honor.

The grandfather had been born on the river island near Arpinum; his
son, Tullius, had been born there. Here, also, little Marcus had been
born. Helvia spoke of the farmhouse as the Villa. The grandfather called
it the House. Tullius, but only to himself, thought of it as the Cottage. So
for once opposing his father and his wife he began to expand the house
to more spacious proportions, and the air was suddenly filled with the
sound of chipping and hammering and the voices of workmen. Helvia,
calmly accepting, came from the women's quarters to inspect and criticize
and assure herself that the workmen, vivacious all, and from Arpinum and
so free men and not slaves, were not overly engorging their stomachs with
fare from the frugally guarded kitchens. She, it was, who sniffed at every
jug of wine taken to the workmen by the happy female slaves from the
house, who had not seen such activity in a long time, and rejoiced in it.
At sunset, she would perch on a big and comfortable stone nearby and

inscribe the hours the men had spent at their labor and their exact wages, to the copper. They began to complain of the quality of the wine, but she calmly ignored them. They muttered that this must be a vulgar family, because of the food and its quantity; Helvia inscribed the food in her books to the last fish, bean and loaf of bread. By the time the enlargement of the house was complete she had gained the sullen respect of the workmen who, however, vowed that never again would they visit the island with a hammer or saw.

The workmen were also acutely aware of the presence of the "old father," who scowled at stone and wood and avoided his daughter-in-law with her account books. Like all workmen, they were gossips. The family, they told themselves, was not truly a knightly one, but was completely plebeian. None of its sons had held a curule office, not even an aedileship, and so could not ride in an ivory chair. The "old father," it was rumored, boasted that the Cicero family belonged to the Equestrian class, and that the Tullii were of old Roman royal ancestry, and were sons of Tullius Attius, ruler of the Volscians, who had won an honorable war against the crude early Romans. By the time the last wall was in its place the workmen openly scoffed at such pretensions, and in the hearing of Helvia, herself.

She spoke of it to the "old father" with indulgence. "Is it not strange that the meanest of men, who are boastful of their lowliness, take umbrage at employment by those they fear are not as far above them as Olympus is above the plain? In truth, their arrogance is in ratio to their worthlessness."

"It is because, sorrowfully, they believe that they are worthless," said the gentle Tullius, who had not been included in the conversation. His father and his wife had recently begun to be startled when he spoke and to be surprised at his presence. "It is sad," continued Tullius, as the two frowned at him, "that no man in these days is proud that he is just a man, who is far above the beasts, and has a soul and a mind. No, he must have pretensions of his own."

Helvia shrugged. "There is only money," she said. "One can buy illustrious ancestry, I am informed, in Rome, by the rubbing together of money. The keepers of the genealogies will invent noble blood for the lowest of freedmen, if the weight of the gold is enough."

This pleased the "old father" who was thankful that the daughter of the Helvii was not impressed by patrician lineage, and thought only of money and accounts. But Tullius must spoil this tranquil occasion by remarking that a man's nobility came from ancestors of noble mind and heroic character, however obscure. He retreated more and more to his library, and moved his books to the new wing of the farmhouse. He was hardly aware any longer of anything except his books, his secretly written poetry, his walks along the banks of the turbulent river, the trees, the peace, and his thoughts. It was when his son, the little Marcus, was in his second summer that the isolated young man turned to his first offspring with some tremulous hope.

Little Marcus, though slender as his father and subject to inflammations, had walked alone at the prodigious age of eight months, and at two years had mastered a formidable vocabulary. The latter had come from secret visits of his father to the nursery. Tullius, even under the fierce eye of old Lira, had dandled the babe on his knee and had taught him to speak, not in infant accents, but in the accents of a learned man. The child would stare at his father with his mother's large and changeful eyes; in his case, the eyes were eloquent and mystical. It pleased Tullius that his son otherwise resembled himself. He was convinced, by the time Marcus was but twenty-four months old, that the young child understood him completely. Certainly, Marcus listened to his father with a grave and thoughtful expression, his small thin face tight with concentration, his rare smile sweet and dazzling when Tullius made a little jest. He had Tullius' long head, fine brown hair, gentle chin, and sensitive mouth. He also had an air of resolution at times, which escaped his father, and a look of determination, both of which he had inherited from his grandfather. Little Marcus had inherited, together with his eyes, the calmness and steadfastness of his mother.

Helvia thought the child too fragile, too like his father. Therefore, as she indulged her husband with maternal fondness, she indulged Marcus. She petted him briskly. To her he was a little lamb who needed strength, fond but firm handling, and no pampering. When he would babble at her earnestly she would stroke his silken hair, pat his cheek, then send him off with Lira for an extra cup of milk and bread. She believed, with all sincerity, that the strugglings of the mind could be soothed by food, and that any anguish of spirit—which she never experienced herself—was only the result of indigestion, and could be cured by a goblet of country-brewed herbs. Tullius and little Marcus, therefore, were frequently forced to drink appalling infusions of herbs and roots which Helvia gathered herself in the woodlands.

The sweet and spicy ominousness of autumn lay on the island, and cool mists, though it was hardly past the noon hour, were floating in the immense branches of the oak trees, the leaves of which were scarlet as blood. The poplars were bright golden ghosts, fragile as a dream, but the grass remained vividly emerald. The waters ran wildly and darkly along the banks of the island, those cold and brilliant waters which Marcus was to remember all his life and whose mysterious colloquy was always in his ears.

Here, on the banks, stood clumps of tall yellow flowers, or uncultivated bushes of crimson blossoms, or small purplish lakes of lavender. Bees still murmurously pursued their industry in spite of a sharp hint in the breeze, and clouds of white and orange butterflies blew up before one's footstep like delicate petals. Birds still cried stridently in the trees; a vulture or two hovered in the vast and deeply blue vault of the autumnal sky. The distant Volscian Mountains stood in bronze against that sky, furrowed with dark and brownish clefts and erosions; if one looked across the river one could see Arpinum climbing a flank of a mountain, walls white as bone, roofs the hue of cherries in the strong sunlight.

There was no sound in this peaceful spot, at a distance from the farmhouse, except for the conversation of the joined and hasty rivers, the challenges of birds, and the faint whispers of fallen oak leaves which ran before the occasional breeze like dry, red little animals, seeking shelter here and there along the roots of shrubs, in tiny gullies, against the trunks of alders, or, taking flight, hurling themselves upon the water to be borne off like the bloody stains of a wounded man. The fallen poplar leaves were less turbulent; they were pulling themselves into small mounds of fretted gold. And everywhere was the intense spice of the season, springing from tree and grass and flower and sun-warmed air, the ripened fruit in the orchards beyond, burning wood and pungent pines, darkening cypresses and heavy grain.

To Tullius, seeking his little son today, the scene seemed caught in a still and vivid light, rustic and remote, far from those cities whose pulses could not be felt here, far from the quarrelsome men he hated, far from ambition and force and the politicians whom he detested, far from splendor and grandeur and courts and multitudes and crowded edifices, the restless days of other men, and loud music and trampings and banners and walls and chambers and echoing halls, far from the voice of pride and the bustling of those who believed that action only, not meditation, was the true vocation of man. Here there were no temples built by the hands of men, but temples built by nature for nymphs and fauns and other shy creatures who, like Tullius, himself, dreaded and avoided cities. Here a man was alone, truly alone, his essence held within himself like perfumed oil in a vessel. Here no one demanded that he pour out that sacred essence to mingle with the careless outpourings of others, so that it lost its identity and the vessel was empty, drained of that most precious thing which distinguished one man from another, in scent and texture. Men had strong color when they stood alone. Cities destroyed the faces of men, rendering them featureless. Tullius' opinion of civilization was unflattering. He never longed for Rome. He wanted nothing of the theatre or the circus or gaiety or hectic exchange. Only here, on his paternal island, did he feel free and, above all things, safe. Since the new addition to the house had been completed he had taken a small room for his bedroom, with a strong door which was always locked.

He stood on the bank of the river and listened to all the sounds which enraptured him, and here he could believe there was no Rome, no cities of the sea, nothing which could engage him against his will. Then he heard the laughter of little Marcus near at hand. He walked toward the sound, fallen leaves rustling under the soles of his shoes. The breeze had fallen; the air was warmer. Tullius removed his white woolen cloak and let the sun shine on his thin legs which moved rapidly under his woolen tunic.

He found old Lira sitting with her mantled back against a tree, watching her charge, Marcus, who was trying to catch butterflies in his little hands. The child, hardly out of infancy, was tall and graceful; he did not stumble as other children did, clumsily. Tullius paused for a moment, still unseen, to watch his first-born with pleasure. Yes, the boy resembled him closely, though he admitted that Marcus' chin was more resolute than his own, and that he had a kind of latent strength revealing itself about his sweet and eloquent lips and in the carving of his nose. Here was one, Tullius reflected, who would never be much afraid of anything, and Tullius felt the smallest of envies and then the greatest of prides. For this was his son, with his own brown hair curling over his brow and on his nape, with his own form of body and molding of flesh; though the profile was clearer than his own, it was still his own. The boy stopped for a moment in his play to stare at the river, and Tullius could see his eyes, changing always in color like Helvia's. They were amber, now, in the mingling of light and shade, a clear amber like honey. They did not stare, like Helvia's. They contemplated, and lightened or darkened with silent moods.

The child was clad in a blue woolen tunic, for Helvia believed in wool even in the height of summer. The air, now that the breeze had fallen, was very warm, and little drops of sweat lay on Marcus' forehead; the moisture had matted the fine hair into ringlets on the brow. Tullius thought of nobility of soul, of regality of spirit.

"Marcus," said Tullius, and came into the open, and the boy turned and looked at him and gave him a smile that was truly dazzling. He ran to his father with a murmur of glee, and Lira turned her Fury's head and compressed her old features grimly. "We were about to return to the house, Master," she said in a forbidding voice. She began to struggle to her feet. Tullius looked at his son, who was embracing his legs, and he put his quiet hand on the child's damp curls. He longed to be alone with his son and kiss him as no stalwart Roman should kiss a child, particularly a male child, and he wanted to press him to his narrow breast and pray for him silently as he held him.

And why not? he thought, as Lira swayed heavily toward him. He felt a rare anger and repugnance. He said, "It may be that the Lady Helvia needs your assistance, Lira. Leave my son with me for an hour longer." He tried to make his voice stern and dismissing. Lira glowered at him, and sniffed loudly.

"It is time for his sleep," she said, and put out her gnarled hand for the boy.

It was not often that Tullius asserted himself. He had found a precarious peace in avoiding combat and dissension in his house, even from childhood. He had always been surrounded by strong characters. But when he did offer opposition he succeeded, partly because the others were so astonished and partly because they saw something in the flash of his eye which made them suddenly respect him.

Tullius said, "I shall return him soon to his bed. I wish to be alone with my child for a little time. Go to your mistress, Lira."

She did not give ground at once. The seams of her face became deeper and darker; her eyes peered from folds of old flesh with a gleam of pure malignancy. She folded her arms upon her sunken breast and eyed Tullius, and he brought up all his strength and kept his eyes on hers until she dropped them sullenly, and silently mouthed an imprecation. Then, without looking back at father or son, she stumped off, her garments catching on bush or low twig. She snatched them away with a gesture suggestive of what she yearned to do with Tullius, himself. He watched her go, smiling a little. Then he sat down on the warm grass and pulled his child into his lap and kissed his cheek and damp brow and neck, and held one little hand tightly.

The boy's flesh was fragrant as young earth is fragrant in the spring; yet there was the spicy scent of the season on him also. He stroked his father's face, and was delighted with caresses, for it was in his nature to love. He leaned back in his father's arms to study his face with a sudden gravity, for he had intense sensibility. He poised his head as if listening to Tullius' thoughts, and finding them somewhat sad.

Tullius embraced him again. My son, he thought. Where will you be, and what will you be, when you are a man? Will you flee the world as I have flown it, or will you challenge it? Above all, what will the world of men do to your spirit, which is now as a cup of clear water? Will they make your spirit turbid and murky, filled with the offal of their evil imaginings, as the Tiber is filled with offal? Will they taint it with their lies and their malices, as a well is tainted by the bodies of serpents and dead vermin? Will they make you as one of them, the adulterers and thieves, the prideless and the ungodly, the brutal and the unjust, the false and the traitors? Or will you be stronger than your father, and surmount them all, despising them not in silence as I have done, but with words like burning swords? Will you say to them that there is a Force that lives not in weapons but in the hearts and souls of righteous men, and cannot be overthrown? Will you tell them that power without law is chaos, and that Law does not come from men but from God? What will you tell them, my son?

The child appeared to be listening to the young father's urgent and desperate thoughts, for he slowly raised his hand and touched Tullius' cheek with the palm. Tullius could feel the littleness of the hand, but he also felt a strong warmth, a comforting, a promise. It is only my imagination, for he is still a babe, thought Tullius, whose eyes filled with unmanly tears, unworthy of a Roman. He cannot understand what I have asked him in my soul, yet he keeps his hand on my cheek like the hand of a father and not a child.

Tullius lifted his eyes to the sky and prayed. He prayed as the "old" Romans prayed, not for wealth or lustre for his child, not for fame and glory and the snapping of banners, not imperial power or lustful ambition. He prayed only that his son would be a man as the Romans once knew a man to be, just in all his ways, resolute in virtue, strong in patriotism, ardent in piety, courageous in all adversity, peaceful of temper but no secret server of wrong, protector of the weak, prudent in decisions, eager for justice, temperate and honorable.

Tullius offered his child to God, pleaded for mercy for him that he might be kept from dishonor and greed, cruelty and madness, that he avoid no battle but engage in it in the name of right, and that he fear no man ever, and fear nothing but that or him who can maim the soul. He prayed as fathers had prayed before, and was comforted.

CHAPTER THREE

When little Quintus Tullius Cicero, brother of Marcus and four years the latter's junior, was born Helvia did not deliver her child easily as she had her older son. She was in travail for many hours, which made Lira look very knowing and caused her to nod her head wisely as though Juno, herself, the mother of children, had given her some secret information. "No doubt it is a maiden," said the old father, who was afraid of women and therefore despised them. "No one but a woman could cause such misery even before her birth." But the child, delivered when the redoubtable Helvia was barely on the edge of excruciating consciousness, was a boy.

He was much larger than Marcus had been at birth, much heartier and noisier, and he was handsome and looked exactly like his mother. He had her curling dark hair, her lusty coloring, her broadness of shoulder and plumpness of limbs. He had, from the moment of birth, a stentorian voice which he exercised constantly. He was very robust, in appearance, a miniature soldier, and the old father, who was disappointed in the reserved and gentle-mannered Marcus, rejoiced in him. "This is no epicene creature," he said, holding his grandson in his arms and jolting him up and down, to the howling of the little one.

"It is a riotous animal," said Lira. Tullius looked at his son and was immediately both in awe of him and intimidated. Tullius went back to his son, Marcus, and his books. The old father said, "He will be a Consul at the very least. He is worthy of his ancestors." Lira, though solicitous of the child as her beloved mistress' fruit, was not impressed by him. She saw him as a farmer, or as a mere soldier.

As for Helvia, she looked on her second son with delight, though she would have preferred a daughter. He was her image, even if he lacked her composure. Her relatives visited her, including her parents. Her mother swore that were it not for a certain masculine vigor the child could have been her daughter, Helvia, at birth. Quintus, roaring in his cradle, sucking prodigiously, and waving little fists and broad strong legs, was a marvel to his older brother. By the time Quintus was a year old the two were dear friends and companions, and Helvia, who approved of family spirit, was pleased. She did not feel any twinge of jealousy when Quintus appeared to prefer Marcus above others in the house, including herself. Quintus, toddling, followed Marcus everywhere and doted on him, laughed with joy to see him, and held out his sturdy arms for an embrace. "He is a pleasant little man," said Tullius, who felt some jealousy.

When Tullius discovered his favorite artlessly offering his bulla to the tutelary gods of the household in behalf of his brother, the father of both decided that Marcus should have intenser education than he had been receiving at the hands of his male parent. Marcus had more than the ordinary sensitiveness to language and was picking up the doubtful vulgate of the slaves in spite of the purist training of his father. It was also time for Marcus to learn Greek, the language of gentlemen. So Tullius journeyed to Antioch, in which city Tullius had learned of a Greek poet and scholar, Archias, and induced the teacher to return with him to the family island to teach his older son. The old father and Helvia were startled again, as they always were, when Tullius evinced independence and proceeded to accomplish acts without consulting others. Archias, who called Rome "the nation of grocers," as did all his countrymen, was nevertheless enticed by the large fee offered by Tullius, and he was impressed by Tullius' gentle manner and unworldliness and scholarly attainments. It would not be entirely a barbarian household, Archias thought, and the fee would enable him to buy prized books and the delicately depraved little figurines he loved, and the isolation of the island would be conducive to meditation. So Archias arrived to meet the distrust of the old father, the staring indifference of Helvia who was presently absorbed in the manipulation of stocks—having taken to business when it became evident that Tullius was not a particularly shrewd investor—and the antagonism of old Lira who could not bear that her little Marcus was to be shared by still another in the house.

Archias was at first dismayed by the simplicity of the household and its lack of ornamentation and its crude statues and its uninspired country meals. But introduced to rooms of his own in the new wing, close to Tullius who intended that the poet should edify him, too, and given honor, and lured by the amazing fee and the beautiful natural surroundings, he was soon content. Marcus' perceptiveness and sweet nature, thought the poet, had not been exaggerated by a fond father. Nor was it always offered to a poet the opportunity to take a very youthful mind like Marcus' and train it to lofty goals. Archias settled down on the island and conceived a deep attachment to his small pupil, an attachment which was to continue all the life of the poet.

Archias, like all Athenians, was quick of motion and speech in spite of his contemplative nature, and had a great sense of humor and an air of repose when he was teaching. He was also judicious and wise and intuitive. His protection against loneliness was his very young Cretan slave, Eunice, who was fair and blue-eyed like all her countrymen, and was pleasantly stupid, a virtue not to be despised by a poet. She attended her master and enhanced his meals in the kitchen under the frugal eye of the composed Helvia, and became one of Marcus' most avid playmates, for she was but twelve. She was much taller than the short and slender Archias, and her golden head appeared over his dark sleek one like a miniature sun. Docile, and adoring Archias, who had fine dark features and glowing black eyes, she was soon the favorite even among the household slaves. She considered Helvia a noble lady, to be admired and imitated, and was immediately a pupil of Helvia's in the art of weaving sturdy linen and wool garments, and in frugality. Eunice was a magnificent success, and Marcus was one day to write of her: "Though ignorant and unlettered and of a simple mind, her presence was a delight, so warm was it and so sincere and loving.

There are many of our fine Roman ladies who could have emulated her to the satisfaction of their husbands."

Marcus, as Tullius had told Archias, was indeed of a prodigious mind. He accepted Greek as if it were his native language. Archias' kindly and humorous nature soon inspired the boy with affection, and Marcus early learned to appreciate his teacher's subtleties. When he was six Marcus was writing poetry, which Archias considered one of the first attributes of a civilized man and one sadly lacking in Romans. The Greek and the old father were mortal enemies from the beginning, for Archias, so daintily depraved in thought and secluded act, and disinclined to much physical activity, had early dismissed the eldest Marcus as a mere farmer and a typical Roman. He could not, he would aver just to annoy the old father, himself tell a sheep from a goat, nor was he interested in crops except for the grape. Once he told young Marcus that the grape seed was the prophecy of the vine, the grapes themselves, and ultimately of the wine which would delight and soothe the soul and inspire it with wisdom beyond that ever known by an abstemious and sober man.

He was also an agnostic, a matter he prudently concealed in this pious household. But his intimations to young Marcus during the lessons were to teach the boy skepticism of all insistently stated opinions, though Archias wisely did not impair the boy's natural piety and earnest devotion to God. Archias, it was, who introduced him to the Unknown God of the Greeks, and Marcus adored Him at his prayers.

"He does not live on Olympus," said Archias, with a smile. "Nor does He live in Israel, though the Jews assert He does, with arms, when necessary." Archias found the Unknown God easier to believe in than in the multitude of Eastern, Grecian, and Roman Gods. Obscure, hidden, but mighty, Lord of the Universes, omniscient and powerful, Creator of all beauty and wisdom, He appealed to the subtle Greek.

Seeing the little Quintus as he exactly was, the poet felt some annoyance at the love between the little brothers. How was it possible for such a one as Marcus, profound, searching, and perceptive, to love a small soldier who was as active as a cricket and as noisy as a crow? He discovered Marcus tutoring his brother in Greek. This did not touch Archias, who wondered at Marcus' young patience and tenderness. The two little boys would train together in leaping and wrestling and discus-throwing and exercises with the spear and the bow. It annoyed Archias that Marcus appeared not to object too much to this sweaty business.

The more or less tranquil household soothed the innate irascibility of the civilized Greek. He found himself able to turn out cantos with which he was satisfied, and which he published in Rome. Quietude brought him some small fame, and he was gratified. He and Tullius became friends. He told himself that he had another pupil in the lonely young father, and out of compassion he sought Tullius' company even though he preferred to be alone at night. But he would not be present at the family dining table. He had a horror of the smell of baked beans and fish dripping with oil and garlic and pasta smothered in grated strong cheese. He also had a horror of the household wine, and imported his own for his own secret palate.

"A civilized man is known for his sensitive appreciation of good food," he would tell Marcus.

"Your son has character, noble Tullius," Archias told the father. "It is firm but not dogmatic. It is tolerant, but not weak. It is tenacious but not stubborn or obstinate. In his soul he has set the highest standards, and the gods help those who will oppose virtue before him."

So Archias delighted in his pupil, and wrote much poetry, and conversed with Tullius in the quiet dark evenings, and fondled his Eunice in ways which would have shocked Helvia and would have caused his dismissal had she known.

When Marcus was seven years old he wrote, "The best architecture arises when the architect raises his temples with consideration of how they will appear to the eye of God, and not how they will appear to the eye of man. Buildings created only in accord with the nature of man are gross. They reflect the urges of his body and not the urges of his soul." Archias was happy over this small philosophy and congratulated himself for being an excellent teacher, though he pursed his lips amusedly at the mention of souls.

"The Greek gods are poetry," said Archias one day to his pupil. "The Romans appropriated our gods, and renamed them. But they removed their poetry. Minerva is a bad-tempered shrew and her virginity astringent, but Pallas Athene is armed and noble wisdom and her virginity like marble in moonlight."

Marcus always listened uneasily to any attack on Romans, however good-natured.

"Our gods have been perverted by man," he said, "and given man's temper by man. It was not always so in our history. Why must man eventually degrade even his gods?"

"It is man's temper, as you have wisely said, my Marcus," Archias agreed. "Only the Greeks have not done so. Perhaps this arises from innate wisdom, or perhaps it is because Greeks love poetry and let their gods alone. Man must not impudently dissect God, and make Him anthropomorphic. Socrates understood that, and that is why he was condemned by city fathers grown provincial and mean, and, in their hearts, atheistic. It is the man unsure of his faith, and uncertain of the existence of the Godhead, who is the most intolerant."

"You are not intolerant, my teacher," said Marcus with his charming and mischievous smile.

"Never despise inconsistency. It is man's best safeguard against tyranny. God's Law"—and here Archias hesitated for a moment—"is believed, and probably rightly, to be immutable. But the laws of men can never be dogmatic or they become like insentient stone."

"What is God's Law?" asked Marcus.

Archias laughed. "I am no authority. The Jews believe they know; I spent two years in Israel. But it is not possible for man to know God's Law, though the Jews say they are explained by one Moses, who delivered his people, with the crown jewels of the Pharaohs, from Egypt. The Jews, by the way, believed they were forced from Egypt because of their devotion to their God. I disbelieve that. I am of the opinion that the Jews, being clever and astute and wise and manipulating by nature, and great natural philosophers, became too powerful in Egypt in finance and politics and involved relationships. Nothing annoys a man so much as having a more subtle neighbor. He will tolerate vices and even emulate them. But to be asked to think enrages him.

"The Jews, incidentally, are imminently expecting a Savior. The Jews are a very mysterious people. They believe that man was originally perfect as God intended, and unacquainted with death and evil, but that by his own will he fell from perfection and into the power of evil and death. I find this very unbelievable and mystical. In any event, they expect their Savior to make clear to them the whole of God's will with regard to mankind, and all His Law, so that never again can they go astray. It is written in their strange books, which they study unremittingly. They also believe that man's soul is immortal, not to wander after death in pale shadowiness in some Plutonian underworld, but to be conveyed by the Savior, or the Messias, as they call Him, into bright and eternal Isles of Bliss. And the body, they say, will on the last day be joined to its soul and the whole apparatus delivered intact into their heaven. I found the conception very entertaining. Their God is not gay and beautiful as are our gods. He seems of a most unpleasant temper."

But Marcus thought of the Messias of the Jews and of the imminence of His manifestation. Was it possible that he, himself, would be alive on that momentous occasion? Excitement shone in his changeful eyes as he wondered.

"He is the Unknown God," he said.

Archias shrugged. "Let us continue with what we know and not annoy God with our monkey inquisitiveness," he said.

Eunice, who was permitted in the schoolroom by her master because he enjoyed looking at her beauty and was made tranquil by it, was sewing silently and apparently listening to this exchange. She lifted her large blue eyes, which shimmered with intrinsic innocence and foolishness, and said, "The gods do not like to be understood."

Archias laughed and put his hand on her bare and rosy shoulder. "She has not the slightest idea of how subtle she is," he said. "She has not understood our conversation in the least; therefore, she is wise also. There is something very silly, beyond the silliness of my poor Eunice, in the pronouncements of scholars and learned men. Let us hope that scholarly men, in their narrow view of life and entangled in their obtuse theories, and enmeshed in their unrealistic dreams, will never attain to power in government. If they do, then madness will seize mankind and the Jews' Messias will find no sane creature to greet His arrival. But when I speak of scholars I do not mean the philosophers of whom Plato wrote."

Despite Archias' hopes Marcus did not become a true lyric poet. But he early began to write marvelous prose, and would read what he had written in a voice that enchanted his teacher, so powerful, so sure, and so eloquent was it. It had overtones of passion, but was never irrational or too filled with random emotion. Archias informed Tullius that the household harbored an embryo Demosthenes.

"I should prefer that you define your terms more closely, in the Socratic manner," said Archias. "Nevertheless, Marcus, you bewitch me, and against my logic you convince me. Do not be sure, however, that evil is evil and virtue is virtue. The two embrace each other inextricably."

Even as a child Marcus did not believe that. There was the iron of the old Romans in his character, though his nature was still buoyant and as airy as powdered gold.

CHAPTER FOUR

Archias, the city man, full of urban whims and urban appreciations, was dismayed when it was announced that the family would move to Rome.

He did not like Rome. He disliked Rome as a principled Greek. There was to be no dispute if a superior nation conquered an inferior, but to be conquered by Romans was intolerable. He complained of the move to Tullius, whom he bullied because Tullius could rarely bring himself to disagree with anyone even on such an abstract topic as a discussion of philosophy. "I love this island," said the sophisticated Greek. "Permit me, Master, to quote Homer: 'A rugged soil, yet nurse of hardy sons, no dearer land can e'er my eyes behold.' Why must we go to Rome?"

"It is my health," said Tullius with apology, as if his increasing frailty was his personal error. He hesitated. It was almost beyond him to hurt the feelings of anyone, and caused him pain when he had to do so. But Archias, ever alert, had fixed him, upon his hesitation, with his glowing black eye, and Tullius tried to smile as he said, "And my father believes that it would be best for Marcus to study in a school with other boys, as well as having private tutelage at home. The boy has no mates here but young slaves. He must meet others of at least the same family knighthood as ours."

Archias had his own opinions of Romans and the Roman heritage. "Rome is vulgar," he said. "It copies Greece slavishly. If one cannot have the original does it profit him to have a dull imitation?"

Tullius' mild face flushed; for a moment his gentle eye sparkled with patriotism. "That is not entirely correct, Archias. Our architecture is our own, though it is true that in many instances we have borrowed some of the nobler aspects of Grecian architecture. Consider what we have done with the arch! Moreover, though you often speak of the glory of Greece, one must remember that at its height, when Athens numbered some quarter of a million people, only forty-seven thousand of them were free men. Such disproportion is not true of Rome, where for the smallest fee children of the most modest families can attend a school, even if they are sons of former slaves. Polybius, a hundred years ago, advocated free public schools; it is possible that they will be established soon for the children of all men in Rome."

"The gods forbid," said Archias, fervently. "Can a sane man envisage a nation educated by fixed theories of education, artificially established and uniform in all cases? There is nothing so dismaying and repugnant as an average mind which has been forced to acquire knowledge against its inherent capacity. It can never be wise, for all it may be able to quote the philosophers and repeat a canto from the *Iliad* and specify the age of Pericles. Knowledge should not be thrown away on those who cannot, by their nature, convert it to wisdom. It is like the unassimilated food in the belly of a slaughtered pig."

"The Lady Helvia, though no Aspasia, is nevertheless a boon to this household because she was taught her mathematics," said Tullius. "There are uses for education besides the acquisition of wisdom. Would you like to have a school of your own in Rome, Archias?"

The Greek considered this magnificent offer. Then he thought of the mediocre minds he would then be forced to encounter and teach, and he shuddered. He shook his head, but with gratitude. "If I be permitted to remain with this family, Master, I will be content."

Tullius, who usually took men at their word and believed that most men preferred to speak the unequivocal truth rather than half-lies, was touched. In consequence, he immediately increased Archias' fee, and embraced the teacher, grasping his upper arms in his narrow hands.

"We shall return to this island often, Archias," he said, "for my heart is here though the winters are unbearable to me. We shall see each spring and summer in Arpinum."

He is a good man, thought Archias, and has a tender heart and a heroic if gentle soul. How rare is a good man! The gods themselves are not more admirable, for it is almost impossible to be good in the face of mortality and the omnipresent evil of the world of men. You, Archias, are not a good man and it is very wrong of you. I am happy that you suppressed, almost from the beginning, any soft ridicule of Tullius' piety. It may be sadly in error, but what a fine race men would become if they embraced such error—if it be indeed an error! I must think about it.

Marcus, now nine years old, was elated by the adventure of going to live in Rome. He said to his five-year-old brother, "Quintus! We are returning to the capital of our fathers, where we shall see wonders!"

Quintus, however, being a conservative soul like his mother, was opposed to change. "I am satisfied here," he said. "My father does not like the climate, but my mother says it is his imagination that he is sick in the winters. Grandfather does not wish to go to Rome, where all men are very wicked and the streets are hot and filled with people and there are smells."

He threw a ball to his brother, and the two boys raced over the warm summer grass. It was nearly autumn. When the leaves fell the family would leave for Rome. Marcus, holding the thrown ball in hands so like his father's, was suddenly melancholy.

"Throw!" shouted Quintus, who was never depressed, and had his mother's nature.

"I am tired," said Marcus, and sat down on a sun-warmed stone and looked at the river nearby.

Quintus had never had an ailment and had never been tired. "You are not coughing, like my father," he grumbled. If a person was ill he coughed; if he did not cough he was not ill. He waited impatiently, standing on his sturdy brown legs, his yellow tunic blowing back on his thick thighs, and he was as handsome as Helvia with his crisply curling black hair and his square and highly colored little face. Helvia's eyes in Marcus were thoughtful but in Quintus they were quick and impatient. He threw himself on the grass at Marcus' feet and began to chew a blade of grass and wriggle restlessly. He loved action; he delighted in physical movement and games.

He could swim far better than Marcus, who thought the water of the river too cold. He could climb far faster, for he did not have Marcus' fear of heights; he could run easier and could outrace his brother. When he threw a ball he threw it surely and with strength. He loved to wrestle with an infant bull. Yet, even at his early age he considered these accomplishments as nothing before the accomplishments of his adored brother, whom he would have gladly followed into any danger. He looked at Marcus now, his eyes very brilliant, and he said, "I shall be a general in Rome."

"Excellent," said Marcus. "I shall be a lawyer, and perhaps a Consul."

Quintus did not know what a lawyer or a Consul was, but he gazed at Marcus admiringly. "You shall be whatever you wish," he said. Then he scowled fiercely and held up a brown fist to shake it. "And let that man beware who stands in your way!"

Marcus laughed and his melancholy left him, and he tugged at one of his brother's curls with affection.

"There is nothing nobler than law," said Marcus. "It distinguishes men from beasts, for beasts are ruled only by instinct and man is ruled by the law of his spirit and so is free."

Quintus did not understand in the least. He jumped to his feet and began to climb the tree under which his brother sat. Bits of bark and twigs rained down on Marcus' head as the energetic feet scampered along woody limbs. Then the bright face of his brother peered down at him, laughing, from the green leaves. "Catch me," he said. Marcus, always obliging though he did not like climbing, rather awkwardly began the ascent, scraping his knees in the process. But he loved his brother, and Quintus had no playmate but himself. Rising as high as he could, he seized Quintus' sandal and then his sturdy calf, and the boys laughed together.

Then Marcus slipped. Instantly and easily Quintus, feeling the grip loosen on his leg, reached down and seized his brother's hand and held it strongly. Marcus was left dangling from the tree like a swinging fruit, held from falling only by Quintus' vigorous grip. Marcus looked down at the formidable gulf below him and clenched his teeth; his wrist exploded in pain.

Then Quintus, who was always laughing, was very serious and very manly. "Do not be afraid, Marcus," he said. "Grasp my hand with your fingers, very tightly, and I will climb down until you can drop safely."

Marcus was too frightened to utter a sound. Then he felt himself being slowly lowered, inch by inch, as the strong child above him carefully descended, holding by only one hand to the branches of the tree. Within a few minutes Marcus was close enough to the ground to be dropped easily and without damage. He fell into the deep grass and rolled lithely as he had been taught by the slave who trained both boys in physical accomplishments. Instantly Quintus was on his knees beside him, full of anxiety. Marcus sat up and laughed. "You are a Hercules, Quintus," he said, and kissed his brother.

From some reason in far later years he remembered that day vividly, and he thought his heart would break with the remembrance.

"I had the happiest of childhoods," he would write in later years. "I had a father who was not only wise but was good and loving and tender. I had a grandfather who taught me never to compromise with evil, and whose shouts were harmless. I had a steadfast mother, who was always patient and calm. I had Archias, my dear teacher. And I had Quintus. My Quintus, my brother, my beloved!"*

Helvia considered it all nonsense that the family must move, for the winters at least, to Rome. Tullius merely pampered himself. He refused any longer to swallow the concoctions she brewed for his cough when the snow was high on the hills. If Tullius would only learn to enjoy the brisk cold winds and labor with them and shout with them his cough would disappear and his appetite would increase and there would be more flesh on his bones. With this the grandfather agreed. It was unfortunate that Tullius did not like hunting, and he a Roman. How had he endured the army?

"Will power," said his son, with some grimness.

"Fine words for a Roman," said the grandfather, scornfully. "I remember my own days with my legion. I enjoyed every hour I fought for the Republic."

He found a good sound house, almost new, on the Carinae, the southwestern hip of the Esquiline hill. It was of a modern style, unique in Rome, and resembled the keel of a ship, as did its neighbors. Unfortunately, the neighborhood was no longer fashionable, as prospering families were moving nearer to or even on the Palatine hill, itself. This did not disturb the grandfather, because the price asked was modest for such a big and practically new house. The atrium was commodious, much larger than the one in the house at Arpinum, the family's apartments pleasant with an agreeable view of the city, the slaves' quarters more than adequate, the dining room well situated and airy, the garden as large as could be expected for a city house. Its mortar was an attractive Pompeian red, and it had a white tiled roof. The floors shone with bright mosaics and the columns were snowy. While the grandfather haggled over the price with the agents of the owner, Tullius wandered outside to gaze upon the city of his fathers from this height.

Tullius was not happy that his health demanded that he leave his beloved island for the winters. He shrank from turmoil, from heated streets,

* Letter to Sallust.

from noise, from stenches. But he understood that man cannot remain a recluse forever, that his interests steadily narrow during constant isolation, and that he loses the capacity to be a man. There were also his sons to be considered. They were not lonely peasants whose life would forever be circumscribed. Marcus' gifts of rhetoric and prose and philosophy and learning should not be starved or abandoned among trees and grass, pleasant though they were and reposeful, nor should Quintus, the lively, passionate, and life-loving, be deprived of companions and variety. A man owed it to his world and his status as a man to share with his brothers those gifts with which he had been endowed, and every man in Tullius' opinion had a unique gift whether he were noble or humble. There was a time for retirement and a time for the market place, a time to contemplate and a time to participate, a time for peace and a time to take up arms, a time to sleep and a time to work, a time to love and a time to refrain from loving. And a time to live and a time to die.

The summer was over and autumn lay on the gigantic and pulsing city below Tullius. The sunset stood over it, murky, brownish-red, lurid, dusky, the sun like an evil scarlet pupil between eyelids of crimson, brown, and dark gold. These colors were reflected on a city whose own colors, broken and chaotic, were ochre, Pompeian red, gray, light-brown, and yellow. A most vehement city! The steep and narrow streets, resembling canyons, shining with reddish light from the sunset, raced up and down the seven hills, surging with great crowds of hurrying and noisy Romans. The roar was constant, accented by the thick scurrying of vehicles axle to axle and front to back, and shouted oaths at the density of the traffic and loud threats from those who drove chariot or wagon or car. Tullius could see the Forum, teeming and restless with heads. Near and far distances were hazed over with a muddy mist, and the air was full of the smell of burning, the stenches of sewers, heated stone and brick and autumnal earth and dying vegetation. A pale and rising moon was just visible in the sepia west, shining faintly like a skull. Tullius could hear, behind him, his father's bargaining voice as it quarreled with the agents who were becoming sullen and irascible, and the tinkle of two leaf-filled fountains in the walled garden. Uproarious though the city was, the gloomy light and threatening sky gave an air of melancholy to the scene. A wind blew, astringent, smoky, with an edge of warning in it. Now torches and lanterns began to glow redly in the murk, to move restlessly from street to street. The noise increased as Romans left their government offices, their shops, their places of business, their temples, for their homes in various parts of the city; the din of traffic rose like a harsh clatter over all.

Tullius sighed. He liked to think, while at Arpinum, of Rome as a polished city and not as a city of brick and dull stone. (He was not alive when Gaius Octavius, Caesar Augustus, was to make it a city of marble.) He looked about him at the small lawn before the house, which was not walled, the modernist architects having decided to make an "open" city where they could. He saw the small figure of a child watching him keenly on the lawn of the house next door.

Tullius was always intimidated by children, except Marcus. Even Quintus, the assertive and voluble and simple, intimidated him. He looked away from the little boy, who appeared to be about Quintus' age, hoping the child had not noticed him. But the child came nearer, inspired by curiosity. "Greetings, Master," he said in a high and piercing voice.

It was not customary nor polite for a child to address an adult first. Tullius wondered who was responsible for the child's sad lack of manners. He tried to make his mild voice stern, and dismally failed. "Greetings," he murmured. The child came nearer and Tullius could see his face more clearly, pointed, lively, somewhat overexpressive, with dancing black eyes and thin, smooth black hair. He gave the appearance of never being in repose, but imbued with restlessness beyond the mere animal restlessness of little Quintus. He seemed to move in every muscle though now he stood still a few feet from Tullius, and regarded him with deep interest. He was not overly tall.

"Are you buying the house, Master?" he asked in that shrill and insistent voice.

This was more bad manners. Tullius was very uncomfortable. Children were so exigent and bold these days. Their parents were remiss, and their teachers.

"I do not know," said Tullius. He wanted to retreat, but the boy's fierce if smiling eyes transfixed him. It was as if he was amused by the man and was gloating over his evident discomfiture. To direct the child's attention from himself only, Tullius said, "What is your name and where do you live?"

The boy said in surprise, "I live in this house, next to yours. My name is Gaius Julius Caesar, and my father is named the same and my mother is Aurelia. I go to the school of Pilo, the freedman. Do you have any little boys like me?"

Tullius did not particularly like the house over which his father was now triumphantly in the last stages of victorious bargaining, and he liked it less at the thought of having such a neighbor for his well-behaved children. He tried to look formidable. "Two little boys, Gaius," he said. "Well-mannered, and one is very studious. They have been carefully nurtured."

The boy's eyes did a hilarious dance. He knew timid adults when he saw them and liked to plague them. "They call me Julius," he said. "Will your boys go to school with me?"

Tullius wanted to flee from those mocking eyes, but he was always helpless before bad manners in child or adult. So he said, "I have a little boy of your age, Quintus Tullius Cicero. My older son is Marcus Tullius Cicero, but he is nine years old and so would not play with you."

Julius laughed raucously. "Cicero! Chick-pea! What a funny name!" He gazed at Tullius with delight. "It is a plebeian name, is it not? Mine is very old and noble. As for your son, Marcus, who is nine years old, he is not too old for me though I am but five. My best friend is even older, eleven, and his name is Lucius Sergius Catilina. He is very patrician, even more patrician than my family is. We are all patricians."

It was foolish to feel so stung at the heedless words of a child, Tullius told himself. "We are not plebs," he said, with some annoyance. "This is not a fashionable neighborhood," and he hated himself for speaking so, "so why are you patricians living here?"

"The money," said the child, loftily, "has left us. But we have not left our names. We shall not always live here. We shall move to the Palatine directly."

"Good," said Tullius, and turned to go. The child whistled loud and derisively, and Tullius went back into the house to discover his father signing papers the agents had presented and writing a draft on his bank for the down payment. "Stay, Father," said Tullius. "I am afraid we have undesirable neighbors."

"The Caesares?" asked one of the burly agents in surprise. "One of the best families of Rome."

"One must think of one's children," said Tullius, who was disliking the house more and more. "The little boy, Julius Caesar, does not appear desirable to me, and as my boys will go to the school of Pilo, the freedman and Greek, they will of necessity be Julius' schoolmates."

"Nonsense," said the grandfather. "It is true that city children are too free in their ways and lack reverence for their elders, but Marcus and Quintus have been carefully reared and will not be polluted by any ragamuffin like that—Julius? Caesar? I have heard of the Caesares. They are a good family. Besides, I have made an excellent bargain."

"Too excellent," said one agent, who smarted at being bested by a countryman.

Nothing could turn the grandfather from a bargain, even if it were not appetizing. So Tullius surrendered as usual. The grandfather, who had been denigrating the house to the agents, now enlarged on its desirability. "Look at these rooms!" he exclaimed, to the dissenting face of his son. "The hall, the atrium, the sleeping rooms, the dining room, the slaves' quarters, the gardens, the space! Large! Commodious! Airy! And what a view of the city from the outdoor portico! Observe this vestibule! These fine floors, these glassed windows, as fine as any Alexandrian glass!" He scowled at the silent Tullius. "It was not my will that we leave Arpinum. It was in behalf of your health. We could find no more suitable house in all of Rome, Tullius, so why this whim of yours against a child?"

Tullius thought, Chick-pea! He said, "One cannot be too careful about one's children. Very well," he sighed. "It is truly a fine house." The agents grunted. "The balance of the payment," they said to the grandfather, "is due when you take possession."

"You will find my banking affairs to your satisfaction," said the grandfather.

He rubbed his hands together. "It is a great bargain," he said. "Even Helvia will be satisfied." He looked at the agents. "My daughter-in-law, my son's wife, is of the noble Helvii."

Tullius was mortified that his father should try to impress agents. They looked properly impressed which mortified Tullius the more.

"Noble is as noble does," he said, but no one listened to him, as usual.

CHAPTER FIVE

The family was well settled in the Roman house before the first snow appeared on the hills. Helvia was pleased with the house, especially when she discovered that it had indeed been a bargain. She liked the Caesares, whom her parents knew well. Of noble birth, she did not care that the neighborhood was rapidly becoming less fashionable month by month. Even Tullius became reconciled. In the city no one urged him to take long brisk walks for his health, and he could huddle undisturbed around the biggest and hottest brazier without encountering arguments. It was understood that the city was dangerous and the traffic a curse, and as the family did not pamper itself with effete litters Tullius was left in peace in his library and among his books and in his conversations with Archias.

Marcus went to the school of Pilo, the Greek freedman, and was tutored by Archias after his return. It was decided that Quintus should be tutored completely by Archias for at least a year. This pleased Tullius, and he thought of little Julius Caesar next door whom he was disliking more and more as time passed. He never could bring himself to like any of the Caesares, especially the overweening Aurelia. The father, Gaius Julius, was a taciturn man who had business in the city, and had a sour face and was evidently no scholar. He and Tullius encountered each other rarely, for which Tullius was grateful. But little Julius invaded the house freely and the good-tempered Helvia did not care, for she was not afraid of children. She would slap Julius as readily as she slapped her favorite, Quintus, and the boy would laugh heartily. The grandfather found cronies, old veterans like himself who had gathering spots in the city, the Tonsoria for one, and he would drive the one chariot himself to the Forum, or walk hardily down in good weather, to mingle with his peers and exchange stories of dead old campaigns. Everyone, then, was satisfied, though Tullius longed for the spring and the island, and quiet. His life, in spite of his original resolutions, had become almost a replica of his secluded existence in his beloved Arpinum.

Young Marcus found the city exciting and full of wonders, and lingered to look at it on his way to school and on the way home. There was a smell about the city which invigorated him and which lay under the welter of stenches. He loved the shops, the fora, the sound of life and bustle, the teeming people, the façades of temples, the lofty single pillars bearing upon their tops the statues of heroes or the figures of winged deities driving chariots, the mighty fanned steps rising everywhere from street to upper street, the odors of frying fish and baking pastries and roasting meats and wines that gushed from the doors of inns, the crowded porticoes, the sudden brief clamor of music coming from small theatres as the musicians practiced, the air of might and business, the government buildings swarming with avid bureaucrats, the circuses always surrounded by mobs holding tickets aloft no matter the hour of the day, the clangor of traffic daily growing more dangerous, the whinny of horses, the clatter of wheels, the shouts, the rushing of women from doorway to doorway, the sight of the sun on red brick, the well-paved streets on which children played at all hours, and the general vociferous and roaring voice of power.

It was the city of his fathers. He knew what it was to be a Roman, living in Rome. He longed for Arpinum, which seemed far away and beloved, but he also loved Rome and felt himself at home here in the bustle and the sleepless noise. He was lulled to sleep by the sound of traffic and restless feet and alert voices on the street below his house. He waked with excitement to each new day.

But he did not like his school, though he did not worry his father with complaints.

Pilo was an austere and dogmatic man with many airs, for he had once been a slave and now felt his importance, and was unbending and had a slavish respect for those with great names. His attitude was compounded of authority and servility toward the boys of noted family if depleted purse. To those of more plebeian origin and better purses he was condescending.

They were upstarts and should not be permitted to forget the fact. He and Archias had had an encounter which had left the proud and stiff-necked Pilo shaken. "I have never been a slave," said Archias who had brought Marcus to school on the first day, "so," he added pleasantly, "I am democratic. The fee paid you for the teaching of this boy—who is sent here not because I am inadequate but because he needs the company of his mates—is more than customary. I have made enquiries. Therefore, in order that I not inform my employer of this fact you will divide the fee with me. I do not need it, but you need a lesson. Remember that Marcus is the son of the Helvii as well as the Tullii, who claim ancient ancestry also. Do not teach Marcus affectations and improper attitudes toward superiors and inferiors. Do not despise him because he comes from the country. After all, Cincinnatus, the father of his country, was also a farmer. He has an excellent mind; see that you do not corrupt it."

He rubbed a delicate finger around his lips and smiled at Pilo, who was tall and thin and withered. "We are Greeks," he said, in conciliation. "We are captives of barbarians. I am training Marcus to respect what we represent, though our glory is long passed even if our memory is like a golden glow on the horizon. Remember you are a Greek. I have heard you have forgotten it in the presence of these Romans."

He both frightened and pleased Pilo, who at first was determined to be kind to Marcus. He did not find it too arduous. The boy's calm, firm, and pleasant temper caused him no trouble, and his appearance was ingratiating, with all that fine and curling brown hair and the strangely colored and shining eyes. Too, Marcus had an air of gentle authority, and his profile, Pilo conceded, was definitely aristocratic.

As he was far advanced over boys his age Marcus was placed with older boys. Pilo's schoolroom was large and airy, and he had two tiny rooms behind it for his own quarters and a slave to prepare his meals and do the cleaning. Marcus liked the school, itself, but not some of his classmates. He came to hate with a lifelong hatred the great friend of Julius Caesar, Lucius Sergius Catilina. Lucius was favorite of Pilo's, for his family was both ancient and aristocratic and led almost all other names in Rome, though the family was now impoverished.

Lucius was above all an extremely handsome boy, not in a pretty, effeminate fashion but with intense and delicate virility. He had enormous personal magnetism which most people found irresistible, even his enemies, of whom, considering his character, he amazingly had few. He was a natural leader, and even those wary of him and disliking him followed him. Marcus learned for the first time that virtue and good manners did not necessarily draw friends to one, nor did greatness of heart and mind. In fact, he discovered, these very qualities often had a repellent effect, most men being what they are by nature. An evil man was more bearable to the majority of men than a good man, who was a constant reproach and therefore to be despised.

He was never to understand the motives, in entirety, of those such as Lucius Sergius Catilina. Like everyone else he was fascinated by the appearance of this patrician boy who was two years his senior. Lucius was taller than the average and had a graceful figure. He looked like an accomplished dancer, which indeed he was. He was accomplished in everything, including sports. He was eloquent and had an exquisitely beguiling voice which enchanted friend and foe alike, for it was full of nuances and murmurs and extraordinary humor, and very musical. For the rest, he had a smooth dark face, finely molded and beautiful with a noble brow, thick silky black eyebrows and lashes framing extraordinary blue eyes which were large and brilliant, a nose with sharp nostrils, a mobile mouth as red as a berry and dimpled in the right corner, glittering white teeth perfect as pearls, and a rounded chin like a Greek. He carried himself perfectly, as if aware of his unusual beauty and evil charm, which he was. His manners were fastidious, his smile seductive, his taste impeccable. He learned easily and quickly, and engaged Pilo in subtle arguments. His intelligence was far above the ordinary, and in fact, at eleven, he could have bested many of the minor philosophers.

Marcus conceded his fascinating gifts and his beauty. He could not endure what he innocently guessed lay under all that enchantment: that Lucius was corrupt.

Hatred was unknown to Marcus; he had never encountered it before either in himself or in his family. Therefore, he was stunned when he early discovered that Lucius' baiting of him was not mere schoolboy taunting founded on good-nature, but was inspired by a baffling rejection extended to the stranger and especially to the virtuous. All that Marcus was, generous, calm of temper, patient, kind and studious, persistent if a little plodding, aroused Lucius' enmity and contempt and laughter.

There were adolescent boys in the school, older than Lucius, and many younger. He was unchallenged leader of them all. He borrowed money and never repaid it, and the donor felt himself honored. He had no rings, no golden armlets, no fine shoes, and his tunics and cloaks were of the simplest material. Yet the richest boy felt himself singled out for favors if Lucius noticed his existence. He insulted Pilo with lazy grace, and Pilo smiled sheepishly and goggled at the boy as a silly father would goggle at his only, long-awaited son. The slave served him the best tidbits and wine.

It was inevitable that such as Lucius Sergius Catilina should persecute such a one as Marcus Tullius Cicero. Their eyes had only to meet for them to understand at once that enmity stood between them, that their natures were antipathetic and in violent opposition. Even so Marcus could have tolerated and endured Lucius and even admired him at a distance had Lucius not always sought him out to heap detestation and ridicule on him. Years later Lucius was to say to Marcus, "I hated you, Chick-pea, the moment I saw you, and why that was so I do not know. You made me writhe in my bowels."

Being surrounded by boys of the same age or just a little older or younger was a new experience for Marcus, whom Lucius early called "the bumpkin." He discovered shyness. The boys stared at him with open appraisal. It was immediately evident to them that here was no sophisticated city boy, but perhaps even a simpleton. His gentle appearance amused them. His quietness, his earnest devotion to study, his way of effacing himself, his respect for his teacher, vexed them. He had no news of the city, no scandal to report, no gossip. He had not learned to dice, to play adult games; he knew no lewd stories. He did not laugh at the pain of others. He did not like to throw stones at birds or a sick horse drinking in the gutter. In consequence the boys made him the target of their jokes. Why, they said, little Julius Caesar was more of a man than this milk-fed scion of the far countryside. Pilo could find no fault with him, which was the worst fault of all.

For the first time in his life Marcus came face to face with the evil that was man, and it sickened him. When he said to himself, Evil, too, must be endured, he entered manhood long before adolescence. His young lips became less soft and their outlines stiffened.

Helvia said, "He needs a tonic," and as she had brought many bags of her herbs with her from the country she set herself to brewing concoctions that made the boy retch. He did not complain; the bitter taste in his mouth was no bitterer than his new knowledge of his fellowman.

There must be something wrong with me, he told himself. I am not like the others. He had always had the assurance of a child dearly loved by family, but now his assurance became less certain, especially at school.

He and little Julius Caesar went to school together, swinging their books. When away from his idol, Lucius, Julius was a good companion and full of his own charm, and inclined to a great wit. He was much older than his years; he found Quintus, of his own age, tedious. In his precocious way he liked Marcus, whom he considered a little foolish. But Marcus was always kind; he could always be coaxed out of a few coppers at recess when the vendor came to the door of the school with sweetmeats and hot small pastries full of spiced meat and sugary dates and rich nuts and golden fruit.

At first Marcus could not believe that the eleven-year-old Lucius could really be a close friend of the five-year-old Julius, for all Julius' precocity of mind and speech. But it was quite true. Julius adored Lucius and plagued him, and Lucius would cuff him with an appearance of fondness. They had many things in common, such as lack of money to spend freely, and their parents were old and affectionate friends, and they were both sophisticated and without scruple. Julius was never driven from a gossiping group of older boys, because Lucius was his protector in spite of his frequent blows. There was much that was evil in Julius Caesar, for he always wanted to be foremost and was sometimes unbearably domineering, but there was much that was good, such as humor and sudden surges of generosity.

Julius laughed the loudest when Lucius baited Marcus, but away from his idol he showed Marcus considerable affection and kindly took it upon himself to enlighten Marcus about the ways of city life. He was very ambitious, even at five. His family had little money; he would become rich, he confided to Marcus. He would also be famous, he asserted. Marcus would smile down at him with the superiority of years, and Julius would scowl up at him and shake his head fiercely, his fine black hair flying. "You must study harder," said Marcus.

"The boy is too wise for his years," said Archias. "It is not the kind of wisdom which is reassuring, however. It is rather a shrewdness, an ability to use others, a cunning understanding of the weaknesses of those about him. He will exploit his fellows when he is a man."

But Julius was already gayly exploiting his fellows, and most particularly Marcus.

When the boys walked to school together and Marcus remarked on an aspect of the city or on a passing face, Julius had a witticism at once.

One day the child said to Marcus while they were halting to watch a flight of doves around a statue, "You should not be so afraid of Lucius."

"I am not afraid of him," said Marcus with vexation. "I am just afraid of what he is."

"What is he?" Julius asked, intrigued.

But Marcus could not explain. "Look at those doves circling the statue's head. It is Pollux, is it not? Why are they congregating there?"

"It is their latrine," said Julius, and made an obscene sound and Marcus found himself laughing. "That is irreverent, Julius," he said.

"It is true, however," said Julius. "Is truth always irreverent?"

Marcus thought and then said with wryness, "Very often, it seems."

Julius skipped ahead of him for a moment, then paused to make the captivating obscene sound again, to the amusement of some hurrying men. It was late December now, and the time of the Saturnalia, and the weather was cold. Waiting for Marcus, Julius performed a dexterous dance on the pavement, and more men stopped to watch. Marcus was embarrassed. He thought that Julius' merry face was old in appearance for all the childish features. It had a certain cunning sharpness such as street boys have, a certain satyrism and wildness which made Marcus think of Pan. Then as Marcus came abreast of him, Julius suddenly changed and took his hand like a little boy.

"I like you," he said, and smiled up at the older boy with an artless glance. "I think," said Julius, kicking at a slinking street dog, "that you are not quite such a fool as Lucius thinks you are."

"I do not care what Lucius thinks," said Marcus, coldly. He stopped to fasten Julius' cloak with brotherly hands. The wind was bright and strong.

"Yes, you do," said Julius, lifting his chin to facilitate Marcus' efforts. "You do not know what he thinks and that makes you afraid. But I know what he thinks!"

"What does he think?"

Julius laughed. "He hates you because he knows what you are."

"And what am I, Julius?"

"I like you," said Julius, evasively. "How much money do you have in your purse today?"

Once in school Julius forgot Marcus until recess, when the vendor arrived. He had especially fine treats in honor of the coming holiday, such as cakes in the shapes of fauns and centaurs with raisins for eyes. There were also little hot meat pies cut in phallic forms which were supposed to be amusing. Marcus bought some of the dainties for himself and Julius. All the boys were standing before the school on the pavement, which was not crowded at this hour, and Lucius was at a distance with his particular cronies. His beautiful face was illuminated by the strong winter sun. He turned his head and saw Marcus putting an extra pastry into Julius' voracious hands. He sauntered toward the two.

"How now, Julius," he said in his charming and lazy voice, "are you so stricken by poverty that you can bear to receive gifts from an inferior?"

Julius was afraid that Marcus would snatch away the treasure, and so he said impudently, "What is an inferior? One who has no money."

Lucius' blue eyes flashed dangerously, but laughing he struck down Julius' hand so that the dainty fell to the rushing gutter, and then he hit Julius' dark little face with a casual viciousness. Julius did not mind the blow but he did mind the loss of his pie. Losing his quick temper he did the incredible. He kicked Lucius in the shin.

Amazed, the other boys gathered around. No one had ever objected to Lucius' easy cruelty before, and certainly not the besotted Julius. Lucius could not believe it for a moment. He stood while his dark curls, touched with ruddy shadows, were ruffled by the wind. Then, without visible effort, he snatched Julius in his hands and threw the little boy on the pavement and kicked him in the side. Julius, considerably hurt, howled in pain. Lucius, laughing now, lifted his foot again.

"Stop," said Marcus. His face had turned very white and he involuntarily clenched his hands.

Lucius looked at him disbelievingly. "You will stop me?" he said with contempt.

"Yes," said Marcus, and put himself between Lucius and his victim.

Lucius actually stepped back, but it was with astonishment. He was older and taller and heavier than the seemingly frail Marcus, and he was an expert boxer.

"You?" he exclaimed.

"I," said Marcus. He could feel his heart beating with outrage and a sudden loathing for this handsome boy with the wicked and beautiful face. Never before had he wanted to strike anyone. All the weeks of frustration and pain and humiliation gathered like a knot of iron in his chest, hotly pulsing.

Lucius looked about at his fellows and raised his eyebrows. "This baseborn dog dares to defy me," he said, and then moving like the flash of a sword he was upon Marcus without the preliminary and honorable challenge. He struck one foul blow and Marcus bent over suddenly and gasped for air and felt the exploding anguish in his bowels. Lucius cried out with pleasure, and was on the other boy before he could recover.

Forgetting honorable fighting because of his pain and his sudden hatred and detestation, Marcus grasped Lucius to him and bit his neck deeply. Lucius reared back. Then Marcus seized his ears in his hands and pulled hard and fiercely. Instinctively he brought up his knee and gouged Lucius in the groin. Lucius staggered. Again, Marcus gouged him, then as Lucius fell back he kicked him surely and with all his strength in the delicate spot. Lucius collapsed on the ground. The boys raised a great shout.

"Foul fighting!" they cried.

"You did not think it foul when he attacked me foully!" Marcus cried back. He stood over the writhing Lucius and so incited was he that no boy approached him. But he made no sound. Pilo, hearing the commotion, hurried outside, and when he saw Lucius and Marcus above him he stopped short in stupefaction. Julius ran to him.

"Lucius hit me and kicked me when I was lying down!" he said. "And I am only a little boy!"

"Foul," said the other boys. "Marcus gouged Lucius foully. It was not Roman."

Pilo seized Marcus by the arm and dragged him inside the school. The other boys followed, two supporting the silent Lucius. Pilo thrust Marcus before him and addressed the boys in a shaking voice.

"The honor of the school has been violated," he began.

"Lucius kicked me foully," said Julius from the throng.

"Silence," Pilo commanded.

"He kicked me!" shouted Julius, prancing forward and holding his side pathetically. "As if I were a dog."

Pilo breathed heavily, his hand grasping Marcus' shoulder. Marcus was trembling, but again it was with loathing that he looked at Lucius. "You must have provoked your friend," said Pilo to Julius, "beyond endurance. Besides, you are lying, my child."

"I never lie!" protested Julius, who usually lied.

Pilo ignored him. He looked at the other boys, who were crowding eagerly toward him. "What is the truth?" he said.

One of Lucius' most devoted friends, and an older boy, took it upon himself to enlighten the teacher. "Julius was impudent to Lucius, and Lucius punished him with a slap. Julius fell. Lucius did not kick him. And then—"

Julius screamed, beating his breast with his small fists in his rage, "Lucius kicked me! And then he hit Marcus without challenge and foully, because Marcus told him to stop doing it. And then Marcus protected himself!"

"Is that the truth?" asked Pilo of the others.

It was Lucius who spoke, in a sick voice. "No, it is a lie."

The boys closed their mouths and could not look at each other. They let their heads drop, and their faces reddened. Before honor, they loved Lucius who loved no one.

Pilo understood instantly. He was in a quandary. He loved the popular Lucius with his beautiful face and voice and Apollonian charm. He dared not question Marcus because Marcus would tell the truth. He shook the boy helplessly while he considered. If he punished Marcus there would be no reprisals. Marcus was no tale-bearer.

It did not make Pilo very happy to do as he did in all expediency. He thrashed Marcus before the class with utmost severity, and the boy took the lashing of the whip in utter silence, staring before him. Lucius watched with delight, laughing silently so that all his fine teeth were visible.

The boys were ashamed. When Marcus returned to his bench they could not raise their eyes to his face. But they loved Lucius. They hastily opened their books and engrossed themselves in study.

Marcus and Julius walked home together as usual, and each step caused Marcus to wince. Julius held his champion's hand like a trusting little brother. "I hate Lucius now," he said with vehemence. "I will never like him again."

"Do not be too sure," said Marcus, who had learned even more painful lessons during those weeks.

Julius stamped angrily. "I will never like him again."

"You will not speak of this at home," said Marcus, sternly. "You will forget it."

Of course, Julius told his mother at once, and Aurelia went immediately to Helvia. "Lucius' mother is my best friend," said the stout little lady in outrage, "but Lucius never entranced me as he entrances others."

Helvia sent for Marcus to come to the women's quarters, and the boy entered and saw Aurelia and colored angrily. "Remove your tunic," said Helvia. Marcus, looking at Aurelia with fresh anger, removed his tunic and Helvia inspected the welts on his young body. She called to a slave for hot water and ointments. With no comment she rubbed the pungent oils into the welts, after bathing them until they were fiery. Then she said, "You will not return to that school."

Marcus was greatly disturbed. "Mother," he pleaded, "that will be shameful of me. The other boys will laugh at me for a coward, believing I came whining to you like a pampered infant."

Helvia considered, her teeth worrying her ripe under lip. She looked at her friend, Aurelia. Aurelia was nodding with approval. "He speaks as a Roman," she said. "You can be proud of him, Helvia."

"I was always proud of him," said Helvia, to Marcus' surprise. She smiled at her son and pushed his shoulder fondly. "I am glad that you fought Lucius and overcame him, and I am proud even of your welts which you received in silence and in honor and in the defense of one younger and weaker."

"Lucius is larger and older," said Aurelia. "It is not foul to defend yourself foully against a foul man, if only foulness is the answer and the only possible way."

"Lucius is not truly a Roman in spirit," said Helvia.

"But you will not speak of it to anyone?" Marcus said to his mother as he carefully resumed his tunic.

"To no one," Helvia promised. She smiled again at her son, and her handsome face shone.

"And I will thrash Julius if he utters another word," said Aurelia. She had thought Helvia unfortunate in her older son, who was so quiet. She had believed him girlish. Yet he had not only defended her petted Julius, who was her delight and pride, but he had vanquished the haughty Lucius whom she disliked. She fished at a golden chain about her short and rosy neck and pulled up a medal engraved with the likeness of Pallas Athene from her warm bosom.

"The goddess of wisdom and law," she said. "This medal represents her

as she appears in the Parthenon in Athens. You are worthy of it, Marcus."
And she put it in his hand.

"It is a marvelous gift," said Helvia.

"It is from a grateful mother," said Aurelia.

Marcus could never remember when his mother had kissed him, but now
she pulled down his head and kissed his cheek, then patted it. "I am
proud," she repeated. She sat there beaming at him pridefully, the pleated
ruffle of her stola falling over her plump feet.

The enmity between Marcus Tullius Cicero and Lucius Sergius Catilina grew prodigiously. But never again did Lucius ridicule Marcus before their classmates.

Marcus wore Aurelia's gift all his life, and years later he showed it to
Julius.

CHAPTER SIX

Long before he was ceremoniously initiated into the status of adolescence
Marcus was made further miserable at school by the entry of two others
such as Lucius Sergius Catilina: Cneius Piso and Quintus Curius, who
were Lucius' devoted friends. Cneius, too, was of a charming and patrician
air and countenance, but he was smaller and quicker than Lucius and
even more haughty, less interested in leading the school, more thoughtful
and scheming. He had fair hair and gray eyes and somewhat girlish man-
nerisms, and high light laughter like a maiden's. In many ways, however,
these were deceptive, for he had no fear of anything whatsoever, so proud
was he of his patrician family, which was as poor as Lucius'. He demanded
servility in all save Lucius and Curius, and he invariably received it except
from Marcus and little Julius.

Q. Curius was a grim, dark-faced youth, surly but intellectual. He
would inherit a seat in the Senate, and all were soon appraised of the fact.
Tall and athletic and slender, he stood even above the tall Lucius in height,
and had a glowering look, and a sullen, prominent face. His family had
more money than did the Catilinii and Piso families, and he was the heir of
his rich grandfather.

These two joined their contempt with that of Lucius for Marcus, who,
as Lucius informed them, belonged to the class of "new men," that is, the
middle-class. "Do not cross him," said Lucius in Marcus' hearing, "he is a

foul fighter, a fool, and a person of no importance or principle. Should one associate with such?" The two agreed that one should not.

Little Julius Caesar, now almost nine years old, laughed at what he called "the triumvirate." "One of these days," he said to Marcus, "when I am a man, I shall make public idiots of them, for they have pretensions. Are their families better than mine? No. Only Curius is richer." Julius smacked his lips. "Curius has a cousin, an orphan girl, of much beauty. It is said she will become a Vestal Virgin, but Lucius wishes to marry her. Her name is Livia."

Once Curius brought a bundle of filthy garments belonging to a slave of his household to school, and tossed them at the feet of Marcus. "Your family are fullers, are they not?" he asked in his deep, fifteen-year-old voice. "Excellent. Take this then, to your father, for washing."

Marcus looked at him long and silently, then went for a bucket of water and put it at the feet of Curius. "A man is a slave who insults another without provocation," he said. "Therefore, slave, wash your clothing."

"He gouges at the genitals, with an eye to unmanning, because he has no genitals of his own," said Lucius. Marcus, only past twelve, continued to stare at Curius. Curius turned away with an obscene sound of contempt. "I do not fight cats," he said. But the school knew that Marcus had won this engagement.

Marcus' integrity, discerned angrily by all three youths, did not make them feel kindly toward Marcus. They called him upstart and pretender and the mimic of his betters. Fortunately, Curius' father decided that his son must have a private tutor, and included Lucius and Cneius generously in his invitation. Marcus was overwhelmingly relieved. I will never encounter them again, he thought. When he heard, later, that they had gone to Greece to complete their education, Rome, to Marcus, seemed cleaner for their absence. The world was less bright because they lived in it.

Years later, when a mature man, Marcus wrote, "It is wrong to bring children up in an atmosphere solely of family and fraternal affection, without enlightening them that beyond the safe walls of home there lives a world of Godless, dishonorable, and amoral men, and that these men are in the majority. For when an innocent youth must inevitably encounter the world of men he suffers a wound from which he will never recover, and a sickness of heart which will permanently sicken his soul. Better at once, even from the cradle, to teach your son that man is intrinsically evil and that he is a destroyer and a liar and a latent murderer, and that your son must be armed against his brother lest he die in body or in spirit! The Jews are quite correct when they declare that man is desperately wicked from his birth and evil from his youth. Possessing this knowledge, your son can then say to himself, 'With the help of God I shall be kinder than my brother, and shall strive for virtue. It is my duty to aspire above my human nature.' "*

The year after Lucius Sergius Catilina and his companions left the school of Pilo a new student took his place, a boy of fifteen, one Noë ben Joel, the son of a rich Jewish stockbroker. He became a general favorite at once, though Pilo sarcastically observed that half the great Roman families were in pawn to him. Pilo, of course, charged Joel ben Solomon more than he charged the majority of fathers, just as he charged Tullius Cicero more for his son, the reason being, as he would say loftily, that those who had should share with those who had not. This peculiar philosophy was one with which Archias never agreed; charity was excellent, but it should be voluntary and not arbitrarily imposed by those whose purses were not touched, or in the name of "mankind," a word to which Pilo was much attached and which cost him nothing but made him feel excessively virtuous. ("Deliver me from the hypocrites," said Archias.)

Noë immediately took an enormous interest in his fellow students, in Pilo, and even in the slave who cared for the noonday wants of the school. Nothing was too minute for his inspection and curiosity. He was affable, generous with his purse, amusing and irreverent. He rarely appeared to study yet he was soon Pilo's favorite student. He was formidable in mathematics, philosophy, languages, science, rhetoric, poetry, and mimicry. He could imitate anyone, to the screaming laughter of his mates and even to the one mimicked. But he was never cruel or vindictive, nor did he mimic to ridicule.

"Why so grave?" he asked one day, coming on Marcus alone in the schoolroom with his books while the other boys were outside wrestling and boxing and eating forbidden sweets and drinking their noonday wine.

Marcus blushed. He was about to murmur an evasive word or two, then looked up into the large and shimmering brown eyes directed down at him with a kindly smile. Then he said, "I am no favorite, except with that little boy, Julius, who is an actor like you. He is always on your heels, is he not?" Marcus continued, hoping to direct the other boy's intent inspection from him.

"He is an incipient actor. I am an accomplished one," said Noë. He had his delicacy basket in his hand and lifted the white napkin that covered it. "Hammantashin," he said to Marcus, who bent his head to look within the basket on the table before him. He saw little triangular pieces of pastry which gave forth a delectable smell. "Have one," invited Noë. "Have two, three," said Noë, largely. Marcus took one; it was filled with sugared fruit. Marcus, due to his mother's cooking, rarely was interested in

* Letter to Terentia.

food. But these were delicious. Noë watched him with pleasure as his hand dipped in the basket again for a fresh pastry. "We have three cooks," said Noë, "but my mother presides. We are all fat," he said, as he patted his lean belly. "My father is at the mercy of all the doctors in Rome. He has indigestion. My mother says he has a Gentile stomach."

Noë was not a handsome boy. He merely had a pleasant and happy and alert appearance, with a very long profile. His eyes were as gentle as a girl's, with thick fringes about them. His mouth was mobile, always changing expression, and in spite of close cropping his hair was thickly curling. His ears, unfortunately, were very large and stood far out from his head. No one mocked him about them, for he jested about them himself. His skin was very white, and so his dark hair and eyes were emphasized.

He sat down beside Marcus, and they inspected the crannies of the basket together until not a crumb remained. Marcus was suddenly aware that he felt at ease, as he felt with none other of his schoolmates. He was astonished when he heard himself laughing, not reluctantly but with openness. For Noë could change his voice from the highest pitch of a hysterical woman to the deepest tones of an adult man. He used his voice as a musician uses his instrument. He talked of the play he was directing, one of Aristophanes', which was not liked by Pilo. Marcus was one of the few who had declined parts in the play.

"Why?" said Noë, today.

"I should feel foolish," said Marcus.

"But folly is not always foolish," said Noë, wisely. He looked in Marcus' delicacy basket, then hastily but politely replaced the coarse napkin. "I hear you are decided to study law. How will you face judges, then, and courts, if you are afraid to stand up and speak? A successful lawyer is always an actor."

"I was thinking of jurisprudence," said Marcus.

Noë leaned back on his seat and studied Marcus critically. Noë's garments were of the finest linen, his sandals beautifully ornamented. He wore a big amethyst ring surrounded by small emeralds on the long white index finger of his right hand. He pointed the finger at Marcus. "You? A miserable law clerk, advising fat judges who half-snore in their chairs after their fatter meals? Ridiculous. You have the face and bearing of an actor."

Marcus did not know whether to be offended or flattered. Noë said quickly, "It is not that you are flamboyant or of a stage presence or like a preening actor, who is all gestures and alluring gurgles and appeals to the ladies. It is your eyes, your voice, and especially your eyes. They are very strange, very compelling. And when you speak it is with authority and eloquence."

"I?" said Marcus, amazed.

Again Noë pointed at him. "You," he nodded. "I have watched you. I am an actor of no mean accomplishment, and that is what I will be, though my father beats his breast and threatens to take us back to Judea where I must grow a beard and study the word of God exclusively and marry a fat Jewish girl and have ten sons, all rabbis. I will produce plays; I write plays, too. My accomplishments are not to be despised. A sincere actor, like yourself, my grave Marcus, is beyond rubies."

Marcus, blushing again, considered all this.

"You can make the dullest philosopher sound like pearls of wisdom," said Noë. "I know Plato's *Republic* to be all nonsense, and I will tell you later why I think so. Nevertheless, when you spoke of it last week you almost convinced me. You believed in what you were saying, no matter if Aristotle was quite correct concerning Plato. Your voice," said Noë, "is far better than mine. You are convincing. I am only a comedian, though I am now interesting myself in more serious plays, such as Sophocles' *Antigone*. It is absurd that Romans will permit only prostitutes to appear on the stage. To return to yourself, Marcus: You could convince even Pilo he is a fool if you tried, though I regret, at times, your modesty and shyness when you first stand up to recite."

He was so kind and so earnest that Marcus knew he spoke without malice.

"You do not appreciate yourself," said Noë. "You have had unhappy experiences. Does your father beat you very much?"

"My father?" cried Marcus, thinking of his beloved and gentle parent. "He is the sweetest of men. I have never been beaten in my life but once, and that was by Pilo."

"I have heard of that," said the other boy, pursing up his mouth. "You were much admired for your fortitude but considered stupid under the circumstances. That Lucius must be a scoundrel. I am sorry he is no longer here. I should make him the buffoon of the school. My father knows his family well; Lucius' father is trying to regain a fortune long lost, but he is not a man of astuteness. I have seen your Lucius at a distance. I admit his beauty, but still he must be a scoundrel."

"I am glad that I shall never see him again," said Marcus. "He is without honor and principle. He is no true Roman though he is considered a patrician."

"The apple," said Noë, "is a noble fruit, but when it is rotten it is only a rotten apple. Let us consider patrician families. Do they become decayed when they lose their fortunes or do they lose their fortunes when they decay? My father believes the latter and I agree with him. He has a hard hand, and I am his only son, and the object of his constant prayers. I love him so I do not cross him often. Besides, I am his heir and I will need money for my plays. But will he be proud when he sees my plays in the theatre? He will not." Noë struck the palm of his hand flatly on the table and squeezed up his eyes ruefully.

"I have a brother, Quintus," said Marcus, and did not know how his eyes could change so brilliantly from light olive to passionate gray with love.

Noë was touched in his volatile heart. "I see we have no Cain and Abel here," he said.

"Cain and Abel?" asked Marcus.

Noë told him of Adam and Eve and their sons, and Marcus moved eagerly in his attention to the edge of his bench, and he nodded over and over. The story entranced him. At last he said, "Tell me of your Messias."

"Ah!" said Noë. "We expect Him hourly, for are not all the portents here concerning His coming? My father prays for His coming at dawn—and Jews rise even earlier than do Romans, a barbaric custom—and at noon and at night. He will deliver Israel from her sins, so say the rabbis, and be a light unto the Gentiles. But my father and his friends believe He will give Israel rule of the earth, including Rome and all her legions, not to mention the Indus, the Greeks, the Spaniards, the Britons, the Gauls, and lesser tribes and nations."

"So small a country?" said Marcus, feeling a Roman's incredulous surprise.

"A pearl, however small, is more valuable than a handful of the most polished glass," said Noë, feeling a Jew's pride. But his restless mind left the subject. He picked up the purplish edge of Marcus' tunic. "You are not yet a man," he said, "though you have the mind of a man."

"I will soon be invested," said Marcus. "I am nearly fourteen."

When Marcus announced to his family that he wished, at his adolescence, his emergence into manhood, to take Pallas Athene rather than the Roman Minerva as his patroness, Archias chuckled under his clever nose, Tullius smiled in pleasure, the grandfather roared his horror, and Helvia said, "He is fourteen years old, and therefore he is no longer a child and must make his own decisions. He is certainly, however, displaying that effete preference for things Grecian which is scandalous. But, he must live with the scandal. What is in a name? Pallas Athene is the same as Minerva."

"You are inconsistent!" exclaimed the grandfather. "First you speak of scandal, and then you say, 'What is in a name?' I consider names sacred."

"Minerva is more sinewy than Pallas Athene," said Helvia, unmoved. "She has more masculine attributes. Nevertheless, Marcus must do as he wishes."

"To such degeneracy has Rome fallen!" said the grandfather. "In my day the father had the power of life and death over his children, as inscribed in the Twelve Tables of Law. But now sons, hardly removed from the breast, presume to announce their learned decisions to their parents. When children decay—"

"The nation decays," said Helvia, with patience. "We hear that daily, do we not, Grandfather? Marcus, you wish Pallas Athene?"

"Not if it will cause so much distress," said the boy, who did not like to see his grandfather empurpled of face.

"I am not distressed," said Helvia. The Greek teacher, being a Greek, was not asked for his opinion. Helvia reached up from her spinning wheel, which she was almost always industriously employing, to smooth her older son's curling brown hair.

"Pallas Athene," said the devoted Quintus. The grandfather cuffed him. Helvia ordered him to bed as it was now dark, Marcus pushed his shoulder affectionately, and the Greek teacher dared to think Quintus was not entirely stupid. Tullius gave him a surreptitious pat, but very timidly. He was still afraid of all children except Marcus, who was now no more a child.

Then came the discussion of sacrifices on the occasion when Marcus would assume the toga of manhood, the manly gown. This would not be for over a year more, on the Liberalia, festival of Liber, the sixteenth of the Calends of April. However, all arrangements were long in the planning. Lists were made of guests and distant relatives to be invited. Helvia had to choose the flax to weave the robe, which, as Tullius was a knight, and therefore mandatorily in possession of four hundred thousand sesterces, would be of purple striped with scarlet and draped to the right shoulder. This robe would be of the utmost importance, would need care in selection and sewing and dyeing. All other garments must be freshly made, as for a bride. But not, thank the gods, thought Marcus fervently, the woolen trousers in which my mother insists on enveloping my legs in the winter, so that I must, in shame, wear a longer tunic than other youths in order to hide my infamy.

It was not strange that there was more discussion concerning the sacrifices to be offered up to the tutelary gods in Marcus' behalf than in deciding upon the guests, and the entertainment, which would inevitably be frugal. Tullius recklessly suggested four hecatombs, which caused his father and his wife to fix him with stern frowns, he compromised, as always, and there would be two, not with gold collars but with silver. On the great day Marcus would take off his bulla, and be officially called by his name, Marcus, though he had been called so from birth. His name would be inscribed in the public records. As this was the day on which all youths of approximately Marcus' age would enter into adolescence (a stage which would continue until the thirtieth year) it was a national festival. Priestesses of Bacchus would offer white-honey cakes to the god in behalf of the new young men, and the god would accept no other on the grand occasion. A long procession would accompany the youths to the Forum, where they would be ceremoniously presented to their countrymen, and to Rome. Old women and maidens with heads wreathed in myrtle would sing praises, and the youths henceforth would be known as citizens of their nation, with the responsibility of Romans. They would then return to their homes and there would be a feast, during which they would be permitted to become drunk. Marcus doubted that anyone would become drunk, due to his mother's frugality. He would be lucky to have two goblets of the precious wine which had aging for just that day.

"It will be like a Bar Mitzvah, then," said Noë to his friend. "But mine was at the age of thirteen." He made his face into a mimicry of avarice. "Will you receive many gifts?"

"Not from the Helvii. Not from my grandfather, who watches every sesterce, but who will probably invest in a few shares of stock for me, which will be kept at his bank until I am truly at an age of prudence. Otherwise," said Marcus, "I should inevitably squander it on wild and dissolute occasions." He smiled. "From my father I will receive a fine ring; I have already chosen the gems, and it will be made by one of your countrymen. This will occasion accusations of extravagance against my poor father. Quintus has been saving his small allowance for three years and is very mysterious about his gift. And as guests usually match a family's gifts in price, I can be certain to receive very useful but very dull and not very expensive gifts from family friends. My mother? Like my grandfather, she will part with a few shares of stock, put them in my name, then seal them away, probably until I am a parent, myself. Archias will give me rare books."

"And the feast?" asked Noë, fascinated at this glimpse into Roman life.

"Wholesome," said Marcus. "That is, no confectioner will be called to contribute his talents. There will, doubtless, be a roasted tough ox, or a bull, but not one, as will be rumored among the disgruntled, recently killed by a gladiator in the arena. There will be plenty of bread, baked into appropriate shapes, the nature of which I will not tell you for fear of embarrassing your Jewish ears, many vegetables with no sauces, perhaps a little game, some cakes baked in my mother's kitchen by slaves trained in economy, and the cask of wine which has been waiting, and, if that runs dry too soon, by the family wine which is execrable."

Then he said, "Before all this, there will be long discussions with me on my coming new state."

"I remember similar from before my Bar Mitzvah," said Noë, with sadness. "I became so intimidated that I expected that the day following that great one would dawn in thunder and I would be tossed by tempests. At the very least the world would be tremendously changed. Portents had been hinted, stern faces had been directed at me. I was quite astonished to discover that there were no thunders, no tempests, no changes, the day after my Bar Mitzvah. It was disappointing. Life proceeded as usual and my father boxed my ears for my stupidity because I forgot the exact wording of one of the Psalms. Is life nothing but anticlimaxes, therefore? Shall all our years be spent in expectations, to arrive at nothing but another dawn, another lesson to be learned, another vexation to be overcome, until the final day arrives when we are gathered to our fathers?"

His mobile face expressed melancholy, and Marcus became depressed. Seeing this, Noë said, "But you shall go to Greece. Not that the men there stand in the postures of gods but at least it will be another country." He knew very well that all men are the same but he was remorseful that he had made Marcus dejected.

"And you shall be a famous lawyer, Marcus," he continued.

"To what end?" asked Marcus, who was feeling the dark pangs of adolescence.

To no satisfaction of the spirit, thought Noë, but he said, "It is very important to be a man of law, for is not justice everything and the noblest attribute of God?"

"Do not lecture me," said Marcus. The two boys were sitting alone in the school, as they often did. "What did your mother pack in your basket this morning?" They forgot the dread premonitions of their manhood in exploring the delights of the basket and enjoying them.

Noë began to instruct Marcus about the religion of the Jews, not because he wished, being an irreverent young man, but because Marcus was endlessly inquiring.

"We shall circumcise you yet," said Noë.

But Marcus said, "There is only one God, and He is the God of all men, and not solely of the Jews. Did He not make me as He did you also? He lives in our hearts. Repeat to me the prophecies of the Messias and His coming. I cannot hear enough."

Noë was abashed. He did not truly believe with all fervor in the faith of his fathers, and thought the prophesied Messias a pathetic and dismal hope of his people, never to be fulfilled. But he told Marcus all he knew, because he was kind, and he applied himself to his sacred books—to the joy of his innocent father—to give Marcus fresh information and lighten that face which was too grave for a youth so young.

" 'A Virgin shall give birth to a Son,' " Marcus would repeat, and he would know that that Virgin was not Minerva or her Greek counterpart,

Pallas Athene, nor Diana nor Artemis. "'And He shall be called Emmanuel, for He shall deliver His people from their sins!'"

He pondered on the Virgin and he did not know why, and he wondered if she were already among the living, perhaps a girl as young as himself. Once in a temple he went to the altar of the Unknown God and laid a sheaf of lilies upon it and said, "It is for Your Mother." The worshipers about him looked at him strangely, they carrying their living sacrifices to the various priests.

From Noë, he learned the Hebrew of the Jews, the language of the learned men, which was a muscular tongue like Latin.

CHAPTER SEVEN

The family as usual went to the island near Arpinum for the summer where the air was fresh and cool, unlike the murky and smothering winds of Rome. Here among the sacred oaks and poplars, the cypresses and the wooded paths, Marcus would wander alone or with his father or his tutor. Here he began to write his first true poetry, and he would despair of ever being able to put into words the color of the sky, the sound of the waters, the intricate green of leaves, the fragrance of grass and flowers. There were tremendous movements in his heart, large and bursting thoughts in his mind, and painfully, to him, they were rendered banal on parchment and on tablet. Was it possible, he thought once, that that which one so dearly and passionately loves is beyond speech, beyond word? His prose, Archias would tell him sincerely, was even better than some of his own and more eloquent. "Suffice yourself with that," he would say. "But amuse yourself with your poetry, for poetry is natural to a young spirit." Archias would take a pen and deftly replace a word with a singing other and Marcus would watch in envy and in delight.

"Only poetry is immortal," said Marcus.

Archias shook his head. "Thought is immortal. Look upon man, Marcus, and observe how weak he is. He has no scales like the fish to armor himself, he has no wings with which to fly from danger; he has no hide like the elephant to guard him against stings and thorns; he has no claws and teeth like the tiger, and he is not terrible as is the lion. He is not so agile as the monkey, nor so clever as the fox. He is not carapaced like the insect. He cannot live without shelter nor survive long without food, as does the bear and the other hibernating animals. He cannot swim very far or for prolonged periods. He is the prey of the poisonous fly and of many animals. In all ways he is lesser than the beasts, if one thinks only of his flesh and his life.

"Yet, vulnerable though he is, and weak, and as frail as grass and as tender as the weed, how great is man! He thinks. Does the wolf think as a man thinks? Can the crow build a Parthenon? Can the whale encompass the idea of God? The serpent is wiser, I have heard, but has the serpent ever raised a monument to truth and beauty? Is not Socrates, ugly though he was, mightier than the noblest mountain? Is not Aristotle greater than the physical world and all the creatures upon it? Has not the weakest babe a more enormous value, because he is a potential man, than a grove of the highest trees? It is because man can think, and out of his thinking create heaven and Hades, and stand with the gods and say, 'I have a mind, therefore I am one of you.' "

He touched Marcus on his arm. "Thought comes in many forms, as life comes in many forms, and who shall say which form is the more marvelous? There are Homers and there are Platos, there are Phidiases and there are Archimedeses. Be thankful that you can command prose, that you have an eloquent voice which can induce even the Lady Helvia to part with an extra sesterce—and I stand in admiration."

"I should still like to write poetry like Homer," said Marcus.

"Then, write poetry for your own pleasure," said Archias. "I have not said it is bad poetry. I have written worse, some of which has been acclaimed. But your destiny lies elsewhere."

He went on, "I have long wanted to give you the advice which is so necessary for a young man in his adolescence, and which will serve him well all his life. Man, as you know, is a cataloguing animal. He is a creature of reason and rationality, if he cultivates those gifts. Beware, Marcus, of the fervent and enthusiastic man, for he has lost his reason and his rationality! He is hardly more than the exuberant dog, which rushes and barks at every sound and is excited by all things. The truly civilized man is immune to passing exclamations, novelties and fashions in thought, deed, or the written or spoken word, and emotional storms. Be not zealous, Marcus! Be temperate. Cultivate contemplation. Be reverent before the wisdoms and traditions garnered as painfully as grain through the centuries.

"The true man stands apart from the vociferous market rabble, which is constantly acclaiming and then in the next breath denouncing. The man of the street can never be trusted. Consider the noble and tenderhearted Gracchi, with whom I have never been in agreement. (Nevertheless, they were good men and gave all their spirit and their hearts to their people.) The very rabble they wished to elevate and raise to the stature of true men destroyed them in the feverish rage and passions so typical of the common man.

"However, beware as much of the man of the colonnades, who can be trusted no more than his comrade of the streets. The first is like a stone, immured only in his thoughts, which, as they have no contact with reality are dangerous. The second is like a mindless tempest, roaring and uncontrollable, uprooting forests and drowning in tidal waves. The man of the colonnades thinks men are purely thought; he forgets they are also animal with animal instincts and passions. Nothing to excess. The Ionic League brought luxury to Greece, and also her destruction, for then Greece had the leisure to cultivate the body—the idol of the gross and common man—who thinks man's meaning lies in physical beauty, strength, athletics, sports, feastings. There is nothing wrong in the cultivation of the body so long as it is one step behind the cultivation of the mind, and is always obedient to the will.

"But Greece became like a woman with a mirror, or a man glorying in his muscles. I see these signs of decay in the Roman Republic also. Rome admires her image as seen in the eyes of subject people, and is enamored of her power. Like Greece, she will become subject to a hardier race, and all her splendor will be buried in her own luxuriant dung."

He picked up a leafy twig and held it out delicately on the cushion of his thumb. "Balance," he said. "It is the law of nature. Let that man beware who disturbs it. It will crash to the ground. The pedant and the common man—they are the disturbers of the scales, the first without a body, the second without a soul."

Mindful of his duty, the grandfather sought Marcus out one warm and golden day as he wandered beside the river, composing ardent poetry in his mind.

"It is time," said the grandfather, "for me to put into brief words the things a young man must know."

Marcus privately discounted the brevity of the grandfather's words, but sat down on a smooth stone after courteously putting his cloak on the grass for the old man. But the grandfather shook his head with a mention of rheumatism, and leaned on the staff which he was recently affecting. He stroked his beard, which was showing hardly a trace of gray and contemplated his grandson with a sparkling and youthful eye. His long tunic —for he did not wear a toga in the country—molded itself against strong and heroic limb and broad breast. He studied Marcus, the boy's smooth forehead, the large and changing eyes under thick dark brows. The excellent nose with the sharply defined nostrils, the grave and almost beautiful mouth, the firm line of the chin and throat, and the long brown hair which rippled below the ears. What he saw pleased him and made him proud, but he kept his Cincinnatus face stern. One should never let the young know of one's approval.

Marcus smiled up at his grandfather and waited. Then he looked at the river which was all shades of running green under the shadows of the trees, and he looked at the distant bridge which led to Arpinum, cherry-red and white and gold on the flank of the hill.

"A man," said the grandfather, "is known by his character, by the essence of his God-given manhood. If he honors his manhood and the manhood of others he will be just, brave, patriotic, reliable, strong, inflexible in the right. He owes it to his manhood to be healthy of body, prudent, full of fortitude, honest, proud of himself, fearless, worthy of his ancestors and his history, patient in adversity, intolerant of weakness of character, spare, ascetic, frugal, courageous. He must be honorable, because to be dishonorable is to lower his status as a man. The cowardly man is more to be feared than an evil man, and, by governments, to be feared even more than the traitor.

"Beware of the mendicant mind, the dependent soul. They destroy empires. They will," said the grandfather with bitter sorrow, "eventually destroy Rome, as they destroyed other nations. They have no honor; they have no patriotism; they have no manhood."

"Yes," said Marcus, as soberly as his grandfather could have desired.

The grandfather turned his head and looked at the sky and the river and the earth, but he was seeing a dolorous thing in his mind. "In our history," he said, "there have been times of danger when we needed swiftness of action, swiftness of thought, unfettered by law in the pressing hour. So, we appointed dictators. But, we were wise then. When we appointed dictators we removed temptation from them by denying them honors, luxuries, and pleasures, and even the decent furniture of life. We prohibited them from riding a horse, or even possessing one. We needed their superior will to action, their speediness, their minds, their indomitable courage. But we did not need the power for which all men lust, the power over the destiny of men's thoughts and lives, except for the hour. When they had done what they must, we removed all power from them and made them simple and unassuming men again.

"But the day of the dictator is almost upon us again, not the dictator of old, but the dictator who wishes illimitable power, prolonged power, over Rome. Rome is not what once she was. We are fast approaching the day when Rome will not be swayed by the temperate middle-class but by the rich, who will preside over whining and bottomless bellies, and slaves. Each serves the other, satisfies the other's appetite, in an evil symbiosis. For the rabble's votes the powerful man will betray Rome. Though Marius has lately pushed back the hordes of Germanic invaders, we have not done with turbulence, and turbulence is the climate in which tyrants flourish. Therefore, I fear for my country.

"I have seen a noble Rome, a nation of free men. But you, my grandson, will see terrible times, for Rome has fallen in her spirit and there are fierce carrion birds poised even now on our walls, and within the walls of great rich houses, and in the alleys and crowded back streets of our city. It is your duty, as you stand on the doorstep of your manhood, to hold back the enemy, as Marius held back the Germanii. If enough of you do this thing, resolute and brave and with honor, Rome shall yet be saved, though the hour is late and true patriotism is sickening under our very martial banners. Have you courage, Marcus?"

At first Marcus had listened to his grandfather with youthful indulgence, remembering his age and homilies, of which he had unceasingly heard many. But now his mind was captured and fired; his heart was swiftly beating. "I think I have, Grandfather. I pray I have."

The grandfather studied him with a deep and passionate intensity. Then he nodded his head. "I believe you have. I have watched you these past two years, for in you is my hope, and in your generation. When you encounter the evil men—and surely you will!—you must say to them, 'Here I stand, and here is Rome, and you shall not pass!'

"You will look at the faces and the monuments of your country, and you will remember what they mean. You will look at the inscriptions on our noble buildings, and at the arches of our temples. This is the inheritance I leave you. You must never betray them, not out of fear, not for a woman, not for gain, not for honors and powers. This is Rome. Remember always that it once took only three heroic men to save her. Stand on the bridge with Horatius and swear by our gods and by the name of Rome that no one shall reach her heart and halt it. You are only one, but you are one. And remember, above all things, that never was a government but that was a liar, a thief and a malefactor.* When power lies only in the people, and their government is restricted, then that people flourish and no wicked man can conquer them."

He raised his own hands, and his eyes glittered with tears. Abruptly, then, he turned away and marched off with his long and youthful stride. Marcus watched him go. Then he stood and lifted his hand and swore solemnly that never, so long as he lived, would he forget his grandfather's words, and that never, so long as he lived, would he forget that he was a Roman.

---

* Thoreau quoted this often.

That night Marcus sat with his father, Tullius, in the latter's pleasant country library, small and warm and lamplit, with the odor of parchment and vellum about them, and the sweet fragrance of the dark earth and water flowing in the opened windows. Here Marcus had spent some of the happiest hours of his happy childhood. But now, as he looked at his father's gentle and haggard face, he knew that the happiness of those years was passing and that never again would he know their innocence and simplicity and trust.

Tullius did not possess even the strength of his earlier years. He had suffered many attacks of malaria. His kind brown eyes were sunken, his nostrils sharpened. The bones of his face were tight and hot under his drawn skin. His hand trembled as he poured wine for himself and his son. His feet, in their open sandals, were corded and skeletal. His fine brown hair was thin and graying at the temples. His long tunic seemed hung on slats of wood.

Marcus said, "You seem sick, my father."

Tullius replied, "Not more than usual, Marcus. What! Do you think me dying? Not yet. Not yet," he repeated, and his voice was weary. But why am I weary? he asked himself. My life has not been arduous. I have known few storms and no hardships.

He lifted his goblet of wine and saluted his son with the sweetest of smiles. The wind brought in the scent of jasmine, passionate and vehement, and the dark trees murmured in the night wind. "To you, my dear son," said Tullius. "To you, in your young, fresh manhood, and may God be with you always."

Marcus sat forward in his chair, his goblet in his hand, and he said, frightened of the answer, "Phelon is a country physician. Why have you not consulted the physicians of Rome, my father?"

Tullius hesitated. How and in what words did a man tell his son that he was tired of living? What words were these to pour into an ear that heard only the song of youth and the Circe of a golden future? I wish, thought Tullius, that I could say to him, with truth: I have labored hard and long and my life has been burdensome with toil and trouble, and now I wish for my rest. But that would be a lie. I have spent a serene life with my books and my thoughts, and have loved my dear birthplace and the water and all the things about me. I have known no turmoil, no heartbreak, no real despair, no anguish of body or spirit. I have lived in the peace of a quiet bay, in temperate sunshine, and no storm has ever blown upon me nor shattered my lamp or put out my light. Yet—I am tired of living.

Tullius said soothingly, "I have consulted the physicians in Rome. I have malaria. The attacks are very debilitating. Do not be distressed. I have had them many times."

Marcus put the wine to his lips and it tasted as bitter as death. No matter how much we have talked together, thought the youth, we have never said the things that lie closest to our thoughts.

Years later, remembering that night, he wrote to a friend: "Man lives in an awful isolation, imprisoned by his flesh, unable to stir his tongue of flesh to pronounce the words in his heart, unable to show that heart of flesh to anyone, neither father nor child nor brother nor wife. That is man's tragedy, that he lives alone from the moment of his birth until the hour he lies upon his funeral pyre."

Then Tullius, who had been wondering what to say to his son tonight, suddenly thought: I am weary for God! The thought flooded him not with melancholy but with a kind of exultant joy, somewhat sad but all comprehensive. I have loved beauty too much, he thought. I have been engrossed with God from my earliest childhood, therefore I could take no real pleasure in the world, for I was always filled with nostalgia for Him. The world of men was always at variance with what I spiritually understood, therefore I withdrew from it. Now I am weary of the days and hours away from my home.

His pale drawn face filled with radiance and seeing this Marcus was again afraid. It was as if his father had withdrawn from him to a place he could not yet follow and could not understand.

"Let us talk about you, my dear Marcus," said Tullius, and his voice was youthful again and eager. "For what I must tell you now is the only surety you will ever have, the only certitude. You will have duties in the world, but your first duty is to God. For that He created you, to know Him, to serve Him above all others in this your life, and to join Him forever after death. The world is truly an illusion, for no man sees it as does another man. His reality is not yours, nor yours his. There are some who will say to you: 'Politics are the most important, for man is a political animal.' Others will say, 'Power is the driving force of all men, therefore to be important, seek power.' Still others will say, 'Money is the measure of mankind, for only a poor thing of no consequence is content with poverty and obscurity.' And yet still others will say, 'The love of your fellows is all that is necessary, therefore seek popularity.' These are their realities. They may not be yours, nor will they be the realities of millions of your fellows.

"To a good man happiness in this world is of no importance, and has no reality. This is not our home. A good man can find happiness only in God and in the contemplation of Him, even in this world. Even then, it is a happiness overlaid with sadness, for the soul cannot truly be happy separated by its flesh from its God."

Marcus leaned toward his father and without knowing it he placed his hand on his father's bony knee. Tullius laid his fingers over those of his son and pressed warmly, and his mild eyes flooded with tears, and he sighed and smiled.

"Man must have a frame of reference," said Tullius. "Once Rome had a firm frame of reference compounded of God, country, and just law. So she became strong and mighty, upheld by faith, patriotism and justice.

"The nation which drives out God drives out its soul, and without a soul a nation cannot survive. We have a Republic, but the Republic is declining. The evil heads of plotting men are already outlined against the sunset of our life, and their swords are visible. What is it that Aristotle said: 'Republics decline into democracies, and democracies degenerate into despotisms.' We have approached that day.

"Wicked men are born every generation, and it is the duty of a nation to render them impotent. When you discover a man who seeks power for himself, out of hatred or contempt for his fellows, destroy him, Marcus. If a man seeks office because he secretly despises what he calls 'the mass,' and wishes to control them into slavery, with promises of luxuries they have not earned, expose him. You must consider Rome."

Tullius sat before his son and clasped his hands urgently together and said eagerly, "Do you understand, my son?"

"Yes," said Marcus. "You have spoken of it often, but I did not understand it fully until tonight." He wanted to rise and kiss his father on the cheek. But he was a young man now. However, he could not entirely restrain himself, so he took one of his father's hands and laid his lips against it, in a filial gesture. Tullius trembled, closed his eyes, and prayed for his son.

Tullius again spoke of God. "While a knowledge of God brings an ineffable joy, it also brings pain. When I look upon the beauty of the world which He made I am filled with sadness, for it is impossible for me as a mortal man to retain that first moment of exultation and awareness. I know that the beauty I see is only a reflection of greater and more immortal beauty.

"There are moments when the very thought of God fills me with sharp ecstasy, beyond which rapture purely of the senses and mind is feeble. It is an ecstasy self-contained and complete, needing nothing else to ornament it. It lies in the heart like a globe of fire, giving life and joy and radiance as it burns and consumes that which is gross and unworthy. What is this thing beyond the imagination of men, so that it cannot be put truly into words? Memory of life before birth, when the soul recognizes the hand of the Creator? Nostalgia for the celestial vision, long lost, and forever mourned? Or of an existence of man from which we have fallen? If so, how great was that fall from knowledge!

"Pray that you will never forget that without God man is nothing, and all the affairs of his life have no significance and are like the dust of the desert which blows without a destination."

He was suddenly exhausted. He lay back in his chair and fell at once into a deep sleep. Marcus rose and covered his father with a blanket and put a hassock under his feet and turned the wick of the lamp lower. I will remember, Father, he swore to Tullius and lifted his hand solemnly in the gesture of an oath.

Many years later he was to write, "How can I recapture the surety and the unquestioning knowledge of my youth? The world is too much for us. It not only destroys our youth but destroys our certitude. Nevertheless, I must act as if I still possessed it. God can ask nothing more of us than our intention, for we are essentially weak and must rely upon Him for all things, even our breath."

The next morning Tullius was very ill, and Phelon applied his potions and his medicines.

"He has been this ill before," Helvia said. "He will recover." She put aside her distaff, dismissed her maids, and said to Marcus, "Sit down. I must talk with you. You are a most unworldly young man and you must be sensible."

Marcus obediently sat down. He looked at his mother, and saw her olive-tinted face flushed with rose as a girl's. To him, she was young as ever. She has her certitude, thought Marcus. Her hair was bound about her head tightly, that hair so like Quintus', turbulent and unrestrained and thickly curling and very dark. She was plumper than in her early youth, though she was still but thirty-two. Her massive breast pushed against her yellow chiton, and her waist was thick under its girdle. She looks like Ceres, thought Marcus, the mother of the earth and all that grows.

"Your grandfather and your father have talked with you, and your tutor," she said. She moved her hand a little as if dismissing the vagaries of men. "Now you must have a woman's wisdom and rationality. Men have dreams; women have reality. Both are necessary.

"What is a true man? I have heard discussions of this in our household, and sometimes I have become impatient. What would these men do if I left my distaff and my kitchen and sat at their feet? They would have no linen and no wool to cover themselves, and their plates would be empty. In spite of their dreams and their lofty periods, men are tremendous eaters. They eat much more than do women and can become querulous over a sauce or a lack of one, and are very petulant at the table."

Marcus, in spite of his anxiety about his father, began to laugh. His mother laughed with him, comfortably.

"Your grandfather is all patriotism and declared there is nothing else. But if a slave is neglectful about a seam he flies into a rage. Your father thinks only of God, but if a dish is undercooked he rejects it with distress. One would think such mighty thinkers above mundane little comforts. But a man cherishes his comforts and is offended if they are overlooked. If women ever become philosophers or scientists or artists and neglect the loom and the frying pans, who will raise the loudest plaint, in spite of their previous admiration of female prodigies? Men."

His mother's commonsense was like a warmth to Marcus' heart. "We are creatures of the earth as well as creatures of the mind," said Helvia. "The grandfather scoffs at what he calls my materialism and preoccupation with daily things. But he is the first to complain if the household does not run smoothly. Your father, when we were young, offered me books of poetry and philosophy, no doubt hoping I would be another Aspasia. But if his boots were not skillfully lined with fur in the winter and his blankets were threadbare and none other available, he would eye me with reproach. What patience women have with these childlike creatures! I wonder not that some women murder their husbands but that more of them do not."

Marcus laughed again. He said to himself now, Why is it I never really appreciated her before but accepted all she did for me as my due? Did I think my comforts sprang automatically out of the air? Did I think invisible hands wove my garments and cooked my food? He looked about him at the room, which was filled with instruments of industry, looms and distaffs and sewing tables and needles and lengths of linen and wool and cotton. The room had a cheerful and bustling air. Here, thought Marcus, is truly the heart of the household. If Helvia never noticed the changeful greens in a tree nor was never uplifted at the trill of a bird, she moved the house purposefully and presided over it like Juno, the mother of children. A world where women neglected their duties would be a world without neatness and overcome with chaos. Women were the balance wheel of life, and if that balance were no more man would revert to beasthood.

"I will speak of men," said Helvia, "and in this I include women for we are part of mankind, and perhaps the most important part. The male gods disport themselves; one discounts Venus, who caters only to the passions of men. Wisdom is with women, as it is with Minerva. Self-control is with women, as it is with Diana. The care of men and children is with women, as it is with Juno. You will observe that those goddesses most preoccupied with the passions of men, and the satisfying of those passions, are the unproductive goddesses. They contribute nothing to the orderliness of life. They are disrupting forces. A woman never stepped into a man's shoes without throwing life into upheaval. There is a place for everything, including the roles of men and women. You will observe the order of life, each thing in its place and doing its duty. Only man is disorderly, with his inordinate demands. He will bend even God to his will, if he can. That is not true of women. Women are the servers of God. We are the dutiful."

Marcus was amazed. From what source did his mother derive her wisdom?

"The modern Roman woman," said Helvia, reaching for a length of linen and beginning to apply her busy needle, "has been seduced by men into the belief that she must take a part in the affairs of men. With what result? Modern woman has become as full of vagaries as men are. She has taken on the evils of men, and the trivialities. She has not absorbed the loftiness of some men. She has absorbed only their childishness. She is demanding, insistent, vengeful, enamored with her body which appeals to lust. In all ways she has become a slave, not an emancipated woman as she believes. She is a toy, and a boresome one after her first youth, and not the Aspasia she thought. Once her youth has gone, and her charms, what is left? She has no household arts, she is no comforter. She is an aging harpy. If she meddles in politics, it is with disaster. She corrupts, does not uplift. She neglects her children for games and sports and the market place. Her children reflect her disorder and her silly crimes. They have no respect for her, for she does not deserve respect. Her husband dishonors her, for she was never a wife."

"But surely there are wise women," said Marcus.

"Certainly, there are wise women," said Helvia, biting off a thread. "They are those who no matter where life throws them remember always they are women. Let us consider Aspasia again. She was beloved of Pericles, and he consulted her because he was a wise man and needed the sound wisdom of a woman. Never did she forget that she was a female, unlike modern women, who have created only misery. She gave to Pericles, and did not demand things beyond her nature. She was always a woman. But how many are there like Aspasia in Rome?"

"You, Mother, are interested in business and investments," said Marcus.

"So I am. When was a woman not interested in money? That is not invading the interests of men, who are frequently gamblers and improvident. Men are taken with flights of fancy, even your grandfather. I invest prudently, for I am a conserver. I prefer a small sound return to promises of fools' gold. It is no accident that Aspasia was a mathematician. Women are always for totals and balances. They have orderly minds. Did Aspasia die on the streets? No. One can be sure she had sound investments.

"My son, when I advise you concerning your future it will be well if you listen. A true man is known by his control of his appetites. He is characterized by devotion to family and family affairs, does not lose his temper easily, honors money because it represents labor and confers honor on the possessor, rejects all things which reflect badly on his country, his gods and his family. He has endless patience and calm, and always brings matters to a satisfactory conclusion, good for himself and his family. He is a good husbandman, careful in all things, long-suffering and indifferent to pain. He is never disillusioned because he has never suffered illusions and false fantasies and improbable dreams. He does his duty. Above all, my son, he does his duty, prudently and after long thought."

She then dismissed him. There was work to do.

Years later Marcus wrote, "I received different advice from my tutor, my grandfather, my father and my mother. Yet, like the four petals of the sweet-smelling wild rose, they were one, and made a perfect flower. In all essentials, they did not disagree. Blessed is that man who had a wise tutor, a stern grandfather, a spiritual and tender father, and a prudent mother!"

CHAPTER EIGHT

There will never be a place so lovely to my heart as this island, thought Marcus as he stood on the bank and looked at the rivers and the illuminated distant view of the hills.

It was near sunset. He gazed at Arpinum. It was a rising line of broken, golden radiance, brilliantly gold, brilliantly light, against the shining bronze mountain on which it lay. The time was early autumn, with all the trees burning red or gold or copper on the island; the rivers were blazingly blue. The waters chattered busily, or murmured against the bank on which Marcus stood. The birds conversed; the wind was sweet with brazen grass and ripening fruit and heavy grain. Blue haze enveloped distant trees and distant water. A heron paused on its stilts to look at the youth, then fished in the water. Three crows, gossiping merrily, laughed among themselves on a branch. A cow lowed; a sheep called to her young. Somewhere goats exchanged a burst of mirth. Why do all things laugh innocently, except man? thought Marcus.

He saw the bridge leading to the mainland. No one had been there before, as it arched over the waters, for this was a private island owned by the grandfather. But now a figure stood on it, looking down at the rushing river, the figure of a maiden. A slave from the household? thought Marcus.

A wanderer from Arpinum? But girls of discreet family did not wander. They were always chaperoned, and slaves from the household were kept busy by Helvia. It was approaching the hour of dinner. Curious, Marcus sauntered diffidently toward the figure, squinting his eyes against the red sun.

He reached the approach to the bridge. The young girl, who was leaning on the stone ledge, turned to look at him idly, and without apparent curiosity. She did not speak. Marcus hesitated. Should he tell her that the bridge was private, as was the island? But she did not stir in confusion, nor remove her folded arms from the parapet. It was as if he, not herself, was the intruder.

"Greetings," said Marcus at last, setting foot on the bridge.

"Greetings," she responded in the softest and clearest voice. She looked down at the river then at the island, then at Arpinum. "It is beautiful," she said.

Marcus slowly approached her. She smiled at him without shyness. She was tall and graceful, almost as tall as himself, and near his age. She wore a green chiton and a filmy white palla, and from her dress and her ornamented sandals he guessed she was no servant girl. She had an air of assurance and simple dignity. Then he could see her more clearly, and he thought he had never seen a girl so lovely. She was like spring, exquisitely formed and budding. Auburn hair flowed far below her waist, burnished in the setting sun, and rippling like water. It seemed to catch fire around her face, which was luminously pale. She had eyes of so deep a blue that the color overflowed, and her lashes were as auburn as her hair, as were her brows. Her nose was fine and slender and like marble, and so were her chin and throat. Her mouth was sweet, as full and fresh as raspberries, with a deep indentation on her lower lip as if laughter had kissed it.

"I am Marcus Tullius Cicero," said Marcus. He could not look away from this entrancing creature, and stared openly.

Her face changed, but only a little. She smiled; she had teeth like shining porcelain. "I am Livia Curius," she said. "I am visiting family friends in Arpinum. This is your island, is it not?"

"It is my grandfather's," said Marcus. He wondered why the girl's face had changed so subtly when he had told her his name. "Did you not know?"

"Yes," she said. She turned her profile to him and studied the river. "But, is beauty forbidden? Do you feel offended that I am here?"

There was spirit in her voice. "No," said Marcus. Her name hung on his thoughts. Then he remembered. Quintus Curius, the formidable, dark and intellectual youth who was the friend of Lucius Sergius Catilina, the sullen and hateful youth who was his, Marcus' enemy, solely because Lucius was his enemy!

"Is Quintus Curius your cousin, Lady Livia?" asked Marcus.

The girl shrugged lightly. She still contemplated the river. "A distant one," she said. "I am the betrothed of Lucius Sergius Catilina. I believe you were schoolmates?"

What else has she heard about me? thought Marcus, disturbed. He wanted the girl to look at him, to see him as he was. Then he thought: Betrothed!

"Is Lucius here also?" he asked.

"No. He is again in Greece." Her tone was indifferent. "Do you not correspond?" Now she looked at him fully and the blue of her eyes lilted.

"No," said Marcus. "We are enemies."

He knew he was blunt. He stood near the girl and stared at the river. "You must know that, Lady Livia."

"Yes. I know. Even if I also know that Lucius is a liar." She spoke calmly. "But a delightful liar. He is marrying me because I am an heiress. Let us talk of pleasanter things."

Marcus was silent. Was it his imagination only that the colors of land and air became suddenly more vivid and brighter and warmer? He let his glance move sideways. He saw the white and dimpled arms of the girl lying on the arched parapet. He saw her dainty hands and the rings upon them, and the bracelets and the colored fingernails. The wind lifted her veil and it blew across his face. It seemed to have a natural scent of its own, as sweet as spring.

"Why are you marrying Lucius?" he asked, understanding he was rude, but an urgency was upon him. "You say he is a liar."

"But a delightful liar." She turned her head and looked at him and she was laughing. "And, is he not marvelous in his appearance?"

"Fascinating," said Marcus, wryly. "But something more is required in a husband." The girl's smile was a little mocking as she surveyed him.

"Show me your island," she said, with a quick maidenly hauteur.

"It is sunset," he said.

He hated himself for being so abrupt, but he wondered where the guardians of the girl were, and why she moved about so freely. Now she was openly laughing at him, and dimples flashed about her mouth. "I heard you were very circumspect," she said. "Lucius and my cousin do not speak of others often, but they spoke of you, as if you were irritating them constantly."

"I was not brought up to hate, but I hate them," said Marcus, and he disliked her laughter which seemed directed at him.

Her face changed again. "I dislike my cousin, Quintus," she said. "A sour and savage youth. I am not offended by what you have said. And, as you said yourself, Lucius Catilina is fascinating. Moreover, my guardians have arranged and approved the marriage, and what have I to say? I exchange money for a great name. It is a fair exchange."

A sensation of calamity came to Marcus. He wanted to seize the girl's arm and shake her and tell her she must not marry Lucius. But she was gazing at him with coolness as if affronted. "Show me your island," she said again to him.

Before he could say another word she had run behind him and was racing down the bridge to the island, her palla floating behind her like a sunlit cloud. Her spirit, her quick changes of mood, her subtle expressions, dazed Marcus. He followed her more slowly. She stood on the bank as if with impatience at his delay. "Look at that heron!" she cried, and waved her hand at the silent and impassive bird. "He is not afraid of us."

"Why should he be afraid? He knows I will not hurt him," said Marcus.

The girl was still again. The blue of her eyes dwelled on his face thoughtfully. Then, just as he believed that he had made her understand she laughed merrily at him, and ran back from the bank like a flash of quicksilver. She made hardly a sound; she was like an unpredictable wood nymph, illusive at one moment, too open and free the next, quiet for an instant, then mocking. Marcus followed the faintly fragrant movement of her into the small forest of the island. She was nowhere in sight. Had he dreamed that he had seen her and had talked to her? He looked about him through the dim aisles of poplars and oaks. Behind him the waters plashed and revealed themselves like blue and racing light, but here it was dusky, the silence broken by the rushes of forest creatures and the slow falling of vivid leaves.

"Livia?" he called.

There was no answer. Had this baffling girl circled, returned to the bridge and crossed it, forgetting him or dismissing him as of no consequence?

"Livia?" he called again, less surely now. Why did the forest aisles appear so empty now, so alien, as they had never appeared before? Why was the fragrance of autumn less, and the wind cooler?

A piece of bark fell smartly on his head, and he uttered an exclamation. He looked up at the tree and saw Livia perched as agilely as Quintus on a high branch, laughing down at him like a wood nymph indeed, her green dress vivid against the scarlet leaves, her palla like mist floating about her, her lovely face shining with beauty.

"You are no woodsman," she said in her sweet and penetrating voice, "or you should have found me at once." She threw another piece of bark down on him, gleefully, then like Quintus she called, "Catch me!"

Marcus did not pause to consider it unseemly that a betrothed girl should behave like a boy. He was up on the first branch before he realized it. The girl bounded higher above him and his face became hot at the sight of suddenly revealed and beautifully formed smooth young calves and thighs. She seemed to climb without effort, without tearing her clothing, without uttering irritable noises at any scraping of rough twig or branch. Then she was easily at the top of the tree, swinging lightly. She did not look down at the climbing youth. She looked, from her perch, at some distant scene and began to sing in soft voice, some weird, hardly heard melody. Marcus paused halfway to gaze up at her, full of wonder. Never had he met such a strange and delightful creature, untouchable, removed, full of fantasy. She gave the aspect of one alone, unaware of man, clothed in secrets, immortal. The high light flashed on her uplifted face and in her wildly blue eyes, and Marcus, for an instant, was conscious of a little fear. Her veil, freed at that height from restraining foliage, lifted and blew in the wind, concealing her features one second, like a nymph in moonlight, revealing them the next. Her hair was a glow of fire on her shoulders and breast and back. She swung and sang, detached from the earth, in an aloneness that defied the youth, or separated him from her.

Then she glanced down at him and her face changed again, became solemn, almost cold.

"It is dangerous," said Marcus. "For a girl."

She regarded him musingly as if he spoke in a language she did not know, as one listens to the conversation of creatures not of one's kind.

"Shall I help you down?" he asked, afraid of her remoteness.

She did not answer. Without visible effort she stepped down through the branches, balancing gracefully, descending without sound, never once slipping or clutching. She passed him and did not look at him. She fell to the ground from the last branch as lightly as a falling leaf. Then, her head drooping a little, she stood as if waiting, and Marcus, climbing down, wondered if she waited for him or for some voice he would never hear, or some call beyond his ears.

Then he stood beside her. They did not speak. They did not look at each other. They only looked through the arches of the trees at the incandescent water, now tipped with crimson on the hurrying crests. All at once a sense of peace and fulfillment came to Marcus. It was rare for him to make an overt gesture to anyone, out of his shyness and his respect for others. But his hand moved a little and took the hand of the girl. He expected her to change her mood again and snatch her hand away, offended or laughing. But her hand lay in his, smooth, cool as leaves.

"What were you singing?" asked Marcus in as low a voice as he could.

The girl said nothing.

"It was the sound of the wind in the spring," said Marcus, "or like a fountain at night when everyone is asleep."

"It is my own song," said the girl. She looked at him again, and again he was startled by the absolute blue of her eyes, darkened faintly now by her lashes. "They say I am a very peculiar girl. They do not know."

"Then I am peculiar also," said Marcus. The girl smiled at him. "Yes," she said. "Were you not I would not be standing with you now." Her young breast, just rising under her dress, lifted and trembled. "They do not know," she repeated. "I have never told them. My dear mother had a mortal disease and while she was dying my father plunged his dagger into his breast and died with her. They think I did not see them, but I stood in the doorway in the moonlight. When my father was dying he held my mother in his arms, and they died with their lips together, and my father said, 'Where you go, my beloved, there will I go also.' I have never forgotten. I sing my song to them, so they will hear me in the Elysian Fields."

Marcus thought the story not horrifying, but infinitely moving. The girl said, as if she heard his thoughts, "I was five years old, my mother was but twenty, and my father a year older. I did not grieve for them; I do not grieve for them now. They could not endure to be separated. Not even the gods could part them."

Marcus thought of his own parents. Was it possible that disparate as they were in character they were one flesh? Was marriage truly sacred, as the old laws asserted?

The girl startled him by speaking in a different voice. "Why was the heron not afraid of you? They are the shyest of birds."

"I have never hurt one of them, nor any other creature," said Marcus. "Surely God loves them also. I respect that love in them."

The girl dropped his hand. She bounded ahead of him, her palla caught by the evening breeze. Marcus did not follow her. She raced to the bank and the bridge, and then she was upon it.

"Will you come again, Livia?" he called after her.

But she did not answer. She disappeared as a nymph disappears, and he was alone in the forest, to wonder again if the brief and baffling encounter had occurred at all. He was only sure of it when he felt a sharp abandonment as though something ineffably lovely had left him after the smallest of glimpses.

At dinner that evening he was unusually silent among his grandfather, his father, and his adoring brother, Quintus. His mother, as befitted an old Roman, did not dine with the men. Tullius had recovered, as Helvia had predicted, from the bout of illness which had brought him close to death.

"Something has disturbed our Marcus," he said.

"It is the pangs of youth," said the grandfather. "How I remember them! All things seemed wondrous and engrossing to me at that age. Yet, in the light of years, how ordinary they truly were!"

But Tullius was not satisfied, because he still had dreams.

"Do not let your dreams die, Marcus," he said in a low voice to his son.

Marcus could not understand his curious unease and his inner excitement. He knew these had been aroused by the strange girl he had encountered—if he had really encountered her at all. But what they portended, what they meant, he did not know. He thought about her betrothal to Lucius Sergius Catilina, and his mind recoiled incredulously. It was something out of place, out of reality, not to be accepted. A marriage between those two would be like a marriage between a nymph and an evil centaur. A marriage between a stone and a flower. A marriage between a dryad and a wolf. He put down his knife and stared emptily at his plate.

"What is it, Marcus?" asked Tullius.

But Marcus could not answer. For once, he could not speak to his father, nor to anyone. Something was sealed within him. So, he thought, there are times when there is no communication, not even among those who love. Could he speak to Archias, who was a poet and wise? No. All at once he thought, I am sure of nothing, and he passed completely into manhood.

Then Quintus, who was feeling his own first surges of adolescence, said, "Marcus is in love." And he grinned delightedly at his brother.

"Nonsense," said the grandfather. "He knows no girls, and he has not yet passed through the ceremonies of his age."

"He is in love with life," said Tullius, remembering his own youth.

I am in love with Livia, thought Marcus, and suddenly he was taken by ecstasy and by desolation and a sense of loss which in itself was pleasurable.

CHAPTER NINE

The news from Rome was grievous and the family wondered if they should return. There was long discussions between the grandfather, the father, and the tutor, Archias.

"Why is not Marcus interested in his country in these days of crisis?" asked the grandfather.

"At present, he is dreaming," said Tullius with apology. But he did not know of what his son was dreaming. "Let him be for a little." He was hurt that his son had not confided in him.

Each day Marcus haunted the bridge, the banks, the forest paths where he had seen Livia. But she did not appear. With less than half an ear he heard the agitated discussions in the family circle about Rome; for once he was not eager or listening. All his mind and heart and body and soul were involved with one mysterious girl whom he had seen but for a few minutes. He began to write poetry at a tremendous rate. He was like a young tree growing and absorbed in itself at the edge of a battlefield, aware only of sun and wind and the stretching of its limbs and the thrusting of its leaves. Even Quintus, his playmate, found himself avoided. Seeing his dreaming expression, his vagueness and absent eyes, Helvia thought, with the knowledge of women, My son is in love. With a slave girl? She did not approve of a man of a family cavorting with slaves, though she understood this was done in Rome. To her it was supremely immoral and distasteful and not to be countenanced. But all her discreet watching did not bring her enlightenment. There were pretty little slave girls of ten and twelve and even Marcus' age; he did not look at them.

The autumn was drawing to an end; only at noon was the sun warm and golden; the wind had a sharpness in its edge. Marcus began to think that he had dreamed of Livia Curius, for sometimes his dreams were very vivid and on rousing himself from them he had a momentary difficulty in separating fact from fantasy. Once, he remembered—and it was only this summer—he had been half-sleeping in the warmth, deep in the wild grass, his back against a tree, while Quintus had circled about him examining, climbing, exclaiming to himself in his usual exuberant fashion, sometimes hurling himself on the ground in somersaults, sometimes leaping up a great tree to inspect a bird's nest, sometimes imitating the vociferous crows, sometimes just broad-jumping or throwing a wooden spear.

Then it appeared to Marcus that the sun darkened and a host of men, fierce in armor and with violent faces, suddenly emerged from the forest and set upon Quintus and did him savagely to death. Marcus could not move; he heard Quintus' cries; he heard the clash of swords and the movements of terrible enemies. He tried to rise, but iron lay over his flesh and held him down. He tried to scream, and not a sound left his lips. Then all was quiet again and Quintus was lying dead and shattered in his blood near his brother's feet. A hideous darkness fell on Marcus' eyes. When he could open them again he saw Quintus crouching to spring on a grass frog, and all was light and serenity once more. Marcus uttered a great cry; he struggled to his feet, dazed, his heart pounding madly, and he seized his brother to him and embraced him tightly, to Quintus' innocent amazement. Quintus stood still and let Marcus weep over him and hold him.

"You were asleep, Marcus," he said at last. "It must have been a fearful dream."

Marcus let him go. Yes, it had been a most fearful dream. Marcus was not overly superstitious, though he possessed considerable mysticism. Archias, when he scoffed at omens and portents as unworthy of a civilized man, yet admitted there was a vast area beyond the sight and ear of man to which man was blind and deaf. From whence had the gods arisen? Who had set the boundaries of the world? Who had fashioned everything in its intricacy and delicate precision? Who had created Law? Man, Archias said, truly knew nothing at all.

"Superstition rises out of lack of knowledge," Archias would say. "Nevertheless, millions of things will always be beyond man's comprehension. The scientists say that birds hear sounds and see colors we shall never see; the dog hears what man's dull ear will never discern. The stars are beyond us; what are they, more than what the scientists say they are, which may be their error? Man cannot comprehend God with his senses; it must come from his soul. What little comprehension man has of God comes from something intuitive in himself, more profound than instinct. It is that intuition which is the civilizing agent in man, the source of pillars and columns, painting and music, the foundation of Law. But we ponder on it—unless we are an Aristotle or a Socrates—only to our confusion and dismay."

Where does fantasy end and reality begin? Marcus would ask himself, haunting daily the places where he had seen Livia. Now he could believe in wood nymphs and strange spirits and apparitions very easily. What of the voices of Delphi? The books of the sybils? There were intellectual and worldly men who, if they did not actually believe in these things, admitted that man knew very little and that it was arrogant of him to think that reason explained all and that ultimate knowledge will ever be the possession of mankind. Archimedes had said that with a lever of a certain length, and standing in a proper place, he could move the world. Some day man indeed, as the ancient books said, would fly the oceans and the continents like a bird of passage, and might invade the moon. But what would these things tell him of the deeps and chasms and strangenesses that lived in his soul and defied the philosophers?

All Marcus' senses were heightened in these days. He saw lights on leaves he had never noticed before; the feeling and texture of rough bark under his hands excited him. The cry of migrating birds filled him with ecstatic loneliness. He was exalted at the sight of the last flowers. The river spoke to him in mysterious tongues. He wanted to be alone at all times, to feel the exaltation that kept sweeping over him. He longed for Livia, fantasy or no fantasy. He was like one exiled, yet rejoicing in exile, feeling a delightful melancholy. He looked at the moon, and it was no longer a mere satellite of the world, as the dull scientists said, but a huge golden secret on which golden men dwelt and uttered mystical words. It lay on branch and fading grass and on the rooftop, and on Marcus' hands, and he trembled with joy and with sadness. He thought of God, and God seemed nearer than ever, more imminent, all pervading.

In short, he was in love. The gods stood all about him.

He had never considered Venus and her son Eros as worthy deities. Venus was a wanton. Eros was simply the Roman Cupid. Marcus had been bored earlier by love stories. Why did men let themselves be seized by folly, so that great men became fools and less than beasts? Archias had said that the most immense poetry came from the heart of love, but Marcus had been incredulous. Archias had smiled at him with amusement. "You are confusing love with lust," he had said. "Ah, my pupil, you will learn in time."

Now Marcus understood. It was useless for him to tell himself that it was impossible to love a girl he had seen but once, and she so peculiar and so elusive and not to be understood. But in the very moment of his rationality and his ridicule of himself, he remembered the coolness and smoothness of her hand, the blue of her eyes, the fire of her hair against the sun. A mere chit. He would die if he did not see her again. A weird and laughing and indifferent girl, content with her betrothal to a moral monster; she was not worthy of consideration. He would die if he did not see her again.

"In these days of Rome's peril, we must return," said the old grandfather, and spoke of Drussus who was yet but a name to Marcus. Marcus haunted the thinning forest. He did not truly expect to see Livia ever again, but he searched. What songs the rivers sang! What eternal mystery lay in a blade of grass! How tremendous was the light of the sun! What beating heart waited in the forest! How blue was the autumnal sky! What a thing it was to be a man, conscious of firm young limbs and young body and prehensile hands! Each day was a marvel. Each step was an exultation. Each vista was filled with half-seen shapes of beauty. It was glorious to draw breath. It was a rapture to be alive. Why had he never known this before? His eyes swam with dreams.

Then one day he came upon Livia again. She sat on a pile of crimson oak leaves under a thinning oak tree, singing softly to herself and running her hands through the leaves. Marcus had passed that tree scores of times. Yet, there was Livia in a white dress with a mantle of blue wool over her shoulders and a blue silk cloth rippling over her hair. But they were not so blue as her eyes, which shone and sparkled in her luminous pale face. He stopped and looked at her, and it seemed that all creation rushed to this one spot and held its breath, waiting, and never had he felt such joy and delight and fear.

"I have been here every day but you have never found me," said Livia, gravely. "You were looking everywhere, but you have not seen me; have you forgotten I lived?"

Marcus stepped slowly toward her.

"For what were you looking, as you dreamed and walked?" asked Livia.

"You," he said.

She shook her head in wondering denial. "But I was here all the time."

"If you saw me, why did you not speak?" asked Marcus. He sat on his heels and looked at her, afraid to breathe loudly for fear that she would disappear and she would be only a fantasy again.

"I do not speak to men who ignore me," she said in a lofty tone.

Then she laughed, her whole face sparkling. "I was in trees and watched you from above. I was behind a trunk, and you passed within paces of me. I sat in grass and felt your footsteps. But you did not find me!"

She has a voice like summer water, thought Marcus.

She was not a girl like others he had seen, in the women's quarters of his grandfather's houses, or in the streets with their mothers or servants about them. She was not like the girls he had glimpsed in temples, quietly extending their offerings, and praying. He was a youth and he had been stirred by rounded limbs and rising young bosoms and smooth necks and arms. But it had been a passing emotion, which had embarrassed him later when he had looked at his mother and had wondered about her and his father in bed. In some way the very excitement in his loins had seemed shameful and disloyal to his parents.

But he looked at Livia openly, without embarrassment, and only with the most urgent longing and passionate love, this girl he had seen so briefly once, this girl who might have been a fantasy. He looked at her lips, red and indented on the lower lip. He looked into her eyes, and at the curve of her throat. He looked at her breast and the slenderness of her waist. He looked as a man looks, forgetting everything else.

"You hid from me," he said. The thought was a delight.

She let leaves slide through her fingers, and her mood changed again and she was serious. She appeared to forget him, as she watched the leaves. The light trembled on her throat, her cheek, her hands.

"Why did you come at all?" he asked her, enchanted.

"I do not know," she answered. "Who are you? Lucius calls you Chickpea, or Vetch. You are not rich; you are not noble. You were not born in Rome, but in this lonely place. You are not so handsome as Lucius, who looks like a god. You are not worldly. Your clothing is not rich. You are a country youth. Your conversation was not learned when I saw you last.

You will never be invited to great houses; you will never stand in the Forum before multitudes. You are, as my cousin has said, of no consequence."

She gazed at him candidly.

"Nevertheless, what I have said is of no importance, nor what the others have said. Why have I come here today, and all the other days, to see you even if you did not see me? I do not know."

She pushed back her masses of glowing hair with restless hands and stared into the distances. "Why did I tell you about my parents? I never speak of them to anyone. Why is the look of you pleasurable to me, and a comforting? Why do I think of you when I awake, a youth I spoke to but once?"

She looked at him and frowned, as if he had offended her.

"Tell me, Marcus Tullius Cicero."

"I do not know, either," he said. "But you have seen me searching for you. Why did I search?"

"We ask each other only questions," she said. "It explains nothing."

"Nothing can ever be explained," said Marcus. There was no world; there was only this girl on the pile of crimson leaves, with her white wool chiton outlining her body as noble marble outlines a figure on a monument.

She considered. Then she said, "It is because you speak like me, and think like me. No matter what I say you do not smile as if at folly. When I am with you it is as wonderful as if I were alone. I am not conscious that you are another being."

Marcus, who was never in love before, said a wise thing: "That is the essence of oneness, that one is not alienated, not aware that another is a separate being, but only one with one's self."

He was suddenly dazzled, for the girl's face was radiant. "Yes, it is so," she said. "It is what my parents must have known."

She held out her hand frankly to him, and he fell on his knees before her and took the white and slender fingers. She made a murmurous sound of satisfaction and she smiled at him tenderly.

A ragged oak leaf, large and scarlet, drifted down from the tree and settled directly on the girl's left breast and lay there on the whiteness of her clothing like a splash of blood. It was a little wet and it moved with her breath and she was unaware of it.

Marcus was a Roman, and Romans are superstitious, and a long stiffening ran over his body as he looked at that leaf which resembled nothing more than a bleeding wound. It was nothing to him that his logical mind cried that he was absurd and that this was only a leaf. A curious darkening seemed suddenly to invade the forest, in which the girl's face was as white as death and her eyes too still. The evil splash on her breast appeared to expand ominously. Marcus felt all the fear and dread that he had experienced when he had dreamed of the violent death of his beloved brother, Quintus, and he shuddered.

"What is it, Marcus?" asked Livia.

He reached out and took the leaf, and she watched in wonderment, bewildered by the pallor of his cheeks and the trembling of his lips. He flung the leaf from him, and it was as if he had removed something evil and hideous. "It was only a leaf," he said. He clasped the girl's hand firmly; he was sweating a little even in the coolness of the forest and he could hear his heart in his ears. The girl's eyes narrowed with curiosity and they were brilliantly blue. "Something has disturbed your mind," she said. "Has a god whispered something to you?"

This disturbed Marcus even more. He knew of premonitions; he had had them on several occasions and Archias had scoffed at him. Only a short time ago he had dreamed that the gutters of Rome were filled with bleeding and howling men, and Archias had laughed. Yet something was now happening in Rome and in Italy, and he, heedless youth! had not been listening to the alarmed conversation of his grandfather. His thoughts had been with this girl.

She suddenly pulled her hands from his and jumped to her feet, even while he was struggling with his thoughts and trying to control them. She ran from him through the aisle of the forest, and it was some moments before he could get up and follow her. Now she was waiting, in full autumn sunshine, on the bridge, leaning over the parapet and watching the green water.

"Listen to the rivers sing," she said as he joined her; she did not look at him. "They are singing of the mountains and the forests and the ferns, of nymphs and satyrs and Pan with his pipes, and they are singing of the winter which is coming."

Marcus had regained some control over his emotions. He watched the green and rushing water; it was full of the voices of Echo, melancholy yet tumultuous and full of longing. The bridge appeared to move and the water to carry it along. The sun was hot on Marcus' face but there was a cold wind about his shoulders. Livia's white elbow was near him and he put his hand upon it with something like fierce protection. She began to sing with the rivers, a strange and murmurous song, and she was far from the youth at her side.

"You must not marry Lucius Catilina," he said.

She sang a little more, then turned her head idly and looked at him.

"But I have been betrothed to him since I was ten years old," she said. "Why must I not marry him?"

"He is evil," said Marcus.

The girl half-turned her body and gazed at him thoughtfully. "I do not find him so, Marcus. The opinions of one man are not always the opinions of others. To me, Lucius is very amusing and full of enchantment; he looks like a god. He has a great name. I am rich. It is a fair exchange."

"Nevertheless, he is evil."

"Because you two are enemies?" The girl's eyes were a little mocking.

"No. It was my belief from the beginning, before we fought. He is cruel and without mercy. He strikes at the weakest and the smallest. He has the fascination and beauty of a deadly animal." Marcus paused. "He will cause you suffering, and that I cannot bear to contemplate, Livia, because I love you."

She shook her head in denial. "You must not say that to me, for I am betrothed. My guardians have arranged it. It is a matter of honor; one does not repudiate such. No, you must not say you love me, for that I must not hear."

She laughed sweetly, and the blue of her eyes glittered. "You have not yet gone through the ceremonies of adolescence, but Lucius is a man, and it is to a man that I am betrothed. I am fourteen years old, and of an age to marry. Should I repudiate Lucius my own honor would be lost, and I am an obedient girl and my guardians know best. You must not speak to me of this again."

Marcus was desperate. "But, in the forest you declared that what we felt for each other was what your parents felt for each other! Shall you deny that?"

Her face became clouded. "What has that to do with marriage? It is good and beautiful to dream, but marriage is not for dreamers. My mother was a willful girl; she was betrothed to another, and then she loved my father. Against all the wishes of her parents she married him, against the tears of her mother who had seen an omen. She offended the gods, and especially Juno, the virtuous matron. I have told you how they died, my parents. I dare not invoke the wrath of the gods against us, Marcus."

"You will invoke calamity," said Marcus, still gripping her elbow. The feel of her warm white flesh in his hand made him reckless.

"So you say." The girl was curious again. "Are you a seer, Marcus?"

"I do not know! But I have strange dreams and premonitions!"

The girl made the sign against the evil eye and she was troubled. But she said, "Let us be sensible, for a moment. I am betrothed; you are not even a man. We must not speak of it again. You frighten me."

She pulled her elbow from his hand and ran from him down the arch of the bridge to the mainland, her clothing whirling in the wind. She did not look back.

"Come tomorrow!" cried Marcus after her. But she did not answer. As quickly as she had disappeared before she disappeared now, and there was only sunshine and wind with him and he was alone on the bridge.

Desolation sickened him. He looked at his hands on the parapet and he had the sensation that they did not belong to him because they were empty and meaningless. He heard the rustling of dead leaves; a cloud of scarlet oak leaves fluttered in the air and fell on the green water and they were washed away. Somewhere a bird called. The forest lay on either side of the bridge, gold and red and dark purple, filled with hollow bluish light. But it was no longer beautiful to Marcus, overwhelmed as he was with his terrible forebodings. He believed that in some way he could and must rescue Livia from awful danger. He thought of Lucius Sergius Catilina and so intense were his emotions that he was seized with a desire to kill and destroy, a desire so alien to his nature that it appeared to him that he must be going mad. He thought of all that Lucius was, and he said aloud, beating a clenched fist on the parapet, "No. No!" He looked at Arpinum on its hill and at the silver of the olive groves about it and its cypresses, and it took on a sinister light to him in the autumn sun, as if it hid evil secrets.

Then heavily he returned to the island and walked miserably along the bank, occasionally glancing at Arpinum, which changed its aspect as he walked. Whom could he consult? What god should he invoke? To whom could he tell his desperate fears and his crushed longing? There was his mother. She knew or knew of all the great families of Rome. He experienced a sudden relief. He did not need philosophy now, from Archias, nor the latter's poetry; he did not need the stare of his grandfather's eyes and the mention of honor and the pledged word; he did not need his father's faith in God and obedience. He needed the sensible advice of his mother, who had no philosophy except that concerning a woman's household, no poetry except work, no hopeless resignation.

He came on Quintus, squatting and fishing on a steep bank. He was dropping the bait into the rustling water and swinging it about. Beside him lay a basket of reeds, and in that basket writhed a number of jeweled fish.

Marcus was always happy to see his younger brother. Quintus' olive-tinted face, smooth and bright, was flushed with rose. His eyes were almost blue in the sunshine, for they were as changeful as his mother's, but more lively and vigorous. His thick black curls poured over his sturdy round skull and down his nape. His shoulders were broad and muscular under his brown tunic, and his bare knees were domes of strength, his toes clutching the muddy bank.

"Why not use a net?" asked Marcus. He looked back over his shoulder and saw the bridge clearly.

"Then I should have only fish," said Quintus, reasonably.

"Is that not the object?" said Marcus, squatting beside him and looking with distaste and pity on the dying fish in the basket.

"Not at all," said Quintus. "A net gives fish no opportunity; they are merely dragged from the water to be eaten. But this pole makes the contest between me and them equal; it also gives me pleasure to outwit a fish and deceive him and lure him to my bait. Fish are very clever, indeed, and are not easily deceived."

He sounded, thought Marcus, with affection, exactly like his sensible mother. At that moment Quintus gave an exultant cry, flung the pole up into the air. A fish had taken the bait, and it was a wet, gemmed flash of colors against the sky. It struggled in the air. Quintus deftly pulled in the thin flaxen rope, seized the fish and disengaged it and dropped it triumphantly into the basket. "We shall have a good dinner!" he exclaimed. The fish plopped desperately on the bodies of its mates.

"It seems cruel," said Marcus.

"You did not say that a few days ago when they were broiled in fat and lay on your plate," said Quintus.

"I did not know how beautiful they were," said Marcus.

"You need not eat these," said his brother, casting his bait again. "There will be more for me. Do you prefer to eat weeds? Like our father, who shudders at meats since he became fond of a little goat?"

Marcus did not answer. Quintus said, artfully dangling his bait, "I saw a spider a moment ago devouring a beautiful butterfly, a harmless creature all red and white. The spider was ugly. Nevertheless, it lives according to its nature. When the butterfly was only a worm it devoured fruit, and left the fruit worthless for our eating. That was its nature. The hawk takes the pretty rabbit, and the pretty rabbit destroys our mother's garden, which she lays in the spring. The eagle takes the hawk, which eats vermin."

"A philosopher," said Marcus with indulgence. "Is Archias teaching you well, then?"

Quintus made a comical face. "Archias has only thoughts. I have observation. What a thing it is to be a philosopher! One's stomach is never revolted."

He caught another fish and Marcus averted his eyes. He saw the distant bridge. He remembered Quintus' arch, sly glance. "Did you see me at the bridge?" he asked.

"With that girl?" said Quintus. "Yes. Who is she?"

"She is visiting in Arpinum. Her name is Livia Curius."

"You were very interested in her," said Quintus, preparing new bait. "I could see that she seemed pretty. Are you going to marry her?"

Marcus felt a deep convulsion in his heart. "I wish to," he muttered.

"She ran away," said Quintus. "Like a nymph. Girls are tiresome. And, is she not very free, to be wandering away alone from her relatives? She ran wildly, too. Did you offend her?"

"I do not know," said Marcus.

"You have seen her before?" asked Quintus, with deep interest.

"Yes."

"But we do not know her."

"I do."

"Then you must speak to Grandfather and our mother, Marcus."

"To our mother, Quintus. I have already decided that."

"She is wiser than Grandfather, our father, and Archias put together," said the young boy. "There is no folly in her. If you want that girl and mother is pleased, then she will contrive that you have her."

"It is not so easy. She is betrothed to Lucius Catilina."

Quintus frowned. "She is content?"

"She obeys her guardians."

Quintus shook his head. "Then you must seek another wife."

Marcus stood up. He looked down at his brother's head, then tugged playfully at the glossy black curls. "It is not so easy," he repeated, and went away. He thought that Quintus immediately forgot him in his sport. But the younger boy looked after his brother and his face was disturbed. Quintus knew of the stern stubbornness of Marcus and his quiet resistance when opposed on important things. It was far less arduous to move a heavy stone than Marcus when his will was set. He had the strength of ambushed armies.

Marcus found his mother as usual among her slave girls, spinning industriously, for she was preparing the new blankets for the winter. She saw his face and dismissed the girls kindly, twisted a recalcitrant thread then remarked, "You are troubled. What is it, my son?"

He sat on a stool near her and she stopped spinning for a moment or two. "Do you know the Curius family, my mother?"

Helvia considered, then she inclined her head. "Not closely, but enough. They have fallen on degenerate days, all but one branch of the family. What have they to do with you, Marcus?"

He found, to his astonishment, that he could speak freely to his mother and tell her of Livia. The spinning wheel was humming again; Marcus could see his mother's profile, thoughtful, full of life and youthful vitality and color. Her expression was never mobile; once she frowned slightly at the mention of Lucius Sergius Catilina. Otherwise she listened with calm passivity, sometimes smoothing a thread. Her plump feet never stopped at the wheel. The late sunshine touched her riotous black curls, as glossy as Quintus'. Then when he had finished she dropped her hands in her lap and fixed her beautiful eyes on her son and considered him.

"You will not be a man until the spring," she said. "Yet, you are in love. I speak no ridicule. I saw your father from behind a curtain in the women's quarters of my father's house. He had come to visit with his father. When I saw him I fell in love at once. He seemed a young Hermes to me, and I was no older than your Livia."

"Hermes? My father?" said Marcus, who thought the imagery very humorous. She was smiling at him, as if following his thoughts. "I, too, was young," she said. "I told my father that night that there would be no other for me. I was not betrothed to another; no word of honor had as yet been given. My father was not agreeable, but I was his only daughter and one knows how men dote on their daughters. It was much of a surprise to your father," Helvia added, her eyes fixed on those days. "I think it frightened him. He was hardly older than you. If he could indeed have taken flight I am certain he would have done so. But wiser heads prevailed. Including mine."

I, too, have been wise, in consulting my mother, thought Marcus. But he could hardly believe that once springtime had run wildly in his mother's veins.

Helvia said, "But in the case of your Livia—and how fearful it is now that young girls run about so freely and meet strangers in strange places —the honorable pledge has been given. She is betrothed. Troth is not pledged lightly, even in these days of the decline of our country. You have not said she is unwilling."

"No," said Marcus. "But she is young. She does not know Lucius."

Helvia smiled. "Women know more than you know. However, I agree with you that the Catilinii, though a great patrician family, have become very wicked and decadent. Still, wicked men have been known to adore their wives. Moreover, she spoke of honorable troth, did she not?"

"Yes, it is so. But she does not know truly of Lucius' character. She spoke of him as enchanting."

"All the Catilinii are remarkably handsome. And remarkably vicious." Now Helvia was no longer detached. "That girl is not for you, Marcus. I know of the tragedy of her parents. The girl spoke to you of her parents and did not reproach her father for his willing death. Nevertheless, though she spoke bravely, and with the innocent heart of a young girl, she did not truly forgive her father for deserting her, and she a child of but five years."

She looked at her son straightly. "The girl is afraid to love. She does not love Lucius—therefore, troth or not, she prefers him to you. Love would engross her, enchain her. She would marry one who merely attracts her pleasurably with his appearance. But, if she loves you, and if she married you in two or three years, it would make her miserable. She would live in terror of your death. It is not well to have such passion, and children inherit their parents' passion. There is violence in your Livia, a recklessness which was her father's. No, Marcus, she is not for my son."

Marcus was sick with wretchedness. His practical mother seemed to have become his enemy. "But I love her," he said. "I shall die if she marries Lucius."

"What nonsense," said Helvia, beginning to spin again. "Let us consult together, Marcus. You are going to Greece to study; it is your father's wish. It was his own wish, too, and his father opposed it strenuously. Your father thought that he would spend years roaming the Acropolis at Athens, and wandering through the colonnades of the Parthenon, in eternal blue sunlight, among wise men, conversing. Even when your grandfather said he would give him no money he was not disturbed. Where he would sleep, where he would be sheltered, with what he would buy bread and books, did not occur to him. He would merely gaze, as he said, 'upon the silver city on the silver sea.' It took a long time to convince him that silver cities on silver seas require drachmas also, and the Greeks would not feed him for nothing, nor would they shelter him without money. What dreams men weave, beyond the boundaries of commonsense and finance! He still remembers his dreams; he wishes them fulfilled in you.

"Moreover," said Helvia, "you are not like your father. You are more like your grandfather, whom I respect for all he is a fractious old man. He is sensible. I, too, believe that you will not wander, dreaming, on the Acropolis. You will learn from the wise men. I have not underestimated you, though I worry about your health.

"You have said you will die if you do not have your Livia; men do not die for love. That is but poetry, and life is not poetry. You will go to Greece; your Livia will live in your mind as something sublime and I will not quarrel with that. In the meantime, she will become a factual matron. To you, however, in Greece, she will remain forever young, forever inaccessible, forever lost, and that will bequeath you a beautiful memory. The gods grant that you never encounter her later, surrounded by children, and gossiping merrily with her friends!

"You have work to do in the world. You are a Roman. It is the duty of a Roman not to forget his country for any girl. You must be intelligent and worthy. And you must remember that Livia is honorably bound to Lucius. Honor, above all, is the way of great men."

Each of her sensible and forthright words was a stone falling on Marcus' wounded heart. "I shall never forget Livia," he said.

"Do not forget her, then. But do not forget your duty and your future, and your father's dreams for you. And, for that matter, my dreams for you, and your grandfather's. You owe that duty to your family. You owe it to Rome."

"I shall never forget Livia," Marcus repeated.

She looked at his locked, pale face, and for a moment she was afraid.

"Do not forget her," she urged. "But never try to see her again. Let her be for you forever the silvery Artemis, the unconquered, the adorable one. It will light the dull days of your future life, and there are many dull days in living. What is a life without a dream?"

"What dreams do you have, my mother?" asked Marcus with resentment.

She smiled at him with wry wonder. "My dreams are the dreams of Cornelia, who had her jewels in her sons. What more can a mother ask, that her sons will never dishonor her, but that she may move among her friends and hear their praises? For what else do I dream?"

"You have left out love," said Marcus, stubbornly.

"Do I not love your father and his children?" said Helvia, with a rare anger. "What would your father be without me? I have given him sons; I attend to his household and make him comfortable. I let him go his ways with his books and his esoteric conversations with that Greek poet. I conserve his substance. His life is pleasanter for me, and easy. Because I love him."

She smiled. "I have never disturbed his dreams. I have never shattered his illusions. He should be grateful to me."

Then she became stern again. "There is more to a man's life than the love of women. Go to, Marcus, and become a man."

Marcus, in his despair, thought of speaking to his father, and Helvia must have heard his thoughts. "Speak to Archias if you will, and he will write a poem for you which you may cherish all the days of your life."

She recalled her slave girls. "In the meantime, there are blankets to make and your clothing to be finished for the great festivities. Go and lay flowers before a statue of Venus and sacrifice a pair of doves to her, and tell her of your love for Livia. On second thought, no. Venus is a dangerous divinity and brings disaster to mankind. Did she not give Helen to Paris, and in that giving did she not give death to Troy? What fearful things has she not wrought among men! I think," said Helvia with compassion not untouched by maternal malice, "that it would be better to sacrifice to your patroness, Pallas Athene, and implore her to send you the wisdom you need."

Marcus, dismissed, left the women's quarters in anguish.

"I shall never forget Livia," he vowed to himself. "Nor shall I relinquish her so lightly. Do not Romans say, 'He is able who thinks he is able?' Yes. I have not seen the last of Livia, my love."

But Livia never came to the island again.

In the meantime even the miserable youth could no longer escape the news from Rome, and he listened with great and starting fear for his country. The family returned to Rome. It was no longer safe for them in Arpinum.

CHAPTER TEN

Years before young Marcus Tullius Cicero had been born the desperate people of Italy had tried repeatedly to redress their wrongs under Rome. Flaccus, their champion, had attempted to secure the franchise for them, and had failed. They were governed by all the laws of Rome, but could not defend themselves against martial law; their officers, serving in the very armies of Rome, could be executed at the whim of any capricious Roman court-martial. They could not vote, yet they were taxed even more than any citizen of Rome, their goods confiscated undisputed by any venal tax-gatherer who believed he had not been bribed enough. The dependent communities of Rome were forced to give up their sons to the Roman armies, far out of proportion to those of Roman families. If the Italian sons became officers, even of the highest rank, they were held in lower esteem than a Roman foot soldier, whose word was always taken before theirs. Roman magistrates, seated in Rome, could impose laws on communities they had never seen, and enforce oppressions. A Roman Consul held the power of life and death over Italian provinces, could seize and plunder and rape at will, or impose a sudden regulation, unbearable and unjust, on his fellow Italians, because they were not citizens of Rome. Citizenship alone conferred immunity from the caprices of the army and the magistrates and the Consuls; without that citizenship all men were dogs and soulless, at the disposal of their masters. At one time Roman citizenship was the privilege of all worthy Italians, as well as Romans, but the sturdy rise of the middle-class in the provinces and the communities aroused the fear and anger of those Romans who considered themselves (by virtue of long residence in the city) patricians and nobles and men of consequence, not to be compared with their fellow Italians in remote areas of the peninsula.

The middle-class, by their honor, industry, and finally their money, found it easy, at first, to become Roman citizens upon application, and they brought their virtues, their love of freedom, to a city long grown arrogant, corrupt, and overbearing through conquest and gold. The Urbs resented those who believed that all good men deserved liberty and the rule of their own lives without interference from government.

It was the hatred and fear of the virtues of the provincial middle-classes which eventually caused Rome to make citizenship difficult if not almost impossible to anyone who had no distinguished forebears, had not been born in Rome, and knew no powerful Senators, and despised bribes and resented oppressive taxes which were used to gain the votes of Roman mobs and confer advantages, circuses, free food, and housing on those mobs. One Roman patrician said contemptuously, "If the middle-class has any function at all it is to work to provide us with taxes, with which we can bribe the mobs of Rome and keep them contented and docile. It is true that the plebs of Rome are mere animals, but there are so many of them and we need their votes for our power! Let the middle-class be our servant to that end, for the new man is enamored of work and saving and industry and all the other vulgar pursuits."*

The middle-class in Rome, largely without the franchise, and the middle-class in the provinces who had no franchise at all, were in despair. They needed the votes. Possessed of the vote they could control taxation, force the "old" aristocrats to practice, or seem to practice, the ancient virtues of Rome, remove from them privileges which they had arrogated to themselves, control their licentiousness and ambitions and criminal subornation of the laws of Rome, and in all ways compel them to act as men and not as tigers. On the other hand, the vote in the power of the middle-class would mean that the howling Roman mobs, who lived without work or industry or pride or responsibility on the taxes wrung from their betters, would have to become industrious and responsible men again, rather than dependent beasts, slavering for free food from the hands of the rulers of the city, devourers of the flesh of those who stood upright in their souls and did not crawl on their bellies.

"It is hard to say which is the more evil," said Marcus Livius Drusus, tribune,† "those who bribe the masses, or the masses who receive the bribe. It is true that the briber corrupts; it is also true that he who accepts the bribe is the greater criminal. (But then, when was not government a liar, an enslaver, a murderer and a thief and an oppressor, the enemy of all men, in its lust for power?) He who receives a bribe, so he must not work to cover and feed and house himself, is less than the amiable dog

* Gaius Julius Caesar, the Elder.
† Letter to Crassus.

who at least gives loyalty and protects the household. The mob protects nothing but its belly, and he who caters to that belly for its grunted approval must stand before history as lower even than the basest slave, no matter the greatness of the name of his family or his standing among bankers."

The noble Drusus was himself an aristocrat, and held the name of one of the oldest and noblest families in Rome. Above all, he loved what Rome once was: proud, free, virtuous, clothed in honor, industrious, frugal, just, temperate, honest in thought and speech and act. His fellow aristocrats considered him a traitor to themselves. They sought to defame him, but the purity and nobility of his personal and public life were beyond their most frantic searching. "He believes," said Lucius Philippus to the exigent Quintus Scaepio, "that all men are worthy because they are men, even the middle-class, and perhaps even the mobs of Rome!"

But the noble Drusus believed that all men possessed souls and were therefore beloved of God, and that he who degrades a human soul or despises it would be eternally condemned.

His friends, patricians and conservatives like himself, were such aristocrats as Marcus Scaurus, and Lucius Crassus the great and heroic orator and defender of the rights of man. They, too, were men of the most exemplary lives and the most earnest virtue; they were also lovers of liberty and of their country. It was agony for them to perceive the modern criminality of Rome, the powerful politicians, the craven Consuls, the venal and detestable Senate, "the tribunes of the people" who betrayed the people, the vice and the lasciviousness and cruelty of those who ruled, the luxury that corrupted and was corrupt, the death of all honor in public life, the enslavement of the masses who had begged to be enslaved in order that they need not work, the paternalism and the crushing of the human spirit which paternalism invoked, and the oppression of those who wished to live in peace and work for their families and be good citizens and uphold the gods and practice the virtues of old Rome. "It is by taxation that a cruel and monstrous government can allocate power to itself," said Crassus, "for then it has a system of rewards and punishments: rewards for those who will permit tyranny and punishments for those who oppose it."*

"Nations have foundered and have passed away in dust for the same crimes now committed in Rome," said Drusus. "But we still have time to save Rome, to draw back from the abyss."

He could not know that nations never draw back from the abyss, for he still had illusions, he still believed that a corrupt nation could become pious

* Letter to Scaurus.

and virtuous again, "if the people willed." Not until the moment of his assassination did he realize that corruption is not reversible, when that corruption was deep in the bowels of a nation.

(On learning of the assassination of Drusus his brother said bitterly, "So is the end of all men who truly love their country and love truth! What other than death should be their punishment?")

Once the Senate had had the function of juries, but the Equestrian Order had taken most of the duties, "in order," it said, "to relieve the Senate of the mere ritual of law." The Equestrian Order, then, had begun to interpret the Twelve Tables of Law as it wished and imposed meanings on the law which had never existed before and were in violation of the Constitution. Drusus planned to restore the total function of jury to the Senate, and also proposed that the Senate be increased by three hundred more members in order to deal with new obligations and restore the Republic in full, and its law. He wished to set up a special tribunal also, to investigate all jurymen who took bribes or were swayed by political advantage. "The watch dog of the Republic," he declared. He proposed currency reform, so that Rome could retain her gold, which was her power, and prevent it from being drained away by foreign dependencies and nations in the name of loans. His heart devoured by anger and pity, he also proposed that the oppressed middle-class, notable for its virtue, its conservation and its industry, be given underdeveloped land in Sicily and parts of Italy. But, above all, he demanded the franchise for all Italians beyond Rome.

Nimbly, and with the wisdom of the noble, he combined all these ideas in one bill to be presented to the Senate. They could not approve one part without approving the whole. As tribune, and in furtherance of his reforms, he imprisoned Philippus. But the Senate released him, as it was wavering and uncertain and confused. It was one thing to deal with the Gracchi, who had appealed only to the plebs of Rome, and the honor they did not possess. It was quite another thing to deal with such as Drusus, who appealed to all men, and was therefore suspect. The Senate began to listen to tales that Drusus was a traitor to Rome, that he was inciting other Italians to revolt against the city, which was high treason. The Senate trembled; finally it disapproved the law which Drusus proposed on the mere ground of "informality." They surrendered to the aristocrats. Drusus was murdered.

The Social War broke out, between the city and the men of the provinces.

The grandfather had known Lucius Crassus, the great and heroic orator, personally, and when Lucius Crassus died, too suddenly, in September, the grandfather was overwhelmed with grief. "So perishes another man of honor!" he exclaimed. "When great men die, then a nation is truly bereft."

The Cicero family, though Roman citizens only by virtue of the franchise originally granted to the people of Arpinum, was in danger of the terrible anger of their surrounding countrymen, who were not Roman citizens. "It does not matter that our sympathies lie with them," said the grandfather. "It does not matter that our hearts burn with theirs for justice. How frightful it is that men of the same blood must challenge each other and destroy each other, for are we not all Italians? War between nations is evil enough, but war between brothers will never be forgiven by man or God."

Marcus thought of the story which Noë had told him, of Cain and Abel.

The Italian peoples, outside of Rome, founded the Confederacy, which included the Marsians, Paelignians, and many others. The Marsians were the first to declare war on the central government in Rome, and in addition to the Paeligni the Marrucini, the Frentani and the Vestini joined them. There was also the more southernly group, the Samnites, from Marcus' beloved river, the Liris, to Apulia and Calabria. The central government in Rome, however, had the support of the rich, including Umbria and Etruria which had eliminated their middle-class entirely. It also had Nola, Nuceria, and Neapolis in Campania, the Latin colonies such as Aesernia and Alba. It had Rhegium, and neighboring states. Nevertheless, the middle-class, believing that right was on its side, refused to give up hope; the farmers were with it. But, in Rome, there were the wealthy and the patricians who hated all but themselves, they the men of the cities.

"What can prevail against money and corruption?" asked the old grandfather in grief.

"A great man will arise who will restore justice," said his son, Tullius.

The grandfather looked at him with sparkling eyes. "You are the father of sons, one who is almost a man, yet you can speak as a child! When Rome was virtuous, she had her Cincinnatus. But, she is no longer virtuous. Therefore, there will be no great man to restore her. Rome is doomed. I am a Roman citizen, but I was born in Arpinum. I weep for my country."

Young Marcus' heart burned with agreement. In Rome, he prayed for his fellow Italians who were attacking their own government. He heard that all Italy intended to secede from Rome; it intended not only to march on the capital but to crush it and formulate a new nation under justice and law. Corfinium received the new name of Italica, and would be the head of the aborning nation. The government of Italy centered there, a Senate building was raised, the middle-class and the farmers were called citizens of Italica. The ancient laws of the Republic were revived again, and oaths sworn to the ancient Constitution which Rome had been so busily destroying over the past years. Fortresses of the Romans, scattered over all Italy, were seized and new banners lifted. An air of joy and freedom blew over Italy. The meddling and corruption of Rome, men believed, was at an end. No longer would the states and provinces have to endure oppression and disdain and murderous taxation and cruelty and condescension.

But the capital city was not idle in the face of the revolt of the states. Rome declared that her enemies were rebels (dediticii) to be at the absolute mercy of Rome when Rome conquered. They had forfeited rights under the Constitution.

Marcus found that the Caesares had left the old neighborhood for the Palatine Hill. They had always proclaimed that they were not only patricians (though fallen on financially evil times) but that they were descended from Iulus, who was alleged to be the semi-divine grandson of Venus and Anchises. Young Julius' uncle had just been appointed a Consul, and his father a praetor. They declared that they belonged to the Senatorial Party (Optimates). Therefore the humble neighborhood of the Ciceroni was not worthy of them any longer.

"Exigent rascals!" said the old grandfather. "For a miserable honor they have deserted Italy, in the name of a Rome which no longer exists! So the father now announces he belonged to the Senatorial Party! Did he not often nobly insist to me that he was a popularis, in spite of his aristocratic origins—which I do not believe exist at all!"

Helvia said, "Man must come to terms with circumstances."

"Ridiculous," said the grandfather. "I am amazed at you, Helvia."

"The Caesares are not criminals, except in your eyes," said Helvia. But she sighed. "There was a time in our history when men preferred death to dishonor. That is no more. If one is to survive, to exist, one must compromise these days. I do not recommend it. If I were a man I should prefer to die, but I am a mother of children, and a wife. What says Tullius about all this?"

"He believes a noble hero will arise to bring justice once more to Rome and to unite all Italy with Rome again under our Constitution," said the grandfather, spitting. "We shall not see Rome die tomorrow, but surely she is dying. For she has forgotten what once she was, or she laughs at it. We shall be enrolled among the nations who died by their own will and their own mischief."

A short time later, Rome, yielding to expediency, and alarmed by the resolution of the rebels, issued the Lex Plautia Papira for all allies who came before Roman magistrates within sixty days, and sought Roman citizenship. The war continued.

CHAPTER ELEVEN

"We have come," said the grandfather, "on the age of tyrants. Governments use national emergencies to restrict and then to destroy liberty. Tell me not of Sulla, the 'moderate!' Why was he not banished permanently with the true moderate members of the Senatorial Party who were struggling to compromise with our Italian communities, now in revolt? Tell me not of General Marius, who speaks of freedom from one side of his mouth and then supports the oppressive central government! One has only to consider that both Sulla and Marius have now offered their services to Rome. What is the result? We are now restricted in our food and our drink; the military rules Rome, and the vile politicians who lust for power. Our comings and our goings are curtailed, in the name of Roman security. Taxes are onerously raised, in the name of national emergency. These taxes will never be lifted, for once government imposes a tax it finds excuses to retain it forever.

"And the mobs of Rome—do they care that war between brothers is threatening Rome, freedom and the enfranchisement of all Italians? While our rations of corn are restricted, the mobs discover their own bowls are overflowing. While we tighten our girdles, as so nobly pleaded of us by the government, in order to save money and supplies, the mob finds itself clothed handsomely, and is arrogant in consequence, deeming itself superior even to its rulers, and shouting in the streets that their day is come, and writing on the walls at night; 'Down with the privileged!' No one, certainly, has ever told the Roman mobs that privileges are earned, and that those bestowed by a venal government are deceptive, hypocritical, and false. For what is not earned has no verity.

"If the military had imposed military discipline on the city, and upheld justice, there would be no complaint. But they impose discipline only on us, who need no discipline, for we are aware of our duties. The mob is unrestrained. The manufactures who supply military materials fill the hands of the mob with gold, so that they roister at night in the brothels and wineshops, and know no self-control. Who will restrain them when this war is ended, and teach them sobriety and honest labor again? They do not know even the meaning of this war, nor are they concerned! It is enough for them that they are suddenly rich and pampered by the government. Will the fumes of riotous living subside in them when peace is declared? No!

"They have been creatures of the politicians for a long time, even before this. Now they will become their legions of disaster, violence, decay, and decline. Honorable, fair work is distasteful to them; they will demand leisure without working; they will shout that their betters must support them through taxation. Mendicants! Betrayers! Slaves! But the government is worse than they are, for the government is responsible. It now wishes unlimited power. The Republic is doomed, and all our democratic principles. Politicians and greedy mobs—this has been the history of catastrophe forever."

His son, Tullius, was vaguely stirred from his illness and apathy in spite of himself. He said, with piteous hope, "Wars always bring excess; so history teaches us. But Romans are Romans. When this is over order will be restored, our liberties returned to us, our taxes reduced, the mobs restrained, the exigent men retired."

"It is related," said the grandfather, "that a lion, once he has tasted the blood and the flesh of a man, will eat no other meat. Our government has tasted the blood and the flesh of the people; it has tasted, suddenly, unlimited power. It will not be appeased except by more. May Jupiter have mercy upon us! But I fear he will not, for we have permitted the excesses of our government and have set up no safeguards against it."

Archias said to his pupil, Marcus, and with cynicism, "Does your grandfather believe that any nation remained virtuous and just and free? He is in the tide of history, and struggles against it, and dashes himself against stones. The Rome he knew is dying. Shall I weep? It happened so to Greece, and I weep for her in poetry. Marcus, let us write our poems. Consider Homer. The Greece he knew is dead, and all her glory. Troy has disappeared. Ulysses has long expired. The Parthenon echoes with alien feet. My people are enslaved and despised. But Homer remains. Long after Rome is rubble the schoolboys will read Homer and rejoice in his poetry."

Outside Marcus' schoolroom Rome presented a picture of riot and disorder; the war rang beyond her walls. There was nothing in this which could engage a schoolboy, except his fears and anxieties. Because of the national emergency and the terror in the streets, there was little social life but what could be accomplished during the day. There was little feasting, due to rationing, except among the powerful and the mobs who honored no law. Marcus' life, as part of the middle-class, had always been serene and steadfast and virtuous and circumscribed by duty and worship. Now more and more he was driven in upon himself, in the very height of his youth.

He wrote poetry—and thought of Livia Curius. Were it not for this war, he assured himself, he would have sought her out, ceremony or no ceremony. There were rumors that many of the rich, fearing the new and onerous laws of Rome, had fled to quiet spots throughout the world, mostly to Greece. It was very possible that Livia's guardians had taken her to safety.

He had, heretofore, worshiped Pallas Athene almost solely. Now, when he could make his way among the seething mobs of Rome, and among the refugees of the countryside, he went, unknown to his mother, to the temple of Venus. It did not occur to him until many years later that it was ironic that only in the temple of Venus was there no altar to the Unknown God. He sacrificed doves to Venus; he prayed at her altar. He gave almost all his frugal allowance to the priests for special prayers in his behalf. She was, above all, the deity to be invoked by those who loved. He forgot that she was also the goddess of concupiscence, of licentiousness, of all venereal excesses. To him she seemed most beautiful and compassionate and understanding.

"You are pale and withdrawn these days," said Noë ben Joel to Marcus at school. "Is it the war?"

Marcus was embarrassed. He could not look into Noë's shrewd and gentle eyes, which saw so many things, and say, "I am in love." It was true that Noë was almost espoused to a Jewish banker's daughter, and was vigorously opposing this in his house—for he had a mind to be free for some time and it was rumored the girl was unprepossessing—but Noë, in spite of his love for poetry, comedy, and tragedy, had an objective and somewhat skeptical view of passion, derived from his study of the stage if not yet from personal experience.

No, he, Marcus, could not tell Noë of his pain. He was overwhelmed with fresh embarrassment when Noë thoughtfully said, "If I did not know your life so well, my Marcus, I should say you were in love. Love! The fetter of the free spirit! The enslaver! The traitor! You are too wise—and what an eloquent voice you have!—to love anything but poetry and the virtues."

I am not wise, then, thought Marcus. I am a slave, a slave to autumn hair and blue eyes and a wild, young spirit. I have no dreams but of Livia. I hear no girl's voice, but I compare it with Livia's. I see no girlish mouth but what I think how mean it is compared with hers. I hear her laughter in every girl's laughter. I walk the streets, and she is beside me. I lie down at night, and she is with me. I rise, and I think of her with my first thoughts. Her face is imprinted on my books.

"You are dull and inattentive," said Pilo, the schoolmaster, to Marcus who was his most ardent student and the most erudite. Marcus knew that

Pilo disliked him, for he had placed Pilo in a position of dishonor years ago, and men do not forgive those whom they have injured.

The vast and clangorous city about him, murky, fuming in its ochres and yellows and reds and bronzes, the banners unfurled everywhere, the hurrying legions carrying their eagles and their fasces, the sounds of war drums, the galloping of couriers' horses, the rattle and uproar of increasing traffic as more loyal refugees flooded into Rome in their chariots and cars and litters, the crowded temples, the ominous and bloody sunsets, the air of haste and disaster, of comings and goings, the endless mutter of millions of people within the gates, the clash of fright after the dark—all these things became dreamlike to Marcus in the pain which did not recede from him but daily was augmented by his despair.

"He needs a tonic," said Helvia, looking at his stern pale face. She brewed the blackest and vilest of her herbs and administered them to her son. It is strange, thought Marcus, that only my mother knows in some manner of my suffering. He drank her infusions with a vague gratitude. He understood that Helvia gave not only her herbs but her sympathy, and that the infusions were an offering. She never spoke of Livia, but her beautiful eyes would beam on her son, half in admonition, half with sadness.

Even Quintus, his beloved brother, could no longer amuse him. Quintus was now at Pilo's school, and unlike Marcus he was much admired, not for his scholarship which did not exist, but for his good humor, his amiability, his willingness to engage in combat, his attitude of self-assurance and heartiness. He became involved in the gossip of the school and all its affairs. As he was taller and stronger than the average, and excellent in sports and in all physical games, he soon acquired a measure of leadership. He brought his little treasures of scandal home to Helvia, who loved him deeply. Where does he pick up these morsels? Marcus would ask himself, listlessly and without interest. No one had ever gossiped to him, nor had he been concerned with scandal.

One day Quintus said to him as they walked home through the crushing crowds which seemed everywhere, "That Julius! Now he has a tutor, Antonius Gnipho, a Gaul, of whom he boasts that he is wiser than Socrates. But Julius was always a boaster, as are all the Caesares. His father is a great man; his mother is a lady beyond compare, though we all know what a heavy hand she had upon him. All that is related to Julius is magnificent, noble, arrayed in grandeur, splendid beyond speech, important, marvelous, too awesome for a common mind to appreciate."

Marcus smiled a little. "Where do you meet this paragon, since he no longer is our neighbor and our schoolmate?"

"At fencing school," said Quintus, and he smiled with enjoyment. "At another hour than yours. He is a bad fencer. It enrages him. But he smiles. Gods, how he smiles!" But Quintus spoke without malice, and laughed. "However, there are few who can approach him in words. His voice is like honey when he wishes. He is very exigent and without scruple."

Quintus sniffed. "How incense clings to your garments, Marcus! You are always in the temples. Are you aspiring to the priesthood? Or, do you mourn that girl still?" His tone was derisively kind.

Marcus forgot that his brother was very young and far from adolescence. He lost his temper because of his great and hidden suffering. "You are impertinent and I detest impertinence!" he exclaimed. For the first time in his life he wanted to strike Quintus to relieve the pangs in him, but he only clenched his fist under his mantle. The dull February day was darkening, and torches and lanterns and tapers were scurrying everywhere up and down the steep and narrow streets, between the high buildings. Marcus quickened his step. It was intolerable to him that this child should mock him.

"I did not mean impertinence," said Quintus, alarmed at the glimpse of his brother's set profile. "I did not truly believe that you still remembered that girl. I do not even remember her face, though I saw it clearly! You must forgive me."

"It is of no matter," said Marcus, ashamed of the anger he had felt. But his emotions were still turbulent. He thought with despair, Even if she is in Rome, how shall I find her? She is barred against me.

The porticoes of jutting temples swarmed with late worshipers, who descended the steps to mingle with the crowds on the streets. Quintus caught his brother's arm and pulled him sharply into a doorway, for a detachment of soldiers were marching with rapidity up the hill, their iron-shod sandals clanging on the stones. They moved like an inexorable phalanx, their drums beating, their banners flying. They had inhuman faces, fixed and apparently unseeing. They were on their way to one of the gates, and they carried packs on their backs. They rushed by the two youths in the doorway with a sound like wind and thunder. Other doorways were crowded with people caught in their passage. Marcus watched the soldiers march, and thought of his own coming military service with some disquiet. He was not of the metal of soldiers. If the Social War did not end soon he would be called, and his adolescence was almost upon him. The pillars and columns of temples and public buildings glimmered in torchlight; it had been raining; the crimson light was reflected in small pools on the stones. In the west there was a bloody giant thumbprint as if Mars had carelessly paused to smear it there.

Quintus was deeply interested in the soldiers. His eyes sparkled in the last sullen twilight of the day and in the flare of the torches. "The drums stir me," he said. "I regret I am not old enough to be a soldier."

"I am glad that you are not old enough to murder your brother in a social war," said Marcus. The soldiers disappeared at the end of the high street, but their drums echoed behind them.

"It is for the preservation of Rome," said Quintus, who had apparently never heard a word his grandfather ever said.

"It is for the advancement of despotism," said Marcus. "Never was a war but for that."

They went on in silence. Quintus touched his brother on his arm. "I shall sacrifice for you in the temple of Leda, the mother of Castor and Pollux," he promised, in an attempt to appease his brother's misery.

"For what?" asked Marcus, faintly amused in spite of everything. "I am not Zeus, in pursuit of a maiden, as he pursued Leda." Then he blushed. He glanced quickly at his brother. It was impossible for Quintus to be subtle. Nevertheless, he said, "Neither am I a swan."

Quintus was somewhat offended, and this was unusual. He felt Marcus' patronage. "Sacrifice, then, to Pluto, that he return your Proserpine to you," he said. "Then there will be springtime in your heart." His quick umbrage rose. "Do you not know that you sadden the house, and no one knows the cause? Our father has not risen from his bed for weeks, yet you rarely visit him now in his cubiculum, as once you did every night. You are engrossed only in your wretchedness."

A little darkness of remorse and alarm fell over Marcus' mind. "Weeks? He has another attack of malaria. It was only a few days ago that he was at the table."

"Weeks," said Quintus, shortly.

And I did not miss him, thought Marcus, sorrowfully, suddenly aware that those stricken by love become, in a way of speaking, monstrous, immured in themselves, unaware of the life about them.

"You have not seen the physicians, nor questioned them," said Quintus. He loved his father, which was dutiful, but he thought him strange, too self-effacing, too modest, too quiet.

"There have been physicians?" said Marcus, and despised himself.

"And he has been bled several times," said Quintus. "Do you know that you barely touch your plate at dinner, and that sometimes our grandfather talks for hours and you do not hear him? You look at him attentively, but your thoughts are far away. You distress our mother."

Marcus was ashamed. He was also embarrassed because Quintus had seen these things and noted them. If Quintus, who saw life singly and found it good, had noticed his brother's abstractions then the affair was indeed serious. Marcus steadied himself. He could not overcome his pain, but at least he could pretend that it was not so great, or that he could endure it.

He had, he confessed to himself, forgotten even God, his dedications, his hopes, his ambitions. He had been like Orpheus, futilely wailing. Yet, he could not help himself. However, he could muster some decency and remember those he should remember. He began to trot up the Carinae to the house, where lamplight was already glowing, and Quintus trotted more easily beside him. The hill, as everywhere, was crowded. Water from puddles splashed on the youths' long tunics, and their shoes were thick with mud.

Even up on the hill the smothering stench of the city reached them, following them like a miasma of pollution. Romans, though they had homes with latrines, flooded with channels of water, were often careless about using them, and though almost every street had convenient public latrines, also flooded with water, a man caught in an emergency used an alley. Gutters ran with filth; the law demanded that every householder and every business building and temple keep premises clean, and there were swarms of guards about to see this was done. But Romans exerted their independence and their considered right to urinate and defecate wherever the urge took them, especially at night.

The air was heavy and ponderous and the stenches were more intolerable as the youths approached their house. Even Quintus, the accepting, said, "The city stinks like an abandoned pit full of dead bodies and offal. How I yearn for our island, where the wind is pure and sweet! Yet, I have heard you say that you love this city, Marcus."

It occurred to Marcus that it had been considerable time since he had even looked at his city, and he was more wretched. And he was sick with shame that his first terror for his country had lessened with the months.

That night, as Marcus ate his frugal dinner with his grandfather and his brother, he forced himself to notice many things of which he had heretofore been obstinately blind. His mother and two slave girls ministered to the men at the table in the dining room, and Marcus saw that Helvia's serene face was less richly colored and that there were two lines between her remarkable eyes and that though she was composed as always she appeared abstracted. There was but one oil lamp on the wooden table instead of the usual two—how long had it been since the other had been removed? Marcus looked at his father's empty place. He was afraid to ask of his father's health for fear of a deserved rebuke for his past indifference. Then he remembered that there had been no overseer in the hall. When had the man disappeared? The voices of slaves were fewer than he had remembered. Marcus glanced furtively at his grandfather and brother, and as they did not observe these things he concluded that this was now an ordinary occasion to them. He freshly despised himself.

He studied his grandfather's gloomy face. It had never been one of gayety, but now it was much older, thinner and more sombre. The old man appeared absorbed in wretched thoughts. How long had this been so? Even Quintus was subdued. I have seen nothing for I have seen only Livia, thought the youth. I have been pining away my life, and have neglected those dear to me. He wanted to ask with full desperation, and did not know how to begin. After a while, as he ate a tasteless dish of boiled meal sweetened sparely with honey, he tried to speak casually.

"Grandfather, do you think this war will last much longer?"

The grandfather laid down his spoon and regarded him with exasperation. "I spoke of that fully only last night, Marcus," he said. "I spoke for an hour, by the clock. Were you not listening?" Quintus stared at his brother with wide eyes, and there was a twinkle of compassionate mockery in them.

"You said nothing," said the grandfather, "so I assumed, perhaps foolishly, that you were considering my words."

Marcus drew on his subtlety; he had never been devious and it was a struggle to be so now.

"But affairs change day by day," he said.

The grandfather grunted, and wiped his beard. "Not so fast as that. The sheets of broadcast are fastened to the walls but once a week, and it was only yesterday that I read the latest and discussed it with you. Do you think Mercury flies to my side each night with fresh news of importance, for me alone?"

He stared at his plate. "There are always rumors," he said, grudgingly. "But I give no heed to rumors." Marcus wished fervently that he did, so that at least he could come abreast of the news and discuss it intelligently.

"It is but the beginning of disasters," said the old man. "The tribunes and Consuls of the people, elected by them, are betraying them more and more to curry favor with the state. The day of the city-state is over, but fools will not admit that. We have grown too complex for city-states. We need but one large nation, with localities individually administered by elected neighbors individually accountable to their people, but all under one national government, which must be restrained, however, lest it become tyrannical, centralized power. The authority must be completely defined and never be permitted to expand, or we shall have despotism by a few."

"Does not Plato in his *Republic* agree?" asked Marcus, striving to be interested.

The grandfather snorted. "Plato still thought of the republic as a city-state. I am speaking of a national state."

"An empire," Marcus suggested.

The grandfather was aghast. "Never an empire!" he exclaimed. "May the gods preserve Rome from ever becoming an empire! Rome is bad enough now, with her thieving and oppressive bureaucrats and politicians, her immorality and her degeneracy, the wantonness of her people, her Godlessness and her materialism, her ambition and her tyranny! She needs but the sword of empire to become utterly depraved. She needs but to crown a single man and call him 'Imperator' to sink her last virtues into the pit. Let one man rule a state and that state is doomed."

He shook his head mournfully. "But, we proceed to death. As men die, so do their nations. I have no hope for Rome, for I have no hope for men. Only a nation governed by God and His laws can survive the centuries. Once we were such a people, but are no longer."

Marcus was deeply depressed. He drank a little wine. The grandfather did not like subjects of conversation to be changed abruptly, so Marcus waited until the slaves brought in little earthen bowls of water for the fingers of the diners. Then the youth said, "How is my father tonight?"

"He is not improved from yesterday." The grandfather added sardonically and with considerable shrewdness, "But it is possible that you do not know how he fared yesterday, for you did not visit him last night."

Marcus colored. He did not know where to look, and he reproached himself with shame. His mind whirled with questions which he dared not ask. He looked about the dim bare room and it was full of shadows. His heart became sick with misery, and try as he would he could not banish the brilliant face of Livia which seemed to haunt every corner.

He said with bitter honesty, "My mind has been engrossed, and I beg your forgiveness."

The grandfather considered this, and then said, "I have noticed for a long time that your thoughts were far away. Traveler, have you considered the plight of Rome, and your family? Or, have you not known of them?"

Helvia appeared from behind the gray woolen curtain and looked at her men. She had been listening behind the curtain and she took compassion on Marcus. She inspected the lamp in that heavy silence of reproach, and shook her head a little. Then she fixed her eyes on her older son and said, "We must be even more frugal. The economic state of Rome is now desperate because of this war. This family is even more desperate. The value of our investments has declined almost to the point of vanishing. Our greatest investment was in the maritime shares. It is strange, but during periods of war the elements, themselves, are convulsed. Nearly half the ships in which we were invested have disappeared with their cargoes or have sunk or been seized by pirates and lost. Our other investments have declined in proportion, due to the war. Several of the mines in which we have invested have dwindled to almost nothing. Like many of our friends, we have been unfortunate, and it is not our fault. Your grandfather was judicious in investments, and had it not been for war we should have prospered exceedingly. He long ago assumed the burden of the moneys I brought to your father as a dowry, Marcus, for your father, many years ago, began to withdraw his interest." For a moment her youthful and impassive face dimmed in color.

"War," she resumed, "brings not only calamity to nations but to individuals. Only those directly concerned with supplying instruments of wars and the necessities of soldiers are making fortunes in these days. They are even challenging the patricians with their new gold, and invading the old families with marriages of their sons and daughters. It is necessity. One gives a name, the other gives money, and one cannot live without money no matter how exalted the name. But this dilutes noble blood and noble principles, for those of new riches have no heroic impulses but only appetites for the outward display of a nobility they do not possess. A pleb in rich raiment and with a chariot beautifully embossed, and with an entourage of slaves, is still a pleb. Though he has Senators at his command for his gold, he is still despicable. His urges are those of a beast, for a beast he is."

The grandfather nodded gravely. "When a beggar ascends to horseback and takes the rod he is far worse than a proud old patrician who at least has a history of honor and the ways of a gentleman and a tradition of nobility. I am of the middle-class. If I had a contest at law I should prefer that patricians judge me, and not an inflated man of the street, who has no frame of reference concerning honorable justice and the methods of honorable men."

He shook his head. "But there are the exigent even among the patricians and the noble, who lust for power. They know that power rests with numbers, and they now cultivate the plebs, the common people, of whom every government is justly afraid, for they have appetites and bellies, and like beasts they have no restraints and no self-control. So the patricians, if this war ever ends, will turn their attention to the plebs and use them to restore their fortunes and to seize power."

"Perhaps you are too despondent," said Marcus.

"No, no! I am not. For, we have rejected and turned away from God."

Marcus could now understand the shadows which had lain over his family and to which he had been blind. It disturbed him that his mother, always so contained and so imperturbable, now felt despair. He could not remember a time but that Helvia was always judicious and a little indulgent with the grandfather.

"I fear," said Helvia, preparing to retire again, "that you will not go to Greece as soon as you expected, my Marcus. We are bare put to it to keep the four hundred thousand sesterces which maintain your father in the knighthood. That must not be used."

"We have sold half our slaves," said the grandfather. "We could not do otherwise. It was my wish to state in my will that my own slaves be freed on my death, and it was in your father's will. Now we cannot afford this noble luxury."

Marcus had never thought about money at all. He had known that his grandfather and his mother were penurious and excessively frugal. It had amused him. But it was one thing to be penurious and frugal when rich, and another to be so out of desperate necessity.

"I shall be a soldier, a general," said Quintus. "Then I shall be rich, my future assured. I do not intend to be poor."

Helvia, at the curtain, smiled fondly at her favorite. The grandfather rose after a brief invocation of the gods and left the room silently, still exuding reproach. Quintus yawned and said, "I must go to Archias, who loses more and more respect for Pilo, if he ever had any. Nor does he have respect for my mind."

"I shall go to my father," said Marcus, hating himself.

He went first to his little cubiculum, which was dark. He did not light the lamp. Oil, he had discovered, was precious these days. He knelt beside his narrow bed and prayed. He did not pray for money, for that was an insult to God. He prayed for wisdom and courage, but his heart was not in it. He was frightened. He thought, I am no longer a child. I am a man. Then he prayed for his family's peace, and for his father's health. He prayed that he be given the fortitude to endure whatever was to come. But he prayed without fervor. He suddenly remembered that his prayers had been lacking this virtue for some time. He had thought only of Livia, and all his prayers had been directed to Venus.

He beat his head on his bed and muttered aloud in his agony, "Oh, if I could only forget her! Am I a child still, that I cannot control my emotions? Oh, that I were like Zeus, able to fall upon Livia, like Daiene, in a shower of gold!"

His tears fell on his clasped hands. He knelt in sudden silence. Never would he forget Livia. That was impossible. However, he would try to live with his anguish and never again let it blind him to other matters. The Spartans held foxes against their bellies and permitted the animals to gnaw at them. That, however, did not prevent them from being excellent soldiers and conducting their lives normally. Was he less than a rude Spartan? He was a Roman. To be less was not to be a man.

He then went to his father. His hatred for himself gave him strength and equanimity. He fixed a smile upon his face as he drew aside the curtain to Tullius' cubiculum.

Tullius had had his meagre supper and his wine, and lay exhausted by the effort of dining. Here a smoky lamp burned on the wall; his chest of small belongings stood against another wooden wall, and there was a chair. He turned his haggard head feebly to the curtain as Marcus entered; the rays of the lamp showed his gaunt and sunken face, his fallen eyes. But he smiled with radiant sweetness; his brow stood thick with large drops of feverish water, and his lips were broken and parched. To Marcus, it was as if he had been absent a long time only to return to discover someone he had left in health devoured by sickness.

"My son," said Tullius, and Marcus' heart quickened again with hatred for himself for his father's weak voice was the joyful one of one who greets a returning traveler. He sat on the chair. He could not apologize for his neglect, for that would hurt his father more. So he merely inquired about his health. Tullius smiled again, as if amused.

"It is my malaria," he said. "Do not fear, Marcus. I shall not die. I shall see you with these eyes when you are a great man, with your wife beside you and your children."

Marcus looked into those fever-stricken eyes sadly. And then he saw the spirit in them, powerful against the flesh. His misery lifted. If his father decreed life for himself then he would live. Feeling forgiven and reprieved, Marcus talked to him of his school.

"We shall remove you soon," said Tullius. "We must have still another tutor for you, as well as Archias. And you must begin to study law."

He talked serenely. He did not speak of the war or the economic situation of the family to Marcus. He held his son's hand in his own hot and skeleton one and boasted of Marcus' future, and the pride he would bring his family. The plight of his country was far from him. He had always lived in a very small world of dreams, sometimes jogged out of it by his father.

"I regret," said Tullius suddenly, in a voice hardly audible, "that I was ever born."

Marcus thought of what his mother had said of her husband when a youth: "He was like a young Hermes." There was something spiritually fleet and airy about his father, something not to be touched by the gross world, something winged and remote and elusive.

He is in love with God, thought Marcus, with profound intuition. He is sick for a home only he knows.

The youth thought of the altar of the Unknown God. He had forgotten in these last months. He thought of the lilies he had placed on His altar, in honor of His Mother. He had also forgotten what Noë ben Joel had told him, of the Messias. And why? Because of a girl with autumn hair and eyes as blue as an autumn sky. Somewhere, at sometime, thought Marcus, I lost the way. Somewhere I lost the truth.

But still, he could not understand his father's desire to leave the world.

He looked again at his father, who had fallen suddenly into a sleep that was like death, but he smiled in his sleep. Feeling heavy and cumbrous Marcus blew out the lamp, drew his father's coverlet over the thin, linen-covered breast, and left the cubiculum. He was both thoughtful and despondent. He went to Archias with his books. Archias was cheerful.

"The news is disheartening from the provinces," he said, as if imparting good tidings. Marcus frowned.

"Does that please you?" he asked.

Archias chuckled. "Am I to grieve for Rome's troubles?" he asked. "Oh, Rome will not collapse within her gates so soon or be overrun by the barbarian! She will have a splendor yet, but it will be like the phosphorescence that glows from a decaying corpse. Man is the most risible of creatures, though pathetic. Can you not be a spectator as I am, my Marcus? Look you, life is the most dangerous of experiences, the world the most dangerous of places, and man the most dangerous of animals. To contemplate it is the essence of wisdom; not to become involved in it is the wisest course of all."

"You have never become involved in it?"

"Never," said Archias, emphatically. "I stand apart. I love poetry and philosophy. But even these amuse me. They are man's attempt to come to terms with what is hidden from him forever. Does the eagle or the lion wonder from whence he came or what his end is? Does the mouse contemplate and try to solve riddles? Does the flower wonder what lies beyond the sun? No, they are content to be, as I am. They accept. They fear neither life nor death. They are wiser than we."

"Once you said, Archias, that it is impossible to ask a question, by the very nature of things, if there is no answer. The very existence of a question poses a reply."

"I was engaging in a metaphysical exercise," said Archias. "You must not always take me seriously, especially if my stomach is upset, as it must have been when I uttered that absurdity. But now to our lessons. What did that fool of a Pilo tell you today?"

"He knows I am to be a lawyer. And so he remarked that laws must not be static or unchangeable, but must advance as man advances."

"What a sophistry!" said Archias. "Does man advance? No. His nature

remains the one constant in life. He creates inventions; he raises larger
and larger cities. He establishes governments. He exults in the phantas-
magoria of change. He imagines that mere movement is advancement, and
that activity in itself is mutability. If he runs, he believes, he will reach
a higher place. But he cannot escape himself, however he shouts, however his environment changes. Therefore laws based on his fantasy of
change are ridiculous. He will achieve novelty, but that novelty will not
be wisdom, no matter how he glorifies himself, and boasts. He will exchange one opinion for another, forever; he will change his gods and call
them by other names. But always, and forever, man will be the same. It
is on that truth that law must be built and enforced."

Marcus listened intently. Then he said, "Noë ben Joel speaks of the
Messias of the Jews, Who will change men's hearts."

Archias made a superb gesture. "These Jews! And where is this famous
Messias? Why does He wait so long? If He comes, which I doubt, He will
understand men. But I doubt He will be able to change them."

Marcus had had many disturbances of his emotions this night and now
his head began to ache. He became inattentive, and in impatience Archias
dismissed him. Marcus went to his cubiculum but could not sleep.

He lay uneasily and listened to the huge and sleepless roar of the mighty
city about him. He thought of her vast subject territories which embraced
the world, and her countless millions of subject people of multiple races
and tongues. He thought of her power, growing more tremendous every
day. Yet, as she now struggled with her own people in her own land the
subject lands and nations stirred restively, hoping that the eagle's wings
would be torn, her head severed, and that then they would be free of the
short sword and the iron claw that held it. Roman banners on endless
walls and on distant fortresses were eyed with speculation; lips were
wetted. The fasces were secretly cursed. The Roman legions which
marched everywhere were gazed on with hating and hostile eyes. If Rome
were weakened and divided, then the jackals would move upon her
wounded members.

It was true that Rome had established her alien law in conquered lands
and introduced her alien customs and her alien gods. But the law was
still fairly just though the taxes were growing more onerous. The pro-
consuls were as honest as could be expected, considering the local pres-
sures which were exerted upon them and the mighty bribes which were
offered by princes and chieftains and tax-gatherers. To a world simmering
with constant war Rome had brought a peace, a precarious one, but still
it was a peace. The short sword was hated, but it kept the law, and it enforced order. Rome had been wise enough not to impose her gods upon
conquered nations. She had been shrewd enough even to accord alien

deities a measure of honor and to introduce many into her own pantheon.

In all of history, then, there had been no ruler so comparatively benign before. The Roman passion for jurisprudence had relieved populaces from a constant siege. But if subject nations showed signs of rebellion they felt the crushing weight of the Roman fist. Romans considered this only reasonable. They also considered that national pride and natural patriotism in conquered lands to be reprehensible, for did they not threaten the peace of Rome? The world was Roman; let it beware of dreaming of its own hegemony again, its own independence. What had independence wrought in the past? Wars, competitive ambitions, destruction, disorder.

Marcus, lying on his hard bed considered these things. He considered the Pax Romana, enforced with cold and efficient ruthlessness. It was against nature! Nations could not be welded together like bits of iron! They were composed of men, of different races, tongues, customs, gods. They had a right to their land, and only they had a right. Rome strove to destroy individuality and variety, in the name of peace and in the name of Rome. But men persisted in being born with features of their own and souls forever alien from the Pax Romana. It was a mad and unnatural dream—that all men should have one government and look to that sole government for law, and pay their taxes to that government. Dead empires had had that dream before, including Greece, and it had destroyed them, for man's spirit will not be mocked. What was it Noë ben Joel had quoted to him, Marcus, from the writings of the Jews? That God had set the boundaries of the nations and had created the various races, and no man should intrude upon them.

"Of one thing you can be certain," Archias once had said. "Men learn nothing from the past. They tread the same old paths to death and are blind to the warnings."

And today, as Rome struggled with her brothers on Italianate land, conquered nations hoped and prayed that she would fall, and that they would be free of her onerous peace and her taxes and her law once again —for these were alien to their spirits.

Marcus' thoughts became more and more uneasy. He wondered if he were being disloyal to his country. He rose and lighted his lamp by the one in the corridor and then looked at it aimlessly, and with inner disquiet. He was proud of his country. But other men had a right to be proud of their own countries, too, and to maintain their own laws.

Marcus' head buzzed with many thoughts and ached more fiercely. Archias had a low opinion of mankind, he mused, thinking of Archias' words tonight. To Archias man was amusingly evil, and completely evil; he was at his worst when he pretended to virtue. Yet, truly, Marcus said to himself, there is some virtue in man. He had magnanimous impulses as well as cruel ones. He built hospitals for the poor and the slaves, as in Rome. He protected slaves with various laws. (Romans did not consider slaves mere "things," as the Greeks had considered them.) He had an ineradicable honor for truth and justice, even when he was a liar and unjust, himself. He respected virtue, though often lacking virtue.

Marcus found himself in the cold atrium, and wondered vaguely how he had come to be there. No slave slept in the hall any longer. The youth opened the strong oaken door and the chill February wind struck through his woolen shift. But he looked down upon the city. Romans went to bed early, but many were still abroad on their feasting and their revels. The dull mutter of hurrying chariots came to Marcus in a metallic thunder of wheels. The city looked as if on fire in the murk, for the torches affixed to stone walls fluttered for miles like a flaming and restless sea. Lanterns still bobbed everywhere. And the winter sky, lowering in clouds over the city, reflected the torchlight. Near and distant shouts, laughter and heavy voices were borne on the hovering fog. Marcus closed the door.

He had reached the curtain of his cubiculum again when he heard a hoarse groaning. He halted, straining to hear. The groan was repeated, then a faint and strangled cry. Marcus' first thought was of his father, and he was suddenly sick with dread. But when he reached his father's cubiculum he heard no sound from within except a restless turning. The groaning was suddenly loud again, full of distress, and Marcus ran down the cold and narrow hall to his grandfather's cubiculum.

"Grandfather?" he asked in a low voice.

The old man cried out again, and Marcus threw aside the curtain and entered the cubiculum. It was as black as a hole within. Marcus hurried to his own cubiculum and brought his lamp. He held it high over his grandfather.

He had never seen the face of death before, or its shadow. But the old man was sitting up in bed, clutching his throat, and his eyes rolled wildly and dimly in the faint light. They fell upon Marcus. He swallowed convulsively, and his gray beard rippled. His hands dropped.

"I am dying," he said in the faintest of voices.

"No," said Marcus, in terror. He raised up his own voice and shouted for Phelon, the physician, who slept nearby. Phelon came into the hall, naked and drowsy, and blinked at the lamp.

"Help!" said Marcus.

CHAPTER TWELVE

The cypress of mourning stood at the door of the house of the Ciceroni. "You are sixteen, Marcus," said Helvia, whose plump face was serious and pale. "You will not assume the manly robe for seven weeks. Nevertheless, you are now the man of the family. There is none else."

To a young man whose life had been serene, only once or twice lit by passion or anger, who had led a most bucolic existence in the heart of a peaceful family, whose days had been quiet and full of affection and without true responsibility, the situation seemed formidable. Not for him had been the uneasy and turbulent days of those engaged in war or who had warriors in the family; not for him the days of anxiety which attended those whose income was uncertain. As he was no patrician, he had been subjected to no arrogances, no insistences on protocol, no heart-burning honors, no strivings, no tremendous ambitions, no struggling for political power, no schemes or plots, no mingling with Senators or Consuls or tribunes, no terrors, no suspicions, no grandeur. "In all ways," he wrote many years later, "my early life was the golden mean of the Greeks, without excess. But, alas, I do not admire it. Experience makes the man, and if it be fiery, then is the metal tempered. The quiet river moves through peaceful country, but it makes no living estuaries, it does not thunder in green fresh violence over stones. If it has no turbulence, neither has it life. It is stagnant."

Marcus could not weep for his grandfather, for he was too stunned, too incredulous that one so colorful and so majestic would be heard no more, would offer no hand to assist youth, would have no words of explicit advice. Marcus felt some bitterness against his father, Tullius, who wept like a child now, and hid his head under coverlets and cried that the family had been cast into ruin. When Marcus visited him in his cubiculum, the father would extend a trembling thin hand to him for help, for reassurance. It was some time before the distraught youth could bring himself to touch that hand, which should now be the firm rudder of the family and not the hand of a child. "If only I had died, and not my father!" Tullius would cry, and in his misery and confusion Marcus once or twice echoed the thought in his mind.

Young Quintus gazed at his older brother with the respect due to the head of the family. The slaves deferred to him. Archias held his mocking tongue for some time. Helvia eyed him sternly, and waited. And he did not know what to do first. His own grief was overpowering; he was not permitted to indulge it, for the family waited on him.

His grandfather had died in his arms, and it was only then that Marcus had realized how much he had loved the old man, who had stood in the family like a great oak among saplings. His branches had sheltered them from violent winds; his leaves had preserved them from scorching suns; his trunk had been their refuge. Now, in one instant the oak had been felled, and the saplings were exposed. For many mornings, when he awoke, Marcus would cry aloud, "It is not possible!"

The terrible panoply of death had to be observed, sacrifices made, the temples visited, prayers said for the repose of the grandfather's severe and virtuous soul, money to be distributed to the poor in his honor, priests to be recompensed, offerings made for the prayers of the Vestal Virgins, candles to be lighted in the grandfather's name at sundown—lighted by Marcus—exhortations, and money, given to the slaves for their prayers and the remembrance of their duties, visitors to be greeted, condolences to be endured, the grandfather's will to be listened to as it was intoned gravely by lawyers, and above all, the disposition of his gnarled and stately body. A man does not die simply, and disappear.

Helvia prudently did not advise her son or even help him. He was now a man, and must assume a man's responsibilities. Helvia was an "old" Roman. The sooner a youth became a man the better. She merely laid her books before him, explained their significance, and then referred Marcus to the lawyers and the bankers. Marcus on more than one occasion wished to turn to her, but her calm set face warned him that he was no longer a child, and all this was his duty.

He felt soft, weak, and vulnerable, but, as Helvia waited for him to assume his burden his wings hardened and grew strong, as the young wet wings of a butterfly must do when it emerges from its chrysalis. Otherwise, it will never fly, and would be at once the prey of any bird, helpless and pulpy. There was no time for weeping, no time to pity one's self. The days crowded on Marcus like encroaching walls or advancing armies. He must deal with them. He could deal well enough with large problems, for there were lawyers and bankers. The small problems tormented and infuriated him. He found himself losing his temper even with the meekest of slaves. His books were dry as powder. He, who had rarely made a decision, must now make all decisions. "I have the most helpless family!" he exclaimed once to his mother. Helvia merely smiled faintly. "Did you wish always to be a child?" she asked.

The grandfather's will was simple enough, at first glance. The income of his investments was left to Tullius, but Marcus was the residuary beneficiary as the older son. The house was affectionately bequeathed to Helvia. Quintus, as became a future soldier, was left the old man's mementoes of wars, his cherished short sword, his shield, his armor, his bust of Mars, his citations for gallantry in the field, his medals. The grandfather had made Marcus his executor; he had also left to him the paternal island at Arpinum.

For the first time Helvia offered advice. Who knew what had happened to the ancestral home on the island? The family, she pointed out, needed money because of the failure of many investments. When would the family be able to return to the island? Who knew how long the war would last? In the meantime, the property was heavily taxed, due to the war, and the taxes were increasing. Marcus should sell the island.

"No," said Marcus.

Helvia compressed her lips.

"We shall return," said Marcus. "Even wars must end sometime."

Helvia noticed, for the first time, that Marcus had very prominent brows and for a moment she was startled, for it was as if the grandfather were looking upon her with his own eyes, though their color and shape were hers.

"I will take his ashes to the island and bury them there, in the spot he loved," said Marcus. "In the meantime we must live as sparely as possible, to meet our taxes. Strange, is it not?" he asked with bitterness, "but the powerful seem unaffected by taxes, and they flourish even during wars."

"They have Senators as friends," said Helvia. "The corrupt and the influential are never burdened as are the responsible and the just. It is the price we pay to venal government, which protects its favorites and punishes those who despise it."

"It was not always so," said Marcus. "Our history teaches us that when a government is honest and just and virtuous taxes are light. But when a government becomes powerful it is destructive, extravagant, and violent; it is an usurer which takes bread from innocent mouths and deprives honorable men of their substance, for votes with which to perpetuate itself."*

He talked of this to Archias, who shrugged.

He smiled wryly at Marcus. "Now you must become interested in politics, for he who refrains with lofty words has no patriotism and no honor. It was Pericles who said, 'We do not say that a man who takes no interest in politics minds his own business. We say that he has no business in the world at all.'"

Marcus discovered that the father of Noë ben Joel, Joel ben Solomon, had been the grandfather's investment counselor and advisor. So Marcus

* From *De Republica*.

visited Joel ben Solomon, for whom he had a filial affection, having dined at his sumptuous table on many occasions. The elderly man, the father of many daughters—whom he had finally succeeded in marrying off—and one incomprehensible son, received him kindly in his offices in the Forum. His gray beard reminded Marcus of his grandfather, and the shrewd bright eyes also. Marcus looked at him and for the first time since his grandfather's death his eyes filled with tears. Joel ben Solomon appeared to understand. He sat patiently at his ebony table and regarded Marcus paternally. Finally he spoke.

"I have you to thank, Marcus, that my son now takes interest in religious matters. I had despaired of him."

Joel ben Solomon smiled benignly. "I have hopes also that he will enter this counting house," he said.

Marcus returned home to inform his mother that modest though the household was in all its ways more stringent methods must be put into practice. She inclined her head seriously. "Tell me," she said. "Was I ever profligate? Do I possess a slave whose sole duty it is to anoint me after the bath and arrange my hair? Do I have three cooks in my kitchen? I am the cook, my son. Is my dress extravagant, my shoes jeweled? Do gems lie upon my throat or against my ears? What few slaves we still possess are necessary; moreover they are old and have been in my service, and my mother's, for many years. Shall we sell these miserable and ancient creatures? Who would buy them? Shall we give them their freedom, and so loose them to starve on the streets? Their manes would curse us! You must tell me what we must do."

Marcus hesitated sadly. "There is the stipend of Archias," he said. "We cannot afford it."

"Socrates has said that a man to be of value to the world must have education," said Helvia.

"Quintus is no scholar," said his brother. "He detests books. His tuition at the school of Pilo is half Archias' stipend." Helvia sat with her books and waited while Marcus, shrinking inwardly, went to Archias' quarters to impart his decision. The Greek listened in silence.

Then he said, "Your father has paid me generously all these years, and I am a man of few wants, except for an excellent wine, which I buy, myself. Moreover, my Eunice is invaluable to the Lady Helvia. I have saved my money; knowing the ways of men, I have invested it in certain ventures. Therefore, permit me to remain with you, my dear Marcus, without a stipend at all. I have no other home." He hesitated. "If my poor funds will assist you in this crisis, you may call upon them."

For the second time that day, and the second since the death of his grandfather, tears filled Marcus' eyes. He fell upon Archias' neck and embraced him. "Do not depart from me, my dear teacher," he said.

"Tut," said Archias. His brow wrinkled. "Withdraw Quintus, that amiable dunce, from the school of Pilo. I will teach him for not a penny at all, though I confess that I wince at the thought. But he has a cheerful nature, and that is not to be disdained. He will be in the army in a few years, for which I offer up my pious gratitude."

"And I begin, in a few weeks, to study law," said Marcus. "It is no longer necessary for me to go to the school of Pilo. He has taught me all he knows."

"Which is of no great magnitude," said Archias.

Marcus returned to his mother, more than a little happier. She smiled without surprise. "Without the help of Eunice," she said, "it would be impossible for me alone to clothe this family. I judged that Archias would do as he has done."

"We must still peel to the meat, as a knife peels through the skin of a turnip," said Marcus, seating himself beside her again.

"I have a plan," said Helvia. "We must arrange for your betrothal to a girl who will bring you an excellent dowry. I have a girl in mind— Terentia."

For the first time since his grandfather's death Marcus permitted himself to think of Livia Curius. Her memory had lain in his distraught mind like a dull ache; now it flamed into fire. "No!" he exclaimed.

"Why not?" asked his mother with tranquillity. "She is twelve, and of an age to be betrothed. She is not of a very handsome countenance, but she is the only daughter of her family, though she has a half-sister of no importance. The very rumor of your betrothal to her, after you assume your manly robe, will bring us good fortune. The marriage can take place in two years."

"No!" cried Marcus, again.

His mother eyed him strangely. "There is no necessity for such vehemence. Is it possible you are still thinking of Livia Curius? I have been informed by Aurelia Caesar that her marriage to Lucius Catilina is to take place this summer. He has returned from Greece. He returned to assist his country—so he said."

Marcus felt acutely sick. He clenched his hands upon his knees and stared blankly before him.

"It does not matter," he said at last in a low voice. "No matter if she marries another I shall never forget her, nor marry anyone else."

Helvia shrugged. "We shall see," she said. She bit her lip thoughtfully. "You cannot go to Greece, as you had planned, Marcus. Nor have you any military gifts; the army is not for you. I have arranged for you to study law with old Scaevola, the augur and pontifex. This is an extraordinary privilege, and you owe this honor to my father, who is his friend. However, he is a dicer, also. Do not let him entice your allowance from you!" She smiled again.

But Marcus, though suddenly excited by the thought of studying with Scaevola, the famous old lawyer, could not be induced to smile at his mother's sally.

"I cannot forget," he muttered. "Before Zeus, I cannot forget."

"You can endure," said Helvia. "More than that, even the gods cannot do."

Quintus was joyful at the news that he was to be released from school, though he regretted the gossip of which he would be deprived. Now it was the spring of the year, and he would not be engaged in the sports of the school, and this was his only dismay. "And the fencing?" he said to Marcus.

Marcus would gladly have dispensed with the fencing. He was an excellent fencer, for he felt it was his duty to be so. Helvia said, "We must continue the fencing school. What is a man if he has no means of self-defense? Moreover, to withdraw from all things will cause unpleasant rumors."

Soft airs blew from the Campagna now, and the swallows were cheeping even in the most crowded streets, and the little red poppies were appearing on every spot of unused ground. Helvia worked with Eunice very industriously in her small garden, for food was expensive in the war-stricken city. She bought a goat for its milk, and its incipient young. Marcus often saw his mother in the garden, her stola draped high over her sturdy legs, her bare feet in the warm earth, a hoe in her hand. The golden-haired Eunice labored with her. An old slave assisted them, twittering like a swallow himself.

Helvia would not let Marcus help her. He must study his law. She did not speak of her husband, immured again with his books, and now also with his grief. But Quintus, after his lessons, happily wheeled manure to the vegetable plot and dug with zest. Archias condescended to plant onions. "What is a dish without a savor?" he asked, squatting on his haunches, his lean dark face sharp in the sunlight.

Helvia drew from her own secret account to provide Marcus with the proper ceremonies of his adolescence, though he protested at the expense. "I have saved a little money," said Helvia. "We cannot celebrate as we wish, because of the war, but we must do what we can. How otherwise shall we retain our honor?"

So Marcus, to please her, pretended interest in the ceremonies. His father came from his library and his cubiculum, wan and lifeless, to greet the guests, and to drink to his son's future. Once Marcus thought, It is unmanly to withdraw from life and its responsibilities. He was at once grieved and horrified at this disloyalty to his beloved father. And then he knew, with fresh misery, that he had been impatient with Tullius since the death of his grandfather, for was it not the father's place to be a rock of refuge and comfort to his family? Not once had Tullius asked about the family's affairs. He had always consigned them to his father and his wife. He appeared not to wonder how the family was faring, though once he complained of the inferiority of the wine. Helvia had said without perturbation, "We are fortunate even to have this."

"Ah, the war," sighed Tullius. He promptly forgot the war. It did not interest him. He envied his father who was finished with living.

Marcus had now assumed the manly robe. It lay on his shoulders like a weight of iron. There is much of my father in me, he thought with some ruefulness, and was again miserable.

But his studies were beginning to absorb him. He was gone from sunrise to sunset. Even his pain concerning Livia diminished in the midst of his duties and his arduous books.

Then one day in the temple of Venus he saw Livia.

CHAPTER THIRTEEN

Years later Marcus wrote of the Caesares: "They will be remembered as great, yet no one will be completely certain in what their greatness lies. I believe I have solved the riddle: They loved no one but themselves. At no time did they forget their duty to themselves, or their own advantage. By this magic they convinced every man that the Caesares were uncommon men, indeed, and deserved honor and love."*

To the powerful, the Caesares were flattering, deferential, sincerely devoted, self-sacrificing, loyal, eagerly serving. To their equals they were kind and considerate, but faintly aloof; always, they were agreeable and entertained well, rarely engaging in argument, agreeing even when they secretly disagreed, gracious, hypocritical, not opinionated in speech, dishonest, charming, totally insincere but flexible, open to gossip which they could turn to their advantage, but speaking admiringly of friends and

* From: Letters to Sallust.

neighbors. To their inferiors—who loved them most—they were cold and demanding and arrogant, impressing upon them the mighty superiority of the family, making each man believe that a mere condescending word from the Caesares was a favor equal to a favor for the gods, themselves. The powerful, then, advanced the fortunes of the family, for the powerful love sycophants; the equals wished to reward them for their kindness; the inferiors wished only to serve ones so noble and so above ordinary mankind.

"It was an art they practiced," Marcus wrote with some ruefulness. "It is not an art I admire."

Helvia, too, was not deceived by the Caesares. Her family was superior to Aurelia's. She ignored the male members. She was unimpressed by their weighty impressiveness, and laughed at their charm. Consequently Aurelia was her great friend. Even when the family moved to the Palatine Hill Aurelia visited Helvia for the pure relief of not being compelled to be charming, gracious, insincere, agreeable, and on guard.

Aurelia, who had a heavy hand on the young Julius Caesar, did not trust him out of her sight, so she invariably brought him with her when visiting the Ciceroni, saying that her son remembered his old playmates with affection. Marcus found young Julius, now twelve years old, irritatingly amusing. Quintus thought him affected, which he was. In the art of sports Quintus was superior. Julius spoke of the military with enthusiasm and declared he would be an officer of importance. But he displayed a great care for his person and preferred strategy to tests of strength. He was nimble and graceful, and was always able to evade Quintus' suggestions for wrestling and boxing. "I am no gladiator," he would say.

Young Julius was a fascinating conversationalist, but even the simple Quintus suspected that many of the tales he told of his encounters were gay lies. Nevertheless, Quintus liked to hear them out of sheer enjoyment. "You are a Homer, Julius," he once said. "But, speak on." Julius did not take offense or protest that he was speaking the truth. Truth, to Julius, was a most confining thing and frequently dull. His lively and imaginative mind, his genius for invention, made him leap over truth as one leaps over a stolid boulder in one's path.

He, however, had as sincere an affection for Marcus as he was capable of, and preferred his company to that of Quintus. For Julius, at twelve, had the mind of a man, a subtle and devious mind. He did not believe in Marcus' protestations that he disliked gossip. What was more interesting than a malicious tale of others' defections, faults, and sins? There was no rumor of any shocking proportions in the city that Julius did not know, and he loved to annoy Marcus by recounting them. He also invented. So when Julius spoke of Livia Curius' approaching marriage to Lucius

Sergius Catilina and Lucius' behavior among the more complaisant young ladies of Roman society, Marcus discounted the tales of Lucius' prowess. Was not Livia enough for any man? Julius thought him naïve. Then he observed Marcus' sudden pallor with the shrewdness and intuition for which the Caesares were famous.

"You have seen the maiden?" he asked.

"Twice," said Marcus, shortly.

Julius sighed. "Were I older," he said, "I should challenge Lucius, whom I now despise, for all he is a captain. I should challenge him for Livia, who is virtuous as well as beautiful. But she is very strange. He is strange, himself. They share the same blood."

Marcus had not known this. He was horrified to learn that Livia was related to Lucius. "How is this?" he demanded.

"It is not a close relationship," said Julius, pleased at Marcus' sudden attention. "I believe they are third cousins."

Marcus remembered, now, the extraordinary blue of Lucius' eyes, a color that appeared to fill all its socket. So were Livia's eyes. But he said to himself, "It is only the color and the shape. The expression is not the same."

Nevertheless, he was disturbed. It was evil enough to think of the approaching marriage; it was even worse to think that those two shared a blood relationship however remote. To Marcus, it were as if a profane hand had dared to lay itself upon the flesh of a Vestal Virgin. Remembering that Julius was a liar, Marcus asked his mother for the truth. She thought, then nodded. "It is true, Marcus. I did not think of it before, or I should have told you. You would then have forgotten the maiden sooner, for the Catilinii have evil blood."

But there is nothing of the Catilinii in Livia, thought Marcus with the stubbornness which was characteristic of him. He now knew the date of the wedding. It was in less than four weeks. He had tried to resign himself, had engrossed himself in his duties to his family and in his studies. There had been hours when he had not remembered Livia at all. Now the agony returned.

Early summer heat had come upon the tremendous city, and great storms blew over it, reflecting the storm of war. Never had the crowded streets been so impassable with bodies and so pervaded by the stench of sweat. All colors appeared too vivid, from the smoldering blue of the sky to the reds and saffrons and yellows and ochres of the steep buildings, from the teeming plazas to the temples, from the hills to the Forum. Sunlight glittered from the soldiers' armor and helmets. Chariots stood motionless for many minutes in their passage, wheel to wheel, while the drivers cursed furiously and wiped their running faces. Banners hung limply from standards. There was no alley in which to pause, no empty doorway. Sometimes Marcus, heavy with his books, stood panting and immobile in the press of the throngs, deafened by the uproar of clamorous voices and curses, his eyes blinded by the hot sunlight. He could not lift his arms or move his feet. It was as if the whole world had moved to Rome. There was not a spot of refuge from humanity. Slaves shouted for the passage of the litters of their masters; the throngs heaped imprecations upon them; the curtains remained discreetly closed. Tribunes and Consuls on horseback waited with false smiles of patience, their horses snorting. Then the ranks of litters, chariots, soldiers, horses, and people would move along again, to be stopped at the next intersection.

Those who had villas in the suburbs, or farms, could not now go to them because of the war. They added to the crowded conditions, as did the endless streams of refugees and the soldiers. It was intolerable. Roman tempers, never very tolerant, seethed. The sewers, always stinking in the summer, stank worse these days. Rome was one vast stench of sweat, humanity, and offal. Marcus thought of Arpinum with acute longing and pain.

He had ceased, since his grandfather's death, his visits with doves to the temple of Venus, for his hope for Livia was gone, and he was too harassed. One day, as his sweltering legs moved obediently along with thousands of other legs on the street—when the traffic could flow again—he saw the cool dark entrance to the lovely, pillared temple. It was a refuge from the heat and smell and press, and he darted within. He took a long free breath. The temple was not empty; in peaceful days it would have appeared crowded. But compared with the street without it was silent and the worshipers were few. Marcus leaned against a white marble column, and wiped the sweat from his face and shifted the books on his arm, and shook out his wetly clinging tunic. The coolness of the marble invaded his grateful back; the scent of incense was delightful to his nostrils. The marble under his feet eased his hot soles. He looked at the goddess on her altar, and her great calm beauty assuaged his wretchedness. Candles burned before her like silvery stars. There was an odor of flowers.

Many girls, approaching marriage, or in love, stood or knelt before Venus, offering up their prayers. They were like young flowers, themselves. Doves fluttered in their hands. Their varicolored hair streamed down their backs, held with ribbons of different hues. Their small breasts heaved under their chitons. Their chaperones stood beside them, severe in their mantles. It suddenly occurred to Marcus that there were always more women and maidens in the temple of Venus than there were men and youths. He thought, with sudden cynicism, that this was because men did not confuse concupiscence with love, as women did. War, money, ambition, power, glory, conflict: these were the realities of men. Love, or lust, was only their dalliance.

It was then that he saw Livia among the other maidens, offering up her doves.

He had seen her so often in his dreams and in his waking imaginings that he thought this only another delusion. The candlelight flickered on her pale cheek and exquisite profile, in the pools of blue which were her eyes, on her ruddy hair flowing under its white veil, on her high young breast under its yellow covering, on the white ribbons which bound her waist, on the sparkling bracelets on her long white arms, on the glittering betrothal ring on her finger. She seemed absorbed by the face of Venus. She held the doves close to her breast, her chin uplifted over the wings. Behind her stood a very elderly lady soberly but richly clad.

It seemed to Marcus that he froze like a statue, himself. But he heard a thick pounding in his ears. Joy, like a light, burst over him. Then he began to tremble and to breathe quickly, as if he had been running. All the past dreary months fell from him like dried mud; his barren life rushed into scent and greenness. Promise and hope bloomed again on the stark mountains of his existence. He thought he heard music. He had endured; he saw how empty and desperate had been that endurance. He thought he had almost forgotten; he knew that he had only smothered his thoughts of Livia. He saw himself like a turbulent river, rushing toward the girl, pouring over her, swirling her to himself.

The priests moved among the worshipers with baskets in which they gathered the doves. A faint sound of lutes filled the temple, and the softest of singing voices. The girls and women rose from their knees and prepared to leave. Marcus, shaking as if with fever, removed himself to the portico, and awaited Livia and her guardian. A musical storm of female voices burst about him; his eyes probed the ranks of young and old famales. Then Livia and her guardian appeared. The girl's face was aloof and grave.

"Livia," said Marcus. She did not hear him. He spoke her name again as she was within hand's reach. She started and glanced up. Immediately her face became scarlet; her lips trembled and her blue eyes brightened. She hesitated. He narrowed the distance between them and said urgently, "Livia?"

He saw her struggle. He knew she wished not to speak to him, but to pass him in silence. So he stretched out his hand and touched hers. She shivered, then stood mute, not looking at him.

"Who is this impudent person?" asked her guardian in a harsh voice. The older woman's eyes swept over Marcus' modest tunic, his plain sandals, and noted his lack of jewelry. "Who is this slave?" asked the woman.

"He is my friend," said Livia, in the lowest of voices. The guardian stared, then cupped her ear, under its white hair, with her hand.

"Eh?" she said in her parrot voice.

"My aunt, Melina, is deaf," Livia said to Marcus. But still she would not look at him. She put her red lips to her aunt's ear and almost shouted, "My friend! Marcus Tullius Cicero!"

Those passing gazed at them curiously and circled about them.

"I know no Cicero!" shouted the aunt. "Cicero! Chick-pea! What is this, my girl?"

Livia said to Marcus in a quiet and rapid voice, "I am sorry that your grandfather died. I am sorry—" She drew a quick breath, and now her blue eyes were full of pain. "Do not delay us, Marcus. Do not touch me. We must go."

"Livia," he pleaded.

"What is it that you wish of me?" the girl cried, despairingly. "What can you say to me? There is nothing, Marcus."

"I cannot forget you. I live only by the thought of you," said Marcus. The aunt was tugging at the maiden's arm. Her old eyes fixed themselves angrily on the interloper.

"Nothing, nothing," murmured Livia. "Forget me, Marcus."

"No. That is beyond me," he said. "Livia, tell me that you remember me, that you think of me."

He felt, if she left him like this, he would die of his desolation. "I come here often to pray that Venus will have mercy on us," he said. He spoke hoarsely, out of his anguish.

"I pray that I will love Lucius," said Livia. "What is fated must come to pass. Not even the gods can avoid fate."

Now she looked at him sternly. She seemed to tell him that she was no servant girl who could flee with a groom. The circumstances of their lives were inexorable.

"Say only that you think of me," he pleaded.

Her eyes suddenly pulsed with tears; her raspberry lips quivered. But she said, very quietly, "I think of my bridegroom, Lucius."

"Livia!" he exclaimed, clasping his hands as if praying.

Her lids covered her eyes, and her white face became rigid with suffering.

"I beg of you, Marcus," she whispered. "Depart from me."

"There is nothing impossible, so long as we live," he said.

Livia gathered her filmy cloak about her, and turned to her aunt, who was staring at Marcus in umbrage. The girl took the older woman's arm gently. They passed Marcus and Livia did not glance back at him. A double litter awaited them below. They entered, and the slaves carried them away. Not once did the curtains move. Marcus watched the litter until it had been swallowed up in the press of traffic.

He leaned his forehead against a pillar and he wept as he had not wept at his grandfather's death. He knew now that the Lady of Cypress was the mightiest of all the goddesses, that she was mightier than Zeus. The cynics and the skeptics might sneer or utter profanities or obscenities. Venus remained unchallenged, immortal, never to be overcome.

If only I were rich and powerful, he thought in his agony. If only I had a great name! But I am nothing, nothing.

He returned home in a daze of torment. He could see nothing but Livia's blue eyes.

CHAPTER FOURTEEN

The family did not notice Marcus' pallor that night, for Tullius had again sickened with the prevailing malaria. Helvia had just returned from one of the three temples to the Goddess of Fever, and was in the kitchen hastily preparing the evening meal. Quintus was glowering miserably over his books. Only Archias saw Marcus' face.

"How goes it with the honorable Scaevola?" he asked in the atrium, shrewdly speculating about the reason for Marcus' overwhelming aspect of distress.

"I did not see him today. He was busy defending the Carpenters' Guild from charges brought by the Senate for overcharging the government," Marcus answered, listlessly. "There were other cases also, involving the Harness-makers Guild, and the Shoemakers. Extortion against the government in time of war."

"As the government practices extortion against almost everyone, it is only just that others engage in the practice against it," said Archias.

Marcus tried to smile. "Scaevola says the law is a donkey, and its only permitted rider is government," he said.

"But who won in this case, or cases?" asked Archias.

"Scaevola." Now Marcus truly smiled. "He has secret histories of all the Senators, most of the tribunes, and many of the Consuls. So they listen seriously to his arguments. The carpenters, the harness-makers, and the shoemakers were acquitted of extortion. Scaevola warned them privately, afterward, that they must be less greedy for a time. He received, as usual, vast gifts." Marcus paused. "He has only to look straightly at the faces of the Senators for them to cower."

"It is well for a lawyer to have dossiers concerning the powerful," said Archias. "Ah, men! An honest lawyer, believing in honest law, would die of starvation for lack of clients. He would never win a case."

Marcus frowned. "Then I shall starve," he said.

Archias chuckled. But his keen eyes dwelled on the youth's face. He is sickening of something, he thought. And of what do men sicken the most? At his age? Love. It is foolish, but nevertheless it is true. He pulled Marcus aside and said, "Listen to me. You are approaching the age of seventeen. Yet never have you known a woman."

Marcus' pale face colored deeply.

"At your age," said Archias, "one feels ready to die of love. I am a poet. I do not laugh at love; at least, I do not despise it. But it has other agreeable aspects. They soothe the flame; they temporarily quench the burning. They stun the feverish mind for a time, which is engaged in the contemplation of one image only."

"You recommend a brothel?" said Marcus.

"Not in these days, when the mob has gold and soldiers from every part of the world are frolicking in the city," said Archias. He said, blandly, "I recommend my Eunice."

"You are not serious!"

"I am very serious. I am not a young man, my innocent Marcus. And Eunice is young, amiable, and tender and versed in the arts of love. I taught her, myself, when I was potent. She is voluptuous and ripe life pulses in her. She is faithful to me; she adores me now as a father. But her nature will not be denied. Take her to your bed. I should prefer that to having her secretly romping with a gladiator or a slave, who might make her unclean and unsafe in this household."

Marcus stared at him. He felt violated. Archias stared back at him, smiling.

"Are you a panderer?" said Marcus, almost hating him.

Archias pursed his lips. "Your words are harsh. Therefore, it means that you are deeply wounded. Apparently the beloved maiden is unavailable. I would be your benefactor. I know, from experience, that women have a sameness when the lamps are out. You have only to pretend that you embrace your beloved. I will send Eunice to you tonight. You will be conferring a benefit upon her, and upon me."

Marcus was silent. Archias rapped his knuckles on the young man's chest. "Aphrodite is the goddess of love. She is also the goddess of the arts of love, and concupiscence. As an experienced goddess, herself, she does not admire those who keep themselves inviolate because of the unavailability of one beloved woman. Such self-castration is abominable to her, and to all sensible gods—and men. Should you offer up your testes to her she would reject them, and rightly so. Go to, Marcus, and become a man."

Marcus thought, If I could lie with Livia but once! Perhaps then I could forget her! The very thought of embracing Livia set his loins on fire for the first time. He colored violently. Archias grinned under his long nose, and seeing this Marcus turned on his heel and left him.

But when Eunice was assisting Helvia at the table that night Marcus could not keep his glance from her. She was only a few years older than himself, and ripe and golden-haired and rich of lip. She caught his glance once and smiled at him affectionately. She caught his second glance, and her smile was no longer sisterly. At the third glance, her smile was provocative. Marcus then attended to his supper, despising himself. But he could not stop remembering that Eunice's breasts were full, her hips rounded, her arms like those of a statue. Her cheeks were like pears. When she served the wine she leaned toward Marcus and exuded a fragrance like sweet clover. He became dizzy with his first true desire.

When he lay in bed that night, his whole body throbbing, he tried sternness with himself. A Roman controlled his impulses. Still, they had female slaves. He, Marcus, had no wife. He would probably never possess one, because of Livia. Should he deny himself? Should he detest his natural nature?

He struggled with these thoughts, wakeful and tossing. Then in the darkness he heard the rustling of his curtain, and the softest of laughs. A moment later the warmth and fullness of Eunice was against his body, and her arms about his neck and her lips pressed to his. There was an innocence about her, a lavish giving. There was no vileness. He forgot she was a slave, belonging to another. She was a gift, and she alone gave that gift. While he took it, awkwardly, he forgot Livia.

A few days later Archias took Eunice to the praetor and gave her her freedom. He also gave her—after some struggle with his Grecian thriftiness—one-third of his small fortune. The girl went to Helvia who felicitated her upon her good fate. "You can now procure a husband for yourself, Eunice," she said. She had a great affection for this sweet if stupid young woman, whose delight it was to serve.

"Permit me to remain with you, Lady," Eunice implored.

"I cannot pay you in these days, Eunice. You are no longer a slave. Would you work for your mere bread and bed, and an occasional mantle or sandals?"

"Yes," said Eunice with deep earnestness.

Helvia shrugged. There was little in the household which escaped her.

"I will keep my accounts," she said. "One day we will not be so poor. I shall then repay you."

Eunice kissed her hands and was full of rejoicing. Helvia sighed. She went to her lonely cubiculum and studied herself in her silver mirror, a gift from her mother. I am old, old, she thought. I am thirty-three; the juice of life has left me.

She knew that Eunice would do Marcus no harm. She hoped, however, that he would do Eunice no harm, either. That would be unpardonable.

In the meantime, Marcus' pallor lessened. He appeared less abstracted. He grew in stature. His voice steadily deepened, and the brows over his eyes became more marked. There was an authority, even a tranquillity about him which pleased his mother.

Old Scaevola resembled a gigantic coin. He had an enormous round bald head, no discernible neck, three vast chins which rolled on his broad chest, a huge belly, and short fat legs. He had a remarkably small satyr's face, full of lewd knowledge and intellect. His eyes were excessively minute, but resembled pieces of brilliant blue glass, and overlooked nothing. It pleased him to be told that he had the ugly snubbed nose of Socrates above thick and smacking lips. His complexion glowed like a pomegranate, and was full of winey threads. He possessed a voice like a bull and though he had grandsons he had an intense passion for life and a bounding zest.

He thought earnest and sincere young men to be fools; he thought those who believed man had the capacity for virtue to be even greater fools. He did not hold the wicked in contempt, nor did he revile them or denounce them. He accepted the evil that was man with good humor and laughter. To him law was an exciting game, even more exciting than his beloved dice. It was a matching of the wits. If he loaded his dice against magistrates and Senators with his knowledge concerning them, he did so genially. He knew they carried loaded dice themselves. His were only infinitely better and he could throw more shrewdly. He loved his clients though he rarely believed in their innocence. "You say you are no murderer, my dear," he would remark to a man who had been caught almost red-handed by the guards. "I am prepared to believe that, though we both know it is a lie. Let us see what we can do."

He defended everyone who came to him, even those who had no money. He was rich, himself, and a patrician. He was adored by multitudes for what was believed his charity and his ardor in defending the accused. He accepted plaudits happily. He had won his game. There was not the most obscure of regulations, invented by some faceless bureaucrat, of which he did not know. His library was famous even among other illustrious lawyers. He had concocted a game of his own—a board on which pellets of various colors could be moved or taken on the throw of a die. It was hard to say which he preferred more: winning a lawsuit or winning a game at his own table. His students, like Marcus Tullius Cicero, were always forced to play with him after lessons. He invariably beat them, to his almost childish delight.

In the beginning he had looked incredulously at Marcus who sincerely believed that law was the foundation of nations, and that rule by law was true civilization. He would shake his head over and over, as if dazed. Once he said to the youth, "You quote your grandfather copiously. He must have been remarkably innocent, as well as a good man. But he put his trust in what does not exist; disinterested justice. By Apollo, my child! That has never been so in man's history! Is not justice depicted as blind? You speak like a drooling infant."

He thought he had disposed sensibly of this nonsense. But Marcus returned to it obdurately and finally Scaevola had to take him seriously. The old man was aghast.

"You have been with me in the courts. You have seen me defend all manner of men. Did you believe my clients innocent? One in a thousand, my dear, one in a thousand! I was merely more adroit than the magistrate, or those infernal Senators. Law is a harlot; she smiles on those with the fattest purse."

"It should not be so," said Marcus, stubbornly.

Scaevola threw up his hands and his eyes. "It is a fact of life!" he roared. "Am I, or you, to oppose it? What an imbecile you are. Retire to the desert, or go to the Indus and contemplate your navel. You are not of the stuff of lawyers."

"I am," said Marcus, setting his mouth firmly.

The tiny blue eyes studied him with diamond hardness and thought. "Why do you want to be a lawyer, my dear?"

"Because I believe in law, and justice. I believe in our Twelve Tables of Law. I believe that all men have a right to be represented before their accusers. If we have no law then we are beasts."

"That is the very point," said the old man. "We *are* beasts."

"You have said yourself, Master, that one in a thousand of your clients is innocent. Is that not enough, that one man escape injustice and punishment? Is that not why law was written?" Marcus hesitated. "My grandfather always asserted that when Romans are governed by men and not by law, then Rome must fall."

The old man belched loudly and Marcus was enveloped in a wind of garlic. Scaevola scratched himself through his soiled tunic. He contemplated Marcus again.

"Rome has already fallen," he said at last. "Did you not know that?"

Marcus was silent.

"Even if you become a lawyer you will have no clients—if you take only those you believe are innocent. Why, then, do you study law?"

"I have told you: I believe in the rule of established law. I also wish to make an honorable living."

Scaevola shook a thick finger in his face. "You are doomed to bitterness, and probably to suicide, or even to be murdered," he said. "That is always the fate of men who espouse virtue, or believe in justice. You are also doomed to penury. You are wasting your money sitting with me here and in the courts."

"Do you wish me, then, to leave?" asked Marcus.

Scaevola grunted, scratched his head. Then he said at last, "No. I have had all the amusements that men know in my life, and still have them. Save one. I have not seen an honest lawyer in my life." He laughed uproariously.

He disliked his students on principle. He found himself disliking Marcus less than he did the others. This was because he admired intelligence, and he found intelligence in Marcus' eyes, stern lips, and wide brow. Once he even said, as if conceding a game, "It is possible that without the little law we do honor we should have chaos, and even a bought harlot is better than no woman at all. But I tell you that the day is coming when Rome will have no law whatsoever but the decree of tyrants."

Once Marcus brought up the subject of the Ten Commandments of Moses. Scaevola knew all about them. "You will notice," he observed, "that almost all of them say 'Thou shalt *not*.' If there were any virtue in men this would not be necessary. If men were *not* by nature murderers, thieves, adulterers, liars, enviers, blasphemers, betrayers, the Commandments would not have been given to that Moses. If any men obey them it is out of superstitious fear, and not from any good inclination of their hearts. Let the pious once be deprived of superstition and religion, then you will see chaos, indeed. The tiger is not more fierce than man, the lion not more terrible, the rat not more cunning and blood-thirsty, the leopard not more wild. Let us bless the gods, even though they do not exist," said Scaevola, rolling up his eyes solemnly.

In the meantime, Marcus heard of the marriage of Livia Curius to Lucius Catilina. He heard of it even over the thunder of the war. Scaevola and his family were invited to the festivities, and the old man spoke approvingly of the viands. Usually so acute, so instantly aware of any change of expression in anyone, he did not see Marcus' whiteness of face nor the agony in his eyes. "I do not trust the Catilinii," he said. "Of course, I do not trust any man, but I mistrust that family more than most. Young Lucius is ambitious. I do not decry ambition, for did it not raise me to my present eminence? But the young Catilina is without a single virtue, except for his appearance. He does not even pretend to have a virtue! So long as men pretend to some goodness we can plod along in a measure of safety, if only by appealing to pride. Even a demon wishes to stand well in the estimation of others. The young Catilina does not even desire that."

"Yet, he is greatly loved," said Marcus.

Scaevola nodded, and frowned. "Perhaps it is because a totally evil man has an irresistible charm, and excites the envy and admiration of those who dare not display themselves so completely."

"Then total evil has a kind of virtue of its own," said Marcus. "An honesty."

Scaevola was delighted, and struck Marcus on the shoulder so heavily that the youth reeled in his chair. "My dear, you have spoken words of wisdom! An old man is enlightened by a youth who is still comparatively beardless! For this, I shall reward you with three of my games instead of one."

Marcus was so wrapped in his anguish and so abstracted that he was not aware of the boring game and the fall of the dice. In consequence, he actually won two games out of three. Scaevola was astonished; his lips pouted as if he were about to weep. He said, "I am becoming old. I am not so keen any longer."

It was the last game with his mentor that Marcus won, for in a sort of revenge Scaevola plied him with books and took him on an endless round of the courts. It seemed to him that he came to know every stone in the Basilica of Justice, and the face of every magistrate.

But regardless of what Scaevola never ceased from informing him, he never was diverted from his belief that law was inviolate—in spite of the evidence. It was a matter, he was convinced, of proper presentation. It was a matter of believing in the ultimate triumph of justice, however it was perverted. It was a matter of truth.

Once Scaevola said to Marcus, "You have a presence, which is invaluable in law. Handsomeness is no asset; were it so, I should not be a lawyer of success. I do not know what it is, but in your jejune way you are impressive. Nevertheless, you display too sincere a modesty and humility. It is no paradox for me to assert that modesty and humility are worthy in a lawyer. But they must be theatrical—and false! True modesty and humility excite contempt, as does all truth. It is affectation, and histrionics, which impress even the intelligent. Think always that you must impress magistrates, then hypocrisy will come naturally to you. Remember that a lawyer, to be successful, must be an actor, with an actor's sensitivity for his audience. Do I speak in riddles?"

"No," said Marcus.

"First, my dear, you must impress others that you have some secret power—then you may be as modest and humble as you please. Be confident; tell yourself that Marcus Tullius Cicero is an important man, and tell yourself that constantly, even while you still lack importance. What is importance? A man's belief that he has more wealth, power, intellect, learning, family or whatever, than his antagonist. It is not necessary for this to be true; one has only to believe it, and by osmosis the belief extends itself to others. It is not even necessary for you to be fully informed in the law; one's clerks can seek out the dusty knowledge when it is needed." The fat old man shook his head and recited from an essay Marcus had just written:

" 'True law is right reason consonant with nature, worldwide in scope, unchanging and everlasting. We may not oppose or alter that law, we cannot abolish it, we cannot be freed from its obligations by any legislature, and we need not look outside ourselves for an expounder of it. The law does not differ for Rome and Athens, for the present and the future, but one eternal and unchanging law will be valid for all nature and for all times. He who disobeys it denies himself and his own nature.' "*

Scaevola pursed up his fat lips and spat. "Nonsense," he said.

But Marcus said, "Why is it nonsense?"

"For the reason that men make laws which are convenient for their political factions and for themselves, when it is necessary. 'Unchanging law!' Laws change as men need them to change; as I have said, law is a harlot."

But Marcus kept his notes and later used that when writing his history of Roman law. He was never to deviate from his belief that law was above man's exigencies and his lusts. Violent events and lawlessness did not shake his convictions; they only proved them.

"Where did you learn this presence you possess, for your neck is too long and you are too slender to be naturally imposing?" asked Scaevola.

"My friend, Noë ben Joel, the actor and playwright and producer of plays," Marcus confessed, blushing. "He has taught me the posture, the gestures, the motions of an actor."

"Excellent," said Scaevola, inspecting him critically. "You see then, my dear, that histrionics are the most important things in a lawyer's career. Your voice, when you forget to be respectful, is mellifluous. Can we attribute that also to the astute Noë ben Joel?"

"True," said Marcus. "I have a wonderful teacher, Archias. We quote long and sonorous poetry."

"I recommend poetry for a lawyer," said Scaevola, approvingly. "He can

* From Cicero's *Law*.

learn his speeches, then, by rote, perfecting and polishing them in private, and then delivering them in public without stammering and hesitation—as an actor speaks his lines. While so doing, he can think of his gifts, and thoughts of large gifts can put eloquence in a man's voice. Money is better than a woman; it never betrays a man. Therefore I disagree with other lawyers who recommend thinking of one's mistress when pleading a case. It is money which puts fervor in a man's tones, and passion in his eyes. You will observe that the majority of cases which come to law concern money and property. These are the greatest preoccupations of men."

The Social War was succeeded immediately by the war with Mithridates VI. The newly enfranchised Italians discovered that far from being truly enfranchised by Rome, the central government, they could vote in only their localities, and among their tribes. The picture became more acute, more violent. The virtuous P. Sulpicius Rufus, the tribune, attempted reforms in the Senate and sought to bring amnesty to all Italians who had been accused of complicity in the Italian revolt against Rome. "They acted according to their honorable convictions, and there was much justness on their side," said Rufus. "What more can be asked of a man? And, have we not now given them the franchise, and should we not now extend it to all franchises, and recall the leaders who fought for their honor and justice from exile?"

Despising the corrupt Senate, he proposed that all Senators who through their profligacy had fallen into debt be removed from their seats. He championed freedmen. He urged that the command of the armies be given to General Marius, who appeared to him less venal than Sulla, though Sulla was legally the general in command of the armies against Mithridates. But Sulla's fellow Consuls thought they themselves were attacked, when this proposal was suggested against one of them. Now Romans within the gates eyed each other with fury, and prepared for the utmost violence. The Consuls, to add confusion to what was already confused, declared a public holiday. Rufus then armed his followers and drove the Consuls from the Forum. Sulla, in command of the legions in Nola, advanced on Rome to overthrow Rufus. Later he was to enter the city in triumph and in the name of the Republic—which he secretly despised. Marius and Rufus were to flee in disgrace and in fear of their lives. But that was two years later in the war.

Scaevola had his opinions, but as they were satiric and fatalistic, and amused, his pupil, Marcus, could not sort out any coherence from the general terror and confusion of the Social War. "Have no opinions if you value your future, my dear," said Scaevola to his favorite pupil. "Agree with Sulla, then again with Sulpicius Rufus, in a temperate voice at all times. But never disagree with them, either! A lawyer, being only a man, naturally has his opinions. But never must they be known, if he is to be successful—and above all, to survive. Let him say, 'Yes, you are correct. But on the other hand, if you will pardon me, there may be something else in favor of the opposite opinion.' Let him then be vague and pliant, and appear to be convinced by his opponent. Always must he smile agreeably. He will then become famous as a level man of wide tolerance, and no politician can then accuse him of anything disastrous. He will not only survive; he will become prosperous."

"I commit the first sin, then," said Marcus. "I disagree with you that a lawyer must be a hypocrite."

"Then, invest what sums you have in a manufactory of bricks," said Scaevola. "Do not be a lawyer." He glared at Marcus. "I have prophesied it before: you will not die peacefully in your bed. Manufacture blankets if bricks do not appeal to you. But, alas, even manufacturers of blankets and bricks are now the servants of politicians! If you do not agree with the current masters you do not receive contracts. It is best to hold your tongue, whether in law or in manufacture. In fact," said Scaevola with a gloom rare with him, "it is better if one has never been born. How is it possible for an honest man to endure his fellows? By compromising with them. By silencing his own thoughts. By pandering. By becoming an adroit liar. By never offending, even when in opposition. This is called fine manners. I prefer to call it prostitution. But forgive me, my son. I have lapsed from my own convictions, which is not to have any convictions at all, and only to laugh at mankind."

He shouted irascibly, "Confusion on you! I am too old and too learned to be depressed by a schoolboy's candid eyes!"

He shook his head. "Of one thing we can be certain: war never leaves a nation where it found it. What the shape of Rome will be when this is over I do not know. But it will not be good."

To punish Marcus for having shaken him even a little, he forced the youth to play four games of dice on the board with him.

The early autumn twilight was gray and dull and chill when Marcus was finally released from the dice and the board. It was a long walk home to the Carinae from the house of Scaevola. Torches had not yet been lit, lanterns were not yet moving through the teeming streets. But the noise and the smell and the traffic were omnipresent. The gray sky loomed overhead, sombre, unlit by stars or moon. Marcus could not tell if the cold that enwrapped him came from his heart or from without, but despondency slowed his steps and bent his head. He had rarely smiled since the marriage of Livia. He thought each day would lessen his pain, but it did not.

Sometimes he thought that his burdens were more than he could endure. Legally his father was his guardian until he came of age, but Tullius had no part in the decisions of his son and knew nothing of the finances of the family. He appeared to be less and less engaged in living, and an invisible cleft widened between father and son, which bewildered and pained Tullius but at which Marcus could only stare in suffering and in impatience and with a sense of wrong. Marcus, bereft now of the strength of his grandfather, felt his callowness and his aloneness. He would not be seventeen until the month of Janus, three months in the future, yet he had investments to consider, a household to guide, a younger brother to oversee, a mother to advise, a career to undertake, studies that became daily more complicated. He had also his private grief.

As he walked home tonight his desolation almost overwhelmed him. His life was narrow and restricted, full of duties. There was none of the lightness of youth to give his days any gayety; he had no friends; the family could not entertain because of its recent bereavement and the war and lack of money. There were no warriors in the family, none of the excitement of war. There were only taxes. Marcus felt as hopeless as the grave.

He suddenly remembered that he should be at his fencing class, before going home. Sighing, he pushed against a slowly moving wall of humanity in another direction.

The fencing school was patronized not only by young boys but by officers and men in their middle-age, and was famous. The master was one Gaius, and he had several teachers, all masters of the art. The school was lighted with lanterns, and when Marcus opened the door he felt a blast of warmth from sweating bodies. The teachers were in full occupation; the air was filled with shouts, admonitions, the clash of guarded swords. Gaius moved about from group to group, watching, shaking his head, advising. Marcus put his books on a stool, removed his mantle and long tunic, and stood in a short tunic of gray wool. He took his sword from its peg on the plastered wall and looked about for an unengaged teacher or a skilled opponent. He felt very tired and isolated.

Three officers were laughing heartily at one group. They were young men in full armor, and helmeted. They stood with their thumbs in their leather belts, their armored legs apart. They joked, goaded the sweating men and youths, taunted, uttered lewdnesses, and swaggered more than a little. The wooden floor throbbed with the best of many dexterous soles.

One of the young officers took off his helmet, and Marcus, who had just finished assuring himself that the guard was firm on his sword-point, glanced up. He saw ruddy hair and a handsome profile. He had not seen these for years, but his heart lurched. He recognized Lucius Sergius Catilina immediately, and also his companions, the slight fair Cneius Piso and the tall, grim and dark-faced Quintus Curius, cousin to Livia.

Lucius wiped his magnificent face on a kerchief, which he then carelessly tucked in his belt. The three friends were intent on a group of three fencers and teachers. Marcus stood, rigid, and watched them, his face very white and still. If he could have moved he would have hung up his sword again, snatched on his long tunic and mantle, seized his books and fled. But he could only stand there, paralyzed, and gaze at the husband of Livia and hate him with a wild and desperate hatred. His heart trembled and roared in his ears; his lungs seemed to have shut themselves off from air; his flesh crept and shivered, and his blood pounded. There was a stricture about his throat, like fingers of iron, and sickness crawled in his belly.

If Lucius had been handsome years before, he looked now like a god, like a young Mars. He did not pose; his body was full of the lines of heroic grace. He had an aura of intense magnetism about him, which held the eye. When he threw back his head to laugh his brilliant white teeth flashed in the lantern light. He stood with his hands on his hips and shouted mockeries, or turned to his friends for a jest.

Gaius, the master, a short fat man, paused before the three, and Lucius clapped him affectionately on the shoulder. Marcus, through all the roaring in his ears, heard his voice clearly. "There is not one here that I should recommend to my general, Gaius," he said. It was an insult, but the master only smiled, not obsequiously but with genuine amusement and liking.

"You were one of my best fencers, Lucius," he said. "Why do you not show my pupils, the younger ones, a display of your talent? Or you, Cneius, or you, Curius?"

"No, no!" cried Lucius. "These are but schoolboys! There is none here we know; we but paused on the way to a fine dinner." He looked about him with his tremendous, smiling charm, and his eyes reached Marcus against the farthest wall. The smile did not disappear; it only changed, lost its charm, and became ugly.

"Ah!" exclaimed Lucius. "There is one we know! Look, Cneius. Look, Curius. Do we not know him, or am I mistaken? Is it a freedman, a fuller? I seem to remember those undistinguished features. Quick! You must tell me."

His friends swung about and stared at Marcus and recognized him.

"It is the vetch, for a certainty," said Curius. "Chick-pea," said Cneius.

They burst into loud laughter, and stared at Marcus who could only stare at Lucius, with the terrible hatred growing in him, with the terrible urge to kill taking over his senses. He had felt it only once before, when he had been but nine years old, and he had felt it for this man. His hands sweated. Not looking away from Lucius, he rubbed his palms on his tunic. The sword in his right hand felt as light as a wand; it shook in his fingers as if it had a life of its own and wished to leap straight at the heart of young Catilina. For here was the desecrator of Livia, and the despoiler of his, Marcus', life and hope.

"You have frightened him, Lucius," said Cneius in a soothing voice. "His loincloth is now probably overflowing."

Marcus heard the words; his nostrils distended, and now his tight lungs expanded in a great breath. But still he could look only at Lucius in a deadly silence. Gaius was staring at him. The master was fond of him, and his sharp eyes narrowed in uncertainty, both at the youth's expression and the faces of the three friends.

"What is it, Marcus?" he asked.

Lucius replaced his helmet. He strolled toward his old enemy then paused before him, looking him up and down as if he were a base fellow, an intruding slave. "Do you have such as this fuller's grandson in your school, my Gaius?" he asked.

"Marcus Tullius Cicero is one of my most talented pupils," said Gaius. Now his round face flushed with annoyance. He felt danger in the air.

"Then you have fallen on evil days," said Lucius. His friends moved to his side, laughing. "I thought you accepted only men and boys of family and name, and not such as—this." He lightly extended his booted foot and tapped Marcus on the knee with it, as one would touch a dog.

Without consciously willing it Marcus slapped aside the foot with the flat of his sword. He said to himself, with calmness, I must kill him. I shall surely die of frustration if I do not kill him!

As if a signal had been given, or a command, the room fell silent. The teachers and their pupils stood with half-raised swords, and stared at the group. The lanterns flickered; dust swirled in the air.

Then Lucius, his teeth glittering, drew his sword, and the sound was a clash in the silence. Gaius caught his arm, in dismay.

"What is this?" he exclaimed. "This is my school! This is no arena, Lucius! Are you mad?"

"It is but an animal," said Cneius with contempt. "Let Lucius run him through, and then bury him in your garden."

Gaius was frightfully alarmed. "Stop!" he cried, seizing Lucius' arm more tightly. "I will not have murder done in my school! Marcus Cicero is one of my honorable pupils; I knew his grandfather well. Will you force me to call the guard? In the name of the gods, gentlemen, leave my school at once!"

"We are officers of the army of Rome," said Curius. "Lucius has been insulted by the son of a slave, or worse. Is he armored? Is he a man? No. Is he a soldier? No. And Lucius has been offended by such as he."

"Murder!" shouted Gaius. "Would Lucius, who is an honorable man, murder a younger who is but a pupil, and has a guard on his sword, which is only a light shaft?"

Lucius did not look away from Marcus. But he sheathed his sword. "Give me one like his," he said through his teeth.

"One with a guard," pleaded Gaius, desperately. "This is but a school."

"With a guard," said Lucius, nodding. "As you have said, my Gaius, this is a school, not an arena or a battlefield or a field of honor. I will bring this low-born rascal to his knees, and it will be enough for me."

He lifted his hand and struck Marcus across his cheek. "There is my challenge, Chick-pea," he said.

Still not looking away from the tense quiet face of his enemy, Lucius stripped himself quickly of his armor until he stood only in his boots and his red tunic. His friends deftly accepted the armor from him, and began to laugh again. Gaius thrust a light, guarded sword into Lucius' hand.

"On guard, Chick-pea," said Lucius, and fell at once into a strong and graceful posture of attack. He was smiling once more, his teeth flashing.

I must kill him, thought Marcus. But there was the guard on his sword. Then he thought, I must humble him at the very least and drive him to his knees.

The teachers and their pupils, wide-eyed and holding their breath and their faces shining with excitement, spread themselves against the walls. There was a sudden wide and open space about the antagonists. Their swords crossed at once.

Marcus was more than two years younger, and much lighter. He had had no training in the army and he was no athlete. He felt the pressure of Lucius' sword on his, a strong and steady pressure beyond anything he had ever felt before. This man was not only a soldier, trained in the legions and on the battlefield. He was one of the finest athletes in Rome, one of the most notable swordsmen. He had killed before.

They sprang apart, their swords whistling. Marcus knew only one thing: that he must drive this hated man to his knees. His purpose was like a power in him, a drive, a lethal determination. He experienced no fear, no dismay, no hesitation. His muscles tightened lustfully; his knees, which were his weakest point, pulsed with alien strength.

Lucius' sword moved like a thin streak of lightning and the guarded point stung Marcus' left shoulder. Had the point been bare Marcus would perhaps have been fatally wounded. Lucius laughed with delight and his friends raised a cry of pleasure.

He is like a snake, thought Marcus, giving way a little. But, like a snake, he must have a weak point. Lucius struck at Marcus' throat but this time his sword was dashed aside. He is reckless, thought Marcus. Lucius was frowning. Yes, he is reckless, said Marcus to himelf. I will goad him to more recklessness. So Marcus, suddenly bending his knees, reached under Lucius' guard and struck him full in the chest.

Cneius and Curius raised a shout of anger and outrage. But Lucius was silent. He actually fell back. Marcus did not pursue him. He waited.

As if seized by a disgusted impatience, Lucius lunged forward, seeking by sheer force to drive Marcus back, to cause him to stumble and fall. Marcus deftly stepped aside, and Lucius ran several paces with his sword into emptiness.

"What?" said Marcus, tauntingly, as Lucius recovered himself. "Did you see a mirage of me?" It was the first word he had spoken.

Lucius could not believe it. His face turned a deathly white with fury. He was incredulous. He must have done with this at once! He sprang at Marcus with all his strength now, refusing to believe that the younger man had actually reached under his guard, refusing to believe the blow he had felt. No one had pierced his guard before.

I will madden him, thought Marcus. He saw no one but Lucius; his quick eye held itself on the other's sword. When Lucius, who was beginning to lose his head with umbrage and loathing, plunged his sword directly at Marcus' face the younger man struck it aside with an easy motion. The clashed weapons made a plangent sound, loud in the breath-sucked silence.

I am dreaming, thought the intent Gaius. This Marcus had always been bored by fencing. He fenced as a duty, as something without pleasure or interest. Truly, I am dreaming. He is like a dancer. There, how nimbly he danced aside at that lunge! But what is wrong with Lucius, who won all the prizes in this school when I taught him personally?

Gaius had been wounded many times on the field, and he had scored many hundreds of times with the finest fencers in mock fights. But he had never been spurred by hatred; he had never experienced the deadly hatred that Marcus was experiencing. Even in battle, he had wanted only to disarm, for he was a good-tempered man.

The swords clashed, crossing. Marcus and Lucius stared into each other's faces. "Am I on my knees?" asked Marcus, gently.

Lucius sprang back. His teeth clicked together. He was wild with mortification before his friends, who were muttering uneasily. He must have done with it at once! This slave was weaker and younger, though he danced like an actor. And, he was mocking Lucius Sergius Catilina, and that was not to be endured. He, Catilina, an officer in one of the finest legions, experienced, dexterous, a man who had killed easily face to face with the most skillful foes! This was not to be endured.

Now he ran at Marcus in a very blaze of lightning moves, acid on his lips and in his throat, as if he were about to vomit. His eyes sparkled with rage. His attack was so fierce that Marcus indeed fell back, circled, stumbled once or twice, was stung several times on shoulder, on the breast, on the arms. But never once did he feel uncertain; never once did his hate lessen or his determination. He fell back and around; he retreated, only fending off the blows aimed at his face. Lucius pursued him, smiling again, sure of victory. His friends applauded, howled with laughter, as the two circled the room. Sweat stood on the antagonists' faces in great drops, then rolled down their cheeks and into their eyes.

Marcus was not wearying, though he moved back dexterously, and merely defended himself. During lessons, he would have exhausted long ago. But this was no lesson.

Again their swords crossed, halfway up the hilts. Marcus said with that soft gentleness, as they stared at each other, "What! Did they not teach you better on the field, or did you fight with unarmed men, or maidens?"

They sprang apart. It was then that Lucius suddenly struck the floor with his sword and disengaged the guard.

Gaius shouted, "No, no! This is but fencing, not murder!"

But Lucius' friends roared with blood-thirsty joy, and the teachers and pupils screamed. The sword came lancing, naked, at Marcus' breast. For the first time fear touched him lightly. Lucius meant to kill him. He fell back, and as he did so he struck the guard from his sword also. Now they faced each other with shining and flickering death.

Gaius groaned. But all the others were seized with blood lust. This was no game any longer. It was serious; it would end, if not in death, with desperate wounds. This was the sport of the battlefield, of the arena.

"Dishonorable wretch!" cried Marcus. "Liar! Coward!"

But Lucius smiled. His tongue licked over his lips. He was now so sure that he made a deadly mistake. He lunged, and his foot slipped. Instantly he felt the sting of naked metal in his right shoulder. Before he could recover himself Marcus' sword was at his throat and he was on one knee. Marcus' sword flashed, hurled aside Lucius' sword, and the point returned to his throat, at a fatal spot.

The room roared with voices. Gaius came plunging forward. Marcus said in the most quiet of voices, "No. Let one man move and I run him through and that will be the end of him."

He meant it to be the end in any event. But he wanted to savor this moment of victory over this cruel and vicious man. He wanted Lucius to know death before he actually experienced it. He said, "I will kill you in a moment. But I must enjoy the thought first."

Lucius' stiff arms were bent straight backward and he was supporting himself now on the palms of his hands. He looked up into Marcus' face and saw the joyful hatred, the contorted mouth, the exultation. And he knew he was about to die.

"It was your choice," said Marcus. "You struck the guard off your sword. You meant a fight to the death. You have had it. Now you must die, you, the great and noble Catilina, the liar, the coward, the bruiser of children, the fool and the detestable slave in his soul."

Lucius said, "Kill me. Have done with it."

The point edged gently into his flesh. "Not too swiftly," said Marcus. "I am taking my pleasure, and my pleasures are slow and calm. A little more, now," and the sword slipped in just another fraction.

Never was anyone to say that Catilina was not a man to face death bravely. He did not wince before the metal. He even tried to smile. The pain was like a fire in his throat.

And then Marcus saw his eyes, wide and unblinking. He saw their full intense blue, fringed with ruddy lashes. And they were the eyes of Livia.

Agonizing grief smashed upon Marcus' heart, causing it to cringe and shake. His own eyes filled with tears and despair. He stepped back, withdrawing his sword. He could not speak.

"Noble fighter! Gracious victor!" shouted Gaius, and flung his arms about his pupil. He wept aloud with joy and relief. "Magnanimous warrior! He restores life; he does not take it, for all he was challenged to the death! I salute you, Master of all!"

The pupils and the teachers raised their voices in salutation and embraced each other as if they had won the victory themselves.

Cneius and Curius came to their friend and in silence helped him to his feet and pressed a kerchief against his bleeding throat. But Lucius put them aside after a moment. He looked at Marcus, standing at a little distance, and saluted him mockingly.

"I felicitate you, Chick-pea," he said.

Years later Marcus said to himself with anguish, "I should have killed him. I should never have let him live. Livia, Livia! Let my hand wither, that I betrayed you."

In those later days, Catilina said once to Marcus, "Why did you not kill me, Chick-pea? Were you seized at last by the knowledge that one who kills an officer of the Republic, a mere nameless citizen, would be punished and put to death?"

But Marcus was not able to answer.

The news went about the city, which desperately seized on trifles to give it relief from the gloom of war. The noble patrician of the house of Catilinii, Lucius Sergius, and an officer of the army and of one of the most famous legions known for its valor, had been overcome in a duel with bare swords by an unknown law clerk, the son of a humble knight, a country youth born not in Rome but in Arpinum, and of a family distinguished for nothing! (It annoyed the gleeful spreaders of the news when they learned that Marcus' mother was one of the noble Helvii, so this was not mentioned as of anything important.)

There were those who delighted that Lucius had been so humiliated, even among his friends and fellow patricians. Marcus often saw faces peering at him from rich litters, and smiling. Groups of artisans and shopkeepers, thinking of him affectionately as one of them, waited on Scaevola's doorstep for him to emerge.

Scaevola was silent about it all for several days, then he said to his pupil, "Tell me, my dear, did you refrain from killing him out of mercy?"

Marcus shook his head.

"No?" cried the old man, with pleasure. "Why, then?"

Marcus had now a deep affection for his teacher. He could not offend or disappoint him by telling him the truth, which would have seemed unmanly to Scaevola.

"Not," said Scaevola, losing his pleasure, "because you feared punishment as a civilian who killed a notable officer, and a patrician?"

"No," said Marcus.

"Good! Then you spared him so that he might suffer mortification, which, in a man like Lucius, would be unbearable?"

Scaevola was so pleased by his own reasoning and so delighted with Marcus that he embraced the youth.

"Lucius will never forgive you," said Scaevola, showing all his old yellow teeth in a joyous smile.

Helvia said to her son, "Did you spare Catilina because you feared the consequences of his death?"

"No," said Marcus.

Helvia meditated. Then she smiled. "You had disarmed him. You could not kill an unarmed man. You are a hero, my son. I am proud of you."

"I, too, am proud," said Quintus, his brother. "I did not know you were so splendid a swordsman."

I did not know, either, thought Marcus, with some wryness.

"Why did you not kill him, my friend?" asked Noë ben Joel. Noë's bright brown eyes began to dance. "Not," he exclaimed, "that you were remembering the Commandment, 'Thou shalt not kill'?"

"No," said Marcus. "I wished to kill him."

Noë clucked mockingly. "Then, why did you not?"

Marcus felt that Noë, an actor, an artist, a lover of plays and romances, would understand where others would not, and wished to unburden himself.

"Because he has the eyes of the girl I love, for he is distantly related to her, and has married her. Had I not seen those eyes fully, an instant before I was prepared to thrust the blade into his throat, he should have died."

He had not been wrong. Noë was delighted. "What a play this would make!" he cried. "Fear not; I will not give the hero your name nor the vanquished Catilina's. But someday, I will use this episode." He said exactly what Scaevola had said: "He will never forgive you."

"Nor," said Marcus through his teeth, "will I ever forgive him."

PART TWO

The Man and the Lawyer

Protexisti me, Deus, a conventu malignantium, alleluia; a multi-
tudine operantium iniquitatem——

"There is but one thing certain," said old Scaevola wrathfully. "What these new rascals call democracy is only confusion! You will discover this for yourself, if your life is spared, which I doubt. You are not likely to enjoy an old age like mine, with your absurd theories of the rights of man and democracy.

"Look at the law of Sulpicius, which granted to the freedmen—the base freedmen!—equality with the old citizens of Rome! Cinna, who prates of democracy and liberty and the Constitution of our nation and who is a monstrous despot, revived that law for he knows where his power lies, the exigent rascal! He nominated himself Consul every year, without consulting the people whom he alleges he loves. He will reduce taxes and debts, he declares, and he has done so, to our economic ruin, and the bareness of our treasury which has been looted for wars and the benefits of foreign dependencies and nations. We can be certain of one thing, my dear: this temporary alleviation of taxes will result in greater taxation and final collapse. It is pure bookkeeping. But are the people concerned with budgetry, and the hard fact that one cannot spend what one does not have, without bankruptcy? No! They cry 'Hail!' to the tyrant, Cinna, for an immediate gain at the expense of the nation."*

The noble old pontifex maximus shook his head despondently. "Marius, another famous democrat, spared my life, after the massacres he instigated when he returned to Rome. Why, I know not, for I detest all hypocrites. It was no accident that he was one with that vulgarian, Lucius Cornelius Cinna, who now so oppresses us in the name of democracy." He scratched his ear and chuckled sombrely. "Nevertheless, I am sometimes inclined to believe in the old myth that there is some wisdom in the people. When Marius died in his bed—very sad, he should have been murdered as he had murdered thousands of others without mercy—there was no public mourning on the part of the people for their self-appointed liberator. All Italy, and Rome, herself, raised their heads as if a sword had been lifted and deliverance announced. It is very puzzling. Those who shouted the loudest for the franchise and freedom are quite content with the bloody oppressions of Cinna—"

* Letter to Scaevola's son.

"They need to breathe, to collect themselves, after all these years of war," said Marcus. "They are exhausted. But surely we will rid ourselves of Cinna!"

"No," said Scaevola. "A restoration of the Constitution will only breed fresh social wars, and dumbly the people realize this. Better oppression with peace, they say, than freedom with war. This is the voice of the new freedmen, who strut about Rome and know nothing of her history, and rejoice in Cinna the tyrant, who embraces them in his vulgarity, with cries of 'democracy!' I am disappointed in our provinces, where I thought some manhood remained."

"They wish peace," said Marcus, again.

"Ha, ha," said Scaevola, in a voice of gloating. "There is still Sulla, in exile, in the East! Has he forgotten? No. We shall hear from him soon. Wars breed wars, as locusts breed locusts, and there are always ambitious men.

"In the meantime, let us consider that tomorrow you present your first case to the Senate. I will not plead with you, but I will be in the audience. You are twenty-one years old, and I have taught you conscientiously, for you have been less stupid than my other pupils, who are still only clerks. I have informed a number of my friends, and they will be there to applaud you—"

"If I win," said Marcus. He stood tall and thin and long-necked and quiet before his mentor, who narrowed his eyes upon him and tilted his great old head.

"A lawyer must not permit himself an 'if,'" said Scaevola. "Have I not told you? You cannot appeal to any established law of Rome in the case of your client, for there is no such law. Your client was a small farmer, a husbandman, with a wife and two young children, and three slaves who assisted him on his farm. But, like all of us, he fell on evil times and economic ruin. He could not pay his taxes. Therefore, the tax-gatherers have seized his small property, have imprisoned him and are prepared to sell your client into slavery, and his wife and children into slavery also. That is the law: a bankrupt, one who fails to pay his taxes, or cannot, or has debts he cannot pay, is seized, his property confiscated, and himself and his family sold into slavery, to satisfy his debtors or his avaricious government. That is the law of Rome, and who is not always celebrating the laws of Rome but you, my dear?"

"Once the heart of Rome was humane," said Marcus, in distress. "That evil law should have been repealed, and that it would have been done had it not been for the Social Wars. It remained for decades on the books without being enforced."

"The government needs money. That is always its plaint," said Scaevola, with contempt. "Let us translate that properly: Tyrants need money with which to buy votes and influence. Ergo, they revive evil laws. Their bureaucrats delve into dusty manuscripts and come upon a regulation or a little obscure law which will justify their oppressions. It is all very legal, and very virtuous. When that law appeared on the books, centuries before this, it was to discourage profligacy and irresponsibility in our then new nation, and to impress men that they must not undertake more than was consistent with their abilities, and the intelligence with which nature had seen fit to endow them. But now the government, eagerly seeking revenue, exploits an ancient law which was never enforced because the people were frugal and provident and their rulers humane. Now it is being enforced because the people are profligate and irresponsible, and their rulers monsters. It is a paradox, but governments are not noted for consistency. And, does not the government need money? Your client is but one of thousands."*

Marcus sat down and leaned his elbow on the marred table where so many pupils of Scaevola had studied. He bent his chin into the palm of his hand and stared at the table.

"I shall appeal to the humanity of the Senate," said Marcus.

Scaevola rocked his fat buttocks with mirth on his chair and slapped the table in an ecstasy of laughter. "Humanity? The Senate? My dear, you are mad! You appeal to a government for clemency, the very government which is a destroyer by nature? The government, you remember, which needs money—the money of your client? You are appealing to a lion to release a gazelle, for which it has an overpowering appetite, being eternally hungry. No, no, my downy-bearded one. You must seek another passage than that of appealing to the lion."

"What?" asked Marcus in despair. "I have searched."

"I look upon your case," said Scaevola, "as only an exercise for you. I have not the slightest hope that you will win clemency for your client. Let us be objective. Romans are natural actors. I hope you will move them with your eloquence, for all you are but a fledgling. I hope they will listen to you seriously. I hope they will applaud you. But they will not relinquish that power they have just discovered through their bureaucrats—the government needs money. Or, am I growing monotonous in my reminder?"

"'Only an exercise' for me?" asked Marcus, flushing. His eyes became cold and gray, flecked with amber.

"Only," said Scaevola. "I look upon your pleading tomorrow as a critic regards a new actor."

"You have said I must not permit myself an 'if,' Master," said Marcus.

"I am thinking of you only. You will be a success if you move your audi-

* Letter to Scaevola's son.

ence to tears. If you do not, then you are no real pleader. The fate of your client is secondary, for you cannot win for him."

"What is the new passage you mentioned, then?"

Scaevola shook his head. "There is none. Unless your divinity, Pallas Athene, can grant you a miracle."

"Power and the law are not synonymous," said Marcus.

Scaevola regarded him with mock admiration. "You must tell that to the Senate," he said. "They have never been presented with such a unique argument before."

"Where power is exercised in an unlimited fashion, there is no law," said Marcus, stubbornly.

"True. But the Senate wants power. Does not every government? Will you deprive it of its life's blood? My metaphorical lion, my dear, represents all governments."

"I shall rescue my gazelle," said Marcus.

Scaevola burst into fresh laughter, and wiped genuine tears of mirth from his fat and oily cheeks. "Bravo," he said. "Brave words. But they never moved a lion."

Marcus went into Scaevola's library again and sought, again, for an avenue of justice for his client. He found none. At noon, he went to the temple of Athene, and prayed. He paused at the altar of the Unknown God, and suddenly knelt before it. "Surely, You are justice," he whispered. "Surely, You will not abandon Your children. Have You not told it to Your prophets?"

It was his first case of single pleading. His heart was afire with anger and burned for righteousness and honor and just law.

He returned to the house of Scaevola. Rich litters before the door were no novelty to Marcus, who saw them regularly. But when the curtains parted and Noë ben Joel emerged with a white and desperate face, the matter was quite different. Marcus ran to him and held out his hand. Noë took it. He tried to speak. Then he burst into tears and leaned his head on Marcus' shoulder. He caught his breath while Marcus, astounded and fearful, held him. "My father," he groaned.

A few months before, in the spring of the year, Joel ben Solomon had summoned his son, Noë, and had said, firmly, "I gave your sisters large dowries, for God, blessed be His Name, did not see fit to endow them with the countenances of angels or the souls of a Rachel. Who are we to dispute His will or question His judgments? Nevertheless, the dowries, and the loss of many of my investments in these wars, have depleted my coffers. As my only son, I had thought to leave you a vast fortune. It is true that I am not a poor man, but my conscience now forbids me to continue to fatten your purse in order that you may produce plays and pay actors. I had hoped," said the elderly man, sighing, "that you would join me in my counting houses and in my offices of investments. You did not, exclaiming bitterly that gold meant nothing to you, that you were a man above such a gross pursuit.

"Had your plays brought you a profit I might have been somewhat reconciled. Alas, they did not. And this is very strange, for during wars a people seek entertainment. I have heard that the circuses do not lack audiences—"

"They are free. The government provides them," said Noë, with an ugly premonition coming to lie like lead on his heart.

His father closed his eyes for a moment, then resumed as if he had not been interrupted. "Your plays must be marvelously dull. I am no critic. I have never attended a play. But I have read those you have left in this house—"

"They were written only by Sophocles and Aristophanes," said Noë, with a wave of his large but delicate hand, "and a number of other notable Grecian artists."

"Marvelously dull," said Joel, smoothing his beard wearily. "Romans have more intelligence than I believed, if they did not patronize your productions of these plays."

"The plays are art," said Noë. "I must sadly admit that the mobs prefer bloody spectacles in the circus, and gladiators and wrestlers, and boxers and dancers, particularly those of more depraved character."

His father shuddered. "Art or not, they have brought you no sustenance, but my coffers have dwindled. I had believed that in these degenerate days in Rome it was necessary for a young man to have his will for a time, though it was not so in my day. In my day—"

Noë listened dutifully, his eyes glazing with boredom. He had heard about his father's day all his life.

"I have apparently offended the God of my fathers," said Joel. Noë judged that his father was approaching the climax of his story and shook himself awake. Joel always concluded his lamentations with that phrase. Then Noë's heart sank. His father's eye was cold and bright and was fixed on him. He was not going to dismiss his son after the conclusion of his lamentation as usual.

"Therefore," said Joel, "I have arranged a marriage for you with the daughter of Ezra ben Samuel. The dowry—"

"She resembles a camel!" cried Noë, in horror. "She is older than I! Not even her dowry could persuade any man to marry her!"

"She is but twenty-four, which is not elderly," said Joel. "A camel? The maiden is no Judith or Bathsheba, but she does not offend the eye, though, of course," the old man added ironically, "as I am not an artist and but a gross man of business I am no judge. She is a gentle daughter of Israel, of much virtue, and is not a good wife above rubies? She has been taught well by her mother—"

"A camel," said Noë, desperately.

"Speak not so," said his father with unusual sharpness. "Her nose could be more shapely, resembling your mother's, and her eyes could be larger, resembling your mother's, but she is of a fine complexion and possesses excellent teeth—"

"A man does not take a wife for her teeth, as if he were purchasing a horse," said Noë, refusing to believe in this calamity. "She is also fat."

Joel said, "It seems to me, though I may be wrong—and correct me if I am—that you are not purchasing a wife. Leah is purchasing a husband. You."

"No," said Noë.

"Yes," said Joel.

Noë reflected. He saw his father's firmness. He saw how steady was the knotted hand that stroked the beard. If he did not agree to this marriage to this camel, there would be no more purses. If he did marry Leah bas Ezra he would have her dowry. The maiden had an agreeable nature, soft and pliant and would be devoted to the man who would clasp her hand under the canopy.

"I," said Joel, "have also arranged with Ezra ben Samuel that his daughter's dowry be soundly invested. It is true that foreign investments at this time are disastrous, and therefore I have advised Ezra ben Samuel to buy property in Rome for Leah, and to invest in gold. The income from all this will provide a pleasant house for you and Leah and two or three servants, and your future sons."

I am undone, thought Noë, and wanted to tear his hair and heap ashes upon it. However, a little more reflection caused him to reconsider. The income would be very regular, unlike his father's purses, weighty though they were. He could still produce his plays and pray that Romans be lured by pure art.

However, Noë appealed to his mother whom he could always influence. But it was most apparent that she and Joel had discussed this matter thoroughly before. So she merely sighed and spoke of the will of God, and remarked that Noë was twenty-three and long past the age of usual marriage. "The girl is not uncomely," she urged. "Do you have another choice?"

Noë took his woes to his friend, Marcus, who was heartless enough to laugh.

"It is easy for you, who are a Roman, to howl with mirth," said Noë, bitterly. "For, though your marriages are arranged, you have other consolations if your wife displeases you. It is not so with Jews."

"You have regaled me with some very notable stories from your holy books," said Marcus. "Was there not David, and Solomon, to mention but two? And what of Sodom and Gomorrah?"

"Nevertheless, it is expected that Jewish husbands be virtuous," said Noë. "Or at least those Jews who move in the immaculate company of my parents—and Ezra ben Samuel."

Marcus was a guest at the wedding. He thought it sumptuous, and he also thought that Noë had done his bride injustice. Leah was no seductress, and she was too plump even for a voluptuous taste. She was also short in stature. But she had pink cheeks, a charming smile, demure eyes, and gentle manners. She also had a fat dowry, even by Roman standards. These were virtues not to be despised.

Noë apparently came to this conclusion also, for Marcus did not see him for two months. When Noë arrived at the Cicero house one evening Marcus noted that he was less lean than before and had a somewhat contented expression. He talked of a new play with animation. He had also procured the services of a handsome prostitute to act in his play, which he had composed himself. "A pig of a woman," he said, happily, "but of such allure! I am also considering her for *Elektra*. She is rich, herself, and was once the mistress of a Senator."

Marcus had not seen Noë until this late summer day, when he had fallen, weeping, into his friend's arms, speaking of his father, Joel ben Solomon.

Noë sat, his face streaming with tears, in the company of Scaevola and Marcus, and told his story.

A number of Senators, whom he had named, and who had been of Marius' party and therefore had not had to flee with Sulla to the East, had done much business with Joel in the past before the wars. They had invested heavily in stocks which he had recommended, and had gone into debt to him. He kept the records in his counting houses, in which he employed clerks of the best reputation. Had the wars not interfered the Senators' investments would not only have been safe, but they would have been purchased at last in full, and the debt to Joel would have been paid. However, in common with all Romans of property, the Senators were unfortunate in their investments, most of which had been in ships and in mines and properties. Some of the investments included money invested in manufactories supplying the government with war materials.

As the wars continued, the government paid less and less to the manufacturers, and even threatened, when they protested, to confiscate their property during the emergency. So the Senators lost money here also.

Too, much of their land, including vineyards, had suffered during the wars and were lying fallow, awaiting the day of peace. Only now were they beginning to yield again.

Cinna, that dangerous man, had reduced debts, it was true. But that reduction was a two-edged sword. While it measurably reduced what a man owed it also reduced the sums due him from his debtors. So the new law was of no tremendous help to the Senators, who found themselves not only in debt to bankers and brokers like Joel ben Solomon, but in debt to many others because of their profligacy which had not been prudently restrained during the wars. Many of them, of former great fortune, had lived like potentates in their Roman houses. Among them were clients of Joel ben Solomon.

The Senators considered that the debts they owed to Joel were the less onerous, for he did not press for payment, understanding their predicament. However, the debts, despite the reductions by Cinna's law, were still formidable. So the Senators concocted a vile plot: They announced that Joel had not delivered to them the stocks for which they had fully paid, but was asserting that they had paid but a fraction! With one blow, then, they not only schemed to be rid of their debts to him, but to seize his property and all the money he owned—thus enriching themselves— and throw him into prison for embezzlement.

He had been taken but that morning. Upon his seizure he had fainted and had been carried roughly away. His wife and his family were in despair. The daughters and their husbands consulted together, and the fathers of the husbands, to consider how much money they could bring together to free their father from the accusations; perhaps that would satisfy the Senators if the sum were large enough. Several of the young husbands of Joel's daughters had then gone pleadingly to the Senators, offering a magnificent sum "in payment in full." But the Senators had laughed at them. They wished to appear virtuous in the eyes of their clients. Therefore, Joel must be punished.

While Scaevola listened like a huge fat toad in his chair, keeping his ear keenly on Noë's broken words, he studied Marcus' face, which was frozen in white horror and incredulity. So, thought Scaevola, this will at last teach this young donkey—for whom I have an unaccountable affection —that what I have been relating to him is the truth.

After Noë had concluded, and had buried his face in his hands, Marcus stammered, "It is not possible! Does your father not have lawyers of his own, Noë?"

"No," said the unfortunate son. "He is honest. He has always proclaimed that an honest man needed no lawyer. He was safe from all injustices."

"Hah!" exclaimed Scaevola. "Joel ben Solomon, of course, is a prodigious fool. You are serious, Noë? He has no lawyers? No!"

He could not believe this folly. Noë was compelled to repeat the truth over and over. Then Scaevola threw himself back violently in his chair and shook his head like a dazed gladiator, unable to speak for a moment.

Marcus said, "But your father has his records, has he not, Noë?"

"All of them," said Noë, in an exhausted voice. "We offered them to the Senators for their own perusal."

Scaevola came furiously back to life and struck the table with the flat of his hand so that it roared like a drum. The old man leaned toward Marcus and shouted, "Imbecile! Of what use are records presented to tribunes, Consuls or Senators if the government is determined to rob and destroy a man who has displeased them, or who possesses what they want? Oh, gods," he groaned, "have I truly wasted all these years on such a stone-assed idiot as this Marcus Tullius Cicero! Those years of my old age!" He clenched his fists and shook them in the air and cursed himself for his stupidity.

Noë, during this rich flow of imprecations, blinked emptily at Scaevola, and then at Marcus. The noble pontifex maximus finally came to himself. He glared at Noë. "I assume that your father is also being accused of defaulting on his just taxes?"

"He is. I had forgotten that in the larger enormity," said Noë, with a hopeless expression.

Scaevola nodded with a wise and bitter smile. "That was added further to proclaim the Senators' virtue. They were also the victims of what they call necessary taxes. But, were they not patriotic, did they not love their country and respect her laws? Thrice thousand times they did! They paid their taxes to the last penny. They will have forged records to prove it, and where is the tax-gatherer who will dare dispute their assertions? He knows he would not be safe from poison or more unpleasant means of assassination or reprisal. It is understood by all reasonable men that the powerful do not pay taxes in the fashion of helpless citizens." Scaevola looked at Marcus, "You will remember your own client tomorrow, my Marcus, when you plead his case before these selfsame Senators, and ask for their clemency. For, are they not honorable Romans of much virtue? Are not taxes the lifeblood of a government? He who defrauds his government, you will hear tomorrow, defrauds every citizen of Rome who has met his just obligations!"

"Let us think, now, of Joel ben Solomon," pleaded Marcus. "Surely, Master, this injustice cannot be allowed to take place. Surely, we have law."

Scaevola implored Noë for condemnation of this ape-brained idiot. "Listen to him," he urged. "He speaks of law! Is there anything more contemptible in these days? In all these years he has sat at this table, in all the years he has accompanied me to the Senate and the courts, he has heard, with those brazen ears of his, that there is no law save that which is graciously vouchsafed by tyrants—for a price. Long before his grandfather's grandfather was born, I have attempted to teach him, Rome was already corrupt and depraved. The Republic had died of fatness and riches and swollen belly. It had died because the people did not insist that law be honored, and justice be observed and the Constitution upheld. Yet, he still speaks of law, in face of what Aristotle has said concerning Republics —that they decline into democracies and degenerate into despotisms. He has had all history at his hand, and he has been as blind as stone and as deaf as mud."

Marcus said with all the stern quietness he could bring to his voice, "Nevertheless, the laws are still on the books. My grandfather, of whom I have told you, Master, believed that vigorous and honorable men could still restore them, and the grandeur of Roman justice. How else can I live if I did not believe that, also? If men ignore law, it is because the venal and the contemptible despise it and circumvent it, and ridicule it, and profit by it. Men may throw filth on the white garments of Justice, but they cannot overthrow her or move her from her place."

"Oh, offal!" screamed Scaevola, almost beside himself. "They have thrown filth on her for nearly two hundred years, and have overthrown her and have moved her from her place! Will you not, in the name of all that is sane, recognize the great truth that confronts you, you pitiable creature? You cannot live, you declare, if this truth is not false. Then drown yourself. Fall on that sword with which you defeated Catilina five years ago. Borrow your grandfather's rusty dagger and thrust it into your vitals. This is no world for you, Marcus!"

Scaevola's breathing was like a gushing wind in the library. He stared at Marcus' bent head. He groaned like a defeated gladiator, who welcomed death.

"Bribes?" asked Noë, uncertainly.

Scaevola laughed. "Not a penny. What is more valuable to a powerful scoundrel than money or bribes, however seductive? His public image of virtue."

He waved his hand contemptuously to Marcus. "Here is a key. You will find a strongbox under my bed. What it contains is not only there. It is hidden away, far from Rome, in secret recesses not available to the keenest fox. In the meantime, my Noë, write on this papyrus the names of the Senators who owe your father money, and whom you have seen this morning. However— There are some whose crimes I do not know, myself. It is of no matter. Every notable politician and scoundrel, every powerful man, has secrets he would die to preserve. One has only to hint that one knows them. And they know Scaevola!"

When Marcus, moving like one stricken, but not mortally, returned with the box Scaevola regarded it with rich pleasure. He patted it paternally. "Here is my power, my reputation, all that makes Scaevola formidable, all that throws the evil men into a dance which would be the envy of Pan, himself." He bent and kissed the box, smackingly.

He said, "When the wicked attack you, do not boldly front them and attack them honestly, believing that you have justice on your side. Discover their secrets." He unlocked the brassbound box and contemplated the contents with delight. He then removed scrolls and studied one, first glancing at Noë's list, then nodding happily.

"The first, Noë, and my Marcus. He is not only the grandfather of his grandson, but the father, also. He seduced his daughter when she was but twelve years old. He poisoned her mother, who threatened to destroy him publicly. He married off the girl to a man without the ability to lie with a woman, and who prefers little boys. The Senator does not wish his beloved daughter to be polluted by another man; so, he arranged this marriage. The girl is exceedingly beautiful, and stupid, and under her father's influence, for she adores him. The Senator is, at the present time, arranging to have his daughter divorce her husband in name, so he may return her to her house, there to shelter her—shall we say paternally—and protect his grandson, who is also his son, for he loves the boy. It is not often," said Scaevola with enjoyment, "that a besotted man can arrange matters so neatly and agreeably. We shall see."

Scaevola was studying another scroll with satisfaction. "Ah, we have a rare rascal here! He had the noble and virtuous Drusus murdered. The people of Italy have not forgotten Drusus, whose assassin has never been apprehended. They would, even at this date, tear our fine Senator limb from limb for this."

He plucked out still another scroll, over which he almost drooled. "My dear Senator! You shock this leathery old heart! You have seduced the young wives of four of your most devoted colleagues in the Senate! Tut, tut. A wise man does not seduce the wives of his friends, who could ruin him. Are there not other women in Rome? If your fellow Senators ever learn of this they will murder you, themselves, each pleading for an opportunity to bury their daggers in your carcass."

He took up another. "Dear friend, you have had six wives, and not one produced a child for you, not even a daughter. But your loving friend Scaevola knows why. You are not capable. Five wives were ladies of family. They would never reveal their mortification and the insult to their womanhood. Yet, you have two fine sons. Whence did you receive them, handsome friend? They are the children of your slave girls—who have long disappeared into the silence of death. They were begotten by male slaves, who no longer speak, either. It was necessary for you to have these sons, for your patrician name depends on their being, and also a great fortune. I do not wish to injure innocent children. It will be your choice if they are injured. Your nephew, whom you despise, will then inherit your seat in the Senate, and your fortune. And think of the laughter of Rome, which loves a joke."

"But his wives divorced him. How then, does he explain these sons?"

"He took unto himself a sixth wife, a young girl of obscure but excellent and impoverished family. A very young girl. He threatened her that if she denied the first child was hers he would destroy her father. He threatened her again when the second was born. But, as women, even the most intimidated, have a habit of tattling under the proper circumstances, it was unfortunate that the very young sixth wife died at the birth of the second son. It was said she had a hemorrhage."

"But the physician," Marcus began, then stared at Scaevola as at a basilisk.

"It happened when our friend was alone with his little wife," said Scaevola, in a tone of commiseration. "Oddly enough, is it not? that both children appeared to have been born so rapidly that the physician, when he was summoned, found only the little girl and a newborn babe in the bloody bed. Ah, the sadness of life!"

Noë and Marcus exchanged aghast glances. Noë sucked in his lips; Marcus swallowed dryly. He had known of these dossiers, that they existed. But he had not known what they were. He thought he could no longer endure the litany of these horrors, of these monstrous things. He made a motion to leave, but Scaevola impaled him with a fierce and malevolent eye. "I am doing this to purge you of your nonsense," he said.

Scaevola continued in a rich and purring tone. Then finally he laid down the last scroll. Each had been more terrible than the one before. Scaevola clasped his hands over his belly and contentedly began to scratch his navel through his tunic. He surveyed the two pale young men with benevolence.

"I have brought these matters to the attention of the unfortunate Senators before," he said. "On several occasions my house has been broken into. The Senators know that these dossiers are only copies. After my house had been attacked four times I let them know the discreet facts. Nor would they attempt to murder me, or my son. I have two friends who detest these Senators. They have my orders to deliver the facts to a public which still retains some loathing of crimes, in the event of my death or the death of my son, by violence."

Noë, in a weak voice, said, "How did you obtain this information?"

Scaevola made a gesture of rubbing finger and thumb together. "Ah, what gold cannot do! And I have the best spies in Rome, whose names I shall not tell you. You have only to believe in the truth of my information."

Marcus seized his head in his hands and cried, "To what Rome has fallen!"

"To what man has fallen, from the day he was created," said Scaevola.

He summoned messengers, and he addressed a short and respectful letter to each Senator he had named. It reminded the Senator discreetly that he, Scaevola, still possessed his information. And it also urged the Senator, in the name of justice, to consult with his colleagues and have the charges removed against Joel ben Solomon, and the banker returned at once to his house. "Does not the passion for law still burn high in your breast, dearest friend?" Scaevola asked in his letters. "One knows of your devotion to law, especially this admiring pontifex maximus, who is honored to be one of your friends."

To the Senators on which he had no information of a frightful kind, he merely wrote, "I am in possession of two of your secrets, which distresses me. I should like to confer with you about them, so that you, in your majesty and honor, can deny them. Scandal and libel should not be permitted to exist."

Noë almost forgot his reason for being in this library as he considered. Then he said, "Has any Senator or notable man of affairs or politician ever challenged you, as you suggest in this letter?"

"Never," said Scaevola, emphatically. "Because no man is innocent, and no powerful man is anything but guilty. Each of these Senators, on whom I have as yet no information—though I shall have, eventually—will scan his life thoroughly on receiving my letter, and will be fearfully alarmed and wonder what crime I have stumbled upon which he has committed. He will decide that it is the very worst."

Noë now believed without doubt that Scaevola would rescue his father at once. He could bring himself to smile. "It is not a pleasant thing to contemplate that justice must be brought about by such means," he said.

"It should not be so," said Marcus. "I should have listened to my grandfather with less boredom. He was the wisest of men. He believed," the youth added with a sad smile, "that I could help to rescue Rome and restore the rule of law and abolish the rule by men." He looked at Scaevola fully. "I shall try."

"Good," said Scaevola, winking at Noë. "You will try. That is why I have often prophesied that you will not die peacefully in your bed, as evil men die."

Suddenly he pulled himself upright in his chair and beamed upon Marcus. "I have it! You will have your miracle for your client, tomorrow! For, I shall be sitting near you and I shall look upon the faces of my dear friends, the Senators."

"I should wish to win on the merits of my case," said Marcus, with a bitterness in his tone that his teacher had never heard before.

Noë was deeply interested so Scaevola benevolently outlined the case to him. Noë said, "It is not unlike my father's in many ways. But this man is but a humble farmer. Why is his case not tried before a local magistrate in a local court? Why is he brought before the Senate?"

"As I have explained to our innocent friend, Marcus, the government needs money. Therefore, above all crimes, it considers the crime of inability to pay taxes almost the worst of all. It is even worse, in their opinion, for a man to attempt to keep a portion of the fruit of his labors for the benefit of himself and his family. So the Senate wishes to make a public example of Marcus' unfortunate client, for, you will understand, as matters go on and the government becomes more powerful it will need more money for its own evil purposes. It cannot be certain that its demands will be met if even a single man is permitted to keep what is his own, and for which he alone labored."

Noë turned in his chair and studied his young friend. "I have been occupied lately, Marcus, and so have had no opportunity to tutor you as before. Stand up, then, and show me how you intend to present yourself to the Senate tomorrow."

"I am interested," said Scaevola, and looked benignly attentive. Marcus hesitated, embarrassed. Then he reminded himself that an advocate should be prepared to address any audience at any time without embarrassment, so he slowly rose and faced the cynical old lawyer and his watchful friend.

"Think, first," said Scaevola, "of Joel ben Solomon. Never let him leave your mind tomorrow, as you address my dear friends, the Senators. Think of him now."

Marcus' slender shoulders straightened, his long neck became a heroic column, his face flushed with outrage and passion. He looked at his audience, and his eyes sparkled. Before he could say a word Noë applauded with enthusiasm, and Scaevola was delighted.

Noë pointed to Marcus' legs. "But a longer tunic," he said. "Your legs are not your most endearing feature, Marcus. Wear a robe to your insteps. It must be a faultless robe, with intimations of a marble toga. It must be fastened with a dignified pin, severe yet expensive. Your shoes must be white, white as your robe, to indicate unsullied justice—faced with unsullied justice." Noë made an obscene grimace. "I have the very robe you need, voluminous, of the finest linen. Permit me to send it to you, out of my love for you." He put his head on one side, critically. "A girdle, too, of finely wrought silver. I shall include it. And armlets of the same. Ah, and I have a ring of magnificence! The one touch that will heighten the aspect of austerity!"

"They know I am but the son of a poor knight, and of no great name," said Marcus, with fresh embarrassment.

"Then, they will wonder who is your secret benefactor, your unknown but powerful client," said Noë. "It will shake them."

"Excellent!" cried Scaevola, enjoying himself.

Noë became warmer under this praise and with the thought that his father would soon be restored to his family. His actor's soul brightened. He shone with enthusiasm. Never had he prepared an actor for such a role before. He leaped to his feet and circled Marcus, scrutinizing him from every point, lifting an elbow here, dropping a shoulder there, turning the chin in this direction, shaking his head, rectifying a fault. Scaevola watched, entranced. Before his eyes his somewhat stern and diffident pupil became a statue of avenging and youthful justice.

"Do not jerk your head too suddenly," said Noë, absorbed in his work. "Let your head move nobly, heroically. When you reach the height of your plea, let your voice break and tremble with emotion. Be overcome with the thought that you are addressing men dedicated to law, and of the most scrupulous honor."

Scaevola clapped his hands gleefully. "I shall enjoy this tomorrow!"

He ordered the best wine for his young friends and himself, and a dish of fine cheese and grapes and plums and olives from Israel, and bread as white and soft as silk. Marcus, thinking his mournful thoughts, was silent.

He thought, I am certain that I will win. But what is not certain is that I will win on the basis of justice—for justice has departed from Rome. How shall I be able to live with this knowledge, which came to me fully only today?

CHAPTER SIXTEEN

The house of the Ciceroni was quiet. Helvia, finally unable to struggle against her sense of justice, had persuaded Archias to seek another client in the city. "The gods alone know when your stipend in this house can be renewed," she said. "Your presence here, good Archias, is only a painful reminder to me of our state, and of what we owe you."

So Archias had departed for the house of a rich client who had several sons. He had done so reluctantly, but he honored the self-respect of the Lady Helvia. He also suspected that Helvia had finally lost patience with Tullius and was determined to force him to engage in life once more. So Tullius dragged himself painfully each morning from his cubiculum to teach his younger son. As Helvia had hoped, his health improved and he became interested, if only a little, in his son's lessons.

Helvia, two years ago, had married the golden-haired Eunice to the freedman, Athos, who was overseer of the island near Arpinum. It was safe now, in a measure, to return to the island. Athos and Eunice were busily engaged in restoring the household and the farms.

Quintus, now seventeen years old, had been invested in the manly robe the year before. It became him. He was determined to be a soldier. Helvia was seeking a commission for him among the friends of the Helvii. In the meantime, Quintus with good humor, but also with impatience, studied Greek with his father and tried to understand philosophy. He considered neither necessary for a good Roman. But he could not explain this to his father, for he had, above all things, the kindest of hearts. The cantos of Homer left him bewildered, and dismayed. He smudged Tullius' precious parchments with blunt and sweating fingers. His highly colored face, so like his mother's, would become crimson with effort. His beautiful eyes would film with tears of vexation against himself for his inability to understand what his father described as the noblest of sagas. Though he admired Achilles as a soldier, he thought him somewhat of a fool not to have taken precautions concerning his vulnerable heel. He considered Paris an idiot to have plunged his country into ruin and fire because of a mere woman, however beautiful. But what could one have expected of a man who preferred to be a shepherd rather than a soldier? Priam, the silly old father, should have cut Helen's throat immediately or have returned her to her lawful husband. Hector, the noble soldier, alone excited Quintus' admiration.

There was, thought Quintus, absolutely no Roman logic in the *Iliad*. The *Odyssey* was little better. How could, in the light of reason, Ulysses have been seduced by Circe? It was surely not possible for rational men to be enticed out of their wits by a mere woman. Quintus, advised by his mother to look about him for a suitable wife, had not as yet seen a maiden who could cause him to be indifferent to a single meal.

Quintus, though he had long left Pilo's school, still retained his friends who greatly admired and loved him. Among them was Julius Caesar. They had assumed the manly robe together in the same ceremony. Julius thought

Quintus to be not overly intelligent. But he had other virtues which Julius admired in others though he refrained from cultivating them in himself. Quintus might be simple, but he was loyal. Quintus' conversations might sometimes be naïve, but he was never a liar. Quintus might lack much in the way of imagination, but Julius had long ago learned that it is best for ambitious men to surround themselves with followers who have few fantasies, for fantasies begot speculations and speculations could rise to experimentations and experimentations to direct action—all of which was dangerous to an ambitious man.

Quintus had told Julius that Marcus was about to undertake his first and solitary case himself, and, before the Senate. Julius considered this thoroughly, as he did all things. He was very fond of Marcus, though he often thought Marcus to be, at times, even more simple than his brother. Nevertheless, he was aware of Marcus' intellect and honorable conduct and virtue, and his tendency to protect the helpless. These were not matters to be despised in potential followers. Ambitious men, more than any other, needed a façade of public nobility and integrity. Moreover, Julius suspected that Marcus represented a still potent if minor part of the population which had rejected corruption.

When Marcus, dejected and stern, returned home the night before the trial, overcome with the horror of what he had learned that day, Quintus greeted him with enthusiasm. His friend, Julius, would be present to applaud his dear friend, Marcus Tullius Cicero.

"Julius?" said Marcus, a little diverted out of his misery. "When was Julius ever interested in justice?" But he smiled. Once Julius had teased him by calling him Endymion. "So," had said Marcus, "I am a silvery poet, my soul seeking in vain for what can satisfy it?"

"You will never be satisfied," Julius had said.

Marcus turned to him and studied him acutely. "Nor will you, dear young friend. Your desires are the highway to death."

Julius was very superstitious. He shivered, made the sign of averting the evil eye. He did not like the glow between Marcus' lashes. He said, insolently, "And are your desires the kind that lead to an honored old age and death in a peaceful bed?"

"I am a lawyer, Julius. I will never seek to control men."

"You are also virtuous, and when did a virtuous man ever die tranquilly?"

It was such exchanges, mysterious to Quintus, that paradoxically nourished the real affection between Marcus and Julius.

Tonight, he proudly exhibited a small ivory and silver rod which Julius had sent to the house on the Carinae for Marcus to hold when he addressed the Senate. It was a rod of authority, lent to Marcus for the occasion. Marcus examined it with admiration and amusement. "It is very like Julius," he said. Quintus was puzzled. "It does not resemble Julius in the least," he said, baffled. Marcus laughed. "He could have presented this to me as a gift, and not as a loan. Was he consciously subtle in this, or unconsciously so?"

Quintus abandoned this unfruitful discussion. "A slave from the house of Joel ben Solomon brought a gift wrapped in white silk for you. It is in your cubiculum. There is also a letter from Noë."

Marcus took a lamp from the atrium and carried it into his cubiculum. He opened the sealed letter. Noë had written: "Rejoice with us, dearest of friends! Scaevola is indeed powerful. When I reached home my father had already been delivered from prison! The Senate, on occasion, can act with dispatch. I will be present tomorrow to watch my friend, and bless him. You have my prayers."

Marcus closed his eyes and thanked his patroness, Pallas Athene, for her mercy. Quintus had followed him and was inquisitive about the contents of the parcel. "Ask our mother to come here," said Marcus. Quintus ran off to summon Helvia, who returned with her younger son. She was thirty-seven years old now, but there was only an occasional thread of gray in her abundant black curls, and she was as calm, as plump and composed as ever and always, forever, an "old" Roman matron whom life could never overcome.

When Marcus unrolled the parcel she could not restrain her admiration for the pure white toga contained therein, the armlets, the shoes and the ring. She looked at Marcus proudly. She threw the toga over his coarse long tunic. She clasped the armlets on his arms and put the dazzling ring on his finger. She stood back to admire him. Quintus was overwhelmed with pleasure and pride. He showed his mother the delicate rod of authority which Julius had lent Marcus. "Marcus says it is very like Julius," said Quintus, frowning in renewed bafflement.

Helvia laughed, understanding. With the intuition of a mother she knew that something had freshly unnerved her son. She said, watching him, "You have no fear that you will forget portions of your address?"

Marcus removed the ring of Noë from his finger, then held it in his hand and stared at it emptily as it shone and glittered in the lamplight. "No," he said at last. "I am not going to give that address. What I say will be entirely different."

She waited. But Marcus only silently refolded the toga and neatly covered it with the silk.

"Then," she said, "you will write it tonight and memorize it. You must have quiet."

"I shall let myself be moved by the power of Athene," he said.

Helvia frowned. She considered that most imprudent, and very dangerous and uncertain. The gods did not always come when summoned, not even at the imploring of their most devoted servants.

"You think that wise, Marcus?"

He suddenly spread out his hands helplessly. "I do not know," he confessed. He opened his small chest of treasures and took from it the round amulet Aurelia Caesar had given him so many years ago, and he hung it about his neck. Helvia thought, so, it is very serious, and he will not tell me.

That night Marcus followed his father into Tullius' cubiculum. Tullius was both overjoyed and amazed, for it had been a very long time since Marcus had freely sought him out. Tullius sat in his plain chair, but Marcus stood before him.

Marcus said, in a low voice, "I have learned much today. I knew from the discourses of my grandfather, and yours, my father, that Rome had fallen far from her original innocence and republican glory and virtues. But not with all my flesh and blood and understanding; not with all my knowledge and my mind and acceptance. Today, I learned it all."

"Tell me," urged Tullius. But Marcus shook his head. "I cannot repeat the infamy. But this I can say: My address to the Senate tomorrow will be another than the one I wrote. However, I must have a starting point." He sat down on the wooden stool near his father and looked into Tullius' gentle brown eyes.

"You wish me to give you a starting point, Marcus?" asked the father, flushing with pride and pleasure. "You are to defend an honest farmer who cannot pay his taxes. The government has seized his small farm, has imprisoned him, and will sell his property and force him and his family into slavery." Tullius shuddered. "You have already told me this."

"What shall I say?" muttered Marcus in despair. "The Senate represents my country."

"No!" cried Tullius, with sudden vehemence. "A government rarely represents the people! Love of country is often confused in simple minds with love for one's government. They are rarely one; they are not synonymous. Yet," he added, mournfully, "the evil men in government are compelled to show a public face of sympathy for the oppressed and must pretend, at all times, to be one with them, seeking to rectify the very wrong they have secretly committed."

Marcus stood up so suddenly that the stool fell over. He cried out, "I have my starting point!"

He moved toward the curtain. Tullius said, wretchedly, "I have not helped you, though you are my son."

Marcus came back to him, his eyes shining and he bent and kissed his father's cheek like a child. "You do not know how much you have helped me, dear Father!"

Tullius was dumfounded. But he placed his hands on Marcus' shoulders and returned his kiss, with humility.

Helvia knelt before her son and tried to drape the toga majestically. "I am no handmaiden," she said, wielding the ivory instrument with some clumsiness. "When I was a girl a man's success did not wait on the way his toga was folded and arranged; it did not wait on foolish externals. If Cincinnatus appeared today before the Senate, as once he did, in his dusty rough tunic, with bare legs, his bare feet brown from the fields, the Senate would be outraged and would call for the guard to throw him out. He had, the Senate would declare, offended their august dignity. But now a man must dress like an actor and decorate himself like a woman with jewels, before he dares plead a simple case."

"In those days," said Marcus, "Senators represented the people. If they offended the people, they were removed or exiled. They did not inherit their seats. Nor did the retention of their seats depend upon base creatures and the passions of low and greedy men."

Helvia nodded. She sat back on her plump heels to regard the toga. She also glanced up through her lashes at her son's face. It was still very pale. But now the misery was less upon it. She was satisfied. She said, "Quintus' great friend, that antic Julius, has procured a place for him to hear you. He will bring back the news. I wish we had a litter to carry you to the Forum. But we now have not even a simple chariot." She studied Marcus again. "That ring is very theatrical. It does not become you."

"It will become me today," said Marcus, with some grimness.

"I have no doubt," said Helvia.

But one of the few slaves left in the household now appeared in the doorway of the cubiculum, to announce, with proud excitement, that a rich litter was awaiting the noble Cicero, carried by four magnificent slaves wonderfully dressed. Marcus, forgetting that he was noble, and Helvia forgetting that she was a dignified matron, ran into the atrium and then to the strong oaken doors, which stood open to the hot late summer air. There, almost on the threshold, waited a litter, the curtains of fine blue wool embroidered in silver, the carriers arrayed like minor princes, their black faces shining like polished ebony.

"Noë!" exclaimed Marcus. The curtains parted and showed the smiling face of Noë ben Joel. Noë lifted himself out of the litter and came to embrace his friend and bow over the hand of Helvia. "Did you expect to walk to the Forum, like a peasant?" asked Noë, grasping Marcus' arms in another embrace.

"Cincinnatus walked all the way to the Senate," said Helvia, but she smiled.

"These are not the happy days of Cincinnatus, Lady," said Noë. He looked at Marcus. "My father sends you his blessing, and his blessings are not to be despised, for he is a good man."

When the young men were in the litter Noë said, taking his friend's arm, "My father owes his life and reputation to you." His voice trembled. "It was an impulse from God which sent me in search of you yesterday."

"Your father owes me nothing," said Marcus, with amazement. "It was Scaevola, and he alone, to whom you must direct your gratitude."

Noë shook his head. "Who is my father? A banker, a broker, a man of no importance to such as Scaevola. To such a patrician my father is nothing. You will remember his metaphor about the use of a keen sword. He would not have used it for my father—but for you."

"I?" cried Marcus. "He dislikes me only a little less than he does the other young lawyers."

"You are wrong," said Noë. "He loves you like a father, or a grandfather. It hurts, not offends, him that you are unworldly and have defenseless virtue and still believe that man is ultimately good. He fears for your peace of mind, your ultimate reason, your future, your fate. He would have you protect yourself with knowledge; he would have you close your open gates. Or, he fears, you will be destroyed."

"No," said Marcus, after a little thought. "He is a roaring bull from Spain, but he loves justice."

"He knows it does not exist in Rome."

Marcus said, "Tell me of your father. Did he suffer greatly?"

Noë replied: "He said that when he was in prison he prayed for God's justice, but above all, that His will should be done."

"So it was," said Marcus, with some uneasiness.

"Without intention," said Noë. Marcus looked at him sharply. Noë was frequently irreverent concerning the God of his fathers, and confessed to an enormous measure of doubt. He moved as if throwing a burden from his shoulders. He lifted aside a curtain to gaze with full light upon his friend. "You are marvelous," he said. "When you stood on the threshold of your door you were like a hero, a statue, come to life. But, I was not surprised. What is this curious rod you hold so tightly?"

Marcus told him. Noë took it in his hand and examined it. "Julius Caesar," he said, thoughtfully. "But I have no affairs with those who live on the Palatine."

"You will hear of that young man in the future," said Marcus. "I have come to believe it, for Rome today is his perfect environment."

He pulled aside the curtain and stared out at the vehement faces and the press of bodies that surrounded the litter, at the many-colored tunics, at the violent hot sunlight on the sides of red and yellow and lemon-hued buildings, at the pylons with their winged heroes or gods or goddesses, at the surging stairways that went up and down, at the crowded porticoes of temples, at the throngs already hurrying to the theatres and the circuses. He was accustomed now to the uproar of the titanic city, the thunder of chariots, the screaming of multitudes of children, the shouts and whistles and oaths, and the shrill cries of pigeons. But now the noise appeared too acute to him. Had he been alone he would have covered his ears. He looked at the fierce blue of the sky, at the distant glitter of the Tiber, at the bridges massed with hurrying people. He smelled the pervasive stink of the giantess on her seven hills.

Noë looked at his pale profile and thought, My friend is greatly disturbed today, even more than he was yesterday.

Noë tried to divert him. "I have some gossip for you," he said.

Marcus tried to smile. "You remind me of my young friend, Julius, who has every man's name on his lips, and knows every man's most vicious secret."

Noë laughed. He said, "You will remember your famous duel with Catilina. I have heard he is with Sulla, in Asia."

Marcus said with slow quietness, "I had hoped he was dead."

"Unfortunately, no. The spear and the sword do not impale themselves in such as he. This frequently urges me to believe in the old Jewish story of Lucifer, who protects his own, a method I highly recommend to the Almighty, Who seems less conscientious in these matters. I understand that Catilina is one of Sulla's favorite officers. If Sulla ever returns to Rome— and he cannot be worse than this Cinna who afflicts us now—the Catilina will be in a fine position under his general. It is unfortunate."

"I have wished to kill him many times," said Marcus. "There are moments that I regret that I did not."

His white face flushed with hatred.

"But you spared him, and so acquired a reputation, which is not to be disdained. It is believed, as you know, that you could not bring yourself to kill an unarmed man, or that you spared him out of magnanimity. Either is excellent for a reputation."

"His—wife?" asked Marcus.

"She is certainly not with her husband on maneuvers in Asia! So, she must be in Rome."

"Then she is in Rome," said Marcus, and all at once his sense of futility and exhaustion lessened. He knew that there was no hope for him, that Livia was forever lost. But the thought that she looked upon this very sky on which he looked, that he might even see her face in some temple, lifted his heart. He wanted to know that all was well with her.

The litter descended toward the Forum. Here the crowds were thicker and noisier. Litters carrying other lawyers moved rapidly toward the Basilica of Justice. Marcus' breath came faster, and his hand gripped that lent rod of authority. He fumbled for the amulet under his tunic. The kingly ring on his finger flashed with a thousand lights.

Now they were in the Forum, entering down the steep slope of the Sacred Way. It was all familiar to Marcus, but he looked on it today with new eyes as though he had never seen it before. For today he was part of the Forum, and it was his arena of ordeal.

Here was all vast and colorful and uproarious confusion under the brilliant sky. Markets, temples, basilicas, porticoes, government buildings, and arches crowded together in the urban structures of red and citron and brown and pale yellow and white and gray; walls of brick and mortar and stone crushed furiously on each side of the road as if wishing to surge upon it and inundate it. Banks and brokerage houses teemed together in arches, shouldering one or two small theatres whose porticoes were even now seething with those in search of entertainment. As the great Forum lay in a hollow, the air sweltered with the stink of latrines, oils, incense, human sweat, animal offal, perfumes, dust, and heated stone. The markets were a clamor; bureaucrats with grave faces strove for an air of menacing dignity in their togas, but were often thrown from their feet by the sheer excited mass of fellow Romans, bent on business in the offices or counting houses or Senate or temples or shops. Chariots churned and lunged amidst a turmoil of litters and people on foot; horses screamed, wheels hammered, whips cracked, guards, attempting to control the turbulent traffic, waved wands or staffs, and strove to keep on foot. At times, they had to leap for a spot on the branching stairways, to avoid being kicked by a horse or trampled by the throngs.

Romans, having lost Republican simplicity, now tried to outdo each other in the violence of the color of their tunics, long and short. There was not a color nor a tint nor a hue which did not flare in the seering sunlight, from scarlet and crimson and blue to yellow and white and rose and green and orange. It was like a thousand rainbows gone mad and whirling and hurrying and rushing and leaping on the road and in the alleys between buildings. And above it all spread the hills of Rome, glaring in the light, jumbled with the high broken mass of multitudinous buildings, and all streaming with countless people. The incredible noise stunned the ear, drowned out an individual voice and the dim patter of indolent fountains before the temples.

Noë eyed the impassable mob dubiously. The Senate stood at a distance, tall, severe, straight-lined, of yellowish brick. It was as high as it was long, with thin windows of clear Alexandrian glass. It was fronted by several white stone steps leading to four stone pillars guarding the entrance. More than any other building in the Forum the Senate Chamber informed the eye that here was a nation not of poets and artists, but engineers, scientists and businessmen and soldiers, vigorously materialistic and bustling and energetic and ambitious. It was a nation of people alleged to grow rapturous over Grecian art and beauty and philosophy, but in its soul it regarded these things as somewhat effeminate and best left to elegant gentlemen whose thoughts did not encompass large and precise designs for a world order, precisely governed, and realistic in all its plans.

While only lawyers and advocates and those necessary for the conduct of law were permitted within the Senate Chamber, it was usual for lawyers who had tried cases previously that day, or were about to try cases, to stand near or within the entrance of the chamber surrounded by clients and well-wishers and paid applauders and friends. A few, but very few, like the famous pontifex maximus, Scaevola, could even bring their own chairs on which to sit, basking in the midst of their entourages, uttering witticisms or wisdoms, sometimes enjoying sweetmeats from little silver boxes. Those who could not get inside sat in their chairs with small awnings against the sun held over their heads by slaves. Therefore, the noise outside was far greater than within the dignified precincts of the Senate Chamber itself.

Scaevola, held in such terror by the venal men among the Senators, sat to the left of the entrance, just inside, sprawled in his chair, his admirers clustered thickly about him. Among them were Julius Caesar, Quintus (who had raced so fast to the Forum that he had passed Noë's litter), Archias, Marcus' former tutor and now a famous personage in Rome because of his published poetry, several strange youths, and a mass of admirers, fledgling lawyers and old lawyers, pupils and devoted friends. His entourage was far larger than the entourages of other lawyers, almost as distinguished as himself, and there was a constant migration of men from the circles of others to that of Scaevola. One could always be sure of a bitter and acid witticism from the lips of the formidable old man, who in his dress despised dignity but possessed it in his person, whose great bald head shone like a moon.

Marcus knew that Scaevola was not there today, personally, to "use his sword to move a pebble." Nevertheless, he was joyous to see him. He announced his business to the guards at the entrance, then hastened within with Noë, and went at once to his old teacher. Scaevola was sprawled in his chair, at ease, scratching at the large mole on his cheek, which, because it sprouted black hairs, resembled a spider. His entourage was laughing heartily at some joke. They all turned to stare at Marcus and Noë as at intruders. Scaevola regarded his pupil with those amazingly small but vividly blue eyes of his, and smiled faintly, showing his long yellow teeth.

"Greetings, Lord," said Marcus, formally, bowing.

"Greetings, Marcus," said Scaevola. He studied the young man. "We are splendidly arrayed this day. I did not recognize you."

"Greetings, Lord," said Noë, bowing also.

Scaevola inclined his head without reply. He resumed his study of Marcus. "No," he said, "I should not have recognized you. The Senate will think you a patrician." He spoke with satire. But Quintus, standing beside Julius Caesar, beamed proudly upon his brother.

Archias said, "It is a proud occasion for me, my dear Marcus," and embraced his former student with deep affection.

The mass about Scaevola stared curiously at the young lawyer. Many eyes were respectful.

Then Julius said, "Dear Marcus, I have invoked Mars in your behalf."

"I am not about to fight a battle," said Marcus, unable to keep from smiling at that mischievous and attractive young face.

"Are you not?" said the young man with impudence.

"This Julius," said Scaevola, with a wave of his fat hand. "His uncle was the great Marius, now—eh, unfortunately?—dead. What will happen to him and his family when Sulla returns, as he most surely will?"

Julius had a beguiling voice. "Do you think my family, Master, places all its money on one chariot in the races—or all its influence?" He was thin, not as tall as Marcus, and gave the impression of intense vivacity. He turned to the watchful youth beside him, who was very handsome and who had alert gray eyes of a peculiar luminescence. "Permit me, Marcus, to present my friend, Gnaeus Pompey (Pompeius). His father is a dear friend of Sulla's," he winked with good temper. "We are like brothers. Speaking in confidence, Pompey fought with Sulla, also."

"Aha," said Scaevola. He moved his massive shoulders in slight laughter.

Pompey bowed to Marcus, who was his own age. "I pray you all success, Marcus Tullius Cicero," he said, gravely. "He who is a friend of Julius is a friend of mine."

"Always make as many friends as possible," said Scaevola. "Then, in an emergency, if you have a score of friends, you can count on one. Sometimes."

"I have many more than a score of friends," said Julius, raising his voice above the clamor about them within the portico of the Senate, and without. "I am devoted to the human race." He spoke in a serious voice, and with a serious expression, but his black eyes danced.

Marcus had been gazing at the young Pompey, and he could not tell whether or not he liked the young man's appearance. He was no non-entity, though he wore no insignia which could identify him. From Julius' air of patronage Marcus came to the conclusion that Pompey was plebeian. Yet his dress, a simple white tunic bordered with the Greek key in crimson, was not coarse.

"I am here," said Scaevola, "because I have concluded some cases before the Senate, and because I have a number more at noon."

So, thought Marcus, he is now making it plain to me and to the others that he will give me no assistance. "Should you win," said Scaevola, with a supreme air of neutrality, "I shall lead the applause, however." He scratched the mole again, not taking his eyes from Marcus. "You are not nervous? You have memorized your address fully?"

"I am not using the one you have heard," said Marcus, bending to speak in his teacher's ear. Scaevola's mighty head jerked backward, and he stared up into the young man's face and despite himself his eyes showed sharp concern.

"No? And your first case? This is folly. You will ruin it all in confusion."

"I think not. I hope not," said Marcus.

Julius, who always heard everything, said, "Who can listen to Marcus' musical and compelling voice, touched both with hauteur and majestic humility, and not be moved?"

Archias deftly rearranged a fold that fell from Marcus' shoulder. He said, "One is moved, most of all, by his passionate sincerity and his belief in ultimate justice. One can question that innocence, but one must respect it for what it is."

But Scaevola, for all his air of neutrality, was disturbed more than any of those present could guess. Because he was disturbed, he was angry at Marcus.

"Take your place," he said abruptly, waving Marcus on to the end of a line of lawyers waiting to be called. There were four before him, and he joined them. He was taller than any; his long neck lifted his well-formed if somewhat small head; the sunlight from the open doors behind him gilded the back of his head, which rippled with soft brown hair. It gave his profile, with its long nose—and because of that profile's pallor—the aspect of a statue. His shoulders were too narrow, but the heavy folds of the toga draped them gracefully. Once he turned a little, and the sunlight behind him struck on the ball of his eye, showing its mysterious and changing colors. He will do, thought Scaevola, and though he did not believe in the gods at all he angrily invoked several. Would nothing, he reflected, ever change that serene and petrified brow to one plowed with wrinkles? Would the years—if he survived—remove that glow of light in his eye? What a thing it is, thought Scaevola, with irascible pity, to observe a man of principle in these days! It is like coming upon sunlit Apollo when one expected dark Pan with his smells, his dancing hoofs, his goatish legs, and his maddening pipes.

There were only thirty Senators present today. It had alarmed Scaevola that a few of them—if only a few—were men of integrity and honor, with no blemish on their public or personal lives. The Senators knew that the pontifex maximus was there; the evil ones among them would be uncertain concerning Marcus, wondering if Scaevola's hidden sword guarded him. The Senators of integrity would be indifferent.

Moreover, the Senator Curius was present, a most evil man, the father of Marcus' old enemy who was a friend of Lucius Sergius Catilina. Curius would remember the story of Marcus' defeat of Lucius; he was a proud as well as a vicious man, and was closely attached to the Catilinii, and was a relative of Livia. Out of spite alone—for vicious men in high positions were notorious for spite—he would be hostile to Marcus first because he was a son of an obscure knight who had not even been born in Rome and second because of Lucius.

Scaevola turned to Noë, who was standing at a little distance watching Marcus closely. Scaevola beckoned him to his side, and peremptorily waved away a number of clients, friends, and admirers, indicating that he wished to discuss a private subject. Noë bent over him. Scaevola said, "Your father has returned to the bosom of his loving family. Does he know how it was done?"

"The Almighty and merciful God delivered him," said Noë.

"Ha," said Scaevola, shaking his head. "You have not disillusioned him?"

"He would only then repeat his belief in the mercy of an Almighty God, who uses His creatures to establish His will."

"Ha," said Scaevola, again.

"He believes in the honor of Rome," said Noë, winking. "He is proud that he is a Roman citizen, that his son is so, and that three of his sons-in-law are also Roman citizens."

Scaevola sighed. "Nevertheless, my dear Noë, he and his wife, your mother, must fly Rome at once and return to their beloved Jerusalem. It will be fatal for them to remain here. I may die tonight, and who knows if my son will have the courage to use what I have used?"

"The old story, again," said Noë, frowning with distress.

"The Jews are a wise and ancient race," said Scaevola. "Therefore, they have prudently concerned themselves with assets which can be removed with expedition and at a moment's notice."

"My father," said Noë, "frequently quotes the old Hebrew saying that an ungrateful son will bite the edge of the table. I am his ungrateful son, according to him."

"Gods," said Scaevola, impatiently. "How can I endure any longer these innocent ones? I care not how you do it, Noë, but your parents must flee Rome almost at once."

"Will they be safer there?"

"Yes. Your father's presence in Rome is a reminder to these scoundrels of the infamy of their lives, which I had brought to their attention. Your father is an old man; he may have a convenient failure of the heart, or an accident, or a slave could poison him, or he could fall down a flight of stairs in his offices, or a serpent, crawling into his cubiculum, could attack him."

He irritably waited to see Noë's expression change to one of horror. But Noë's face was only thoughtful and alarmed.

"I will study this matter," said Noë. "It must be expeditious?"

"Yes. Ha. Our Marcus is now second in line. Does he not look magnificent, arrayed like this?"

Noë, after a quick glance at Marcus, bowed his head, covering it unobtrusively with a part of his toga. He had not prayed sincerely for years. He found himself imploring God with fervor.

"He is now first!" cried Julius Caesar, with excitement.

"My noble brother," said Quintus, and softly clapped his hands.

Marcus had begun to tremble in the last moments; his sweating hand clutched Julius' ivory rod. A streak of moisture ran down his right cheek. Light fell from the high windows; huge though the chamber was the heat was frightful. The immensely high roof was painted white and was of wood smoothly joined, and bore a design of carved squares in which a decoration like a rose had been gilded. The effect was calm and monumental. The walls, too, were of wood, laid over the brick, and these also were painted in purest white ornamented with lines and scrolls of gold. The floor glimmered like a lake, for it was composed of elaborate mosaics laid in swirling patterns of white, gold, blue, and purple. Oval niches, tall and with backgrounds of mosaic, and guarded by slender white columns, appeared at intervals along the walls, and in these niches stood beautifully executed statues of heroes and gods, mostly purloined from Greece. Before each statue was a narrow altar on which incense burned, filling the heated air with thin blue coils of smoke and intensifying the heat with odors. At the end of the Senate Chamber was a high stone platform on which stood a huge marble chair, cushioned in velvet. Here the Consul sat in state. He was a small dark man with a face resembling a gloomy ape, but his eyes glittered with intelligence and an irascibility worse than Scaevola's. His white toga was wrinkled; his scarlet shoes appeared to annoy his feet.

Three broad marble steps, like podiums, stood shallowly along two sides of the chamber, and on these sat the comparatively few Senators who had appeared today, formidable in their white robes, golden girdles and armlets, and ornamented scarlet shoes. They sat with weary negligence, their chairs at different angles. It was apparent that they were bored and hot and impatient. They chatted indolently together, and yawned.

In the center of the floor stood Marcus' manacled client, Persus, and his more lightly chained young and weeping wife, and his little children, also with chains on their wrists.

Marcus did not at first see his wretched clients. He was looking at the Senators, and his heart quailed. One of the Senators, he saw with alarm, was regarding him very closely and with a tight and vindictive expression, as if already exulting in Marcus' approaching defeat. He scrutinized the patrician with sudden attention. His face was familiar, yet he was certain he had never seen him before. Then, with another lunge of the heart, he saw that the Senator bore a remarkable likeness to Curius the younger, and he knew this was Senator Curius, the father.

He directed his eyes to his clients, who were all gazing at him beseechingly, their tear-wet white faces lighting up at the sight of their supposed deliverer. It was their abject suffering, the chains upon them, their helplessness before tyranny, their slight and emaciated bodies, their wide and stricken eyes, which made him momentarily forget the Senators and even Senator Curius. He went at once to the side of Persus, and laid his hand gently on the prisoner's shoulder. "Be comforted and of hope," he said, and despised himself for his words. For he did not believe in them, himself.

The aedile was droning in a bored voice, "Prisoner, one Persus, plebeian and small farmer outside the gates of Rome, and his wife, Maia, and his two children, a boy of ten, a female of six years. The charge is failure to pay just taxes levied upon Persus by the authority and law of the Roman Republic, and to have evaded those taxes justly levied, to the scandal and hurt of his countrymen, and in defiance of the majesty of Rome. The farm of Persus has already been seized in part payment of the just taxes, and the slaves also, three of which he possessed. His household goods and cattle have also been seized. Nevertheless, the debt is less than half paid. The prisoner is guilty of all charges."

He was an insignificant man, and he mimicked his ennui-saturated lords obsequiously. He flicked the scroll from which he had been reading with a contemptuous finger and paused, and looked at the lofty ceiling.

"The lawyer. Surely there is a lawyer," said one of the Senators, who had a face like a sharp coin and was of a distinguished appearance.

"One," said the aedile, peering at his scroll as if he were having difficulty in deciphering so unworthy a name, "Marcus Tullius Cicero, son of an obscure knight, born in Arpinum." He paused to let this ridiculous fact impress itself on the Senators. He added reluctantly, "He is the son of the

Lady Helvia of the noble Helvii family, and student of the pontifex maximus, Scaevola."

"His qualifications are accepted," said the old Senator.

"I crave your pardon, Senator Servius," said Senator Curius in an acid voice, as thin and poisonous as vitriol. "Is it indicated that this—this advocate—is a citizen of Rome?"

The question, of course, was superfluous, and the Senator knew it. Senator Servius looked at his younger colleague haughtily, and said with vexation, "Certainly! Who can plead before us who is not?"

Curius wishes to humiliate me, thought Marcus.

"Cicero," repeated Senator Curius with the slight inflection that made the name absurd. "Chick-pea. It is extraordinary."

"When we consider the lowliness of all our ancestors, who founded Rome, then it is most extraordinary that we sit here at all," said Senator Servius, and Marcus knew at once that the old worn man was no friend of Curius, and he took some heart. Scaevola had taught him that it was necessary for a lawyer first to establish sympathy with at least one of the judges.

In turn the Senators saw a very young man, tall and too slender, with too long a neck and with long and narrow hands. His face had much virility, though it was tight with anxiety. His eyes were beautiful. His brown and waving hair clustered about his pale cheeks. His dress, the Senators observed, was dignified and rich and there was a costly ring upon his left hand, and he held a rod of authority in his hand richly chased in bright silver. His shoes were as white as snow. Above all, his brow was noble.

Then they saw his resolute expression, the carved firmness of his lips. Senator Servius leaned forward in his chair the better to observe him. This movement seemed friendly to Marcus and he smiled. Instantly his face was charming, tender, almost dazzling with a light of its own. He did not know the value of his smile.

So once was I, thought the old Senator, Servius. But it is I no more. So was my son, who died in the Social War, and who believed in man's inherent nobility. It is always innocence which dies, and it is always evil which prevails.

Nevertheless, the Senator was an honest man and celebrated law as strictly as did Marcus.

The aedile said to Marcus, hardly glancing at him, "What is your plea, Master?"

"Not guilty of any crime against Rome," said Marcus.

The Senators stirred in umbrage. The crowd in and without the door raised a buzz of voices. A guard quieted them sternly. The prisoner and his wife and children wept; the little girl, in her coarse tunic, raised a tremulous cry and tried to reach her mother and could not.

"Not guilty of a proved crime?" demanded Servius. He scowled at the scroll in his hand.

"He is not."

"The law is specific," said Curius, with a gesture of disgust which indicated the baseness of the advocate. "Does this farmer owe taxes or not? He does. Does the law state that in this event his goods and his properties shall be seized in satisfaction of the debt? It does. Does it also say that if the goods and properties are not sufficient he and his family shall be sold into slavery for further satisfaction? It does. It is the law.

"Yet, this Cicero would declare he is not guilty!"

"It is the law," said Servius. He was a little sorry for Marcus, but also irritated. "Do you wish to reject the law, Cicero? Have you no respect for it?"

"Lord," said Marcus, in a fervent voice which rang through the chamber, "there is no one more devoted to honorable law than I, no, not in all of Rome! For men without law are animals, and nations without it fall into anarchy. I bow before the Twelve Tables of Roman Law. No one serves them with more profundity and pride and solicitude. And so I say my client is innocent."

Servius made a grimace, while the other Senators smiled at the young man's presumption.

"The law concerning your client exists," said Servius. "Therefore, according to what you have said you must respect this law also."

"I respect just law," said Marcus, and now his heart felt as if it were about to burst. "I respect the laws of Rome, which were founded on justice, patriotism, fearlessness of spirit, a proper regard for liberty, and charity and manhood. But I respect no evil law."

Servius frowned. "Nevertheless, no matter your opinion, Cicero, this is law. It is truth. Truth is that which exists, and this law exists."

He had a fondness for syllogisms. He added:

> "Truth is that which exists.
> This law exists,
> Therefore, this law is truth."

Again, he was sorry for Marcus. He considered the case concluded. He glanced at the Consul in his chair, waiting for the signal. Marcus held up his hand.

"Please, Lord, let me add one thing. You have made a valid syllogism. But validity is not always truth, as you know. Let me give you another, which is not only valid but true:

"A reality is that which exists.
Evil exists,
Therefore evil is a reality."

"It is true that evil exists. It exists as objectively and as fully as does good. It is at least as powerful as virtue, and in many cases it is more powerful, for there are more evil men than there are virtuous.

"But who, if he is a man of probity, will hurry to embrace evil because, in philosophy and in fact, it exists, has reality and has its measure of truth?"

His fine voice, youthfully sonorous, soared through the chamber, and all were silent, even the crowds within and without the portals. Scaevola nudged Noë with his elbow and smiled slyly.

The attention of the Senators was fully caught. The venal ones glanced uneasily at the distant Scaevola and wondered how much he had told his pupil.

Marcus resumed, his large eyes flashing like pale gold: "Pestilence exists, therefore it has verity. Do we hasten, therefore, to throw ourselves into pestilential circumstances and contagion, because of the true existence of the terror? For again, there are evil truths, and there are excellent truths. We sedulously avoid the one, with regard for our very lives and our spirits, and we embrace the other which makes us fully men, and preserves us as a nation.

"We hasten to eliminate pestilence. Therefore, we should hasten to eliminate evil laws. The evil of this law, under which my client was seized, is an old one, more than half-forgotten, and found not very long ago in some dusty archives."

"Do you wish to abolish taxes, on which our nation subsists and which cannot subsist without them?" demanded Curius with contempt, and in a rising voice of passion.

"No," said Marcus, with a calm that contrasted with the other's fury. "Permit me to recall to you why that law was promulgated in the very beginning. It was to prevent the people of the infant Republic from falling into loose and easy debt, and abandoning responsibility. It was to teach them thrift and sobriety, the sanctity of the given word. Without these an individual perishes. Governments also so perish."

He paused, and looked slowly from one Senator's interested face to the other. His stern eyes came to rest on Senator Curius.

"It was the intention of that law to offer a warning not only to profligate citizens but to profligate governments. For, is it not the foundation of Roman law that the government is not more than the people? If the government is guilty of criminal acts is it not the duty of a people to restrain it and punish it, as if it were a lawless individual? So it is written; so it is truth. A body of powerful men sitting in government are no less guilty than a single man of crimes common to them both, but in the case of government the crime is greater and more heinous, for it strikes down the walls of a city and lays it open to the enemy."

"Gods!" groaned Scaevola.

"Romans," said Marcus, and now his face was high and flushed with his own passion, "have always taxed themselves from the first days of the Republic, for good taxes are necessary for survival. But for what were these taxes invented? To pay for soldiers to protect us from enemies without our walls. To pay for the guards within the city. To establish courts of justice; to pay the stipends of the lawgivers, the Senate, the tribunes, the Consuls. To build convenient roads and temples. For the maintenance of sewers, the raising of aqueducts to bring us the blessing of pure water. To create a department of sanitation to guard the people's health. To impose a tariff on nations who deal with us—and that tariff has served as well." He smiled charmingly again.

Then suddenly his face changed and was full of high and heroic anger.

"But the law was not passed—and it fell into obscurity because Romans obeyed that law even while not knowing it was a written one—for the purpose of foreign adventures; not to extract a man's industrious substance to support the deliberately idle, the worthless and the abandoned and those without responsibility toward neighbors and country! It was not passed to purchase a depraved rabble with free food, free shelter and free circuses. Not for their envious lust was this lax passed! Not for the purpose of buying their votes was the law written! For when our fathers hewed a civilization out of rock and wilderness and forest and wild beasts and barbarians the market rabble did not exist, the cowardly were not yet born, the thieves were not clamoring at the treasury, the weak were not whining at the doors of Senators' houses, the irresponsible did not sit idle on the streets and on the land.

"We had a law for such people. We put them forcibly to work for their bread. We gave them no solicitude because they were of low intelligence and base passions and craven spirits. We said to them, Work, or you shall not eat. And they worked, or perished. They had no voice in our government, and were despised by heroes, and our fathers were heroes."

He had to pause to get his breath. He was panting. Sweat was pouring down his face and he did not heed it. He bent his head to facilitate the movement of his lungs. His hand gripped the rod of authority.

And there was silence in the chamber, silence on the steps and at the entrance. Scaevola was no longer glowering and rolling up his eyes.

Then Marcus raised his head again. He had long forgotten that he was addressing dangerous Senators who could destroy him. He spoke to the soul of Rome, as a Roman.

"We are taxed in our bread and our wine, in our incomes and our investments, on our land and on our property, not only for base creatures who do not deserve the name of men, but for foreign nations, for complaisant nations who will bow to us and accept our largesse and promise us to assist in the keeping of the peace—these mendicant nations who will destroy us when we show a moment of weakness or our treasury is bare, and surely it is becoming bare! We are taxed to maintain legions on their soil, in the name of law and order and the Pax Romana, a document which will fall into dust when it pleases our allies and our vassals. We keep them in precarious balance only with our gold. Is the heart-blood of our nation worth these? Shall one Italian be sacrificed for Britain, for Gaul, for Egypt, for India, even for Greece, and a score of other nations? Were they bound to us with ties of love, they would not ask our gold. They would ask only our laws. They take our very flesh, and they hate and despise us. And who shall say we are worthy of more?"*

"They will kill him," said Scaevola. "For he has spoken truth and when shall a man be permitted to live when he speaks the truth?"

But the Senators of probity listened with pale and severe faces. The Senators who were venal sneered silently at each other.

Marcus went on in a voice that trembled yet was loud. "Then, for the base within our gates, and our potential enemies throughout the world, Rome is slowly but surely being destroyed. For votes. For a peace which is without honest foundation. Was ever a nation so dishonored and threatened from within and without before, as Rome is now threatened? Yes, Greece is only one. Egypt is only one. And those before them. And they fell; they died. It is a law of nature. It is also a financial law. Debt and profligacy lead but to despair and bankruptcy. It was always so.

"This law, under which my client has been convicted, is an old law. Let us remember the intentions of those who wrote it, and let us beware of the dark intentions of those who use it today. For the first were heroes. Those who use it today are criminals."

"He will not see the dawn," said Scaevola.

"Treason," muttered Senator Curius. "Let us throw him in chains."

One of his friends whispered behind his hand, "Let him continue. Let Servius and his friends listen to this monstrous affront to the government and the people of Rome, and let them learn for all time what it means when such as this Cicero afflicts us. Let Servius and his fellows condemn him, themselves, then that Scaevola cannot blame us."

* From *De Republica*.

Servius and his friends had listened with pale faces and gathered brows and in total silence. They waited for Marcus to continue.

His voice dropped eloquently. He held out his hands to the Senate, and the magnificent ring flashed on it like a myriad of colored stars.

"My lords, let us consider just law. Does it bring tranquillity, good order, piety, justice and liberty and prosperity to a people? Does it nourish patriotism and the way of a manly and upright life? Then it is a good law, and deserves our utter obedience.

"But if it brings pain, intolerable burdens, injustice, sleepless anxiety and fear and slavery to a people, than it is an evil law passed and upheld by evil men, who hate humanity and wish to subjugate and control it. If this be treason on my part, lords, accuse me then of it, and say why it is treason. Let those who listen, hear your accusations before them and before God."*

He fell into silence. He clasped his hands tightly before him. His piteous clients huddled behind him and tried to touch his garments with their timid hands. Then he brought forward his client, Persus, and stood him before the Senate.

"Look upon this man, lords," said Marcus. "His fathers fought with ours, for Rome. His fathers gave birth to the Republic, as ours did, also. His forefathers built our walls, and struggled with hardships and the wilderness, as did ours. He is bone of our bone, flesh of our flesh. But his spirit, though independent, is yet humble. It never sought for power. It loved the land, and a little peace, and the sun on a few acres. It asked little of life but the comfort of a wife and industrious children. If this man gave birth to no Senators, no Consuls, no tribunes, he yet gave birth to the ancient strength of Rome. He, more than many of us, is Rome, herself.

"What crime has our brother committed against neighbor and his country? Has he taken illicit bribes? Has he been guilty of treason? Has he run with the enemy one day and then pursued him the next, for money? Is he a murderer? Is he a thief or a pervert? Has he betrayed friendship or a trust? Has he practiced simony or subornation, or any other evil? Is he vile, detestable, an adulterer, a dangerous liar, a blasphemer of the gods?"

Marcus paused, and then he raised his fists and cried, "No! He is only not able to pay his taxes, which you say are just! For that shall he be defamed, punished, destroyed, starved, driven into the earth which is more merciful than we?

"Of what crime does he stand committed? He could not pay his taxes!

"Is a little money greater, then, to a government, of more importance, of more value, than a human life, a Roman life, and above all, human

* From Cicero's *Law.*

dignity? Is a Roman citizen less than his house and his cattle, his humble lares and penates, his small furniture?

"God gave this man his life, yet you would destroy it for a few pieces of gold. Do you believe, then, that you are wiser and more urgent than God, that gold is more valuable than a human soul? Then, my lords, you have uttered the most terrible blasphemy of them all!"

"Treason!" cried Curius, and started to his feet and glared with violent fury on the lawyer. "Dog! You have taunted us with your obscurities, your maudlin pleas, your lies, your insolence! Guard!"

Servius rose also. He turned to Curius and said, "You lie, yourself, Curius. He has spoken but truth. And may the gods defend him. Surely man will not."

A great hubbub rose in the chamber and at the doors, and there were distant shouts of "Hero! Noble Marcus Tullius Cicero! Free the oppressed!" For a great mob had suddenly gathered at the doors and were now shaking raised fists and showing their turbulent faces.

"Sit down," said Servius to the other Senator. "Do you want insurrection, while we are in the midst of war? You know how volatile and easily aroused is the Roman rabble. Take care! This man can destroy you with his tongue."

Curius sat down, but he clenched his hands on his knees and regarded Marcus with hatred, and there was murder in his eyes.

Marcus waited. He put his arm tenderly about his client. He prayed inwardly. Then, suddenly, he was overcome, his heart swelled. He could not restrain his tears. His sobs were clearly heard. His whole body shook and quaked with his emotions. And the Senators watched, some with hard and bitter faces, and some with compassion and shame.

Then Marcus could speak again. He put his hand again on his client's shoulder and displayed him to the Senate.

"Look upon a fellow Roman, lords. He is a victim of these gold-devouring wars. Just as you are victims. He had a young son, hardly more than a child, who died in the Social War, full of patriotism and the love of his country. Just as some of you have lost sons in the war.

"But—he lost all he had in this calamity! It was little—but he lost it. But you did not lose all you had. There was much you retained.

"Persus has nothing left but his wife and his remaining children. Shall you deprive him of that little? Shall you take from a Roman brother that which is dear to yourselves? Only the Fates prevented you from being born in his bed, and with his destiny. It was no worthiness on your part. It was a throw of the dice."

Then Marcus flung out his arms and advanced a step or two toward the Senators. He did not hear the dull and roaring clamor near the doors, as more and more men crowded to hear him. He was not aware of the tension in the chamber, the unbearable passions, the quickly beating hearts of pity or rage.

"Do justice to my client. It is said that the gods love to see mercy in man, for mercy gives a godliness even to the most humble. Be magnanimous. Let the news of your charity and your kindness reach the gates of the city, and beyond. Are you not honorable men, Romans, revering your fathers? Is not virtue the most becoming toga a man can wear? What is more shining? What is more laudable? What arouses admiration most of all in the breast of all men but examples of goodness, mercy, and justice? What do men reverence more than power? Honor and nobility and right doing. For, no matter how base the man, he adores virtue."

The majority of the Senators then remembered writings at midnight on the walls of the city. Their names had been vilified. They had read inscriptions in red: *"Adulterer! Murderer! Traitor! Seducer! Libertine! Thief!"*

Roman mobs were never truly friendly, not even to a hero. They had sly eyes and ears for the peculiarities of those in power. They were a lion, held precariously by the tail. What had the sybils written? That Rome would fall first from within, that Roman streets would run red with blood, that Rome would burn. Romans might fawn for corn and a purse, and might give their votes to a benefactor. But it was in the nature of men to dislike the powerful, whether out of envy or out of suspicion.

A thousand legions would not be able to restrain them if they revolted, nor a thousand prisons contain them.

The venal Senators pondered. They needed new adulation in these days, new clients, new followers, new voters. All these were now difficult to obtain. But, if their virtue were broadcast from this chamber, carried on the wind of many voices, then they could rest secure, at least for a little while.

And there was Scaevola near the door, watching them with mocking eyes, his thumb turned up, Scaevola who knew too much.

The Senators of integrity had been deeply and profoundly moved by Marcus' words. They wrinkled their brows over the law. They, too, thought of rumor from this chamber. Would others default on their taxes, hoping for mercy, if Persus were freed?

The Consul then rose, and all rose with him. He said, in an old man's voice, but in a steady one: "You have heard. I recommend that this prisoner be set free, and his wife and children with him. As he has lost all, through our command, I order that that which we have taken be restored to him. Of what use are more beggars in the streets?"

He looked at Persus and his wife and children, who had fallen on their knees at these words and had lifted their hands in tearful adoration to him. His face was stern.

"You have been freed not because you were a victim of a law which does not exist. It exists. To your lawyer I say that this law cannot be removed, however his eloquence. To abrogate this law would be to destroy all our elaborate legal structure and its many ramifications, which certainly to many sober citizens would be most salubrious." He paused to purse his mouth in a dry smile. "It is said that for the sake of Rome we are committed to the world, which needs the money of Roman taxpayers, no matter the desperate burden on our people. What matter if a Roman starve or despair or lose his faith in just government? Who is the modern Roman? He is a slave to countries who regard him only as a means of soft subsistence and protection and endless bounty. He is a slave to the ambitious in his own nation, who use his own money to buy personal power and maintain themselves in office.

"I have said this law cannot be removed. I will amend that by saying that it can only be removed when Romans, aware of their extreme peril, demand that it be removed. Alas, a people never awake to their danger until it is too late."

He looked at Persus and his wife and children and said in a sad voice, "Go in peace. Be industrious as always. Implore the gods that they, and your fellow Romans, visit no more affliction upon you. Have not all of us Romans suffered in these years? May God have mercy on us all."

He stepped from his high stone platform, set his face forward and moved without a glance through the aisle of the Senators, who stood like statues on each side of his passage. The guards cleared a path for him and he left the chamber.

Immediately on seeing him the people shouted, "Hero! Hercules!" He smiled darkly and contemplated them for a moment. Then he inclined his head in a godly fashion and the mob screamed at this acknowledgment of their existence and tore garlands and ribbons from their heads to hurl at his feet.

"Jove!" the mighty cry went up. The object of this salutation smiled from right to left, musingly and with some satire, and went into his waiting litter. But before he closed the curtains he caught the eye of Scaevola and gave him an ironic bow.

The Senators, hearing the salute to their leader, came out eagerly in a dignified body and were gratified to be saluted as heroes also. They would be forgotten tomorrow, but as no politician believes that in his heart, they accepted the adulation. It was only Senator Servius who asked himself,

"Do they know why they acclaim us, or what occurred this hour, or what is the meaning? No."

Marcus remained behind to console and congratulate his clients, who knelt about him to kiss his hands and his feet and his garments. He gave them his own meagre purse. Roman lawyers did not receive fees from clients, but only random gifts if the beneficiaries were grateful enough. Persus wept. "I will send you two of my new kids, blessed Master!" Marcus said, "Then send them to my paternal island in Arpinum, if you can spare them."

He suddenly thought of Arpinum, and he was filled with so powerful a nostalgia for that peaceful spot that he immediately vowed that, danger or not, he would visit it soon. He stood in meditation and it was only after a considerable period that he looked up to find himself alone, confronting the vast statue of the blind goddess of Justice, with her scales in her hands.

He thought: There are many who make sardonic remarks on the blindness of Justice. But she wears a blindfold not for the obvious reason. She wears it that her judgment shall not be swayed by the mere "appearance" of those she judges in her balances, by overt and false pathos, or pleasing but meretricious distress. At all times she is impartial. That is the meaning of Law.

He walked slowly to the great doors, to find only his friends waiting for him. He smiled on them a little grimly.

"To whom do I owe the honor of the motley Greek chorus which seethed about this door only a short time ago, hailing 'heroes'?"

Scaevola, in his chair, assumed an injured expression. "I am the pontifex maximus. My fledglings are not to be ignored. Therefore, I asked my former students, who are grateful to me, to send their clerks to salute you. Ungrateful one!"

"And I," said Noë, also appearing indignant. "My people love my father, and if they desired to hail his savior, shall they be restrained?"

Archias winked at his beloved pupil, and said, "The Greeks admire those who admire them. Do you not admire the Greeks, my dear Marcus? Shall you deny them the opportunity to express their affection for you?"

Julius Caesar said, "My friends on the Palatine adore a just man." He smiled broadly at Marcus, and nudged him in the ribs. "They also adore me. They are young men, and love a frolic at Senators' expense. Did you wish to deny them amusement?"

"And each of these devoted men brought with him the scourings of rabble from the alleys and the wine shops," said Marcus.

Scaevola became extremely virtuous. "Is it not better for a mob to howl exuberantly for justice than to howl for the death of a fallen gladiator in the circus—though I admit they do not know the difference?"

"I should have preferred that my eloquence had moved them, or that justice had stirred their hearts," said Marcus.

Scaevola rolled up his eyes as if desperately imploring that the gods give him patience. He could find no words. He said only, "Bah."

"Do you not realize," said the young Marcus, with heat, "that at a word from all of you that mob would have assaulted, and perhaps killed, a number of the Senators, without knowing why they did it?"

"Excellent," said Scaevola. "I overlooked an opportunity."

Noë, in his litter with Marcus, said, "You forget that you won your case. Is that not of some satisfaction? Many who heard you were not mindless, in spite of Scaevola's remarks. They are serious young men. They will remember."

Marcus was a little relieved. Also, he was exhausted by his own emotions. He said, "Remain for a cup of wine with me, while I receive my mother's and father's felicitations. I see my brother has already raced home with the news." He paused. "And then I will return to you all this magnificence with which you arrayed me. Did you notice that young Julius deftly removed his lent wand of authority from my hand?"

Noë laughed. "It is symbolic of the young Caesar. I hear he has developed epilepsy, and you know the superstitious believe that it is a divine gift, for one hears strange things and sees even stranger during convulsions. No. You must not return what I gave you. It is a fee from my father and myself, for what you have done for him."

"I did nothing," Marcus persisted.

"You did it all," said Noë, with considerable impatience. "What is this modesty? It is said that God loves modesty in men. But mankind despises it."

Later, Marcus embraced his father, Tullius. "It was your words that inspired me," he said. He kissed his father's hands, and his father tenderly blessed him.

"I have had few moments of pride," said Tullius, weeping. "But today I am a proud man. I have not lived in vain."

CHAPTER SEVENTEEN

Marcus stood in the spring sun that flooded over the gardens in Arpinum. He leaned against an oak tree and reread a letter from Noë ben Joel, who had lived for over a year in Jerusalem with his family.

"Greetings to the noble Marcus Tullius Cicero from Noë ben Joel:

"I received your last letter with delight in your increasing success. Fortunate it is that you have obtained clients who can enrich you with gifts. As a remembrance, and in eternal gratitude to you, my father is sending you several jars of those little black Judean olives which you appreciate, and several kegs of costly oil—which you cannot obtain in Rome under present conditions, and which are worth their weight in gold. Moreover, I am sending you many lengths of Egyptian white and colored linen, a scroll of the Phaedo inscribed by a Jewish scholar of singular note, and quite excellent, for your father, two bracelets of silver wire encrusted with precious stones—an art in which my countrymen excel—for your lady mother, and a shield embossed with the arms of your family for your brother, Quintus. Accept these, dear friend, from the hearts of those who love you and who yearn to look upon your face again.

"We have just celebrated the first birthday of my son, Joshua, in my father's house where, as you know, we all live. It was a tranquil occasion. The Roman proconsul, a worthy man, and a friend of my father's, attended the festivities. He presented my son with a beautiful Roman short sword sheathed in a jeweled scabbard. My father was uncertain how to express his gratitude—if he possessed any—but as usual I was swift with my fluent tongue and the innocent Roman was pleased. It occupies a place of honor in the household.

"I am not sorry to linger here awhile, in the golden shadow of the towered Temple and among my people. I had feared, as you know, the stern life and presence of my countrymen in Jerusalem who are enamored of God and not of life. But the Hellenistic influence is very powerful among the younger Jews of family, who have many friends among the Greeks householded in the city. They speak Greek more often than they speak Aramaic, and Latin more than they speak Hebrew, the language of the learned men. My father was perturbed in the beginning, and he fears for his country. But the Hellenistic spirit receives sympathy here. There appears a greater similarity between the arête of the Greeks and the spiritual virtu of the Jews than between the cool unity of the classicism of Athens and the heated versicolor of Rome. Even my father perceives this, though he is a man of singular stubbornness. He spends hours each day in the gates with the wise men, who discuss the almost instant arrival of the Messias, who will, of course, drive every Roman and Greek and other alien from within the sacred precincts of these yellow walls, and lift up Jerusalem on the wings of archangels to rule the lesser tribes of the earth. I think of Rome, and smile.

"I have done as you requested and have sought out more prophecies of the Messias for you. There are many Egyptian merchants here, and I have made their acquaintance, for they must be civil in Jerusalem while conducting their business. They tell me that an ancient Pharaoh, Aton, prophesied that Horus will descend from heaven to take on the flesh of a man and lead all men to justice, love, peace and faith, and reconcile them to their God. I have also made the acquaintance of Indu traders who linger here awhile, resting between their ships, and they have informed me that their Gita, which vaguely resembles our Torah, declares that man is corrupt from his conception, and by no effort of his own can he elevate his state. He is evil from the hour he draws breath, for he was conceived in evil, he lives in evil, and he dies in evil, and shall suffer death, except that on some far day God may rescue him from his foreordained wickedness. Again, possibly, when some god takes on the flesh of man and leads him to grace.

"I have heard that Hammurabi, the great Babylonia king, says in his Code: 'How can man free himself from the evil of himself? By contemplation of God, by penitence and penance, by confession of sins, by the power of God, only. On a fated day God will manifest Himself to the eyes of men, in their own flesh.'

"You will observe the entwining theme in these prophecies and words of wisdom: The wickedness of man, his lack of grace, his sentence to eternal death, and his possible rescue by a compassionate God who will take on the flesh of mankind. You will recall, in this frame of reference, the words of Aristotle: 'There is no good in mankind, save that which is vouchsafed it from God, by virtue of God and by His loving kindness. For man was born to evil, and he cannot free himself from the web of iniquity without God, no matter his striving or his good will.'

"My father delights that I seek the company of the wise men in the gates, but I seek it to gather news for you concerning the Messias. I have read the books of Isaias pertaining to Him, He Who will be born of the Jews. Writes Isaias: 'For a Child is born to us, and a Son is given to us, and the government is upon His shoulder, and His name shall be called Wonderful, Counselor, God the Mighty, the Father of the world to come, the Prince of Peace. His empire shall be multiplied, and there shall be no end of peace. He shall sit upon the throne of David and upon his kingdom, to establish it and strengthen it with judgment and with justice, from henceforth and forever.'

"However, alas, it appears that, according to Isaias, there will be few who will know Him and follow Him, when He has taken flesh, and when He dwells among men. Isaias writes: 'Who hath believed our report? And to whom is the arm of the Lord revealed? And He shall grow up as a tender plant before Him, and as a root out of a thirsty ground. There is no beauty in Him, nor comeliness, and we have seen Him and there was no sightliness that we should be desirous of Him. Despised, and the most abject of men, a Man of sorrows and acquainted with infirmity, and His look was as it were hidden and despised. Whereupon we esteemed Him not.'

"But, my dear Marcus, when have men esteemed the truly great among them, and when have they honored the just and the noble? They prefer those who come with heralds and banners and the thunders of the drum, and with servants before them, crying out the praises of him who rides in the gilded chariot behind several horses with gemmed harness. If the Messias appears, as Isaias prophesies, as a Man of humility, not overwhelming in beauty, not with the hosannahs of angels echoing on all His steps, He surely will be despised and rejected by those whom He has come to save. For man strikes the Image of God on the base metal of his own heart. Would God descend to man in mercy and love without clouds of angelic attendants, armed and terrible, crowned with the sun? No, He would not!

"Isaias continues: 'Surely, He hath borne our infirmities and carried our sorrows, and we have thought Him as it were a leper, and as one struck by God and afflicted. But He was wounded for our iniquities, He was bruised for our sins. The chastisement of our peace was upon Him, and by His bruises we are healed. He was offered because it was His own will, and He opened not His mouth. He shall be led as a sheep before His shearer, and He shall not open His mouth.'

"Apparently, then, the Messias will be done to death in a most dreadful fashion by blind and ignorant men, for He will not come with panoply and in the company of the Seraphim and with the cloak of celestial majesty on His shoulders. What shall He say, in those days, and who will listen? He is the Covenant between God and man. He will be, as Isaias writes, 'a light unto the Gentiles' also. But who will know Him?

"It is possible that I shall see Him, and you. By what mark shall we recognize Him? Shall we remember the prophecies? Or shall we say, 'There is no beauty in Him—no sightliness that we should be desirous of Him?'

"I have heard these prophecies all my life, and have not credited them, for I am a skeptical Jew, and a Roman citizen acquainted with many religions. Nor do the aristocratic and the men of religion in Jerusalem give heed to the prophecies any longer. It is only the old men in the gates of the city, who ponder and look at the dark heavens, and wait with growing impatience. Will they recognize Him when He comes? The children read of Him in their books, and recite the prophecies. Will they know Him?

"Yes, there is an air of excitement in the city, as if news of a mighty King has gone before Him. Who can understand this?

"You, I believe, my dear Marcus, would find Israel not only interesting but agreeable, in climate and in atmosphere. Joppa, on the Great Sea, is worth a visit of a month at the very least, if only to contemplate the sunsets each day. Regarding the celestial conflagrations, the great and silent awesomeness reflected in the sea, one can repeat with David, '—the work of His fingers, the moon and the stars which He hath ordained—what is man that Thou are mindful of him, and the son of man, that Thou visited him?' Even I ask that unanswered question. Surely it is presumptuous for us to believe that God cares for us!

"Jerusalem is the heart of our nation, a dusty, colorful, teeming, crowded, odoriferous, noisy heart, intolerably hot during the day, and deserty-cool at night. Here are many peoples, not only Jews; traders, merchants, scoundrels, mountebanks, bankers, historians, soldiers, sailors, businessmen, antiquarians from all over the world, Syrians, Romans, Samaritans, Jordanians, Egyptians, Indus, Greeks, and only God knows what else. So long as they observe the Judean law, they are ignored and despised. The Jew, like the Roman, loves Law. 'God has said, He has revealed,' state the wise old men dogmatically, and let that alien beware who disputes it! The Jews have no laws but the Law of God. We are a Theocracy, and it is wonderful to observe. One would think that in a Theocracy there would be no disputations. But the wise old men in the gates weave commentaries and subtle webs over the simplest of the Commandments. God speaks plainly, but man must always be devious, and ask a thousand 'whys' and give a thousand answers.

"As Jews are violent and intense by nature, the Romans respect their convictions. A dead people are not profitable to Rome, so Romans are careful not to insist on what the Jews call idolatry in Jerusalem. Coins struck here bear the head of no god, and Jews are not pressed into the Roman armies as they are in other countries. So long as Jews pay reasonable taxes the Romans do not disturb them. On the contrary, they are friendly, and many Roman officers are married to Jewish girls.

"Your Polybius would have delighted in Judea, where we have free schools for all youths and where universal learning is obligatory. I am not certain this is wise. It puffs up the ignorant who are incapable of true learning. If they acquire the words of the Law they do not understand its spirit. Many are there who are born mentally illiterate, and they have a place in the world. But they are like ravens, whose tongues are split, who learn words but not their meaning. Who is more dangerous than a man who can quote wisdom but who does not know how to apply it in his own life, and in his government? But at least we are profound in one way: we insist that all men, even the rabbis, must learn a trade and must work, no matter the wealth of the family. Beware of the man of the colonnades, who does not labor at anything with his hands! Beware even more of the rich and idle man, who has time to develop a lust for power to fill his empty days! The Jews know this. Therefore, we work. I manage my father's gardens, I who knew nothing of the earth and the seasons and growing things until I came to Jerusalem.

"It is much more vociferous even than Rome, for we are a small country and are desperately crowded in the city. Jerusalem is like a hive of bees; one cell is packed upon another; one could run over the whole city on the rooftops without touching one's feet to the ground. In truth, from the top of our yellow walls we seem to see nothing but heaving roofs extending into the gold and dusty distance, broken here and there by groves of cypresses and carob trees and palms, like oases. All the roofs are yellow or white, rising and falling blankly, except after sunset when they are crowded with people sitting or standing on them to catch the evening air. Then music bursts forth from various houses and the city resounds with a vast humming, and a trumpet shatters at intervals from the temple. We are locked within our yellowish and twisting walls, and hear the calls of the guards who pace the tops.

"Beyond the gates are the theatres which the Greeks or the Romans have built. The Greeks produce plays; the Romans produce bloody spectacles. One would deduce that the one was civilized, the other barbarous. This is a superficial judgment. Greek cruelty shines and glitters and sparkles in the erudite comedies. Who was it that said all laughter is cruel, even when it appears most harmless? For laughter must have an object, preferably man or men, to excite it, and who but an obtuse man can contemplate the predicament of humanity without compassion? There is no compassion in laughter. Gayety is an entirely different matter; it is innocent and does not caricature, does not mock, does not deride. It is amused at the antics of man, but not man himself. You will see that I have changed. I, being only a man however, delight in the Greek plays, tragic or comic. I attend the presentations regularly, and so do other young Jews influenced by Hellenism. But not even the Greeks attend the Roman spectacles, except to observe, and deplore with disgust. As you know, crucifixion is a Roman method of execution. The Romans regularly produce spectacles of mass crucifixion of criminals, including Jews. They ask the Jews who violently object: 'Is this worse than your method, which is stoning to death?'

"I have written several plays, in which comedy is entwined with tragedy, and the Greeks have received them with considerable acclaim. But I must do it all anonymously, because of my parents. I have made parodies of the most weighty of Greek plays, including *Oedipus Rex* and *Elektra*, and even the Romans laughed at them heartily, though Romans are not notable for their sense of humor. They prefer buffoons and clowns and broad situations to subtleties, and does this not argue that there remains some primitiveness in them? The Greeks love games, but they prefer the games which display the human form in agile grace, and are not mainly tests of strength. But then, in Rome power rings on stone. In Greece beauty stands in marble.

"Still, I long for Rome. My father wishes to see his daughters there, and their husbands and children. He intends not to engage in business on his return. He said to me, 'If one is to live to a peaceful old age, one must not become known to governments. Let not the eye of politicians alight on you!' I believe him.

"Dear friend, be cautious and circumspect. Do not arouse more animosity than you can afford. We send our affection to you, and our blessings."

Marcus rerolled the letter with a powerful feeling of love for his friend. But he also smiled. Noë's concern for him was ludicrous. He was only a modestly successful young lawyer, now almost the sole support of his family through the gifts of grateful clients. (Some could not give him a copper.) He had practiced his profession for hardly more than a year. Clients came to his house on the Carinae, or to the house of Scaevola. The old pontifex maximus had given him a small room in his house, austerely furnished with but a table and two chairs, and shelves for his books of law, and with no window and no light except for a dim lamp. For this, Marcus paid his mentor a little but regular fee. The room was stifling even in the winter, for no air came except that which wafted through the door, which must be closed during consultations and confidences. Inevitably, it stank of sweat and parchment and damp stone and burning oil. "The odor of learning," said Scaevola with a solemn face. "Or, perhaps, the odor of perfidy. When was a lawyer not perfidious, especially in these days?"

He had had many arguments with Marcus concerning clients. "What?" he exclaimed. "You will not take a client who is overtly a criminal? But, have you not agreed that even criminals are entitled to just representation before the law? What a fool you are, Apollo. But I should not call you Apollo. The Apollonian light shines without restraint on all men, but your light would shine only on the just. Pah."

"I have no hesitancy in defending criminals," Marcus had protested. "But I must be assured that in the particular crime under discussion the man is innocent of it, no matter his past. How, then, can I defend him with all my might?"

"He is still entitled to representation. Put aside your scruples, or you will never be a rich man. But you do not care for riches!"

In this, Scaevola was wrong. Marcus had begun to care for riches, for he was by nature prudent and did not deprecate the idea that a man was worthy of his labors. He had a family which must be protected. Still, he could not bring any eloquence to his command in behalf of a man obviously guilty of a foul deed.

"It is the credo of lawyers that no man they defend is guilty, in spite of the facts," Scaevola said. "It is a matter of a little juggling in your mind."

Marcus could not toss clubs in his mind to form a pattern he desired. "I am no juggler," he said, to which Scaevola replied, "Then, you are no lawyer." He added, "If you defend only those you believe to be guiltless of the crime of which they are accused you will want for bread. Remember, a man is innocent until proved guilty before a magistrate. That is Roman law. Law is an exercise in wits. It is like a combat in an arena, my simpleton."

Marcus understood, and it caused him anxiety for his future.

"A lawyer must believe he is cleverer than other men, and particularly that he is more astute than a magistrate. But, you have no sense of irony. Who knows what was the intention of the formers of the laws? An intelligent lawyer must interpret them for the benefit of his client."

But Marcus was tremendously concerned by the fact that the tyrant, Cinna, was reinterpreting the strong, masculine, and just laws of old Rome. Even Cinna did not dare flout the written law and Constitution, but he had a host of subservient lawyers eternally busy in the reinterpretation of them. This would lead inevitably to chaos, injustice and outrage, and inevitable tyranny. The law stated that a man's property was inviolate. But Cinna's new tax laws violated that ancient provision of a proud country. A man's property, it now appeared, was inviolate only against private thieves. But not against the government, which was engaged in constant and giant theft, sucking up the people's substance and returning only sewage and debt. It did this with unchallenged impunity, and modern Romans did not protest; this demonstrated the pusillanimity to which they had descended. The populace now extolled the Gracchi, who had robbed the industrious of corn for the idle and profligate. No doubt the Gracchi had been virtuous men in their private lives. But their minds had been corrupted by sentimentality. They had been stoned to death by an infuriated people, and for a long time their execution had appeared just. Now they were heroes of a degraded populace, which despised honorable labor and preferred free bread and circuses.

Not for the first time did Marcus realize that governments are enemies of the people. Now, as he stood in the spring sunshine on his paternal island, he considered the Theocracy of Judea, of which Noë had written him. Laws not based on the Law of God were evil laws. The end was national death.

How long would Rome endure, his beloved country?

He held the letter of Noë in his hand as he leaned against the sacred oak, and looked with trouble at the rushing river, lemon-colored in the light of spring. But a musing part of his brain engaged itself in admiration of the scene and the season. Spring was golden, not green. The tender tufts of trees gleamed with yellow, and shrubs and bushes burst into the fair light in all shades and hues from amber to primrose, from delicate gilt to glimmering honey. The whole appeared to have been plunged into aureate springs, then lifted again into place between its two rivers which reflected it and the daffodil-tinted sky. Only the grass, faintly emerald, disturbed the gilded appearance, the frail golden showers drooping from willow and birch, the tight golden stars of poplars and oaks. The view of Arpinum across the river seemed drenched in shadowy gold as it climbed hills still brazen from winter. Summer and autumn were not so fragrant as spring, so jubilant in the renewed celebration of life. The earth exhaled and the heart stirred, even the heart of a young and troubled and somewhat despondent Roman.

He looked at the bridge that led to the mainland, the arched bridge of memory, and he thought of Livia. He thought of her as he remembered her more than ten years ago, a maiden of wildness and fragility, with glowing hair and strange blue eyes and virgin breast. As his mother had prophesied she remained forever young and chaste to him, safe from years and time, safe from sorrow and change. The faint spring wind sounded like her remembered song, unearthly and pure and pondering. Like the nymphs on many Grecian vases she was pursued but forever uncaught. She was a dream that did not pass, and she left no shadow.

As he thought this the old savage sickness took him again, the old unappeased longing. He felt that he was in a large vessel, inexorably moving down the river while Livia stood on the island as a maiden, with hair and palla flowing in the wind, her hand upraised in farewell. He fled with time; she remained as a pure hue always imprisoned, yet shining, in Alexandrian glass. All about him was in activity, but where Livia stood the trees did not change their color, the sky did not darken or flame in dawn and sunset, the sun did not arch from horizon to horizon. It was always

spring, and she was forever young and forever lost. The river took him
away, but Livia sang her song to the wind and eternity.

He had learned sternly to shut the lid of his mind upon Livia, as one
shuts the lid of a jeweled box upon a treasure and then forgets it for a
while. But there was something about the light today, the descending sun,
the scent of the earth, that held up the lid against his pressing hands. Livia
lived; she was not a dream at all. It did not matter that no one spoke her
name to him in Rome, that he did not know where she dwelled, or even
if she lived at all any longer. She was a breathing presence to him; he
heard her voice, clear and a little mocking, as he remembered it. He felt,
if he only turned his head quickly in that Umbrian light he would see
Livia again, like a dryad under the trees, fleet as a breath, as radiant as a
vision. "Livia," he said aloud. He did not turn his head, but he was certain that some emanation of her was near him, like the dear ghost of one
who was dead yet lived. The Livia he knew and loved was not the wife
of Lucius Sergius Catilina, having an existence under some unknown roof,
forgetting him, busy with random things and apprehensions. She was
Livia, and she had no other name. She was bound to his spirit as a vine
is bound to a tree. His mother urged him to marry, for Quintus was in
the army and he might be killed. The name of the Ciceroni lived still
formless in his loins.

He knew, however, that he must marry some day, for the sake of unborn
sons. But that time was not now, while Livia still embraced him in dreams
and fantasies. To marry would be to commit adultery. He had a fear that
marriage would take from him something ineffable, something poetic
which fell like a brilliant shower still on the mundane city of reality. The
random woman in Rome, yes. But—not yet!—a wife on the hearth and at
a loom in his house. Livia still occupied all the rooms of his heart.

The spring wind was becoming cooler; he could feel it even through his
wool cloak and in the folds of his long blue tunic and in the crevices of
his leather shoes. The light was not so ardent now; it was fading from the
walls and cherry roofs of Arpinum. The river sang; it was darkening to
hurrying brown. He could hear the lowing of distant cattle as they came
from the meadows. He heard the lonely voices of sheep. Eunice and Athos
would be directing the five slaves who lived with them on the duties of
the evening. He must leave this bank, this golden forest, and return to the
farmhouse for his supper. And then, silent and bereft, he would sit in what
once was his father's library and read before retiring to his empty bed.

Yet, as if imposed on this scene, on this time, the aureate island remained, with its lovely dryad who never departed. It was to know this vision again that he had returned to the island through dangerous villages
and towns, in this most dangerous time, against the pleas of his mother

and her warnings. But no one disturbed Eunice and her diligent Athos. They lived in peace, and it was this peace he had sought. There were moments when he had found it. There were moments when he forgot the war, when he forgot the courts, forgot even his parents and his brother. He lived in amber. Each night he said, I must return, and each morning was a new day that was a replica of the one that had gone before. It was not only love for the island and its tranquillity that held him here. It was a dream and the dream was all that mattered. Eurydice was here, in fields of asphodels, and he recoiled from climbing up to a world of clangor and duties and grief, and the harsh ring of power and the hot exigencies of men. He must return, as did Orpheus, leaving Eurydice forever behind. But not today! And surely not tomorrow.

Loneliness, with diaphanous forms of delight, was to him as yet preferable to plangent life. He had not come in vain. The island of dreams was more real to him, more desirable, more blissful, than anything the world of Rome could offer him, even if it were power and fortune. Here he could write the poems and the delicate essays that had gained a publisher for him in Rome. He wondered, sometimes, if all men kept a dream within them even to great age, if all had a secret island where their limbs were free and they looked upon other suns and stared at other moons. If they did not, then they had truly died.

He did not hear the stealthy glide of a large boat near him. He did not start at the fierce eyes that gazed at him. He was listening to the choruses of song in the trees; he was watching the urgent flight of birds against the sky. So he heard no hushed footstep creeping upon him. The citron light was sparkling on the upper houses of Arpinum, and the west was a lake of gold on which floated rosy mist.

When he felt iron arms suddenly seize him he could not believe it. So, at first, he only dimly struggled, numbly outraged. He was not frightened. He turned his head and saw four men in cloaks about him, the hoods falling over and concealing all but their mouths, which were cruel and triumphant. One of the men struck him sharply in the face, and he tried to recoil. But they held him. Another spoke angrily, "No, there must be no mar, no sign! Restrain yourself."

He did not recognize the voice. For an instant he thought these men were his own slaves; there were rumors that slaves were in revolt all over Italy against their masters. But another man said, "We must do what we must do, as it was commanded. Let us be quick about it, for I hear the bark of a dog, and who knows what brute will burst out upon us." The voice was not rude as the voice of a slave. It had the cultivated accents of Rome. He, still incredulous, looked down at the hands that held him in such an immovable grip. They were not the hands of slaves, though they were strong. In a wildly clarified light he saw that one hand bore a ring, and it was a handsome ring artfully contrived.

"What is this?" he cried. "Who are you? Unhand me, animals!" He thought of thieves, of vagabonds, of criminals from Arpinum. He opened his mouth to shout for help, but instantly a wad of cloth was forced between his teeth.

It was then that for the first time he thought: Death.

He struggled with all his strength, forcing his feet into the cool and yielding earth. Now he cursed his former supercilious attitude concerning physical prowess and dexterous throwing and heaving by using the strength of the antagonist against him. However, sudden and terrible fear gave him some strength; once he actually broke away from his captors, but they soon seized him again, laughing gleefully between their teeth. Panting, he tried to see their faces in the shadow of the hoods, but he saw only their violent mouths.

They began to strip him, very carefully, holding him strongly against his struggles, as if they wished not to tear his garments. One removed his cloak, folded it and laid it down neatly on the grass. Another took from him, very dexterously, his long tunic and unfastened his leather girdle and purse with its few coins. These were placed in an orderly fashion on his cloak. They unlaced his shoes, put them side by side beside the heap of clothing. Marcus was so fascinated by this meticulous arranging of his effects that he stood still to watch in the clutch of the restraining arms. One man reached for the golden amulet of Pallas Athene which Aurelia Caesar had given him so long ago, but another man said, "No, he would not remove that, his amulet, while swimming. It would be his protection."

Then Marcus understood that he was to have an accident, and that explained the fact that no sharp knife or dagger had been used to dispatch him surely and at once.

"His feet must not be soiled with earth or scratched with stones," said one of the men who was apparently the leader. So Marcus was lifted in strong arms and carried to the bank of the river, which was now suddenly on fire with the sunset. He was laid almost lovingly in the boat, his ankles and feet held in hard hands. Then two of the men stealthily rowed to the middle of the river, while Marcus looked despairingly at the flaming sky and prayed for help and life. Death, in the abstract, had never seemed horrible to him, for he could philosophize with Socrates that a good man had nothing to fear in this life nor the next. Now, in his youth, he was overwhelmed with terror. Nothing mattered to him but that he must survive. He felt the sliding of the boat over the hurrying waters; the current was very swift here and would be arduous even for the most accomplished swimmers, and as the river had been fed by icy springs from the mountains it would be deathly cold and paralyzing even to one of great muscular power. Quintus, himself, the mighty swimmer, never ventured into the river until summer was on the land.

"The current is furious," said one of the rowers in a tone of satisfaction. "He will not linger long."

The air was already chill upon Marcus' bare flesh, but he sweated with fear and dread as he was held in the bottom of the boat. Two of the rowers were carefully examining the island to be certain that there were no watchers, no one who could raise an alarm. Now the waters rocked the boat impatiently, and waves slapped the sides.

"Would it not be better to wait for twilight?" asked one of the men.

"No, for at twilight he would be missed and there would be searchers, with dogs," replied another impatiently. "It must be done speedily."

The rowers had reached the center of the narrow river. They turned broadside to the current to hold the vessel. The four men regarded Marcus without animosity; he could feel the intensity of their hidden eyes. They smiled at him almost in a friendly fashion. "Drowning," said one, "is not an unpleasant death. There are worse ways to die. Be grateful that we did not disembowel you or strip your flesh from your bones."

Marcus' eyes, staring and changeful blue as they faced the sky and his captors, looked fearfully on the men. They reached for him and lifted him again in their arms and slowly slipped his body in the water, maintaining hold under his armpits. Then, quickly, one pulled the gag of cloth from his mouth. But before he could shout they had pushed his head under the bitter water, and one grasped his long brown hair by the crown. Instinctively he had closed his mouth the moment the river had covered it and held his breath.

He could see his white body flowing and bending in the water like the body of one who is already dead. He could see a school of silvery fish and scaly bodies scraped his own in flight like birds. The river instantly numbed his flesh with its cold so that it had no feeling. His lungs began to strain so that he hardly felt the pain that flashed through his scalp. Then he came to himself madly. In some way he must tear himself loose from the grip in his hair. It seemed most necessary to do this, if only to avoid the ignominy of being passively drowned, though surely he would drown on the moment of escape. He was not a good swimmer, though Quintus had vainly tried to teach him, and had been offended at Marcus' jest that there was no Hero waiting to greet him with loving arms. He cursed himself for his past stupidity.

His lungs swelled in protest at the inheld breath and his ears appeared to be on the point of bursting. What! Was he to die without fighting for his life at the very least? He flexed his muscles in a spasm of frightful panic; he pretended to go limp, glancing with half-shut eyes at the distorted figures of his murderers through the upper water. They were not speaking now. They were only waiting for him to die.

They had judged him as a poor and flaccid thing, so that argued that they knew of him if only by report. He made his body waver feebly in the river, as if already dead. He closed his eyes. He opened his mouth, but shut larynx against the water; the river lapped his tongue and his palate. As he had hoped and prayed, the hand that gripped his hair relaxed a little. Instantly, he wrenched his head down and forward; agonizing pain lanced through his skull as some of his hair was detached. His heart roared and thundered in his breast. He sank down into the waters, which were partly obscured by the mud torn from the hills. Then the current seized him and he was swept away.

But now he must breathe for his life's sake. He thrust out his legs, and cramps bound them. Nevertheless, he was in such terror that he came to the surface. He could think of nothing but expelling his breath and inhaling the air of life. The sky above him was a sheet of flame and reflected on his bluish face. He drew in a deep breath with a strangling sound. He heard a subdued yell. His murderers had seen him and he turned his head as he instinctively trod water. All four men now had seized oars and were rushing down the river toward him in their boat. He heard them cursing. He wanted to shout but knew he must spare his breath, and he was too far from the shore to be heard. The torture of his spasmodic muscles almost killed him as it was. Only by the most superhuman efforts could he keep them moving. He prayed frenziedly as he had never prayed before.

He waited until the boat was almost upon him before he let himself sink below it again. The current spun him as a wounded bird, falling, spins in the vault as it plummets to earth. He saw the murky water, felt the pounding of it against his icy flesh. Above him, he saw the shadow of the searching boat, like an avenging cloud. Forcing himself, he swam deeply away from it. His arms and legs screamed like separate entities, and he needed air again. If I live, he thought dimly, I shall become a veritable Leander!

The water was so muddy that he could no longer see the bottom of the boat, and he struggled to the surface again. To his horror his shoulder, uprising, hit the side of the boat. Then his head emerged from the river, and he drew a groaning breath.

The men, now infuriated at his escape and intent only on his death, lifted oars to smash his skull. He saw the wet blades, bloody in the light of the sunset, upheld over him. He let himself sink again. His heart labored. He could endure this little longer. Vague thoughts brushed through his mind soothingly. How easy it would be to die, to hold himself far down in the water and sleep, to escape this horror, to drift down the river—and to sleep, alone and in peace. Why should he struggle? What was life? A dream, a painful fantasy, a delusion, a weariness. He let his body drift with the hastening current, and jagged splinters of red and gold light flashed behind his closed eyelids.

Then his grandfather's voice—that voice stilled years ago—thundered in his dulling ears. "You will die supinely, like a slave? You will not fight for life, as a Roman and a man?"

His feet brushed the stony bottom of the river. His grandfather's voice was all about him, imperative, full of scorn. But, I am tired, my body is numbed and dead and full of agony, his mind replied. "Arise!" cried his grandfather. He could not disobey. He moved his legs and his arms feebly, and rose sluggishly to the surface. His glaucous eyes saw that the boat was at a considerable distance. But the men had seen his wet head, as one sees the head of a seal. They swung the boat about and pursued him. Again, he waited until they were almost upon him, and again he bent his body and let himself sink.

How long could this deathly game continue until he died? The shore had appeared miles away. He had drifted and swam near the keel of the island. For one instant he had seen the quiet meadows, the tops of distant trees scarlet in the sunset, the toy white farmhouse, the inflamed hills. Never had they appeared so dear, yet never had they appeared so like a mirage. He was like one who gazes on the precious earth for the last time before retreating into the darkness of death. Surely, he could not resist the pull of the river. Even if he lived a while longer he would be swept into the main river, too far to reach any shore again.

His failing lungs demanded air. But he could hear the boat above him, the swishing of oars, though he could not see them.

"God!" his failing mind prayed. Now he must come to the surface again, even at the deadly risk of a quicker murder than drowning. The water appeared alive with rainbows, rushing and merging into each other, embracing him, heavily dragging him down. But he moved; he drifted to the surface. To his fainting surprise he saw that he was some distance from the boat. However, the men had seen him. He breathed deeply. The island was a golden ship moving away from him. Again, filling his lungs, he waited until he saw the upraised oars, then bent his head and let himself fall.

The current, hastening toward the sea, was a wall of force. He let himself be carried by it, under its roof. He began to dream, long soundless dreams. His body no longer tortured him; his lungs no longer seemed to shriek for air. He was like a wisp of cloud, floating mindlessly. He no more had any identity.

Then, there was a savage tug at his throat, a ripping along his flesh. He opened his mouth to cry out and water rushed into it, strangling him, setting him to flailing. A second later and the blessed air succeeded the water, and he was coughing and choking, but helpless to move. Something had seized him brutally, had lifted his lips horizontally above the water. It was still tugging at his neck. The back part of his head was below water, and his ears. Only his eyes and his lips and nose had emerged, so that he remained unseen in the waves.

He was so dazed, so exhausted, so dulled, that he could do nothing for a while but float like a cadaver, held by that which forced his mouth above water. He could not see; clouds moved over his eyes. He felt disembodied. The river flowed about and around him but could not take him again. He forgot his murderers; he forgot the boat and even why he was here. His body relaxed, conscious only of a cutting sensation and grip at the base of his skull, and something scratching along his flesh as if he were being flayed alive.

Then he remembered. He turned his head in the water and saw the boat, diminished and tiny now, at a long distance. It was being rowed toward the bridge, the bridge that was so small that a man could hold it in his hand. The sky was darkening to deep and misty crimson. The island was a little ship with foam at its keel. The waters had many manly voices, questioning, drumming answers, crying, chuckling. And Marcus floated, helplessly, held by he knew not what.

Then, as if something had struck his mind like an impatient fist, he came alive once more. He saw that a great tree had floated down the river from some place far in the hills, and its trunk had been lodged in rocks at the bottom of the river. It was not visible from the surface. But the highest twigs had caught Marcus' amulet as he had drifted, had lifted him so that his lips and eyes had emerged. This had saved his life; his murderers had finally been satisfied that he had drowned, for his head had not risen again. They must have waited for some time. Marcus was conscious that many long minutes had passed while he had been held, like some dead bird, at the top of the tangled tree. His cautious eye saw the boat land on the Arpinum shore, though all was cloudy dull crimson now. He saw the men pulling the boat up on the shore, little figures so far that they were scarcely longer than one of his fingers. Then they were lost and gone in the thickening fog of land and water, and he was alone with only the thousand voices of the river in his ears.

The river was a heavy green here, smoking with mist. Marcus' body began to smart unendurably. The dead twigs and branches of the top of the tree had torn his skin, and no doubt he was bleeding. His arms felt like iron, but he forced them to move, to grasp the blessed tree. He clutched relieving the tug on his neck of the chained amulet. He wound his legs about a branch. He waited, and rested. Now the water no longer seemed cold as circulation returned to his body. Then his heart shivered once more.

He was so very far from the island. Twilight was falling rapidly. Only a smudge of reddened light illuminated the west. Stars were creeping out, and the edge of a rounded moon. The water lifted and dropped him, and the tree wavered.

"Be reasonable," he said aloud in a thin voice. "You cannot remain here. You will die of exposure. What then is left for a sensible man? He will swim to the island. Oh? It is impossible? But God saved you, therefore it is not impossible."

Noë ben Joel had said that nothing was impossible with God. God had preserved him, therefore he must labor with the hand of God, in gratitude. Nevertheless, it demanded all his courage to disentangle the chain of his amulet from the saving twigs. His fingers seemed three times the size of normal fingers; they groped thickly and heavily. At last he was free, but he again embraced the branch. A curious fish nudged his toes and nibbled at them. The darkness came down on the waters like a cloak. He must go now, or be lost in the night forever.

He turned on his side and moved away from the tree toward the island. He was a poor swimmer, and he was swimming against the current. But Quintus had taught him how to float; he remembered how indulgently he had resisted the lessons and considered how stupid his resistance had been. All that a man saw and learned and heard was valuable, no matter how much he had deprecated it, had undervalued its importance. Marcus, when he was exhausted, floated, and regarded the passionate blaze of the stars. Never had he felt so close to God. No longer did he feel insignificant, hidden in his insignificance from the eye of the Eternal. God had desired his continued existence; therefore, there was a reason.

He swam doggedly, in increasing darkness. He was only a man, of no importance. He had been set upon, however, by men who had deemed him dangerous for some mysterious reasons. Had they mistaken him for someone else? No. One of them had mentioned his name, mockingly. It was a great mystery.

He was enormously tired. The current resembled a limitless wall which he must climb. What had Noë said of God, in his letter? "God, the Father." "Father," prayed Marcus, "help me, as you saved me." For an instant he remembered that even the sons of the gods did not dare address their progenitors as "father." It was blasphemy. Yet Marcus prayed, "Father, uphold me with Your Hand. Bear me upon it."

The stars dazzled him; the moon-edge bewildered him. All seemed to swing in circles. Silver light raced fleetingly on the river. Forms, created from the mist, strode the water, light in the folds of their garments, light on their heads. They moved on the river, bent on mystic missions, unaware of the man weakly striving. There was a swiftness to their movements, as if they were bearing momentous tidings, and preparing a way.

He could not believe it, but he was upheld by something more than water. A rock. A heavier darkness was before him. No, he could not believe it, but he must accept it. He was near the shore of the island.

Warm salt tears ran over his wet face. He walked the shallow waters and reached the beautiful dry land. He fell upon it, kissing the earth, rubbing his outstretched hands on the warm soil, smelling the fragrance of bruised grass and herbs. It surely was too early for jasmine, but he had the illusion that he could inhale it, sweet and comforting and pervading. Joy overpowered him, like a shattering wave. He could not have enough of embracing the blessed earth.

CHAPTER EIGHTEEN

He must have slept a little in his crushing weariness, for he came to consciousness with a profound start. The edged moon was higher over his head. He contemplated it for a while, too broken to move, then he stirred his arms, stiffened them, got up on his hands and knees, shaking his head like a wounded dog. The night wind was merciless on his naked flesh. Nevertheless, he began to consider.

His assailants now considered him dead. They had taken care to give his death the appearance of accident. They had not harmed the other dwellers on the island, Eunice and her husband, Athos, and their newborn infant, nor the slaves who worked in the fields. They had not set fire to the farmhouse. Their only object had been himself. Marcus remembered the magnificent ring on the finger of one of the hooded men. He would remember it forever as it had glittered in the sunlight. Someday he would discover that man by that ring.

Was anyone watching the farmhouse to be certain that he had not, after all, escaped the death planned for him? No. Too much time had elapsed; he had not appeared; the night had protected him. Then, all at once he heard a faint calling, the glimmer of a distant lantern. It was Athos' voi—

he heard, and the voices of the searching slaves. There was despair and
hopelessness in their faint shouts. So, they had discovered his clothing on
the bank of the river. He wanted to shout in reply, but restrained himself
in the very vague event that there was a watcher. However, the slaves
would be armed, or at least Athos would have a dagger. Slowly, as silently
as he could, he crept on his hands and knees through the flowering bushes
and rising grass toward the lantern, keeping his eye upon it as a man
watches a lighthouse. The voices came nearer; the lantern flashed from
side to side.

Now, it was very close, and he could see it glancing from shoulder and
hip and hand. He called in a subdued voice, "Athos." The men halted.
He called again, "Do not raise your voices, in the name of the gods!"

They murmured joyfully among themselves, knowing him to be safe.
But they came cautiously in his direction, their instincts alive, their eyes
watchful, searching for him. He crouched on the grass, then lifted his
hand and the light of the lantern brushed it. Athos came running to him
at once, breaking away from the others.

"Put down your lantern, and leave it," said Marcus. Athos obeyed instantly. Like a tracking animal, he came to Marcus, fell on his knees and
embraced him, saying tearfully, "Master, Master! We thought you were
dead, that you had drowned!"

"Hush," said Marcus, and raised his head to listen. Athos listened also.
The frail moonlight glimmered on his melancholy barbarian's face.

Marcus found it difficult to speak, out of his exhaustion. "I was set upon
by those who wished to kill me as if it were an accident, and I had died
in the river," he said. "You must not question me more. The less you know
the safer you will be. I must return to Rome at once. My presence is a
deadly danger to all of you. If it were known that I had lived and had
returned to the house, they would bar the door and set the house in flames,
and all would perish. Therefore, I must go." He paused to pant.

"Master! We will find them and kill them!" Athos cried.

"You cannot find them. They planned this well. You must know nothing. Are you armed? Excellent. Remain with me, and call a slave to you,
so that we will be three and not two. Order the other slaves to go to the
house and bring me clothing and shoes, a cloak and my sword, and the
best horse, and a filled purse which they will find in my chest in my cubiculum. Have another slave prepare me provisions—"

He could say no more. He rested in Athos' arms, and closed his eyes and
tried to gather his strength. Through wavering dimness he heard Athos
call the slaves and give them orders. The slave who remained threw his
rough woolen cloak over Marcus' naked and shivering body. Athos chaffed
his hands, then lifted his own in horror. "Master, you are bleeding!"

"No matter," said Marcus in a faint voice. "I am only scratched. Athos, if men come tomorrow and ask for me, tell them that I did not return from my ramblings, that you fear I am lost. For many days, then, do not enlighten Eunice, for she is a woman and may speak inadvertently. Let her believe I am dead for a while, so that her grief may seem convincing. You must consider your child, and the lives of all of you."

"Master, you cannot ride through the night in this condition," said Athos, tenderly wiping Marcus' bleeding body with his tunic.

"I can. I must. There is naught else for me to do." Marcus closed his eyes once more and rested. His heart thudded wearily in his breast. He said, "You must command the slaves to be silent, to pretend that I am dead. They can be trusted."

"Should one speak, I shall kill him with my own hand," said Athos, dashing away his tears. "Oh, Master, how fearful it was to find your clothing and to believe you were dead! I will burn a votive light to Neptune every night, that he preserved you from his own waters."

"Thank Ceres that one of her trees caught me, and thank Minerva that her amulet lifted me from the river," said Marcus. "Good. If any see the votive light they will believe you burn it in my remembrance and for my soul."

"Let me ride with you, Master, as a guard in the night and in the day, to Rome."

Marcus considered, then shook his head. "Your absence, then, might be noted. To be safe only a little I must go alone. Once I am in Rome I will not be unguarded. You can be certain of that! Moreover, I have friends of influence in the city."

"But the country is disturbed, Master, and dangerous."

"It was when I came here also. It is not more dangerous now."

Again, he marveled that he had been attacked at all. Who should want him dead? And, if they wanted him dead, why had they arranged so elaborate a plot? Such plots were born only against the powerful and influential, to avoid the appearance of overt murder and thus challenge revenge. He, Marcus Tullius Cicero, was not of importance to anyone, save his family.

Rome had seized all the best horses for the war. Therefore, the one which would be brought to him would not have great stamina and youth. It was not a pleasant thought for a fleeing man. Athos gave voice to it, and Marcus assented. The best horse available arrived, saddled, led by a slave, and another slave brought warm clothing and food and a sword and Marcus' purse.

Athos helped him to his feet. It was only then that he realized how wretchedly weak he was, and his heart failed as he swayed in the freedman's arms. "You cannot go! Master, come what may, you must return to the house and rest for a day and a night."

Marcus reluctantly shook his head. "No. Your lives would not be safe. I must go at once. Do not restrain me, Athos."

The freedman and the slave dressed him. His whole body trembled with his exhaustion. His bones seemed to shake in his flesh; his skin was sore and wounded. The woolen tunic and the heavy dark cloak with its hood could not warm him. His feet were swollen from the water, and he struggled to pull on his high leather shoes. Athos clasped his waist with the silver girdle Noë had given him, and affixed thereto his sword, which he rarely wore, and added his Alexandrian dagger, the gift of Quintus on his birthday so long ago, before the rites of manhood. His purse was attached to the girdle also. Marcus looked at the horse, a poor and docile creature of many years, used more to the plow than to carrying a horseman. He patted the horse as if to reassure it. It snorted once and nuzzled his hand. The bag of provisions was lifted and tied to the saddle.

It took much effort, even with the aid of Athos, to climb into the saddle and thrust his feet into the stirrups. He took the reins. The moon was much brighter now for all it was only a crescent, and there was a wide shimmer of starlight. Worse, the only exit from the island was the bridge. He leaned from the saddle to press his hand on Athos' shoulder. "Come with me, until I have crossed the bridge. I may need your daggers."

Athos walked on one side, the slave on the other, and the horse nervously ambled forward. He was old, and he was tired from the fields and he had been too early aroused. The men did not speak as they moved toward the bridge. They held their breath, and kept glancing from side to side, daggers in their hands. Marcus held his unsheathed sword.

He heard only the sound of the horse's hoofs and the rustling of grass and trees and the mutter of the river. No one spoke. They reached the bridge, and the horse awakened a small thunder on it. Athos and the slave moved closer to the animal and its rider. But no one approached them. Arpinum, asleep, was dark save for moonlight flowing wanly over its climbing roofs. The dark river hurried in broken silver. Then the three men were across the bridge and the road to Rome lay before them, smooth and straight.

"Will you take the road, Master, or keep far from it?" asked Athos with anxiety. "Your enemies may, themselves, be upon it, and may hear your approach."

"I have no choice. I must take the road or be lost. If my unknown enemies are upon it, they must have better horses and be long gone. I doubt they would reveal themselves as strangers, in Arpinum, for fear of suspicion."

Marcus thought of the long ride. He had come on this very poor horse, and it had taken two days and a long night. He had not dared to stop at any inn, for the country was in chaos still, and there were armed men and scoundrels everywhere, taking advantage of any traveler who came alone. The only men who dared to travel casually were the legionnaires, and they rode in company, armored and with unsheathed swords. With the exception of fools like me, thought Marcus. At night, he had slept in his cloak far from the road, his horse tethered near him, his sword in his hand. And, as tonight, he had carried his own provisions. He had encountered stray fellow travelers, and they had stared at him with hostility, and he had returned it, for strangers were suspect. Even couriers rode in company. He had escaped any attack because he was dressed humbly, and his horse was not notable, and his purse had been hidden, and he had halted nowhere. He hoped that he would escape so easily again. In many ways it was safer to travel at night, for marauders considered that only soldiers would be abroad.

He leaned from his saddle to embrace the frightened Athos, and to kiss his cheek. Athos gripped his hand. "Master, I am afraid," he said.

"So am I," said Marcus. "Pray for me. I must go now. Return, and keep silent."

He gathered up the reins, remembering dismally that he was a poor horseman also, and was always chafed by leather. It was excellent to be a man of books. But in these days a man with sturdy thighs and buttocks and a strong back was even more excellent.

"Do not sheathe your sword, Master," said Athos, holding to the saddle.

"Not for an instant," Marcus promised him. He was still trembling, but his heart was steadier. Then he lifted his hand, spurred the horse gently, and rode away down the glimmering road that led to Rome, the horse raising echoes in the night silence. Marcus did not look back at his faithful servants. His hair was still wet under the hood, and streaked against his cheeks. He tried not to remember how long was the way to the mighty city on her seven hills, and how dangerous was his passage.

He encountered no one coming or going, and he began to breathe more easily. He did not goad the old horse. Sometimes he spoke to it kindly and with encouragement. "At least," he said, "you have had a little sleep. You have also had your supper. That is because you are wiser than I."

He did not halt until the horse was panting and lathered, and that was at the darkest hour near dawn. He alighted and led the horse to the river that ran near the road, and let the poor creature have his fill. Now utter weariness took him also. He must rest or fall from the saddle in a stupor. He took the horse across the road and into a small forest, where tree frogs piped for Pan. When he was certain he was hidden, he wrapped himself in his cloak, and lay down with his sword in his hand. He was instantly asleep.

He awoke to full sunlight. The forest was in fuller leaf than the little forests of the island, for all he was traveling north. Marcus saw precious greenness about him, and sharp golden shadows which broke through the trees. His horse had slept also; it was cropping the lush grass. It turned a mild eye upon Marcus, and snorted affectionately. Marcus scratched his mosquito bites, yawned, and rubbed his aching head. He untied his bag of provisions, ate some bread and cheese and cold meat, and drank a little raw red wine. In a few minutes he was on the way again, riding not too fast, hoping that he would be taken for a rude bumpkin by any wary traveler. But he encountered no one for several hours.

The sun was hot for all it was only spring. Marcus dismounted once to refresh himself with a clump of forgotten dates on a palm, and to bathe his drawn face in the river. The horse ate also, and drank. "You are a true Roman," Marcus addressed the animal. "You live off the land, but I am too effete to have that knowledge for all I was born in the country." The horse replied with a soft neigh, and nodded his head as if he understood. "But still, dear friend," said Marcus, "I must be grateful enough to you to pause to buy you some oats, even if it is dangerous."

He mounted and rode down the empty way again, the horse's hoofs ringing on the stone. "Ah, you are a brave one," said Marcus. "I give you my solemn promise that never shall you work again, but shall browse in green meadows for the rest of your life."

He looked about him now for a lonely and isolated farmhouse where he could purchase some oats for his horse and perhaps replenish his own store of food. For the horse was slightly lame, and could not travel fast any longer. The countryside was green and gold and silent. There were cultivated fields on the right, but no houses. On the left, the river hurried. Finally it disappeared as the road struck more surely north toward Rome.

Marcus drowsed in the saddle, awakening briefly to full consciousness. His body throbbed; his thighs and ankles were already badly chafed. He had not thought to ask for ointment to relieve them, and the slaves had packed hastily for him and had too much to remember. Moreover, they were not depraved city men like himself. They could travel for days without discomfort. Horse and rider passed olive groves, silvery and gnarled in the bright spring light, and fragrant citrus groves, and meadows full of sheep and goats. But there were no houses.

Then he heard the thunder of horses behind him. He pulled up his own horse, and began to tremble with fear. He spurred the horse off the road and into a copse of trees, and he put his hand on the horse's nose to keep him quiet. But he also heard, as the riders came nearer, the rumble of a chariot, and the rude voices of men. He peered through the trees and saw a detachment of legionnaires sweep by him grandly, banners blowing behind them, faces lifted. They surrounded a car of respectable ornamentation, guided by a soldier; on the seat within sat a centurion in his cloak, his helmet glittering bravely.

Forgetting that his horse was lame and old Marcus goaded it onto the road again and raised his voice in a shout. He shouted over and over, until a riding soldier finally heard him, and turned his head. The soldier evidently spoke to his companions, for they slowed, and all heads twisted to survey Marcus gallantly riding up. The chariot halted, and the centurion, a bearded man like a barbarian, scowled upon the approaching rider.

"Hail!" cried Marcus with gratitude, lifting his right hand in the stiff military salute.

"Hail," said the centurion without notable enthusiasm. He scowled more forbiddingly.

"Marcus Tullius Cicero, lawyer, of Rome, and of the Ciceroni and the Helvii," Marcus said, smiling with delight.

"Ha," said the centurion, looking at the other's humble cloak and tunic. His brown eyes sharpened as he saw the unsheathed sword. He was suspicious. The soldiers did not stir their harsh faces but stared straight ahead as if Marcus did not exist. "Why have you halted us?" the centurion demanded.

"For safe passage into Rome," said Marcus, too happy to be daunted by the soldier's manner. Never had he been so happy to see the banners of his city and the countenances of his grim countrymen. "And oats for my horse," he added.

"We carry provisions only for ourselves," said the centurion, who evidently considered Marcus a poor fellow indeed. He glumly looked at the horse. "That is not a fine steed, Cicero. He would not keep pace with us. You said you were a lawyer? Why are you abroad these dangerous days, and alone?"

"A sensible question, but I must confess, alas, that I am not a sensible man," said Marcus. The centurion did not smile. The many horses snorted impatiently. Marcus became aware of the unfriendliness about him. He said with some haste, "My brother is Quintus Tullius Cicero, a centurion himself, and now in Gaul."

"Ha," said the centurion again, as if he considered this a likely tale. Marcus was a little dismayed. He studied the centurion, who appeared to be a man of fifty years or more. He said, "My grandfather was Marcus Tullius Cicero also, and a soldier and a Roman, a veteran of many wars."

"Marcus Tullius Cicero," repeated the centurion, mouthing the words.

Then his browned and sullen face relaxed a little. "He, your grandfather, was from Arpinum?"

"Yes."

"I remember him well," said the centurion, and he began to smile. "I was only a subaltern, but he was my captain. A noble soldier."

His men began to notice Marcus' existence, but their eyes were full of wonder at his appearance and at the condition of his old horse.

"Why are you not a soldier yourself?" asked the centurion.

"I am a lawyer," Marcus repeated. Then he said, "I intend to volunteer my time in the legions." This was meretricious, but it served to make the centurion smile again.

"With your brother, Quintus," he said.

Marcus said gravely, "With my brother, Quintus."

"In Gaul."

"In Gaul," Marcus echoed, shuddering inwardly.

The captain grinned, and his bearded face was suddenly fatherly. "You are a liar, Cicero," he said. "Your buttocks, no doubt, are already raw. You are no horseman. I observe that, from your seat. But I do not doubt that you are a lawyer, for all you appear as a peasant. Who is your mentor in Rome?"

"The great old pontifex maximus, Scaevola," said Marcus.

"Scaevola!" cried the centurion. "My dear old friend! What a scoundrel he is, may Mars protect him! Is he still alive? I have been long away from Rome."

"He is alive, and he will thank you for protecting me," said Marcus.

The centurion sobered and grunted, annoyed with himself for his momentary pleasure. He sighed. He moved on his seat. "You may as well ride with me, and we will lead your horse, who would do better in the market as meat. I still cannot understand why a lawyer, a subordinate of Scaevola, a member of a great house, and a grandson of my captain, should be abroad under such circumstances, and have such a dirty and haggard face. I cannot understand."

"Nor can I," said Marcus, joyfully dismounting and hobbling to the vehicle. "It is a long and sorrowful tale." He climbed into the chariot.

"I have no doubt," said the centurion. "It is possible that you are again a liar. But it is more probable that you are a fool."

"I agree with you most heartily," said Marcus, subsiding with a wince on the wide leather seat. "I am a total imbecile. I should be imprisoned for my own sake."

"And I agree with you even more heartily," said the centurion. "Let us be gone. You have delayed me enough."

So Marcus, despite his earlier fears, rode with majesty into Rome the next day and for the first time in his life blessed the military. He was to bless them many times more, but not so fervently as this.

CHAPTER NINETEEN

Helvia was astonished to see her son, for she had not expected him for some more days. Marcus, not to alarm her—for his father was ill with malaria again and his mother appeared tired for all her resolution—did not tell her of his encounter with his unknown and mysterious enemies. He merely said that he had become anxious to see her again, and had yearned to return to his family. Helvia was skeptical. She stared acutely at her son.

"One understands that you love us," she said with shrewdness. "But one understands that you also love the island. Moreover, you appear exhausted and too sombre. But I suppose I cannot expect confidences." There was considerably more gray in her luxuriant hair, and lines in her ruddy face, all appearing in the last year.

She was suddenly anxious. "There is no calamity on the island?"

"No. All is well." He embraced her again. She accepted his embrace and smiled, and her countenance was mischievous. "The less a woman knows of the antics of her men the more serene she can be," she remarked.

Scaevola was as astounded as Helvia when Marcus walked into his house the next day. "You rascal!" he cried. "What is this that I hear from my old friend, the centurion Marcius Basilus, that he encountered you on the road to Rome, in vagabond attire and with a limping horse and the face of a criminal in flight? Is that an appearance for one of my lawyers, furtive, dirty, clandestine?"

"Let me tell you," said Marcus, seating himself. His manner was so serious and grave that Scaevola forgot both his umbrage and his secret pleasure at seeing his favorite pupil.

He listened, at first with incredulity, his eyes fixed disbelievingly on Marcus' face, then with blank bewilderment, then with rage, then with renewed astonishment. When Marcus had done, he sat sprawled fatly in his chair and scratched the mole on his cheek, pulled his heavy underlip, blinked, muttered. He considered the whole story in silence.

Finally he said, "If anyone but you, imbecile, had told me of this I should not believe him! Have I not always said you were as bland as milk and as harmless as a dewdrop?"

Marcus no longer considered this complimentary, in view of the lack of athletic prowess which had almost resulted in his death. Once he had been pleased, for he believed that men, to be civilized must not be dangerous; they should be conciliatory, concerned with peace and justice, kindly to all men, tolerant and urbane. Such men, he was almost convinced now, incited attack and murder.

Scaevola tried to hide his concern with a short laugh. "You have not been seducing the wife of a Senator or other prominent man?"

"Certainly I have not," said Marcus. "My ladies are for hire."

Scaevola winked. "What ladies are not, especially the wives of these Senators? What enemies do you have? Whom have you offended?"

"None who would be so infuriated as to plot my death so carefully, in order that it seem an accident. None of the clients you have referred to me is rich or important, and I have usually won their cases. Nor do I engage in politics, nor am I ambitious, like our Julius Caesar, nor am I rich so that heirs are greedy for my fortune. I have not been lured into intrigue either for or against Cinna; I am too busy. I have offended no husband, I have betrayed no woman. I am not a powerful soldier."

Scaevola raised his hand. "In short," he said impatiently, "you are a pure draught of water in an earthen cup. I understand. Still, someone wished you dead. Your attempted assassins, you have related, appeared men of culture and refinement, and one had a marvelous ring. Repeat to me again the appearance of this ornament."

Marcus said, "It was of heavy yellow gold in the form of two scaled serpents whose mouths were joined together by a round large emerald, which shone like green fire in the sun. The stone itself was carved, intaglio, with a figure of Diana holding a crescent moon in her lifted hand."

"I have taught you well to be observant," said Scaevola. He reflected in silence again. "I do not recognize that ring; I have not seen it myself. Yet it was so valuable to the owner that he still wore it when attacking you. He would not be without it. Therefore, he is a devotee of Diana, the nocturnal one. Hum. He is no Asiatic; he is a Roman. You saw no other details of their faces but their mouths? Could it be that you should have recognized any of them?"

"No. I heard their voices, and none was familiar."

"And they wished not to do a clean murder, which might be investigated by me, but an apparent accident brought upon yourself by an injudicious dip in the river. Could it be possible that it was some enemy of my own?"

Marcus thought of this dubiously. Then he shook his head. "They thought they would kill me, and so they spoke freely. They did not mention your name, nor the name of anyone else. But they mocked me with my own name. I, alone, was the object of their intentions."

"Incredible," muttered Scaevola. Then he slapped his knee and laughed obscenely. "I know! It is that infernal poetry of yours which you have published! It enraged a true devotee of the arts!"

Marcus did not think this humorous, and he frowned. He said with stiffness, "I have thought of Senator Curius, whom I offended so deeply nearly a year ago."

"Nonsense!" exclaimed Scaevola. "Curius is a scoundrel, but he is also a patrician. He does not order the murder of mice, such as you. Moreover, he knows that I am your mentor, your protector. A poor and insignificant lawyer would be regarded by him, if he thought of you at all, as one regards a gnat."

Marcus' natural vanity was offended. He said, "My friend, Noë ben Joel, has written me that it is unwise to attract the attention of government, or to make it aware of you."

He waited for Scaevola's burst of ridicule and his exclamation, "And how have you attracted so malignant a notice?" But, to his surprise, Scaevola's broad smile disappeared and Scaevola's brilliant little blue eyes fixed themselves keenly upon him in deep thought. At last he said as if to himself, "They will soon know, if they do not even now, that you escaped, that you are alive. Therefore, your danger is still extreme."

"But why?" cried Marcus. "What have I done?"

Scaevola turned to his table and began to pick up books and lengths of parchment and papyrus, and pretended to study them as if forgetting Marcus entirely. Marcus waited. Scaevola belched, rubbed his ears, pulled his lip, scratched under his armpits, his great gross body billowing under the short and deplorable tunic he insisted on wearing. Then the old man pretended to start, and become aware of Marcus again.

"What! Are you still here? You have a client waiting."

When Marcus, nonplused, began to rise, Scaevola waved him down. "I am not done with you. How many slaves are in your house in Rome?"

"Only four, and all of them are old men, members of our family, long in our service. My will sets them free with an income—if ever I have any."

"You have no young muscular slave, deft with dagger, strangling hands, or a sword?"

"No. Not even in Arpinum. We are rural people, peaceful and harmless."

"It is apparent, my dear young fool, that someone does not consider you harmless at all! He considers you potentially most dangerous. Whom, potentially, do you threaten, now or in the future?"

"No one," said Marcus readily.

Scaevola made a mouth of disbelief and vexation. "You are such an innocent. Potentially, you are extremely dangerous to someone, and he would have you dead. It is someone powerful. You have not irritated our young Julius, have you?"

Marcus smiled. "No. We are the dearest of friends."

"Do not underrate him. Not long ago he publicly demonstrated his epilepsy. He spoke mysteriously of a strange vision to everyone who would listen, but he would not enlarge on the vision. He now goes about with a most abstracted air."

"He was always an actor," said Marcus.

"There is no one so dangerous as an actor who is not employed openly as an actor. The most brilliant and malign of tyrants have been gifted mountebanks. I am exasperated. Someone wishes you dead, by an apparent accident. Therefore, it is suspected that you have powerful friends who must not be offended and seek revenge. What powerful friends do you have? The situation must be remedied. You must have many powerful friends. I will give a dinner for you. I have an excellent cook, a Syrian, who does remarkable things with grape leaves. He stuffs them with an exotic mixture which makes the palate delirious with joy. He is no Roman chef. Therefore, my table is always honored by important men.

"You are under my protection. I will persuade others to protect you. In the meantime, you need a guard." Scaevola raised his voice in a bellow and a young male slave hurriedly appeared, a Nubian black as night, and tall and powerful and armed. Scaevola pointed to Marcus. "Syrius," he said, "behold your new master. Leave him not for an instant, anywhere. Sleep at the door of his cubiculum. Keep your dagger in readiness at all times."

Marcus looked at Syrius with dismay, and calculated the amount of food he would consume, and the state of the larder of the house on the Carinae. Syrius bowed to him deeply, lifted the hem of his tunic and kissed it in a sign of complete obedience.

"How can I feed him?" asked Marcus, bluntly.

"Syrius is a rascal, and a bettor. He will soon have all the slaves on the Carinae, and the masters, too, betting with him on the races and the games. He inevitably prospers. Like a Roman, he lives off the available land. Force him to share his ill-gotten gains with you; you will find yourself in possession of some luxuries."

Scaevola waved at Marcus as if vexed. "Why do you devour so much of my time? Go, both of you, to your office, together. Syrius will stand at your side, and that will be most impressive. There is a client waiting, a small, miserable divorce case. Hereafter, to suit your new status, my Marcus, I will refer more elaborate cases to you, though it will cost me a pretty penny."

For the first time Marcus was nervous. He had thought he would be safe in Rome. But Scaevola had disagreed. The hidden murderer would become more bold. Marcus was grateful for the presence of Syrius, whom he had always liked, and who was already devoted to him. But how explain his acquisition to Helvia? She must be enlightened, unfortunately.

The attempted murder remained a mystery. And Marcus always looked at the hands of men for a serpentine ring.

It was summer again, and the Social War continued sporadically all over Italy. But the Romans had lived long with war and accepted the stringencies and inconveniences of their lives as a matter of course, grumbling and fatalistic. Fatalism was not part of the Roman nature, which was pragmatic and materialistic and expedient and optimistic. Marcus felt with alarm that the nature of his countrymen had already begun to deteriorate in that it had apparently accepted an Eastern philosophy now, and he recalled that many wise men had been concerned about this in the near past.

As for himself, he doggedly pursued his law career. More and more magistrates became acquainted with his strong and mellifluous voice, his air of integrity and authority, his manner which conveyed that he honestly believed in the innocence of his clients.

One day Scaevola brought him a new client. The old pontifex maximus said to him, with an air of contempt, "Here is a strange one for you. I cannot bring myself to defend him, but your devious mind, it is possible, will find some reason for your own defending."

The man's name was Casinus. He was middle-aged and of a sturdy and obstinate appearance, and his clothing though of good quality, considering these days, was not elegant. He sat down before Marcus and studied him with an air of rebellion and suspicious challenge. It was evident he did not consider him of much consequence, seeing that Marcus was thin and slender and had a mild expression and did not look belligerent. He said, "I doubt if you can help me."

"Tell me about it, Casinus," said Marcus, and gave the other all his attention.

The man muttered restively, and moved in the chair and frowned. Then he burst out: "I hate this war! I have lost a son and two brothers in a fraternal struggle. While we quarrel among ourselves and drain our blood and decimate Roman ranks, our enemies abroad deride us and wait for our destruction. But, it is a war for freedom, and my heart is with those who so fight. Why is it not possible for our government to come to terms with our brothers, and grant them true liberty and equality, as once we knew?"

Marcus gazed at him reflectively. He said, "I have asked myself that question many times and have found no answer. But there are evil men amongst us who promote dissension for gain or ambition. What is the fate of Rome to them? However, let us judge your own case. What is wrong?"

Casinus owned a manufactory which made fanciful things of all metals, from copper and tin to brass and silver and gold. Until the Social War he had prospered, contriving objects from the most intricate and valuable jewelry to plowshares and cooking vessels. He employed forty able craftsmen. He had no objection to making implements of war to order for the government, from shields and lances to the short sword and daggers and armor. It was part of his business.

"I am the best in Rome," he said proudly. "There are others, but none can match me; my furnaces are beyond compare. I own several mines here and abroad. Therefore, what I make is much desired. For several years I have been in great demand in Rome; the government conscripted many fine workmen for my manufactory. I paid them excellent wages. But still, I regarded the implements of war as only one of my arts, and not the most pleasing to me. After all, I am an artist."

Then, several weeks ago he had been ordered by the tribunes, and even by Cinna himself, through a bureaucrat, to cease the production of all but war material, and to concentrate on that alone.

"My men have been trained by me over many long years of apprenticeship, Master. There is none to compare with them in artistry and design and beauty of concept. The noblest ladies wear their creations; their hands are delicate; their eyes preternaturally keen. To set them manufacturing rude articles of war would ruin them. But the government has demanded that these artisans, exquisite and profound craftsmen and artists, go into the smoking manufactory and labor rudely, stiffening the fine muscles of their fingers, burning their hands irredeemably and callusing them beyond repair. Surely, there are coarse workers the government can send me! If art is destroyed, is not a nation's soul destroyed also? The government will not listen. I will not obey!" shouted Casinus, his broad face flushing with rage and disgust.

He flung a papyrus on the table before Marcus, and Marcus saw the great eagle seal of Roman power waxed upon it. Marcus studied the peremptory order. Then he turned in his chair and brought down a book of law and opened it. He read thoughtfully for some time. He said at last, "It is written in the law that no free Roman citizen shall be conscripted against his will to do anything he does not desire, with the exception of duty in the armed forces or during great emergencies when the national existence is at stake."

"I know that, Master! But there have been exceptions. A competitor of mine, one Veronus, has been exempted from that law; his wife inherited a fortune. I do not suggest bribery, Master! I assert it! Veronus produced implements of war, as I do, but his jewelry shops have not been closed. Moreover, one of my foremen came to me and whispered that Veronus has already approached him with an offer of a large competence—and this was before I received my orders from the government! Is this just?"

The summer day was hot and Casinus, overcome with outrage and heat, wiped his face and hands with a big linen kerchief, then stared at Marcus with bulging eyes of wrath and indignation.

"My jewelers love my foreman. Moreover, they would follow him into the employment of Veronus, if only to preserve their distinction and their clever hands and their way of life. But I protest at this arbitrary command of my government, which is supposed to protect my liberty and my dignity and not to encroach upon them!"

"Hah," said Marcus.

"I am willing to accept many more workmen and have them trained to make the materials of war. But I will not, I cannot, obey this demand that I send my artists into the pit and the foundry, to the destruction of their art and their livelihood in the future. As Veronus has been so successful in evading the precious law—through bribery, I swear—he will be in a position to command the market for all artifacts and jewelry later. I have even heard a rumor that if he gains my artists he will not send them into the murk and the blistering heat to make war materials, but will quietly let them pursue their trade, even during this war!"

Marcus thought a little. He said, "I should like to see that foreman of yours who was approached by Veronus."

Casinus jumped to his feet. "He is here with me." He ran to the outer door and called, and a moment later a tall, dark-faced and sombre man joined him, obviously nervous and alarmed. Casinus put his hand proudly on the man's shoulder. "My foreman, Samos, a Greek of great skill and an artist beyond compare!"

Samos looked down at his long folded hands with an expression that betrayed his uneasiness. "Samos," said Marcus, "you have been approached by one Veronus to join his manufactory?"

"Yes, Master," the man muttered.

"You have been promised, by Veronus, that you will continue to employ your art, and that the men who will go with you will also be left in peace?"

Samos hesitated. Marcus saw his fear. The man moistened his lips, glanced sideways at the stern Casinus, and murmured, "It is so."

"You are a Roman citizen, Samos?"

"Yes, Master."

"You do not desire to labor for Veronus?"

"No. But a man must preserve what is best in him, even if he must compromise to do so."

"A hard choice," said Marcus. "It is an evil situation." He reflected again. "Samos, you will swear that Veronus approached you if we take this case to the magistrates?"

Fear flashed on the man's dark face. "I am afraid of law and lawmakers, Master! I am afraid of lawyers; I know how devious they are. I wish to avoid controversy. There is only danger in it."

"I agree," said Marcus in a dry tone. "Nevertheless, if every citizen acted only on that conviction justice would die and chaos result, and there would be no law whatsoever, and no government. Was it not Aristotle himself, who said that only gods and madmen can live safely without the law?"

"I am a man of peace," Samos repeated. His eyelashes became wet. "I am a loyal man, but I am afraid."

"You will have more to fear, my Samos, than appearance before magistrates, if law collapses."

"A noble sentiment," said Samos, who was evidently a man of some culture. "But thousands have died in the past for noble sentiments, and what did it profit them?"

"It profited their children. You have children, Samos?"

The man nodded in misery.

"Then, as a father, you wish justice for them. What harm can come to you if you uphold the law in the case of Casinus, your employer?"

Samos sucked in his lips, and fright brightened his eyes. Marcus waited. Then Samos stammered desperately, "Veronus has hinted to me that he has much influence and if I refuse him it shall go ill with me, and I shall never be able to employ my trade again."

Marcus frowned. "It is couched as a threat, but it is a reality nonetheless." He considered while the two men watched him anxiously. Then he said, "I will take your case, Casinus. As for you, Samos, I will call you as a witness. I promise no harm will come to you."

"Promises," said Samos with gloom, "resemble the fruitless flowers of the wild cherry tree."

Marcus went into Scaevola's offices. "You are familiar with this case, lord. What is your advice?"

"Do not take it," said Scaevola, promptly.

"Why not?"

Scaevola stared at him. "Do you wish another accident?"

Marcus was astonished. "That is surely a non sequitur!"

"Is it?" Scaevola scowled. He sighed. "Never mind. You will take the case?"

"I have already done so."

"I think you are a fool. However, I congratulate you, though it is apparent that you are doomed to die at an early age. Are these not evil times? Is not the government seizing more and more power? When you oppose government now, even in the smallest matter, you place yourself in the deepest danger."

"Then you advise me to give up the practice of law?"

Scaevola slapped the top of his table violently. "There are thousands of cases to take that do not dispute with government! Do all your cases come to you with a parchment on which is affixed the seal of authority? No!"

"I have taken this case," Marcus repeated.

Scaevola groaned and lifted his eyes to the ceiling.

"You were always obdurate. Never let Syrius leave your side, not even in the courtroom. And before you appear in court, enlighten me as to what you wish me to say at your funeral pyre."

Marcus laughed. "That is surely an exaggeration. The order that came to Casinus was signed by a petty bureaucrat—"

"The pettier the bureaucrat the more danger, for petty men are remorseless and malicious, and are jealous of their authority."

Marcus maneuvered in the next days to place his case before a magistrate of noble family and position. But this was impossible to do, for all was now in confusion. It was rumored that Sulla would soon return to Rome in triumph, and that all who had opposed him would meet with dire misfortune if not with immediate massacre. In consequence the noble families of Rome, who stood with Marius, were in a state of alarm and overwhelmed with premonitions of disaster. Many of them were preparing for flight, among them a number of Senators and others of the noblest and most patrician of families. Only the "small" men were not unduly affrighted, including the petty bureaucrats. Changes of government meant nothing menacing to them. They would serve one government as faithfully as another, so long as it meant their meagre retention of individual power and their stipends and the ornamentation of petty authority over others.

Marcus reluctantly called upon his young friend, Julius Caesar, who had only a few months ago married the daughter of Cinna, a very young girl named Cornelia. Julius was now a flamen Dialis, or priest of Jupiter, and a member of the ruling populares party. He professed to adore Cornelia, and was apparently devoted to Cinna. Marcus, who loathed Cinna, had avoided his old friend as much as possible. So it took a profound effort on Marcus' part to go to Julius one hot summer evening.

Julius greeted him with affectionate mockery. "What! You have brought yourself at last to endure the company of one you believe has betrayed Rome?"

"Each man to his own convictions," said Marcus, now forcing himself to keep reproach from his voice.

Julius smiled at him. The younger man was very elegant these days, and was rapidly polishing that inclination to sophistication and artfulness with which he had been endowed at birth. His sleek black hair, always thin and fine, was perfumed. His toga was of the finest linen, violet in color and beautifully embroidered. All the hair had been plucked carefully from his slender and graceful arms. He had a long neck, and he wore about it an Egyptian necklace of many gold layers encrusted with gems, and he also wore armlets of jeweled gold and a girdle to match them. His shoes were of golden leather with sparkling thongs. His face, mobile and dark and mischievous, expressed his great intelligence and humor, and had a way of changing rapidly in expression. His lips were bright red. Marcus hoped he had not tinted them in a new depraved fashion now going its rounds among the younger patricians. But there was certainly kohl around his shimmering black eyes.

"You are late for dinner," said Julius.

"I have dined," said Marcus with some formality. He looked about him at the large and gracious house, now lighted with Alexandrian lamps of glass and brass and silver. Moonlight lay in warm pale shadows on high Corinthian columns in the atrium and in the portico. Lamplight shone on tables of lemonwood and ebony on which were arranged luxurious flowers. Oriental carpets bloomed on the marble floors; marble busts of heroic families and heroes peered from corners. The furniture was elaborately carved. There was a splashing of fountains everywhere.

"You have done well for yourself, Julius," said Marcus.

"Ah, you speak with reserve! But you were always too sober." Julius wound his thin arm through that of Marcus. "Let us go into the gardens and drink wine."

They went into the gardens and Marcus was taken aback by the formal splendor of cypresses and scented trees, by red graveled paths, by many fountains in which stood marble nymphs and satyrs, and arbors and terraces meticulously maintained to add the greatest beauty and sweetest line possible. Jasmine flooded the air intensely; here the moonlight washed over all objects in a luminous tide, and the wet statues gleamed like white still flesh in it. But beyond the gardens the hoarse and ceaseless voice of mighty Rome rumbled insistently, like the voice of a giant who would not sleep, or muttered in his sleep.

A female slave of marvelous beauty brought them wine as they sat on a marble bench side by side. Cornelia, of course, was rich, and her father was present tyrant of Rome. Still, Roman vessels were not engaged these days in the carrying of luxuries. Julius, watching Marcus, embraced the waist of the slave with a negligent arm. "Is she not delightful, this pearl of Cos?" he asked. "I bought her only yesterday."

Marcus did not look at the girl, and Julius laughed with delight. "I forgot you were an 'old' Roman," he said.

Marcus held his tongue, for he feared that if he spoke now he would speak sententiously and that Julius would mock him in consequence.

"Are you a Stoic?" asked Julius, lovingly dismissing the slave.

"No. Nor am I a priapist," said Marcus.

But Julius laughed. Laughter always came easily to him, and that was part of his charm. This annoyed Marcus more. He could not restrain himself. "Do you think you will retain all this grandeur and luxury, and your new power, when Sulla returns?"

"He will not return," said Julius. He reached to a marble table for a dish of figs and early grapes and citron and dates. He insisted that Marcus enjoy himself with some. "Sulla," he said, "will not dare to attack Rome."

"No doubt Cinna has assured you of that," said Marcus, chewing a fig.

"My father-in-law is a man of much wisdom," said Julius, drinking more wine. "Did he not choose me as the husband of his daughter?"

Marcus could not resist smiling in spite of his efforts. He was always amused by Julius' insouciant utterances, and his high-hearted impudence. Too, he had a great affection for him. He looked at the expressive and youthful face in the moonlight and discreetly sniffed at the perfume which wafted to him from that gay person. Archias had been correct: republics are austere, august, temperate, and masculine, but when they decayed into democracies they became vulgar, base, irrational, feminine, luxurious. Cincinnatus had spoken of the "ideal man," who could appear only in republics. The only men who emerged in democracies were disheveled creatures, given to recklessness of principle and act.

"You were always one who had a reason for everything," said Julius, refilling Marcus' goblet, which had not only been chilled but was affectedly wreathed in fresh ivy. "So, I do not flatter myself that you have come here tonight merely to renew sweet acquaintance and to inquire concerning my health. You have a purpose."

"Yes," said Marcus.

"Has it aught to do with the fact that you take a bodyguard with you always, as I have noticed, in the person of that huge Nubian slave with the suspicious eye?"

Marcus hesitated. Slowly, he fumbled for the amulet Julius' mother had given him and he decided that it was time to abandon his usual prudence and recklessly confide in another, even if Scaevola had warned him not to tell of his encounter in the spring.

So he told Julius. Julius listened. The smiling face became quiet, still, intent. The black eyes dwelled fixedly on Marcus' face. But Julius made no comment. Then Marcus showed him the amulet of Aurelia and said, "Had it not been for this, given to me by your noble mother, I should be dead."

"They must have been mad," said Julius in a low voice, staring at the golden amulet quivering with light under the moon.

His voice was peculiar, and Marcus gazed at him. Julius still contemplated the amulet, and his mirthful face was hard and dark. "How could you harm them?" Julius continued, as if questioning himself.

"Who are they?" asked Marcus.

Julius averted his head and answered, "I do not know. Why should you think I do?"

He stood and began to walk up and down a path, the gravel scraping under his feet. He folded his arms across his breast and bent his head in deep thought. Marcus watched him, then said, "I did not tell you all. One of the men who attacked me wore a magnificent ring, two golden serpents joined at the mouth by a large carved emerald. It possessed some significance for me."

Julius paused on the moonlit path but did not turn. "And that significance?"

"I do not know," said Marcus. "Is it possible you do, Julius?"

But Julius shook his head over and over in silence.

"Scaevola said he believed I was potentially dangerous to someone," said Marcus. "To whom, Julius?"

The young man turned and his face was smiling and gay and he came back to the marble seat, sat down and put his hand on Marcus' unyielding shoulder. "To whom could so kind and amiable and peaceful a man be dangerous?" he asked. "You are a lawyer. You plead undistinguished cases in the courts. You are not possessed of great wealth nor do you know men of power. You are an 'old' Roman—" He paused, and the smile left his face and it was as if the moon left it also and it was obscured.

"Yes?" said Marcus. "I am an 'old' Roman. What else?"

He was startled at Julius' sudden loud laugh, for it was not mirthful at all. "Therefore, though you are eloquent, you are dangerous to no one! But, tell me. Why did you seek me out tonight?"

Marcus was so perturbed that he could not reply for a moment. Then in an abstracted voice he told of a search for a magistrate of noble family who would not be swayed in his opinion and justice by any oppressive government, but would be fearless and adhere to the law. He told of his client,

Casinus. "I ask only justice," said the lawyer. "If Veronus is exempt from this law, then it is because he has bribed someone of importance. Are we to be ruled by favor, and not by impartial law? By exigency and extortion, and not by honor?"

Moved and disturbed, his voice rose and filled the garden with strong and musical fervor, and Julius listened rather to that eloquent voice than to the words. For it had the power to move the heart, to stir it. It was enforced by manly passion and the trumpet of reason, by the thunder of indignation and righteous probity. I see now, thought Julius, why it was judged he must die. Nevertheless, though I am one of them, he must not die. I need him for my own purposes. Does not every ambitious man need a follower beside him who is all sincerity, all justice, all burning with truthful rage?

He became aware that Marcus had fallen silent. He beamed upon him, struck his arm lightly and affectionately. "My dear Marcus," he said in the richest tone, "I shall find you the magistrate you desire! A man," said Julius, his mercurial face changing again to one of deep soberness, "who will hear your case on its merits only, who cannot be moved aside by random interference, and not even by my father-in-law himself!"

Marcus was a trifle incredulous. "I thank you, Julius," he said. "My case comes up in the Basilica of Justice, itself, and many will be there to listen."

"And they will be touched to the heart by your fire and eloquence and rhetoric," said Julius. "You will defend the laws of Rome, and demand their equal application to every man. I shall be there, myself, to hear you!"

Marcus, though still namelessly uneasy, was grateful. Julius clapped him again on the shoulder, and refilled his goblet. He lifted his own. "To Rome!" he exclaimed, and laughed in the face of the moon.

"To Rome," said Marcus. "May she outlive any tyrant."

"Ah, yes," said Julius, drinking deeply.

He accompanied Marcus arm-in-arm to the atrium. "What! You came through these dark streets on foot, with only one slave with you? How imprudent. I will send you home in a litter, carried by six armed men. We cannot lose you, my dear Marcus."

While being carried home Marcus arranged his thoughts. Julius, for all his openness and gestures of friendship and love, had become ambiguous and disturbing. There had been about him, for all his youthful laughter, the dangerous scent of power. That may have come from the knowledge that he was Cinna's son-in-law. Then Marcus, in the darkness of the litter, shook his head. Men like Julius Caesar did not depend upon mere influence and favor. They depended only upon themselves, and therein lay their mysterious and terrible force.

In the meantime Julius was writing a hurried letter. "Therefore, he must not speak, for he can move all hearts. But it must be remembered that he is under my protection henceforth—"

He sent the letter by a slave at once, while the sand still clung to the ink.

Two days later Casinus came rejoicing into Marcus' office in the house of Scaevola, waving a document high in his hand. "The order has been withdrawn, Master!" he cried in jubilation. "Gaze on this, and see for yourself! Ah, what wonders you have accomplished!"

Marcus read the order of withdrawal. He could not understand it. He was not a famous lawyer, before whom a bureaucrat would facelessly cower. He was unknown to the vast government power of Rome. He took the parchment to Scaevola.

"Um," said the old pontifex maximus. "Now why was this so hastily withdrawn? Veronus has friends of importance."

"It is incomprehensible," said Marcus. "Still, who knows the ramifications of a bureaucrat's mind?"

"That bureaucrat," said Scaevola, "was acting under orders, himself." He turned and scrutinized Marcus. "To whom have you spoken lately of this case?"

"But to you, and Julius Caesar. I know no one of importance in Rome, save he, and yourself."

Scaevola's huge fat face with its many chins tightened, became strange.

"What is it?" asked Marcus, again obscurely alarmed.

"Nothing at all. I was merely thinking," said Scaevola. He tossed the parchment from him. He stared at it from its distance. Then he added, "What else have you told him?"

"Julius? I told him of the attempt on my life. I was imprudent; I disobeyed your suggestion not to speak of it."

"I see," said Scaevola. "What did Julius say?"

Marcus' conjectures of two nights before returned to his mind. "He said, 'They must be mad.' I questioned him, but he said nothing more. I possibly attached more significance to that phrase of his than what lay in it."

"Certainly," said Scaevola, after a moment. He gave Marcus his satyr's grin, and dismissed him.

Marcus wrote a letter to Julius Caesar explaining why his case would not be brought before the magistrate at all. He was about to send it by a slave of Scaevola's when a letter from Julius arrived.

"Greetings to the honorable and beloved Marcus Tullius Cicero.

"I have written here the name of the magistrate you desire, and I have spoken to him of your client. You will have justice."

For some reason Marcus was so relieved that that night he called on his young friend again, and was received with even greater affection. "I thought to send you a letter," Marcus said, as he walked in the garden once more. "But that would have been a surly return for your kindness. You see, it is no longer necessary. The demand on my client has been withdrawn."

"Now, that is astonishing," said Julius with a bland and innocent countenance. He shook his head merrily. "It was a mistake from the beginning. But matters are somewhat chaotic these days." He insisted on Marcus sharing wine with him and sweetmeats. Nightingales sang to the moondrowned night, poignantly, and suddenly Marcus was mysteriously relieved of his nervousness which had haunted him since that day at Arpinum.

"I shall never forget your kindness, dear Julius," he said, and his heart was warm with love for his lively friend.

Julius became grave and quiet, and Marcus looked at him questioningly. But the younger man was staring into his wine cup. At last he said, "No, you will not forget. All others might, but you will not, Marcus Tullius Cicero."

CHAPTER TWENTY

There were rumors in the startled city that Sulla was returning by land and by sea, and the rumors were everywhere like affrighted pigeons. To Marcus they were of little interest. He had never admired Sulla, whom he knew only by reputation. And he, himself, was too obscure and of too small a significance to come to the attention of any Sulla. The famous Roman could not be worse than Cinna, he reflected. In any event, it would mean the end of war. When he mentioned this to Scaevola, the old man said harshly, "One ambitious mountebank is no different from another. The people love mountebanks, and they are worthy of them. How does your charming young friend, Julius, receive these rumors of Sulla's return?"

"I have not seen him for several weeks."

"There are others I have not seen lately, either," said Scaevola, grimacing. "If Sulla returns and Cinna falls, then Julius' life will be in danger."

Marcus went to see Julius and was informed that he was visiting friends for some time. Marcus did not know whether to be relieved or to be alarmed. While he was hesitating before the chief of the atrium, wondering if he should leave a message, Julius' young wife appeared, a girl-child hardly past puberty, and of a sweet and innocent appearance. Her small and slender body seemed virginal, and her blue eyes were clear and interested. Her dark hair flowed unrestrained down her back, as if she had come from the schoolroom.

She smiled at Marcus. "Julius is concerned with many things," she said. "He has told me much of you. I am glad you are his friend."

Marcus was touched, and he colored. "An insignificant friend," he said. "You do me much honor, Lady."

The daughter of Cinna was like a flower. When he left her he could not help remembering the brightness of her eyes, her sweetness, her innocence. If Sulla returned, what would be her fate? She, even more than Julius, would be the object of Sulla's revenge. In what fearful days do we live! thought Marcus. Once Rome was safe for any honest man, or any helpless woman. Now we live constantly under the shadow of violence and death.

There had been no letter from Quintus for some time and Helvia was anxious. "He is safe, in Gaul," said Marcus. "Let us be thankful that he is not in Sulla's path! Our Quintus is totally without ambitions."

"Someone, my Marcus, believes that you have ambitions, or you should not have been attacked on the island."

"I?" cried Marcus, in amazement. "I have no ambitions but to be a better lawyer in order that our financial condition be improved. I also have ambitions to be considered at least a minor poet and essayist. Are these things inciting to murderers?" In order to cheer his mother he ruefully told her of Scaevola's remark concerning his poetry. Helvia laughed, but to Marcus' pleasure she also showed disapproval of Scaevola's witticism. "Your last poems, and your essays, received much critical approval," she said.

"And two hundred sesterces," said Marcus. "With which I bought several cows for the island. By the way, my poor Casinus, believing that in some occult manner I had brought about an improvement in his affairs, insisted upon giving me a purse of one hundred sesterces. I will buy more sheep."

But he, too, was uneasy about his brother and he paused one hot afternoon in the Forum to visit the temple of Mars to say a prayer to that furious god in behalf of Quintus. The temple was crowded, as usual during wars, and he had difficulty in purchasing a votive light. When he emerged from the temple he saw that great livid storm clouds arched and piled over the city, gathering themselves together like enormous armies. As yet they had not merged. The Forum was plunged into brown gloom, but translucent and umbrous in its shadows. However, the columns and buildings on the high hills glowed in vivid gold from the sun which was not yet obscured. Marcus stood in the portico of the temple, watching the clouds, many of them deep purple or almost black. Lightning was already flashing in their ominous depths. He said to Syrius, "We must move quickly to the Carinae or we shall be caught in the storm."

But they had hardly reached the temple of Vesta, reflecting brilliantly white in the long blue pool before it, when the storm incontinently broke and with ferocity. Marcus fled into the temple. Instant by instant, clear columns became shadowy and unsubstantial in the growing darkness. Shafts of fiery lightning exploded into the temple, lighting up pillars and floor and altar like a conflagration. Thunder roared simultaneously with the lightning, and the temple trembled a little. The wind had come on wings of destruction, screaming in the sulphurous air. Roman storms were notoriously intimidating, but this was extreme. One could not see the scene without because of walls of glittering rain. Marcus did not enjoy storms, and he shuddered at each roar, at each burning blaze. He leaned against a cool marble wall and his arm touched another arm, soft and yielding.

He turned his head and looked into the eyes of Livia Catilina, illuminated by lightning.

He stood absolutely still, forgetting the storm, forgetting everything but that sudden wild vision, believing it a dream, a fantasy. His heart began to stroke with sickening speed; his knees felt soft; a heavy lump rose in his throat. Before the next flare of lightning, he turned his head and saw a dim mantled form beside him, tall and slight, a form so still and unmoving that it was hardly more than a shadow in the darkness. Then another blaze of light lit up Livia's face, which was turned upon him, and he saw it with savage clarity, and he saw her eyes.

Once her eyes had been extraordinarily blue, large and passionate and intense, full of young life. They were still large and blue. But it was as if sapphires, glowing and vital and intact, had been smashed into a thousand infinite crystals so that though they still reflected light they reflected it in cold and meaningless ruin, ready at an instant to disintegrate. He had a horrible sensation that the young woman was blinded, for there was no recognition in those calamitous eyes, no start, no widening. Her face remained blank and empty and it was as pale as sorrow, even to her lips. A few strands of her autumn-colored hair escaped the hood of her cloak and lay about her neck as if all life had gone from them.

So would she look at the hour of her death, untenanted, lost, forsaken.

Now it was dark and dull in the temple again. A few people near the altar murmured prayers. A few small votive lights burned before the marble goddess. The thunder prowled savagely outside, invaded the temple like a beast, searching. And Marcus stood as unmoving as Livia, his mouth open to take smothering air.

The lightning flashed again, and again Marcus saw her, and again his heart plunged and he was as sick as if dying. Surely this silent woman, this woman who appeared not to be alive at all, this abandoned woman, was not Livia, his dream, his beloved, the haunter of his nights, the radiant companion of his days! He pressed his back closer to the wall, and felt the ice of sweat on his forehead and on his lip.

The storm was retreating as fast as it had come, like all summer storms. Now the lightning came rarely, though the thunder roamed as if seeking a victim, like a lion hungry for that which had escaped. Still Marcus could not stir, nor did Livia stir. They stood alone with no one near them, shadows in the depths of shadows.

Then Marcus murmured, "Livia?"

She did not reply. A random shaft of lightning touched her, raining down upon her from the high round hole in the painted ceiling. It was surely Livia. He stretched out his hand. It encountered soft but lifeless flesh that did not start away, did not respond to his touch. It was the hand of one dead for hours, chill and quiet. He found himself squeezing it; it was limp in his fingers. "Livia!" he exclaimed. "Livia?"

She said nothing. He continued to hold her hand frantically, as if he were willing to infuse it with his own warmth and blood. She did not resist, did not withdraw. She was like one unconscious, drugged beyond hearing or speech or awareness.

Suddenly the hot red sun lighted the drenched Forum outside and the rain ceased abruptly. The worshipers at the altar rose with mutters of relief, and came toward the door, passing the two shadowy ones against the wall. The people stepped outside, and the noise of the refreshed city came vehemently to Marcus' ears.

Marcus turned and faced Livia directly. She looked at him with those awful eyes which had no recognition in them. They appeared not to blink. He put out his hand and pushed back her hood, and his hand brushed her silken hair, which was disordered. Light from the vehement sun above and from outside leaped upon it, so that it began to burn metallically. But it was a lifeless burning. Her face, smooth and fixed, was the face of a statue, and as expressionless. She had not aged; she did not have the aspect of a matron. She had been frozen in her early youth, an embalmed and silent corpse.

Marcus bent his head and pressed his forehead against the wall near her cheek in his agony. He still held one of her hands. Then he heard the faintest sound, hardly even a murmur: "Why do you weep?"

"For you," he whispered. "For you, Livia, my beloved. And, for me."

She sighed. It seemed that the sigh rose not from herself but from the underworld the dead roam speechlessly and sightlessly.

"Oh, Livia," said Marcus.

"Do not weep," she said, indifferently. "There are no more tears to shed. I have shed them all." She paused. "I have had a message from—him. He will return with Sulla very soon. He will return to me, and our little son. Where shall I flee? Where shall I go? Where shall I hide myself? Where shall I hide my child—from him?"

Marcus had the impression that she was still hardly aware of him, and that she was addressing sister ghosts. He thought that he had experienced agony before in his life, but this was beyond all enduring, beyond all expression. He said with incoherence: "Come with me. I shall guard you. I shall keep you safe. My mother—there are places to hide, where no one will find you. Let me be your shield, beloved. Livia, Livia."

She sighed again, over and over, in the barest sound of tragedy. "He will find me. I am afraid. But I am more afraid for my child, my little one."

"Livia, what has he done to you?"

"He took my life from me. Why did he not die?"

Accursed am I, accursed am I! cried Marcus in the depths of his soul. I could have killed him, but I spared him, anathema, anathema!

He did not know that he was embracing Livia until he felt her head drop heavily upon his shoulder. Then he held her tightly to his breast, and he touched her cold cheek and forehead with his lips. What had Catilina done to this girl, this innocent child, this nymph of the forest? What horror had he brought to her that her eyes were shattered, her soul broken, her heart hardly beating against his? Her arms lay flaccidly along her sides. She did not move in his own, did not turn her head. She had closed her eyes, and now she appeared utterly without life, a dead body held upright only by his support.

"Come with me, beloved," he said, brokenly. "I will hide you. I will protect you."

"My child," she whispered, not hearing him. "His uncle possesses him in the house where we live. I am mad, they laugh at me. My child. I cannot flee without him." The head on Marcus' shoulder was like a fallen stone, pressing into his flesh. The girl sighed over and over, dolorously. "I cannot leave without him, for then he would die also. There is no pity in Catilina. He will return to divorce me, and I shall never see my child again. Nor is there shelter for me anywhere. Not anywhere, not anywhere. I died a long time ago."

"He is not here, in Rome, Livia. He may never return, for Sulla may never return. I am a lawyer, Livia. Divorce him! Have you no relatives, no friends?"

"My uncle believes me mad, also," the faint voice continued, unheeding. "They will rarely let me see my little one, who cries for me. I hear him crying in the night, but the door is barred to me. Listen! He is weeping for me now!"

She lifted her head and stared wildly before her, pushing Marcus away with incredible strength. "I must go!" she cried. "I must go! My child is calling for me!"

He could not restrain her. She slipped through his hand like a shade, running from him, stola and mantle flying, hair blowing behind her, feet flashing.

He shouted, "Livia! Livia!"

But she vanished through the door. He followed her. The Forum was crowded again in the raw red sunlight of approaching evening, and the voices of the people rose like a flock of angry birds. But Livia had vanished among the throngs.

"Accursed am I, accursed am I!" Marcus shouted, aloud, and with crushing self-hatred and loathing he struck his breast over and over with his clenched fist. Some of those passing below him, as he stood on the top of the stairs, looked up and stared, then pointed at his terrible and disordered aspect.

He dropped his voice and muttered, "Anathema, anathema."

Syrius, whom he had forgotten, had also been in the temple. He came to Marcus' side and looked into his desperate face. "Master," he said quietly, "let us go."

But Marcus could not return home now. Accompanied by Syrius, he roamed the streets of Rome, blindly, and did not come to himself for a long time. When Helvia saw his face and his eyes, she asked no questions. She knew only that something terrible had happened to her son. She let him go without words to his cubiculum, and then she questioned Syrius.

So, he had not forgotten Livia. Helvia was full of pity, but also full of impatience. But she was a wise woman and she greeted her pale son the next morning in a tranquil tone and spoke of casual things. She saw his eyes, bloodshot and sleepless, and she mentioned that the garden would produce many excellent fruit this year.

CHAPTER TWENTY-ONE

Marcus dined with Scaevola and the other young qualified lawyers at noon. For some, it was the only worthy meal of the day, for they were poor and they ate ravenously of the boiled meat, onions, artichokes in garlic oil, wine, cheese and summer fruit and little hot pastries. Scaevola would watch them with a pursed lip and a scowl, but this was to conceal the fact that he was secretly benign to his fledglings. Marcus, he noticed today, as he had been observing for several days at least, hardly touched the food, and drank unusually large quantities of wine. The young man's face was drawn and haggard and his eyes were heavy and red.

Scaevola said, "I have good news of our Marcus, and I wish you all to share it and to felicitate him."

The young lawyers glanced up alertly, but Marcus, not hearing, poured more wine from the bottle into his goblet, then began to drink it, staring heavily at nothing. Scaevola raised his voice irascibly. "Am I to be ignored at my own table, Marcus?" The young man started so violently at this direct assault that the goblet slipped in his hand and the wine splashed on his fingers. Scaevola glared into his eyes and said with elaborate patience, "I have been speaking of your good fortune, and have been addressing you."

Marcus murmured an apology. He saw the amused and curious smiles of his colleagues. "I was thinking of something else," he said.

"Without doubt," said Scaevola. "And when a man is so absorbed in his thoughts he is not thinking of a law case. He is thinking of a woman. That is stupid."

The young lawyers laughed merrily to please their mentor and because they knew of Marcus' austere life and his very rare excursions from virtue.

"Stupid," repeated Scaevola. "But let me return to the reason for our felicitations. Marcus had occasion to defend a rich old man a year ago from his rapacious sons, who wished to seize his fortune. The old man, the sons declared, was incompetent to manage his own affairs and was entirely mad. Why was he mad? He published at his own expense, a short book of hortatory diatribes and polemics against the corruption and venality of modern Rome. He prophesied the coming age of tyrants in our nation. He cried out against the Senate, once a body of honorable men impervious to bribes and other little peccadilloes of public creatures. He decried the new method of permitting low magistrates to become Senators through wealth and deviousness. In long paragraphs of lamentation, he described how we have fallen from republicanism into democracy, and the results which shall soon come to pass. His pejorative sentences had a vigor amazing in one so old; it was as if he were on fire. He denounced Cinna in furious language. Therefore, according to his wily sons, he was mad. I agree. All virtuous and patriotic men have some madness in them, for it is normal for men to be wicked and to be traitors."

He smiled fiercely at the listening young men. "Nonetheless, our Marcus did not believe him mad. He believed him to be a true Roman, and Marcus loves Rome. Is that not very unsophisticated in these days? So Marcus defended him and so ably that even the magistrate was moved to tears and in that emotional state upbraided the sons for their craftiness and congratulated the old father."

Marcus looked down at his plate, which he had barely touched.

Scaevola exhaled a gusty breath. "The old man died three days ago. He entrusted his will to me. He has left our Marcus one hundred thousand gold sesterces!"

The lawyers shouted and applauded loudly and hailed Marcus as a magnificent success and gathered about him to embrace him enviously.

"So our Marcus is rich. Temporarily. Before taxes," added Scaevola. "I trust he will invest in property if there is any money left after the vultures have calculated how much he 'owes' the government."

Marcus tried to smile. But all his emotions, except for hatred and lust for vengeance, were dulled these days. "It is very pleasing," he said in a dim voice.

"It is excellent!" cried Scaevola. "Let us have another goblet of wine in honor of this good fortune!"

After the wine Scaevola dismissed his lawyers, except for Marcus. "I wish to speak with you," he said. So Marcus, sunken again in his apathy, and incurious, remained behind. He sat like a statue in his chair, and Scaevola, smacking his lips, ate a pastry or two and watched him sharply. Finally, he said, "There are many things which trouble you these days, but one greater than the rest. I suspect it is a woman. I do not ask for your confidences, lest I lose my respect for you. There are more important matters which should disturb us. I have heard, this morning—and the city is only now quaking with the news—that Cinna was murdered a short time ago in a mutiny near Thessaly, whence he had gone to challenge the advance of Sulla on Rome. Now we have Gnaenus Papirius Carbo as our Roman Consul, the colleague of Cinna. He is no improvement over the latter."

Despite himself, Marcus looked up with a change of countenance. Scaevola nodded grimly. "You have despised Cinna. Yet, for all his expedient association with the old murderer, Marius—who decimated the best Senators—Cinna was not entirely evil, and distrusted Marius and his party, including Julius Caesar, the nephew of Marius. We have had worse Consuls than Cinna, including Carbo, our new one, who is considerably of a fool as well as exigent. I say this dispassionately, for as a wise man I do not engage in overt politics. However, I am threatened. Who knows at what hour I shall be assassinated?"

"Nonsense," said Marcus. "Are you not pontifex maximus, and holder of a most sacred office? Who would lift a hand against you, lord?"

"Many," said Scaevola, promptly. "And certainly Carbo, whom I detest.

Let us consider Sulla, who suspects the Senate as all military men suspect civilians. But he is a man of genius, for he had been born poor and rose to riches. If he succeeds in seizing Rome then the Roman mobs will have met their master at last, and for that alone we should wish him well. He is a cold and ruthless general. He will not spare his enemies, especially those Senators of the Marius party, the populares or 'democratic' party of your dear young friend, Julius Caesar. Sulla believes in law, which should induce you to admire him. He especially believes in laws he invents. Young Julius is in hiding, is he not? He will not escape Sulla."

Marcus looked alarmed. Scaevola smiled. "But Julius has the genius for being all things to all men. His nature is serpentine. He may escape, in spite of Marius."

Scaevola ate a handful of fresh grapes and ruminated. "Carbo, who hates me, suspects that I favor Sulla. I do have a weakness for men who know their own minds. Look at me. I have always avoided entanglements with men who lust for power. Nevertheless, I am in danger. I should like a worthy successor for the future. You."

Marcus was incredulous. "I? I am no one!"

"I wish to recall to you that only recently an attempt was made on your life. Those who are nobodies are not singled out for such distinguished treatment. Incidentally, I have come upon a strange thing. You may remember that friend of Julius, Pompey."

Marcus frowned, trying to remember, then he recalled the ambiguous young man, evidently a pleb, who had been the companion of Julius when Marcus had addressed the Senate. "Pompey?" he said.

"Pompey," said Scaevola. "I saw him a month ago near the Senate doors. He was wearing a ring such as you described, when you were attacked."

Marcus stared wildly. Then he exclaimed, "But, I remember his voice! It was not his voice that I heard on our island!"

Scaevola nodded. "Certainly it is not, for you should have remembered. Therefore, the ring symbolizes an arcane brotherhood. I wonder if Julius also possesses such a ring."

"Impossible," said Marcus. But he paled even more as he considered the matter. "Julius shook his head in bewilderment when I described the ring to him, and asserted that he knew no one who possessed such an elaborate article."

"And you believed Julius," said Scaevola with amusement. "That is a great flaw in your character, my dear. You are intrinsically convinced that men tell the truth, and are not inherent liars. Julius is a liar. He manipulates truth admirably, so that it serves his purpose. It is probable that he will survive Sulla."

"I cannot believe that Julius, whom I love, was responsible for the attack on my life," said Marcus, shaking his head.

"I did not say he had plotted against you! I have said only that he is probably a member of that secret brotherhood. Let us consider. Many of our younger Romans are much entranced by the East, especially Egypt. Julius is considerable of an Egyptologist; I know his house on the Palatine is filled with stolen Egyptian treasures. One of the treasures is a small pillar of bronze on which coils a golden serpent with a brilliant crystal in its mouth. You will remember that in Egypt the serpent is sacred and is endowed with marvelous powers, including prophecy and strength. It is the guardian of those on thrones, and those who hold sceptres. It is the nature of the serpent to move in darkness to accomplish his ends, and none can withstand him, for he is obscure and silent and remorseless."

"I did not see such an ornament in Julius' house," said Marcus.

"No. It is in his bedroom. He had bought it for a high price. He was so candid that I became suspicious, remembering the ring you had described. When men like Julius are candid and frank, then it is time to beware."

"It is all coincidence," said Marcus, stubbornly.

Scaevola sighed. "You will believe nothing ill of those to whom you are attached. Suspect all men, and do not overlook yourself. I have survived so far by adhering to that admonition. Let us consider one strong fact: there has been no further attempt on your life. Syrius is a brave slave, but he would be no match for a company of men. Had they not decided to let you live you should be dead by now. Have you not felt safer since you told Julius of your would-be murderers?"

Marcus started. "Strange. It is true. I did not think of it before." Then he cried, "Syrius has protected me, or there have been no more attempts!"

"Believe what you will," said Scaevola with resignation. "Who can put sense in the head of a virtuous man? But I am a mathematician at heart, and I have considered the odds against you. Syrius or no Syrius, you would not be alive now if someone had not interceded for you. I believe that one to be Julius Caesar. I had not thought him a sentimental man."

Scaevola added shrewdly, "Do not struggle against your doubts. Your instincts are better than your intelligence, and your virtues. Once you told me that Julius in himself was a portent. Have you forgotten?"

Marcus said nothing.

Scaevola changed the subject. "I have survived so far by not engaging in factions, feuds, and politics. I watch, with detachment, the steady decline of my country. Who can oppose it? Who can restore the Republic and all its virtues? No one. When a nation becomes corrupt and cynical, and prefers the rule of men and not the rule of law, it has entered upon destruction, notably its own. That is history. We have entered on the age of despots, as other nations so entered. Man never learns from the history of nations which died in the past. He pursues the same path to death. It is his nature, which is inherently evil. Let us consider the tribunes, the representatives of the people. Who receives the votes of the people, the virtuous man or the evil man who is extravagant in his promises? The evil man, invariably."

Marcus made no comment.

"It does not even matter that the evil man does not fulfill his promises! The people do not care, do not remind him. It is enough that he is evil, and reflects themselves. The mobs are more comfortable in the climate of malignity than the climate of good, which embarrasses and discomfits them, for it is against their nature. Let us return to Sulla. I have not the slightest doubt that he will soon seize Rome. Among his followers is your old enemy, Catilina. So, you are in danger."

Scaevola was startled at the sudden change in Marcus. The young lawyer half-rose to his feet. Even when he subsided again in his chair his hands were clenched on the table and he was breathing heavily. Scaevola waited, his gray brows arched, his lips circled in the form of an O.

"I despise myself," said Marcus, in the most quiet of voices. "I should have killed him." He struck the table with his fist. "I should have killed him. I shall never forgive myself that I did not."

"Yet, you spared him. Why are you now so regretful?"

Marcus knew that Scaevola derided sentimentality. But his emotions overcame him and he lost his calmness and his control. In stammering sentences he told his mentor of Livia. His voice rose to calamitous heights. Tears ran down his face. He beat his breast. His tight throat made his words hoarse and terrible. Finally, overcome with his anguish and despair, he dropped his hands on the table, and sobbed aloud. "I am guilty," he groaned. "I, myself, killed her, delivered her to evil. I am the weakest and most despicable of men."

Scaevola looked on that bent young head and Marcus could not see the compassion on that gross satyr's face. Wonderful are the arts of Aphrodite, thought the old pontifex maximus. Desperate are her devotees. She is the goddess, truly, of madness.

He pondered, as Marcus continued to groan and weep, his face hidden. Should not all wise men, and leaders of the people, be castrated by law when they become powerful? Then they would be immune from desire, from insanity, from evil. They would then be governed by reason. Knowing of the law, then, they would accede only if moved by virtue. They would sacrifice their testes for justice and devotion to the welfare of their nation. It was an intriguing thought.

Scaevola waited until Marcus had gained some control over himself.

Not to shame Marcus, he ate tranquilly. When Marcus lifted his head from the table he saw Scaevola calmly devouring dates and drinking wine. This calmness, in view of his own storm, brought rationality to him. He saw the apparently undisturbed little blue eyes of his mentor, and he wiped his own. "I was distraught," he said.

"So you were," said Scaevola. "But you are young. Therefore, I forgive you.

"Let us consider. You have vowed to kill Catilina. That is ridiculous. You would merely remove him from suffering, make him immune to pain. Is that a triumph? A dead man is serene, though his evil lives after him. It is more intelligent to balk such a man, to frustrate him, to deprive him of his ambitions and desires, than to kill him. Then he dies a thousand deaths."

Marcus' eyes became quiet.

"Be sure," said the old man, "that Catilina has desires. He is an ambitious man, like all the Catilinii. He is a patrician, and proud. Discover what he desires, and defeat him."

"Who am I?" said Marcus, despairingly. "I am powerless."

Scaevola rose. "You are many things. I feel the stirring of prophecy in me. You will do what you desire to do. I feel that in my bones."

That night, in the steaming heat of the city, Scaevola in his litter was being carried to the house of his son for supper. He was by nature a fatalist, and though his young lawyers did not know it, he was sickened by Rome and had dire premonitions of the future. Therefore, when his slaves screamed in terror and the curtains of his litter were torn aside, and the litter itself dropped to the street, he made no effort to defend himself or reach for his dagger. By the light of a high-held lantern he saw the faces of his assassins and recognized them. He did not utter a word before he was stabbed to the heart. He died as imperturbably as he had lived, as Romans died.

"Hail, Carbo!" cried the murderers, brandishing their daggers. They fled into the darkness of the night, which was licked by the red flames of the torches thrust into sockets along the walls. When the guard arrived, their iron-shod sandals clattering on the stones, they found disordered and weeping slaves, and Scaevola lying in his blood on his cushions, his eyes staring ironically.

When Marcus heard the news the next morning, on his arrival at the house of Scaevola, he could not believe it at first. Then his grief overwhelmed him. He recalled the prophetic words of the great pontifex maximus, and he hated himself for his impotence. He cried to his friends and to the sons of Scaevola, "Who would kill so noble and wise a man, so harmless, so kind?"

One of his sons said bitterly, "He was not considered harmless. One of the slaves heard the murderers cry, 'Hail, Carbo!' Apparently it was believed that my father was dangerous to our pusillanimous Consul."

I am utterly alone, thought Marcus, understanding that the dead are not to be pitied but those who remain to mourn them. He went into Scaevola's office, which was empty. Scaevola's many friends and clients, whom he had defended, had listened to what was borne on the wings of rumor and were determined not to jeopardize themselves by their appearance in this house. Marcus looked at the long marble table, at the heaps of books, the scrolls, the multitude of signs of the dead Scaevola's work, the bookshelves, and, above all, at the chair in which he had sat. That chair had been Scaevola's one touch of luxury in the bare room, for it was of ivory and teak and ebony, beautifully carved. It had been given him by a client. One of the sons followed the weeping Marcus into the office, and saw him touch the chair.

"He was very devoted to you, Cicero," said the son. "I know his will. He has bequeathed to you fifty thousand gold sesterces, and this chair, and all his books of law. And the slave, Syrius."

Marcus could not speak.

"He shall be avenged," said the son. "Do not weep. He shall be avenged. We will weep later."

But the murderers were never discovered. The Senators and the tribunes and the Consuls expressed their horror and their anger. Few appeared at the funeral. It was Marcus Tullius Cicero who delivered the funeral oration, clothed in his white toga and with his sword at his side.

"It is not Scaevola who shall be avenged," he said, in his powerful orator's voice. "It is Rome who shall be avenged. For a patriot has been silenced forever, and when patriots die the swords of good men must never be sheathed until those swords are scarlet with the blood of traitors. There were three assassins, it has been said. No, there was a nation of assassins. A corrupt and wicked people assented to this death by their apathy, their greed, their malice, their cowardice, their lack of patriotism. He was sentenced to execution a long time ago. The people are not guiltless.

"We shall avenge him by never forgetting him, and by opposing tyrants, and the furies and the treacheries in the hearts of evil men. Let his death not have been in vain."

Those who listened lifted high their clenched fists and muttered that they would never forget, and Marcus was still too young to discount the oaths of men.

Carbo had replaced the Consul, Cinna, after the latter's murder near

Thessaly. His dear friend and trusted colleague was the son of old Marius, and therefore a relative of Julius Caesar. While Sulla fought his way to Rome, Carbo ordered the death of the virtuous Senators who had not been corrupted, and the son of Marius carried out his orders. One by one, in those desperate days, all of note who were suspected of sympathizing with Sulla were ruthlessly destroyed. The end of law had begun, not in secret any longer, but openly.

Julius Caesar had been hiding in the house of Carbo for many days. He said to Carbo, "Scaevola should not have been murdered. I advised against it. The people will remember him; they are already beginning to remember him, if what Pompey has told me is true. He goes about the city. There are outcries against you, my friend."

Carbo shrugged. "Who cares for the outcries of rabble? Scaevola was involved with Sulla. We have the evidence, for all his protestations of neutrality. And, who is raising the loudest cries against me in Rome? That plebeian lawyer, that dear friend of yours, my dear Julius! Why did you intervene for him?"

"Marcus Tullius Cicero?" Julius laughed a little. "That mild and affable man?"

"Did he not humiliate Catilina? Is not Senator Curius his enemy?"

"Cicero?" repeated Julius, with an incredulous expression. "It was mere good fortune that he overcame Catilina. Catilina slipped and fell. Cicero is the enemy of no man, and Senator Curius has probably forgotten even his name. Do not catch at shadows, Carbo. Cicero may raise his cries but none listens. He is but a farmer, and innocuous."

"He is a lawyer. He has inherited Scaevola's clients. The magistrates speak well of him. He is gaining riches. You will see that I am aware of this nonentity of yours, Julius. He is not the dove you seem to think he is."

Julius was inwardly alarmed at Carbo's savage expression. But he continued to smile. He said, "I have known Marcus Tullius Cicero since I was five years old, and he has the most timid heart. He has no stomach for intrigue. He is an 'old' Roman."

"And 'old' Romans," said Carbo grimly, "are our most violent enemies. I say he must die."

"I say he must not," said Julius. "If he dies, then I shall avenge him."

Carbo's eyes narrowed on his gay young accomplice. "You threaten me, Caesar?" he asked in a soft voice.

"Let us be sensible," said Julius. "Let us not indulge in death and carnage for mere sport. We are in mortal danger, ourselves, and there is work for us to do. Berate me for a soft heart with regard to Cicero. I smile sheepishly over the accusation. If I thought him dangerous, however, I should not withhold my hand against him. Have I not proved that with regard to others?"

When Carbo continued to gaze at him in brutal silence, Julius went on, "Scaevola was pontifex maximus, a sacred office. The people no longer believe in the gods, but they fear them. Now they know who fills Scaevola's sandals—Cicero."

"You have said he is not important."

"He is no Scaevola, and I have admitted that I have some affection for him. Let him live in peace. I have heard he has some powerful friends who would be greatly annoyed should he expire suddenly."

"You," said Carbo.

Julius lifted his eyes patiently. "I," he said. "My annoyance would overwhelm my good temper."

"There is more to this concern of yours than I can decipher."

"Sentimentality, Carbo. Let us not descend to butchery for the mere wantonness of it. Sulla is approaching Rome."

Carbo regarded this elegant and smiling young man with an evil expression. Then he made a dismissing and contemptuous gesture. "I have already forgotten your gentle protégé, Cicero. We now have a civil war on our hands, since Sulla landed on the peninsula. Our armies, under our Consuls, are fighting Sulla's forces desperately, and so are our Samnites and other discontented Italians. We shall overcome Sulla. Is not Jupiter your patron? It was said that you would overcome your enemies, and that includes Sulla. And it is also said that Sulla has over five thousand names on his proscription list, and you and I are numbered amongst them. We will choke him with his own list!"

"I detest the military," said Julius. "I detest the Senate even more, for I belong to the populares party." He was relieved that Carbo had forgotten Marcus. "I have had a dream."

As Julius was now famous among politicians for his epilepsy, considered a sacred disease and full of prophecy, Carbo gave him his full attention. Julius smiled musingly. "I saw the shade of my uncle, Julius. He told me that I would not perish. My uncle said I was under the especial guardianship of Jupiter, and that I would be involved in enormous events."

"The events are already at our door," said Carbo with gloom. But he was interested deeply. If Julius survived, then this meant that Sulla would be defeated and his armies with him.

In the meantime, Marcus almost forgot his own griefs in the ominous news that riding couriers brought to Rome. Sulla was advancing steadily. The armies flung against him were retreating. If this were so, then Sulla would be at the gates of the city within days.

Tullius said fearfully to his son, "This is a most direful day for our country. I do not understand this war! Have we not had enough with the Social War? Shall we never be at peace? Where is my Quintus, your brother? Is he still in Gaul, or with our armies, or with Sulla?"

Marcus tried to soothe him, tried to hide his own fears. "Quintus is surely in Gaul. Was not his last letter addressed to us from there? And Quintus is no politician. Let us not become suffocated by the periodical waves of panic which drown the senses of Romans these days. Our family cared nothing for Cinna; we care nothing for Carbo. We are even less concerned with Sulla. We are a quiet family, and we live in peace, and have no enemies. We must work as usual."

Tullius wished to believe all this, and so he assented eagerly. But Helvia was not deceived. She questioned Marcus privately in his cubiculum. "My family is not for Sulla," she said. "You will be known as a member of the house of the Helvii."

"Nevertheless, my mother, I am not alarmed. I am only a lawyer, pursuing his tranquil way in the midst of a storm that does not concern us. In the vortex of screaming chaos we must serve law and order. That is my duty. I am doing it."

He embraced his mother and said, "We are no longer poor. We have thousands of sesterces now, thanks to the noble Scaevola and all my new clients. Let us consider what we shall do with our money when Rome is at peace again. Scaevola advised the purchase of property. I long for a sweet house on the island of Caprae, or near Naples. A villa, perhaps, with farmland. For, you will remember, I am a farmer at heart."

He had many burdens and anxieties, and he was afraid. Often he could not sleep for his dread concerning his brother, his dear Quintus. Was Quintus indeed still in Gaul, or had he been ordered to fight Sulla? Was he, even now, opposing the advance of that formidable man? Was he dead, or in flight?

There was also Tullius, the father, an invalid who must be protected. There was his mother, daughter of the Helvii, whose relatives were fighting Sulla. The affairs of the family were like chains upon him, making him listless and often physically sick. Yet, he must betray nothing so that his parents might have what could possibly be their final peace.

He grieved endlessly for Scaevola. But Scaevola seemed still to live, and was not dead in his thoughts as Livia was dead. His sardonic spirit was always at Marcus' elbow, his voice always in his ears.

"Sic transit Roma," he told Marcus in a dream. "Do not be distressed. Rome will perish, but your memory shall endure."

I prefer not to be a memory, thought Marcus on awakening. I prefer to be potent. I prefer to be a Roman to the last day of my life, and I hope that life will be long in the service of my country. I have no desire to encounter Cerberus and to cross the Styx. So, I will be prudent. One should, perhaps, hide virtue.

CHAPTER TWENTY-TWO

Rome was suddenly in the utmost disorder and terror.

The sweltering heat in the city and the brazen sun of an unusually hot season appeared to confine and contain the great city within her guarded walls, and to imprison the inhabitants who dared now not to go through the gates on any business at all. For Sulla was approaching the very walls of Rome, if one was to believe rumor and the blood-flecked and panting couriers of Carbo's defeated armies who came in desperate gallop to Rome.

There was no reason to doubt the couriers. Rome became an armed camp, swept with violent winds of fear. The mindless mobs, who cared nothing for Carbo or for Sulla, and knew nothing of politics, nevertheless found the vehement climate of terror exciting. They milled through the plazas and fora, streamed up and down the hills, shouting, gesticulating, embracing each other, running everywhere like brainless sheep, laughing, weeping, shrilling, calling sometimes for Carbo—who had suddenly left Rome with a fresh legion to confront Sulla—and sometimes howling for the grim general. Rumor with her thousand tongues flew above their heads in winged madness. They shrieked that when Sulla triumphed in Rome there would be more free grain, bread, beans, and meat distributed to the idle and incompetent, and that even free wine would flow into multitudes of eager goblets. They dreamed of plunder, and slavered. Other mobs hailed Carbo, who had promised as much, or more. Factions sprang up overnight, one shouting that Carbo was the hero, the other insisting that Sulla was the "deliverer." (From what he would deliver the fat and avaricious mobs was not very clear.) There were tumultuous dancings in the streets, day and night, and public drunkenness and riots in the wine shops, and everywhere the exuberant, insane laughter of an ignorant and envious populace. Worthy citizens locked their gates and their doors and set slaves on everlasting watch, fiercely armed. The Senate gathered and for once the doors of the chamber were shut, and the frightened men discussed flight and disappearance. And the gates of Rome opened constantly to admit crowds of refugees from the provinces and exhausted and wounded soldiers.

Marcus Tullius Cicero, attempting to go about his affairs and uphold the trembling law, considered the mobs of Rome with grimness. Should Sulla be successful, they would shout and laugh and dance no longer, nor live easily on the industry of their neighbors. They would work or starve, according to the ancient laws of Rome. Marcus, for the first time, found himself hoping that Sulla would indeed conquer. He was surely no monster like old Marius, the dead uncle of Julius Caesar, no irresolute Consul like Cinna, no bewildered and tyrannical fool like Carbo, whose adherents had murdered Scaevola.

The mighty giantess on the seven hills shook as if with an earthquake during the storm of events, her red, green, yellow, and ochre walls appearing to tremble constantly. The city, the people, sweltered with excitement and the brazen heat. The streets rang with the tread of soldiers preparing to defend the city from Sulla. All waited for news of Carbo. It finally came. He had fought a fierce battle with Sulla near Clusium, but was defeated by Sulla's general Metellus Pius, near Faventia. Then he had fled from Italy. The mobs paused, blinking, to consider this and to give, for the first time, some thought to their own fate. Those who had shouted for Carbo now muttered about the virtues of Sulla. Those who had howled for Sulla were triumphant. They ran in disordered ranks through the alleys and even down in the great Forum before the Senate chamber, carrying ragged banners inscribed with the name of Sulla, and shouting for surrender to him. They roared with wild but empty eyes into the temples, particularly the temple of Jupiter, to shriek their prayers in behalf of the terrible general. Thousands attacked and looted little shops, and struck down the shopkeepers. Armed guards, ready to kill, surrounded larger business establishments, swords unsheathed, and the mobs mocked them and thrust fists into their faces. But the mobs neither understood nor cared for that which they bellowed. They only knew that in their numbers lay terror, and felt invincible, and their excitement grew with their excesses. They scrawled on the walls at night, with red pigments. Sometimes, for no reason at all, they joined hands in the midst of the streets and leaped like dervishes, or the two sexes coupled in alleys in the very daylight in their frenzy of exuberance.

And the intelligent and industrious citizens went about their business, upholding law, and trying, with dignity, to ignore the mobs who roared ceaselessly day and night. Many of the prosperous and sound spoke with quiet dread of Sulla, for it was notorious that he was a militarist only, and despised all but the military. Senator after Senator slipped away from the city in the dead of night, after bribing the soldiers at the gates.

Julius Caesar, in hiding with his little wife, in the deserted house of a Senatorial friend, was always in touch not only with rumor but with fact.

One day he received a letter which made him smile. He went to his wife and said, "Do not fear any longer. I have had a message from my dear friend, Pompey, who, as you know, is now with Sulla. It was Pompey, himself, who captured Carbo at Cossyra only a week ago, and put him to death. Ah, you weep for your father, beloved. But one must be realistic." There were no tears in his own eyes. To Julius, all men were expendable except himself.

He was a member of the populares, or democratic, party, and Sulla despised and hated that party as the ally of the mobs of Rome. But for some reason—which history was never to explain—Julius was not very alarmed. He comforted his young wife. She shed tears for her father, and he wiped them away. When the time came, he assured her, he would offer large sacrifices in Cinna's name and pay lavishly for prayers for the repose of his soul. Sometimes, closely hooded, he ventured forth from his hiding place to visit the temple of his patron, Jupiter, the father of all the gods, the invincible one. There, among the mobs, he would raise a votive light. He was beginning to have faith in Jupiter and to believe his own stories of his remarkable visions. Quite often in the temple he would exchange hurried whispers with others like himself, and messages passed from hand to hand and were hidden in cloaks, to be sent to another destination even beyond the walls of Rome.

One day, when Sulla was within a few miles of Rome, Julius stumbled against Marcus when the latter was leaving the Basilica of Justice. Marcus saw only a slight quick figure cloaked and hooded in that dull brassy light; he was not surprised at the garb, for there were thousands of such furtive figures on the streets these days. He merely muttered an apology, and was startled when a thin brown hand darted from the folds of the cloak and seized his wrist. He turned his head and saw nothing but a faintly smiling mouth in the shadow of the hood, but there was something about that smile and the flash of the bright teeth that was familiar to him.

"Speak not my name, dear friend," said a voice he instantly recognized. "Come. Let us find a secluded spot in which to exchange news of each other's health."

Marcus thrilled with alarm. He glanced about him at the crowds in the Forum hurriedly pushing their way against streams which poured down from the Palatine. But Julius, still gripping his wrist, moved with a serpentine grace and ease through the throngs, and the two young men walked without obvious hurry to the foot of the Palatine and the great steps that rose upon it. The crowds were even thicker here, but Julius found a place behind the monolithic statue of Mars. Marcus withdrew his wrist, and said in a low voice, "This is imprudent of you. It is most dangerous. There are some who would tear you to pieces in an instant if they recognized you."

"True," said Julius, still keeping his face shadowed. His smile was gay and wide. "What is it that your old friend, Scaevola, always said? 'Only in republics and despotisms are men utterly safe, for in the first they are free and in the second they are slaves. In democracies, they are not free and they are not slaves; therefore they live in danger.' But, tell me. How goes it with you, dear Marcus?"

"Well enough," said Marcus, glancing at the streams climbing up and down the stairs. "And you?"

"As you have said, well enough. I am sorry that Scaevola was murdered, for he was dear to you and I admired him greatly. But he suffered the fate of all just men who live in democracies, death by the sword or death by slander. Ah, well. We shall have a democracy no longer when Sulla seizes the government."

"You are not afraid? For you are the nephew of Marius."

Julius chuckled. "I have never been afraid in my life. But you are concerned about my safety, and that touches my heart. Has your concern given you that pallor and those white lips, my friend?"

Marcus was becoming more frightened for Julius at every moment, for occasionally he caught a curious glance from passing men.

"Do not be frivolous," said Marcus, with impatience and growing fear. "I do not wish to witness your death. The mobs are scenting blood in Rome. They need but one bloody spectacle and they will rush roaring like the whirlwind through the streets, killing senselessly and with joy. Do not give them that spectacle in your person. How reckless this is of you! Why have you not fled Rome, as hundreds have done in these days, and hid discreetly until you are no longer threatened?"

"I am not pusillanimous," said Julius, "and I love the smell of danger, though I prefer to smell it from afar. Why should I flee? I am safe enough." His teeth flashed again. "You would not betray me even if a lion were at your throat."

"No. I would not betray you," said Marcus, with increasing anxiety. "Do not be absurd. We cannot stay here. A group has paused at the foot of the steps and are looking up at us with a curiosity I do not like."

"They recognize you, dear Marcus. Ah, I hear tremendous things of you, and I am proud to be your friend!"

Marcus was forced to smile. "What a liar you are. We cannot stand here. Return to your hiding place. Are you often this indiscreet?"

"I go to honor Jupiter in his temple and plead for his protection. No one would believe that one such as I would dare appear on the streets, even in a hooded cloak, in these days when Sulla is being acclaimed from every portico. These volatile dogs! It was only yesterday that they were acclaiming my uncle, and Cinna, and Carbo. Tomorrow, who knows? They will be acclaiming someone who overthrows Sulla."

"True. But I must detain you no longer for your own sake." A vast uneasiness pervaded Marcus. It was obvious that Julius was not afraid of Sulla. That meant that he was either a traitor to his own party and people, or was vainglorious. It came to Marcus that he was probably both.

Julius had now satisfied himself that he could depend completely on Marcus' affection and good will. Such a one was extremely valuable to an ambitious man. He pressed Marcus' hand. Marcus saw the thin strong fingers and felt their grip. "You are comparatively safe?" he asked, annoyed that his voice expressed his deep anxiety.

"I am safe," said Julius. He touched his hand lightly to his hooded forehead in a salute. "I go. But I shall not forget you, Marcus."

Marcus caught his arm. "My brother, Quintus. You have heard no rumors of him? I am fearful for him," Marcus added rapidly, and wondered why he should question Julius who dared not show his face on the streets of Rome.

Julius paused. "He lives," he said, kindly, and Marcus believed him. He watched Julius melt like a mist among the throngs on the steps.

Marcus' heart lifted with relief and became almost light. It was his intuition which had made him inquire of his brother of Julius. Julius was a liar, and that was certain. Yet, there had been conviction in his voice. He would not lie to me merely to soothe me, thought Marcus, as he descended the steps again. Marcus had another and disturbing thought: he was positive, knowing Julius' nature, that had he raised a cry of betrayal on these steps Julius would not have hesitated a moment to plunge a dagger into his friend's heart. He would have killed, and felt no remorse later. He is very ambiguous, thought Marcus, and now his heart was no longer light. He thought of Scaevola's cryptic warnings against Julius, and his description of the golden-scaled serpent in the young man's house.

The ruthless, inflexible general, Lucius Cornelius Sulla, drove the unfortunate Samnites before him to the very walls of Rome, and there they died by the many thousands at the Collina Gate at the hands of the Roman armies, while the armies of the Consuls within the gates prepared to lay down their arms. Sulla's officers and soldiers, resting after the slaughter of their fellow Italians, could hear the roaring of the mighty contained city beyond, and the thunderous shouts of the populace hailing the general. Sulla smiled darkly. He was the man whom his enemies called "half-lion, half-fox," and he had a coldly violent nature which could flush his face purple during frequent rages.

"Had the armies of the Consuls defeated me, and had they seized me, that same mob of jackals would be screaming for my blood and my head," he said to his officers. "Ah, we shall see!" His hard face, carved in tight flesh, flashed as if the blade of a knife had passed over it. He had been born of a poor but patrician family, which had always been of the Senatorial party, as he was, himself. He believed in power; he had come to hate the weak Senators who took bribes and were for sale to their clients and friends. In many ways he was an "old" Roman, incisive of mind, fierce and dedicated of purpose, implacable in his desires and his ambitions. Now, he was determined on vengeance. He would not accept the title and position of Consul of Rome. He would declare himself dictator. "And I shall retain my horse," he said to his laughing officers.

He had been wise enough to promise his fellow Italians that his success over Rome would not mean the abrogation of franchise and liberties all over the peninsula. "I come to restore the Republic," he said, and there was no smile on his lips as he said this.

He entered Rome during the most fiery of thunderstorms, which frightened a people who were acquainted with such storms. But never had any, in their memory, been so huge and terrible. At the moment Sulla, wrapped in his cloak and riding his magnificent black horse, and followed by the ranks of his officers and his foot soldiers and charioteers, reached the Sacred Way, the temple of Jupiter was struck by lightning and the pillars and the walls rose in flame and fell to the earth in shattered and crashing fragments. The temple had been the resting place of the famous books of Sybil, and they burned with the building. Sulla, at a little distance, surveyed the wild and roaring fire, which defied even the plangent rain. Those who had gathered to welcome Sulla, howling tens of thousands of them, were stilled into terrified silence. This was a portent, they cried to each other, their eyes wide and aghast, their ears deafened by the constant thunder that seemed to hover in deadly rage above the city, seeking to destroy it.

Sulla was a Roman, and therefore superstitious for all his intelligence and education. Had the temple of Jupiter been destroyed to reveal to him that he was mightier, in Rome, than even Jupiter, or was it an ominous warning? He, being an egotistic man, decided on the former. When the thunder paused enough to allow him to be heard, he said to his officers near him, who were watching the blazing ruins with awe and with pale faces, "You will observe that Jupiter, himself, has lit a torch to guide me!" They waited for him to follow this remark with his hoarse laugh, but he did not even smile.

One of his officers, Gnaeus Pompey (Pompeius), did not smile either. He thought of his friend, Julius Caesar, whose patron was Jupiter. Was this a portent? Pompey sat on his horse in the dark, flame-filled rain, and thought. His position in Rome until fairly recently had been equivocal; he had pretended to be one of the Marian party in order to preserve his life, though he was of the Senatorial party. He had served Sulla as a spy and liaison officer during his years in Rome, and had joined Sulla later, during the last stages of the war. For all he was a plebeian he had aristocratic pretensions and ambitions. Astute and worldly, cool and immovable, he had always been convinced that Sulla would return from the East and make himself master of Rome. In the meantime, through subtle contrivances, he had been able to leave Rome at will and report to the couriers of Sulla in quiet places, and then return.

Pompey's helmet glimmered in mingled lightning and reflections from the fire. He was a young man, but his eyes were not young. His broad face was impassive, his short nose prominent in its fleshy contours, his mouth heavy and straight and firm. His thick and curling dark hair glittered with raindrops and he moved a little on his horse as he wondered about Julius Caesar. He remembered that his friend's name appeared prominently on Sulla's list of proscriptions; he knew of the imminent slaughter of those men who had espoused the Marian party. He also remembered his dispassionate assurances to Julius; he remembered many things about his friend, among them the fact that Julius had much information about him, Pompey, also. Pompey looked at the burning temple with a smooth, inscrutable expression.

The lightning continued to inflame white column and portico and all the buildings in the Forum; it lighted up the massively crowded dwellings on the hills, so that they appeared to catch fire, and then to be curtained by darkness. Among the officers who watched the awesome spectacle of dusk and fire was Lucius Sergius Catilina, home from the wars, and ceaselessly plotting. He thought of his general, Sulla, and he smiled a little, and considered the murders and the tempests which should now afflict Rome. By craning his head he could see Sulla on his black horse, towering over all others, like a silent god indifferent to the fury about him and even unaware of it.

All that Catilina hated and loathed would be at the mercy of Sulla now, and of his officers. The mobs of Rome! Their master was only resting until he could avenge himself upon them, and upon their craven masters. Catilina felt the serpentine ring on his finger. This, he thought, was only the beginning.

Sulla touched his horse and turned it. His house and all his property had been confiscated when he had fled Rome for the East. But now his house, bedecked with flowers, awaited his return.

The storm had driven the welcomers from the streets into any shelter they could find. Therefore, with the exception of the smashing thunder, there was little sound on the streets as Sulla and his men rode onward. Only their steps echoed.

The remains of the temple of Jupiter sank into embers, expired into blackness, the broken columns strewn far as if hurled by giant hands.

There was no Sybil abroad in the gathering night warning Romans that the Republic, long in its dying, had finally died and had vanished into the sombre shadows of history. There were only the ghosts of the dead to mourn, "Sic transit Roma!"

CHAPTER TWENTY-THREE

Marcus Tullius Cicero had known terror as a wild and flaring thing, as scarlet as a smear of fresh blood, as dark lightning, as a tempest that broke and scattered.

He had never known it as he knew it now, as a vast and silent grayness, as a climate like iron. It held the city in the hollow of its echoing palms; it filled the air with silent and drifting grit. Its shadows fell from all the tall buildings and appeared to obliterate their outlines. It rode in muttering quiet from gate to gate. Its hushed voice was on every threshold; its presence was in the temples, and in the colonnades. Wherever its crepuscular umbra swept men's voices dropped. It obscured the faces of the crowds in shifting swarthiness, made all colors murky; even the noon was dull. Alleys were heavy with gloom; the vast fanlike stairs rising on every hill appeared laden with ghosts; thoroughfares even by moonlight and torchlight seemed shifting with forms that had no substance.

The Roman giantess had never known such terror before, no, not even under Marius, the old murderer, who had slain out of sheer and childish malice, and not with a plan. Sulla killed implacably and methodically. He had posted his five thousand proscribed names in the very Senate, but there were thousands of names more which were not known except to the bereaved. He had announced himself as dictator supreme. He had said, "I will restore the Republic." In the name of the Republic, then, he murdered without emotion, without remorse. He brought to Rome her first experience with true dictatorship, which was lightless and terrible—and almost soundless. Even the mobs were quiet, the emotional and animated mobs whose voices heretofore had never been silent. Their volatile faces were smoothed into masks by the horror that rode through the streets; they blinked emptily at each other, and their mouths opened. They knew they were too unimportant for murder to mark them as her own, that she did not even know their names. But they felt the presence of death everywhere, and saw funerals on every street. They said to each other in low, stuttering voices, "What is this?"

"I feel despair in the city," said Tullius, who never left his home and wandered only in the narrow autumn gardens of his house, listening to the livid patter of the two small fountains, watching the leaves falling one by one onto the silent earth. "You must tell me, Marcus, what is abroad."

But he was an invalid and frail, with strength only to move through the small halls of his house and in the garden, and he must not know. So his son, Marcus, said, "Matters have not settled themselves as yet, under Sulla. In the meantime, I pursue law in the midst of chaos."

"It cannot be as bad, under Sulla, as it was under Cinna, Marius, and Carbo," said Tullius, fretfully. "What tyrants they were! How they profaned the name and freedom of Rome! Sulla has said he will restore the Republic. Is that not what we have always dreamed, you, my son, I, and my father, and his fathers before him?" When Marcus did not answer, Tullius' voice rose. "Is not Sulla restoring the Republic?"

"That is what he says," replied Marcus.

He and Helvia did not tell Tullius that one of Helvia's cousins, a gentle, slightly stupid businessman, had been murdered by order of Sulla. He had not been a man of politics; he had not known one tyrant from another. He had been a man of smiles and great amiability. He had hailed Marius, Cinna, and Carbo out of sheer good nature, and because they were "the government."

He had been an excellent businessman, a merchant of textiles. He had numerous shops throughout the city; he imported silks and linens and the finest of wools. His designers and dyers were the best craftsmen. Therefore, even during the long wars he had become prosperous. "Let us go to the shops of Lynius," the middle-class of Rome would say, and many of the rich. "For there we shall not be cheated; the quality of his goods is beyond compare."

Lynius, like thousands of his kind, did not know that the middle-class was deeply hated by Sulla, as it is always hated by tyrants. He was never to know that an envious competitor whispered that Lynius had been devoted to Cinna. So Lynius was murdered.

Tullius became conscious that his wife's cousin's calm and genial presence was seen no longer in his house.

"Where is Lynius?" he asked of Helvia one night. "Has he deserted us?"

Helvia's dauntless face these days had lost its bright color, and her hair was graying rapidly. She could not answer her husband and so Marcus said smoothly, "Now that the wars are over, Lynius has gone abroad for new and more enticing silks and linens."

On another occasion Tullius wailed, "Why do we not hear from Quintus? Surely now that all is quiet letters could reach us. I fear he is dead."

Marcus answered over his own fear, "Letters are often lost. I have heard a rumor in the city that his legion is on the way home." This was not true, but Tullius, the scholar, the immured man, the God-enamored philosopher, must never be forced to confront the frightful reality of these days. His father had protected him in other years; his wife had protected him; his son, Marcus, must now protect him from hearing the voice of terror that muttered in the streets of Rome.

Marcus himself lived with fear and grief and anxiety. He had so many silent terrors of his own that often he could not endure his father's petulant voice, his demands for an enlightenment which might kill him, his insistence that he be assured that all was well not only with his family but with his world. One night Helvia came into the darkness of Marcus' cubiculum and sat on the edge of his bed and took his cold hand. She tried to speak calmly and with sympathy. She, the strong and indomitable, could only burst into tears. He held her in his arms and she wept against his cheek, "Where is my Quintus? Why should Lynius have been murdered? And many of our friends?"

Marcus began to ask his own wretched questions of his mother. He found he could speak to her of the awful pain of his own heart, and his dread of tomorrow. "I am only a lawyer; I am not a politician. Yet, there is Catilina among Sulla's officers, and Catilina has forgotten me no more than I have forgotten him. I cannot forget Livia, my mother. Does Livia exist, still? Or, has she died of her wounds? Shall I be alive at tomorrow's sunset? If I die, who shall care for you, and my father?"

"Pallas Athene will protect you, Marcus," said Helvia, wiping away her tears and her son's tears also. "The gods do not permit good men to die wantonly." She paused, then added, "What nonsense is this I speak! Still, I believe that Pallas Athene is guarding your days."

"I hope that Sulla is aware of that," said Marcus. "How many names have fallen in Rome, the names of virtuous Senators as well as evil ones! How many men like my cousin, Lynius, innocent and bewildered, have died for nothing! What was their crime? That they did not hasten to make friends with tyrants, or fawn upon them. They wished only to live in peace, under any government which would permit them to earn an honest living. But governments will not permit men to live in peace!"

He had many clients, even in these days, but he had no friends. Men were too afraid to speak to each other in confidence. Sulla had proclaimed freedom, so men trod warily and spoke in low voices behind their shut doors and wondered if they could trust their sons. Sulla had restored peace, he declared, so fathers looked apprehensively at the faces of their young in their cradles. "I will refill our bankrupt treasury," said Sulla, so men whispered with dismay at the rumors of even higher taxes, and withdrew their savings from the banks and hid them in their gardens, or stole from the city at night with their gold. "Justice, at last!" cried Sulla, and the citizens were afraid of each new dawn and held their wives desperately to their hearts, and knew that justice was dead.

"Rome is no longer a city-state," said Sulla. "We are a nation, and we must march on to our manifest destiny!" So thousands of Romans, who had money with which to bribe, fled Rome for quiet spots in Greece or even in Egypt, or lost themselves on little farms in Sicily, praying that Rome's manifest destiny would thunder abroad far from their doors.

One dark winter day Helvia said to her son, "We are no longer poor as once we were. One of my uncles has been wise enough, all these years, to walk prudently, inspire no envy, and hide his wealth. He has offered me a car and two fine horses. Let us go to Arpinum and forget our fear and our grief for a little."

"Our father will suspect that something is greatly wrong if we flee when winter is on the land," said Marcus.

One day he went into the Temple of Justice. He moved silently in the winter dusk to the smooth and empty white altar of the Unknown God. Marcus touched it with his hand; the marble felt sentient under his fingers. He prayed, "Why do You delay Your birth? The world is plunging swifter and swifter toward bloody destruction. Death waits in every shadow. Evil rides triumphantly through the streets of Rome. There is hope for man no longer. Why have You denied us Your salvation?"

The altar glimmered in the half-light; the crimson shadows of the votive lights on other altars licked the quiet marble of this one which awaited the visible sign of its God. It awaited its Sacrifice, its flowers, its vessels, the voice of its priests. Marcus pressed his cheek against the altar, and his tears wet the white emptiness of it. "Help us," he said aloud.

Marcus' old murdered mentor, the pontifex maximus, Publius Mucius Scaevola, had once told him, "We shall not be lost as a nation until the colleges of the Pontifices shall be seized by a tyrant and made to serve his will."

Sulla declared himself not only the dictator of Rome's civil life and government but head of the Pontifices, shrewdly understanding that he who controls the gods controls all humanity. It was not his will which was now being imposed on Rome, he said. He spoke only as directed from Olympus. The patrician Pontiffs did not revolt, or denounce Sulla. They, like their fellow Romans, had long since lost their manliness. "Let us consult together," they said in privacy. "Shall we lead Rome into bloody insurrection and catastrophe? It is in our power, but this we must not do. Let Sulla declare himself privy to the desires of Jupiter. Men of wisdom will merely smile. For the sake of our people we must remain silent." They were, like most Romans, practical men, but they were not practical, or wise enough to understand that when priests abdicate to civil authority and to tyrants they have abandoned God and man.

Now the master of the abject Senate—the once powerful Senate—Sulla appointed his own favorites to that august body, increasing it to six hundred members. Almost all were patricians and men of property, for Sulla mistrusted the masses. The public assembly hastened to confirm those he appointed. Some of the new Senators were prosperous businessmen who had never favored Sulla. They did not know that they had received this honor solely because Sulla wished to gain the favor of the commercial class—so that they would desert their sound interests and pragmatic principles and be his absolute creatures. Unlike Cinna, he did not underestimate the power of businessmen. Contrary to ancient Roman law, which laid all power in the hands of the public assembly, the Senate now was given power over that assembly. All measures, once offered to the public assembly for approval or disapproval, had to receive the approval of the Senate first—a direct reversal of the law. The public assembly regarded this move with justified dread and despair, for now the government no longer represented the people. "I wish responsible government," said Sulla, who destroyed the Constitution with a stroke of his pen. He then attacked the office of Tribune. No tribune, he decreed could ever hold any other office henceforth, and not serve again until ten years had elapsed since the first year of office. The "representatives of the people" then became impotent, and no honorable man, eager to serve his country honestly and under just law, felt any desire to circumscribe his life so stringently.

For the first time in its hundreds of years of life the Roman Republic became a slave nation, answerable only to its master, Sulla, and his creatures. What he had not accomplished through murder he accomplished through flattery and the giving of honors and powers to those who once were his instinctual enemies.

"I am a lawyer," said Marcus to himself. "Yet, we now have no law but Sulla. However, I must behave, as a responsible man, as if law still exists, and I must pray that it will again exist, if not in Rome, in another nation perhaps yet unborn."

That year the Saturnalia was very subdued. Sulla wished the rejoicing to be jubilant, as a tribute to himself, for, had he not restored the Republic? But the people were uneasy, confused, and afraid, though not understanding in the huge mass of them what it was that made them so. Their instincts sniffed out the odor of tyranny long before punitive laws against their public assembly and their tribunes became effective and reduced the power of the populace. Sulla, in honor of the Saturnalia, made a large gesture of magnanimity and generous solicitude for the general welfare. He ordered tremendous amounts of stored food to be given to the people without cost, and arranged for huge festivities, and magnificent games in the circuses.

The people accepted it all. But they were not gay, and they were filled with apprehension. They remembered the first days of terror, the funerals massed on the streets, the gray iron of the climate. It was a long time before they could smile willingly and regain their usual buoyancy.

The month of Janus was extraordinarily cold.

Marcus heaped coals upon the brazier in Scaevola's office, which he now occupied. But still it could not heat the room adequately. The blue woolen curtains were drawn tightly over the windows even at noonday, and the frost penetrated and the cold winds. The floor was like a sheet of ice, and the chill seeped through Marcus' fur-lined shoes. When he paused in his industrious writing of briefs he could hear the great uproar of the savage winter gale and the hiss of snow. He could not recall that he had ever known such a winter before in Rome. It seemed part of the pervading misery and fear in the city.

Now he had students of his own, and he was patient with them as Scaevola had never been patient. His sensitive face might be pale with dread and cold, but it was always kind. His changing eyes dwelled on the students gently. When he spoke he spoke as serenely as possible to these disturbed boys. "In the midst of the wilderness law must prevail or our humanity shall be lost," he would tell them. "But Sulla changes the law," they would reply. To this he would say, "There are the natural laws of God which can never be changed. Let us study them, for we are Romans still, and we have always invoked God." But when he was alone he would bend his head and run his long fingers through his thick brown hair and sigh.

One day while he was preparing a civil case one of his students came to him in great terror and cried, "Master, there is a centurion who wishes to see you, and he is accompanied by his soldiers!"

Everything became very still in Marcus. Yet he could reflect, "Woe to us in these days, that the appearance of our own soldiers can inspire such fright in us!" He said calmly, "Request the centurion to enter, and send us wine."

The centurion, a young armored man with swinging heavy cloak and bright helmet, entered with a clangor of iron-shod shoes, and raised his right arm stiffly in the military salute. Marcus rose. "Greetings," he said. He leaned his palms on his table and smiled inquiringly at the soldier.

"Greetings, Marcus Tullius Cicero," said the centurion. "I am Lepidus Cotta, and I am commanded to escort you to dine with my general, Sulla. At noon, which is now."

Marcus regarded him with astonishment. The centurion stared at him arrogantly. It was this, at the last, which made Marcus' thin face flush with indignation, and which made him remember that the old law placed civilian authority above that of the military.

"It is impossible for me to leave," he said. "I am to present a very important case to a magistrate in the Basilica of Justice within the hour."

The centurion's stare loosened; his jaw dropped. Then he said, "Master, I have only my orders. Shall I return to Sulla and give him that reply?"

Be prudent; forever be prudent, thought Marcus. But his indignation was rising. A man had to stand for his rights or he was not a man.

"Let me think," said Marcus, and sat down. Syrius, the black and faithful slave, silently poured wine into two silver goblets. Marcus motioned to Cotta to drink, then took up a goblet, himself.

"I have had two postponements of my case, Cotta," he said. "The magistrate will not look kindly on my absence. I think it best that I go at once to the Basilica of Justice and present my case as rapidly as possible. Then I will be delighted to accept the honor of Sulla's invitation."

Cotta nodded solemnly. "This is very good wine," he said in a boyish voice. He sat down opposite Marcus and poured his goblet full again. "But we have a litter awaiting you."

Marcus' lips pursed wryly. So, I am not to die, he thought. At least, not immediately. What did Sulla want of him, he a modest lawyer who was of an obscure family and who lived quietly, doing only his duty? Only the magistrates knew of him, and his clients. Then he thought of Catilina.

"Why am I given this honor?" he asked.

The centurion shrugged. "Master, I have only my orders. But I do know this: the great pontifex maximus, Scaevola, was the general's devoted friend, and it is possible that Sulla wishes to honor Scaevola's beloved pupil."

"Scaevola was no politician," said Marcus, with incredulity. The centurion gave him a youthful smile which attempted to be very knowing. Then Marcus thought of something and he burst out laughing. He pictured himself arriving in the Forum escorted by Cotta and the soldiers carrying the eagles of Rome and the fasces, and banners. The magistrate had been obdurate in the matter of his client. But the magistrate was only a man and this magnificent escort would awe him.

The lawyer said to the soldier, "I must appear in behalf of my client.

I accept the courtesy of the litter. And your escort, my good Cotta. Shall we go?"

So Marcus put on his crimson, fur-lined cloak—the first luxury he had ever permitted himself—and pulled the warm hood over his head. Escorted by Cotta, he walked through Scaevola's house and the faces of the law students became blank with fear and astonishment. Marcus said to them, "I shall not be long, lads. Do not be remiss in your studies while I am absent. I am to dine with General Sulla."

Syrius appeared at his elbow, his great black eyes fixed and bright. "Master, I must accompany you."

"Certainly," said Marcus, putting his hand on the other's shoulder. He went outside into the whirling blur of the snow and entered the warm litter awaiting him. Four slaves in scarlet mantles lifted it, and soldiers surrounded it, and led by Cotta they all marched off, Syrius running behind.

As Marcus had suspected, the magistrate was awed; the officers of the court were awed. The magistrate's supercilious voice became respectful. Marcus presented his case ably. The magistrate nodded soberly, over and over. Then he drew the papyrus to him, signed it with a flourish of his pen, and imprinted his seal upon it. "I do not know, noble Cicero, why you should have had difficulty with this case of yours."

Marcus was disgusted. But he bowed to the magistrate and then to the officers of the court, and they bowed to him also. He marched out with his clanging escort.

The streets were sheathed in ice. The watery sun had come out behind dark clouds, and the ice glittered. Icicles hung from the white porticoes of buildings. The river ran blackly between its white banks. Beggars and other riffraff had built bonfires near every intersection and were warming themselves or roasting scraps of meat on the flames. The rushing throngs hurried swiftly through the streets, hooded heads bent low before the wind. Acrid smoke drifted everywhere. The crowded hills shone and sparkled under the new sun, the red roofs gleaming with moisture and snow. Now the sky appeared in small patches, brilliantly blue and brilliantly cold.

It was not far to Sulla's walled house, not a great distance from the Palatine. Soldiers stood at the gates, and saluted. A ruffle of drums announced Marcus. I know now, he thought, what it is to be a potentate. The soldiers and the slaves marched over the slushy gravel of the path that led to the bronze door of Sulla's large white house. The door opened and more soldiers appeared, fierce-faced youths, black of eye and eagle of countenance, the sun glinting on their armor. Marcus alighted. The centurion went before him with rigid steps, and they entered a marble hall, softly warm, with thick white columns, and scented as if with spring flowers. A fountain played musically in the atrium. Somewhere, behind closed doors, a young woman laughed merrily.

Then Marcus was escorted into a spacious room with a floor of black and white marble, and delightfully heated. The furniture was sparse but elegant, the tables of lemonwood and ebony inlaid with ivory. Here and there Persian rugs were scattered. A man sat at an immense table with carved marble legs. He lifted his head, frowning musingly when Marcus entered.

It was as if he had scarcely noticed Marcus' intrusion, nor the centurion, nor the fearful but resolute black face of Syrius peeping over Cotta's shoulder. Cotta saluted. "I have brought the lawyer, Marcus Tullius Cicero, at your command, my General," said the soldier.

Marcus bowed. "I am honored, lord," he said. "Greetings."

"Oh," said Sulla, frowning again. "Greetings," he added, impatiently. He looked down at the mass of scrolls and papyrus and books on his table, then thrust them aside. He rubbed his eyes, and yawned briefly.

He was a man about fifty-six years old, lean, browned with wind and weather, leathery of face, with deep furrows about his thin straight mouth and across his brow. His cheeks were sunken, and this gave him a sullen and hungry appearance. He had very black eyebrows, as straight as a dagger over the palest and most terrible eyes Marcus had ever seen, eyes like ice and bitterly shining. His black hair was cropped short to his finely shaped skull, and his ears were pallid and close to his head. He had a firm and angular jaw, and broad almost skeletal shoulders. He wore a long tunic of purple wool, with a leather girdle which held his dagger. There were no armlets on his arms, no rings on his fingers. Despite his lack of military garb no one would have known him for anything else but a soldier. His voice was harsh and clipped.

He contemplated Marcus without notable curiosity or interest for several long moments. He saw the tall and slender figure in the crimson cloak and hood and the modest dark blue long tunic. He saw Marcus' pale and studious face, the fine features, the large eyes, the mass of curling brown hair on the white forehead. Marcus returned his regard straightly, and Sulla thought: This is a brave man, for all he is only a civilian and a lawyer. The formidable soldier smiled a little, and sourly.

"I am pleased you have accepted an invitation to my frugal meal," he said. He waved a dismissing hand at the centurion. "We shall dine alone, except for my other guest," he said. He noticed Syrius for the first time. "Who is this slave?" he demanded. "He is not of my household."

"He is mine, lord," said Marcus. He paused, then continued: "He protects me against my enemies."

Sulla raised those thick black brows of his. "Is it possible for a lawyer to have enemies?" he asked. He laughed, and the laugh was unpleasant. "Ah, I remember what rascals lawyers are! I had forgotten." He said to Cotta, "Take the slave to the kitchens and let him be fed while I dine with his master."

Cotta saluted, seized Syrius by his reluctant arm, and led him away. The door closed after them. Sulla said, "Seat yourself, Cicero. You must be content with a soldier's meal, not served in a dining room, but at the base of my operations. You have never been a soldier in the field?"

"No, lord." Marcus removed his cloak and placed it over a chair, then sat on it. "But my brother, Quintus Tullius Cicero, is a centurion. In Gaul."

Sulla's pale eyes fixed themselves on Marcus with a curious expression. "In Gaul?" said Sulla.

"Yes, my lord. We have not had a letter from him for a long time. My parents and I are gravely distressed. It is possible that he is dead."

"Death is always the companion of soldiers," said Sulla, contemptuously.

Marcus looked up. "And it is the companion of all Romans," he said.

"And particularly now?" said Sulla. To Marcus' amazement he was actually smiling.

Marcus did not reply. Sulla picked up his pen and tapped the table as if in thought. "I am a man of blood and iron," he said. "I am also a man of grim humor. And I honor a brave man."

Marcus could not speak. He remembered that Sulla had been called half-lion and half-fox, and was a man of no mercy.

"I have brought peace and tranquillity and order to Rome, which she has not known for a long time," said Sulla. "I have brought them to all Italy."

The peace and tranquillity and order of slavery, thought Marcus. Sulla, watching him, was amused.

"I have heard much of you, Cicero," he said. "I have had many letters from my dear friend, Scaevola. Before he was murdered." Sulla's voice became as cold and smooth as a stone. "Did he never speak of me to you?"

Marcus was shaken. "My mentor did not admire the military," he said at last. "I recall that he said that you were preferable to Cinna, and Carbo. He was a man of many acid jests."

Sulla smiled. "He was also very discreet. He was more valuable to me, his friend from our youth, than a legion of couriers. I owe him the largest debt of my life. And you, whom he loved, never suspected it!"

"No, lord." Marcus felt suddenly weary. "And that was why he was murdered. I thought the assassins had destroyed him because he was a man of justice and honor, and Carbo could not endure such men."

"I do not impugn either his justice or his honor," said Sulla. "Who should know more about this than I, his friend? Once he wrote me, 'When one is confronted with two evils, one should choose the lesser.' He decided I was the lesser. He also knew I was inevitable. But more than anything else, he loved me." He turned in his chair and looked long at the many banners that hung from the black and white marble walls. "He had no greater love, except for his country. Nor have I."

Marcus had always thought that only men of profound justice and goodness and integrity could love their country as she should be loved. Yet now he heard the tremor of genuine emotion in the voice of one who was not just, not good, and had only the fierce integrity of a soldier. I am naïve, he thought.

Sulla stared at him again with those pale eyes. "Your grandfather was my captain," he said. "I was his subaltern. He was an 'old' Roman, and I honor his memory. He compromised with no one when he believed himself in the right. Rome is poorer for his death. She has been growing poorer with every year, as her heroes have died. But they were old-fashioned heroes. We live in a changing world, and they would not change."

Marcus said, "Lord, the world is never static. It will be another world in another year. Yet today, on every hand, I hear, 'We live now in a changing world!' This is said as an excuse for excesses!"

"You are disputatious," said Sulla. "That is your lawyer's failing. Let us consider. Do not the people love grandiloquent slogans and jargons? If they shout today that this is a changing world shall we quiet their enthusiasm? They always believe that change means progress. We must not disillusion them." His sharp white teeth flashed in a broader smile. "I admire you, Cicero. You are much like your grandfather. You, too, are a brave man."

"You have said that before, lord," Marcus replied with heat. "Is it so unusual for a man to be brave?"

"Most unusual," said Sulla. "Even soldiers are not always brave." He threw his pen from him. "I wished to know the pupil of Scaevola. I wished to meet an honest lawyer, and to study such a strange manifestation. Ah, my other guest has arrived."

Listlessly, for now his weariness of spirit was very great, Marcus turned his head. Then he started with the utmost astonishment. For, entering easily, and clothed with splendor, was his old friend, Julius Caesar, smiling as gayly as the summer sun.

CHAPTER TWENTY-FOUR

Marcus rose slowly, and Julius seized him by the upper arms in a buoyant embrace, and kissed his cheek affectionately. "My dear Marcus!" he exclaimed. "I never see you without joy and pleasure!"

"And I never see you without amazement," said Marcus. Julius laughed heartily and struck him on his shoulder; he gave Marcus a sly wink.

Julius, though not of notable height, yet gave the impression of grandeur in his snowy toga, his golden armlets set with many gems, his jeweled and fringed golden Egyptian necklace, his glittering rings, his golden girdle and shoes. His gay black eyes, wanton and ancient, sparkled as if at a huge jest. His aspect, as always, was dissolute and depraved yet curiously buoyant and joyously youthful. He wound his arm through that of Marcus, and turned to Sulla. "Lord," he said, "I have learned more wisdom from our Marcus than from all the tutors who afflicted me. He was my childhood mentor."

"To no effect," said Marcus. But, as usual, he could not help smiling at Julius. He added, "I did not expect to find you here."

Julius laughed again, as though Marcus had uttered a tremendous witticism. "Do we not meet in the most extraordinary places? But here we are at home, you and I."

Marcus thought of all the pungent and devastating things he should like to say, but restrained himself. All his suspicions about his dear friend returned to him. He had long ceased to expect Julius to have principles or loyalties or dedications. He knew Julius to be exigent. Yet Julius was the nephew of the man Sulla had hated most, Marius. Julius was a member of the populares party, which Sulla despised. Julius had proclaimed democracy in the most eloquent voice and Sulla detested democracy. They should have been the greatest of mortal enemies, the middle-aged soldier and the adroit and crafty young trickster, whose first allegiance had always been to himself, and his last also.

"I am not excessively surprised," said Marcus, "to find you here. I should not be surprised to meet you on Olympus, or in Hades. You are always in the most unlikely spots."

Julius assumed a very serious expression, but his eyes danced. "As you know, sweet friend, I am under the protection of the Vestal Virgins. Therefore, under their aegis of purity I can appear anywhere." He looked at Sulla again and said, "Lord, is not our Marcus the noblest and gentlest of creatures, the wisest, the most temperate?"

Sulla's pale eyes glinted. "He is noble, but I do not find him gentle nor overly temperate. There is a griffon under that modest manner; a lion peers through his eyes, and not a tender one."

"Lord," cried Julius, "how wisely you have put it! Marcus loves the mobs no more than do we. He is an aristocrat by nature, a fastidious man though a lawyer." He struck Marcus on the shoulder again. "I have a matter of law to discuss with you before General Sulla."

"I doubt you honor the law," said Marcus. "Or, is this a new phase of your nature?"

"The law is that which exists—at a given time," said Julius, laughing. His manner toward Sulla was that of a favorite son, indulged and tolerated.

"Your concept of law is very interesting," said Marcus, coldly. "It is, however, a concept on which too many lawyers base their cases and their pleadings. And too many rascals."

Julius was not insulted. He led Marcus back to his chair and without invitation took one for himself, facing Sulla. "We can always rely upon Marcus' probity. He is no diplomat, therefore he is no liar. Did I not tell you so, lord?"

"Above all things," said Sulla, "I prefer an honest man who does not change his opinions to suit the occasion, and whose word can be trusted." He looked at Julius, and his harsh face was subtly amused. "Nevertheless, men like yourself, Julius, are valuable to men like me. So long as I am powerful you will be faithful, and devoted. I intend to remain powerful."

Two slaves brought in a small table covered with a linen cloth. Gilt spoons and knives with sharp blades were arranged upon it. The three men watched in silence. The slaves went out and returned with trays which were loaded with plates, platters and vessels containing cold veal, cold fowl, cheese, rosy apples and grapes and citrons, clean brown bread, boiled onions and turnips, and wine. "Not a sumptuous feast," said Sulla. "But then I am a soldier." He poured wine, himself, into the three goblets. Then he spilled a little in libation. "To the Unknown God," he said.

Marcus was unaffectedly amazed that Sulla, the mighty Roman, should honor One of whom the Greeks spoke, and not Jove or his patron, Mars. He poured a libation, himself. "To the Unknown God," he murmured, and felt a deep spasm of pain and longing in himself.

But Julius, pouring his own libation, said, "To Jupiter, my patron."

"Whose temple was destroyed," said Sulla.

"But which you will rebuild, lord," said Julius.

"Ah, yes," said Sulla. "The populace was much disturbed that lightning struck the temple on the day I returned to Rome. They found a portent in it. The vulgar masses are always discovering portents, and a wise ruler listens to them. I have proclaimed that Jupiter wishes his temple to be far more magnificent than the one formerly consecrated to him, and that he has indicated his desires to me alone." He did not even smile. "It shall be a glorious temple, as the father of the gods deserves. We shall have a rich lottery to finance it, which will please the masses. It will please the frugal and sober, also, for they know how bankrupt our treasury is, and wish no more drain on it."

Marcus ate little, and in silence. He wondered again, with growing alarm and confusion, why he had been brought here. He thought of Catilina. He listened to Julius' jocular exchanges with the saturnine general with only a portion of his attention. He saw that Julius amused Sulla. Yet, Julius was hardly a buffoon. He was a graceful and intriguing young man, with a voice of marvelous expressiveness. He could be grave at one moment, and full of laughter the next.

I am here for a purpose, thought Marcus.

They had just finished their repast when the door opened and Pompey entered in his military garb. He saluted Sulla stiffly, smiled briefly at Julius, then turned to Marcus. "We have not met for a long time, Cicero," he said. "I remember your miraculous success in the Senate, while defending a client accused of inability to pay his just taxes."

Marcus looked at that broad and impassive face, the light gray eyes which betrayed nothing of the owner's thoughts, the heavy, firm mouth. He glanced at the strong wide hands to see if Pompey wore the serpentine ring of which Scaevola had told him. The ring was not there. Pompey was regarding him seriously. "It should please you, Cicero," he continued, "that law and order are now restored, for are you not a lawyer? At the last, law must rely upon military discipline to maintain and support it, and so you should be grateful." He sat down and poured wine for himself into a goblet a slave brought to him.

Marcus' face flushed. But before he could speak Pompey continued: "True law is impossible without militarism, therefore the army is more important even than law."

I am being goaded, thought Marcus, but why I do not know. He said with quiet anger, "I wish to correct the prevailing prejudice that the work of the soldier is more important than the work of the lawmaker. Many men seek occasions for war in order to gratify their ambition, and the tendency is most conspicuous in men of strong character, especially if they have a genius and a passion for warfare. But if we weigh the matter well, we shall find that many civil transactions have surpassed in importance and celebrity the operations of war. Though the deeds of Themistocles are justly extolled, though his name is more illustrious than that of Solon, and though Salamis is cited as witness to the brilliant victory which eclipses the wisdom of Solon in founding the Areopagus, yet the work of the law-giver must be reckoned not less glorious than that of the commander."*

"So speaks the civilian," said Pompey with some disdain, and giving Sulla a meaning glance.

"So speaks the honest man of conviction," said Julius, and also glanced at Sulla. "And does not Rome need honest men?"

"I speak as a Roman," said Marcus. He was full of umbrage. He looked at Sulla, expecting vexation, but to his surprise Sulla appeared pleased. Sulla said, "We have no traitor here, in the person of our Cicero. Therefore, he can be trusted."

Is it possible that they were afraid of me? Marcus asked himself incredulously.

Sulla said, "Our Julius has told me that you have always mistrusted the masses, Cicero."

"I distrust uncontrolled and vehement emotion, which has its impulse not in reason but in malice and confusion, lord. If man is to rise above mere beasthood then he must obey just law, formulated by just men." Marcus spoke with emphasis. "I repeat, just law, formulated by just men, and not random and expedient law which is the servant of tyrants. That law which appeals to the sentimentality, gross and unlearned, of the masses, or to their bellies, is no law at all. It is only the lust of the barbarian, the scream of the jungle. Such law leads us back to the wilderness of tooth and bloody claw, the service of mindless beasts. Unfortunately, too often, that wild law of savagery is used by unscrupulous men to advance their own interests, and they, too often, find it in the masses. These unscrupulous men discover, to their own ruin, that they have seized a tiger by the tail."

"You will observe, lord," said Julius, "that Cicero has no high regard for the noisy and noisome masses." He spoke with affection.

Marcus cried, "We are not speaking of the same thing at all! The people have souls and minds! I ask that rulers appeal to these things, and not to base appetites!"

"Cicero is not ambiguous, thank the gods," said Sulla. "He is not ambitious." He smiled briefly at Marcus. "I am pleased to find a man who loves the laws of Rome. I can ask nothing more."

Marcus stared at him bitterly. He said, "You killed my cousin, Lynius, a kindly and innocent man who knew nothing of politics, and wished only to live in peace."

* From Cicero's *On Moral Duties*.

Sulla put down his goblet of wine. "I know nothing of your cousin, Lynius." He turned to Julius. "Was his name on my proscription list?"

Julius frowned as if trying to remember. Then he threw up his hands. "Lord, it is impossible to remember all those names. I do not recall the name of one Lynius. It is possible that some informer whispered, out of his own interests, to one of your officers, who then ordered his execution."

"That is militarism, blunt and ruthless," said Marcus. "It is not even aware of its own crimes. It delegates wholesale murder."

"Was his property confiscated?" asked Sulla.

"Yes. As was the property of thousands of men like him, of the middle-class, innocent men who industriously pursued their daily occupation, believing that established law would protect them."

Sulla made a faint sound. He said to Julius, "The property of this Lynius must be returned to his family at once. Cicero is justly distraught."

They are trying to buy me, but why? Marcus asked himself. He said, "Thank you, lord. My cousin has a wife and several children." He was so exhausted by his own emotions that he prayed to be dismissed. He said, "Rome is no longer a nation of law. That is my grief."

"I have restored the law. I have restored the Republic," said Sulla. "I have delivered my people from that which you deplore: Exigency. Lawlessness. I have given discipline again to the populace."

It is useless, thought Marcus with growing despair. We do not speak the same language.

If only I could return to the island, and forget this new world! he cried in himself. But, where is there peace? Where is there a spot which is not invaded now by corruption and violence and lies? He said to Julius, "You have spoken of a point of law. Tell me. I have clients waiting."

But it was Sulla who spoke. "Julius is married to the daughter of Cinna, Cornelia. I wish him to divorce her. I could command it, but you will observe, Cicero, that I am a man of law." He said this without a smile, and only with the gravest face.

Marcus was again amazed. If Sulla wished Julius to divorce that young and beautiful girl why was Julius obdurate? Julius beamed upon him. "I love Cornelia," he said. "What has her father to do with us?"

"You oppose General Sulla?" asked Marcus in a disbelieving voice.

"In this, yes, my dear Marcus." Julius' smile was serene.

"It is an insignificant matter," said Sulla, impatiently. "The girl is not important. Let Julius divorce her and return her dowry. Why should he not, if he is devoted to me?"

Why not, indeed? thought Marcus. He stared intently at Julius. He shook his head in bewilderment. Julius said, "I will give up all else in my devotion to General Sulla, but not my wife."

Hah! thought Marcus, bitterly. I see it now. He will not divorce Cornelia at Sulla's command because he wishes to convince Sulla he is not all exigency, and therefore he can be trusted.

"Let us consider the law," said Marcus. "It is not enough for law to be meticulous. It must be just also. It is not enough for law to be meticulous and just, it must be understanding. It is not enough for law to be meticulous and just and understanding, it must also be compassionate. It is not enough for law to be meticulous, just, understanding, and compassionate. It must also be rooted in absolute truth.

"What is that truth? God alone knows. Laws of men cannot be truly laws unless they are based on, and further, the laws of God. Our ancient laws state that such a man must not divorce his wife unless for total cause, such as adultery or inability to bear children, or for madness or betrayal. Cornelia has committed none of these, of her own will or out of her nature. Therefore, Julius has no grounds for divorce."

"So, you uphold Julius in his disobedience?" asked Sulla.

"It is best, always, to obey God rather than man," replied Marcus.

Sulla turned to Julius. "I did not know that you reverenced the laws of gods and Rome more than anything else," he said, and smiled slightly.

But Julius assumed much gravity. "Lord, I could not serve you well if I did not serve the gods more."

Sulla said, "As a soldier, I am a man of law, a Roman. Therefore, though I prefer a different judgment from Cicero, I bow to the laws I have restored."

Marcus saw then that Sulla was studying him with concentration, that his black brows were drawn together, his hands clasped tightly on the table. Sulla finally said, "As you obey the gods, Cicero, then you obey the law. It is enough for me."

Sulla was smiling his cold and wolfish smile. "And now, Cicero, I have news of great import for you. Your brother, the centurion, Quintus Tullius Cicero, is under my roof at this very moment."

Marcus' first emotion was a wild and stunning disbelief, a sense of profound and numbing shock. He rose slowly, his eyes fixed upon Sulla, then upon Julius, and then upon Pompey. None told him anything; each face was like a bust carved from marble, unchanging in expression. Then a powerful thrill of incredible joy ran like lightning through him, again and again. Quintus was not dead! Quintus lived! In a moment he would hear his voice, embrace him, clasp him to his heart. He swung on his heel. "Quintus!" he cried. His heart trembled.

There was no answering call; the door did not open; no one spoke. Marcus suddenly became conscious of the deep silence in the large white and black room. He swung back, bewildered, to those who sat near him, and he saw their smooth faces. It was then that joy and gladness departed. It was then that he was filled with the greatest fear of his life, far greater than that he had experienced when assassins had tried to murder him. He leaned forward, shaking, and grasped the edge of the table to keep himself from falling. "Quintus," he whispered to Sulla's brown still face. "Quintus?"

Sulla said in a voice that was almost kindly, "Seat yourself, Cicero. You are as white as death. I have a story to tell you."

There is no story to tell, thought Marcus. They are to execute Quintus, as they have executed thousands more. What has my good and loving brother done against them?

"Tell me," said Marcus, forcing the words through a throat that felt like iron and salt. Then he cried furiously, "Tell me! Do not torment me like this!" He struck the table with his clenched fists.

Sulla raised his eyebrows, then looked at Julius. "Why is our Cicero so distracted?"

Julius said very quickly, "Marcus, restrain yourself. Quintus is alive. He is a noble soldier, and we honor him. Sulla regards him as a son."

Marcus' hands slipped from the table and he fell into his chair. His heart clamored at his ribs. He was as weak as death. He stared at Sulla, who frowned faintly.

Sulla said, "I called to the officers of the Roman armies outside the city and in foreign territories to join me against the armies of the Consuls. It was their duty, but many were stupid and obstinate and thought that they should remain with the latter; I do not deplore their loyalty, though it was misplaced. However, your brother was not one of these. He came to me at once, in Asia, from Gaul, with his men. His duty, he understood, was to Rome, not to Cinna, not to Carbo, not to the Consuls."

His pale eyes dwelled on Marcus' face, waiting for a comment. Marcus did not know what Sulla wanted of him; he did not even know that Sulla wanted anything at all. He could only whisper, "Quintus, Quintus."

They waited for him to regain composure. Then Julius was at his side with a goblet of wine. "Drink, dear friend," he said. "There is nothing to fear."

"Why should Cicero fear anything, for himself, for his brother?" asked Pompey in a slow and meaning voice.

Marcus pushed aside Julius' hand and shook his head over and over. He could feel nothing at all now except a vast trembling along his nerves. "Where is Quintus? Why does he not come to me?"

"He cannot," said Sulla, with something like compassion in his metallic voice. "He has lain at the point of death for a long time, and for a long time we despaired of his life. He fought the Samnites with me, to the very gates of Rome, and there fell. He was carried to a farmhouse near the gates, and his men, and my own personal physician, have been in attendance on him from that very moment. Only three days ago was he brought to this house, when we were assured that there was a possibility that he would live. He is still in much danger, and not often conscious. But my physician believes that he will survive."

Marcus turned in desperate rage to Julius, only half-comprehending. "Why was I, his brother, not told? My parents and I have lived in agony for nearly a year! You knew where we live, Julius! A word, a single word, would have alleviated our terrible anxiety, but you would not bring it!"

Julius' face changed. He hesitated. "I was in no position to do so."

Marcus' white lips drew back from his teeth as he regarded Julius with mingled anger and loathing. "No," he said, "I must not ask you, for you will never tell me." He turned to Sulla, again. "Why did we not have letters from my brother, so that we should not have lived in our apprehension and our misery?"

Sulla became impatient. "Have you forgotten my own position with regard to the Consuls of Rome? Have you forgotten that they thought of me as an outlaw, a revolutionary, a traitor to them? Have you forgotten my exile for all those years, while Marius, Cinna, and Carbo ruled Rome and almost destroyed her? Would you have had me betray my own heroic officers, like your brother, so that the murderers within these gates should visit their contemptible and craven revenge on their families? I forbade my officers to communicate with their families, for their own sake. Do you think you should have survived, and your parents with you, if Cinna and Carbo had known that your brother was my loyal officer and had given me his fealty? Consider, Cicero."

Marcus' shaking hand reached for the goblet which Julius had placed near him and he drank all the wine in one long gulp.

"You underestimate your importance in this city," said Sulla, in a fatherly voice. "You are too modest. Your fame is everywhere, Cicero. You would not be alive today if your brother had disobeyed my orders and had written to you, no matter how secretly."

He sighed, and moved irritably in his chair. "Consider Rome. The populace is no longer of the order of the old Romans. Many are composed of the sons and the grandsons of those who were once slaves. They are people of a multitude of alien races and religions, a polyglot tribe. What do they know of the Founding Fathers of Rome, of our traditions and institutions, and our Constitution, and our inheritance? There is no pride in the mobs of Rome, no understanding of the history of Rome. What few old Romans remain are in the minority, and they were hated by Marius, Cinna, and Carbo, for their virtues were a reproach. Have you forgotten, Cicero, the endless massacres which took place in this city while I was in exile? Only the gods preserved you and your family!"*

It was as if Sulla had struck a great bell in Marcus' heart, and he was filled with confusion, for Sulla had spoken the words he had known best, and which he had learned from his grandfather. Sulla said, "It is impossible to restore a nation without the sword. I have used the sword. That is why you detest me, Cicero. But you are still young. Understanding will come to you." He sighed again. "I do not deceive myself that what I have tried to restore will survive. I have only delayed the final ruin of my country."

He motioned to Pompey who refilled his goblet. Marcus was silent. But he was thinking: How intricate is man, how tortuous, how indirect! There are no absolutes in him! All that Sulla has said is in my own spirit, yet he is a ruthless murderer, and he has abrogated the Constitution in many ways and has imposed militarism on my country. How divided are the hearts of men! What confusions dwell in their souls!

Sulla drank his wine, then folded his lean hands on the table and stared at them. "Your brother should have died, Cicero, had not Lucius Sergius Catilina come to his rescue in the heat of battle."

At the mention of that hated name Marcus became very still. He could only stare at Sulla.

"Your brother," the general continued, "had been unhorsed by the Samnites, whom he was battling. He fell to the ground; they pierced him with their lances, in the throat, the arms, the breast. In a moment he should have died. Then Catilina, at some distance, plunged through the fighters, with a few men about him, and slew the attackers. Your brother owes his life to him."

Marcus swallowed over and over, and then said weakly, "Catilina did not know he was my brother!"

Sulla smiled darkly. "Catilina knew your brother, Quintus. They were men-at-arms together. Catilina is a great soldier, above all other things. A soldier of Rome was about to be done to death. Therefore, Catilina preserved him. Catilina has no quarrel with your brother. Is it not time that you forget your boyish disagreement with Catilina, and feel gratitude?"

Marcus put his hands over his face. "Let me think," he muttered.

He felt the silence grow like stone about him. His mind was invaded with clouds that fled when he tried to see them. Catilina had saved the life of Quintus. For that, he deserved gratitude. Catilina had killed the spirit and the mind of Livia, Marcus' beloved. Nevertheless, he deserved grati-

* From Sulla's *Memoirs*.

tude. Had I killed him when I should, thought Marcus, my brother would not be alive today.

"I am grateful to Catilina for this," he said in a dull voice. "However, there are other matters between us, which I cannot speak of, for it is beyond me."

"Life," said Sulla, with considerable grimness, "is beyond most of us."

"Yes," said Marcus. "It is utterly beyond us." Lassitude, like cement, lay heavily upon his limbs. "May I see my brother?"

Julius rose with alacrity. "Dear Marcus, dear friend. I shall take you to him at once. He may not recognize you, but be assured that he will live."

He had to assist Marcus to his feet, and he did so tenderly. Sulla and Pompey watched in silence. Then Julius led Marcus into the atrium. The outer door opened, admitting a white swirl of snow. A young woman, gay, beautiful, laughing, passed over the threshold, throwing back her hood to reveal curling masses of golden hair. Her cheeks were rosy, her lips apart to show dazzling white teeth. She exuded a thrilling air of vibrancy and life and delight. Her eyes, warm as brown silk, shimmered and sparkled. Gems glowed about her throat, on her wrists, on her fingers. Her small feet were shod with gold, and she wore a chiton of yellow wool, embroidered with a colorful multitude of flowers. Her laughter was like a tinkle of lutes.

"Julius!" she cried, extending a perfumed hand for Julius' kiss.

"Divinity!" cried Julius in reply. He kissed the white and extended hand.

The girl eyed Marcus with curiosity over Julius' bent head. Her lips were voluptuous, her breast rich with curves, her arms like snow. She was like full spring, profound with promise, eager and sensual. "Who is this?" she demanded of Julius, in the sweetest of voices, but peremptory.

"A friend of our lord, Sulla," said Julius, releasing her hand with reluctance. "Marcus Tullius Cicero. A lawyer."

The young woman looked disappointed. Apparently she had expected a great name.

"The Lady Aurelia, Marcus," said Julius.

Marcus had never seen her before, but he knew of her. She was a very rich young woman, twice divorced, and licentious and full of notoriety. Her amorous adventures were infamous in the city. There were songs about her, highly lewd. Her name had been frequently scrawled, replete with obscenities, on the walls of Rome. She looked incredibly alive and vital and avid. Her face was the face of a wicked child, smooth and without virtue.

"Where is Lucius?" she asked of Julius. The young man glanced at Marcus out of the corner of his eye.

"He will be here in a moment," he said.

"Catilina?" said Marcus. Julius took his arm like a younger brother. "Do you not want to see Quintus?" he asked. He led Marcus away. He said, "Sulla is also named Lucius."

"Nevertheless, she came to see Catilina," said Marcus, sick with his old hate. "Do not lie to me, Julius. I have been able to read you like a book since you were five years old."

"What matter these things to you, Pyramus?" said Julius.

Marcus pulled away his arm. Julius was laughing softly at him. He took Marcus' arm again. "Women are women," he said. "Let them not distract us. They may be beautiful, but we are men."

As he was guided through long white halls glimmering with early winter dusk, he thought of the presence of Catilina in this house, and his mind was dark with dismay again. Catilina was vindictive and depraved, a man without conscience, a man much worse than Julius for Julius had a humorous attitude toward his own evil, and acknowledged it. Quintus was in danger in this house, from Catilina, for all his rescue by that man.

Julius reached a tall brazen door and knocked quickly upon it. It was opened by an elderly man in an austere white toga, evidently the physician of whom Sulla had spoken. "Greetings, Antonius," said Julius. "I have brought the brother of our Quintus to see the invalid."

The physician bowed to Marcus. "Greetings, noble Cicero. I fear you must be very quiet and not disturb my patient, who still lies close to the door of death after all these months. Only the Great Physician, Himself, has preserved him, and it is a miracle. There were many times when his breath stopped and I was certain he had died. Then his mighty heart rallied. He has a will that is almost superhuman; he refused to die. He is a true Roman."

It was a moment or two before Marcus could make his trembling voice articulate. "I can never repay you for your devotion, Antonius. Will he recognize me?"

"That I do not know," said the physician. "If not today, perhaps on another." The physician was thin and tall and his bald head shone faintly in the pallid light behind him. He regarded Marcus with pity. "You must be prepared for a change in the noble soldier's appearance."

Marcus tried to prepare himself, but his legs were soft and weak under him when he entered a magnificent bed chamber of white marble walls inlaid with lines of black stone; the floor was covered with thick warm rugs of dark red. A carved ebony screen, intricately pierced, partly hid the window. A big wide bed stood in the center of the room, made of the finest wood and strewn with fur robes. Chinese vases decorated the corners, dimly flashing their many bright colors, and a bust of Mars, huge and fierce, stood on a squat marble column near the bed, a votive light burning scarlet before it.

Marcus ran to the bed and gazed at the face on the silken pillows of blue and gold. He had prepared himself for an immense change in his brother, due to his long and arduous recovery, but he could not believe that this emaciated man, hardly breathing, was his beloved Quintus. He appeared old and shrunken, very slight, diminished in body, barely raising the rugs which covered him. The flesh was gray, the sunken eyes closed in shadowy purple, the lips livid and fallen inwards, the brow bony and furrowed. A healed but twisted red scar ran from his left temple to his chin, and it glistened vilely.

"No, no, it is not my brother," whispered Marcus through his tears. His gaze traced the profile, aloof and strong, pure with its fleshlessness. Then he dropped to his knees and laid his head beside that of the unconscious man.

"Quintus," he said. "Quintus, can you hear me? Carissime, it is your brother, Marcus."

The snow hissed beyond the window; the winter wind growled against it. The votive light raised its scarlet beam, then dropped it. Marcus' tears wet the pillow near his brother's head. Quintus did not stir. Marcus took one cold and lifeless hand, all bones and heavy. He pressed it against his cheek. Then slowly the eyes fluttered open, the head turned and Marcus saw the far eyes, filmed and empty, the eyes of one who had looked upon death and still stared at it.

"Carissime!" repeated Marcus. "Dearest of brothers!"

He stared desperately at his brother's skeletal face, and into the distant eyes. Then the hand in his moved only a little, like an infant's hand, and into the eyes came the dimmest of gleams and the dry lips stirred. Marcus bent his ear to those lips and heard a sigh, "Marcus?"

"He knows you!" said the physician, joyfully. "For the first time, he recognizes another! Ah, we shall restore him, deliver him to the arms of his family again."

"Beloved Quintus," said Marcus, his tears falling down his cheeks. "Rest. Sleep." He held the cold hands between his two warm palms, to give them some of his own strength. "I shall take you home. Our mother and father await you. You are safe."

The lips stirred again in the slightest of smiles, the very shadow of Quintus' amiable grin, and suddenly the soldier sighed deeply and with contentment and fell asleep. But his fingers had crept about Marcus' fingers and the pulse was stronger in them. Marcus felt a compassionate hand on his shoulder and heard Julius' voice, "He will live now."

Marcus had determined before seeing his brother that he would take him at once from this house but now he knew it was impossible. Quintus' spark of life was too faint, too flickering for any movement. Any stress would blow it out. Then he became conscious that two young soldiers, armed and helmeted, stood behind the bust of Mars, watchful and silent. He said to them, controlling his voice, "Are you my brother's legionnaires?"

They came forward, saluting. "We are, lord. We guard him day and night, listening to his breathing, and assisting the physician who never leaves him either. He is our officer. He is more to us than our own lives."

"Is—anyone else your captain?" asked Marcus.

"None, lord, save he." Marcus studied the resolute young faces, the ferocious temper of the black eyes. "We love him more than a brother."

"May Mars guard you, and the blessing of Zeus fall upon you," said Marcus, and now he loved all soldiers.

Julius, the subtile and intuitive, said affectionately, after hearing this exchange, "Be not anxious. There is none to harm him. He is under Sulla's eye and protection, for Sulla loves him as a son."

Marcus and Julius returned to Sulla's room. Sulla looked at Marcus' face and his own grimaced in sympathy. "Quintus will live," he said, and poured wine for the young man. "Before the first spring day arrives you will take him home. Had you seen him but a few days ago you should have thought him dying, or dead. Be of good heart."

Marcus was so undone that he could only stammer, "I am grateful, I am grateful." He accepted the wine but before he drank he closed his eyes. Then he said, "I must be truthful. I fear for my brother, that Catilina is in this house."

Sulla laughed shortly. "That is absurd. Catilina saved his life. He is proud that Quintus will live. They are brothers-in-arms, and soldiers love each other. Moreover, I am here. I have promised my physician his freedom if Quintus lives, and a large competence. Do you think he will jeopardize them?"

Julius led Marcus into the atrium again. "The litter is waiting. Go, and give your noble mother the joyous news. I have much affection for her, for she was as a mother to me, herself, when I was a child. Convey to her my greetings."

Marcus glanced behind him, longingly, wanting to return to his brother. Then he saw, in the shadow of columns at the end of the atrium, the Lady Aurelia and Catilina. They did not see him or cared not that he saw them. They were embracing passionately, and Aurelia was murmuring and laughing, her lips against those of Lucius.

"A pretty picture," said Julius, idly. "Ah, how lovely is love."

When Marcus had gone, after Julius had embraced him again, Julius returned to Sulla and Pompey. "Did I not tell you, lord, how inflexible our Marcus is in rectitude?"

Sulla smiled darkly. "How is it possible that such a one can be your friend, Caesar? What magic do you possess? Ah, if only Rome held more of his kind!"

Pompey said, "I had held that Cicero in low esteem, for he is a civilian and a lawyer. Now I feel a kindness for him."

CHAPTER TWENTY-FIVE

Helvia listened to Marcus' story of his encounter with Sulla in silence and in attentiveness. Only the welling gray and olive lights in her large eyes and the convulsive clasping of her hands revealed her joy that her favorite son was safe and under Sulla's protection. She said, "I must go to Quintus tomorrow."

"I have so arranged it," said Marcus. "When he has recovered sufficiently we shall bring him home. Then we must all go to Arpinum. I am weary."

"Yes," she said. She put her hand on his arm. She continued: "I cannot hate that Sulla now. I am a mother, and I rejoice that Quintus is safe. Yet, you hate him still."

"I loathe what he represents," said Marcus.

"We must be grateful to Catilina also," said Helvia.

"He did only as a soldier must," said Marcus. "Do you think that I can forget Livia, his wife, and what he has done to her? Between us there is irrevocable enmity."

"What shall we tell your father?" asked Helvia.

Marcus considered, and he considered with cool bitterness. He shrank from the prospect of his father's lyric cries of joy, his emotionalism, his lavish gratitude to God and man, his sweeping aside of all prudence. He said to his mother, "We must be cautious, for my father is frail and happiness can sometimes be as dangerous as grief for such as he. Let us go to him and tell him that we have had a message from Quintus through a comrade-at-arms, and that Quintus is well and will be with us soon."

Helvia, understanding, smiled a little. "That is best," she said.

But still Tullius' joy was extravagant and childlike. His emaciated face was filled with light. He talked animatedly. God was good; man was good, even in these days. He embraced Marcus during one of his paeans of thanksgiving. "You will see, all will be well," he declared. "Rome is still Rome. Man is still good. But there has come a division between us lately, Marcus. Your face, though young, is often too sombre, your brow often too clouded. Do not expect too much of the world, my son," said the man who had always expected that the world would be better than it had the capacity to be, and was grieved when it had refuted him. "Why do we talk together no longer, Marcus?" he asked, piteously.

"I have the support of the family," said Marcus. "I am no longer a youth. I am a man and a lawyer. When I return to this house at night I am very tired." He watched Tullius for an expression of sympathy, but Tullius only nodded. Men of affairs were necessarily frequently tired.

The winter insensibly began to flow into early spring. Marcus sedulously practiced law. At times he was filled with despair and a sense of the ludicrous. He argued Constitutional law before magistrates while he well understood that the old Constitution had been abrogated and an iron one of mercilessness and militarism substituted. He invoked the honor of judges, when he was aware that honor was dead. Often he felt that he was a grotesque actor in a ridiculous comedy written by a madman. The judges, hypocrites all, would nod seriously, for they liked to believe that they were still men in a world that had become chaotic and filled with beasts. Sometimes Marcus could hardly refrain from bursting into wild laughter. Still, he thought, was it not better for a criminal and a liar to pretend to honor law and justice than to have him openly defy it and sneer at it?

One day Marcus received a letter from his old friend, Noë ben Joel. "Rejoice with me, that I now have a daughter, dearly beloved," wrote Noë. "An infant as sweet as Jasmine. My parents have decided not to return to Rome. But I shall be with you before the heat is on the city, and I am filled with delight." Noë's letters were always discreet, for instinctively he mistrusted other men with good reason. "We hear many rumors of Rome, and Sulla. But still, Rome can be no worse now than it ever was."

One day Marcus returned from the courts in particularly low spirits. A law clerk told him that a mysterious lady had come to Scaevola's house to see him. "She would not leave her name or a message," said the clerk, who was very young and delighted in mysteries. "She arrived in a curtained litter, and did not lift her hood, so I did not see her face. But her voice was not old. She murmured something about her will."

"She will return," said Marcus, wearily, and removed his cloak and contemplated his table heaped with briefs and books.

"I do not think so, Master," said the clerk. "When I told her you were not here she lifted her hands in resignation, and she departed like one who has been refused a last reprieve."

"You have too much imagination," said Marcus. "Ladies are frequently theatrical, particularly ladies who have wills in mind."

The clerk was stubborn. He had undertaken the study of law because he had believed it was inherently dramatic. He thought Marcus prosy. He said, "Still, the lady was young and even her cloak could not fully conceal the beauty of her body. Her hair under the hood must have been disordered, for one loose lock escaped the hood and flowed over her bosom. It had a glorious color, though it may have been dyed. Her cloak was of rich stuff, and her litter magnificent."

Marcus leaned against his table, and his heart jumped. He tried to control his awful excitement. He tried to tell himself that vivid color in any lady's hair was not unusual in Rome these days, when women experimented with curious hues on their locks. Even ladies of great family in Rome now dyed their hair golden, for all it was a sign of prostitution, and evoked shouts of "Yellow Hair!" But Marcus sat down suddenly and stared at his clerk.

"Not yellow hair, but hair like an autumn leaf?" he said.

"Yes, Master," said the clerk, happily. "And her voice was aristocratic and most sweet, though faint and slow."

Livia, thought Marcus. He fought against this incredible idea. Always, even when they had been very young in Arpinum, she had been aloof, strange, not to be reached by touch or voice, a nymph so elusive and enigmatic that she escaped from between one's urgent hands like a mist. There had been a few rumors, coming to Marcus' ears, over the years, that the wife of Catilina was mad, and certainly her manner in the temple, her exclamations, had been disordered and incoherent.

Marcus thought furiously, and with growing emotion. There were many rumors about Lucius Sergius Catilina now, the aristocrat, the consort of the vilest creatures of Rome: the undisciplined sons and grandsons of slaves and freedmen, actors, criminal gladiators, pugilists, wrestlers, thieves, owners of many prostitutes, moneylenders to whom he owed a fortune, dicers, malcontents, gamblers, proprietors of horses and racing chariots, and all the vast and murky underworld of Rome. Roman law stated that a man became the owner of his wife's fortune on marriage, and could dispose of it as he willed. But it also stated that in the event of a divorce the husband must return his wife's dowry.

Rumor said that Catilina had spent the last of his own fortune, and all of his wife's. If he divorced her he must return her dowry. But rumor had not said he was to divorce Livia, for all of his widely known infatuation for the dissolute woman with the wicked child's face, Aurelia Orestilla, "in whom no good man, at any time of her life commended anything but her beauty," as Sallust was to remark later. Even the benefits Catilina had derived from his apparent devotion to Sulla had been dissipated with gay abandon. He had the patrician's disdain for, or unawareness of, the rules of conduct of more plebeian men, which kept them in order. It was notorious that he and his friends, Cneius Piso and Q. Curius, lived a life in

Rome that made even the most indulgent frown. Curius, though loved by Sulla, had lost his hereditary seat in the Senate. Piso was a profligate gambler of many vices. Marcus thought of these sinister three, as he remembered them.

Aurelia Orestilla was a very rich woman, and she loved Catilina. She would marry him, if he divorced Livia. But he must return Livia's dowry. Why then did not Aurelia give Catilina the amount of the dowry, so he could be free? However, the rich, even when touched by the power of love, were prudent concerning their wealth. Too, it was possible that Aurelia did not know that Catilina had dispersed all his money. Wealthy ladies might dally in bed with paupers, but they rarely married them.

Marcus' thoughts rushed on. Livia's fortune had been spent by her husband. But in the event she divorced Catilina she would demand that her dowry be returned, which she could dispose of in her will. In that event Catilina's bankruptcy would be exposed, and Aurelia would be lost to him. Moreover, the law would be punitive. Sulla invariably proclaimed that he had restored the dignity of law in Rome. An exigent man, he would not protect Catilina, for all he was a soldier.

Marcus dismissed his clerk and became absorbed in his thoughts. If Livia divorced Catilina, or he her, then she would be free for another marriage. If he, Marcus, could just reach her! He would tell her that her dowry was of no consequence to him, that he would consider that Venus, herself, had stooped to honor him if Livia consented to be his wife. He would take her and her son to Arpinum, and they would live in peace and joy and ecstasy. He clenched his hands together in the excess of his rapturous thoughts. The spring day invaded his room like a glory, like a shouted promise of delight and hope. He thought of Livia in his arms, her lips against his. He would remove from Livia's memory all the horror of her marriage to Catilina, all her agony. He would hold the elusive nymph to his breast and know the sweetness of her kiss. He sprang to his feet, and looked about him wildly.

He had thought that he had put some restraint on his thoughts and his longings for Livia. Now he knew that the restraint had been false, that the fury of his love had only waited under his self-control for this moment. What had his life been, all these years, but a dullness and a monotony? He had not been alive at all. He had pursued duty, but duty was a grim and penurious mistress, with no flowers in her hands, no light in her hair, no song in her eyes. Men who espoused only duty became eunuchs. They begot no poetry, no grandeur, no splendid deeds. They lived in a gray cell, barred against the morning, and their fingers were smudged with dust.

Marcus walked rapidly up and down his room, stumbling against table and chair and bookcase. "Where have I been, all these years!" he cried aloud to the sun at his window. He was like one who had been sternly dead and had been recalled to the living.

Finally he composed himself a little and sat down, and rang the bell for the young clerk. The youth was intrigued at the sight of Marcus' face, so pale yet so tense. "Tell me again of that lady who came to see me," said Marcus. "Use no imagination. Tell me in simple words."

The clerk repeated what he had said. After he had dismissed the clerk again, Marcus considered. He was certain now that his visitor had been Livia. He must go to her at once! Then his natural prudence, though he now despised it, held him back. It was one thing to be certain in one's mind, and another thing to be certain objectively. Should he send a message to Livia? But if it had not been Livia his message would only heighten her lost confusion. Worse, the letter might fall into the hands of Catilina, himself. If Livia had indeed come to this office, then Catilina could very probably become dangerous.

"What shall I do then?" Marcus implored aloud. He had a premonition that time had become a desperately rushing emergency, like a river in full revolt. He dared not delay, yet he dared not make a move. Then he thought of Aurelia Caesar. She was his friend. Forgetting his lawyer's prudence he wrote a letter to her and called in a messenger.

He had painfully written in his letter: "I have reason to believe that Livia Catilina came to my office during my absence today. I was absent. Dear friend of my mother's, can you give me any enlightenment?" He knew it was an almost hysterical message, but he had no other recourse. He added, "I beg of you that you keep this letter in confidence. You are the friend of the Catilinii, and you would know of the affairs of the family."

Then he had to wait. The red sunset of spring came through his window, and there was no reply. The sunset darkened, and the roar of the city became closer, and there was no reply. At last, when he had given up hope the answer came, written affectionately by Aurelia Caesar. She expressed no wonder at Marcus' letter, for she was a woman who was matter-of-fact. Livia Catilina was not in Rome, and had not been in the city for some weeks. She and her son were visiting relatives near Naples. Aurelia added, "Livia has been strange for a long time, and it was thought by those who loved her that she should rest in the country."

The letter devastated Marcus. He was like the old leather of a wine bottle, which had been drained of its vital and sparkling substance. She had not been here at all. His new life went from him, and he gazed about him with dullness, loathing his existence, his dead hopes.

He could deceive himself no longer. Without Livia, he was nothing. His self-revelation shook him savagely. Was it possible that always, through these years, he had hoped that Livia had not moved away from him forever, that one day she would be attainable? He had thought he had been wounded, but that he could live with his wound as other men lived. But today he had been revealed to himself with starkness. The light, for a few hours, had been light indeed, and life had poured in upon him in ecstasy and fulfillment and brilliant color. How could he endure the rest of his life, colorless, pedestrian, filled only with the things he must do, the cautious words he must utter, the paths he must tread carefully to the grave, the lifeless books he must read, the flaccid cases he must present to judges?

He could afford a litter now with two slaves to carry it. He was borne to the house on the Carinae. He closed the curtains on the short journey. He did not want to see his city, and the multitudes of faces on the streets. He struggled with himself. I did not find my existence too intolerable until today. Surely I can resume it tomorrow. I must be a man.

Quintus was at home, an invalid still, but recovering rapidly. His vital force was returning in great spurts. As usual, he was surrounded, in his cubiculum, by friends, and they were dicing on his blankets. It was a tremendous mystery to Marcus, who had few friends if any, why Quintus had them, and why he rejoiced in their company and found them satisfying. To Marcus, they were strong and vigorous youths, but callow, and expectant of life as all the callow are. They filled the cubiculum, which was the largest in the house, like mighty bear cubs, shouting and laughing and cursing as they threw the dice, and stamping in feigned wrath and drinking wine. They thought Marcus a serious elderly man, though he was but four or five years their senior. He thought of them as one thinks of children. He wished to avoid them and their noise today. But dutiful as always, he paused in the doorway to greet Quintus, and was met, as always, with an invitation to drink a goblet of wine. And again as always, he smiled amiably and refused. Then he hesitated for a moment to gaze at Quintus, and he recalled that not once had Quintus, since his recovery, mentioned the name of Catilina to him.

Marcus' pain of spirit extended beyond himself. The screaming, crashing world: there must surely be an end to the inharmonious roar that proceeds from man! The tiger, the eagle, the river, the lion, the thunder: they were one in enchanted clamor of being. Only man was alone; only man was the discord, the lute out of tune, the torn drum, the broken trumpet. He was an exile on this earth, for only he was afflicted with thought, and thought could kill a man, destroy him. Only man knew true grief. For what had he been created?

The curtain of his cubiculum was drawn aside and Helvia stood there, her hands coarse and scored with her endless labor. She and Marcus looked at each other in silence. He could not speak. She nodded, as if in affirmation.

"Something evil has come to you, my son," she said. "But does it not, to all creatures? We must endure. That is our fate."

"I have lost patience," he replied.

Helvia shook her head. "You will regain it, Marcus." She went away, and he was left alone with his despair.

He looked at his table. He had begun a long series of essays for his publisher. He reached out and swept the scrolls from the table as if he could not bear the sight of them.

CHAPTER TWENTY-SIX

The lightless days went on, relentlessly. Then one morning a clerk came to Marcus and said, with excitement, "The noble Julius Caesar is here and wishes to speak with you, Master! And with him is the great patrician, Lucius Sergius Catilina!"

Marcus was seized with a powerful revulsion and sickness. He shook himself. He warned himself not to be ridiculous. Catilina, who had saved Quintus' life, had merely accompanied Julius out of idle friendship. But was it possible that Catilina had forgotten the old enmity, the old hatred? No, it was not possible. Marcus motioned to his clerk to admit his visitors, and stood up.

It was still early spring, but the sun was hot and the office was flooded with golden light and warmth. Julius entered, flamboyant as always, and full of smiles and affection. "Greetings, Marcus!" he cried, embracing his old friend. He was magnificently attired in white and purple; his laced shoes, purple too, were decorated with gold. His dancing black eyes beamed upon the lawyer. Then Marcus saw Catilina over Julius' shoulder.

Catilina was dressed as a captain, in full brilliant armor, with a helmet shining like the sun and embossed, and inlaid with colorful enamel. His short sword swung at his side. He was as beautiful and as stately as a god; he was a young Mars, but beardless. His extraordinary blue eyes were like glowing jewels. His limbs were clean and marvelously well-formed, like a statue's. His shoulders were broad, his neck faultless. He wore a short crimson cloak over his armor, and there were golden armlets on his arms and rings upon his fingers. He glittered. He exhaled an air of power and splendor and dissolute casualness. He merely stood in silence and studied Marcus. If he felt enmity or contempt he did not reveal it.

Marcus could say nothing at all. Then Catilina, who was subtle, smiled. With an expression of candor he held out his soldier's hand to the lawyer. Mechanically, Marcus stretched out his own hand. But in the second before encounter both hands paused in mid-air and did not touch. Both dropped their hands. The space between them was like an unsheathed sword, glimmering with menace.

"Greetings, Cicero," said Catilina in his musical voice. "How is our dear Quintus?"

"Well," said Marcus. His own voice sounded thin and distant in his ears.

"I must visit him," said Catilina with ease.

Marcus forced himself to speak louder. "I have never thanked you for saving his life, Lucius."

"We are soldiers," said the other. Catilina smiled again. "And, I love your brother. He is artless and of a single mind. He is a true soldier. General Sulla sends him his affection."

It was unendurable to Marcus to speak of his brother to Catilina. He turned to Julius, who had nonchalantly seated himself, and who, during this exchange between the two enemies, had been examining the briefs on the table with no apology and no attempt to hide his curiosity. "Dull," he said. "Here is a shopkeeper suing another man for thirty sesterces! Thirty sesterces! A vile little sum. But vile little lives are engaged with them."

"To a hard-working shopkeeper thirty sesterces are not vile," said Marcus. His cheeks felt hot and stiff. Julius sat back in his chair and beamed again on his friend. Then his face lost its smile and became grave.

"We are here on a matter of importance, Marcus," he said. "You are the tenth lawyer we have visited this morning. Gods! It is very hot today, and the stenches are richer than ever. And, we are weary." His black eyes suddenly were amused in spite of the severity of his face. "Will you not offer us wine to refresh ourselves?"

"You are in difficulties? I trust," said Marcus, striking the bell on his table.

"Always the jester," said Julius. "No, I am in no difficulties that should concern you or fill you with solicitude. But then, have we not always loved each other dearly?"

"Have we?" said Marcus. He kept his eyes from touching Catilina who still stood at a little distance. He said, "You have told me I am the tenth lawyer you have visited today. What? Do you find the others inadequate for your purposes?"

"They had no information for us," said Julius. Syrius entered silently with wine and goblets. He poured the wine and offered it first to Catilina, then to Julius, then to Marcus. The other two men drank deeply, but Marcus could not bring himself to drink with Catilina. He merely touched the rim of the goblet to his lips, then laid the vessel on the table. "What is the information you require, Julius?" he asked.

"The matter of a will. Or possibly of a will not made," said Julius. He glanced quickly at Catilina who was negligently sipping more wine and indicating, by his expression, that his opinion of it was not excessively appreciative.

But Marcus' heart had jumped violently. "Whose will?" he demanded.

"Your taste in wine has improved, dear friend," said Julius, refilling his goblet. He remembered, at last, to pour a little in libation. "To my patron, Jupiter," he said in a religious voice.

"Whose will?" cried Marcus. Catilina, like the leopard he resembled, moved closer. Again, Julius glanced at him, and now as if in warning.

"It is a sad story," said Julius. "I shall be brief. The will of Lucius' wife, Livia Curius Catilina."

Marcus sat down abruptly. Catilina's face became intent. Julius licked drops of wine from his lips, but his gaze tightened on Marcus.

"You know of such a will?" he asked in a gentle tone.

Marcus could not speak for a moment. He knew they were watching him like tigers. He knew they suspected something. He reached out a trembling hand for his goblet and he put it to his mouth and forced himself to swallow. He said at last, in the ominously sharp silence that filled the room, "I know of no such will."

But the two young men still gazed at him, Julius with renewed kindness, and Catilina like a soldier faced with a sudden enemy and prepared for attack.

"You were never a liar, alas," said Julius. "Therefore, I must believe you." He looked at Catilina, and again the warning lit his eyes. "Is it not incredible, Lucius, that there could be a lawyer who is not a liar and a thief? Behold our Marcus. He is probity, itself, and he would not lie to us."

"Why should I lie?" said Marcus. "If there had been a will I should have not said, 'I know of no such will.' I should have said, 'My clients' affairs are confidential and not to be discussed.'" He felt foolish and ridiculous, a countryman and awkward.

"So," said Julius, and lifted another brief carelessly and scanned it. He burst out laughing. "A lady wishes to divorce her husband because he has dallied with her sister! She is certainly of a small mind, and trivial. After all, it is a family affair!"

"Put down my briefs!" exclaimed Marcus, with sudden fury. Julius stared at him with affected surprise. "Accept my apologies, dear Marcus," he said. "I was always curious; it is an old vice of mine."

"Old vices frequently kill," said Marcus. Julius folded his arms and relaxed at ease, but his stare was hard on Marcus.

"Not one of the other lawyers, dear friend, had been visited by Livia. Were you?"

The question was sudden and fierce for all its quiet.

Marcus blurted before he could restrain himself, "How could it be possible for the Lady Livia to visit me, when she is not in Rome?" A second later he was aghast.

Again something flashed between Julius and Catilina. But it was Catilina who spoke softly. "Why should you think that? It is true that she was on one of the family farms for a time. But she returned. How did you know she had been absent?"

"Rumor," said Marcus.

Catilina arched his brows in innocent wonderment. "They speak of Livia?"

Marcus did not reply. Julius was regarding him closely, and with a faint and inscrutable smile.

"Why should Livia be of importance to you, that you should hear of her?" said Catilina. "Did you know her?"

Marcus wished to kill him, as he had wished before. But he said only, "I have seen her."

"And you have talked with her?" The patrician voice probed at him like a dagger seeking his vitals.

"When we were children," said Marcus. He clenched his fists on his knee. "She was visiting in Arpinum, and she came to my paternal island."

"The sweet memories of children," sighed Julius with a sentimental smirk. He saw Marcus' emotion, and he wished to spare him further pain. "Lucius, let us go. There are other lawyers to question."

"I believe," said Catilina in a cold and deadly voice, "that this lawyer with us now knows something we do not know. I desire him to tell us."

Marcus lifted his eyes to that beautiful face and his hatred and loathing were vivid upon it. "I have told you all I know. I have four cases before the magistrate within the hour. I must request that you leave me in peace."

But Catilina said relentlessly, "Did my wife visit you here?"

Marcus got to his feet and faced his enemy. "Had she done so I should not tell you."

"Then she visited you," said Catilina, and his hand stole involuntarily to his sword. "What did she say to you, Cicero?"

"Are you threatening me, you?" cried Marcus, shaking with rage. "Do you wish another engagement, Catilina? This time I shall not withhold my hand!"

Julius put his hand quickly and soothingly on Marcus' arm. "Do not be reckless, and foolish, dear friend. You must forgive Catilina's abruptness. He has suffered a great sorrow."

Marcus started violently. He looked from one man to the other. "Livia?" he whispered.

"Have you not heard?" asked Julius, and now there was genuine compassion in his tone for Marcus. "The unfortunate wife of Lucius has been mad for many years, perhaps even from birth. Did she not appear strange to you, even as a maiden?"

Marcus could hardly speak. "She is not mad. That is a lie. She was a lonely orphan, the child of young parents who had died tragically. She told me of it, when we were children together, on the two occasions I saw her at Arpinum. It is a lie," he repeated. "Livia is not mad."

Julius pursed his lips in an expression of sadness. "Doubtless she told you that when her young mother died her father killed himself on his wife's breast? Doubtless she also told you that one of her aunts also committed suicide, and her grandmother? Livia was mad. It is possible that her young son, and Lucius', had also inherited the taint."

"No," said Marcus. Then he became aware of a peculiar atmosphere in the office. It was as if something inimical had centered upon him.

"You are no physician," said Julius. "But Livia's own physicians have said that she was mad."

"I am a lawyer," said Marcus. He had a sudden thought. "I have known Livia. I saw her in Rome, on two occasions, both in a temple. My reputation for prudence is well known, and my considered opinion. If I were to swear that on my own knowledge Livia Curius Catilina is sane, then my word would be taken."

The quivering sense of danger increased about him. Catilina's face was malign. Marcus thought: I see it now. He intends to bring a divorce action against Livia so that he need not return her dowry. He thinks to succeed in that action; he has only to swear that he will keep his former wife in quiet seclusion, and it will be enough.

"You concern is commendable," said Julius, sighing. "Nevertheless, Livia had been under the care of family physicians for a long time, because of her aberrations. They will swear to her condition. In truth, they have already done so, before the praetor."

So, the action had already begun. Marcus' teeth shone in his bitter smile. "Who would take the word of slave physicians against mine, a citizen of Rome, a lawyer?"

"They were not slaves," said Julius. He put his hand behind him to hold off Catilina who had already half-drawn his sword. "Marcus, you are a man of prudence and sensibility and intelligence. Do not, I beg of you, embroil yourself in this."

"Why should he, except out of vulgar hatred of me?" said Catilina. "I saved the life of his brother. However, he is not grateful. He would destroy me for a whim, for he is but a plebeian and he is envious. What it is to be base!"

"Marcus is not base-born," said Julius, with reproof. "He is of the Helvii. His mother is the friend of my mother. Let us not exchange insults, Lucius." He regarded Marcus with pity. "As one who has loved you from childhood, dear friend, I advise you well. Do not engage in controversy out of vengefulness. It is beneath your dignity, and will bring you nothing but regret. It is too late for Livia. Two nights ago she poisoned her son, the son of Lucius, then attempted to poison herself also. Apparently the poison was too slow, and she feared she would live. So she stabbed herself, and she died."

Marcus listened. He felt nothing at all, except that a great silence and stillness surrounded him. It was as if he stood in a pool of icy water that extended all about him, and nothing moved. The water rose, numbing all his body. It reached his lips and froze them. It reached his eyes, and he was blinded. Then he heard a far and mournful drum beating in the air, in his ears, in his throat, in all the universe, and he did not know it was his own heart. Now he could see Livia again in the forest, seated beneath a tree; a scarlet leaf, like a stain of blood, lay on her bosom.

He could think again, and he thought, I can no longer live in a world that does not contain Livia. Then he had another thought: She is at peace, at last, that strange and sorrowful girl.

He found himself seated again. His head was bent on his chest. Julius was pressing a goblet of wine against his lips. He lifted a hand like iron and motioned it aside. He did not hear Catilina say with incredulous savagery, "Is it possible that this slave dared to touch Livia?"

"Quiet," said Julius. "I know Marcus well. If he loved Livia, it was as a distant nymph, not to be seized, not to be known. You know this is true, and it does you little credit to pretend to believe otherwise."

She is at peace, Marcus thought. The ice and grief were heavy within him, but there was also a great quietude which he did not know as yet was only despair.

Julius seated himself opposite Marcus and put his hand on the other's knee. He spoke gently. "Slaves have repeated that for several nights before Livia slew herself and her son she muttered ceaselessly. She spoke of lawyers, and her will. Then one day she disappeared from her house, and from under the very eye of her anxious guardians. She returned in a state of incoherent distress. She never spoke rationally again. Therefore, you understand, dear Marcus, it was necessary for Lucius to discover if she had indeed consulted a lawyer and had made a will. Who knows what sad absurdities she had written in it, what baseless accusations? What dishonor! It would be an embarrassment to Lucius, as her husband. She had no fortune to leave. She, like so many others of us, had been ruined by the wars. It is a measure of her madness that she did not know this."

Slowly, Marcus' head rose from his chest. But he looked only at Julius, and his eyes were stretched wide with horror. Julius patted his knee, sighed again, and appeared more sad.

"I see that you understand, Marcus," he said. "It is a frightful matter."

Marcus turned his monstrously heavy head to Catilina, and he spoke only to him.

"Yes, it is a frightful matter. Livia wished to divorce you. She planned to dispose of her dowry in the event of her death, after her divorce, for she knew that you would have to return her dowry. But, you had already dissipated her dowry. You had no money at all, except the gifts of Aurelia Orestilla. Livia's public action for a divorce would have revealed all this, to your dishonor and the punitive action of the law. And to the loss of Aurelia Orestilla, who is a rich woman.

"Therefore," said Marcus in a hoarse and laboring voice, "you had to prevent Livia's action for divorce, until you could bring your own action against her for madness. But Livia, you learned, had tried to consult lawyers. What was left to you? But murder?" His voice rose like a screaming eagle's. "You murdered her!"

Julius stood up as if shocked to the heart. "Marcus!" he exclaimed.

But Marcus pointed at the silent Catilina. "Look upon him! Guilt is red on his face, in his black heart! He killed his wife and his son for the sake of a woman who is wanton, and who is rich! The poison was sufficient for your son, was it not, Catilina? But it was not sufficient for Livia. You dared not let her speak in her agonies. So you plunged your dagger into her innocent heart, and then placed it, crimson with her blood, in her hand!" He stood up, still pointing at the soldier. "What did you do then, base and murderous Catilina? Did you flee silently to friends, who would establish that you had been in their presence while your wife and child were dying? Did you suborn those friends?" He swung to Julius. "Are you one of them, willing to swear that Catilina was with you when his wife and son were dying?"

"He was indeed in my house!" exclaimed Julius. "And so was General Sulla."

"Then he came to you, red-handed, after he murdered his wife and son!"

"Libel!" said Catilina. "I call you to witness, Julius, this utterance of vicious libel, this malevolent accusation, this vindictive lie of a man who has always hated me!"

"Let us be calm," said Julius. But his lively face had paled excessively. He looked for a long and considering moment at Catilina, and his mouth had an unreadable expression.

"Yes, let us be calm," said Marcus in a trembling voice. "Let us consider the case of a murderer who must be brought to justice. Livia is dead. But I shall be her advocate." He turned to Catilina. "Have you been turned to stone, murderer, by the Gorgon's head? Or were you born of death? Is there no quiver in you of guilt, of shame? No. You are not a man. You are a vulture, a jackal. I look upon your face and I know you, with all the instincts of my soul, and I recognize what you are. You speak of libel, Catilina. There is a redress for libel. Will you bring suit against me, Catilina? Will you dare let me speak before the magistrates of what I know? Or, will you arrange my 'suicide' also?"

Now he looked at Julius Caesar. "Is it possible that you are a murderer also, in your heart? Will you connive to hide a murder? I have loved you since you were a child, though I have not been deceived by you, Julius. I have thought that you loved me also. I beg of you that you stand with me and speak the truth."

Julius said, "Marcus, I swear to you that Lucius was with me, and General Sulla, and others, at my house when his wife was in her dying agonies, with her child beside her. I swear that a messenger came to us while we were dining, to deliver the message that Livia and Lucius' son had just expired, by poison and the dagger."

"And when," said Marcus, "had Catilina arrived at your house, Julius?"

Julius was silent. He looked at Catilina for a long moment. Then he said in a voice shaken and slow, "He had been with us for several hours."

"You lie, Julius!" Marcus cried.

But Julius said, looking into Marcus' eyes, "I am prepared to swear, and with honesty and honor, and others with me, that Catilina had been with us from the late afternoon."

"Then," said Marcus, "this has already been discussed among all of you, before you even came to me."

He lifted his arms with a slow motion of despair, and held them upright.

"Is there no God to avenge this crime, this murder of a young woman and her child?"

"He is mad, the dog," said Catilina. His handsome face was tense with evil and cold rage. "Let us seek a writ for him, that he be confined in the sanitarium on the Tiber, lest he do a mischief in his madness."

But Julius said to Marcus, who stood like an invoking statue of wrath, "You have uttered a calumny, dear friend, a libel against a gentleman of great family in Rome, against an officer and soldier of Rome, and you have uttered these things on no substantial evidence save your own emotions and your own grief for a girl known long ago, who did not remember you. It is one thing to be romantic and stricken with sorrow, and another to accuse where there is no evidence. I have known Livia for many years, and not in fleeting moments as you knew her. In her calmest moments she was not as other women. In her more excitable—and these I have seen also—she was irrational and distraught. It was not her marriage to Catilina which made her so, for I knew her from my childhood. It was a byword for us boys to say to our sisters, 'You are as mad as Livia Curius.'

"As for Catilina's attachment to Aurelia Orestilla, he has not sought to hide it. His marriage was a calamity to him. When he returned to Rome, eager for the arms of his wife, for the embraces of his son, he discovered that Livia did not even recognize him! She shrank from him as though from the jaws of Cerberus. Seeing this strange affright of his mother's, Catilina's son became wild also. It was a bitter welcome to a hero of Rome. He had hoped his wife had recovered."

"She had reason to be afraid," said Marcus, in a groaning voice and dropping his arms to his sides. "I saw her last in the temple of Vesta, during a thunderstorm. She told me of her terror, of her fear for her child, of the accusations against her of madness. I saw her agonized face, her dead and lightless eyes. She feared, above all things, the return of Catilina, and she feared in truth."

He looked into Julius' face. The younger man's black eyes were flickering in a most peculiar manner, and the black brows were drawn together.

"Julius," said Marcus, extending a hand to him, "in the name of honor, in the memory of our long friendship, stand with me to bring a murderer to justice."

Julius took his hand and held it strongly. "If murder had been done, I should stand with you, Marcus. But the murder of the child was done by his mother, and she in turn killed herself." A veil, like a cast, drew over his eyes. "I am convinced of that truth. And Catilina was with us when these sorrowful crimes were committed. Let the unhappy girl rest in peace, with the ashes of her fathers. To shout out intemperate accusations, which you in calmer moments would be the first to decry, will do Livia no service. We, the comrades of Catilina, have given out, this day—with the assent of the physicians—that Livia and her child perished inadvertently of tainted food. This was done to preserve her own honor. We told you the truth, trusting in your discretion. It is possible that it was an imprudent thing to trust you."

But Marcus said, "Who else perished of that food?"

All Julius' features narrowed and lengthened, and he was like one whom Marcus had never seen before. "Two slaves," he said.

"Four murders," said Marcus.

He turned to face Catilina, who was now leaning languidly against a wall and staring with indifference at the opposite wall. "Behold," said Marcus, "the grieving husband, the sorrowful father! Mark his tears, the lines of sadness on his face!"

Julius said, smoothly and coldly, "He is an aristocrat, Cicero. Would you have him rend his garments in public like an indecent pleb, a slave, a hysterical woman of the streets?"

But Marcus hardly heard him. His lawyer's mind, even over his anguish, was informing him that he was impotent, that he had no proof of any murders, that these men were stronger and mightier than he, that should he denounce Catilina he would put himself not only in danger of punitive laws but of Sulla's anger.

"Catilina is here with me today, searching for a ridiculous will which would sully the honor of his family, for the sake of Livia, herself, and his child. He had no other purpose."

Marcus once more gazed at Julius. "I knew you, Caesar, but never did even I, who was not deceived by you, dream that you would condone the murder of a helpless woman and a little child, who had done no wrong, who had lived their lives in fear. I have a Jewish friend, whom you know, Noë ben Joel, and he has told me of what is written in the Sacred Books of the Jews, and the wrath of God. 'He who lives by the sword shall die by the sword.'"

He glanced at Catilina again. "Long ago I had a premonition that Livia would die as she died, when we were young together on my paternal island. And now I say to you both: You will die as Livia died, in your own blood."

His white face blazed. Catilina lifted himself from his position against the wall. Julius stepped back rapidly from Marcus. As Romans, they were both superstitious. They were transfixed by Marcus' wide and eloquent eyes, by his attitude of an oracle.

Then both made the hasty sign of protection against the evil eye, and Marcus laughed aloud in his despair to see it. They fled from him and he was alone.

He sat down and leaned his elbows on his table and dropped his face into his hands, and he wept.

That night Marcus called his mother and his brother to him. He sat behind a table like a judge, and not as a son and a brother. He told them of Livia's death, and the death of her son, and he spoke quietly for all his face was haggard with suffering.

Then he raised his eyes to Quintus and said, "You are my brother, and I love you more than I love my life. You have not spoken Catilina's name to me, for you knew of my passion for Livia, and my hatred for Catilina. And now I tell you, Quintus, though you are dearer to me than even my parents, I can wish that you had died on the battlefield than to owe your life to such a man."

Later as he lay sleepless on his bed he remembered old Scaevola's wise words, counseling him that for such as Catilina death was not sufficient and was unavailing. There was only one just revenge on Catilina: the destruction of what he desired most.

And, I shall set myself to discover what it is, if it takes all the years of my life, Marcus vowed to himself, lifting his hand in a great oath.

CHAPTER TWENTY-SEVEN

The island lay like a crimson, gold, scarlet, green, and fiery ship on the sea of the warm blue autumn air; a glowing opal in hands of crystal. Peace enfolded it; only the sounds of distant cattle and sheep and goats, and the occasional bark of a dog, and the last wild cries of birds, and the plashing of radiant water, stirred the quietude. Serenely, across the bridge, Arpinum basked under the sun as it climbed the flank of the opposite mountain, its cherry roofs sparkling like broken rubies. The delicate wind fanned scents of late roses and honey and warm crisp leaves and ripe grasses and grain into the silence.

There is much to speak in praise of the country, thought Noë ben Joel as he stood blinking approvingly in the sweet sunshine, and as he listened to the tender music of the basking earth. Nevertheless, it is in a way disquieting. Man realizes his irrelevancy in this world, his brash intrusion, his noisy discord, the absurdity of his meditations and his questions—and the irrelevancy diminishes him and accords him discomfort. The earth is august. It is joyously one with God. It is like a temple at dawn, before man profanes it with his presence. I prefer the city where I can delude myself that I am important and am indeed Jehovah's crowning achievement, where what I say is accorded a measure of respect by my fellow parrots, and where the noise I make—no matter how ridiculous and inconsequential and blasphemous—is considered of worth simply because I am a man! Hallowed Lord, why did You afflict this, Your world, with so ugly a race, and why have You promised to save us and have vowed to give us a Son? It is possibly only a dream of arrogant man. Behold me, Lord, the least valuable of Your creatures, the least comely, the least harmless, the least significant, the least holy, and permit me to say with David: 'What is man that You are mindful of him, and the son of man, that You visit him?' We should spend our revolting lives with our faces in the dust, like the serpents we resemble. I can proffer Lucifer my sympathy, for we deserve his detestation. We are Your most inexplicable mystery, for we are but adulterers, liars, thieves.

In this subdued and uncomfortable state of mind Noë left the farmhouse and looked for company. Quintus, the true countryman, was with the shepherds in the meadows. Tullius was with his books in his cool dim library. Helvia was with her women; Noë could hear the murmur of female voices and the industrious humming of looms. Where was Marcus? No doubt in his mournful solitude near the river. Noë, attracted soothingly by the women's voices, went in search of Helvia, who was fond of him and who smiled at his very appearance and thought of him as a son.

Noë found Helvia and her women taking advantage of the glorious and shining weather in the outdoor portico, where they had set up their spinning wheels and their looms and their tables of cloth. Noë paused for a moment to survey the women with delight, their placidity, their calm faces, their brisk hands, their bare brown feet, their red-lipped smiles, their dark brows and unbound hair. Their gossip was as innocent as bird-song, and occasionally a girl would laugh gently. Once, thought Noë, all Roman women were so, virtuous and simple and kind. It is a measure of the decay of Rome that the majority of her women are now only shrill-voiced imitations of men, busy with banking houses and stock brokers; or wantons, or idle fools concerned only with their appearances, their perfumed hair, their excesses, their scented bodies, their robes, their adventures, their jewelry, their scandal, their noisiness and raucous laughter, their endless follies which are like a stinking corruption.

Helvia saw him. She lifted a hand in greeting from the distaff. Her maternal smile invited him, and he approached her and sat on a stool near her. The mellowness of her coloring had returned in this sublime peace and beneficent air. Her eyes were polished with health and vitality. Her tresses, though heavily streaked with gray now, tumbled riotously on her warm shoulders. Her firm mouth was like a pomegranate, and her tawny hands flew. Noë could not look away from her. The slave women became shy and silent in his presence.

A basket of apples and grapes stood on a table near Helvia. Noë thoughtfully chose an apple and sank his teeth into its luscious texture, and sweetness and crispness, and munched contentedly. The looms and the wheels were a drowsy music. The wind was intoxicating. Long sunny shadows lay on the thick green grass. Hurrying bees paused to loiter over the fruit. The walls of the farmhouse were white mirrors of brightness. Noë thought, as he contemplated the women: these are the women of the dead Republic.

Noë, suddenly gloomy, thought of Sulla and his gray dictatorship. It was, he decided, the prelude to tumult and tyranny. Why had Sulla delayed in declaring himself emperor? Dictators eventually made certain that they would continue, through their sons, through their brothers. Yet Sulla had established none of this. It was possible that some military virtue still living in him shrank from the final crime. But the culmination would not be delayed. There was, in man, a suicidal impulse that led inevitably to madness and death and fury when unrestrained by principle and rectitude. Sulla was apparently holding it back, as a charioteer holds back his plunging horses in the race. I do not despise Sulla, thought Noë. I pity him.

Helvia smiled at Noë inquiringly, as if she had heard his thoughts, and then she sighed.

Noë leaned toward her and bowed and touched the hem of her robe.

He said, " 'A good wife is more precious than rubies, and all the things you can desire are not to be compared with her. Length of days is in her right hand, and in her left hand riches and honor. Her ways are ways of pleasantness, and all her paths are peace. She is a tree of life to them that lay hold of her, and happy is everyone who retains her.' "

Helvia was not a woman of sentimentality; nevertheless, her eyes were suddenly full of tears. She said, "That is most beautiful, and you are a poet, Noë, and I thank you."

"Do not praise me," said Noë. "It was Solomon who spoke so of women, and I think it of you when I see you and remember you, Lady."

Helvia said, "Roman men do not think this of their women."

"Lady, Roman women have abdicated the throne of women, and that is a great sorrow for the world."

"Tell me of your wife, Noë."

Noë stared at the sky. "When Jewish men and women are married it is a holy thing in the sight of God, a sacrament. However, men frequently forget, and God is busy with an eternity of worlds. But Jewish women do not permit their husbands and their God to forget! They are very insistent upon their remembering."

Helvia laughed like a girl, and bit a woolen thread from the distaff. She regarded Noë merrily. "I take it that Leah reminds you," she said.

"Endlessly, Lady."

Noë sprawled his long length on the stool, yawned and stretched with content. His lean and slender face was golden from the sun; his light brown eyes shimmered; his wide mouth parted to show his fine teeth. His waving brown hair was ruffled by the wind, and his excellently shaped nose wrinkled as he inhaled the fine scents of wool and linen near him, and the fragrance of fruit and grass. His big ears appeared to have a life of their own. He wore a short tunic of yellow linen and a leather belt and sandals, as a concession to country life, and thought himself very rustic. However, to his attire, he had added golden armlets crusted with jewels and an Alexandrian dagger also gemmed.

Helvia's face slowly became grave. She hesitated. "Marcus does not speak to you as yet of serious matters, Noë?"

"No, Lady. His wounds still bleed sorely. He talks to me of trivial affairs and comments on the weather only. He is grateful, he says, that I came here. He sometimes smiles at my jests, and for that we should be thankful."

He smiled at Helvia like an older son speaking of a younger. "He should marry. I doubt if he will forget that unfortunate girl, who died so monstrously. If he had married her it would have been tragic, for she was very strange. I have heard she was like wine and fire, and as enigmatic as the shapes of clouds. This is excellent in a mistress, but disconcerting in a wife. Men are poets and speak of nymphs and myrtle and the quicksilver of moonlight. But when they marry they prefer bread and cheese, on their tables. Such will it be for Marcus."

"But, he will not forget her."

"No. He will not forget. He will make Catilina remember and that will be an awful day."

"He saw the girl but four times in his life. I do not understand men. How can Marcus have become so enamored in so short a time?"

"I have told you, Lady. Men are poets. That is why you find us so endearing."

Helvia laughed again, and the girls laughed with her.

"I have two sons of my body," she said. "Yet, when I married I acquired my first son—my husband."

Noë found Tullius somewhat tiresome, for all his goodness. He also found him ethereal. He had met many men in Jerusalem like Tullius, who sat in the gates and discussed God and philosophy endlessly while their wives struggled with households and kept the books and counted the silver and the bales of cloth and ordered the servants, and bore the children these delicate men absentmindedly begot in odd moments of the night. Noë thought of his mother, who so resembled Helvia, and he made a vow that never would he be a husband to Leah as his father was to his

mother, and Tullius was to his wife. He had bought a house in Rome, and
Leah was busily engaged in preparing it for her family. He would write
her a letter and tell her that he would soon return. There was much to be
said in favor of good bread and ripe cheese on a white wooden table. Contrary to the poets, they fed the soul too.

"You will be returning to Rome soon, Lady Helvia?" he asked.

"Yes. The days are drawing in; the nights are cold."

Noë stood up. "I shall try to persuade Marcus to return with me when
I go. Life is calling to him, though he refuses to face it as yet. What a name
he has acquired in Rome! There is none like him, but he does not know
it in his modesty." Noë paused. "I have not yet informed him. Lucius
Sergius Catilina has married Aurelia Orestilla, though the cypress tree still
stands at his door in mourning for Livia."

"What effrontery!" cried Helvia, aghast.

Noë shrugged. "To an aristocrat, none of his desires is effrontery. By
what measure, they ask, can lesser men judge them. Decencies and respect-
abilities are for dull creatures and the market place and the middle-class.
Let those like Catilina beware."

"Of what, Noë?"

"Of the wrath of God," said Noë. Seeing Helvia's sad and skeptical face,
he added, "That is the fate of man, and his ultimate despair, that God does
not forget."

Bowing to Helvia, he sauntered away, musing. He went down to the
river. He saw Quintus at a distance, riding a spirited horse, and he shuddered. He thought of Quintus with indulgence and fondness. However,
he preferred that a man did not sweat and did not smell of hay all the
time, or of oiled iron.

The river ran and sang in purple and silver and gold under the sun.
Noë found Marcus sitting on a bank looking at the water, his hands folded
on his bare knees. His profile was pale and still. Sorrow shadowed his face,
darkened his mouth, made his chin and brow resemble bare bone. But
when he saw Noë he smiled with pleasure. "Lazy one," he said. "You
keep the hours of the city in the country."

Noë sat on the grass beside him. "You rebuke me undeservedly. I have
had a long and fruitful talk with your mother, whose conversation is as
satisfying as an excellent meal. She reminds me of Leah."

"Whom you often forget exists," said Marcus.

"Who does not let me forget she exists," said Noë. "That is my only
objection to good women. They are always nearby. I prefer women who
are more elusive."

"But who do not have ready coffers," said Marcus.

"I am not a bankrupt, Marcus. My profits from my plays in Judea were satisfactory. The Greeks appreciate art. So do the younger Jews."

"I did not mean to offend you, dear Noë."

"Certainly you did!" Noë laughed. "When will your next book of essays be ready?"

Marcus moved restlessly, as if in sudden pain. "I do not know. I do not know if I shall ever write again. My publisher is impatient. I have discovered that publishers believe that writers and poets and essayists have no true existence apart from the business of publication. We are commodities, as are other goods to merchants."

"Without a publisher, Marcus, you could not afford this island, nor the other properties you have acquired."

"True," said Marcus. "But I should like my publisher to realize that I am of flesh and blood, and am not solely composed of paper and ink. Noë, I observed your good father's advice. I bought land and farms and a villa or two, which are now very valuable."

"Which you would not possess without a publisher."

Marcus smiled, and then chuckled. "You see how inconsistency plagues us all. Still, I have received many fine gifts from clients, and three magnificent legacies recently from grateful former clients."

Noë coughed. "I did not tell you. I have had tremendous good fortune! The great actor, Roscius, had assented to appear in my next play. He is a scoundrel and a cheat, a mountebank and a posturer, a man without morals —it was inevitable that the ladies of Rome should adore him. My contract with him, gravely and duly annotated by the praetor, calls for a sum so enormous that I hesitate to mention it to you. But Rome is even now excited over the next exhibition of his artistry, and I confess to you, though I should not to him, that he is in all ways an artist. I adore actors, though I deplore them. They are at once gods and children, and full of malice and envy. Ah, Roscius!"

Marcus was stirred from his apathy.

"Roscius!" he exclaimed. "He can command his own fee!"

"He did," said Noë, ruefully. "And I, needing him greedily, agreed. He is as penurious as a Spartan. His sartorial splendor is paid for by unaware husbands; his jewels are incredibly magnificent, and had their origin in the dowries of wives. One lady whom charity forbids me to name has just bought him a villa high on the Palatine, itself. He has a farm in Sicily, another near Athens, olive groves without count and citron groves to match, statues, Alexandrian vases, crystals beyond compare, stocks and bonds to make a banker lick his lips, carpets to shame the patricians, chariots to suit his mood and horses for the races, slaves by the platoons, and idolatrous women by the multitude. He also owns several theatres of his own. I have rented one from him, so you will understand my position."

"How can you afford such a prodigy?" asked Marcus with amusement.

"It is true that I cannot," said Noë. "What a face he has! He makes Apollo look like a cleaner of the Cloaca. He has but to stride along a street to have every vehicle stop instantly, a matter your dear friend, Julius Caesar, has not been able to accomplish in spite of his stringent traffic laws. By the way, it is possible that you do not know that our young Julius has forbidden the entry of all vehicular travel into the Forum and along the main streets during active business hours, and to give honor where honor is due this has been a law badly needed in Rome for a long time. But to return to Roscius. There is no actor, no athlete, no aristocrat in all Rome to compare with his appearance. I detest him. He has robbed me. As you know, Leah's fortune is carefully managed by her father's lawyers and bankers, and though she is generous to me—God preserve her—I find myself in a difficult position."

"In short," said Marcus, showing increasing interest, "you cannot meet the terms you legally swore to meet."

"How discerning you are, my dear Marcus!" cried Noë. Then his long face became dejected. "I must have an additional forty thousand sesterces before my play opens in Rome. For that ravisher's purse, and if I were not employing him I should heap on him some ancient curses I learned in Jerusalem."

"Forty thousand sesterces!" said Marcus, incredulously. "You are mad."

"Without the shadow of a doubt," Noë agreed. "Do you remember that I said 'additional?' "

Marcus stared at him. "You are to give him more, besides?"

"I have already given him twenty thousand."

Marcus' mouth opened. He began to shake his head slowly from side to side.

Noë became rhapsodic. He flung up his hands. "But I shall gain a profit of five times as much! I tell you, Marcus, I have written a stupendous play, and have engaged musicians who will cost a fortune in themselves. Roscius has already read it, or rather his scribe has read it to him for he disdains to read, he says. It is my belief that he is illiterate. He is as transported as I am over its grandeur. Ah, I have a copy with me for you to read here at your leisure." Noë beamed at his friend.

Marcus became apprehensive. He looked pointedly at Noë, Noë beamed with even more brightness at him. "It is in the Greek style, of course. A marvelous tragedy. But I will not spoil your pleasure by relating it to you now. I prefer that you read it."

Marcus seized his head in his hands and rocked it to and fro and groaned. "Never did I believe that a Ciceroni would be seduced into investing in a play!" he said. "In a vulgar theatre, for a vulgar mob."

"I have not asked you to invest in my play," said Noë. "I am offering you one-third of my interest in Roscius. Why do you call plays vulgar? Socrates, himself, and Plato, and Aristotle, regarded them as the highest art."

"They never knew Roscius," said Marcus, with a louder groan.

"You will admit that it is impossible to buy tickets for his performances. It is a magnificent event in Rome, or in Athens, or in Alexandria, when he appears. It is a holiday."

"How much?" asked Marcus in a stifled voice.

"Twenty thousand sesterces."

"Twenty thousand sesterces!"

"Not a fortune," said Noë. "It is only half of what I must pay that thief in the near future. For that modest sum you will own one-third of Roscius. Only to you, Marcus, would I make this offer. I have only to go to the bankers—"

"Well, why have you not before this?"

"I have already been to them," said Noë, with a sigh. "They agree that my play will stun Romans, that Roscius is beyond compare and will drive the city mad with love and rapture. But, you know bankers."

"I do. I respect their perspicacity. I know of Roscius' reputation. What is to prevent Roscius from declining to appear longer in the play than the first few performances?"

"I have a contract. Give me credit for intelligence, Marcus! If he fails even one performance he forfeits a certain sum. Each failure to appear forfeits him more, and he is as avaricious as an Athenian shopkeeper."

"And as mendacious," said Marcus.

"A lady he greatly admires now owns another third of him," said Noë, winking. "And her husband has a bad disposition, and her brother is one of Sulla's generals. Marcus, this is an opportunity which will never come to you again!"

"For which I devoutly thank the gods," said Marcus, sighing.

Noë ignored this. "You will not only receive the return of your money speedily, but you will then receive a certain amount—an astonishing amount—every week for so long as the play runs, and I expect it to be an astounding success. You will, after this fine fortune which is looming on your horizon now like a galleon loaded with gold, need to practice law only as a diversion."

"Sometimes I think I do," said Marcus. "Noë, did you come to visit me for the purpose of attaching yourself to my purse? Ah, I have hurt you, dear friend. I only jest. I will write you a draft on my bank tonight."

"What it is to have a soul enamored of the theatre!" said Noë, with a blissful moan. "What a moment for the writer of a play when his characters appear on the stage and declaim his lines! He is transported. He is like Zeus, himself. He is a creator. I should have been an actor; I love them all, and execrate them all."

He jumped to his feet and tore off his tunic. "Let us swim in that delightful water. I tell you, I am in a fever of joy. The sun is still hot; the river is filled with water nymphs, singing out their little sweet hearts."

"The river is treacherous," said Marcus. But Noë ran down the steep bank and with a cry flung himself into the waters and began to swim strongly. Marcus, remembering his dreadful experience, hesitated. Then he took off his tunic and more sedately joined his friend, and they frolicked together like young boys. But Marcus judiciously stayed close to the banks.

Eventually, they rose dripping and shining from the river, and lay down on the warm grass to dry themselves. Noë said critically, "Neither you nor I, Marcus, would ever be invited by a sculptor to pose for a statue of Hermes, nor even for a Senator. We have the bodies of scholars and are as wan as larvae, and our muscles are not notable. This would meet with the approval of the old men in Jerusalem, who despise beauty of body and prefer the beauty of soul, which is not discernible. I have told you that Jerusalem is a theocracy. Unfortunately, it is now no longer completely true, for the Pharisees, our lawyers and the guardians of our spiritual laws—and there are no others—are hair-splitters and grim as your Vulcan. Woe to our Messias, if and when He finally appears, if He deprecates one iota of the law as it is written!"

"Do you still expect Him?" asked Marcus in a dull and wondering tone.

"Hourly," said Noë, beginning to chew on a long stalk of grass.

"You believe He will be born?"

Noë considered. "I am no theologian. For myself, I can say neither yes nor no. I can only tell you what I have learned and what I have read in the Sacred Books. 'Who is she that looks forth as the bright morning, fair as the moon, clear as the sun, and terrible as an army with banners?'"

"Who is she?" asked Marcus, with returning interest.

"The Mother of the Messias. And so the holy men and the Pharisees seek her face everywhere, and they declare that they will know her by her beauty and her majesty, this Virgin of virgins, this young Queen chosen by God, Himself. They also declare that they will know her by her 'entourage' but that surely is symbolism, for Solomon was a poet and not a lawyer who concerned himself merely with dry statements. Why should her Son need armies and banners and trumpets and the thunder of drums?"

"How shall you know Him then?"

Noë reflected: "As I have told you before, from the prophecies, it is more likely that we shall not recognize Him at all. He will be known by an act of faith only."

" 'By an act of faith, only,' " Marcus repeated bitterly, and shrugged. "That is too much to ask, of mankind. We are exhorted, in our pain and despair, our loneliness, in our cloud of unanswered questions, in our sorrow, our bewilderment, and with our feet plunged deep in the clay of earth, to rise like a bird and arrow into a light as yet unseen, to fling ourselves on the winds of the firmament, and trust only. So the priests exhort us. But it is too stupendous an act for mere men."

"I understand that it has been done before," said Noë.

"To what avail? What voice replies to us from the tomb? What sign is there in the heavens signaling our vast leap into the silence? Aristotle trusted with explicit ecstasy. He has not returned to enlighten us. There is only a void."

Noë turned his head and discreetly examined his friend's weary face, and noted his exhaustion of spirit which had turned his cheeks ashen. Noë said gently, "If we knew all that was to be known, how could we bear this life of ours another day? We should fall on our own swords, panting to join the glory beyond our sight. Or, we should sit idly, waiting for our deliverance from life. Trust in God is surely not vain. I have seen the transfigured faces of the old men in Jerusalem, when they speak of Him, and they are men worn by living and full of sorrow. Too, there were our prophets. There was Moses, who gave us the Law. These were not foolish men, enchanted by their own invented dreams. They had been given revelations. Aristotle compared God with a perfect crystal, glowing with light, the Giver of life to which all life must return. Were all these deceived, mad, enamored of fantasies?"

"You speak eloquently, for a realist," said Marcus. "As for myself, I have come to the end of hope, as all men must come at last."

"There is no end to hope, for there is no end to God," said Noë, distressed at Marcus' words and what they implied.

"Then, you believe?" said Marcus with a faint smile of sadness.

Noë hesitated. Then he said resolutely, "I must believe, or I must die. I am not insensible to the world's agony. I cannot look upon it with complacence, though my father thinks me facile and without depth. I laugh so I may not weep. I trust, so I may endure. And," added Noë, marveling, "I did not know how much I believed until this very instant!"

He paused, then said, "If you wish, you may withdraw your promise to buy one-third of Roscius."

Marcus stared at him, then burst out laughing, the first laughter he had uttered for a long time. "Ah, virtue and honesty seize you, out of your faith! Noë, dear, beloved friend, I insist on my one-third purchase of that living divinity, Roscius! We shall be rich, if nothing else."

Helvia, still with her women, heard the young men's laughter as they approached the farmhouse, and she closed her eyes a moment to thank her patroness, Juno, for this mercy. Quintus, returned from the fields, stopped to listen with disbelief as he stood in his rough herdsman's tunic of gray cloth. His strong brown feet were dusty. His valiant spirit shone in his beautiful eyes; his arms were like bronze from the sun. He nodded happily and thought, My brother has returned to us. He smiled, pleased, at the red sunset.

Some peace had come to Marcus from the hours at the river with his friend. However, he knew that this was a different peace from any he had ever known before, and he also knew that never again would he know the rapture he had known, the joy, the sudden start of delight at the sound of a name, the passionate wonder at the world. All this had forever gone from him and it would never return. As Noë had said, he could endure. What more could be asked of a man?

Noë thought, as he lay in his country bed: The dead has risen, God be thanked. I thought him prepared to end his life when first I came, and there was a fatality in his eyes, a deathliness on his lips. He had abandoned living, and turned from existence. Now he has returned.

CHAPTER TWENTY-EIGHT

Noë ben Joel's play, *The Fire-Bearer,* was a magnificent success in Rome. This was, to a great extent, due to the vast popularity and adoration which Roscius enjoyed.* Women of all ages regarded him as their divine idol; homosexuals yearned after him without success. Husbands derided him and called him rude names. Fathers declared he was a corrupter of their daughters. Young men and youths imitated his delicate swagger, his poses, and abandoned the Roman way of cropping their hair very short and stiff on their skulls for Roscius' style of gleaming waves and ringlets on the nape of the neck. As Roscius favored soft purples and glowing yellows, every man his age, and younger, favored them also. He loved jew-

* Roscius' position at this time in Rome was similar to that enjoyed by a great actor, John Barrymore, in America. There is a statue in bronze of him in the Vatican Museum.

elry; therefore virile Romans wore Egyptian necklaces like his, and intricate armlets of spun gold and embroidered sandals and shoes. He was watched for every idiosyncrasy of manner, dress, or speech, by the public and by merchants and jewelers.

Lucius Sergius Catilina was noted for his Roman beauty, strong and manly. Roscius had a different beauty, graceful, lithe, and extremely refined. He was tall and slender, and his every movement was poetry. His hair was black and shining, his brows like painted silk. His eyes were an enchanting violet color between lashes as thick and long as a girl's. His features, in his smooth olive face, were clear and sardonic, his mouth like a plum when it is ripe. Women wrote poems to that mouth, and to his dimpled chin and exquisite ears. He had the supple dexterity of a dancer, the strength of a lion, the aspect of a Hermes about to take flight, and a smile so beguiling that even the surliest man was forced to respond to that glow of white teeth and full lip. He was, in addition, a man of natural wit and intelligence and irony, and an actor of immense powers. He had only to speak in his rich and rolling voice to command instant attention from the most reluctant.

Actors were not regarded with much esteem in Rome. Men of sports were lauded far more excessively. Displays of strength and power and crude force and blood-thirstiness were flattered and rewarded. A gladiator could ask his own price; a wrestler had statues cast in his honor. A boxer of stamina could be assured of as many mistresses as he lusted from among the great families of Rome, and all the gold he could desire. Actors were not so fortunate. Roscius was the exception. Roman men could deplore the fact that their ladies had become debased in worshiping an actor rather than a gladiator, wrestler, or boxer, but that did not disturb the ladies nor decrease the lavishness of their gifts to their idol. When Roscius declared he was a patron of the arts, the ladies, and young men, of Rome discovered much merit in Grecian artistry and Egyptian subtlety. If he bought a statuette from some unknown sculptor that sculptor became famous overnight and his wares bought up at once.*

Roscius was also sharp and penurious. Knowing the shortness and fickleness of public favor, he shrewdly invested his money in the best enterprises. Roscius never appeared, feeless, in honor of anyone, not even Sulla, and never graced a banquet without recompense in some form or another. Yet he was always the first to decry avarice and declare his love for the people.

* Roscius, famous Roman actor, can truly be called the father of the modern theatre. All Greek and Roman theatres were free to the public, tickets given in lotteries. But Roscius was the first to introduce privately owned small theatres for which admissions were charged. This resulted in better and more distinguished presentations for more discriminating audiences, besides the general non-paying public.

"Words cost nothing," he would say with cynicism. "Charitable deeds are expensive and despised." Therefore, he wisely kept all his works of generosity—and they were enormous—a secret to himself. He was considered a scandal, and he sedulously spread that lie, knowing that it made him irresistible to women and an object of envy to men.

The Fire-Bearer was based on the Promethean legend of the Titan who had stolen fire from the chariot of Apollo and had brought it down to earth for the use of men, and who therefore incurred the rage of the gods who wished man to be a mere creature and not like themselves. Prometheus' punishment was dire; ravens ate eternally of his liver, and it was eternally renewed. The aspirations and pain of man: the theme had excited Noë. He had decided that the Greek tragedies were too ponderous, the large, wailing choruses tiresome. Therefore his play became the concentrated tragedy of mankind, intense, central, and individualistic. Prometheus had seized the illumination and life of light and desired to place the gift in the hands of his dark-souled fellows, whom he had made. Then the play became symbolic. Maidens flitted about the stage in a frail and poignant dance like blind moths. But Prometheus placed lamps in their hands, and the maidens cried out in joy as the lamps glowed upon their faces, and their eyes opened, and they passed the lamps from hand to hand, and to dancing young men also, and it was like a chain of light. They relinquished the gift to others who ran upon the stage, and they then put on masks depicting decrepit and dying age, and sank into shadow and obscurity, signifying death, and out of those same shadows leaped youth, eager and calling and singing, to receive the gift in turn, to pass it on, and then to die.

And always in the background, the towering and vengeful and silent gods, surveying the creature who had become immortal, the frail and death-stricken animal who had attained a soul. But Athene said, "Man has become like unto us. Therefore, I will give him wisdom." Mars said, "He has become like unto us. Therefore, I will give him hate and war." Vulcan said, "He has become like unto us. Therefore, I will give him labor." Venus said, "He has become like unto us. Therefore, I will give him lust and love."

Apollo said, "He has become like unto us. Therefore, I will give him the glory of the arts and the knowledge of the body, and the power to create beauty from the dust."

But Prometheus said, as he writhed in his agony, "We have become greater than the gods, for we have acquired pain."

Roscius imparted grandeur and suffering and dignity to his role. Never had he been so acclaimed. He received the laurel crown. Some said that in his part as Prometheus, always on the stage and skillfully garbed and illuminated at night by cunningly placed lamps, he portrayed Sulla. Roscius refused to deny this, though he winked at his intimates. Artists were above politics, which was a low occupation. "Money," suggested Noë, "is an even more ignoble quality," but with this Roscius did not agree.

Within two weeks Marcus had been repaid some of his share of Roscius and was receiving a pleasant sum in addition. He decided to retain what he "owned" of Roscius, and as Noë's imagination was constantly expanding to produce new effects and new dancers, the play grew in power and beauty. Before the first snow fell Noë could say exultantly, "We are a success!" and he proceeded to write an even more ambitious play.

When the first snow fell Quintus, restored to full health, returned to the army.

Marcus' editor and publisher was one Atticus, a stout young man with jovial eyes and a solemn face and a round head. He affected togas even in the privacy of his family, and he was always scented with verbena, an astringent perfume which in some manner was meant to convey the loftiness of books. He invariably wore a harassed air, which was only partly hypocritical. He loved writers, for once he had aspired to be one, and he also detested them, which was eminently natural. In their turn his authors pretended that they considered him a thief and a man who had no reverence for the arts, and they respected his scholarship and his integrity. In short, Atticus and his authors were typical of themselves.

He thought that Marcus was wasting his time at law, for was he not a distinguished poet already acknowledged by the intelligent gentlemen of Rome, and was he not an essayist of formidable powers whom politicians regarded uneasily? Marcus should devote all his days to writing. "Excellent," Marcus would say, "but how, then, shall I live and support my family?" Atticus would wave all this away with a superb gesture. "When the gods endow, they should be obeyed." "Let the gods, therefore, pay my taxes," said Marcus. They usually parted with expressions of love and admiration, after some small prodding on the part of Atticus concerning another book, and some mention, on the part of Marcus, that he had not discovered his last volume of essays in certain bookshops.

Just before the Saturnalia Atticus was announced to Marcus as he labored over briefs in his office in the house of Scaevola. Marcus greeted him with pleasure. "Have you some royalties for me, dear friend?" he asked. "I have just received a very disagreeable notice about my taxes."

Then he saw that Atticus was distressed. Marcus helped him to remove his cloak, a cloak of deep blue wool lined with soft fur. He called for wine, then sat opposite his publisher and looked at him with fond intentness.

"You seem like a man in trouble, Atticus," he said. "Have you and the law collided?"

Atticus sighed. It was not the usual sigh of a persecuted publisher when confronted by an author. It was a sigh from the heart, and today the jovial eyes were not smiling. They were filled with pain. He did not speak at first. He drank Marcus' wine, and so disturbed was he that he refrained from remarking on its ordinary quality. He drained the cup immediately. Marcus refilled it.

"In a manner of speaking," said Atticus, absently playing with the long gold and jeweled chain that hung about his neck. "However, I am not in much danger."

"You have published a book which one of Sulla's grim censors have pronounced a danger to youth?" said Marcus, thinking of the lightlessness of the dictatorship.

"In a manner of speaking," said Atticus, sighing again. "But the book is not lewd, which would have been the lesser crime. It was merely honest."

"Therefore," said Marcus, "unpardonable."

"Unpardonable," assented Atticus. His eyes, light blue and protuberant, remained distant and wretched. "It was written by an old soldier, a captain under Sulla."

Marcus became interested at once, and sat up in his chair and smiled joyously. "Ah, Captain Cato Servius! The great blind soldier who lost his sight while fighting with Sulla, and also his left arm. I have read his book. An old Roman, an honorable man of many virtues, Servius. The book was unpolished in many places, and often rude in its expressions, but it was written with fire and passion in behalf of the Roman virtues and against oppressive and all-powerful government. It also demanded a return to national solvency and pride and industry and patriotism—old virtues all, but also vanished. I thought, when I read it, 'Rome is not yet dead when such a man can write and be published and his book can be bought in the bookshops.'"

Atticus gave Marcus a glance of weariness and irony. "That is what I thought also," he said.

"What!" cried Marcus. "Who has objected to it?"

"It is said, Sulla himself."

Marcus was incredulous. "Servius was one of Sulla's most beloved and decorated generals, Atticus! They were schoolmates together. Not once did he denounce Sulla in that book."

"Let me refresh your memory," said Atticus, who had brought a copy of the book with him. He turned a number of pages, then read aloud in slow and emphatic words. Marcus listened, nodding, his melancholy face slowly lighting with appreciation and approval. Atticus closed the book. "That enraged many about Sulla, Marcus."

"That is ridiculous," said Marcus. "We all know—"

"Who?" said Atticus. "Even those who probably know refuse to admit it."

"Sulla is not an ignorant man," said Marcus. "He knows."

"Sulla is not everywhere. He has his captains and his servants and his soldiers about him, and his vile politicians and Senators and bought tribunes. He must, of necessity, leave much in their cruel hands. It was into those hands that Servius' book has fallen." Atticus paused, looked at Marcus sadly. "Cato Servius is now in the Mamertine, charged with treason against the state, charged with subversion, charged with seeking the overthrow of lawful government, charged with insurrection and incitement to riot, charged with violent and extreme prejudice against the people of Rome, charged with contempt of society and authority, charged with incontinent madness, charged with disrespect of the Senate! and, of course, charged with malice against Sulla. These are but a few of the charges."

Atticus smiled drearily. "The Senate has been ordered to try his case, and not the magistrates. And the penalty asked is death. The prosecutors are two, Julius Caesar, your dear young friend, and Pompey, whom Sulla has named Magnus. They will speak for the government against Servius."

Marcus was silent. But his pale face paled even more with wrath and indignation. Then he said at last, "I still forget. I still thought, at moments, that Rome was a free nation, and that books are sacred."

Atticus nodded. "My dear Marcus, you will never forget how dangerous it is to speak the truth, how unpardonable. A liar leads a most comfortable life under any form of government, and dies peacefully in bed. The speaker of truth—"

A nameless sense of calamity and desolation came to Marcus, as if he had heard words of doom which pertained to himself.

"I have come to you," said Atticus, "to ask you to defend Servius. I am not a rich man; I am only a publisher," he added quickly.

"I?" said Marcus. He suddenly thought of his brother, who had returned to Sulla's service. He said, "Quintus, my brother, is commanding a legion in Gaul at the present time. The hand of tyrants is a long hand."

"I had forgotten your brother," said Atticus. He reached for his cloak. "I should have remembered. You dare not jeopardize him."

"Quintus is a soldier," said Marcus, drawing the cloak out of the publisher's reach. "He would have me do what I will. In all honor, as a citizen of Rome, as a lawyer, I can do no else. I will visit Servius in the Mamertine at once."

Atticus' eyes filled with tears. "You are a brave and resolute man, dear Marcus," he said.

"Not so brave, not so resolute," said Marcus. "I have, all my life, walked the prudent way, the way of lawyers. So, in many respects, I have betrayed my country, for he who does not speak out when honor and anger command is as guilty as any traitor. Cowardice is often the companion of lawyers." He repeated, "I will go to Servius at once."

"I do not know how they dared to denounce and imprison him," said Atticus, sorrowfully, "for he is greatly beloved of the people of Rome, and the foot soldiers whom he commanded, and the old soldiers who were his companions and who are veterans like himself of many combats in the name of their country. He is known for his gallantry and uprightness, for his bravery and steadfastness, for his courage, for all the things which make a noble soldier loved by his countrymen. He shared Sulla's exile. His fortune was confiscated under Cinna and Carbo, and his lands. His two sons died in the wars, under Sulla's command, and Sulla loved them also. Sulla restored the lands to Servius, and the fortune, in a speech before the Senate, itself, and embraced the old soldier publicly and kissed him on the cheek and called for all the honors Rome could bestow. Yet, they dared to imprison and denounce such a man—such a man!—for writing an honest book which exposed corruption and despotism in the government today."

"Not a light insult," said Marcus in a dry and bitter voice. "Atticus, I will do what I can. But when governments are determined to defame, disgrace, and murder a hero they do so with impunity in these days. For, we are now ruled by men and not by law."

"You do not think you can save Servius, then?"

"Have you not already implied that as an honest man he deserves death?"

To Marcus' relief, when they entered the cold dank prison, they discovered that Captain Servius had been lodged in a comfortable room, warmed by a small stove, a room reserved for respected public men who had annoyed the government. Moreover, the prison guards did not surround Servius. He was guarded by ten of his devoted legionnaires, who served him with ferocious tenderness. Marcus considered this a good augury. But after he looked at the soldiers' faces he understood that their country came first, even before their beloved captain. If he were convicted of treason they would doubtless weep, but they would sternly bow before what they considered the justice of Rome, which must not be questioned.

Cato Servius was a man about sixty. He was of a poor but patrician family, of the gens Cornelia. His wife had brought him land and a huge dowry, and a deep love. Now he was as poor again as he had been in his boyhood, and he had no wife, no love, no sons, no lands, no fortune. But he sat upright and with great dignity in his chair before the stove, in full uniform. The window of the plastered room was barred, and the iron door was barred. But a bearskin rug was on the stone floor, and the narrow cot was covered with neat warm blankets, and the table held a vessel of wine and two goblets and a basket of late fruit.

Servius turned his blind scarred face toward his visitors, who were silent with emotion, and he said in his short, irascible soldier's voice, "Who has entered?"

One of the soldiers saluted, forgetting that Servius could not see him, and replied respectfully, "Your publisher, Atticus, my captain, and one Marcus Tullius Cicero, a lawyer."

Servius grunted. He extended his right hand, all that remained to him, and said, "Greetings, Atticus. But I do not need a lawyer."

"Dear Cato, you do indeed need a lawyer," said Atticus, seating himself on the cot.

Servius shook his long white head. "Why should a soldier of Rome, a captain of Rome, a citizen of Rome, a man of a great name, who has done no wrong, need a lawyer? I have committed no crime. I laughed in the faces of those who read out a ridiculous list of offenses it is alleged I have committed against my country. Sulla, too, must be laughing now as he reads the letter I dictated to him this morning, and which was delivered by one of my men. In truth, I thought my release had come just now when you entered. Ah, Sulla is very busy these days. One understands that. But"— and the old soldier's voice raised itself to a deep shout of outrage—"when he knows that his captain, his dear friend, has been imprisoned he will have the heads of those responsible!" He paused, and again confronted Atticus with his brave blind face, full of hauteur and umbrage. "He inherited this disgusting government of thieves, betrayers, liars and murderers. I do not agree—and this I have written—with the manner of his efforts to restore the Republic, and I have feared his dictatorship and have execrated it, but I know in my heart that Sulla detests it as I do and with as much passion, and he will dispense with it very soon."

Atticus and Marcus exchanged glances.

The publisher said gently, "Cato, you do not believe all this. You will not let yourself realize that Sulla signed the order for your arrest, though I have seen that order myself, and have told you."

The old captain fell silent. His dark and eagle countenance tightened; his withered lips, so fearless and proud, suddenly quivered. The eyeless sockets appeared to fill with water in the light of the gloomy day. Then he began to beat his bony knees with his clenched fist. He muttered, "I cannot believe. I dare not believe."

"You must," said Atticus. "While you did not mention Sulla by name in your book, he understood whom you meant. This is a strange and degenerate Rome, ruled by rascals and exigent men, and men without honor. They dare not let you live."

"I do not wish to live in this Rome," said Servius in a changed voice. He shook his head over and over. "I do not wish to live in a Rome no longer free, no longer the home of honorable and courageous men, no longer the seat of justice and law and pride."

"You have forgotten," said Atticus. "You have two young grandsons, the bearers of your name. Their fathers died for Rome. Will you leave to your grandsons shame and dishonor, the disgrace of a noble name? Will you let them face a brutal world with the stigma of a grandfather's treason upon them, so that all doors will be barred to them forever, and their name anathema? They have no fortune now. They have no protector but you; they have no name but yours."

The eagle countenance became as gray and still as death, and as wizened.

"Your name," Atticus repeated. "That will live on, in infamy. Is that your legacy to your grandsons?"

Marcus spoke for the first time. "Lord, I am Cicero. But I am of the Helvii family, which you must know. A man does not live only for himself. He lives for his children and his children's children, and he lives in them. If you resign yourself to death without an effort to defend yourself, you disgrace your name, and you dishonor the memory of your sons and the existence of their sons."

One of the soldiers at the door looked at his captain in astonishment, as if realizing for the first time the enormity of this situation. Then he filled a goblet with wine and put it in the officer's veined and only hand. Cato lifted the goblet to his lips, then with a gesture of revulsion he put it down on the table.

He said in a low, stern voice, "You have said I do not believe my own words, Atticus. That is true. I have beguiled myself with falsehoods."

He put his hand over his eyes and groaned, "Oh, if only I had died before this day! If I had only died in battle!"

"Then," said Atticus, "you would not have written your book. Does it mean nothing to you? Would you wish it had never been written?"

Servius did not speak for several moments. It was as if he had not heard. Then he dropped his hand, and lifted his fine head and his lined cheeks flushed with blood.

"No! I wrote it for the sake of my grandsons! I wrote it in the hope that enough good men would read it and would restore Rome for those children! For, I cannot face the thought that they will not live in liberty, as Romans, when I am dead."

"Then," said Marcus, "let us fight for Rome."

"I have no eyes, and, therefore, I have no tears to shed for my country," said Servius. He paused. Then he said, "Marcus Tullius Cicero. The name rings in my ears."

"It was my grandfather's also, lord."

"I knew him well!" exclaimed Servius, and he stretched out his hand, and Marcus took it. "Tell me!" said Servius. "Can you restore my name, Cicero? My life is nothing to me, but my name is everything."

Marcus hesitated. "It is possible I cannot save your life, lord. But I will, with the help of my patroness, Pallas Athene, who wore the helmet, the shield and the sword also, clear your name in Rome so that it is no longer dishonored."

Servius nodded. Then his lips spread in a grim, military smile. "Your voice is like a trumpet, Cicero. It moves my heart. I have lost my eyes, but my ears serve me well. You will save my name, and that is all that matters."

The young soldiers at the door looked at each other, and their faces were harsh with sudden anger.

Seeing this, Marcus had a quick memory of the old augur, Scaevola. When he and Atticus were without the door of the prison room, he turned and looked slowly from one soldier's face to the other. He had to choose his words with delicacy. "General Sulla," he said with deliberation, "is a great soldier, and certainly he rescued us from Cinna and Carbo, for which may the gods preserve his life. My own brother, Quintus Tullius Cicero, is one of his captains, and my brother was like a son to Sulla.

"However," said Marcus, as the young men watched him with intent expressions, "Sulla is not omnipresent. He has, perforce, to delegate authority and responsibility. He has to trust many men about him, and woe to him who has to give this trust! He must rely upon their integrity concerning all they lay before him, and if they are men without integrity, such as politicians and the opportunistic, not only does he suffer but his country, and honest soldiers with him."

The soldiers listened to him in dark and scowling silence. After a few moments Marcus sighed. "Here is one who has given up his sons, his eyes, his left arm, to his beloved country. Here is one who commanded legions who loved him, and whom he regarded as his children. Here is one who never, by unmanliness or cowardice, disgraced Rome, whom we love. Yet, he lies in prison because of some unknown traitor's falsehood, envy, or hatred! To what have the Roman legions come when such a day arrives? We have been ruled by murderers—until the event of Sulla." (Here Marcus refused to meet Atticus' ironic eye.)

Portentously, then, he gazed deeply into each pair of young and violent eyes, and slowly walked away down the stone arches like a man who carries a terrible burden too heavy for his strength. Atticus followed him.

"It is fortunate," said Atticus, "that you did not remain long enough for those boys to ask you why you did not go at once to Sulla to tell him of the imprisonment of his beloved captain!"

"Tut," said Marcus. "A lawyer tries to avoid embarrassing questions. The military mind is single. Do I not have a captain for a brother? There are times when I bless such minds, for they are incapable of duplicity, and above all they love their brothers-in-arms and their country."

Atticus grasped his hand. "I cannot tell you of my gratitude, dear Marcus. Now he will fight as a soldier must. Do you think you can save him?"

"I doubt that they will dare to let him live, for such a hero cannot be silenced. But I hope to have his lands and fortune restored, and the honor of his name, for his grandsons."

Marcus returned to his office and sat, frowning in thought. Then he wrote to Julius Caesar, whom he had not seen for many months:

"Greetings to the noble Julius Caesar from his friend, Marcus Tullius Cicero:

"I have, today, undertaken the defense against the State of one Captain Cato Servius, whose soldiers love him, and whose name is revered among the military, and who was brother-in-arms to General Sulla, and whose inconvenient death, or convenient, if you will, in the Mamertine, would cause the military much grief and set many indignant rumors afloat among soldiers."

Marcus smiled darkly as he appended his love and compliments to Julius' mother, Aurelia, and mentioned the amulet she had given him which he wore always. Then Marcus wrote a letter to Noë ben Joel, and sent him his copy of Servius' book, which he implored Noë to read at once.

Upon reading the book, Noë thought for a long time. Then he went to Roscius' villa, where he found his actor basking in the company of many admiring young ladies, and eating sweetmeats. "Hah," said Noë, "have we not agreed, my charmer, that the sweetmeats are deleterious to one's appearance? Have we not agreed to abandon them?"

"Have some," said Roscius, pushing the silver bowl toward Noë. "You, not I, gave up sweetmeats. What do you want? Are you going to ask me to reduce the price of the rent on my theatre? No."

Noë ate a sweetmeat, then another, then another. He smiled at the handsome Roman young ladies, and openly admired them. He said, "I have a matter to discuss with you."

"That means money," said Roscius, his violet eyes narrowing. "Again, no."

"Not money," said Noë. "Honor. Glory."

"Doubtless," said Roscius, with no belief at all. He looked at the girls. "Run away home, my pets. I have affairs to discuss with this thief." He accompanied the ladies to their litters, swaggering and displaying all his beauty lavishly. He returned to Noë in the hall, and rubbed his hands over the warm stove, and again narrowed his eyes.

"You are up to tricks, you wily Jew," he said.

"As you are a Jew, yourself, I accept that as a compliment," said Noë.

"Then I withdraw it. What is it that is up your sleeve?"

"An opportunity that rarely comes to an actor in Rome. Were we in Greece the whole land would be at your feet, for Greeks appreciate artists. But actors are not held in the utmost esteem in this rude Rome, for Romans are intrinsically vulgar. We are both citizens of Rome but being honest men we know her faults. What is dearest to an artist's heart, such as yours? Money, no."

"Money, yes," said Roscius, becoming more and more suspicious as Noë became more enthusiastic.

Noë waved this away. "You jest, certainly," he said. "Would you refrain from acting if you received no money for it?"

Roscius chewed a stuffed fig, swallowed it, sucked its seeds from his teeth. He said, "Yes."

"I do not believe you!" cried Noë, holding up his hands in horror.

"You are wasting my time. Tell me of your scheme, which I will immediately reject as too expensive—for me."

"I am offering you glory and honor, dear Roscius. That is all I am offering."

"I can believe that," said Roscius.

"A mere mention that you will appear in a certain spot at a certain hour draws all Rome to that spot like flies are drawn to honey," said Noë. "Men and youths rise up from the very stones of the street, as well as matrons and maidens."

"Granted," said Roscius. "What spectacle, in which you are invested, demands my appearance? It will cost you money."

Noë sighed. "Let me continue. As I have said, artists have little true glory and honor in Rome. They are not considered the equal of base gladiators who sweat and grunt and bleed like stuck pigs in the arena. They are less than an absurd discus thrower. Who wants to throw discuses? But that is Rome for you! However, when an actor becomes a hero, even Romans bow before him."

"That sounds very dangerous to me," said Roscius. "Are you plotting my death?"

"I have considered it several times," Noë admitted. "But I have too much invested in you. There is also my dear friend, Cicero, who owns part of you."

Roscius wrinkled his silky black brows. "You put it crudely. Would you dare, in your beloved Jerusalem, to say to another Jew: 'Such and such a man owns a certain part of you?' That is against the Law—"

"I know all about the Law, which I doubt you do," interrupted Noë. "Let me continue. I have decided to present you with an opportunity to be a Hero, in Rome, as well as a beloved actor, and Romans love heroes, and they place their names in history. Think of it, Roscius!"

"I will not perish of grief if that does not happen," said the actor.

"They will cast statues in bronze of you, in your role as Prometheus. They will hail you as a hero on the very streets! You will be greater than Sulla."

"You are mad," said Roscius. But he listened with an actor's profound attention while Noë spoke at length. He took Servius' book in silence into his hands, and scanned a page or two, which surprised Noë who had believed him illiterate, an unusual state for a Jew.

Then, stirred and moved, his actor's soul afire, he began to pace up and down the hall, and he was so enchanting in appearance that as Noë watched him he almost forgot why he was here. Then he stopped before Noë and glared at him.

"Sulla will, without doubt, have me murdered," he said.

"Even Sulla would not dare to do that to the darling of Rome."

"It is too dangerous."

"Heroism is not bought with safety," said Noë.

"I have not implied for a single moment that I yearn to be a hero. I prefer to continue to live."

"I guarantee that you will live," said Noë.

"Oh, and you swear it by your father's head, do you?"

Noë paused. Then he said resolutely, "Yes. Can I say more?"

"You have already said too much," the actor said. "Does Cicero know of this fine theatrical idea of yours?"

"No. I was inspired by it myself."

In the end, however, Roscius agreed. It was an opportunity an actor's soul could not reject. And, as Roscius did not suggest a small token, such as a valuable jewel, in appreciation, Noë left him with a high heart.

Marcus, while this was taking place, was also writing a letter to his old friend and tutor, Archias, who had lately retired to a small villa just outside the gates of Rome, where he cultivated a grove of olive trees and kept a few sheep, and a large garden.

When the letter had been sent off with a messenger, Marcus began to outline his case. An hour before the wintry sunset Julius Caesar arrived, splendid and genial, and full of affection, and clad as a general in full uniform.

"Dear Marcus!" exclaimed Julius, as though they had parted those months ago in utmost felicity. "I have neglected you! Forgive me. You are looking in good health."

"I have learned to endure," said Marcus.

Julius smote him heartily on the shoulder and laughed aloud. "Those are the words of an old man, dear friend. The young celebrate life; only the aged endure."

"I have given up celebrating in Rome," said Marcus. "I take it you have received my letter and have come here to discuss it with me."

"For your beloved sake," said Julius, removing his crimson cloak and sitting down.

"For which you are greatly concerned."

He was startled when Julius' smile faded and the lively black eyes fixed themselves on him with genuine gravity. "Yes," said Julius. "I do not wish you dead, or evil to occur to you, for all you prophesied evil for me."

"There is someone who intends to murder me, then?"

"In these days, Carissime, many men wish many men dead."

"Elliptical, as always," said Marcus. "I shall not die until the gods decree it, so spare your anxiety."

"These are dangerous days," Julius said.

"And who has made these dangerous? Answer me, Julius. Who has made free Romans, proud of their freedom, proud of their invincible law, proud of Rome justice, afraid for their lives?"

Julius shrugged. "I did not make these days. Your mild eyes have a way of lighting up like a bonfire, and it is disconcerting to those who love you."

"Such as yourself."

"Such as myself."

Marcus called for wine, and the two men drank in silence. Then Julius said, "I must send you some from my own cellars. It is not that you are poor. You are now comparatively rich, and prosperous, in spite of the taxes you deplore."

"I save my money. Why did you come, Julius? It was not solely concern for me."

Julius refilled his goblet, drank, made a grimace. He looked at Marcus. "I have discussed your letter with Sulla."

"Naturally. I expected that."

"Sulla, though a military man, wishes peace for Rome. She has been torn too long. And we have still rebellious allies, satellites, and enemies. It is necessary that we present to our fellow Romans, and to those abroad, an image of inflexible power and potency. You are endangering that. You are endangering your country."

Marcus was not alarmed. "It is not I who am endangering my country. The fault lies elsewhere. And of what interest is it to me, as a Roman, what foreigners think of Rome? How long have we been considering their good opinion, which can move wantonly at any change of the wind?"

"You do not understand. I can only say that your defense of Servius will militate against the peace and tranquillity of Rome."

Marcus raised his eyebrows. "How?"

"You know the populace?"

"But of what concern is my defense of Servius to the Roman mobs?"

"He is also a soldier."

"Which Sulla has forgotten. He is also blind, and was crippled in defense of his country."

"You are deliberately obtuse. Let us consider Servius. He is quite mad. One does not deplore patriotism. But these old soldiers, who have been deranged by battle and suffering, are often excessive, and their speech is wild. They rant. They cry despair; they cry ruin. They are extreme in their emotions. But the mob, easily inflamed, does not comprehend."

"In honest words, you do not wish the mob to hear him speak and defend his country and ask that she return to dignity, and valor, and lawful integrity. You do not wish that the people hear his passionate exhortations. You are afraid of them."

Julius was silent. His black eyes sparkled inimically.

"There are also his fellow soldiers, his legions, his officers. You do not desire that they hear Servius. The military is restive these days under Sulla, who has betrayed them."

"That is treason."

"If it is treason, condemn me, punish me."

Julius' mouth twisted. He thought, he is necessary to me. In many ways I love and admire this brave man.

"Is it treason for a man who loves his country to try to defend it in the person of Servius?" asked Marcus.

"You speak as if Rome were a mere weak province, a vulnerable nation, Marcus. She is not."

"Then let her not be afraid of the truth, and Servius."

Julius shook his head sadly. Then he said, "Marcus, we are willing to make extraordinary concessions. The whole city knows of Servius. There are already grumblings. We will return to him his full military honors, his fortune, his lands, and let him go quietly in peace."

"With his name tarnished, and the name of his grandsons."

"We shall give it out that Sulla out of his old love and his sorrow, has forgiven Servius, and will accord him mercy."

"And the people will then acclaim Sulla for his majestic compassion, though he was cruelly offended, and Servius' name will be dishonored forever."

"What is a name?" asked Julius.

Marcus flamed into cold anger. "To you, Julius, it is nothing. To Servius it is the whole world. He welcomes the opportunity to defend himself, and Rome, before the Senate."

"Does he not want, in his age, to be at peace?"

"An old soldier, torn indignantly to his heart, does not care for peace. He cares for honor, a word you do not know."

"I am a sensible and pragmatic man. I move with the times. But you have thrust your feet in the dark mud of the past, and will not move."

"The past," said Marcus, "is also the present and the future. The nation that forgets that is doomed."

Julius did not reply. Marcus gazed at him piercingly. "Sulla is afraid of Servius!"

Julius was still silent. "I have friends also, honorable, upright men. If I am murdered, then they will not keep silent. I have informed them all of Servius."

"You threaten Sulla?"

"I threaten all tyrants."

Julius stood up. He said, "We are prepared to offer you a magnificent sum, not for the betrayal of your client, but for your withdrawal. And we promise to free Servius, as I have said, let him go in peace with his restored fortune and lands."

"I do not want Sulla's money. Let him restore Servius' name, and I will withdraw."

"That is impossible."

Julius turned to the door. "I knew you would be obdurate, for you are an obstinate man. I told Sulla so. So, I bear his invitation that you dine with him tonight so he may lay his own case before you."

"If I refuse?"

"I should not recommend that," said Julius in a soft and menacing voice. "May I recall something to you? You owe your brother's life to Sulla, who cared for him tenderly as a son. Would it not be dishonorable to be ungrateful?"

Marcus' face changed. "How subtle you are, Julius. And"—and Marcus' voice faltered—"if Quintus is made to suffer from my decision I will broadcast the news to the people. He would prefer to die in honor than in dishonor."

"Honor!" cried Julius, struck at last. "It means different things to different men! What a fool you are, Marcus! Honor is the last refuge of the impotent."

He strode to the door, then stood there, cold and implacable. "It is sunset. I order you to accompany me to Sulla's house."

CHAPTER TWENTY-NINE

They went to Sulla's house, Marcus in his own litter, and Julius on a huge black horse and accompanied by three young officers, also on horseback. The last crimson stain of the sun outlined the crowded hills, ran like sanguine water over the roofs of the buildings. The air was crisp and sharp and cold, and Marcus kept the curtains of his litter closed. The horsemen clattered about him; he could hear the roar of the multitude in the streets, the rumble of cars and wagons and chariots, the shrill bursts of laughter, the even more shrill invectives.

Archias had told him that he was, by nature, a politician. At first Marcus had laughed; he despised politics and politicians. But now it came to him that law was not enough, even the grandeur of Roman law.

Sulla's large and beautiful house was warm and lamplit, tinkling with fountains and sweetly perfumed. There was a scent of fern in the air, and freshness. The polished columns glimmered. Marcus' feet sank into thick and brilliant rugs. He was met in the atrium by Sulla, himself, politely cordial. He said, "Greetings, Cicero. I am pleased that you condescended to dine with me."

He even smiled as he lightly embraced the younger man. "We are few," he said. "We are only myself, Julius, Pompey, Crassus, Piso, and Curius. I prefer small dinners. Yes, there are ladies, also, some pleasant young actresses and singers and dancers, who have consented to be amongst us."

"I am not arrayed becomingly," said Marcus, "for I was pressed to come in only my woolen tunic, as you see."

"Oh, we are very informal tonight," said Sulla, who wore his favorite purple robe of wool, bordered with gold. He was as lean as Marcus remembered, and as brown, and his pale eyes were still terrible. Like a fond father, he led Marcus and Julius into the long dining hall. There a table had been spread with Oriental lace and adorned with bronze Alexandrian lamps whose perfumed oil emitted luxurious scents. Fine paintings on wood, and frescoes in mosaic, covered the marble walls. Silk and woolen draperies hid the windows and concentrated the warmth within. The other guests were waiting, Marcus' old enemies, Piso of the fair face, malicious smile and golden head, the surly Curius, and Pompey prematurely named the Great by Sulla, his broad face impassive but friendly, and Crassus with his brown hair arranged in petals over his forehead. They were already reclining on soft divans about the table and drinking wine from beautiful Grecian goblets of gold and silver and sampling the gilded dishes of anchovies, pickled fish, olives, little hot pastries filled with meat and cheese, vinegared veal-heads, sausages in pungent sauce, and little British oysters floating in olive oil and spices. Between each divan was a chair, and each chair was occupied by a pretty girl in a brightly colored long robe, her arms and neck bare, her hair fantastically arranged.

Marcus deprecated the new fashion of reclining at meals, for he was an old Roman. He sat between Pompey and Julius. Sulla preferred a throne-like chair of gilded wood and ivory and ebony, cushioned in scarlet silk with gold tassels. He sat at the head of the table, in his unconscious military posture of straight shoulders and high head. Marcus dubiously sampled the delicacies on the table, decided they were intriguing, ate more, and drank a fine sweetened wine. Three female slaves with zithers and lutes, sitting on the floor in a corner began to play sentimental songs very softly, and one of them sang in a pleasant and mournful young voice.

The young men and the girls about Marcus chattered with vivacity. Piso and Curius ignored Marcus, and when they addressed Julius or Crassus they looked over or around Marcus as if he were an insensate object. His pale and slender cheeks began to burn angrily at this discourtesy. In his turn he would wait to catch the eye of one of his enemies and then would look coldly and contemptuously in it, and shrug lightly. He was pleased to observe that this had a vexatious effect on the young aristocrats, whose eyes, despite their smiles, began to flash. In the meantime, conversation about the table was easy and gay, and the girls chattered, squealed in laughter, and steadily drank wine and licked their fingers with a delicate air.

Marcus had not known that Sulla had a passion for wanton actresses and singers and gayly lewd conversation. But Sulla was enjoying himself. He played with the cheeks, the hands, and the hair of the girls who sat on each side of him. They flattered him; they laid their pretty heads on his shoulder; they teased him; they bridled happily at his touches which were becoming less and less restrained as time passed. They laughed aloud when he bent his noble Roman head and kissed their necks and dimpled white shoulders.

No one spoke to Marcus. He waited until the dishes were removed to make way for the dinner, and then he said in a quieter moment, "I see that our dear friend, Catilina, is not here tonight."

Pompey and Julius exchanged glances. Piso laughed maliciously; Curius scowled at Marcus' effrontery in daring to speak the name of a great patrician. Sulla's light eyes filled with amusement. He said, "No, he is enjoying the embraces of his bride tonight."

"I thought," said Marcus, "that he was mourning the murder of his wife."

"Murder?" said Sulla.

"Does anyone dispute it?" asked Marcus.

"Dear friend," said Julius, "you know this is libel, and we have witnesses."

"Let Catilina sue me then," said Marcus. "I have been investigating." All eyes were on him silently now. He shrugged. "Is the cypress still standing at his door for Livia?"

No one answered him. Marcus wiped his hands elaborately on a linen napkin extended to him by a slave. He took his time. "Murder, in Rome, was once considered barbarian. Murder, in Rome, was once punished by death. But these are new days. Murder of one's wife, even if done crudely as Livia's murder was accomplished, apparently results in high honors, a rich second wife, and favor."

"You are deliberately obnoxious," said Julius, with a faint smile. "Proceed. You have our ears."

"I am a lawyer," said Marcus. "I do not bestow information without a fee."

He looked fully at Piso and Curius. "If there is anyone who desires to dispute with me with his sword, I shall be glad to arrange a time and place."

Julius laughed loudly, and struck Marcus on his arm. "What a jester is this!" he exclaimed.

"I thought we should have an amiable dinner," said Sulla. "It seems we have a bull with us tonight, roaring through red nostrils."

"He is the soul of elegance," said Julius, nudging Marcus sharply in the ribs with his elbow. "My general, your wine must be potent."

"Not as potent as my outrage," said Marcus.

Slaves brought in the next courses, which consisted of a suckling pig, roasted, on a huge silver platter, broiled fishes, various vegetables and sauces, and small white breads rolled in linen cloth to retain their heat. More wine was poured. The musicians sang a livelier song.

"Let us discuss pleasanter matters," said Sulla.

"I am a man who toils," said Marcus. "I do not keep late hours in the modern fashion. I am here for a purpose, and that I know, lord. And the purpose, I assume, is my defense of Cato Servius the next week, before the Senate."

Sulla raised his black eyebrows. He was no longer smiling. "I have a high regard for you, Cicero. It is not well for lawyers to make enemies. They are usually men of great discretion and prudence. It is not their fashion to indulge in extravagances, to make a public spectacle of their cases. Julius has already told you of our offer concerning Servius. Why are you stubborn?"

"You wish to disgrace his name, so that no man of valor and courage who cries out in behalf of his country will henceforth raise his voice, for such a man regards his name as sacred."

Sulla spoke kindly. "He is not young, and he is sick, and has not long to live." He lifted his hand. "You will speak of the dishonor with which his grandsons will have to live. Public dishonor, my dear young friend, is not the stigma it was once in Rome. Men in these days have short memories; they regard honor as old-fashioned and tedious. The grandsons will not suffer."

"Servius will not forget, nor will his grandsons, reared to revere their honor more than their lives. I shall protect him from that suffering."

"You will not succeed," said Sulla.

"I shall try, with all my soul and all the law I know."

Julius clapped with light derision and Piso and Curius laughed aloud.

"Heroic words!" said Julius. "Worthy of a Ciceroni."

"Worthy of a Chick-pea," said Curius in a hoarse voice.

"Worthy of a Roman," said Marcus, "but then, who is here who understands what that means?"

"I," said Sulla, in a quiet voice, and the small uproar in the room subsided abruptly.

Marcus looked at him, startled. "Then you know, lord, that I must do as I must do. For the sake of Servius; for the sake of the dead soul of Rome."

Sulla flung his knife and spoon from his hands with controlled violence. His dark face became sharp and lean with his anger. He leaned toward Marcus. "Answer me honestly now, Cicero, and answer me from your own soul, which seems impregnable and resolute."

His bitter voice filled the room. He pointed a thin brown finger at Marcus, like an accuser. "Let us consider this Rome of ours, Cicero, this Rome of today and not of your grandfather's yesterday. Let us consider the Senators, the red-sandaled Senators in their stately togas, the Senators with their soft litters, soft beds, and soft courtesans, the Senators of privilege and power and money, of rich estates within the walls of Rome, farms in the countryside, villas at Caprae and in Sicily, vast foreign and domestic investments—these Senators who lie in warm, perfumed baths or sleep under the oiled fingers of those who massage their corrupt bodies, and who bejewel themselves and their mistresses before repairing to orgies and banquets, to the theatre, to private exhibitions of shameless dancers, songsters, gladiators, wrestlers, actors—let us consider them!

"Once their forebears, from whom most inherited their seats, repaired to a rude wooden Senate Chamber on their bare feet, to indicate their humility before the power of their people and above all, before the power of the gods and eternal law. They sat, not in embroidered togas, on cushioned marble seats, but on benches of wood, homely fashioned, and their tunics were still stained by the innocent earth and simple labor. The Consul of the people was more than they. When they spoke, those old Senators, they spoke in the accents of the country; they spoke with manliness, learning, truth, justice, and pride. They were prudent; they distrusted all law that did not rise from the natural law, from the heart of the nation.

"Look upon their inheritors! Would our present Senators give up one yoke of their power, half their fortunes to replenish our bankrupt treasury, their vile and extravagant mistresses, the ambitions of their wives, their fawning clients, their idleness and lascivious pleasures, their multitudes of slaves and their rich houses, a measure of their investments, to save Rome and restore her to the stature of their fathers?"

Marcus had paled. He could not look away from Sulla.

"No," he said. "It is true. No."

Sulla's mouth opened for a new breath.

"Let us consider the Censors, the tribunes of the people, the politicians! Is there any man as vain, brutal, or criminal as a man who has a purse filled with a little authority and who can strut haughtily before those who elected him? Is there anyone who can boast of being a more desperate thief than these representatives of the people, one who will not sell his votes for the honor of sitting with patricians at their table, or of kissing the hand of a strumpet of a powerful lord? Who is more of a betrayer of the people than a man who swears that he serves them?

"Look upon them! Will they turn from the busyness of filling their coffers if you cry to them to save Rome? Will they yield their petty staffs in the name of the people, and serve the citizens who elected them without fear or favor? Will they denounce the Senate, and demand of them that they respect the Constitution and pass no self-serving law? Will they cry 'freedom!' rather than privilege? Will they exhort the electorate to practice virtue and thrift and husbandry again, and ask nothing of tribunes but what is only just? Will they face the mobs of Rome and say, 'Be men and not idle cattle'? Will you find one of these among the representatives of the people?"

Marcus put down the shining utensils in his hands, though he had barely touched the rich pork and fish. And he gazed at his plate with desolation. "No, lord," he said.

Sulla lifted a goblet to his lips and drank deeply. No one, not even the light women, moved a hand.

Sulla spoke. "You, Cicero, consider the middle-class, of whom you are a representative. The lawyers, the physicians, the bankers, the merchants, the owners of merchant fleets, the investors, the stock-sellers, the business-men, the shopkeepers, the manufacturers of goods, the importers, the purveyors. Will they, of their own will, serve Rome but a month each year, yielding their profits above taxes, so that we may be solvent again? Will they besiege Senator, patrician, tribune, or Consul with demands that Rome be restored to her ancient grandeur and nobility, and above all, her peace? Will they relinquish the profits of war and not take such a profit? Will one of your lawyers challenge the lawmakers and cry to them, 'This is un-Constitutional, an affront to a free people, and it must not pass?' Will one of these, your own, lift his eyes from his ledgers long enough to scan the Twelve Tables of Roman law, and then expose those who violate them and help to remove them from power, even if it costs their lives? These fat men! Will six of them in this city, disregarding personal safety, rise up from their offices and stand in the Forum, and tell the people the inevitable fate of Rome unless they return to virtue and thrift and drive from the Senate the evil men who have corrupted them for the power they have to bestow?"

"Before God, lord, no," said Marcus.

Sulla closed eyes that appeared suddenly exhausted. "Cicero, let us con-sider the sweltering polyglot mobs of Rome, the men who have smothered her face with their own dung. The mobs of Rome, the cat-mouthed, jackal-voiced mobs! The wall-scrawling villains of the sewers and the al-leys! The bold and insolent people, the enthusiastic and uncontrolled and uncontrollable swill of our towns and many nations! If one honest man implored them to work industriously, and practice austerity, and return to the simple faiths—would they let him live? If a man cried to them that no longer must they depend upon government for their food, their shelter, the tunics that cover them, their amusements—would they harken to him? If a hero admonished them for their idleness and their greed, what would they do?"

Marcus clasped his hands on the table and looked down at them. "Lord, they would murder him, or scream him to silence with their howlings."

"True," said Sulla, with sombreness. "Now let us consider the old Ro-mans, men like yourself, who still live in this city and on the countryside. They are the true inheritors of that for which our fathers died. They boast of the soldiers in their families, of dead warriors borne on their own shields after a battle. They speak proudly of Horatius, of all the heroes of Rome, and consider themselves one with them. Their homes are marked with ancient arms. Their children bear the names of mighty men now sleeping in the dust. They are everywhere these men, in all conditions of life.

"Can you gather together one dozen of these old Romans and ask them to stand on the bridge of Horatius with you, and will they say to the mobs, 'Silence!' To the Senators, 'Honor and law and justice!' To the voracious in the counting houses, 'For a certain time give up your profits for the sake of Rome'? Will they say to the tribunes, 'Represent us or yield your staff of office'? Will they say to me and my generals, 'Depart from us, so that we may regain our liberty and our law'? Are there such a dozen of the old Romans who will cry these things, and pledge their lives, their fortunes and their sacred honor to re-create Rome in her old image?"*

Marcus' very lips were white. He shook his head. "Before God, lord, they would not do that. They are pusillanimous, these descendants of heroes. They are afraid to lift their voices."

Sulla pressed his lean dark hands over his face for a moment. All the others sat transfixed, barely touching the food on their plates. Even the musicians had fallen silent.

Then Sulla said behind his hands in a muffled voice, "Let us consider the farmers beyond our gates, cultivating the land. For many years they have sold their grain to the government granaries and have received large sums for it, and it has been fed to the slothful at their demand. The farmers are happy. It is nothing to them that our treasury is bankrupt.

"If I should say to them, 'Roman farmers, the nation is bankrupt and in danger, and, therefore, I pray to you to decline the bounties heretofore poured in your hands, of your own will, for the sake of Rome,' would they lift their arms in an affirmative vow, for the love of Rome?"†

Marcus' face became full of pain. "No, lord, they would not say that."

Sulla dropped his hands and turned his countenance upon Marcus and it was black with passion.

"Look upon me, Cicero, a soldier, the dictator of Rome! Remember that I am here, in this house, in Rome, with this power, not because I willed it for myself in some dream of fantasy in a lonely night.

"If one hundred men whom I could honor had met me at the gates and had said to me, 'Lay down your arms, Sulla, and enter the city only on foot and only as a Roman citizen,' I should have obeyed in thankfulness. Above all, I am an old soldier, and an old soldier respects the power of established law and courage. Yet, there were not a hundred men to chal-

* Patrick Henry quoted these actual words of Sulla, whom he admired.
† Roman farmers were receiving government subsidies.

lenge me at the gates, or to offer their lives to our swords in the name of their country! There were not even fifty, nor twenty, nor ten, nor five. There was not even one!"

Marcus gazed at him and saw his powerful grief and despair.

"I would, even now," said Sulla, "at the cost of my life, try to restore Rome as she was once, and Roman law, and Roman virtues, and Roman faith, honesty, justice, charity, manliness, labor, and simplicity, if it would avail. But you know I should die in vain! A nation which has reached the abyss which now confronts Rome, by her own willing, her own fatness and ambition and greed, never retreats from that abyss. The leper cannot remove the marks of his disease; the blind man cannot restore his sight; the dead man cannot rise again.

"You have thought me evil, the image of dictatorship. But I am what the people deserve. Tomorrow, I shall die as all men die. But I tell you that worse men than myself will follow me! There is a more inexorable law than any law ever made by man. It is the law of death for corrupt nations, and the minions of that law are already stirring in the wombs of history. There are many who are alive today, young and lustful and without faith. They will not fail. So passes Rome."

He lifted his goblet and drank it to the last drop in a sad and reckless gesture.

"I drink to the corpse of Rome."

He stared at the faces about him, the faces of the vital young men in their narrow silence, the empty faces of their women. "Look upon these, Cicero," he said. "They are Rome's tomorrow. They are her executioners. Well, lads, will you not drink a toast to your gilded, terrible tomorrow?"

Julius met his exhausted eyes boldly with his own. "Lord," he said, "you do us an injustice. We love Rome as you love her."

Sulla threw back his soldier's head and laughed long and loud, and it was a frightful sound in that room. The others stared in each other's eyes with strange smiles, their lips pursed, and their shoulders shrugged slightly.

Marcus stood up, and leaned his hands on the table and waited until Sulla's laughter had died. And then when he had the general's sudden attention, he said in a quiet voice:

"Lord, I stand indicted before you. I was not at the gates to challenge your entry. I was a prudent and careful man, a lawyer. I was the writer of briefs; I was the saver of money; I was the cherisher of my family. In short, I was a coward.

"Lord, I must remove my guilt. If only for that reason I must defend Servius. In his person I defend the Rome I betrayed."

He bowed. Then in the silence he walked from the room and closed the door behind him.

A slave refilled Sulla's glass. He was now sick with wine and his furious sorrow. He said to the young men, "There departs a Roman, marked for death, if not tomorrow, then in the future. It is his fate."

"A traitor," said Curius, with hatred and contempt.

"A fool," said Piso. "A base-born fool."

"A man of emotion, and hasty judgments," said Julius.

"A man of irrelevant passions," said Crassus.

Sulla's mouth opened in a smile.

"A man," he said.

CHAPTER THIRTY

Marcus dined with Roscius in the actor's gem of a house, and Noë was also present. "Politicians," said Roscius, "must be mountebanks, or they are not politicians."

"I am not yet a politician," said Marcus.

"My dear friend," said Roscius, "all lawyers are incipient politicians. And both are actors. It is not what they say before magistrates or the people. It is how they say it, the postures they assume, the manipulations of their voices. One of my early mentors, a very old actor, had the ability to count to ten and so moving was his voice, so tragic his aspect, that spectators burst into tears."

"Marcus has a most eloquent voice," said Noë, "and most moving, and I have taught him to stand gracefully and use certain gestures."

"I have observed him before magistrates," said Roscius, refilling his goblet, and then turning to study Marcus critically. "I have also observed that he wins often after appeals, when the records are read meticulously. Why does he not always win originally, in spite of those fine gestures you have mentioned, Noë? Eheu! He is not much of an actor."

"Thank you," said Marcus. "I know I am jejune, but I was under the impression that lawyers win on points of law and the justice of their causes."

"What nonsense," said Roscius.

"So Scaevola told him, and I," said Noë. "What was our reward? He asked us sarcastically why we had summoned a 'Greek chorus.' Scaevola threw up his hands in despair."

Roscius sighed in sympathy. "Stand up," he directed Marcus. "Consider me a Senator. Walk toward me, as if about to present the case of Captain Cato Servius."

Marcus obeyed, trying to conceal his annoyance. He fixed Roscius with his eyes; he stood tall in his long plain robe with its wide leather belt. Roscius pursed his lips. "I like that fire in the eye," he said. "Can you summon it at will?"

"I did not know it was there," said Marcus. "I was only considering knocking out a few of your teeth, those splendid teeth of yours."

"Excellent," said Roscius, slapping his knee. "Consider the teeth of the venal Senators. Do they not devour the substance of the people? Are they not the curse of widows and orphans. Retreat, and approach me again, so I may observe you more closely."

Marcus did so. He stopped before Roscius who stood to examine him. Then the actor nodded and sat down again. "You have a proud air," he said. "It will not be well on this occasion. You must appear broken. And you must wear the clothing of mourning, and carry a staff on which you will lean as if you need its support. There must be ashes on your brow, and a kerchief in your hand with which you will wipe tears away at intervals, tears which I trust you can produce easily."

He lifted his hand as Marcus began to protest in a loud voice. "Listen to me, my dear friend, and listen intently."

He spoke for some time. Marcus' expression lost its indignation. He began to smile. His eyes sparkled with marveling amusement. When Roscius had done, he laughed with delight, shaking his head. "I shall feel a fool," he remarked.

Marcus gave exclusive thought to the case of Cato Servius in the next few days, and wrote on his address day and night to the point of exhaustion. Nothing pleased him. Then he remembered his first appearance before the Senate, and went to his father and explained all to him.

The pale and emaciated and sickly Tullius listened with new passion. "So, it has come to this in Rome," he said, as he had said so many times before in a grieved and broken voice. "You say it is possible, my son, to save Servius' honor. You think that enough? You must save his life also, for which you despair. His grandsons are very young. Who will be their guardians after the death of Servius? Servius must live, that he instruct his grandsons in fearless pride and Roman faith."

Marcus was silent. Then his face glowed. He put his hands on his father's shoulders and bent and kissed his cheek. "You are right, my father," he said. "But you must pray for my success, for which I fear." And he marveled again in himself that one so secluded and so timid and unworldly could strike so directly at the heart of a matter.

"Men of honor in these days," he said to his father, "are like the bird who feigns to have a broken wing to lead astray the destroyer who would despoil her nest and murder her children. We have but broken wings. The destroyer will prevail."

"Yes," said Tullius, his mild eyes shimmering. "Nevertheless, some fledglings survive. What you save of Rome today will be remembered by a few, who will hand the lamp of truth down through the ages to other men, to light the darkness."

Lucius Sergius Catilina said to Julius Caesar, "I do not know your reason, but you should have permitted Cicero to be murdered. Are you still sentimental?"

"No," said Julius. "But he has a reputation, and there are multitudes who love him."

"Bah," said Catilina. "The people forget their heroes; they obey only their masters."

Julius smiled. Catilina laughed heartily. "You!" he exclaimed. "No, it is something else. You will not tell me, of course."

"No," said Julius. He paused. "But Cicero is still under my protection."

"Though he will oppose you and Pompey in the Senate."

"Though he will oppose me."

"You think you will succeed?"

"Without doubt. Do you not know that he has written to Sulla to say that he will denounce his noble client, Captain Cato Servius, before the Senate?"

"No! It is not possible!"

Julius smiled complacently. "It is true. Sulla showed me Cicero's letter."

Catilina was stunned. "You are speaking truly? Cicero wrote that he would denounce that old fool before the Senate?"

"Yes. I saw the letter with my own eyes."

"Then he is not as formidable as I thought him," said Catilina, still incredulous. He considered, then said angrily, "He is a trickster! I do not believe he is retreating now."

"He was never that," said Julius. He smoothed his thin black hair. "He has respectfully prayed that Sulla be present."

Catilina stared at him, then frowned. "He would never dare, that Chickpea, to humiliate the great Sulla before the Senate," he said.

Julius considered. He said, "I doubt that Cicero would not dare to do anything. You have thought him mild and ineffective, and his triumph over you due only to an accident, the slip of your foot. But I have known him well. He is afraid of nothing. Did he not defeat those who would have murdered him?"

"But he would not dare humiliate Sulla! It would cost him his life."

Julius, who had hardly listened, said, "I may have underestimated him, for I recall him as a gentle and humorous youth, full of honor and uprightness. But what would he gain if he gamble everything in a game he cannot win?"

Marcus sat with his old friend and tutor, Archias, in the house of the Greek, before a round bronze stove containing hot and comfortable coals.

"Your strategy, my dear Marcus, is very dangerous," said the Greek.

"I have always been extremely cautious, to my present regret."

"I have counseled caution, if you may remember, but now I deplore it. Cautious nations become slaves. Let me read, again, your address to the Senate."

Archias shook his head. "My years are heavy on me, otherwise I should be enchanted at all this. Why do I cling to what little time remains for me? It is simple. The known is less frightful to contemplate than the unknown. I pray again, but to whom I do not know." He paused. "You understand, of a certainty, that this cause of yours can result either in triumph or in death—for you?"

"Yes."

Captain Cato Servius turned his face with umbrage upon Marcus, as they sat knee to knee in the prison.

"I cannot do this," said Servius, shaking his head.

Marcus said wearily, as he had said a dozen times, "I am asking you to do nothing dishonorable, for I should not do it myself. The dust of the earth is filled with the remains of reckless heroes. If a man climb to a high pillar and then hurl himself stupidly upon the winds, exclaiming that the gods will uphold him with their arms and their wings, will they do so? No. It is expected of men that they use the intelligence and prudence with which they have been endowed, and not tempt the gods. What availed the recklessness of Icarus? Apollo melted the wax on his presumptuous wings and let him die in the sea."

"You have not talked so to me before like this, Cicero," said Servius.

"I have never advised you to come bare-handed into the presence of your enemies, lord. We cannot come before them like children, pattering and babbling. Again, I implore you to remember your grandsons."

It wounded his soul when the old soldier tried to peer at him from his eyeless sockets. "Lord," he said, sadly, "I am not speaking to you with guile, I swear to you. Did Horatius and his friends stand unarmed upon the bridge they defended? No. You are a soldier. You must meet the enemy on his own ground, and bear the arms he himself bears."

"I shall never be happy again," said the old soldier.

"When your grandsons sit upon your knee, lord, you will be happy," said Marcus.

"I would, almost, that they die," said Servius, "before this day."

"Then Rome would be the poorer."

Servius tried to see him again. "Would your grandfather have advised me as you have done, Cicero?"

Marcus hesitated. At last he said, "I swear to you, lord, I do not know. Do not press me. Think of your grandsons."

"But at what a price I must buy their lives!"

Marcus left the old soldier in a gloomy state of mind. That night he went to his parents' chamber and told them all. Helvia's face became brooding, but to Marcus' astonishment Tullius began to laugh, at first faintly, and then with huge, gathering mirth. Helvia was amazed, and so was Marcus.

"I think it's a marvelous comedy!" exclaimed Tullius. "Ah, Marcus, do not be like the lawyer, Strepsiades in Aristophanes' play, who, when shown a map and observing a dot upon it which his tutor said was Athens, replied in bewilderment, 'It cannot be! There are not, to my observation, any courts in session there!' There is no integrity in session in the Senate in these days, my son."

Helvia looked with pride at her husband, and smiled upon her son. "Your father has put it well, Marcus."

Encouraged and excited by his wife's admiration, Tullius added, "Were this an occasion when a point of just law is to be argued, then I should urge you argue your cause upon it, and then leave it in the hands of the gods. But how can gods prevail when men choose evil in their government?"

Sulla, alone the night before that session of the august Senate which would hear the charges against Servius, considered Marcus' extraordinary letter, written with apparent humility. Sulla was attacked by a strange emotion. Then he, who did not believe in the gods, but only in himself, went to the shrine of Mars in his atrium and lighted a candle before the ferocious statue. He said, aloud, "There are soldiers who never bore a sword, and brave men who died in no battle."

CHAPTER THIRTY-ONE

The wind changed to the north during the night and snow fell, white and heavy over the great city. Seeing this, Julius Caesar, riding in his fine canopied litter with Pompey, said with satisfaction, "There will be few on the streets or in the Forum this day. I fear the mob above all things."

"The mobs care nothing for old soldiers and their fate," said Pompey.

"True," said Julius. "But Cicero cares about Servius, and even I am amazed at the influence my unwarlike friend possesses in this city. He is known as a man of honor, and even mobs respect honor—in others. Do they not salute just men on the streets, before returning to their mendicancy and their pilfering? And do they not shout imprecations upon those who share their own crimes, though in vaster degree?"

They were disagreeably astounded as they descended in the litter to the Forum. The streets all about seethed with cloaked men whose hoods showed glimpses of intent dark faces. The soldiers directing traffic of men—for no cars or chariots or carts were permitted on the local streets or in the Forum during hours of business—were harassed and hoarse with shouting. A veritable ocean of humanity roared into the Forum; endless throngs had already gathered there, shivering and restless. The new waves pressed them closer together. Imprecations sounded furiously in the cold bright air, as each man jostled for space for his feet. Little seething battles rose here and there, when men were pushed from their places by others. Blows were struck. The vast seething pool of sombre heads contrasted vividly with the cold white pillars and columns surrounding them. Some mobs stood on the steps of temples, craning their heads toward the Senate. Some even climbed to the top of porticoes, ignoring the angry commands of soldiers. There they perched, spitting down at the warriors, and darkly grinning. The soldiers put their hands on their swords, threatening, and the men laughed. The Forum hummed like a gigantic hive of bees, a dangerous hum. The steps of the Senate were solidly packed, so that the soldiers had to stand with drawn swords making way for the litters of the Senators, whose faces revealed their consternation.

Vendors of hot sweetmeats and little steaming meat pies and wine and sausages and roasted onions and bread simmering with garlic were dexterously moving among the enormous mob, crying their wares. Men bought eagerly, holding the hot dainties in their cold hands and eating them with relish.

The red roofs of the city fumed as the snow upon them melted under the brilliant sun. The stones of the Forum ran with little black streams of water, in which the people stood heedlessly. The porticoes dripped; the columns were streaked with sparkling moisture. And still the people arrived, pushing in upon the Forum until it seemed that a man could not raise his arms from his sides. The air began to vibrate as if with constant thunder. The soldiers looked at each other helplessly and shrugged.

"Gods!" exclaimed Julius, staring down at the Forum from the parted curtains of his litter.

"Hah," said Pompey. "So they would not be here! I did not know your Cicero was so famous."

The litter had halted near the base of the Palatine, for it could not, as yet, proceed onward. Julius sent a slave with a staff to try to breach that fortress of human flesh. The fortress suddenly parted. A company of men appeared on horseback, with banners. Julius stared incredulously, for the leader was no less than Roscius, the actor, himself, splendidly arrayed, and surrounded by old soldiers on magnificent steeds, veterans of many years. Running behind them on foot was a turbulent river of younger soldiers, armored and helmeted, trotting in unison, their faces harsh with determination. They carried banners and lictors, and colored streamers announcing their legion. The company on horseback swept toward the Forum, unimpeded, carrying those on foot behind them as if by a wind.

"Roscius, and his accursed old soldiers, whom he tenderly patronizes!" cried Julius.

"Were they ordered by Sulla to come here? Of a certainty, no. Then, why have they come?"

But Julius said, "Servius' men. They are on furlough."

"Where is Sulla?" said Pompey. "When he appears, he will order them to leave at once."

Julius smiled grimly. "Even Sulla, especially in these days when he is not very popular with the military, will pause before exercising his right to disperse the soldiers. He will permit them to remain for all they are an embarrassment."

The litter tried to proceed, then was halted again. Another and more determined horde of men poured down into the Forum, well-dressed and even armed with jeweled daggers and swords. Julius peered at them. After a moment he laughed without much amusement. "I know the leader well, in that handsome litter. It is old Archias, Cicero's former tutor, whom I met in the house of the Ciceroni many times. And this mob is his friends, and I recognize the faces of various actors whom I have seen in the theatres. And gladiators! Gods!"

The arriving soldiers mingled with their friends already in the Forum, and the sun began to glitter on a sea of helmets and red plumes. The soldiers conferred. The earlier arrivals glanced over their cloaked shoulders uneasily. The new arrivals laughed. The banners swayed over their heads. The people roared happy approval, and clapped and stamped their feet. The atmosphere was full of the stench of bodies and wool and leather and food and garlic. The sun became brighter.

"Where is Sulla?" asked Pompey.

Said Julius cynically, "It would be less dangerous for him to be absent, than to be present."

Pompey was impatient. "But did your Cicero not write him a letter of capitulation and imploring his presence?"

Julius leaned from the litter and admonished two of the leading slaves to try to force the wall of flesh again. Then he looked at Pompey and raised his eyebrows. "It is true that Cicero wrote that letter. But it was not exactly capitulation."

"What, then, is your explanation, O Oracle?"

"I think," said Julius, "that we are to enjoy a comedy."

Suddenly trumpets shattered the air on the rise of the Palatine Hill, and there was a thundering of imperative drums. The walls of humanity parted. Soldiers rushed down the walls and stationed themselves with drawn swords, and pressed the backs of their shoulders against the screaming mobs. Then through the corridor they had made came a pounding of hoofs and the rumbling of a chariot leading a detachment of armored horsemen. And in that chariot, alone, standing up like Jove himself, stood Lucius Cornelius Sulla, dictator of Rome, whipping his horses, his head bare to the cold sun, and clad in golden armor and golden tunic, with an embroidered scarlet cloak rippling back from his shoulders.

Romans loved a spectacle. They had rarely seen their tyrant, with his pale and terrible eyes and his lean, ascetic face, and when they had seen him he had been clad sombrely and had moved with cold sharp dignity. But now he appeared imperial to them, bright as noonday, magnificent and heroic, and they raised their voices in a roar that echoed back from all the hills in a crash.

Sulla did not look at those who hailed him out of sheer admiration for his appearance. He lashed his horses splendidly. He ran like a glittering wind down into the Forum, followed by gloriously arrayed officers in silver and black breastplates and helmets tossing with blue and crimson plumes, their horses white as snow.

Julius yelled with irreverent laughter. "Roscius has a rival!" he exclaimed, as the litter slaves deftly followed in the wake of the company through the shouting and leaping hordes. Julius threw himself back on the cushions and laughed until his face dripped tears, while Pompey stared at him as one stares at a madman. When they arrived at the steps of the Senate Chamber Julius was still helpless with convulsions of mirth. His dark face was contorted; it began to turn red; a line of foam appeared at the edges of his lips. Pompey, grasping him, shook him fiercely. "Control yourself!" he cried. "Or, you will have a seizure!"

The "sacred illness" was rarely to be halted in its manifestation by an effort of will, and Pompey was in despair. Then, incredibly, he saw Julius deliberately unclench his fists, deliberately open his mouth and breathe slowly and steadily, and deliberately fix his eyes, which had begun to turn up toward the lid. The scarlet hue of his face was replaced with pallor. The foam subsided on his lips, and he licked it away. Sweat sprang out on his forehead. Calmly, he wiped it with the back of his hands, then looked at Pompey with a moment's bedazement. He drew quiet breath after breath, then said, "We are here." While Pompey, who had been trembling, watched in amazement, Julius alighted from the litter and made his way to the Senate steps.

The eager and craning mob saw Julius. They loved his gaiety; they loved and admired his youth; they listened avidly to the stories of his dissipations and his dissolute life, his pranks, his imaginative antics which appealed to the Roman sense of humor. He was a patrician, but he bled in his heart, it was said, for the Urbs, for the plebeians. If his solicitude for them was quite false the myth of it had been spread sedulously by his followers in many places. So the mob was delighted at the sight of him, and roared their joyous approval of all that they imagined he was. Julius paused gracefully on the steps of the Senate, doffed his helmet, and bowed smilingly to his admirers. Then he bounded like a very young man up the rest of the stairs and disappeared within the bronze doors. Pompey followed more slowly.

The Senators were all gathered in the chamber, quiet and serious in their red tunics and their white togas and red boots. Their hands glittered with gems. They gazed impassively at the seat of the Consul of the People, in which Sulla, shining and resplendent, now sat. The incense before the niches of the heroes and gods smoked bluely in the sunlight that penetrated through the doors and the high narrow windows. The cold white air of winter poured in through every aperture. Now, despite the soldiers, the mob thronged the steps and even pressed through the doors, to stand restrained. Beyond them was an endless plain of restless heads and shouting mouths, to the very limits of the Forum.

Two chairs had been placed below the Consul's seat, chairs of fine wood with cushions of blue silk. Gravely Pompey and Julius made their way to these chairs and sat down with slow dignity and stared before them with expressions of aloof severity.

There was a tumult again at the doors and protestations. Then surrounded by the soldiers of his legion, Servius was led into the chamber, his white head proud and high, his features calm and pale, his cratered blind eyes turned straight ahead. He wore his full armor and uniform as a captain of Rome, and he walked steadily as if he could see, guided gently at each step by the touch of a soldier's hand. When he had reached an area before the Consul's seat, a filial hand halted him, and he stood and faced Sulla and his face was as still as stone, and the color of it.

Sulla regarded him in silence, this old friend of his, his comrade-in-arms, his captain. The Senators peered over each other's shoulder to share the sight of this tragic confrontation. They looked from one face to the other, and could read nothing. Sulla's pale eyes were shadowed; he had leaned one elbow on the arm of his chair and his hand partially obscured his mouth. A faint quivering began to run over Servius' features. He could hear the restless mutterings of the huge mob; he could hear breathing all about him; he could smell the incense.

Then Servius said, in a low and questioning voice, "Lucius?"

Sulla moved, as if stricken by that word. The Senators sighed. One whispered to another. "How sorrowful for Sulla!"

Sulla said at last, "Cato."

Servius smiled. He kept his face turned to his enemy while his soldiers rearranged his scarlet cloak and settled his helmet in the crook of his right arm, for he had no left one. All saw his scars, his blindness, his shattered state, and his pride. And all started when he held out his helmet to a soldier, and then struck his breast with his right fist and bent his stately head to the man he could not see, in a salute that had no fear in it and no servility.

"Where is the advocate of the noble Captain Cato Servius?" demanded Sulla, his voice ringing in the comparative quiet of the chamber.

"Here, lord," answered a clear and confident voice at the doors and Marcus entered. A deep rumbling emanated from the Senators, expressive of their astonishment, for Marcus was clothed in absolute mourning and there were ashes on his forehead and he carried no rod of authority. His face was very white. He moved slowly between the ranks of the Senators and came and stood beside Servius and he gazed up into the face of Sulla.

Sulla looked down at him and his long thin mouth twitched in anger.

"What is this garb?" he demanded. "It is an insult to me and to the Senate."

"No, lord," said Marcus, humbly. "It is a mourning for my client's crime."

Sulla raised his fierce black brows. "You admit, before any trial, that your client is guilty of the crimes alleged?"

"I am not completely familiar with the alleged crimes," said Marcus.

The mobs at the doors whispered this astonishing exchange to those behind them, and the message was spread.

"By the gods, read the roll to him," exclaimed Sulla, gesturing down to Julius who rose with majesty and spread out a scroll, holding it high.

In a resounding voice Julius intoned, "Cato Servius, prisoner, is accused of high treason against the State, against Lucius Cornelius Sulla, of subversion, of seeking the overthrow of lawful government, of insurrection, and incitement to riot, of violent and extreme prejudice against the people of Rome, of contempt of society and authority, and of malice."

Sulla listened. The Senate listened. The soldiers and the people listened. Marcus had bowed his head at the beginning of the reading and he kept it bowed when Julius was done and had seated himself again.

"Speak, Marcus Tullius Cicero," said Sulla.

Marcus slowly raised his head in the dramatic manner in which Roscius had tutored him. He lifted his hands with Roscius' own gesture of pleading before the gods. Roscius, standing with Noë ben Joel just inside the doors, watched critically, then nodded with satisfaction.

"I do not know of these crimes," said Marcus, in rolling tones that reached even to many outside the doors. "But I know of a greater crime."

A shadow ran over Sulla's face. He leaned back in his chair. He pursed his lips and considered Marcus. Then he looked at the Senators and at the taut soldiers and then he saw Roscius in his magnificence. His face darkened. He looked down at Marcus contemptuously.

"Are you responsible, Cicero, for this tremendous assemblage in the Forum today? Are you so famous that such a multitude should hasten to hear you?"

"It is said, lord, that Romans love justice before all things, and they have come to hear justice. Law is like eternal granite. It is not an airy butterfly, a creature of the idle breezes, or a wanton of the whimsies and passions and vindictiveness and envies of little men. It is the soul of Rome. The people cherish it more dearly than their lives."

Roscius nodded happily at Noë. "He speaks it well, for all that you wrote it," he whispered to his friend.

"Then," said Sulla, "this—throng—has gathered to celebrate Law."

"Lord, this is a case of tremendous importance to the people of Rome, in whose name we are gathered here together." Marcus' voice rose without effort and penetrated far and wide, and like waves gathering sound and force the people murmured and then shouted far outside the Senate. "And as you, lord, have been so libeled—as it has been said—it has excited the attention of Romans."

"You are ambiguous, Cicero," said Sulla.

"I am but a modest lawyer," said Marcus, in such mellifluous accents that they brought a flush of anger again to Sulla's cheek. "I have some slight fame as an advocate. But it is you, lord, whose name has summoned them here."

He looked at Sulla with solemn guilelessness. Sulla shifted on his buttocks. "You flatter me, Cicero. And I consider you a liar."

Marcus bowed. "I shall not dispute you, though the accusation is unjust."

The countless friends of Roscius, Noë, and Archias, looked for the arranged signal, and when they caught its unobtrusive appearance they raised their voices in an enormous bellow. "Hail, Cicero! Cicero! Cicero!" The shout spread to the farthermost reaches of the Forum, and it was caught up ecstatically even by those who had never heard Cicero's name before and by those who stood a long distance from the Senate. The clamor of their great noise swept the Senate in billows of sound, and Sulla listened intently. Again, he leaned back in his chair and contemplated Marcus darkly.

"It is not my name they are screeching," he said.

"I am overcome with confusion, lord."

Marcus felt Servius move beside him, and he was afraid of the old soldier's impatience and fearful that he would not much longer endure what he had reluctantly promised. He started nervously when Sulla addressed himself directly to Servius. "Cato," he said abruptly, "are you responsible for the appearance of these old veterans of many years, and your own legion, in defiance of the orderly procedure of the law?"

"No, Lucius!" exclaimed the old soldier.

Marcus put his hand on Servius' arm and said, "They have come as a tribute to their old commander, lord, and it is very moving, is it not?"

If Servius should blurt out, in his honesty, what must not be said, then all is lost, thought Marcus, and I with it. He tightened his fingers on Servius' arm.

"I do not find it moving," said Sulla, who had not missed the little play before him. "Have you attempted to coerce the Senate, Cicero, with this appearance of my soldiers?"

"Lord!" said Marcus. "Who am I to command the military?"

"True," said Sulla. His eyes slowly wandered to the soldiers, old and young, gathered at the doors and even within them. The soldiers were watching him with too strong an intensity. He recalled that that infernal actor, Roscius, whose actresses he frequently enjoyed, was a patron of old veterans and loved them dearly and provided for them what the government could not provide. He had built too small sanitoria for them, and paid for excellent surgeons and physicians. For a moment Sulla was moved. The national Treasury was bankrupt still. It would have given him gratification if he could have done for his old comrades what Roscius had done.

Sulla looked down at Julius, whose eyes were leaping with irresistible mirth. "You are the prosecutor, Caesar. Speak!"

Julius rose, every gesture elegant and confident. He waited until he had absolute quiet. Then he held a copy of Servius' book high above his head so that all could see. He struck a statue-like attitude as he rotated on his heels; his long woolen robe was dyed purple, and he wore a wide belt of gilded leather encrusted with gems, and his boots were of purple leather lined with fur.

The merry face assumed an aspect of gravity, though the black eyes continued to twinkle. Julius looked down at the scribes who were busily writing on long scrolls. "Heed it all, lords," said Julius to the Senators, "for this is most momentous. A book that rings with treason, written by the noble Cato Servius, once-beloved captain under General Sulla. With what gratitude has Servius repaid his ruler, his ancient government? He has denounced them! He has accused them of violence against the people of Rome, of tyranny, of oppression, of innumerable crimes, of obscenities committed in the name of the Constitution, of the perversion of our hallowed Constitution, of exigency and expediency, of cynical opportunism, of ruthless cruelties and suppression of freedom, of flagrantly interpreting our laws to their own advantage, of exciting hatred and envy in the mobs, of government by fiat and not by law!"

Marcus listened closely to Julius' voice. An actor! thought Marcus, and in spite of all he felt himself smiling a little with that old weakening affection for his young friend. Then he started, for Julius was looking directly into his eyes, and the eyes flickered with humor.

The Senators murmured angrily; Sulla leaned back in his chair and again his hand half-concealed his cold and savage mouth.

"These are dangerous days!" cried Julius. "We have emerged from an era of tyranny, and I say this who am the nephew of old Marius, who was a murderer! Our noble dictator, Sulla, has restored the Constitution and the Republic, and there is no man of any learning or wisdom who can deny this truly!

"Yet, Cato Servius incontinently and recklessly, a man who has been a soldier nearly all his life and is, therefore, no authority on philosophy or politics or government, has seen fit to attack in all ignorance the heroic labors of Lucius Cornelius Sulla to restore to us all that we had lost under Marius, Cinna, and Carbo! Did he expect that in so short a space of time that all that we had forfeited under tyrants could be completely restored?

Apparently he believes in instant miracles, this man blind in more ways than one!"

He looked at the Senators compellingly. "Shall the edifice that was torn down in many years be rebuilt in a day? It is beyond mortal man's most heroic efforts. If a man is a slave, it is arduous for him to learn to live again in the air of freedom. He must not be incited into the belief that chains and slavery can be overcome in an hour, or the stain on his soul be cleared instantly. He must be taught freedom, as a child is taught his letters, and this is a painful labor which Sulla has undertaken.

"During this labor no excited voice must rise, no ignorant voice, no uncomprehending voice, or we shall fall into chaos again. But more than this, there is the aspect of treason in this book, beyond the mere incitement to riot and subversion, and treason is an old vice."

He paused momentously, and Marcus took advantage of this silence to clap gently and to smile with irony. Instantly the attention, and the frowns, of the Senators were on him.

"Excellent!" said Marcus. "Treason is indeed an old vice, and it is protean. Wise is the man who recognizes it in its many forms. Cato Servius is one such.

"May I ask the noble Julius Caesar to read an excerpt from Servius' book which most illustrates the point he is—attempting—to make?"

Julius hesitated. He glanced swiftly at Sulla, who made no move at all. Then he glanced at the Senators. "Why should I repeat passages from this book, when all are acquainted with it? It is needlessly stealing the time of this Senate—"

Marcus said, with mocking solemnity, "As the advocate of Cato Servius, I am permitted to ask questions even of the Senate." He turned and faced the august body.

"Lords, are you all familiar with this book and its contents?"

The ranks of the Senators stirred, so that the chairs seemed a ripple of scarlet and white. Then an old Senator said with vexation, "We are familiar."

Marcus smiled again. "Lord," he said, addressing the old Senator, "for the sake of many in this assemblage who have not read the book, would you repeat or paraphrase one paragraph or sentence which particularly offended you?"

The old Senator flushed angrily. "I do not care to repeat treason, even if I did not write it myself."

Marcus looked at his servant, Syrius, who had accompanied him, and whose black arms were filled with scrolls. Marcus impressively took one, and then unrolled it slowly. He scrutinized it. Then he bowed first to Sulla, and then to the Senate.

"Lords, with your pardon I will read you a section of the ancient law, still potent, still living, devised by our Founding Fathers whose memory we reverence and for whose souls we pray in our temples, and whose eternal guidance we implore.

"'A man shall not be accused lightly by hearsay, or by intemperate accusations. The witnesses against him, the judges who shall judge him, must at all times present irrefutable evidence and direct testimony, and the judges shall rule constantly that only such testimony be admitted to the books of the scribes and to the attention of magistrates and executioners of the law.'"

Marcus bowed again to the old Senator. "Lord, you have not presented such testimony. We are here to judge evidence given impartially and intelligently, without regard for personalities or sentiments or prejudice." He paused, and looked at Sulla. "That is the Law."

The Senators muttered loudly and furiously. Sulla dropped his hand and said with indifference, "That law has not been abrogated, Cicero." He raised his hand to cover his mouth so that his dark smile should be hidden.

Marcus bowed very low. "I thank you, lord, for this information imparted to the Senate." Here he was interrupted by shouts of "Insolence!" from many Senators, who half-rose in their seats. Sulla was unmoved. He turned his light eyes upon the Senators and that glance quelled them, and they sank muttering into their seats again.

Swallowing a throb of exultation in his throat, Marcus said to Julius, "Caesar, it is apparent that you have read this book, and apparently you are one of the few. May I impose upon you by requesting that you read a section you found particularly objectionable?"

Again Julius hesitated, and he looked at Sulla. Sulla nodded. Julius glanced at Marcus. He turned some pages in the book. Dead silence filled the Chamber. Then Julius began to read. Marcus halted him. "I must beg that you read louder, Caesar."

"Louder!" cried a musical voice near the door, and Marcus recognized it as the voice of Roscius.

Julius shrugged. His expressive eyes danced madly in his grave face. He lifted his voice and read:

"'Worthiness resides in no man, and let that nation beware who discovers itself regarding its temporal ruler as a divinity, fawning upon him, delighting in news of his comings and goings, reverencing him, listening to his words as though they rolled down from Olympus with the sound of thunder, ostracizing those who differ from him, raising up their voices like trumpets hailing all that he does and deluding themselves that he is superior to those who have elevated him by vote or in the name of emergency.'"

Marcus listened soberly, watching the darkening faces of the Senators, and again he felt a throb of exultation. He let a little silence dwell after Julius had concluded his reading. Then he said to the Senators, "Do you object to that, lords?"

"It is an attack on Sulla! The implication is obvious!" cried the old Senator.

Marcus shrugged. He said, "I trust the scribes have recorded that reading in full."

The scribes nodded. Sulla bit his lips to prevent a harsh laugh from bursting from his throat. Marcus spread his hands helplessly and made his eyes wide.

"How was it possible for Cincinnatus, the Father of his Country, who said that before the new Senate of Rome four hundred years ago, to know of Lucius Cornelius Sulla, and to refer to him?"

A great laugh burst involuntarily from the soldiers and the crowds near the door, and the mobs outside caught it up though they did not know the cause. Pompey tugged at Julius' robe and whispered angrily, "Is it so?" "It is so," whispered Julius, grinning.

When the Chamber was quiet again Marcus looked at the nonplused Senators and said kindly, "But certainly this majestic body recognized the words of the great Cincinnatus to whom they daily offer their reverence and to whom they have dedicated their duties?"

Not a Senator replied, but the many eyes fixed on Marcus were inimical.

Sulla said languidly, "There is no treason in that quotation which Servius has used. We honor the words of Cincinnatus."

"And I," said Marcus, "honor you, lord, for your respect for the Father of our Country." He looked at Julius. "Pray continue."

Julius by now did not know what to do. He was inwardly hilarious, for he loved a joke above all things. He looked at the formidable Sulla for a signal, but Sulla's expression was not to be read. So Julius began to quote again:

" 'There are times of dire emergency when power is given to one man, but that time must be limited and that man's days scanned sleeplessly lest he be devoured by ambition. Should he become overweening and tyrannical, should he say, "I am the Law," then you must depose him at once for his own sake as well as your own. For now that man stands on the threshold of death and all bloodiness and is a dreadful danger to all that lives, including himself. Never permit him to say to you, "I am needed by my country more than any other man, therefore, you must not dismiss me." You have corrupted him and he should be removed and avoided, and left to rediscover his soul in silence or—in exile.' "

"Treason!" shouted the Senate with one voice.

Sulla raised his hand and said wearily, "That is also a quotation from Cincinnatus' speech before the Senate."

They subsided, but glared upon Marcus, who bowed again to Sulla.

Marcus spoke delicately to the Senate, "Surely this august body does not believe that Cincinnatus, dead four hundred years, had precognition of Sulla! If they believe so, then there is secret treason in their hearts."

Julius spoke. "Let us leave the divine words of Cincinnatus in peace for the moment. We are all familiar with those deathless words." He coughed.

"Continue, then, Caesar, with other readings," said Marcus.

Julius coughed again, riffled the pages of the book. He darted a look at Marcus which was inscrutable. He read:

" 'If the existence of the state is alone to be considered, then it would seem that all, or some at least, of these claims are just; but if we take into account a good life, then, as I have already said, education and virtue have superior claims among men. As, however, those who are equal in one thing ought not to have an equal share in all, nor those who are unequal in one thing to have an inequal share in all, it is certain that all forms of government which rests on either of these principles are perversions. All men have a claim in a certain sense, as I have already admitted, but all have not an absolute claim. The rich rightly claim because they have a greater share in the land—and land is the common element of the state—they are more trustworthy in general in contracts. The free claim under the same title as the noble, for they are nearly akin. For the noble are citizens in a truer sense than the common or ignoble man, and good birth is always valued in a man's own home and country. Another reason is that those who are sprung from better ancestors are likely to be better men, for nobility is excellence of race. Virtue, too, may be truly said to have a claim, for justice has been acknowledged by us to be a social virtue, and it implies all others.' "

The Senators looked at each other uncomfortably, for all were rich and many were patricians. It was obvious that they agreed with this quotation. Nevertheless, the old Senator lifted up his hoarse voice and said, "That is defiance of the democracy which Sulla has established, and, therefore, it is treason!"

"Treason by whom, lord?" asked Marcus.

The old Senator regarded him with fuming hatred. "By Servius."

Marcus shook his head sadly. "Servius was merely quoting Aristotle, from that noble philosopher's *Politics*."

The old Senator was silent. He looked to Sulla for a gesture, but Sulla remained impassive. Marcus turned to him. "Noble Sulla, is there a law now in Rome which prohibits the study of Aristotle's *Politics*?"

"I revere Aristotle," said Sulla. "You know, Cicero, that there is no such law."

Again the few gave a signal near the door, and the crowd bellowed and the Chamber was filled with the voice of their enthusiastic clamoring. "Hail Cicero! Cicero! Cicero!"

Marcus waited with modestly downcast eyes until the uproar subsided. Then he said to Julius, "Pray continue with your reading, noble Caesar."

Julius said, "Servius tells of a mythological tyrant, who posed as the friend of the common man and democracy, but who in his heart despised both the man and the democracy. He appeared before the multitude with his military scars, and appealed for a restoration of the law, and the populace emotionally voted him a great bodyguard of soldiers, for the protection of himself and the State. The mythological tyrant, then, exultantly proceeded to enslave all the people for his own splendor and power. He promised the greatest good to the greatest number—and went on to subject all to his ruthless and insane ambition, and to plunge his nation into the most abject misery."

The old Senator cried, "He maligns Sulla!"

Marcus reached out to Syrius for his own copy of Servius' book and affected, with frowns, to be searching for the passage. Then he sighed in relief, and looked at Julius, and he raised his brows.

"'Mythological,' Caesar? Ah, has your education been neglected? Servius invented no such character. He was speaking of Peisistratus, the tyrant of Athens, dead these five hundred years!"

Again the young and old soldiers burst into loud and derisive laughter, and the mobs, hearing this, laughed delightedly also though not understanding.

"Surely, Caesar," said Marcus, "you do not equate Peisistratus with our noble Sulla?"

"Why, then, does Servius?"

Marcus again studied the book, then closed it. "He does not! He merely recounts history and permits the reader to draw his own conclusions. The Law of Rome has no objection to men reading what they will and drawing their own conclusions. Or do you, Caesar, wish to control the minds of our free people by censoring what they read and deciding what books they must read?"

"Tyranny!" shouted the people near the doors, and Marcus smiled at Julius.

Sulla said, "There is no censorship of what a man may read in Rome, for we believe in freedom of publication and there are no guards here who read over a man's shoulder. Our law prohibits censorship."

Marcus bowed almost to his knees. "I thank you, lord."

The Senators stared in dismay at Sulla, who smiled enigmatically.

"However," said Sulla, "we do prohibit treason."

"You consider, lord," said Marcus, "that Cincinnatus and Aristotle and the history of old Greece are treasonable?"

Sulla, for the first time, openly smiled. "Do not bait me, Cicero," he said. He looked at Julius. "What else?"

Julius, who had seen Sulla's smile, was greatly relieved. He said, in a voice filled with affected irritability, "It appears that almost all of Servius' book is composed of quotations from worthier men and from great patriots and philosophers, whom Rome reveres."

A deep murmur ran through the Chamber. The Senators stared at Sulla, who was rubbing his cheek and faintly smiling again.

Marcus said, "Is it prohibited to a man to quote honored sources?

"Yes! For it is the Law that if he does so he must give credit to those sources! This Cato Servius has not done. He has written in a fashion that implies he is the author of these noble utterances. Therefore, he is guilty!"

He raised his arms in a gesture of anguish and mourning, then slowly dropped them and let his head decline, as if in remorse, on his breast.

He said, "I have come to denounce my client of a crime. Plagiarism. It is forbidden under the Law of Rome. I ask that he be adequately punished."

Sulla leaned back in his chair and closed his eyes, and all waited breathlessly for his words. But many moments passed and none could read his face.

Marcus spoke again, "Woe unto me, that I have a client who has broken the law concerning plagiarism! Had I known of this crime before I should not have defended him! What is the punishment? Let me read it to you, lords: 'The offender shall be fined from one hundred to one thousand gold sesterces!' I leave the judgment in your merciful hands." He bowed humbly to the Senate, and then to Sulla, and then wiped his eyes with his kerchief. Sulla watched him, and his throat vibrated as if by withheld mirth. A signal was given at the doors, and the mighty mob laughed also with good nature.

Sulla sat forward in his chair and gazed at the Senate. "We have a serious infraction of the law here before us. Senators, what is your judgment?"

They stared at him, and saw his strange smile. Then they stared at each other.

Sulla then said to Julius, "What is your opinion, Caesar?"

The subtle Julius kept his face straight. "Cato Servius is guilty of plagiarism. Therefore, lord, I suggest that his book be seized until such time as he gives credit to his sources. Moreover, he should be punished. Permit me, lord, to leave in your hands the extent of the legal punishment."

Sulla said, "The law is not in my hands. It resides with the Senate. Lords, what is your judgment?"

The old Senator said, "Two hundred gold sesterces fine, noble Sulla."

Sulla said, "It is done.

"As Cato Servius is not guilty of treason, but only of unlawful plagiarism, I order that his lands and fortune be restored to him, and that he be set free."

Marcus nudged his client. Servius started. He turned his blind sockets on his once-beloved general, and his face was torn with emotions. Marcus nudged him again.

Then Servius said in a bitter and despairing voice, "I yield not, unless Sulla, my old general, forgives my—crime! Otherwise, I shall fall on my sword."

All waited, with held breath. Sulla gazed at Marcus, and Marcus returned that gaze blandly. Then Sulla rose from his chair and descended the steps with slow majesty. He reached Servius, and paused, while all watched and craned their necks. Like all Romans he loved drama. He extended his arms and embraced Servius. He kissed Servius' cheek. And then he kissed it again and the terrible light eyes filled with tears.

"I command you, Servius, not to fall upon your sword for any crime you have committed! You are under my protection henceforth from yourself and from all others. I forgive you the crime of plagiarism. Go in peace."

Marcus' friends again gave the signal, and now the crowd screamed, "Hail, Sulla! Sulla! Sulla! Hail, Cicero! Hail! Hail!"

Servius leaned his head in prostration on Sulla's shoulder, as if undone. He said in a voice only Sulla heard: "You are still a tyrant, and the enemy of my country."

Sulla whispered back to him, "Blame me not, Servius, for the people willed it so. On them the curse and the imprecations, and not on me. I am but their creature."

Servius lifted his head suddenly, and his face was moved. For the first time he returned Sulla's embrace and kissed his cheek, in sadness, in understanding pity.

PART THREE

The Patriot and the Politician

Est quidem vera lex recta ratio naturae congruens, diffusa in omnes, constans, sempiterna, quae vocet ad officium iubendo, vetando a fraude deterreat; quae tamen neque probos frustra iubet aut vetat nec improbos iubendo aut vetando movet, huic legi nee obrogari fas est neque derogari ex hac aliquid licet neque tota abrogari potest, nee vera aut per senatum aut per populum——

—CICERO

The summer was extremely hot, and the monolithic city sweltered and sweated under fierce bronze rays of light from the sky. Every sunset was a conflagration, as ominous as a distantly seen fire which inexorably approaches.

Marcus received a letter from his friend and dear enemy, Julius Caesar, in Asia, where Julius was serving his first military campaign under Minucius Thermos:

"Greetings to the noble Marcus Tullius Cicero from his friend, Julius Caesar.

"Carissime, I rejoiced to receive your letter and to hear that all is well with you and that you have triumphed in your last major pleadings before the law. What a man is our Cicero, what a patriot! He needs only to become a politician to be complete, and I am happy that he is considering this matter as a duty. But when shall I have the pleasure of hearing of your marriage? A man is not complete without a wife. Do I not know this? Did I not lovingly adhere to my Cornelia in face of Sulla's threats, even when he deprived me of my priesthood? What is it that you often said to me: 'It is better to obey God than man.' I, therefore, must be virtuous in the sight of God for I honored the sacredness of marriage."

(At this, Marcus made a grimace which reluctantly became a smile as he remembered the dissipations and adulteries of his friend.)

"Alas," continued Julius' letter, "I was grieved to hear of Sulla's death in Puteoli, a year only since he resigned his dictatorship of Rome. But I expected it long before this time, for though his visage and his form did not indicate that he possessed any plethora which would lead to apoplexy he was a man of great passions and inner violences. He detested many, and hated many, but for reasons of state he repressed all expression of these emotions, and such repression has a dread effect upon the body and the soul. It was unfortunate for his memory that he died suddenly in the arms of his latest actress, for it has stained his true image of a spiritually austere and Stoic man. But let us be glad that he lived to complete his memoirs. I am impatient to read them."

(I am certain of that, thought Marcus at this point.)

"In your last letter, Marcus, you wrote that you feared I am ambitious. Is it evil to be ambitious, to yearn with all your might and heart to serve your country justly and bravely? If that be ambition, let Romans again be endowed with such a priceless virtue! You, above all, should rejoice in ambitious men. But why should you accuse me of what you apparently consider an ominous thing? Who am I but a humble soldier, serving my general in this steaming and ungrateful and rebellious province? My ambition is to serve him well. In all modesty I declare I did not seek nor desire the Civic Crown for saving a comrade's life at Mytiline. Laugh if you will."*

(Marcus laughed.)

"My general is sending me to serve under Servilius Isauricus against the Cillilian pirates. What a people are those pirates, a race composed of ancient Phoenicians, Hittites, Egyptians, Persians, Syrians, Arabs, and other maritime scourings of the Great Sea! Nevertheless, one must admire their effrontery and audaciousness, for do they not defy Rome? It is as if an ant would defy a tiger. They do not hesitate to seize even Roman ships and murder Roman sailors and seamen and to rob our cargoes. We shall put them down speedily.

"You prudently do not write your opinion of our present dictator, Lepidus, and I possess discretion also though you appeared to doubt it always.

"However," continued Julius' letter, "though a man of riches he does not possess the wealth that Sulla possessed. You were not then referring to him when you quoted Aristotle: 'It is surely a bad thing that the greatest offices should be bought! The law which permits this abuse makes wealth of more account than nobility in a politician, and then the whole State becomes avaricious. For whenever the chiefs of the State deem anything honorable, the citizens are sure to follow their example, and where ability has not the first place there is no real aristocracy of mind and spirit.' No, you were not referring to Lepidus.

"Or, is it possible that you were warning me? Incredible! It is true that I am not destitute, but it is also true that there is no office in Rome which I would attempt to buy, for I desire none."

(Hah! thought Marcus.)

"I wish you were not always so ambiguous," the letter went on. "But you possess the subtlety of a lawyer, which is beyond the comprehension of a humble soldier like myself."

("O Julius!" exclaimed Marcus aloud, in his office.)

"I had hoped," wrote Julius, "that the paths of your brother, Quintus, and mine would cross, but it was not in our fate though we were less than two leagues apart at one time. I hear of the respect and honor in which he is held by his general. He is a noble Roman, for all his simplicity."

(Which you do not admire, thought Marcus.)

_____
* From letters to Cicero.

"I feel a premonition, Carissime, that I shall soon look upon your amiable face, for have I not always loved you and held you to be a paragon of probity and all the virtues? I hope to return to Rome when the pirates are extinguished, which will be speedily. In the meantime, my sweetest thoughts are of my friend and the guide of my youth. Consider that I have just embraced you and kissed your cheek. I also kiss the hand of your dear mother and the cheek of your father, as though I were their son. May my patron, Jupiter, look upon you with favor, and my ancestress, Venus, grant you the sight of a desirable maiden for a wife, and may Cupid, the son of Venus, pierce your heart with his most delectable arrow."

(And you consider that meaning me well! thought Marcus.)

He put down the letter, still smiling. Then the smile disappeared. He was filled with lassitude and weariness. He was but twenty-nine years old, but he felt aged and heavy. He could not forget Livia, the murdered wife of Catilina. Years had passed since her horrible death, but her face did not leave his inner eye. She remained passionately young to him, beautiful beyond all dreaming, eerie as a Sybil, elusive as a dryad, fleet of foot as a nymph, wild as a spring wind, a wraith from an unknown land.

As a man who analyzed everything, including himself, Marcus still did not know why he loved Livia, and why her face and her voice haunted him, why her whole person was as alive to him as no other was alive. He could recall the sound of her voice and her mystic singing at will, as sharp as if he had just heard it within the past hour. He could recall her smiles, the touch of her leaf-like hand, her faint laughter, the light of her blazing blue eyes. It was as if he had just left her side and then had looked back upon her over his shoulder and had seen her face again.

The fearful events which had shaken Rome, and himself, over these years were not so vivid to him as Livia Curius Catilina. When he visited the island near Arpinum he walked the little forest, and heard her voice echoing to him eagerly from shadows, and sometimes he believed he caught the flash of her hair, the floating of her palla, among the mysterious trees. When the wind ran through the branches he could hear Livia's singing, the murmur of her unearthly song. His arms never ceased from aching to embrace her; he felt the sweetness of her kiss upon his lips. Her shade wandered over the bridge between the island and the town, and the stones whispered softly with her light step. It was on the island that he felt her presence most strongly, and not in Rome where she had lived and died.

He said to his mother, "No, I can never marry. I cannot forget Livia. I have nothing to offer another woman but the very shadow of myself, and that is not enough."

Sometimes it seemed to him that his external life was a dream, and that the only reality he had ever known was Livia and the island, his endless studies, his poetry, and his thoughts. Years later he wrote to Atticus: "I served for a little space in the military service under Sulla (and was not considered the most able of soldiers). Nevertheless, the whole experience appears not to have any verity for me, but only a fantasy indulged in for an hour or more. I do not recall, now, even the name of my general, nor of my comrades—who never attempted any close approach to me. Nor I to them, I confess. They delighted in war, and thought it the noblest and most exciting of sports, even when the probability of death was always present. I found wars no pleasure to an intelligent man, and the short campaign in which I was engaged—Sulla, and my mother, believing I should miss no experience however arduous or dull—drowned me in yawning ennui. I do not decry armies and soldiers, for man, being what he is—a lover of war—can never be trusted especially if he is envious of your nation and lusts for your possessions, or yearns for power over you."

Marcus was still receiving congratulations from many quarters because he had won the case of Cato Servius, and then, a little later, the case of one Sextus Roscius (who was no relative of the actor). Again, in the case of Sextus Roscius, he had had to oppose Sulla before a fearful jury, and he had had to accuse Chrysogonus, the friend of Sulla, and a former Greek slave, during the murder trial of Sextus, for whom he won an acquittal. In conclusion, and in referring to the sad state of law in Rome, Marcus said, "The daily spectacle of atrocious acts has stifled all feeling of pity in the hearts of men. When every hour we see or hear of an act of dreadful cruelty we lose all feeling of humanity. Crime no longer horrifies us. We smile at the enormities of our youth. We condone passion, when we should understand that the unrestrained emotions of man produce chaos. Once we were a nation of self-control and austerity and had a reverence for life and justice. This is true no longer. We prefer our politicians, particularly if they swagger with youth and are accomplished jesters and liars. We love entertainment, even in law, even in government. Unless we reform, our terrible fate is inevitable."*

(In recalling that case Marcus was to write decades later, "It won such favorable comment that I was thought not imcompetent to handle any sort of litigation. There followed in quick succession many other cases which I brought into court, carefully worked out and, as the saying is, smelling somewhat of the midnight oil.")

In short, he became rich. He was not fool enough to despise riches, remembering his ascetic life in his youth, and he never believed that deprivation was nobler than money. "Poverty does not harden the soul, nor strengthen it. It creates slaves."† Yet, with another part of his mind he

---

* Concluding speech of Cicero at the trial of Sextus Roscius.
† Letter to Caesar.

regarded his new wealth with indifference. It was there; he could afford to forget it.

If Helvia, for all her plotting, had not yet been able to find a suitable and acceptable wife for her older son she manipulated the marriage of Quintus, her darling, to Pomponia, sister of Atticus, publisher to Marcus. Quintus, the secretly tenderhearted, had through long labor finally been able to acquire the reputation of being a blustering soldier. But Pomponia, a shrewd and intelligent young woman, had soon succeeded in conquering him, and it was a scandal in the family that he had become a typical Roman husband of modern times—afraid of his wife, fearful of her tempers, and docile, and well governed. In this connection Marcus remembered the angry statement of old Porcius Cato, "Romans govern the world but are themselves governed by their wives." He also recalled that Themistocles, the ancient Greek statesman, had complained that while Athenians governed the Greeks and he governed the Athenians, his wife governed him, and their son governed her. Marcus had no desire to be governed by a woman. He amiably visited the country home of Quintus, when his brother was on furlough, and amiably smiled upon Pomponia, but he shuddered at the awe and terror in which Quintus held his young wife. Quintus the fearless, the impulsive, Quintus whose own temper among men had gained a respectable reputation! As if to balance the oppression of his wife, Quintus often undertook to advise Marcus about politics, about which he was certain that Marcus knew nothing. "One must be a tactician, as in war, and you, dear Marcus, hate war."

At twenty-nine his work, his endless labors, his growing fame, his lassitude and sadness, began to overcome Marcus. He discovered, to his alarm, that that fine instrument of his, his voice—so sedulously trained by Noë and Roscius—was showing signs of failing. There were mornings when he awoke that he said to himself, "It is impossible for me to face the day." Never exceptionally strong, he was aware of weakness in his limbs. He struggled on against increasing pain and increasing disability, and would listen to no advice, not from his physician, not from his parents. "There is so little time," he would say with an irritability foreign to his affable nature.

Then, one hot summer day, he collapsed in his office, and his students carried him to his couch in a fainting condition. His physician was called. The physician said, "I hold no hope for your life unless you leave Rome and your work and rest your mind and your spirit." Marcus scoffed. But in the days that passed he found that he could rarely stir from his bed, that his joints ached and throbbed with anguish. His physician said, "You must go to Greece, to the shrine of the great physician, son of Apollo,

Aesculapius, who is reputed, in dreams, to cure the afflicted. You have rheumatism; your body reflects the weariness and pain of your soul."

Quintus said, "I will go with you to Greece. Have you not always longed for that country?" Marcus smiled at him, thinking that Quintus might desire a little respite from Pomponia. "We shall see Pomponia's brother, who is also my publisher," he said. Atticus had discreetly fled from Rome before the trial of old Servius and had amassed a fortune in Greece by various methods. But his publishing business was still very prosperous in Rome, and he still employed one hundred scribes.

With seriousness, now, Marcus began to plan to go to Greece.

"You shall walk where Socrates and Plato and Aristotle walked!" Tullius exclaimed. "As you trace their footsteps, who knows but what their shades shall whisper to you? Never have I forgotten what Socrates said concerning the Unknown God: 'There shall be born to men the Divine One, the perfect Man, who will bind our wounds, who will lift our souls, who will set our feet on the illuminated path to God and wisdom, who will cherish our ills and share them with us, who will weep with man and know man in his flesh, who will return us to that which we have lost and who will lift our eyelids that we may gaze again on the Vision.'"

Marcus was now so weak, in these last hot days of summer in his bed, that he could not control his emotions. He remembered his youthful dream of seeing the Divine One face to face in the flesh, and he was sorrowful that He had not yet appeared among men. Why did He delay, in this enormous world of confusion and pain and evil and strife, of endless distrust and betrayal and the clashing of arms?

Noë came to see his old friend and to read him his latest play. Roscius, the rascal, was in Jerusalem. "No doubt seeking forgiveness for his many crimes, especially those against me," said Noë. "He has a copy of my play. He demands an extortionate price for appearing in it. He is also growing a beard, as he writes me. I prefer to believe he is growing a horse's tail and hoofs, like a centaur."

Noë was proud and pleased that crowds of former clients and devotees came daily to the house of the Carinae to inquire about Marcus' health, and filled the street before it and even intruded on the gardens in the rear. Noë said, "We are famous, it seems. When are you going to buy a more impressive house, dear friend, and leave this decaying area?"

"When I return from Greece," said Marcus.

Friends of Scaevola visited him, honoring both Scaevola and his favorite pupil. Looking on their elderly faces with the new charity of illness, Marcus began to wonder if they had not, over the years, smoothed his way for him, for many inexplicable things had happened.

One day a slave came running into his cubiculum with the news that

Julius Caesar and Pompey had arrived. Marcus felt the old thrill of fond pleasure and amusement at the name of his young friend, and sat up in bed the better to receive him. He wondered, however, at the presence of Pompey, the strong and taciturn. Julius came in, flowing gracefully as usual in a long rich robe of the finest red silk, and with silver shoes and girdle and silver armlets studded with turquoises. He exhaled his customary air of exuberance and good-will and delight in living. He was also fragrant.

"Dear friend!" he cried, leaning over the bed to embrace Marcus. "What is this that I hear of you?"

"I thought you were still killing pirates," said Marcus. "I thought there was a price on your head—again—in Rome."

"I am a very valuable man," said Julius, sitting down on the foot of Marcus' bed and regarding the older man with deep affection. "I survive."

"That is a great talent," Marcus admitted. He looked at Pompey, in his military garb, standing at the end of the bed, his broad thumbs thrust into his leather girdle. Pompey was regarding him with kindness, and this startled Marcus. Then he noticed the serpentine ring on Pompey's hand. He averted his eyes. Julius was chattering gaily, a habit he had when he wished to conceal his thoughts. "You smell like a rose," said Marcus, a little sourly.

Julius laughed, and slapped Marcus' bare foot. "I am the rose of Rome," he said.

"Rome smells of the Cloaca," said Marcus, and Julius was overcome with mirth. Pompey grinned, and his large white teeth flashed. Julius said, "One would not believe it, but our Marcus is a man of great wit, of subtle wit. He is also an augur."

"So?" said Pompey, with gravity, and Marcus saw that he believed Julius. Marcus said, "Did you come to me for an omen, Julius?"

"I heard you were sick!" cried Julius, reprovingly. "I returned but yesterday to my wife and my little daughter, Julia, but when I heard of your illness but an hour ago I hastened to you. This is your gratitude."

But Marcus said, "Has not Lepidus attempted to assassinate you as yet?"

"I am no threat to Lepidus," Julius said. "I am a man of many parts, and priceless in them all. Besides, Lepidus and I belong to the populares party. I have given up politics. I am but a simple soldier."

Marcus laughed. The two young men laughed with him.

"I respect the Consul of the people," said Julius. "So does Pompey. Did not Pompey help Lepidus to be elected Consul? And Pompey is my friend."

"I discern a winding connection," said Marcus.

"As I have told you, Marcus, I have given up politics."

Marcus watched him as he said, "Lepidus is attempting to overthrow

Sulla's Constitution. The Senate is angry. There are rumors that the Senate
will exile him to his province, Transalpine Gaul. He is ambitious."

Julius sighed. He helped himself to a bunch of grapes from Marcus'
table. A slave came in to pour wine. Julius eyed it mistrustfully before he
drank it, then he shook his head, regretfully. "You are a rich man, it is
rumored, yet your taste in wines is still deplorable. What is that you have
said of Lepidus? That he is ambitious? Ah, to what excesses does not ambition lead! But when were men not ambitious? Except for myself." Pompey
was silent, holding a goblet of wine in his hand.

"You did not admire Sulla," Julius went on when Marcus did not speak.
"You ought to prefer Lepidus who at least is an amiable man regarded
with affection by the people."

"He also is a dictator, and a tyrant," said Marcus. "Sulla forced the
mobs to work at honest labor or go hungry. Lepidus has retired many of
them, again, on the substance of the people, thus raising taxes on the industrious. Must position always be bought, and power, over the bellies of
the despicable, the haters of work, the mendicants? Our treasury is empty
again, thanks to Lepidus and his adoring mobs of rascals and graffiti and
former slaves. It is no marvel that I am discouraged. Nevertheless, I must
still uphold law in the very howling face of chaos, trusting that law will
eventually prevail, and justice also."

The two young men were regarding him in serious silence and intentness. He drank a large goblet of wine, for he was suddenly thirsty. Julius
refilled the goblet for him, and he drank again. He leaned back on his
pillows and wearily closed his eyes.

He said, "I am tired of mankind, and its natural degradation. Do we not
all exalt ourselves when speaking of Socrates and Aristotle and Plato and
Homer, and the other immortals? That is presumption. They are not of us.
They are bright stars of another and unseen world, fallen into our darkness. They walked in our flesh. Still, they are not of us. They were glorious,
but their glory is not ours."

He opened his eyes and Julius gave him more wine. The narrow and
vivid face of Julius was very still. Marcus' weariness returned to him with
powerful force, and again he closed his eyes. A whirling chaos was before
him, shot with sparks of fire and strange half-seen forms and faces. He
forgot where he was, and who was with him. Then the chaos began to
take clearer form and he gazed fiercely at what he saw. Without opening
his eyes he murmured, "There is not one of us in this cubiculum today who
will die peacefully in his bed. We shall be betrayed, and perish in our own
blood." He began to shiver. The wine dulled his awareness of his body and
his bodily senses.

"Who will betray me, Marcus?" Julius asked in a soft voice, leaning over Marcus whose face resembled that of the dead.

Marcus whispered, "Your son."

Julius looked at Pompey, who, very pale, only shrugged. "I have no son," said Julius.

Marcus did not speak. "And I?" said Pompey, speaking at last. "Who will kill me?"

"Your best friend," said the lawyer in that faint and wandering voice.

The eyes of Julius and Pompey locked in hard ferocity. Then Julius said, "He has many best friends."

The sick and dreaming man did not answer. Julius took his cold and flaccid hand and looked at it meditatively. "Who would kill you, Marcus?" he asked.

Marcus whispered, "I do not see their faces."

"You are dreaming," said Julius, still holding the other's hand. "You are sick, and you have the visions of sickness. Do you see Catilina?"

"Fire, and blood," said Marcus. "Livia is avenged at last."

He fell into a deep sleep. The two young men stared at his pale and haggard face, at the dark shadows under the closed eyes, at the white exhaustion of his mouth. The curtain parted and Helvia stood on the threshold. Julius and Pompey kissed her hand, but her anxious gaze was on her son. "He falls, like this, into sudden slumbers," she said. "It is because he is so tired. You must not be offended." Now she looked at the visitors and was surprised at their disturbed expressions. "He is much better," she said, thinking them sorrowful. "Soon he will be able to travel to Greece with his brother. He has not spared himself all these years. He will rest, in Greece."

"He spoke very mysteriously to us," said Julius. "And of us."

"Marcus is superstitious," said Helvia, with the indulgence of a mother. She reached under Marcus' pillows and brought forth a small silver object of much antiquity, for it was worn and shining dimly with ancient scratchings. The young men regarded it with horrified repugnance, for it was the cross of infamy, the top curved into a loop to hold a chain.

"It was given to him by an Egyptian merchant who was his client two years ago," said Helvia, replacing the cross under the pillow. "It came, the merchant said, from some old violated tomb of a Pharaoh, centuries ago. The merchant told my son that it was the sign of the Redeemer of mankind, prophesied eons ago in the mists of the youth of our world. It is, as we know, only the sign of the infamous death of criminals and malefactors and traitors and thieves and rebellious slaves. Yet, my son honors it and tells me, in moments of abstraction, that it is the sign of the redemption of man. He awaits, he declares, hourly for the birth of the son of the gods."

Julius was smiling broadly. "Are the gods coming down from Olympus again for fresh rompings?" he said.

But Pompey, newly fearful, looked back over his shoulder as he and Julius left the sickroom. When they were in Julius' litter, Julius saw, for the first time, the ring on his friend's hand. "How imprudent of you!" he exclaimed with annoyance. "Marcus recognized that ring! In revenge, he deliberately disturbed us and filled us with dismay." Then he smiled and shook his head admiringly. "Marcus is more subtle than even I knew. He wished us, in his gentle malice, to suffer in our minds."

Marcus, unaware that his friends had left him, unaware that he had spoken to them in his half-dream, was dreaming again. He was wandering in a field that was lit by no sun he could discern. There was no limit to the horizon. His feet sank into soft green grass, and there was a murmurous sound of bees and birds in the gentle air. At each step flowers sprang up before him and filled the atmosphere with wonderful fragrance. Suddenly he saw a great city in the distance, bright and shining as if built of gold and alabaster. He hurried toward it, eagerly, but always it retreated, its columns and its glistening domes falling back from him. The breeze rustled as if with a multitude of unseen wings. Just beyond the limits of his hearing he heard singing voices, full of joy and merriment, but when he turned his head he saw nothing but flowers and grass and great stands of trees which were unfamiliar to him. Each tree bore masses of blossoms that exhaled a scent of intense perfume. And the distant city stood in radiance, as if emanating a light of its own and it was this light that lit up the world.

He felt his hand taken gently, and he started and turned his head. Young Livia was beside him, laughing, clad in garments that glowed and with a wreath of flowers on her autumn hair. Her eyes were bluer than he had remembered, and her hand was soft and warm in his. She held him tightly, and he looked at her with ecstasy. "You are not dead, beloved," he cried.

"No, I am not dead. I was never dead, my dear one," she answered in a voice he had never forgotten. She stood on the tips of her toes and kissed his lips, and the touch was like delicious fire. "Remember me, always," she said, and laid her head on his shoulder.

Then a darkening fell over everything and all became wan and far. Marcus, in terror, seized Livia in his arms again. "Tell me!" he cried. "Did you ever love me, Livia? Did you ever know me, and my love for you?"

Her face was becoming the face of a shade, transparent and white, but her eyes lay on him with blue passion. "Yes, but it was not to be. It was the will of God that we did not possess each other in those days, for there is much for you to do and I should have hindered you."

Her words were very mysterious to him and he could not understand them. He tried to grasp her but it was like grasping mist. "Remember me," she said as if she spoke in echoes. "Above all, remember God, and we shall see each other again, and we shall never part thereafter."

The darkness and the wanness fell faster, and now he was alone in a vast darkness, crying, "Livia, Livia!" Only silence answered him. He opened his eyes and saw the anxious face of his mother bent over him.

"I have seen Livia," he said in a weak voice.

Helvia nodded indulgently. "Do we not all dream, my son?" She gave him the elixir the physician had left. "What is life, without a dream?"

CHAPTER THIRTY-THREE

"It is easy enough for you to counsel patience, Julius," said Lucius Sergius Catilina, "for you have more time. But I am thirty-one years old and I am impatient."

The two young men sat in the hot and fragrant garden of the house on the Palatine which the money of Aurelia had purchased. Peacocks strutted and spread their fans in the dark-blue shade, which contrasted with the blinding light that lay on red gravel paths and flowerbeds and glittering fountains and on the tops of dusky cypresses and myrtle trees. A flock of birds as scarlet as blood fluttered in and through the fading leaves of an oak tree, chattering with vehemence as they discussed the coming migration. The first scent of evening jasmine rose on the warm air.

Julius and Lucius were sitting on a cool marble bench in the shade of a myrtle, drinking honey-sweet wine the color of pale roses, and eating figs and grapes and citrons.

"Observe that mountebank," said Julius, chuckling and nodding toward a young peacock who, with an eye to an older one's ire, was tentatively lifting his brilliant, argus-eyed tail. "He wishes to woo the damsels of the flock. But the old peacock looks sternly and warningly at him. His time has not yet come."

"I judge that remark to mean that my time has not yet come, either. Nor yours," said Catilina. "You are still but twenty-five. I am thirty-one. I do not look with equanimity on the fact that my time may arrive when I am a graybeard. We were certain of it under Sulla. But again it has evaded us. Now we have Lepidus. He is like water which runs through the hands before one can drink. Do you know what I have heard? The Senate is weary of him. He restricts their power in behalf of those whom he calls 'the people.' So, the Senate will banish him soon to his province Transalpine Gaul. They love the power Sulla gave them. What, then, of us?"

Julius drank reflectively, then paused to smile again on the young peacock. "Lepidus needs some advice. He is positive the people of Rome are with him. If he should be banished, what if he decides to raise up an army against Rome and march against her?"

Lucius studied him with a faint dark smile. "I assume he has been given this advice."

"Has Lepidus asked my advice? No."

"But you have friends."

"I have friends."

Catilina refilled his crystal goblet, then held it in his hands and looked down into the heart of the glimmering wine. "Well," said Catilina after a moment. "What after that?"

Julius shrugged. "One must observe and consider. One throws the dice. It is in the hands of the gods which way they will fall."

Catilina laughed. "But your dice are always loaded, Julius."

"It is well to assist the gods occasionally."

"You are ambiguous, Caesar. There are times when I do not trust you."

"I am the most loyal of men," said Julius.

"To yourself."

Julius looked offended. "My stars have indicated that those who are born under them are suffused with the deepest devotion toward friends. What friends have I lost through betrayal?"

Catilina considered him. "You have told me that your dear friend, Cicero, has repeated to you that you will die betrayed, in your own blood. If he hints so of your murder, then he is plotting against you."

Julius laughed out loud. "Cicero? Dear friend, you are mad. He may be subtle, as you have seen, but never vicious. He is, above all, amiable and kind and irenic. Jupiter has endowed me with the ability to look into the hearts of men."

Catilina turned his beautiful and depraved face upon him with contempt. "He prophesied my murder, also. Did he not also speak so of Pompey? What is good about a man so openly vindictive?"

"Oracles are moved by no passion nor personalities, Lucius. They speak of the future they see."

"You think him an oracle?"

"No. He has been prophesying the death of Rome for a long time. Is she dead? Have we been murdered? No. He said my son would kill me. Do I have a son? No."

Catilina smiled. "What of M. Junius Brutus? That little boy?"

Julius' face became cold and he fixed his black and sparkling eyes upon his friend. "You defame his mother. And his father, whom I hold in high regard, and who is my friend."

But Catilina smiled even more. "Your friends cannot destroy the rumors that young Brutus is your son. Before your advent, his mother was barren."

"I hear she is devoted to Juno and made many visits to her shrine." Julius' eyes, which had the capacity to look like the points of presented blades on occasion, deadly and violent, now smiled again. "Rumor!" he exclaimed. "If one listened to rumor one would become mad. I prefer facts. On that foundation one can build cities."

"You are building too slowly."

"I build well."

Catilina moved restively on the marble seat. "You are not bold, Julius."

"When necessary I am a lion. The time to roar has not yet arrived. Let us wait until Lepidus has destroyed himself."

"Let us return to that Cicero. He haunts my mind like an evil dream. He is powerful in Rome now. Moreover, he is studying politics. He may rise to confront and challenge us."

"He is very sick. He may die."

"Let us, then, end his pain."

Julius carefully placed his goblet on the table before him. He said, "What do you recommend, Lucius? Poison?"

He raised his eyes slowly and fixed them on Catilina. Catilina's blue eyes shifted, like the flick of a snake's tongue. "Poison is a woman's weapon."

"Ah, so. Livia employed it. I should have remembered."

"Are you threatening me, Caesar?"

Julius was astonished. "I? Why should I threaten you, Lucius?"

"To save your incredible friend, the Chick-pea."

Julius laughed. "It is true that I have an affectionate regard for Cicero, who was my mentor in my youth, and who protected me against you, dearest friend. The loves of one's childhood are not easily forgotten. However, if he rose in my way I should dispatch him. Do you not believe me?"

Catilina gazed at him thoughtfully. Then he said with reluctance, "I believe you. What, then, am I to conjecture? That you think the Chick-pea will be of some assistance to you."

Julius, who was rarely startled, was now taken aback. But he stared into the eyes of Catilina with candor. "How could he assist me?"

"That is what is mystifying. But I feel that you think it."

"You are as fanciful as a woman. My path is not the path of Cicero. They will never cross. I love Cicero, for many reasons which would seem absurd to you. My mother gave him an amulet—"

"Which I believe saved his life."

"You are superstitious. Again, let us consider Cicero. He has many powerful advocates in Rome, if few intimates. Should he die, he would be avenged. His political ambitions, if any, are small. He has made no move to satisfy them. He is speaking of going to Greece. He is a scholar, a poet, an essayist, an orator, a lawyer. I admire him. And his brother is a soldier. Do you think Quintus, who is devoted to him, would accept his death meekly? Let us not complicate our affairs."

"He spoke of his own death, you have told me," said Catilina with satisfaction. "Did he see my face among his murderers?"

"He does not speak of you, Lucius. Now let us talk of realities."

As the hot summer inclined toward autumn Marcus made little progress. His joints were suffused. The physician was alarmed at his heart sounds. "You must go at once to a milder clime," he said.

Now Marcus knew he must go if he were to survive. His young lawyers came to his bedside for advice on law matters which must be brought to conclusion in the coming months. Quintus, eager to go with his brother, and to escape from his young wife, urged haste. He looked at his brother's pale and haggard face with terror.

In the next month or so Marcus almost forgot his pain and his illness because of events. Aemilius Lepidus, the dictator of Rome, was indeed banished to his province of the Transalpine Gaul by the angered Senate. He agreed with apparent meekness. But he stopped at Etruria and began to levy an army amongst disgruntled veterans of many wars, who felt that they had been treated with disregard by the masters of Rome. The Senate declared him a public enemy, and rumor excitedly ran through the streets like a carried torch. Lepidus' army grew daily, and it was said he would soon march against Rome, to seize ultimate power and avenge himself on the Senate.

Pompey was commissioned to meet him in arms, and taking Catulus Pompey met Lepidus on the Campus Martius and defeated him. Lepidus, escaping, fled to join Sertorius in the Spains.

But so long as he lived he was a menace to Rome. "Ah," said Julius, to his many secret friends in the Senate, "if one only possessed a helmet from Hades, so one could be invisible and approach Lepidus at night and destroy this enemy of our nation!"

"We are a lawful body," said the Senators. "Besides, Lepidus still has many friends in Rome, and in the provinces, among the military."

"Am I not a soldier?" asked Julius. "Lepidus does not lack guards. Nevertheless, he must die. He is a traitor."

"True," said the Senators, averting their eyes from Julius' face. "But he still has friends. We have been through a difficult and dangerous time. If he dies, it must be by accident, or in a way so mysterious that his death cannot be laid to our offense."

Julius, satisfied, nodded in agreement. And so it was that Lepidus, who had considered himself a greater Sulla, died mysteriously in the very house of his friend Sertorius, who avowed to avenge his murder by someone unknown. The Senate issued a proclamation in Lepidus' behalf, saying that though he had set himself against the Senate and the people of Rome he had been a noble soldier. It was obvious that he had become deranged. The Senate ordered a period of mourning for him, and publicly honored his family.

Marcus, who had despised and feared Lepidus, who was of an unstable and violent character, was nevertheless greatly disturbed over the murder. It was another example, to him, of lawlessness overcoming law in the name of expediency. When Julius visited him Marcus expressed his alarm. Julius agreed with him.

Marcus looked at him with the acuteness of grave illness. "You never cared about law, dear young friend. There were some weeks, Julius, when you did not visit me. Were you in the Spains?"

Julius was all amazement and offense. "What are you implying, Marcus?"

"Nothing. I was merely wondering," said Marcus, with weariness. Julius' eyes narrowed on him. But he spoke no more of Lepidus.

Nor did Sertorius, the friend of the Consul. Rome subsided. Many old and disgruntled and crippled veterans were delighted to receive handfuls of gold sesterces from a treasury that was almost bare, and they forgot Lepidus also.

Two nights before Marcus left with his brother for Greece, the father visited the older son in his cubiculum. "I have discerned a sadness of the spirit in you, Marcus, that seems even greater than your illness. You speak to me no longer of God; you turn from His name. Why is this?"

Marcus murmured, "I have considered if He is dead. He is silent in the face of enormities."

"He is concerned with man, not with men," said Tullius, seating himself and taking his son's hand.

Marcus moved restively. But Tullius would not free his hand. "Let me repeat to you, Marcus, what Plotimus of Egypt said over a hundred years ago. 'But mind contemplates its source, not because it is separated from it but because it is next after it and there is nothing between.' This is true also in the case of soul and mind. Everything has a longing for and loves that which begot it, and especially when there are only the One that begot and the one begotten. And when the Supremely Good is the One who begot, the one begotten is necessarily joined to Him so intimately that it is separated only insofar as it is a second being."

"The Greeks," said Marcus, listlessly, "knew of Plotimus, and so invented the Unknown God, who would be begotten of the Godhead and would descend to earth. The Jews have that fable, also. It runs through our own religion."

"Because God willed it so, for it is His truth."

But Marcus felt defeated in his mind and his soul and his body, and he did not know why. Always, he had wanted to go to Greece. Now he contemplated the thought with dismay and without desire.

Helvia said to him, "When you return, with your health restored, you must marry. You have waited long enough." He did not dispute with her, for he had no strength.

Atticus, in Athens, had expressed his joy in a letter to his author. Marcus and Quintus must be his honored and beloved guests. Marcus, in that benign climate of sea and sun and cerulean sky and wisdom, would regain his health rapidly. He would also begin to write again, for the edification of mankind. Marcus laughed.

His friends repeatedly brought news of the concern of Romans for the great lawyer and orator. But Marcus looked at them incredulously and said to himself, "Do they speak of me? What nonsense!" He would move his anguished limbs and it seemed to him that the pain of his body was less than the pain of his mind. As for himself, he should prefer to die here in his bed, defeated and alone, and join his spirit with that of Livia's. Sometimes he became petulant in the face of his family's concern and grief for him. It seems he must live for them. Have I not always? he thought, with bitterness. On the night before he left for Greece, he dreamed of his grandfather, who regarded him with sternness.

"Are you a dog, or a Roman?" asked the old man, who seemed of a towering height.

His strength was a little renewed during the night. In the morning he huddled in the family car while Quintus drove the fine horses. In a few hours they set sail for Greece.

Marcus sat on the deck of the galleon and the fair breezes of the sea struck his face and the sun lay on his cheeks. He was very exhausted. Syrius, who had accompanied the brothers, covered him with quilts against any chill. He lay back in his chair and closed his eyes and let himself be carried on the gentle swell. He had never been on the sea before. At last, he opened his eyes and looked upon the water, and for the first time in many months he felt a quickening in his body. He said to his heart, Be still. And to his restless sick mind, Be quiet. It is enough that I have eyes.

When Quintus brought him wine Marcus smiled at him, and Quintus' strong bright face jerked with emotion. "I feel much better," said Marcus. "I am glad that you forced this journey upon me."

He looked at the sea, which ran past the ship in foam and in millions of rainbows. The masts creaked; there was a smell of oil and tar and hot wood. The sails held the red sunlight cupped within them. Sailors sang. Marcus said, "I fear I shall live." But he smiled.

CHAPTER THIRTY-FOUR

"It is a strange thing which I have heard before," said Marcus to his affectionate host, Atticus. "Greek temples and even the great theatres and public buildings have been erected not to please the eye of man but the eye of God. That is why they are so marvelous, so mysteriously fascinating. I have seen magnificent buildings in Rome, overpowering with might and glory and columns and arches. They were built only for the exaltation and panoply of man."

The hot dry climate, parched as the silvery dust of Greece, had restored his health. He had indulged Quintus, and even the skeptical Atticus, by going to Epidaurus, where he had slept one night in the temple of Aesculapius, called by the Greeks Asclepius. Here was the final refuge of the afflicted whom doctors had abandoned for incurability. But Marcus noted that the priests of the divine one, son of Apollo, student of Chitron, the centaur, were all notable physicians also and treated the hopeless not only with solicitude but the best of medicines and their own skills. "It is said," one old priest remarked kindly to Marcus, discerning he was not superstitious—or, rather, not more superstitious than the average Roman sufferer —"that God heals. That is true. He is the Great Physician, as Hippocrates often asserted. To point a lesson in piety He will often cure instantaneously, in a miracle, to bring men's minds to Him. But He has endowed good and dedicated physicians as His deputies, His messengers."

Quintus and Marcus had found lodgings in a fine inn in Epidaurus, among others who could afford it. Many were Roman officers and gentlemen, and their wives and their children. Some were Hellenistic Jews, urbane nobles with pale and learned faces and the delicate features of the well-born, aristocratic Jew. It was obvious that they avoided the company of the Romans, no matter the Romans' station, but they were friendly to the Greeks especially those of wisdom and education. Most were Sadducees, cynical and worldly men, whom Noë ben Joel deplored. When Marcus spoke to them of the Messias, they smiled tolerantly as if a child had spoken to them of a myth. They had made an exception of him, for all he was a Roman, for he was a lawyer and many of them were lawyers.

He would sit with them in the sharp blue evenings, when the sun declined, on the terraces of the inn, looking toward the distant plains. They conversed with him concerning international law, and their respect for him grew. They had heard of him, they said, even in Athens, and even in Jerusalem. But they rallied him somewhat for his dedication. Law, they said, was invented to control the vehement masses and make them malleable to order. They smiled at him, and fingered their necklaces and armlets and rings, when he said that Law was of God, for all men. "Why, then," one asked him, "does your face become so sad and withdrawn when you speak of God? Do you suspect He is dead, or never existed?"

"I was overcome, in Rome, by a sense of inevitable disaster," Marcus replied with reluctance.

"You have come to an answer, then?" asked the Jew, with a smile.

Marcus looked into that fine, grave face with the amused eyes and said suddenly, "Yes. But it is an answer I had forgotten. God will not interfere if man is bent on destruction. He has given us free will."

The Jew lifted his delicate eyebrows. "You are conversant with Jewish theology."

"The theme runs through all religions, from the most ancient Egyptian down. So universal a concept, then, can have no source but an original one, and that one is God."

The Sadducee was disappointed in Marcus, and rallied him a little for his superstition. But others of the Sadducees, men worn with illness, looked on him with some hesitant uncertainty. They pondered. If even a Roman believed what they themselves had been taught as children then they should re-examine their skepticism.

Marcus said, "A very young and still unknown poet in Rome sent me one of his poems. He has read some of my work, and wanted an opinion. May I quote that poem to you, written by Lucretius, who is still almost a boy?:

" 'No single thing abides, but all things flow,
    Fragment to fragment clings; the things that grow
    Until we know and name them,
    By degrees
    They meet and are no more the things we know.

    Thou, too, O Earth—thine empires, lands and seas—
    Least with thy stars of all the galaxies,
    Globed from the drift like these, like these thou too
    Shalt go. Thou art going, hour by hour, like these.

Globed from the atoms, falling slow or swift,
I see the suns, I see the systems lift
Their forms, and even the systems and their suns
Shall go back slowly to the eternal drift.

Nothing abides. Thy seas in delicate haze
Go off; those mooned sands forsake their place,
And where they are shall other seas in turn
Mow with their scythes of whiteness other bays.' "

The skeptical Sadducee thought on that for a few moments. Then he said, "So, as nothing abides, nothing is important."

"Except God, and His children. For they are immortal, though the world and the suns, and their worlds in order, shall pass away." Suddenly Marcus' languor and pain diminished and he was filled with a brilliant courage and new fortitude, as if a divine Hand had touched him.

"I had thought," Marcus mused, "that only Rome was important, that her death would be the death of all mankind. But now, suddenly, I know that even if Rome passes away God will remain, and all His plan for humanity. Nevertheless, that does not give me warrant to cease my personal fight on evil, for those who fight evil are the soldiers of God."

"And you believe that God will manifest Himself through His Messias?" asked another of the Sadducees with intent interest.

"Yes. The belief runs through all religions of the worlds. Socrates called Him the Divine One. Aristotle called Him the Deliverer. Plato spoke of Him as the Man of Gold who would rescue the cities. The Egyptians call Him Horus. We all await Him."

One of the Sadducees, who had earlier expressed his opinion that the story of the Messias was one to comfort the masses, said, "But the Messias is of the Jews only!"

"No," said Marcus. "Even your own Sacred Books speak of Him as a 'light unto the Gentiles.' Isaias spoke so. And your wise men in the gates of Jerusalem speak of Him as imminent."

"Ah, the old men with the rheumy eyes and the white beards!" said the Sadducee. "They dream."

"The dreams of old men are the sunrise of the children," said Marcus, and wondered why he, who had been so sick of soul, should speak like this now.

But the Sadducee, who was mysteriously disturbed that a materialistic Roman should touch his worldly conscience with a finger of fire, said scoffingly, "Romans eat at every man's table and reside in no man's house of philosophy. You have originated nothing; you have only borrowed, a fragment here, an urn there, a law here, a theory from yonder dead mists, a column from a grave, a wall from a lost city, a myth from some forgotten pantheon, a goblet of water from a stream which comes from no source you know."

"But man persists," said Marcus. "His empires die, but he remains. All that man knows is a synthesis of dead men's knowledge. Did you not borrow from the Egyptians, the Phoenicians, the Hittites, the Babylonians, the Persians, and others of the Hebraic peoples? Your Abraham was a Babylonian, but not a Hebrew, as you are not Hebrews, though you call yourselves so, erroneously. You speak of yourselves as Jews, but that is only because your founder, Judah, son of Abraham, claimed that section of Israel now known as Judea. From whence do you come? You men like myself, who were never one with the brown Babylonians, and the dusky Egyptians who ejected you because you clung to the Faith of your Fathers and would have naught to do with local gods? And because your skin is fair?"

"He speaks truly," said one of the Sadducees, and fingered his chin from which the beard had been shaved. "From whence do we come?"

"Who knows?" said Marcus.

He spoke of Athens. "There are many who stand with awe before the Pyramids. They ponder on the dead Egyptians. But what are the Pyramids compared with the Acropolis of Athens? And tell me, why do you people of the Jewish Faith look upon the Acropolis with a lift of the heart and identify yourselves so with it? Because it is your own. It is our own."

He looked at their disturbed and noble faces, and smiled. He stood up. "Pray for me," he said. "I am sorely afflicted."

"We, too, are sorely afflicted," said one of the older Sadducees. "Pray for us also."

The Romans present loved Marcus. But when they spoke of politics to him they could not understand his replies, for they themselves were pragmatic and concerned only with the immediate. He spoke of legal balances, and they spoke anxiously of the rise of dictators. "It is our fault," he told them, "that we have dictators. God gave us the gift of freedom. We have despised it in the name of today's exigencies."

One of the Romans wrote to his favorite Senator and denounced Marcus as a subversive, a traitor to Rome. But the other Romans listened to him seriously, and nodded. He said, "Just as a builder must have a plan on his paper in order to build wisely and well, so must a people have a Constitution in order to guide them. But we have abandoned our plan and our map so painfully wrought by our fathers. Hence, we have dictators, men who lust for centralized power in order to oppress us."*

* From Cicero's *The Moral Law*.

The famous sanctuary of Asclepius, noted throughout the civilized world, was not only a religious and miraculous shrine but a whole community. The inn, or Katagogion, in which Marcus, his brother and his servant lived, was a two-story structure of some one hundred and fifty rooms, the largest building in the sanctuary, and accepted the very poorest, who slept in the kitchens or the stables or even under the outdoor porticoes for a drachma or two. The very rich had several rooms for their families and their slaves. Nevertheless, rich and poor were served the same simple food of the region, with the exception of wines and those luxuries the wealthy could bring with them. For Asclepius loved all men. The inn was built of tufa and had a colonnade about it of squat white columns, unornamented, through which men could walk and converse in the cool of the evening. Surrounding it was a large circular garden in which children played and laughed at the caged birds and small animals, and fed them. Their nurses and their mothers stood among them, smiling.

Marcus was moved to pity by the sight of many of the children, some of whom were twisted and lame, some blind, some deaf, some with the blank staring faces of the mindless. Some had arms like tortured twigs, immovable. Some had sores which would not heal. Some of the young backs were bent as the backs of very old men are bent. But in this clime, in this shadow of one who had so loved humanity and had so preserved them as to incur the wrath of Pluto and Zeus, even these miserable little ones laughed as though they felt the smiling shadow of him who had pity upon them and did not find them contemptible as the other gods found them.

The purlieus of the sanctuary contained a respectable gymnasium and a pleasant small open theatre, where plays were performed every afternoon or beautiful music played, also a temple to Apollo, the father of Asclepius, Doric in style and very white and airy in appearance, a stadium for horse races and athletic events, the shrine itself, buildings for water tanks, dwellings for the priests and the assistants and servants, Roman baths of curative waters, a temple of Hygeia, another of Aphrodite, and still another of the goddess Themis, and yet another of the sister of Apollo, the goddess of chastity, Artemis. Each temple had been built of the purest white marble and was an epic poem in itself, surrounded by terraces and fountains and green gardens alive with the songs of birds. Around the confines of the many buildings were small structures where the desperately sick and the pregnant remained overnight and prayed and were visited by the priest-physicians, for within the sacred building of the shrine itself no one near death was permitted, nor were those about to give birth.

This whole sanctuary and all its outlying buildings lay in a shallow valley surrounded by low hills dark with cypresses and the sacred oak and myrtle. Above it all arched the incredible and shining blue of the

Grecian sky, a blue so intense and so incandescent that Marcus was never weary of gazing at it with something like disbelief. This disbelief had first come to him during his journey to Epidaurus when he had passed over the isthmus that joined the Ionian and the Aegean seas, which were a brilliant violet not to be encountered anywhere else in the world. What mysterious alchemy of earth and heaven had been brewed here to give rise to such a sky, and to the color of such seas? For surely it was a unique phenomenon! He had, on his journey, seen small bays like dazzling amethysts, surrounded by hills a deeper color clothed in mystery. And all the dust had been argent, as pure as snow, under the fantastic hue of the sky. This was surely the land of Apollo, filled with depthless light insistent and burning—the land of the sun. It was no enigma any longer to Marcus that here was the country of the gods, the home of wisdom, of beauty, of poetry, of glory, of a celebration where those on Olympus met those who dwelt on the dusky earth and talked together as comrades. No man could visit Greece, or live in her, without awe. Sometimes Marcus thought that Greece was the Eden of which Noë ben Joel had spoken, flawless, flaming like a diamond, colored with absolute blue and purple and silver. Here human flesh became marble, smooth and gleaming, in the many temples. Here color was not ambiguous, but passionate. Here the sun conferred healing, and the mountains rejoiced. Here it was that Zeus—not the grim Jupiter of Rome—had enveloped Danae in a rain of gold, and Artemis had slept in the radiant forests of the moon. From this land had flashed the light that had illuminated the wilderness of the western world, and had given it thought and philosophy. The harmony and the color and the brightness were portent of immortality, the wisdom the echo of the Lord's voice. There was not an art—and art is divine—which Greece had not produced, whether it was mathematics, reason, the theatre, poesy, sculpture, painting, column or portico, science, medicine, astronomy, philosophy, or symmetry, proportion or music.

Greece enforced upon man the knowledge that without God he was nothing, whether he was a laborer in the field or a dictator on an enameled throne. For, as Epictetus had said, "Whithersoever I go, there shall I still find sun, moon, and stars, there shall I find dreams and omens, and converse with God."

Marcus had always believed this from his childhood, but Rome's might and cynical power had finally confounded him and depressed him. He had been caught up in the whirlwind of despair. He had abandoned hope. He had talked earnestly with man, hoping to enlighten him, when there was no enlightenment. Manhood, he thought now, does not confer wisdom. It often distorts it, for men become too often the slave of the immediate. Again he thought of the words of Epictetus: "Give yourself more diligently to reflection. Know yourself. Take counsel with the Godhead. Without God put your hand to nothing!" And what of my unhappiness? thought Marcus. Epictetus had an answer: "If any be unhappy let him remember that he is unhappy by reason of himself alone. For God has made all men to enjoy felicity and the constancy of God."

Quintus and Syrius carried Marcus one evening to the Propylaea of the sacred precinct, for he could barely move because of the pains in all his joints and the spasms in his muscles. Here servants of the god bathed him in curative waters and dressed him in a white robe. He sacrificed on the altar. The low rays of the sun entered through the beautiful bronze doors, which would not be closed until nightfall; they transformed the clouds of incense into billows of deep purple. Other sufferers were already there, lying on the pallets laid out for them, and among them was the Sadducee, Judah ben Zakkai, who had questioned Marcus in a worldly manner. He suffered from an affliction of the heart, which no physician had been able to cure. He smiled up at Marcus as the latter bent over him. "What?" asked Marcus, with gentle raillery, "is the skeptic here also?"

Judah replied, "Let me remind you of what the Stoics say: 'Let us sacrifice to the gods. If they do not exist, then it does no harm. If they do exist, they will be pleased and may grant our prayers.'"

"Do you pray to Asclepius or to the God of your fathers, Judah?"

Judah smiled, his pale face touched with mirth. "To the God of my fathers."

Marcus became grave. "Men give many names to God, but He is only God, and who knows His Holy Name? Have not my Jewish friends told me that no man knows that Name? Let us call Him what we will; it is of no moment to Him, Who loves His children."

Judah said with sudden intentness on Marcus, "You truly believe!"

Marcus smiled again. "I do, of this moment. But who is not assailed with doubts? Today, I say, 'Blessed is He.' Tomorrow, in any travail, I may say, 'Where is He, if He lives at all?'"

The temple, chastely Doric in architecture, was 25.50 metres long and 13.2 metres wide, and had been built over two hundred years ago by the architect, Theodotus. It consisted of pronaos and cella, and was built of stone covered with white stucco. It was roofed with fir and cypress and in the four corners were statues of nymphs. A large statue of Nike stood on the pediment, heroic and austere. The floor of the temple was paved in black and white marble. The pure white altar burned with a crimson flame day and night and was tended by the priests, a number of whom were always on their knees praying at all hours.

But the great gold and ivory statue of Asclepius remained below the temple floor in hushed quiet. Thrasymedes, the famous sculptor, had carved the statue, which sat upon a throne with one hand on a staff and the other on the head of a sacred serpent. A dog basked humbly at his feet. The face of the statue expressed the calm compassion and wisdom of the physician, his removal from passion, his contemplation of mystery. It was impossible to gaze upon that lofty face without reverence. Marcus, upheld by his brother and servant, looked at the statue and listened to the deep quiet of the sanctuary. Then he was carried upstairs again to the Adyton and laid upon his prepared pallet beside Judah. "It is a beautiful statue," said Judah. "It is true that pious Jews abhor statues of all kinds, for likenesses of anything in heaven or on the earth are forbidden in the Ten Commandments. But I am a Hellenistic Jew, and I admire beauty. Moreover, that Commandment was given because the illiterate and the stupid can rarely distinguish between a mere symbol and the reality it represents. God feared idolatry of man-made things."

"But we, who are so much wiser, do not confuse symbols with reality," said Marcus.

Judah smiled. "You mock me."

"I do not have a good opinion of mankind," said Marcus. "That is, perhaps, a lack of virtue in me. Once someone told me that man and the rat are two creatures who resemble each other more than they resemble all others in creation. They are savage and ferocious, killing for mere sport or wantonness and a love of cruelty; they deface; they destroy. They attack the females and the young of their own species, unlike other animals. They are cannibalistic. Moreover, their dung is poisonous. They leave disease behind them. Was it not Sophocles who said that he had no doubt but that rats have a god, too? I often wonder if their god is not in the shape of a man, for rats have the same hatred of man that we have of God."

He lay down on the pallet. A priest came to him with a cup in his hand, which he presented to Marcus. "It is a distillation of the willow tree bark, which is efficacious in the treatment of the rheumatic diseases. It will, at least, relieve your pain temporarily." Marcus drank the potion, which was both acrid and of a vinegary taste and puckered his mouth and throat.

Judah studied Marcus' face, which had relaxed on the pillow. He saw the contemplative profile, the long nose, the firm, if gentle chin, the faintly smiling lips, the sloping brow, the mass of brown and curling hair, and, above all, the deep line of humor that ran from above the nostril on the cheek to far down below the mouth. The open eyes seemed to fix thoughtfully on the ceiling, and they glimmered changefully in the last sunlight as if endless thoughts paraded before him as in a mural. His hands were folded on his breast. Once or twice a furrow of pain ran over his forehead and twitched his lips, but his attitude was of patience and endurance.

The sun sank away. Now the temple was lit only by the scarlet light on the altar. Others lying on their pallets on the floor groaned feebly. Priests moved among them, speaking in soothing voices, and administering medicines and water. Other priests prayed silently on their knees before the altar. Then they began to sing, or to chant, their voices rising in heroic and majestic cadences:

> "O Thou, Who never abandoned man,
> Have mercy upon us who abandoned Thee!
> O Thou, Whose love is wider than all the universes,
> Have mercy upon us who have returned love with hatred!
> O Thou, Whose Hand is filled with the perfume of healing,
> Have mercy upon us who heal nothing, but only destroy!
> O Thou, Whose other Name is Truth,
> Have mercy upon us whose lips are black with lies!
> O Thou, Who moves in eternal beauty,
> Have mercy upon us who defame the earth with ugliness!
> O Thou, Who art pure and everlasting Light,
> Have mercy upon us who dwell in our darkness!
>
> Have mercy, God!
> God, have mercy!"

Have mercy, God, prayed Marcus silently. He fell asleep. His last conscious thought was that the pain had left his joints and his flesh, and that the continuous chanting of the priests was like a fragrant wave that carried him into peace. For the first time in many months he slept without dreams, as warm and safe as an infant.

The next morning he awoke to early sunlight and marvelous refreshment, and his body, though still weak, was without pain and flexible. The priests were already moving among the awakened patients, carrying tablets in their hands on which they recorded dreams. Many of the patients exclaimed aloud in joy that their illnesses had left them. The priests smiled paternally. They administered more medicines. Marcus turned his head and looked at Judah, who said, "I slept without gasping and without struggle. My heart is still."

A priest came to Marcus who said, "I did not dream at all."

"That is the best of sleep," said the priest, and gave him another potion. "Nightmares are the travail of the mind."

"I am well," said Marcus. "Will this continue?"

The priest was silent a moment. Then he said, "None of the very best physicians know the cause of the rheumatic diseases. But we do know that the rheumatic is a man sad and melancholy of mind, dejected and hopeless of heart. None but the intelligent can feel so, and we have noted that it is the intelligent who are mainly afflicted by this disease. The pain of the mind is often reflected in the body. The sense of frustration in the soul is conveyed in the locked joints. The spasmodic muscles indicate the passionate struggles of the tormented spirit. The rheumatic is a man in a state of constant tension of both thought and flesh.

"I can only remind you, noble Cicero, that if your mind rests on peace your body will so rest."

"But who can have peace in this world?"

"We can have fortitude, and accept what we cannot change."

"But, who knows if we cannot change it?"

The priest laughed kindly. "That is the stigmata of the rheumatic. You can but pray that God will bless your efforts; leave all else in His Hands."

The priest turned to Judah. "Did you dream, my friend?"

Judah hesitated. "I dreamed of my dead mother. She held me in her arms as if I were a child again, and I wept. Then, as I wept, the anguish in my heart subsided and my breath came with ease. When I awoke, my wretchedness had left me."

"You were weeping in your soul," said the priest. "For what do you weep, Judah ben Zakkai? Be reconciled to God."

The two young men left the temple together, after leaving large offerings in gratitude. Their friends rejoiced to see them moving in health and embraced them. Quintus, the soldier, had difficulty in restraining his tears of joy, and Syrius kissed Marcus' hands. The fierce dry heat of the sun made their eyes blink, and flushed their pale cheeks. Marcus sat alone in the inn for a long time, meditating. When he emerged his face was peaceful.

The next day he left with Quintus and Syrius for Athens again.

CHAPTER THIRTY-FIVE

Lucent land! thought Marcus, as he sat in the car driven by his brother. The horses and the wheels created great drafts of white, iridescent dust which remained in the hot and radiant air after them, glittering like pale fire. To their right the Aegean was truly a royal purple, running with argent light. To their left rose the cypress-wooded hills, dark and lush. They passed white walls and meadows filled with sheep and cattle, and orchards of twisted silver olive trees, and gardens filled with green vegetables and burning flowers. They passed little cities, crowned by templed acropoleses, and villages crowded with the white, cube-shaped houses of Greece. Each house had a horizontal trellis jutting from it, laced with fruity grape vines. They entered Nauplia and rested in the noonday in a quiet inn above the sea and among dark-blue mountains. Marcus sat on the high terrace overlooking the colored water and while he dined simply on honey, cold mutton, a spicy salad, brown bread and white, and cheese, he looked at the sky, the incredibly sapphire sky of Greece, depthless and glowing. It was not hard to imagine that that effulgence was the reflection of the gods, themselves. It was easy to understand how that sky, this ardent but stimulating heat, these aromatic hills, this blaze of plum-colored sea, could give birth to the noblest wisdom man as yet had conceived. The sea, at this hour, was dotted with the scarlet sails of languid fishing vessels, and they dipped like dreaming dancers. Somewhere, behind the inn, young men sang, their voices harmonious and full of joy. Bees hovered over the pot of honey on the white table before Marcus, and he watched them with love and peace. A dove swooped down to eat the crumbs of the bread. Birds cried sweetly; the breeze was full of fragrance and spice.

The thought of Rome was a vehement background to Marcus' reflections. But he could think of his city objectively now. It was not such a ferocious pressure on his mind. He must return to it, for it was his, but he would return to it soothed and with greater strength of spirit.

Marcus had dined alone. He preferred this, though Quintus, the gregarious, could not understand. To Quintus, the presence of others was necessary for his ebullient soul. He liked laughter and gay conversation and rude jokes. His handsome, highly colored face would then beam heartily. His jests were the jests of soldiers and virile men. He adored his brother, and was awed by him, but he had come to think of Marcus as somewhat effete, and pale with thought. He had been offended that Marcus had not enjoyed his short, military experience. What was a man except a warrior, delighting in fighting and dying for his country? Those who preferred books and the professions were men of staleness, always complaining that soldiers did not understand the art of civilization. But civilizations were established on war, and conquest. Struggle was vital to life. Men of books preferred their libraries and their dry conversations and their interminable dialogues. Quintus would shake his head, baffled. Still, Marcus commanded his respect and fealty and devotion.

So, while Marcus ate his simple meal on the terrace overlooking the sea, Quintus joked with the men in the stables and with black Syrius, who had a wry humor, and who loved horses almost as much as Quintus loved them. They all drank great quaffs of wine, and told stories which would have made Marcus wince. They breathed in the scent of manure and found it hearty. All in the inn were enamored of Quintus, with his curling black hair and his ripe cheeks and his bluff Roman manner. Even the Greeks forgave him for being a Roman.

"My brother," said Quintus, "knows much about law, but he knows nothing of politics. I am endeavoring to enlighten him."

They set off again, Quintus standing sturdily in the car and whipping up the fine black horses, and Marcus reclining on the cushioned seat and Syrius moving along with spirit on his own white horse just at the side of the car. Quintus sang; Marcus drowsed, wonderfully free from the pain and stiffness that had afflicted him and feeling, even in his doze, the returning health in his flesh. The roads were white with soft dust and fairly even if narrow; the declining sun was now warm rather than searingly hot; the sound of wheels and hoofs lulled Marcus. He smiled drowsily at his brother's loud and ribald ditties, and shielded his face from the light with his bent arm. Sometimes other cars and chariots and horsemen overtook them with a thunder of wheels and a called greeting. They would spend the night near Corinth in a quiet inn.

Toward sundown Marcus raised himself on the cushions and yawned contentedly. The car was rolling along the road in comparative isolation now, between towns. The west was a silent ocean of gold with not even a small cloud rising over it. The sea at the right was the color of wine and very still. Long green meadows filled with cattle spread to the left. A soft and aromatic breeze was rising from the land, filled with the odor of ripening grapes and dark cypress. To the east the sky was a passionate aquamarine in which floated the thread-like curve of the new silver moon.

He heard the ring of hoofs behind him and saw two hooded horsemen swiftly overtaking the car. What magnificent horses, he thought, seeing the gleam of their great white bodies. The horsemen rode expertly, cloaked against the dust. Then Marcus became a little anxious. The road was very narrow here, and the embankment down to the sea was steep and filled with large sharp stones. If the horsemen intended to pass the car they must do it in single file and not side by side as they were riding now. "Fools," said Quintus, glancing over his shoulder. Syrius dropped behind a little to give the car more room.

The horsemen came faster, with a kind of fury, as if the car before them did not exist. Marcus sat up alertly and clutched the side of the car. Syrius shouted. Quintus pulled on the reins. Then, at the last moment the second horseman fell behind the first and the two swept to the left of the car in a rush of dust and thunder. They met together beyond the car. But now they lessened their pace. The air was full of choking and shining dust and

Quintus and his brother and Syrius were momentarily blinded and they coughed.

Suddenly one of the horsemen glanced back at the car, though his face was more than half-hidden in his hood. Like a flash a long spear shone in his hand, or a pike. He flung it backward; it arced in the light of sunset and soared toward the car. There was a dull sound as the weapon struck one of the horses in the breast. The horse reared with a death whinny; he fell in his traces and the car crashed onto his body. The other horse raised himself on his hind feet and cavorted and tore himself loose from the car and raced to the left. The car upended on the dead body of the first horse and Quintus sailed through the air like Icarus. He fell with a heavy noise on the road, and lay still. Marcus was hurled to the floor of the tilted car, then he rolled backward and fell onto the road, his forehead making savage contact with the level stones.

Syrius was more fortunate. He had been riding at the right of the car and almost abreast of it. He had seen the flash of the weapon in the horseman's hand, and had instinctively understood and had slowed his horse and pulled back. So though his own horse stumbled into the car and he was almost thrown, he was able to control the animal and whirl it about on its hind legs. But he was fortunate only for a moment, for just as he was bringing his horse to a stop he felt a deathly pain in his chest and incredulously looked down at a second weapon which had impaled him. Then darkness swept over his eyes and he fell dead from his horse and sprawled in the dust near Marcus.

Now all was dusty quiet. The horsemen halted at a little distance and looked back at the violent ruin they had created. "Let us make sure," said one, preparing to dismount.

The other horseman hesitated. He heard, in the deep stillness, the sound of many distant hoofs. "No!" he exclaimed. "Without doubt they are all dead. Let us run across this field so we shall not be seen by those approaching! They will be on us in a moment." He panted and smiled and wiped his sweating face. "None could have survived that, not even Quintus in his leather armor and with his thick head!"

They swung their horses to the left and plunged into the green grass of the meadows.

Quintus was not dead, but only stunned. His military harness had saved him, though the breath had been knocked from him. His military helmet had protected his head. Never for an instant had he been unconscious. He was a soldier and he was accustomed to these accidents. He heard the voices of the men and understood what they had said. No sooner had they turned their horses into the meadow than he had risen on his knees, shaking his head, spitting out the blood in his mouth. Alertly, he looked behind him, and saw Syrius' horse standing trembling near the body of his master. Quintus' legs were shaking but he ran to the horse and in an instant he was in the saddle. It was a fine horse. Quintus glanced momentarily at his brother and Syrius in the dust, then he turned the horse and followed the attackers, who were small figures racing in the distant meadows. He pursued them, spurring the horse without mercy, and holding his military sword in his hand. His fierce soldier's mind forgot all else, and so he did not see the company which had appeared at a turn in the road and were now approaching the wreck with exclamations of dismay. He had but one thought: Overtake. And kill.

It was a company of merchants and their outriders who had come upon the wreck and the fallen men. They dismounted, uttering sounds of consternation and anxiety. They saw at once that Syrius, the faithful black servant, was dead, the pike standing up from his breast. They examined Marcus, whose face was bleeding and whose left arm was obviously broken. Though badly injured, he was still breathing. The merchants began to minister to him, kneeling about him in the dust and asking themselves what calamity had overtaken this company. "Thieves!" said one merchant, and they all loosened their daggers.

"How fortunate that we came upon them before they could rob and complete the killing!" said another.

"But who is that who is pursuing the murderers?" asked still another, pointing. "Look! He has overtaken them! He is fighting with them!"

Others shaded their eyes from the golden glare of the sunset to stare at the far little figures wheeling in a death struggle and outlined like black statuettes against the background of the wildly illuminated sky. Then, as they watched in breathless fascination they saw one horseman break away and run for his life, leaving his companion to struggle alone with the soldier. An instant later Quintus had plunged his sword into the lone horseman's side, and the man tumbled to the ground. Quintus was on him in a second, again plunging his sword into the body of the fallen man. Then he was bending over him, very still. He glanced just once at the horseman who had fled and who was by this time too far to be pursued again.

"Brave man!" cried one of the merchants kneeling about Marcus. "He fought the two, dispersed one and killed the other! See, he is mounting again and returning."

Marcus painfully awoke to lamplight to discover himself in bed with the bruised and wounded Quintus sitting beside him. His left arm throbbed like a fire and was restrained with bandages which bound it to his side. His face flamed. He could barely open his swollen eyes. For several moments, as he stared blankly at his brother's drowsing and discolored face and at the lip which still oozed a little blood, he did not understand and thought he was dreaming. Then horror overtook him as he remembered the senseless attack on the road. Thieves! he thought. But there, on the table nearby, close to the flickering lamp, lay his purses, his Alexandrian dagger studded with jewels.

"Quintus!" he whispered. Quintus, the soldier, who could sleep deeply one second and be instantly and fully awake the next, started upright in the big oaken chair in which he had been drowsing. His bleeding mouth spread in a smile, and Marcus saw that one tooth was missing. He also saw, with growing dread, that Quintus' left arm was bandaged and that the bandage was stained with blood. He saw the many contusions on his brave brother's face.

"Eheu!" said Quintus. "We are alive, and that is all that matters."

"Thieves?" said Marcus, his bruised throat making every sound an agony.

"No, not thieves," said Quintus. His torn face became grave and heavy. He breathed deeply. "I must make a special sacrifice to Mars, who saved us. We were intended to die." His voice was hoarse and labored. He told Marcus briefly what had happened. Marcus began to weep.

"My poor Syrius," he said.

"Let us be grateful that we, too, were not murdered," said Quintus. "For, our deaths were planned. Had the merchants not approached fortuitously we should now be greeting Pluto in the palace of the shades, for the horsemen would have made sure that we were dead. I never admired merchants greatly, but these were kind and good and thoughtful, and they have brought us to this inn and three of their servants are now guarding our door." Quintus paused. "They, too, understand that we were set upon by murderers, not thieves."

"Who, then?" said Marcus.

Quintus reached awkwardly into his pouch and took an object from it, then opened his big brown palm and showed Marcus something small and glittering.

"Do you not recognize this?" he asked. "You told me of it at one time, years ago. I took it from the dead hand of one of those who wished to assassinate us."

Marcus blinked at the jeweled serpentine ring in his brother's hand, and his dread became an overwhelming thing. He could not speak. Quintus, with a gesture of disgust, flung it upon the table. He said, "When I saw it, I began to understand. You were the object of the attack. It was you they wished to kill."

Now Marcus could speak faintly. "You did not recognize either of them, Quintus?"

"No, I never saw either before, but they were Romans. And, as they fought, I realized they were also soldiers, well-trained and dexterous."

The two brothers regarded each other in silence.

Quintus marveled as if to himself: "You are no great officer who has incurred military envies. You are no general on which his men wish to be avenged. You are but a civilian, a lawyer of Rome. You are not even a politician who has been oppressive; you hold no office. You are no man's enemy, nor have you plotted the death of anyone of consequence. You do not stand in the councils of the mighty. It is true that you have some fame in Rome, as an advocate. Why, then, Marcus, is your death so ardently desired?" Quintus laughed briefly. "You are not a libertine, nor have you seduced the wife of any noble man who wishes to avenge his honor! It is a mystery."

"Yes," said Marcus.

"It was intended to appear as an accident, or an attack by thieves," said Quintus. "Another mystery is why they waited so long. Your death was planned; they could have poisoned your food at Epidaurus."

"Then it would not have appeared as an accident, or as the work of thieves," said Marcus, sick with his horror. He added, "But why?"

Quintus shrugged, then yelped a little at the pain the shrug induced. "Who knows? But it is obvious that your death is greatly desired."

Safe at last in the home of Atticus, his publisher, on the flank of one wooded hill facing the Acropolis, Marcus wrote to Julius Caesar in Rome.

"Greetings to the noble Julius Caesar from his friend, Marcus Tullius Cicero:

"I am returning a ring with which I believe you are familiar. It was taken from the dead hand of one of two horsemen who attacked me and my brother, Quintus, on the road from Epidaurus to Athens two weeks ago. Considering that I have seen such a ring before when my death was attempted at Arpinum, as I told you years ago, I can come to no other conclusion but that the same men again desired my death.

"I have loved you always as a younger brother. I cannot force myself to believe that you are responsible for this second attack on my person, nor that you were responsible before. Nevertheless, I am assured in my heart that you are aware of the persons who wish me dead, and that it is even possible that you are one of the company. Your lies, therefore, will not be appreciated, Julius. I am in no mood for evasions, nor will my suspicions be put aside even by your smooth protestations. I grieve for my devoted Syrius, who was presented to me by my old mentor, Scaevola, and who died in my service. I have sacrificed for the repose of his soul. I shall never forgive those who caused his innocent death. One day I will avenge him.

"Return the ring to your friend, Julius, and inform him I will remember him forever, and that his blood will wipe out the blood of a slave."

Marcus smiled darkly at the conclusion of his letter, sanded the ink, then sealed the letter with the ring his grandfather had bequeathed to him and which bore the seal of the Tullii.

Julius sat at his table in his own magnificent house with a number of his friends. On the cloth of silver which covered the table lay the sparkling ring which Marcus had sent him. Julius looked slowly at the faces of the men who surrounded him, and who had partaken of his fine dinner.

"I have told you all," said Julius, fixing his black eyes on each man in turn, "that Cicero is under my protection. One of you has disdained my requests and has flouted my friendship. You, Catilina? You, Crassus? You, Piso? You, Curius? You? You? You? You? You, Pompey?"

Each in turn stared at Julius with affront or scorn, and shook his head.

"The Chick-pea is of no importance," said Catilina, contemptuously.

"Nonsense," said Julius. "Once you protested to me, Lucius, that he should die, that he is dangerous. Have you changed your opinion?"

"Yes," said Catilina, with a beautiful smile. "You convinced me, Caesar."

Julius smiled in return. "I have observed that none of you is wearing his ring tonight. Have you consulted each other, and have you decided that none must wear it until the guilty one has had another made?"

"Be sensible," said the fair-haired Piso. "We have been with you often in the last weeks. If one or two of us were absent in Greece, his absence would have been noted."

But Julius said, "I have observed, Curius, that you are not in the best of health, that your face is drawn and pale, that you wince if you move suddenly. Were you wounded by Quintus, that brave soldier?"

Curius looked at him heavily, his dark and surly features cold with anger. "I was wounded in a duel between myself and the husband of the lady I love."

"I did not see you for three weeks, Curius."

"I was recovering from my wounds."

"And the husband of the lady—he survived? I have heard of no noble death."

"He is recovering."

"What! He permitted you to live? Do Romans not fight to the death any longer?"

"We thought him dead. Unhappily, he was only sorely wounded. When I left him, I thought I had killed him."

"Who is the gentleman, Curius?"

"Oh, shall we be party to the humiliation of a Roman?" asked Catilina. "Let the man recover in peace with his honor still intact." Catilina put his hand affectionately on the shoulder of Curius. "I trust you see the lady no more, my friend."

"No woman is worth a duel," said Curius, grinning darkly.

Julius was not amused. He stared at Curius. "Have you ever known Quintus Tullius Cicero?"

"No, we have never encountered each other."

"Then, if he saw your face he would not have known it."

Curius struck the table furiously with his hand. "You impugn my word, Caesar! You are accusing me of a lie!"

Julius was not disturbed. "I am seeking the truth. One here is guilty of the attempt on Cicero's life. I warn you again that if he dies, apparently in an accident, or is poisoned—a woman's weapon, is it not, Catilina?—I shall not rest until he is avenged."

He spoke as if with calm indifference. They all gazed at him in an ominous and threatening silence. Then Piso said languidly, "What is this whey-faced lawyer to you, Julius?"

"He is my childhood friend; he is like a brother to me. Who would not avenge his brother?" Julius' antic face was smooth and without expression.

Catilina laughed gently. "You, Caesar, would not avenge your brother, if that brother were a threat to you. In truth, you would kill him, yourself, without rage but without conscience."

"Did you attack Cicero, Lucius?"

"I? Have I not seen you almost daily? By the gods, why do we waste even a moment discussing a base-born petty lawyer who is little better than a freedman?"

"He is not a petty lawyer. Rome rings with his name."

"Let him confine himself, then, to his briefs and to the attention of the magistrates. We have matters of more importance to discuss."

"Very well," said Julius, sipping his wine. "But do not forget that he is under my protection."

When, later, Julius returned to the table to recover the ring he discovered that it was no longer there. He recalled his slaves who had served the dinner. No, lord, none had observed the guest who had taken it.

Julius stood for a long time, considering.

He wrote to Marcus Tullius Cicero who was still in Athens:

"I am at a loss, dear friend, to understand why you sent me that most curious ring, the design of which I have never seen before. It is most beautiful and exquisitely wrought. I am having it reduced in size for presentation to a lady whom I greatly admire and who is addicted to jewelry of an Egyptian nature. I assume you did not desire its return.

"I am greatly distressed that you suffered such an attack, which was doubtless the work of thieves. It is very possible that one of the thieves had stolen the ring and was flaunting it. Please accept my expressions of alarm, and my condolence that you were so afflicted. I am happy that your brother, Quintus, survived with you, for is he not a mighty soldier and beloved of the legions?

"Your harsh letter wounded the heart of one who loves you dearly; your implications astounded me. It is true that you told me of a similar ring on the hand of one who attempted to murder you years ago at Arpinum. But never have I seen it on the hand of any man, and so I do not understand your letter.

"Who could desire your death, you a lawyer of integrity who has made no enemies and who has inspired the admiration of multitudes of men? Your name invokes reverence, and I am proud to be your friend. Rome is smaller for your absence. I pray to my patron, Jupiter, that your health has been restored and that you will soon return.

"I have recently visited your beloved mother, who is like a mother to me. She is in excellent health. Your father speaks of you with pride and joy. What a treasure it is to parents to have such a son as you! There is nothing else of importance to convey to you. Democracies are notable for no excitements. It is well, I assume. We have lived through a stormy period and peace is very welcome.

"Dear friend, these eyes will be the brighter for looking upon your face. I pray for your return. I embrace you and kiss your cheek."

Marcus, on receiving the letter, showed it with a wry expression to Quintus. Quintus read it seriously. "I am afraid you have offended Julius," he said.

Marcus burst into laughter, which baffled his brother.

CHAPTER THIRTY-SIX

The Roman Proconsul was displeased with Marcus. Marcus in turn was displeased, particularly with his brother, Quintus, whose tongue in the taverns had brought the Proconsul here to the lovely house of Atticus, on one wooded hill which looked upon the Acropolis. Quintus stood somewhat sheepishly beside Marcus in the breezy portico of the house while the Proconsul sipped wine and darted looks of displeasure at both brothers.

"I cannot believe that they were Romans who attacked you, noble Cicero."

"I did not see their faces," said Marcus. "Nevertheless, Quintus who fought them, and heard their voices, says they were Romans."

"You were stunned," said the Proconsul, an irritable little man with a huge hauteur and fussy arrogance.

"I am a soldier, and accustomed to being stunned yet retaining my wits," said Quintus, who had learned that the Proconsul had never been a soldier. "This, I confess, is beyond the power of a civilian."

Marcus glanced at him admiringly, and smiled.

"I should prefer, for the sake of peace and tranquillity in diplomatic concerns to believe they were not even Greeks," said the Proconsul.

"They were not Greeks. They were Romans," said Quintus.

The Proconsul coughed. "The Greeks admire your brother, Captain. But, on the other hand, they do not love Romans. They are already singing —in the taverns with which I believe you, Captain, to be familiar—of the inability of Romans to endure each other and their eagerness to destroy their virtuous and distinguished men. One of the least offensive verses in the newest songs concerns cannibalism and barbarism. You can understand why I am offended."

"If you had examined the body of the man I slew you would have discovered he was a Roman," said Quintus, who had begun to frown.

"I have told you. When the company I sent from Athens reached the spot the body had disappeared. Who bore it away? We have nothing but your word, noble Captain, which I regret you spread through the noisome taverns of Greece. The merchants saw the men in flight; they did not see their faces nor hear their voices. One was an Egyptian of noble Alexandrian family. They admired you, Captain, who, wounded and injured, pursued the—robbers—and overtook them and slew one and put to rout the other."

"It is neither my will nor my desire that the authorities pursue this matter any longer," said Marcus. The Proconsul fixed his eyes on him reprovingly and said with a weighty intonation, "You forget, noble Cicero, that we are people of Law. If I ignored this attack on you, and thus gave credence to the rumor that your attackers were Romans, the Athenians would be delighted. They have a saying, 'The wolf protects his own cubs,' thus implying that Romans can murder each other and rob each other with impunity, in utter lawlessness."

"In my experience," said Marcus, who was weary, "the more a wound is probed the more inflamed it becomes."

The Proconsul became fretful. "But if I ignore this then total disregard for law will result. I thought better of you, Cicero, who are a lawyer."

The Proconsul paused to sip at the excellent wine again. "I should like to see that famous ring which the noble Quintus Cicero removed from the hand of the—robber."

Marcus looked at his brother with anger, and Quintus blushed and moved uneasily. "What ring?" asked Marcus, with apparent amazement. "I know of no ring!"

"No?" said the Proconsul, with obvious relief. "Why, then, do I hear rumors that the noble Quintus Cicero tore it from the hand of the dead man?"

"Rumor has no legs, therefore it cannot walk, but it has wings, therefore it can fly," said Marcus.

The Proconsul was no fool. He had seen Marcus' expression of vexation. "There is but one thing which I trust you can explain, noble Cicero. You have affirmed your belief in your brother's words that the attackers were Roman. Why, then, considering that you were almost killed, are you protecting those who wished you to die? Is it possible," the Proconsul continued, "that you know their identity or have some suspicion?"

"I do not know their identity."

"But you protect them by your denials. Have you forgotten that as a Roman and as a lawyer it is your duty to uphold the law?"

"It is also my duty as a lawyer not to make wild accusations without proof," said Marcus. "It is also my intention to face those murderers one day, myself. I will deal with them."

"Then it is a private quarrel!" said the Proconsul, who loved vendettas.

The Proconsul rose. "Then, noble Cicero, you will not object if I give out the rumor that you were attacked by thieves of an alien race who spoke in an alien tongue?"

"Considering," said Marcus, "that we Romans in Greece are an alien race and speak with an alien tongue, you will be quite correct."

The Proconsul was not certain that this pleased him. He took his leave with much ceremony and expressed his hope that Marcus would enjoy his visit to Greece. He also implied by looks and gestures that he hoped Marcus would leave promptly so as not to be the cause, again, of a deplorable incident. When he had gone Marcus said to his brother with renewed anger, "What a babbler you are, Quintus, especially in your cups!"

"I regret that I was the cause of your embarrassment," said Quintus, in a somewhat surly tone. He scratched his thick curls. "Why did you wish to protect those murderers, even if they are Romans?"

"We do not know who they are."

"But you recognized the ring."

"True. But I have seen only one man who wore that ring and whose name I know. I doubt that Pompey was one of those who attacked me."

"You have always thought me a fool!"

Marcus was immediately contrite and put his hand on his brother's arm. "No, Carissime, that is not true. I have always considered you truly an 'old' Roman, and I can think of no greater compliment."

He went out into the beautiful garden of Atticus' house and raised his eyes to the distant Acropolis and was again overcome with the same profound wonder and awe which he had at first experienced. The lucent air was so clear, the extraordinary cerulean sky so brilliant and sparkling, that the Acropolis appeared almost at hand, distinct in every detail, confounding the senses, diminishing all men in its aspect of total grandeur and heroic beauty, calling attention to the ephemeral life of man yet emphasizing his importance. For, had not man created this?

It was strange that man had, centuries ago, reared this splendor in honor of the gods, who had always hated him and had wished to destroy him. Zeus had decreed the extinction of man, in outrage that such a creature of mud should resemble the immortals. But Prometheus, the Titan, immortal himself yet of the Mother Earth, had taken pity on mankind, had brought it eternal fire, had inspired it, and had been chained to rock to expiate his crime of mercy and compassion and love. He had wept in his agony, yet had challenged the gods who would have driven man from the world, and had at one and the same time defied the gods and implored their pity both on himself and the creatures of their loathing wrath. They could no longer destroy man, for he had learned the secret of immortality and knowledge.

The challenge between the gods and men would never end, until the gods repented their disgust and hatred and man repented his bestial enormities. It was rare that the gods intervened in the affairs of man in the name of justice and truth and law. It appeared that they intervened only in malice and to protect their own majesty, or to extend their own private quarrels which they had with each other. Ah, sometimes the gods were more malignant than men in their petulances! For men sometimes had mercy.

The garden in which Marcus stood was radiant in the first rosy rays of sunset. The fountains, in which nymphs or statues of Eros stood, sang musically and plashed their rainbow waters into smooth marble basins where gold and silver fish darted, catching light on their metallic scales. The paths of the garden were of red gravel winding among flowerbeds, and myrtle and fir and cypress trees mingled together in cool clumps. Here was a marble outdoor portico to protect one from noonday sun and to rest the weary mind. The columns shone against the dark background of the trees, and the floor was paved with snowy marble. The sweetest voices of birds sounded in the golden air and rose against the absolute blue of the sky. Soft and scented breezes mounted from the hills surrounding the Acropolis.

Marcus looked down upon the crowded city, whose façades glowed with blinding yellow light and whose flat white roofs ran with scarlet and whose colored gardens were like gems set in the dusky shadows of the trees. He saw the hurried teeming of men in the many streets; the men were already leaving their shops and the Agora, and the faint clatter of their voices and laughter could be heard clearly. The heat of the day still lingered in the city and ascended the hills, a hot breath with many fragrances of heated stone and dust and dry spice and a new scent of water, and the arid aroma of palms freshening in the effulgent air. Through the surrounding hills Marcus could glimpse the purple water of the sea, already fuming with silver mist, and the crimson sails that peopled it. And he saw the narrow marble roads rising up through the hills to the Acropolis, filling with pilgrims who sang in far and melodious tones.

Marcus again raised his eyes to the towering Acropolis, and the mighty Cyclopian abutments, built by men, which sustained it. Crowning the abutments, and circling them, glimmered walls of marble, flashing with the red and gold and violet beams of the sunset. Far below abutments and white walls lay terraced gardens filled with white shrines and little temples and fountains and flowers and green grass and dark trees, until they met the city streets. And there on the hill, under the walls, stood the white and rising circle of the theatre of Dionysus, round rank upon rank of empty stone seats where the immortal plays of Greece were produced daily for the delight of the Athenians. Here Antigone had pleaded that the rights of the individual superseded the rights of the government, and that liberty should never be threatened by the evil laws of prideful men who wished to buttress their rule and advance their ambitions and silence the cry of freedom. Here, in the words of Antigone, had dictatorship by one man been denounced and defied, and here Antigone had died, as all free men must die at the whim of tyrants. But the dictator had perished in infamous exile and the call of Antigone still rang through the modern world which unendingly disputed the scream for power uttered by wicked men. Man and the State. Always must they be enemies, for men had been given freedom by God and the State hated God, and loathed men and everlastingly fought against the rights of men. The liberty of the individual defied the luxury and the privileges of those who deemed themselves greater and wiser than their fellows, and wished to enslave their brothers. The gods hated man, but how much more did man hate man!

But it was within the glistening walls above that man both adored the gods and challenged them, attempted to appease them and glorified them.

The agony of man met the cold silence of the gods, and here in pale sentience the mystery remained to defy the philosophers who had once walked in those lofty colonnades, and to confuse them. The antagonism endured, sculptured in unanswering stone, colored in the friezes of the pediments, struck into marble. The question remained.

It was not answered by the imperial glory within the white walls, nor by the aspiring columns between which the vehement sky, flaming like intense blue metal, shone with hard incandescence. Temple and Parthenon, the white fire of colonnades, the paved marble, the stupendous majesty of façade and pillar, the grace of crowding statues: none answered the mystery that lay between man and God. The little dark figures of men roamed among all the vast buildings, which were total in their perfection. Men walked the colonnades where Socrates and Plato and Aristotle had meditated, and all the poets and the marvelous playwrights of the grandeur of Greece. They brought offerings and flowers and incense to the crowded temples. They stood, looking up in awe, at the tremendous statue of Phidias' Athena Parthenos, which faced the east, that figure of pure gold and amber ivory many times the height of the tallest man, helmeted with golden plumes, her left hand resting on her glittering shield which was ornamented with the coiling sacred serpent, her right hand embracing a gilt and marble pedestal on which stood a little winged figure. Her vast and virginal face gazed unmoved at the centuries; her attitude of repose was undisturbed by the eons of men who had come and gone. The great calm eyes contemplated the east where always a tomorrow would arise and announce wisdom, austerity, self-denial and justice and purity. The mighty statue flashed against the peacock sky as if it breathed or stirred, guarding the temple behind it and lifting eye and spirit beyond the borders of the world.

Pylons with their winged charioteers, gleaming column, rounded temples, the Parthenon, the statue of Athena Parthenos, the many other statues and the small sanctuaries, the structures of buildings of learning and music, the white paths, the ascending stairs, the glitter of white roof: All these stood within the walls, and all these denied the truth that man, and not the gods, had created this titanic marvel, this climax of the ages, this crown of glory, this celestial chorus caught in marble. The terrible and monumental beauty affirmed the dream that lay enclosed, like a gem, within the small skull of man. It reflected the splendor of heaven as it had shone in the eyes of a few men, whose hands had re-created that splendor in the chastity of stone, that the vision might endure, that man might remember that not only was he an animal but that he was also clothed with divinity.

No wonder, thought Marcus, that men from all over the world came to look upon this Acropolis, to climb its stairs, to linger in its gardens and on its flowered terraces, to enter within the walls to bow before Athena Parthenos, to wander along the colonnades of the Parthenon, to halt before shrines and there leave an offering, to retrace the footsteps of the philosophers and the poets whose like would never be known again, no, not through the endless centuries to come! Let the men of the future admire their own science and their own wisdom and their own law and their own philosophies. Let them boast, as they would. Never again would any race of man raise such a marbled glory of absolute perfection and nobility under the sun. Man had reached his apex of loveliness and wisdom on this Acropolis. Henceforth, he must decline and become the smaller.

The west became one arch of golden light, and the fragrance of the garden rose more intensely about Marcus as he sat on the stone seat and looked at the Acropolis. He was invariably both depressed and exalted at the vision, depressed that man was now so little and exalted that man had once been so great. What was the power of empire compared with this? If men remained stupid then all their bannered and shouting armies were but the senseless march of the jungles, all their laws would be inscribed in dust, and all their boast would be but the echo of beastly voices, and all their cities would be inevitably inhabited by the lizard and the owl, the wild ass and the snake, the silent rubble of fallen pride.

Daemon and god: man was a greater mystery than even the Acropolis of Athens.

Now all was scarlet and purple and silver over and within the city. Marcus did not feel the chill of evening. He was sunken in himself and his meditations. He started, therefore, when burly Quintus brought him newly arrived letters. "I am to be a father!" he shouted, and struck his breast with his clenched fist in the military manner. "Rejoice with me, Marcus!"

Marcus rose and embraced him and kissed his cheek. "Have you told Atticus?" he asked.

"No," said Quintus, "he has not returned from the city, and his speculations."

"Let us pray you will have a fine son," said Marcus.

Quintus swaggered boyishly up and down the garden paths while Marcus watched him fondly. Quintus breathed deeply; he stared at the Acropolis but it was evident that he did not truly see it. He said, "My son will be a brave man, a man of Rome. I will teach him well."

Marcus did not suggest that the coming child might be a girl. For a moment he was envious of his brother. Pomponia, the young wife, might be oppressive and inhibiting, but she loved her husband and he loved her, if he also feared her. He would always return to her arms, to be chided and admired, to be admonished and advised, to be enjoyed and cherished. What had he, Marcus, to return to in Rome? Law would endure without him and Helvia had her favorite son and soon she would be a grandmother. She also had her husband, wise and lonely child though he was. For the first time Marcus thought seriously of marriage. Surely, in Rome, there must be one woman who would love him above all others and keep his new house and supervise his servants and bear his children, who would be a joy to him. She would not be Livia. But she would be a beloved woman on this earth where Livia no longer dwelled. He was tired of the random woman whose embraces meant nothing, and whose bed gave him no real ease. He was tired of changing faces, no matter how lovely or intriguing. Casual love, or bought love, was no love at all. A man needed a woman who loved no one but him, whose arms were a shelter for his despondencies, whose smile was a cure for his melancholy, whose eyes darkened with compassion for his pains. There was, after all, no substitute for marriage.

"You have not read your own letters," said Quintus. "There is a letter from our mother, and many others."

Marcus opened his mother's letter. It was full of commonsense, as usual. Helvia had visited Marcus' various villas in the countryside and had even gone to Sicily to see his farm and order it. She did not particularly approve of the "luxurious new house" in Rome, but at least she was supervising the gardens and purchasing the furniture. She and Tullius had gone to the island for a few weeks. She missed her sons. She rejoiced, pointedly, with Quintus that his wife was about to bear him a child. She had reviewed Marcus' speculations in the stock market and now advised the sale of some holdings which appeared precarious. The interest on moneys had risen in the banks, which was an occasion for gratification. Tullius, the father, had become less secluded; he often visited the city and he had acquired a few congenial friends, who had even given him an interest in games. The olive groves and vineyards which Marcus owned were bearing well and were being harvested. In short, matters were going excellently.

She wrote with a firmness that was most penetrating:

"I have long sought to have you look upon the Lady Terentia as your wife, for not only is she of a patrician family but is sister to Fabia, the Vestal Virgin, which augurs a divine blessing on the marriage of Terentia, and her husband. Terentia is possessed of a dowry of one hundred thousand sesterces, a not inconsiderable fortune even in the light of your own possessions, and is mistress of several houses in Rome, from which she obtains a respectable income, and a farm near Arpinum. She is most virtuous, and no scandal has attached itself to her name, and she is in all ways a desirable wife for all she is past the age of twenty-one. Her household accomplishments meet with my approval, for her family is truly Roman with all the virtues of the past. She is modest and pleasant and her intelligence would delight even you, Marcus. She is of an attractive countenance, and she has never dyed her hair which remains its natural brown. Though a shrewd woman of investments in the city, she still retains the old Roman aspect of retirement and gentle deportment and does not possess a sharp tongue, as does my daughter-in-law, Pomponia, sister of your dear friend, Atticus. It is true that she does not boast the regal beauty of her sister, the Vestal Virgin, who could have chosen among the noblest families in Rome for her husband, but beauty is often cursed by the jealous gods."

Marcus said to his brother, "Do you know the Lady Terentia?"

"Hah," said Quintus, who had been staring up at the Acropolis. He turned on his heel and looked at Marcus. "Her sister, Fabia, the Vestal Virgin, is of a most remarkable loveliness! When she passes in procession with her virgin sisters to the altar of Vesta the people bow more in awe before her face than before her divine condition. What glorious eyes, beaming like the moon! What magnificent hair, even if half-hidden by her veil! It is the color of gold. Her neck is like a column, her waist—"

"We have a poet," said Marcus. "But we were not speaking of Fabia. I believe I mentioned the Lady Terentia. I surmise she is not so beautiful as Fabia."

Quintus thought, puckering his lips and rubbing them with a blunt brown finger. "She is a friend of my Pomponia. She has visited our house. Her appearance does not come readily to my mind, but I recall that her voice was amiable but firm, her demeanor retiring and truly old Roman. Ah, wait! I remember her more clearly. She has brown hair and brown eyes and a pale complexion. I thought her an invalid but Pomponia declares her in excellent health. She speaks softly."

"Brown hair, brown eyes, and a pale complexion," said Marcus. "They could be the attributes of a beautiful woman or a young Fury. It is no description at all."

But Quintus was thinking seriously, and he shook his head once or twice. "Her appearance is pleasing; she is not lovely, but is of a mild countenance. You will recall that my Pomponia has a mild countenance, also, and a tongue like a viper."

Marcus laughed. "Do you suspect that Terentia has such a tongue also?"

Quintus grinned. "I invariably suspect these soft-spoken women with downcast eyes and sweet manners and glances that prettily invite but promise nothing. I believe Terentia is very virtuous. How could it be otherwise with a sister who is a Vestal Virgin? Delightful Fabia—"

"It is not Fabia I am considering marrying," said Marcus.

"You! Marrying!" cried Quintus in astonishment.

"I am not decrepit nor of a great age, Carissime. Nor am I a male Vestal Virgin. It would please our mother if I married Terentia."

"This is a grave matter," said Quintus, seating himself on the parapet that contained the garden. He eyed Marcus seriously. "One does not marry casually. When one enters upon marriage his whole life is changed, curtailed, ordered. There is no more freedom, no more frolicking, no more adventure. One, it is suggested, becomes circumvented."

Marcus concealed his mirth. "You do not consider it a happy estate, and do not recommend it."

Quintus glanced cautiously at the door of the house, then leaned forward and spoke in a low voice. "There is not a husband, who, though possessed of a handsome and virtuous wife, often does not wish he had never laid eyes on her!"

Marcus could no longer hide his smile. "Ah, traitor! I consider Pomponia adorable, and you the most fortunate of men! If Terentia resembles Pomponia—"

"She does," said Quintus in a somewhat sad tone.

"Then, I will give the matter the most earnest thought. I am weary of having no intimate attachments. My new house on the Palatine needs a mistress."

"Our mother is not extraordinarily old," said Quintus, in a last heroic effort to save his brother from disaster. "She is but forty-four or forty-five. There are ladies in Rome who have had four or even six husbands at that age, and are still merry and vivacious and desirable. Our mother could be mistress of your house."

"You are not encouraging."

"There are times," said Quintus, "when I envy you." His short red tunic hardly covered his big thighs; he slapped one of them with the air of a tragic man.

When Marcus did not answer, Quintus said, "You are serious! I had hoped you were jesting."

"No."

Quintus sighed, as if accepting inexorable fate. "Then, marry. Terentia is as good as any." He paused, and gave his brother a long sharp stare. "You have—no regrets?"

"Do you speak of Livia Curius?"

Marcus stood up, and supported the elbow of his broken arm with the palm of his right hand.

"I have not forgotten Livia. I can give no woman what I gave that maiden. My heart remains in Livia's dead hands. But my life does not lie in them also. I am no longer a youth. It is true that at times my life seems a very weary thing to me, but a man has no choice but to live until the gods decree his death, and the Fates cut the thread of his existence."

"You speak as an unhappy man speaks," said Quintus with affectionate concern, and he put his hand on his brother's shoulder. Marcus looked at him with surprise.

"Unhappy? No, I do not think I am. I am not a child. If we are here for any purpose at all it is not happiness, which is the condition of little children."

"There is no purpose," said Quintus. "Or, if there is, it is not possible for man to know."

CHAPTER THIRTY-SEVEN

Marcus and Quintus remained at the house of Atticus for six months. During that period Marcus studied at the School of Ptolemy. His voice restored to its old vigor, he took lessons in elocution and rhetoric from the famous Syrian, Demetrius. Antiochus of Ascalon was delighted to instruct him in philosophy. He had also inclined to the school of Epicurus, and was taught by Phaedrus and Zeno. Never, in Rome, had he dreamed of the full majesty and learning of the Academy. He had known of the Academy's tremendous importance in the world and had long yearned to attend it. Still, it surpassed his expectations.

He wrote to his parents, "I had earned some fame in Rome with my oratory. But what a squeak and a squeal I really possessed in Rome compared with the eloquence of my noble teacher, Demetrius! His voice makes the air stir in grand periods; I swear that even the birds listen, enchanted. When he quotes Aristotle I feel that it is Aristotle speaking in accents that resemble shining marble, for they seem to gleam and glisten, visible to the dazzled eye. —How delightful it is to be a student again! Men should never cease from studying, from returning to those springs which so intoxicated their youth, for in books there is much wisdom and there is no end to what a man can acquire in knowledge. All surfeits but learning. All becomes stale and jaded that is of the body, but that which is of the mind and the spirit is never satisfied, never satiated, never exhausted. It is as if one possesses eternal youth, for one is always discovering and is always elated at some new treasure revealed to him. Every path is a pristine one; it has been touched by no foot before. Every portal opens on a new vista, never gazed on before that hour by another man. The words of Socrates or Plato mean something unique to each student, for he brings to them a unique mind and a novel soul. So must the Isles of the Blest be, never explored in full—horizonless, swept with winds that come from eternity.

"We go next to Asia Minor, and to Rhodes, for new studies when these are completed, if one can say with truth that study is ever completed. When I return, I will marry the Lady Terentia, for, as you have written, she is agreeable to the marriage. Embrace her for me, and induce her to give her final consent, and implore her sister, Fabia, for her divine intercession in our behalf."

The winter in Athens was unusually mild. Only on a few occasions did snow fly. It was then succeeded by radiant skies and new warmth. Once or twice there were heavy and thunderous rains which filled the streets of the city with rushing floods. But it was not a winter like Roman winters. Marcus had no return of his rheumatism. His health quickened daily. His voice was stronger than he had ever known it. It rang with music and large power. His declamations had always been arresting. Now Quintus would urge him to recite poetry or some phrase from the *Phaedo* and would listen with a touching ecstasy. The soldier did not always understand. It was enough for him to hear Marcus' voice soaring and commanding, spoken as if with no effort. It was like wine that is poured easily from a jeweled goblet.

When Helvia wrote that Pomponia had miscarried, Quintus was much grieved. He said, "It is the will of the gods. The soul of my child has ascended to bliss, for he had done no wrong. Who knows but it will be as the Indus say, that he will be born in another body given him by Pomponia and myself, or to better parents?"

It was Quintus who induced Marcus to learn much of the physical arts, which strengthened him even more. His arm had healed. For the first time he found pleasure in boxing and fencing and wrestling and running and leaping, though his slender form never became muscular. The sad mists which had enveloped his mind the last years in Rome lifted from his brain and there were moments when he must admit to himself, "I am happy! It is not the joy of the child or the youth. It is the joy of full maturity and tranquillity and acceptance." He began to teach himself not to be as compromising as his nature leaned; he began to discover that prudence can sometimes be compliance, and that just anger should not be always restrained in the name of reason. The world had need of ruthless and even raging fire as well as the sweet voice of rationality and diplomacy. "I hope," he said to Atticus a little ruefully, "that I will remember to be so dauntless when I return to Rome!"

A few days before he left Athens he had two visitors. The first, to his amazement, was Roscius, the actor, bearded and browned by Palestinian suns, but as graceful and as handsome as ever. Marcus hardly recognized this *elegante* who had assumed the swagger of a mature man, and he greeted him with delight and embraced him heartily. "Noë," said Roscius, "wrote me you were in Athens, and I disembarked to visit you. Dear friend, how burly you are! You are a veritable gladiator." He pinched Marcus' enlarged biceps, which, though harder, were not very notable even now. "And you have lost your backside, which sometimes would swell through your long tunic in a most distracting way," the actor continued.

"You have not lost your own Apollonian figure," said Marcus, "for all the excellent victuals of Jerusalem. I thought you had spent your time in the gates of the city with the wise men."

"No. I enchanted the ladies. I was a vision in the theatres which the Romans were kind enough to build in that God-obsessed land. Judea is very effete; the younger Jews are now more Greek than the Greeks. It was not necessary," continued Roscius with virtue, "to imitate the Greeks in everything. Did I tell you that Noë has written a new play for me?"

"He always does," said Marcus. "But you will have to remove that beard, which you grew as a devout Jew."

"Not so," said Roscius. "I grew it because the play that scoundrel, Noë, has written concerns Job. You know of Job? A most dolorous man, most persecuted, defamed, reviled, and suffering. And a man of the most furious and affecting eloquence. He was just and virtuous, above all other men, yet God permitted Satan to afflict him in order to demonstrate to Satan that some men cannot be moved from their seat of probity and devotion and morality. The contest was very unfair. Job was but a man, the mouse between God and evil. You would think they would not descend to the torment of so small a creature. I feel very strongly about Job; my heart burns with indignation and compassion for him. Do you think the Romans will like that play?"

"The contest between good and evil is not unknown, even to Romans," said Marcus.

"I see you still possess your old stinging tongue," said Roscius, with approval. "You know how the story of Job ends?"

"I believe God answered him with majestic questions," said Marcus.

"Yes, yes. But what an answer! In Noë's play, God does not answer at all. The questions Job hurled at Him remain unanswered, and the predicament of man still stands as an indictment against heaven. What do you think of it?"

"Aeschylus wrote something resembling that. I prefer the authentic version."

They were sitting in the mild noonday on the terrace of Atticus' house. Roscius was very splendid in silken robes and with a cloak of the softest fur. His noble head was the head of a heroic statue, enhanced by the brilliantly black and curling beard. He resembled a prophet. He considered Marcus' words, then shook his head in denial. "God does not answer, except in riddles which no man can decipher. He is the original Sphinx. The old Jews disapproved of me. They uttered the great rolling words of God to Job. 'Where wast thou when I laid the foundations of the world? When all the morning stars sang together and all the sons of God shouted for joy?' And so on. Job should have reminded God that indeed he was not there, but that the question was a non sequitur, and should not be asked of a bewildered and suffering man who was anguished with boils and had lost all that he held dear. If Job was small and blind and confused and knew no celestial matters—was that his crime, and for that should he be rebuked? Did not God create him so meagre and so without knowledge? If a man makes a wheel that is not round and true and with a weak hub that breaks at the first stress—shall that man curse that wheel and cast it into utter darkness and absolve himself of the blame?"

"That," said Roscius, "is the heart of the matter." When Marcus did not speak, Roscius went on. "I am astounded at Job's answer to those incredible questions. 'Wherefore, I abhor myself, and repent in dust and ashes.' That was unworthy of Job, who had endured so much. I suppose the wheel of which I have been speaking should have abased itself before its creator and have dashed itself against a stone in repentance for being what it had been made!"

"You have become a philosopher," said Marcus. He pondered. "The eternal question of Job is always asked. Men should gaze on the marvels of the universe and consider the stupendous laws and the miraculous intricacy of creation, and the evidence of immortal power and glory. That is the divine answer."

"That does not heal a man's boils or restore to him his lands and his fields and his wife and his children and his treasure. It does not give him the return of his youth and his strength."

"But, it gives him peace." However, despite his words, Marcus felt melancholy.

"The peace of resignation. That is not enough."

"Nevertheless," said Marcus, "it is a great boon. Come, come, Job was a man of tremendous courage, before which the courage of a gladiator is nothing. It is the fortitude of man which inspires the respect and love even of God. For it is the measure of man how he can overcome fear and gird up his loins, as Job was commanded—and be a man. No, no. I do not like Noë's conclusions. Man was not made to pity himself before the Eternal, and to describe himself as a weak thing and not responsible for his condition of mind and soul and body. He was made to become like one of the gods, himself."

"What a Jew in your soul you are!" said Roscius, admiringly.

Marcus smiled. He felt a sudden curious exaltation. "God needs not to justify Himself to man. Man has no rights except those rights bestowed on him freely by his Creator, out of that Creator's love and mercy. He never earned those rights, for he has not the power to earn them. They are a gift, granted out of an affection beyond understanding. For, what is man? A little creature of mud, doomed to disintegrate. But God, out of His boundless and incomprehensible love, gave him a soul as well as a body. Man should spend his life in utter gratitude for that immeasurable gift. Is it not enough that he be alive and is able to contemplate the inexhaustible treasures about him, and the wonders and the glory and the beauty? That would be sufficient, even in the face of unwaking death. But God has promised immortal life, too. Why? That is the real question, one that should shake us to the heart."

Roscius reflected, his fiery blue eyes on Marcus' face. Then he exclaimed, "You believe it! Ah, that stupid Noë! He thought himself very wise and sophisticated. Men who consider themselves so are such piteous fools, are they not? Their mouths are full of cynical words and they believe them so subtle, whereas they are the whinings of imbecile children, and the smirks of idiots. Why should Noë have written such a play? It is maudlin, and false."

"He thought it would be more comprehensible to Romans, who love to weep at tragedies, though they prefer dancing and comedy and brawling laughter in the theatre. We are a meaty race." Marcus smiled. "We do not even question or defy the gods, as the Greeks do. We are very satisfied with our life, and remain satisfied so long as we have enough food and drink and a good shelter, and concupiscence and all the other delights of the body. We are complacent. We rejoice in our power. We love women and gladiators, sports, songsters and dancers and taverns and the wine shops and jewels and fine horses and decorated cars and soft carpets, and all the lustinesses. We wish only that the gods remain on Olympus and refrain from meddling in the affairs of men."

"That would perhaps be wise of the gods," said Roscius, eating dates and spitting out the seeds. "I was not very happy in Israel. There was too much talk of souls and God. What a quandary is our life!"

Marcus hesitated. "Do they still speak of the Messias in Israel?"

Roscius winked. "Yes. They expect Him every morning. They are not discouraged."

Marcus enjoyed the brief visit of Roscius. Quintus, as usual, was jealous.

Atticus was captivated. He gave banquets for the actor, who soon acquired adorers in Athens. After some persuasion, and a sound indication that something of worth would accrue to him, he condescended to appear in the theatre of Dionysus in *Antigone,* which he favored. He was a marvelous success. He departed from Athens in a state of high elation. He also carried letters from Marcus to his parents and his friends.

A few days later a servant came to Marcus who was reading on the sunlit terrace and basking in the hot spring sunshine. "Master," said the servant, "there is one Egyptian merchant to see you, who gives his name as Anotis, and who claims to have rescued you from thieves."

Marcus rose and exclaimed, "Bring him to me, and he must dine with me on the terrace!" He had seen none of his rescuers though they had left messages of solicitude with Quintus after accompanying the two brothers to an inn and securing a physician for them.

The Egyptian was conducted to the flowering terrace, and he and Marcus exchanged deep bows. Then Marcus embraced him in the Roman manner and kissed his cheek and said, "Noble Anotis, you did not linger so I could thank you for saving my life and the life of my brother. How can I repay you?"

Anotis smiled. "I did not know at first that we had helped the famous lawyer of Rome, Marcus Tullius Cicero. You have never left my mind. You have haunted my thoughts."

He was a tall and very thin man of middle-age, clad in long full robes of crimson, green, and yellow linen with a cloak of blue silk over his bony shoulders. His shoes were of fine blue leather ornamented in gold boss, and he wore a girdle of the same about his narrow waist in which was inserted an Alexandrian dagger encrusted with gems. His long black hair touched his shoulders and his narrow head was bound with a gold band with a strange large medallion which hung over his forehead to his brow and glittered in the sun with its many jewels. He was magnificent, but Marcus found his face more interesting than his garments or even his air of enormous dignity and quiet power. That face had been browned by the sun, but the eyes were a clear and pellucid gray, the features delicate yet strong, the mouth indicating both aristocracy and noble pride. From his chin grew a thin black beard, trimmed closely to a sharp point.

"I am at your service, Anotis," said Marcus, seating himself near his guest. "You will see that my arm is completely sound again. I should not be here today but for you and your friends."

Anotis smiled a little. "You owe me nothing. It was a privilege to assist you."

He paused, and those shining gray eyes fixed themselves on Marcus' face.

"I have some training as a physician. For, I am a merchant only by necessity, for my family's fortune, as were the fortunes of all Egyptians, was seized centuries ago by the Greek Lagidae, when Alexander set the Greek Ptolemies on the throne of my sacred country, Khem. We do not forget. I have been trained in the ancient mysteries of medicine and my ancient religion."

He paused. Marcus waited. "I accompanied you, who were unconscious, to your room in the inn near Corinth. I helped undress you. I saw a strange object about your neck, on a fine chain which was ornamented with the holy falcon of Horus."

"Ah," said Marcus, bringing forth the chain from under his tunic, and showing the scarred silver cross. "You mean this? It was given to me by an Egyptian client who told me it was the sign of the Holy One who shall be born to men. It was taken from an Egyptian tomb and is millennia old."

Anotis looked at the object, touched two fingers to his lips, then reached out and applied those fingers reverently to the cross. "It is so," he said.

"I wear it as a promise," said Marcus, "and as a hope." He was deeply interested. "You must tell me. I think always of the Messias of the Jews. Does this represent Him?"

But at this moment servants brought a small table to the terrace and began to serve the noonday meal. Marcus and his guest lifted their goblets in a silent and mutual salute, and then poured a little wine in a libation to the gods. Marcus was fascinated by the fine profile, brooding and meditative, of Anotis.

"Let me tell you, Cicero," said the Egyptian, as they dined on the excellent viands of Atticus' house. "It is possible that you know the story of our ancient gods, who have been supplanted by alien others, notably Serapis whom I do not honor. They were brought to Egypt by the Greek Lagidae, and we Egyptians of ancient family and ancient knowledge do not worship them. We remember our own.

"You may recall the Holy Isis, our Mother, the spouse of the Osiris who was murdered by men and who rose from the dead in the springtime of the year, when the Nile is at its full and giving life once more to the earth." Anotis brought forth a medallion from under the cloth that covered his breast. "Behold the Holy Mother and her Holy Child," he said, and Marcus, leaning forward, could see that upon the golden medal there appeared a beautifully enameled little painting of a sweet-faced young woman with a man-child in her arms. The painting was not only of great artistry but of immense charm and loveliness and immediately inspired reverence.

"Isis, the Holy Mother, and her Holy Child, Horus," said Anotis. "They have left Egypt forever, for they could not endure the Greek Ptolemies who infest our sacred land. They have passed from the memory of most of our people, who worship the Greek gods or strange ones who have been imported.

"The sign of Horus was not only the falcon, Cicero. His sign was also that cross, which appears in our old pyramids and represents resurrection of the body as well as the soul. And the old priests have foretold that He will be born of woman and lead mankind out of darkness. He will be born in a strange country of which we know not."

"It is said, in the Holy Books of the Jews, that He will be born of the house of David, in Bethlehem," said Marcus. "That is what I have been told."

Anotis sighed. "There is not a race who does not have the legend that the Holy One will appear on this earth," he said. "Therefore, the occult knowledge must have come from Ptah, God, the Creator Almighty. He must have imparted it to all nations, for do not the Greeks speak of Adonis who was incontinently killed and then rose from the dead during the celebration of Astarte? I have been in many countries, and the legend is there in their religions.

"When I ascertained this, then I became full of doubt about Isis and Horus. I no longer believe that Isis is the Holy Mother and Horus her Holy Child. I believe that we Egyptians, too, were given the prophecy as were other nations. If Isis and Horus had truly been those prophesied from the ages then never should the worship of Horus have ceased, no, not even under the oppression of the Greek Ptolemies. Therefore, the Holy Mother and the Holy Child are still to come. There is also the mystery of the Cross. How does it really apply to Horus? It does not. So Horus is not our Savior, as once we thought. He has not yet been born. My medal, which I wear about my neck day and night, is still only the prophecy of she who is not yet known and the Holy One still in the breast of Ptah, the Creator."

Marcus thought. "I, too, do not believe that Isis and Horus are of the prophecies," he said. "They are to come. But when?"

The Egyptian was silent for some time. His eyes lifted and fixed themselves on the glowing Acropolis whose walls and buildings flamed like pure white light under the sun.

Then Anotis said, "There are some of our priests who are still hidden in the land of Khem, our sacred land. As I am of a priestly family I am sometimes admitted to their presence as they brood and pray in the fastnesses of our crumbling temples. They tell me of great portents and omens." He hesitated and looked at the Roman as if waiting for a smile of ridicule. But Marcus' eyes darkened with emotion and he put down his knife and spoon and leaned toward his guest.

"Tell me!" he cried. "For my heart hungers and thirsts for hope!"

The Egyptian's eyes glazed and brightened as if overlaid with tears. He bowed his head a little. "It is unlawful for me to tell what has been told me, and we do not love the Romans. Nevertheless, because of that holy thing which you wear constantly, Cicero, as an amulet, and which you love, and because of what I have heard of you, I will tell you a little.

"The priests have told me of strange visions they have perceived in the fires of their secret altars. They have seen a woman clothed with the sun, as bright as the morning, crowned with stars and with a serpent under her foot whose head she is crushing. She is great with child, and her face is like the moon. She is very young, a mere girl-child, but all wisdom and beauty lie in her eyes and all tenderness, and all promise. When the priests saw this vision quivering with intense light above the altar fires they cried aloud and fell on their faces and murmured, 'Isis! She comes again!'"

Anotis shook his head. "But she is not the Isis we have worshiped in our far past. For I have discovered that the Jews have had a similar revelation concerning one they call a Virgin who shall bear a son and He shall be called Immanuel, for He shall deliver His people from their sins and be a light to all peoples."

Marcus felt a sad despondency. "Could it be possible that the Jews acquired the story of Isis and Horus during their slavery in Egypt, and then incorporated it into their own beliefs?"

Anotis shook his head. "No, for they came to Egypt with that prophecy. They abhorred our gods, and never knew them. They lived in Chaldea before they ever saw Egypt, a white mysterious race walling themselves away from their brown-skinned neighbors whom they called Babylonians. The Chaldeans had that prophecy also, of the Holy Mother and her Holy Child, but the Hebrews never knew the Chaldean gods as they did not know ours.

"I, too, have read the Holy Books of the Jews, and she described in them is one whom the priests I know have seen in their visions above the flaming altars."

Anotis paused again. "And they have seen other visions, of the glorious One hanging from the sacred Cross, dying, with the light of Ptah, the Creator Almighty, pouring down upon Him. This, the priests are unable to interpret, and they are baffled, but when I read the Holy Books of the Jews, the prophecies of one prophet, Isaias, I understood but I kept the knowledge to myself. I have read, also, the Books of David, the ancient king of the Jews.

"And let me tell you of a matter most strange. I am a merchant, and I meet fellow merchants from all over the world. The Persians are full of excitement. They tell me that their god will soon be born to all men, for their salvation and their hope and their joy. They tell me that their astronomers have seen the omens in the skies, and their priests have gazed upon the beautiful child's face of her who will bear the Holy One in their visions. But they, too, are puzzled, for their priests have had a vision of the Holy One dying infamously by the hand of man. How, they ask, can the Holy One be killed by men, He Who is immortal? They have no interpretation. Have you, Cicero?"

"No," said Marcus. He moved restlessly. "But, when will He be born and where is she who will bear Him?"

Anotis sighed. He spread out his hands. "That I do not know, as you do not know, nor the priests. But it cannot be too far in the future, for all nations are suddenly and impatiently waiting. Except," said Anotis in a wry voice, "the Greeks and the Romans, who honor their gods skeptically, the Greeks, because of their love of beauty whom their gods embody, and the Romans because of their love of power, which Jupiter embodies. In truth, the Greeks and the Romans do not believe in God at all. Is it not peculiar that those who deny God in their hearts nevertheless are full of superstition? They listen eagerly to the divinations of their atheistic priests, and visit Delphi, which is a fraud, and they visit astrologers and soothsayers. They believe these. But they do not believe God."

"The Jews are the people of the Book," said Marcus.

Anotis smiled and inclined his head. "And to them, who are of the Book and have never forsaken their God, the Holy One will be born. He will delay not much longer. Let us pray that our eyes will behold Him."

They stood side by side and gazed at the Acropolis. Anotis said, "And when He comes, who will recognize Him? There is but one thing certain, that He will pass away never from the minds of men, as Horus passed away from the memory and the worship of Egyptians. No, never will He pass away though men will despise Him as they have always despised God and have fled from Him. It is in our nature to hate and execrate that which is good and immortal, and to deify that which is evil. Who can fathom the darkness that is man, and the dark impulses of his spirit? Yet it would seem that God loves him and will visit him. It is not to be understood."

Anotis took the chain and the medallion from his neck and gave it to Marcus. "Keep it in hope, and wear it in faith, Cicero. I do not know why I give it to you, but I came for that purpose. Her name is not Isis, nor His name Horus. Their names are still hidden in Heaven."

CHAPTER THIRTY-EIGHT

Quintus rejoiced to return to Rome after the long sojourns in Greece, Asia Minor, and in Rhodes. He declared he could not wait to embrace his wife, Pomponia, whom he had not seen in over two years. Nevertheless, he continued to warn Marcus concerning marriage. "A man is no longer a free entity when he has a wife," he said.

"I am nearly thirty-two years old," said Marcus. "It is time I took a wife and had children."

When he and Quintus returned to Rome they found their parents in good health. Helvia was now a plump matron with whitening hair but with her old sturdiness of spirit and strong tranquillity and humorous short laughter. Tullius embraced his sons happily, but his eyes were anxiously upon Marcus. "Tell me of Greece," he implored. But he wished only to be told of the Greece of his dreams, where the gods walked in the streets of Athens. He did not want to be told of the Agora and the shops and the vivacious Athenians who loved money and laughed and were black of eye and skeptical and lively. He wished to believe that the Athenians were uniformly fair and did nothing but posture in togas and utter philosophies, and quote Homer, and Socrates and Plato and Aristotle. It is apparent, thought Marcus with some irritation, that my father desires to believe that Athenians do not have any of the concerns of humanity. Athenians do not have bowels and bladders; they do not itch and scratch; they do not fornicate or spit. They are clothed in marble and their accents are poetry. Alas, thought Marcus, why do men have such silly fantasies?

Marcus loved his father, yet he was annoyed at his innocence and annoyed with himself for his own annoyance. It came to him again, as it did too often for his comfort of mind, that man lived alone in his own sad, dread loneliness, and no other could enter into it with him and warm him from his cold predicament. He was closer in temperament to his father than to his mother or brother; it was possible that the very similarity of nature, the very awareness that there was some of his father reflected in himself, aroused his irritability. Both were inclined to compromise, to seek the middle way, and Marcus deplored the fact even if it were often wise.

Marcus might have hesitated about marrying had not his dear young friend, Julius, called upon him in his usual state of gay exuberance and affection. "Ah, how I have missed you, these nearly three years!" cried

Julius, embracing him heartily and then holding him off to examine Marcus' face. "You have recovered, thanks be to the gods! I have sacrificed to Jupiter, my divine patron, on many occasions for you, Carissime."

"I doubt it," said Marcus. "To whom did you give that ring?"

"To a lady."

"I doubt it," said Marcus. "I hope you warned your friend that some day I shall meet him sword to sword."

"A gladiator!" exclaimed Julius, clapping him on his shoulder. With a silken swish of garments he flung himself into one of Helvia's solid wooden chairs and beamed.

"I am serious," said Marcus.

"I doubt it," mocked Julius. "But what is all this about rings? Tell me of Greece, and the ladies of Greece."

"I met very interesting people," said Marcus.

Julius grimaced. "And philosophized with them."

"That was my purpose."

"No banquets, no revels with the nymphs?"

"The ladies of Greece are very satirical."

Julius kissed his bunched fingers and tossed the kiss into the air. "Ah, I love ladies who are satirical! There are only two kinds of women in Rome, the stolid lumps of lard and the lascivious. No wit, no sparkle."

"Which is Cornelia?"

Julius' face changed. "I endure," he said. "I honor her. But tell me, did you not enjoy yourself, did you not feel the wine of Greece and youth run through those austere veins?"

"Sometimes. But I prefer not to talk of bedrooms. How is your daughter?"

Julius' face became tender but whether or not this was sincere Marcus could not tell. "She flourishes like the rose! I am already thinking of a husband for her, though she is still but a child. But let us speak of you again, my dear friend. Rome was lesser for your absence. There is no lawyer like you."

"What have you been doing, Julius?"

"I told you before! I am no longer interested in politics. I live, enjoy, laugh, love, sing—and do not avoid those bedrooms you mentioned. Is that not enough?"

"I do not believe a word you are saying. What have you been plotting?"

Julius sighed. "I plot nothing. You have always had the direst opinion of me. I am a man of peace, except for my yearly services in the legions." He stared at Marcus with his brilliant black eyes but as always those eyes, in their pretense of candor and openness and simplicity, hid many murky things. He said, "Your house on the Palatine is very handsome and elaborate. You have become luxurious. Do you know that your neighbor is now Catilina?"

Marcus frowned. Julius grinned. "He bought land near yours; he, too, is building a new house, not so fine as yours. Aurelia's investments have not yielded much lately. Her fortune is still large, but apparently not so large as Cicero's." He peered at Marcus inquisitively but Marcus did not rise to the provocation.

Julius, watching him closely, drank some wine and said boyishly, "Ah, this is excellent! How your taste has improved since you sojourned in Greece! Moreover, you have a polished manner. I observe your clothing. It has distinction. It no longer serves merely to cover you. It has style and grace."

Julius drank again. Then he looked into the depths of the goblet. "I hear a rumor which I trust is absurd. I have heard that you are to marry Terentia."

"What is wrong with Terentia?" asked Marcus.

"She is not the wife for you, in your new state, O Bacchus! You have not seen her?"

"Only when she was a very young child. She seemed fair and amiable enough."

"A woman is not a child. She is not a beauty; she has no enticements. I do not say that she is a Hecate, or a Gorgon. She speaks very softly. I do not trust women who have soft voices and rarely laugh, especially if their faces are too composed and too knowledgeable. Her air is mild; it conceals granite. She is also uncomfortably shrewd. As she has influence in the city she is much admired by ambitious men. There is not a day that her litter does not go to the Forum, for visits to the counting houses and the banks and the brokers."

"Aurelia Catilina does that also."

"But with what a difference! Aurelia has solid knowledge of affairs also, but you must admit that she is a desirable woman, of warm flesh and warm breasts and extreme beauty. Aurelia arrays herself like a goddess, with silks and brocades and velvets and furs, and is always scented provocatively. Terentia dresses soberly, wears few jewels, no perfumes, and her hands are large and knotted, like a man's. This contradicts the mildness and modesty of her countenance. Never marry a woman with masculine hands. Others, though admiring her mind and her astuteness, have not sought to marry her, an old maiden in her twenties, far beyond the marriageable age. There must be a reason."

"She is patrician."

"Is that everything?" cried Julius, who loved only aristocrats. "When one is in bed with a woman one desires soft limbs and palpitating breasts and rounded arms. Terentia has none of these."

"How do you know? Have you been in bed with her?"

"The gods forbid!" said Julius, with horror. "I hear she is still a virgin, at her age!"

"Your description of her convinces me she will be an excellent wife and mother."

Now to Marcus' astonishment and curiosity Julius put down his goblet and became very serious. "Do not marry her, Marcus. She will make you wretched. She is virtuous and has character. A man needs more than that. He needs laughter and sweetness. He needs a woman who is at once a mother, a companion, a dear sister, a shy nymph, a concubine, a mystery, a woman of gentleness and delicious surrender. I can imagine what Terentia will be as a wife! It is rumored she has a violent temper and unwomanly ambition. Will you be less wise than other young men, who respect her but avoid her except when she can advance them?"

"In short, it is your great concern that I do not marry Terentia."

"Do I not love you?" cried Julius, slapping his hand on the table. "Do you wish me to contemplate you as a harried and frightened husband? Pomponia, the wife of your unfortunate brother, is a veritable Leda compared with her, yet she is famous for her temper and her rude manners. I fear for you."

"I am overcome by your solicitude," said Marcus. "But you must tell me the real reason for your aversion."

"Oh gods!" said Julius, raising his eyes imploringly. "You will be the most pitied man in Rome if you marry her. It is true that in her youth she still possesses the fresh attributes of youth. But in a few years she will be a dragon. She will haunt you as Juno haunts Jupiter, my unfortunate patron. You will never be able to indulge yourself with more enticing women."

"I intend to be a virtuous and faithful husband."

"Excellent. Except that virtue and fidelity should be a man's own choice, and not forced on him by an exigent wife. You will be found creeping fearfully in alleys and conducting secret delights in the utmost fear and secrecy."

Marcus smiled. "Can you imagine me a furtive husband?"

"You will be compelled to be furtive out of self-defense. Terentia will busy herself with all your affairs. She will give you sharp advice and strongly upbraid you if you ignore it. She will know all that you do. She is domineering and penurious. She will decide your friends. Your children will be hers, not yours. You will be a veritable slave to her whims. She will soon convince you that you are a fool."

"Is there someone else, dear to you, who wishes to marry her?"

"No! None will have her, for all her virtues and her money and her family. They are more perceptive than you, Marcus."

"You must let me decide. I will keep all you have told me in my mind, and judge for myself."

"I foretell disaster, from which I would save you." Julius paused. "Have you seen her sister, Fabia, the Vestal Virgin, in whose prayers I bask?"

"No, but I understand she is very beautiful."

"Yes. Though her hair was cut off when she was initiated into the sacred virginal rites, it has grown again. We have, happily, now permitted this in contradiction to earlier and more severe days. Her hair is like the shower which embraced Danae. Her pure face defies my poor descriptive powers. Her nature is as sweet as balm. But I must not speak so," said Julius, his black eyes sparkling, "for are not the Vestals sacred and is it not blasphemous to speak of them in terms which one might apply to other women?"

"So," said Marcus. "Moreover, a Vestal caught in unchastity is buried alive, and her lover beheaded at the very least. What has this to do with Terentia?"

But Julius was watching him closely. After a moment he appeared satisfied and relieved, which puzzled Marcus. Julius said, "When you see Fabia you will discover such a contrast with her sister that you will not consider marriage."

Marcus smiled impatiently. "Let us not discuss my affairs, dear young friend. I am sorry that you failed in your prosecutions of the Senatorial governors, Cornelius Donnabella and C. Antonius for extortion in Macedonia and Greece."

"Ah, well," said Julius, appearing diverted and cast-down. "I do not have your gift for forensic passion. That is why I intend to go to Rhodes to study rhetoric under Molon. Unless, of course, we do not have a third Mithridatic war." He stood up.

"You will find Rhodes very beautiful," said Marcus. The two friends embraced again. Before leaving, Julius said, "I pray that you will not marry Terentia."

This conversation was one force that determined Marcus to marry his mother's choice. The next was brought about by the death of old Archias, Marcus' beloved tutor. They had not seen each other for a long time, though they had corresponded when Marcus was in Greece and Rhodes and Asia Minor. Even before then, they had encountered each other infrequently. Nevertheless, Marcus had felt that the old Greek poet was a fixture in his life, a statue in a hall he did not visit often, but which was recalled lovingly and regularly. Now that statue in the hall of his mind had fallen into rubble and was no longer part of his existence. No matter

how crowded that spiritual corridor would become in the future there
would be one face and figure forever missing. Marcus was impressed with
a sense of bereaving time, with a sense of rapidly passing years and the
impermanence of living. If he did not marry and have sons there would
be nothing of him to remain for the future.

Julius said to Catilina in the latter's house, "Let us go far into your
gardens so we may converse where the lovely Aurelia will not hear us."

They went into the warm gardens under the yellow moon, and found
a secluded spot in a grotto. The moonlight was like poured honey and in
it Catilina was so handsome that Julius marveled again that the other
man seemed so unaware of his masculine beauty and dangerous charm.
Catilina had passed his thirty-fourth birthday; he still appeared like
Adonis, timeless, virile with youth and passion. The light from the sky
glowed in his blue eyes, brilliant and alert; his profile had imperial majesty, though the lines about his mouth were depraved. He is like Hya-
cinth, who has become a pimp, thought Julius with a small envy for that
extraordinary face and magnificent body.

There were times when Julius wondered uneasily, after his conversations with his friend, if the madness that had been Livia's had not been
inherited by her distant relative, her husband, also. Certainly there was
very often a light in Catilina's eyes which was not quite sane, and often,
in spite of his cold detachment, he was given to bursts of fury. His voice
never lost its hard contempt for everything and everybody, even when he
was amused or most beguiling.

"Have you persuaded Chick-pea to relinquish the fair Terentia?" asked
Lucius.

"Unfortunately, no. Your wife, Aurelia, has failed also in her counseling
of Terentia, and her hints that Cicero is impotent or lacks true virility and
that he has secret, unspeakable vices, and that he is not so rich as rumored,
and is of base family, and a dull temperament. Terentia is obstinate; she
is not very young."

Lucius said with scorn and quick anger, "Aurelia, herself, is becoming
curious about my insistence that she must induce her friend not to marry
the Vetch. I have convinced her so far that it is because of my immortal
hatred for him."

"If he marries her"—and now Julius dropped his voice to a whisper—"it
is more than possible that he will discover your infatuation for Fabia.
Deprecate him if you will; he is subtle and discerning. I beg of you to
relinquish the pursuit of Fabia. It is more than dangerous, more than
calamitous. The girl has not yet yielded, you have told me. How unfortunate it is that our later laws now permit the Vestals to appear in public
only partially veiled and to attend the games even if in a secluded box! Our

future is too valuable to jeopardize. You will drag down your friends with you, for even today Romans will not suffer the desecration of the Vestal Virgins."

Lucius smiled coldly. "Yet I have seen you gazing at Fabia with lustful eyes."

Julius lifted his hands and dropped them. "It is permitted a man to look upon a woman, even if she is a Vestal Virgin. If evil comes to Fabia, or even fulfilled joy in your arms, then she will inevitably confide in Terentia, who is known for her rigid virtue. She would not spare the man responsible for the deflowering of Fabia, even if that meant the destruction of Fabia, herself. Or Cicero will discover the crime, and tell his wife, for he, too, would be horrified beyond expression. That is what you have always feared, is it not?"

"True." Lucius rose and began to pace the warm and scented grass of summer. He said, in a low voice, "I still insist he must die, if necessary, to prevent that marriage."

"Do not weary me again with your arguments, which have continued over the years. What is a woman, even one so lovely as Fabia? Are we men, or youths enthralled by restless passions? We have too much at stake to endanger it. I beg of you to halt your pursuit of Fabia."

"For one who has a legion of beautiful women you are strangely virtuous now," said Lucius.

"None is a Vestal Virgin. None is threatened by a terrible public death if discovered in delicto. Who threatens you? All of Rome, for though few Romans believe any longer in the gods, all believe in the sanctity of the Vestal Virgins. I beseech you, forget Fabia, if not for your sake for hers, and the sake of your friends."

"No," said Lucius, and shook his head over and over. "Never have I so loved and adored a woman as I do Fabia! She is in my blood, my heart, my organs, my brain, all my thoughts. I am beset; I am undone. I must have her, or I must die."

Julius stared at him reflectively. He thought, that would not be a very bad idea. Regretfully, however, Julius shook his head to himself. Catilina was most valuable. His following in Rome was too important, too tremendous, among the wicked and secret mobs who lived in the subterranean world of Rome.

Catilina turned on him so suddenly and with such a flare on his face that Julius was alarmed. It was as if Lucius had read his dark thoughts. "Well?" said Lucius. "Are we to move, ever? The years go by and we accomplish nothing. Even you failed in your prosecutions of the Senatorial governors. The success of such a prosecution was to establish ourselves in public opinion. I am weary of all your patience! Let us strike and have done with it."

"Were the pyramids and the Acropolis of Athens built in a day, or the hanging gardens of Babylon, or the lighthouse of Alexandria, or the nation of Rome? What we propose is too enormous, too tremendous, for hasty action. Forget Fabia."

"Never," said Lucius.

Julius sighed and stood up. "I can only implore Jupiter that he defeat you."

"I can only implore you to permit the death of Chick-pea."

"Let us change the subject. I am alarmed at the indiscretion of Curius. He has threatened his mistress, Fulvia, that if she does not remain faithful to him he will revenge himself upon her, 'when some great thing will have happened.' Fulvia is a very clever woman. Curius drinks too heavily. It is possible that in her arms he may reveal that which will lead to our executions. He is more to be feared than Cicero. He is your relative, the distant cousin of your dead wife, Livia. Talk to him sternly. I warn you that this is of the utmost importance."

"Chick-pea must die, before he marries Terentia."

"No," said Julius. "If he dies, I will have my revenge also."

Julius left him then. He looked back once. Lucius was staring after him with a black and enraged expression.

Helvia and her son, Marcus, went to the large but modest home of Terentia, where she lived with her relatives, her guardians. "You must make a good impression immediately. It is fortunate that Terentia looks upon me even now as a mother. It is not true that she has not been sought, as that lively Julius has told you. Your grandfather would have approved of her."

"And, my father?"

Helvia smiled in the shadowy confines of the litter. "She intimidates him. He once told me that she resembles me. Am I so formidable?"

Marcus kissed his mother's cheek. "If she resembles you, my mother, then she has already won my heart."

The hot late summer evening had drawn to dusk, and low dark clouds were streaming over the sky, threatening storm. Marcus and his mother entered Terentia's house in that steaming gloom. They were informed by the overseer of the atrium that the Lady Terentia was in the garden with the sacred Vestal, Fabia, her sister, who was visiting her. The Lady Terentia had ordered that her guests be conducted to the gardens, where a breeze was arising. Marcus was impressed favorably by the austerity and taste of the house. He went into the gardens with his mother.

The sweltering gloom was thickening rapidly. The visitors walked over grass that even now smelled bruised before a coming storm. Shadows rushed over the earth. Two ladies rose from a marble bench on which they had been sitting close together. At that moment a flash of brilliant lightning lit the air furiously, and Marcus saw Fabia glowing in it like a dream of Astarte. He forgot her sister. He could only gaze on Fabia.

He had never seen so lovely a woman. She was very young and tall and graceful, clothed in white linen that flowed about her like marble. Her blue veil only partially concealed the web of soft and shining golden hair that fell to her shoulders, frail as butterfly wings, and the shape of them. Her face was oval and tender, flushed with coral shades on smooth cheek and full lip, and her eyes, almost as golden as her hair, beamed sweetly and were large and shadowed by thick dark lashes. Marcus could only guess at her figure, swathed in the garments of the Vestals, but by her pliant motions he could surmise that it was heroically young and rounded. Her expression was childlike, trusting and pure, and, in its purity, unbearably enticing yet inspiring the awed reverence of the beholder. She seemed less girl than Artemis. Her brow resembled the brow of Athene. The shyness of her smile revealed small teeth like iridescent pearls. She stood meekly, her hands clasped before her, hands as white as snow even against the whiteness of her garments. She was untouchable, divine.

"Terentia," said Helvia, pinching her son's arm, "my son, Marcus Tullius Cicero."

Marcus, the bemused and enthralled, started and turned to his hostess, his face becoming heated in his confusion and embarrassment, for he had been staring at Fabia like one possessed. He remembered to bow.

Terentia was not so tall as Fabia nor so slender. The crimson linen of her long robe showed a figure matronly in its outlines. Her face was somewhat narrow and her complexion pale. Her hair, dressed severely, was of a medium brown in color and rippled with waves which were not of the art of the hairdresser. She had a nose somewhat too large and strong, and a mouth, though pink, somewhat too tight. Her eyes, however, were a clear and steadfast brown, and her best feature. They revealed great character and intelligence, despite what Julius had said of her. Her chin, very long, expressed firmness or obstinacy. She wore no jewels and her hands were big.

My wife, thought Marcus with conviction, and felt depressed.

Terentia's voice was low and quiet but not hesitant. Fabia's shy voice was a flute. Terentia behaved toward her sister as a cherishing mother. Fabia blushed constantly. A sister Vestal Virgin arrived for her almost immediately and bore her away to those secret quarters reserved for the servants of Vesta. Terentia said with extreme affection, "My dear Fabia wished to look upon you, noble Cicero, for we are like one flesh." Her reserved voice trembled and now her brown eyes were truly lovely.

"One knows how dear Fabia is to you, Terentia," said Helvia.

"It was a great honor to the family when Fabia became a Vestal," Terentia said with gratitude. "Nevertheless, there is not a man of the noblest family in Rome who did not desire to marry her after puberty. But her heart has always been so singular, so chaste, so devout, that she could not conceive of a fate better than this which she has chosen."

"She is a very Europa," said Marcus, still bemused by the vision he had seen. He became conscious that Helvia was regarding him with reproof and that Terentia was coloring. "Without the bull," he added hastily, thus making matters much worse. "I should have said Leda," he blundered on. Helvia took Terentia's arm in a maternal fashion and led the girl toward the house. Their robes swept the grass. The clouds swelled with storm and turned livid and a sharp wind rose. "You will observe, my dearest Terentia," said Helvia in too audible a tone, "that my son is awkward with women. That is because he is a great scholar, a Stoic."

"Do I not hear the applause for him in the city?" said Terentia. She leaned on Helvia's arm like a daughter. Then she glanced over her shoulder at Marcus and all at once her big brown eyes were kind and warm. It was all settled. It seemed he had no choice in the matter.

The first drops from the clouds were falling when they reached the portico. The lightning was nearer. Suddenly Marcus thought of Livia and could have wept.

CHAPTER THIRTY-NINE

The betrothal was very sensible and without illusions. Marcus was to write later to a friend, "It set the tempo of my marriage."* He gave Terentia many gifts, according to custom. He should have preferred to give her jewels and lengths of silk, in a last sad effort to infuse some romanticism into the situation, but Terentia told him, though with modesty, that she would like gifts to be "useful in our new home on the Palatine." She had visited that home in its last stages of building with Helvia during Marcus' absence abroad, and her definite mind had not entirely approved. She gazed at the many treasures Marcus had brought

* Letter to Atticus.

home and though she smiled amiably enough it was evident that she thought them somewhat decadent. Just as she concealed her capacity for ruthless and even violent temper from Marcus now so she concealed her aversion for lavishness and too exotic beauty.

Marcus, who was so perceptive, guessed at much she kept hidden, but Terentia had so many virtues that he hastily decided that those virtues must overwhelm any faults. However, he discovered a dismaying lack of humor in the young woman. When he tried wit, she smiled pleasantly. When he made an epigram of his own invention, she would look artlessly at him. All her learning was practical and pragmatic. She liked to discuss the cargoes of the ships in which she was invested. She was composed and somewhat complacent, but the discussion of money made her face sharpen. She was never tired of hearing of Marcus' influential friends in the city, and a gleam of calculation brightened her eye. She had an attitude of confiding affection toward him, almost sisterly. Once he took her hand and then kissed the bend in her plump arm. She started and turned very red and gave him an outraged look, and drew her sleeve over the offended member. Am I repugnant to her? he asked himself dismally. He bluntly put the question to his mother who arched her thick black brows at him.

"Did you expect sophistication in these things in Terentia?" she asked him reproachfully. "She will come to your bed a virgin. That is not to be despised."

"Am I marrying a bookkeeper or a woman?" he returned.

Helvia said, "She will be the good keeper of your purse and the keeper of your hearth. The lares and penates of your household will never be dishonored by her. What more can a man expect of a woman?"

The marriage was old Roman. On the wedding day Terentia arrayed herself, with the help of female relatives and slaves, in her robe of white linen, a long tunic without a hem. It was fastened about her short waist with a woolen girdle knotted in two knots, the cingulum herculeum. Over this she wore a palla of pale yellow with sandals of the same hue. Her hair had been dressed in the old manner, covered by pads of artificial hair bound to her head in a crimson net. Upon all this was placed a veil of bright orange, which flowed over her face. And still over this she wore a wreath of marjoram and verbena. She displayed no jewelry but a collar of finely spun silver which Marcus had persuaded her to accept and wear. (She would have preferred the traditional iron or copper collar.)

This garb was not designed to make a bridegroom wait impatiently for the bridal chamber. Marcus thought that Terentia appeared hideous, for all the weddings he had attended in his life had been gay and beautiful and the bride had arrayed herself more in the modern fashion and her hair was scented and free and her lips were tinted with red and she glistened with the jewels of both her family and her bridegroom's family.

Terentia stood in her house with her relatives and received Marcus and his relatives. Quintus was struck with consternation at the sight of Terentia. His own young wife, Pomponia, was a veritable nymph in comparison. He thought Marcus to be greatly pitied and he was so desperate that sweat broke out over his face, though the early autumn day was cool. Tullius, who had displayed much indifference about his son's wedding, vaguely believing that something would intervene from Olympus to save Marcus from such a dire fate, felt wretched. Now, as he glimpsed her strong and uncompromising features through the meshes of the flammeum he was more than apprehensive, more than dismayed. The girl was a stranger; her manner was formal. She was not the shy bride of fable and men's pathetic hopes. Competence radiated from her like hard light. Tullius wanted to cry to his son, "Fly, while you have time!" He saw Marcus' pale and sober face and shook his head desperately, and with amazement. Of all the women in Rome had it been necessary for his son to marry such a one, excellent in all ways surely, but with such large and ugly hands and such a severe countenance?

The wedding party adjourned to the atrium where a sacrifice was offered to the gods. It was a tender ewe. All partook of it with their fingers. After this was consumed the witnesses affixed their seal to the wedding contract. The auspex, though he possessed no priestly office, declared that all the omens were auspicious, and that the entrails of the unfortunate ewe had indicated a long and happy married life for the principals. Then the couple exchanged their vows before him, "*Ubi tu Gaius, ego Gaia.*" (There thou goest, Gaius, there go I, Gaia.) The witnesses, friends, relatives, members of the bridal party, then raised a hearty cheer and showered blessings and congratulations on the couple.

Fabia was not present at the wedding of her only sister, for the Vestals, as yet, took no part in festivities or open feasts. But she had sent her prayers and an affecting and touching letter which Terentia now proceeded to read as she stood regally among them all. For the first time her face softened; her cheeks flowed with tender tears. Suddenly, she was charming and young, and not a woman full of certitude. She turned to Marcus and laid her head on his shoulder in order to gain control of herself, and he involuntarily took her in his arms and felt affection for her. She was, after all, still young, and she was his wife and he vowed that he would love and cherish her and hold her dear, even if her conversation was hardly stimulating and her manner hardly seductive.

The feast lasted until long after night fell. It was not a remarkable feast nor inspiring. Marcus drank the wine until his ears rang and his mind grew dull. Now it was time to take the bride from her home and carry her to her husband's house. Musicians, led by torchbearers, marched before the newly wedded couple, and sang discreet songs and not the naughty and lascivious ditties of modern weddings. They sang of home and hearth and the virtue of the bride and the nobility of the husband and of the heroic children who would be born to Rome and to the worship of the tribal gods. Passersby halted to watch this procession of the littered couple and friends and relatives, and they thought it a plebeian wedding for there were no pretty dancers and fauns rioting in the procession, and there were no sweetmeats or coins tossed to eager hands. No one in the procession laughed or showed signs of drunkenness. The litter's curtains were closed. It was all very solemn and decorous, in spite of the leaping young boys who waved twisted hawthorn twigs as an augury for unborn children.

Marcus' fine new house was lighted throughout with many lamps, and all the servants were lined along the blooming path to the door, whose threshold had been spread with a white cloth, signifying that a virgin bride was to pass over it. Marcus descended from the litter and gave his hand to his wife, and she emerged with the orange veil still partly hiding her face. Now it was his moment to carry Terentia over the threshold. The company beamed on him and waited. He put his arms about Terentia and lifted her. And staggered. She was unexpectedly heavy and solid. To assist him, and to prevent impropriety, Terentia wound her arms about his neck tightly. His gait was not very steady, and he was sweating in an unseemly manner, when he finally delivered Terentia over the threshold. Then the bridesmaids followed, carrying Terentia's distaff and spindles, and they sang a song of the matron's virtues.

Marcus offered his wife fire and water. It was noted that he was very pale indeed and that his eyes were glazed. Tullius watched him mournfully at a distance; Quintus was obviously in misery. Helvia watched her son and then fixed her gaze determinedly on the eminently suitable young bride and hoped the girl would display a little fire of her own later. Marcus, she thought, had the soul of a tender lamb. But, she reflected, men were of a fragile nature, easily hurt, easily wounded, for all their swagger and their deep voices and their mastery of affairs. Women were made of iron in comparison.

It was customary for some older female to whisper to the bridegroom, if he was of her blood, "Be gentle! Be patient!" But Helvia went to the composed young wife and whispered, "Be kind, my dear one, for he loves kindness above all things." Terentia turned and stared at her, not in confusion, but with blankness. Even newly arrived in her husband's house she was not displaying any blushes or shynesses or sweet alarms. She was already mistress of this house; surety shone from her brow.

The chief bridesmaid then took Terentia by the hand in the very center of the company, and led the exceedingly calm and confident bride to the nuptial chamber. The curtains had no sooner fallen over the door than the guests and the wedding party abruptly left Marcus to the delights of his bed. Where there had been singing and voices there was now silence, and the ruins of a last libation and pastries and sundry cakes. Marcus heard the overseer close and bolt the bronze doors of the atrium, doors which he had imported from Rhodes. Even the voices of tired slaves had become silent. The lamps glimmered palely and the scent of their oil became sickening and cloying. The overseer returned from the atrium and bowed and said, "Master, is there aught else?"

He was a middle-aged man of immense dignity. Marcus said in a desperate voice, "Aulus, drink a cup of wine with me!" Aulus smiled respectfully, filled Marcus' wreathed goblet and filled a goblet for himself. They drank in a profound quiet.

The overseer dropped his eyes. "May the gods bless your marriage, noble lord, and preserve your happiness." He began to fill trays with plates and goblets. The lamps flickered. Soon it would be morning. And Marcus' wife awaited him in the bridal chamber.

Aulus left the room and Marcus was totally alone. Never, surely, had there existed so reluctant a bridegroom, he thought. He was steeped in anxiety and was fully frightened. He contemplated his state. What madness had webbed his brain that he had married? He was tired and more than a trifle dazed and he had drunk too much wine. If I close my eyes, he thought childishly, I will then open them and discover I have had a nightmare. He could not recall Terentia's face or form. A strange woman awaited him, whom he had never seen before. She had gone with steady serenity to the nuptial chamber, as no doubt she went to her banks. Why had he ever thought that she resembled his mother, Helvia? Helvia had humor and her strength was warm like the earth. The strength of Terentia —and who in the name of Hades wished for a strong wife?—was the strength of concrete.

Then Marcus threw back his slender shoulders. Am I a man or a youth previous to puberty? he asked himself with sternness. I am years older than that poor girl who is probably quaking in my bed and staining my pillows with her virginal tears. He strode manfully out of the room and went to the curtains of the bridal chamber. He swung them aside with a virile gesture.

The chamber was large but snug. It was finely furnished and the mosaic floor was covered with a carpet of many radiant Persian colors. The bed was of ebony and mahogany, inlaid with ivory and highly gilded, and had been brought from the East. The chairs were of lemonwood and so were the delicate tables. A fragrant lamp burned dimly near the bed. Terentia was fast asleep. The blue and yellow blankets were drawn up almost to her chin. It was evident that she wore a modest shift of white linen, for one arm had been thrown without the coverlets and the sleeve reached to the large wrist. She slept deeply and soundly as a child sleeps, her braided brown hair spread on the pillows.

Marcus stood and contemplated his wife. Tears? Eheu! Quakings? Eheu! A bride, and she was asleep and had not waited for her bridegroom! A virgin, and she had no tremors, no fears. Her profile was quiet; it was evident that she was enjoying her slumber. The lamp shone on the mild pallor of her smooth cheek, the shadow of her pretty lashes. And, unfortunately, on her redoubtable nose and her long, determined chin and her short neck.

I should be grateful she did not blow out the lamp, thought Marcus. Was it possible that this girl had not the slightest knowledge of the marital act? The idea stimulated Marcus. He removed his clothing, lifted the blankets, lay down beside his wife after blowing out the lamp.

He could hear late revelers singing and talking and laughing as they climbed the Palatine Hill to their homes. He caught breaths of spicy autumn air and wind through the open window. He put his hand on the shoulder of Terentia, then bent over her in the darkness and sought her lips. She came murmurously awake, not with anticipation and love, but with vexation, as a child is vexed. It was most evident that she understood completely where she was and who was searching her body.

She caught his hand in a very competent grasp. "It is late," she said with firmness, "and I am weary, Marcus."

He wanted to strike her. He had discovered that she had warm full breasts and this had excited him. He sought them again. And again she caught his hand.

"Tomorrow," she said.

"No!"

"Yes. Now let me sleep for I have much to do in the morning."

And, incredibly, she fell asleep again, turning resolutely on her side and leaving only her back to him.

Marcus, outraged and burning with humiliation, decided he hated his wife, and that he would divorce her at once and return her to her records and her stockbrokers and bankers on the morrow. He feasted on the joyous idea of driving his unwanted bride to her house and relatives, rejected and mortified and weeping.

Then suddenly the humor of the situation overcame him and he burst out laughing, and settling himself comfortably fell asleep, still chuckling. At some time before morning Terentia, in her warm slumbers, must have taken his hand, for when he awoke to the blue and gold dawn he found his fingers clasped with hers. He was touched, and kissed her cheek, and sighed a little.

Later Terentia responded to her husband with competence, as she did all things. The act of love was no more significant to her than her other affairs, and had its place in her life, and must be attended to with dispatch and with thoroughness. Moreover, it was her duty, and she valued duty above all things.

Marcus did not know whether she loved him or not. She had a strong affection for him. Did she enjoy his body? He was never to know. She looked on him amiably. He was sure she was his friend.

CHAPTER FORTY

"That accursed Chick-pea!" exclaimed Catilina. "He is now a politician, and you have declared him harmless for years! Is a politician ever harmless? Who knows where his career will end, if we do not destroy him? I have known from my earliest youth that he was a threat to all we are, and all we desire."

"A mere quaestor," said Julius, "the lowest of the low political offices to which to be elected. And he goes to Sicily, which in my opinion is the anus of Hades. Unfortunate Cicero. At his age, he expected a son. The Lady Terentia presents him with a daughter. You were tormented, my dear Lucius, when he rose higher and higher in the esteem of the people through his forensic oratory. You saw shadows of him everywhere, avenging. He obsesses you! There are times when I am so struck with hilarity over this absurdity that I cannot control myself. Never does he speak your name.

"It is no secret that he despises you, Apollo. It is no secret in Rome that you detest him. You have said that he remembers Livia. On what proof? He is a gentle, married man, loved by the people of Rome because of his virtue and probity and his eloquence and mastery in the courts, where he always is the gladiator defending justice. And now he is a quaestor, a most modest position. Still, you fear him!

"Let us speak of more important matters. Such as Fabia."

Catilina's expression changed subtly, but he stared directly into the lively black eyes staring into his. "And what of Fabia?"

"Are you not my dear friend? Do I not visit Cicero and his tranquil household—or it would be very tranquil except for Terentia's ambition— and do I not see him carrying his child peacefully in the gardens and does he not talk to me of his infernal law, or his books? But I visit him, not only because of old childhood affection, but because I wish to catch rumors, to watch any change of his countenance. I speak of Fabia to him in the most casual manner, inquiring about her sacred health. He answers kindly enough, and mentions that the girl visits her sister often. Do you not understand? You wished him murdered to prevent him from marrying the redoubtable Terentia, who is Fabia's sister. Yet he knows nothing. Am I to congratulate you on your discretion during your meetings with Fabia, or am I to be relieved by hearing from your lips that you have abandoned the girl?"

Lucius was silent.

Julius' house was a splendid new one he had built outside Rome, full of fountains, statues, marble, gold and silver, Alexandrian glass, wrought copper and bronze candelabra, flowers, blue pools, gleaming carpets, silken hangings, marble floors, murals, paintings and books, and artifacts from every country in the world. The two friends were together in the gardens, blossoming and green and shadowed with myrtle and oak and cypress, under a fairer and clearer sky than that of the city. In the very center of the lawns stood a gigantic black metal statue of the Egyptian god, Horus, son of Isis, in the form of a falcon with wings outspread and shadowing the grass. The mighty beak lifted itself arrogantly; the enormous wings appeared to quiver in the sunshine. Julius had a weakness for Egypt and its arts, and he possessed many stolen Egyptian treasures, and not only the one of the sacred serpent which he kept hidden in his chamber. He liked to look at the great falcon, and watch its mounting shadow on the earth. At those moments he felt inspired.

He gazed insistently at Catilina. Then Catilina said, "You may choose your own deduction."

"This is not a private affair! What any of us does now becomes momentous. If Fabia has succumbed, desert her at once. If she has not, forget her. Listen to me! Do you know what I have heard in the city? That Fabia has suddenly turned pale of face, and that she fainted before the very fires of Vesta and her sisters had to bear her away, and that but a few days ago. The people thought that an omen of disaster, for all know Fabia, the most beautiful of women, and all know her sweetness and swear that her glance restores them. Therefore, when she fainted it lighted rumor. Are you concerned with this, Lucius?"

Again Catilina's face changed, and now his terrible blue eyes flashed. "I will not permit you to question me, Caesar! Be done with it."

"The Vestal Virgins are my guardians, the guardians of my ancient house. They are the guardians of the hearth fires of Rome. A Vestal who is seduced, whose name becomes defamed, is a scandal and a horror to the people. The people have vengeance on men who corrupt a Vestal, and they also have vengeance on the Vestal who permitted that corruption. It is a capital crime. How long must I continue to remind you?"

"You may cease immediately."

"Gods!" cried Julius. "Do not speak to me with such contempt! Speak to your slaves so, or your wife, or your precious companions. But not to me, Catilina, not to me."

"We have become insolent," said Catilina.

"Insolent? I? To you? Am I your inferior?"

Catilina smiled grimly. "You wish to be my superior. You are ambitious, Caesar, and there are times that I do not trust you."

"Do not divert me. Let there be no more rumors of Fabia."

Catilina turned to him quickly. "Rumors? The maiden fainted; the days lately have been hot. On this small premise you build a tower of iniquity and lies."

"Is she a maiden still, Catilina? Are my suspicions iniquitous, and lies?"

"To all, certainly. You spoke of rumors. What other rumors?"

Watching him closely, Julius said, "She weeps at night, among her sister Vestals, and wakes groaning from dreams, accusing herself of vile but unnamed crimes."

"Ah, you sleep among the Vestals!"

Julius sprang to his feet and a line of foam appeared about his lips and he turned deadly pale. He struggled visibly to control the emotions which were about to culminate in the syndrome of his disease. So great was his will that after a moment or two, while Catilina watched him uneasily, he was able to suppress the onrushing attack. He sat down again and dropped his head on his breast. Then he slowly put his hand to his head in a dazed fashion. He stared about him. He said, as if alone and as if speaking to himself, "What is that which I saw?"

Lucius Catilina went to a marble table and poured a goblet of rosy wine and brought it to Julius. Julius took it like a man in a dream. His face was the color of lead. Sweat streamed from his brow like tears. He began to drink the wine very slowly and gazed before him as if attempting to catch a glimpse of some horror he had seen before.

Then he said in a dull voice, "There must be no more of Fabia, if there has been anything in truth."

Now he raised his eyes, which were filmed yet full of power. "I do not threaten rashly nor out of passing anger." His breath was slow and panting. "There is another matter. It is rumored that you are a dear associate of that Thracian, Spartacus, and of those slaves, Crixus and Oenomaus, whom he incites. We live, in Rome, now terrified of the slaves. Are you one of the plotters, Catilina? I do not expect to hear truth from your lips. But beware! The time is not ripe. A revolt of the slaves will not lead us to power."

"Something must," said Catilina with bitterness. "The years go on, and we remain the same, like schoolboy conspirators."

"You wish to see Romans, your fellow citizens, murdered in the streets by revolting slaves?"

Catilina's eyes shifted but his face took on a dark expression.

"Let us use reason," said Julius. "We want no massacres of our own people. It is true that we expect to use your own influence over your monstrous friends to make us irresistible, so that for fear no one will dare oppose us. But we wish no Roman blood to flow in the streets."

Catilina's arrogant mouth stirred, but he still did not speak.

Julius continued, "Yes, I can see that Roman blood means nothing to you. You hate all things; that is your nature. There is too much violence in you, and violence was always your first love—violence for its own sake. If I should give one word to Crassus you would not live to see another sun, or seduce another woman."

Catilina's hand flew to his dagger. But Julius, now recovered, rose to his feet and smiled at him with sincere amusement. "Be valorous, Catilina, when our day arrives, but do not be violent. I love you. I should not like to offer sacrifices to your manes."

He walked steadily if a little slowly to the black and enormous statue of Horus. He looked up into the ferocious beaked face. When he turned away at last he saw that Catilina had left without a farewell.

Terentia, who believed that no room in her house should be sacred from her presence, came into the library where Marcus was busy with more essays he had promised Atticus.

She had not knocked upon the door before entering, and Marcus started with nervous annoyance and frowned. He was not sufficient of an "old" Roman to believe that his wife should restrict her presence to the women's quarters, and to the company of her slavewomen and her mother-in-law and the nursery where slept her little daughter, Tullia, and to the outdoor porticoes reserved for females, and to their private courtyard. But he did believe that those who invaded another's privacy should beg the pardon of those invaded, or should first ask permission.

"I have asked you, dear Terentia, not to invade my library when I am occupying it," said Marcus, with as much severity as he could summon, which was not very much.

"Pish," said Terentia. "What is that which you are writing? Obscure essays for idle men to read in their baths? There are more important matters."

As it is axiomatic that every writer believes that what he writes is deathless, Marcus was justifiably vexed and irritated. He was more vexed than ever when Terentia seated herself without permission—she who would not sit in the presence of men at the table but kept herself discreetly near the door to supervise the dishes in the hands of slaves before giving her approval. He was very fond of Terentia. He was to write her from Sicily, "You are more courageous than any man," and "the truest of helpmates." But for some reason he was happier in her absence than he was in her presence. He was always trying to put her out of countenance because she was always so certain that all she did was perfect and not to be disputed by a mere man. For an "old" Roman matron, Marcus would think, she has a low opinion of my sex. But, was it possible that the "old" Roman matrons did have that low opinion and so avoided men?

Sighing, seeing that Terentia was firmly fixed in her chair and with a look on her face that indicated she would not be intimidated by anyone, Marcus put down his pen.

"I am engaged on an essay which I believe will cast some light on a most important subject," he said with much weightiness. He never did quite know whether he talked intellectually to Terentia in order to enlighten her or whether it was to define the line between her mind and his, to the denigration of hers. "Where does reason end and emotion begin? Who can say that he thinks rationally on most subjects, which is estimable, or is impelled, unknown to himself, from some deep force hidden in his nature which has nothing to do with his intellect? If so impelled, how can he advance the idea that his 'reason' is objective and therefore to be accepted without quibbling by other men? I love law because I am disgusted with and fearful of lawlessness. But, is that pure reason? There are men who instinctively love lawlessness and recklessness, and find rational reasons for being so—such as the apparent anarchy they find in nature and the disregard of nature for our human ideas and motives. We say law is sacred. But nature regards nothing as sacred. We abhor murder, but nature regards it with tranquillity. We have compassion on the weak—but nature ruthlessly eliminates them because weakness begets weakness and there is no place in the world for those who are not strong. Shall we quarrel with nature in that she has decreed that the advancement of men and animals and vegetables depends on the elimination of those not endowed with the genius to survive? She has shown that she does not desire the survival of a weak babe. But we use our arts of medicine to ensure that survival. Are we wrong, or is nature? Do we use reason? Or are we merely emotional?"

"Tullia is not weak; she is a very strong babe," said Terentia. "Therefore, I do not see that she should be made the subject of one of your essays."

Marcus raised his eyes to the ceiling with a deliberate patience that never failed to exasperate the pragmatic Terentia. "I was not writing of my little daughter, Tullia," he said in the voice of a martyr, of a greatly misunderstood husband, of one who is patient even with idiocy. "I see that I cannot reach you."

"Let me attempt, then, to reach your exotic mind, O Master," said Terentia, with that rare satire of hers which always startled Marcus disagreeably.

"It is true," Terentia continued, "that I cannot write essays nor conduct a case in the courts with subtlety and abstruse arguments. But I can read account books, and I can take the measure of our situation. Though of an inferior mind, I am able to judge whether or not to sell a certain investment, or whether or not a certain bank is worthy of my patronage. I know who of my friends can advance us, and I know those who are a hindrance. I know to the penny our present balance in the counting houses, and the value of our holdings in land.

"But certainly, all that is contemptible to your magnificent mind, Marcus."

"What is wrong now?" asked Marcus in a resigned voice.

Terentia helped herself to a handful of figs and dates. She engulfed her choices audibly and contemplated the wall just over Marcus' shoulder. Her eyes were large and thoughtful. She chewed with enjoyment.

"Almost everything," she said, after swallowing with much deliberation.

"Can you not talk about it with me tomorrow, when I am less engaged?"

"When? In your courts? In your offices? No. It must be now." She fished among her voluminous and unbecoming garments and brought forth a paper. "I have marked these down in an orderly fashion. Master; spare your slave a few moments of your valuable time. I will be brief."

"Please," said Marcus, in an elaborate tone of politeness.

"You have told me that you wish a dinner for certain gentlemen. Master, the dinner will be served as you desire. I have noted the names of the guests. Almost all of them are dull lawyers and businessmen. I do not deprecate them; they are your associates. But none is a man of real importance, and if you are to advance you must seek important men."

"That dinner was designed for an exchange of opinions on law, Terentia."

"Life is too short for mere self-indulgence," said Terentia firmly. "You take pleasure from such discussions. Pleasure is suspect. You have been elected a quaestor. You are now a politician. Who can advance your political fortunes?"

"Who?" echoed Marcus with even more elaborate patience.

"Julius Caesar, Pompey the Magnus, Lucius Catilina. The noble Licinius Crassus, the triumvir, the richest man in Rome, the financier. These are but a few."

Marcus leaned back in his chair. "I find Julius annoying and too adroit. I find Pompey heavy of intellect. I need not tell you again how I loathe Catilina. As for Crassus, I despise him in my heart, for he made himself rich through the expropriation of the estates of the unfortunate when Sulla returned from Asia. He is an exigent man; he can buy offices for himself and his friends at will, and he who buys offices is despicable."

"All politicians buy offices," said Terentia, with her own patience. "Do you think men are elected because of their probity and their intelligence and their devotion to their country and their hope to advance their country? All political offices are for sale, and all successful politicians have laid down the necessary gold."

"I did not," said Marcus, angrily.

Terentia shrugged. "You should have been a proconsul at the very least. You should have bought office, as do all intelligent men. I can name you a dozen triumvirs who bought offices or whose fathers were rich enough to buy them for them. Virtue has nothing to do with it, nor suitability, nor worthiness. If virtuous, suitable or worthy men were the only ones to be elected, then surely half the offices, or more, of Rome would be vacant!"

"A people should search for their best men," said Marcus.

"But who, in their opinion, are the best men? The men who promise them labor and struggle for the sake of their country, or the men who promise them gifts?"

Marcus took his eyes from the ceiling and stared at his wife with respect. She smiled at him maternally. "I have been reading some of your old essays," she informed him. "I did not come to these conclusions through the power of my poor female brain."

"You are my apt pupil," said Marcus, taking up his pen again.

"Wait. Do you insist on those dull men for your dinners? Or will you take my advice? If you do not wish those four I have mentioned, there are others."

"List those, O Terentia, you consider important. Except for Catilina."

Marcus was very kind and he had a deep affection for his wife if not love. Terentia was relieved. "Let us return to the number of your guests, dear husband. I have added other names," and she named them. Marcus scowled. Then he stared at his wife.

"I have discovered that my bronze statue of a nymph and a faun have disappeared from the vestibule."

Terentia smiled at him sweetly. "My list is very comprehensive, regarding your guests, my dear one. I thought the statue indecent. Nevertheless, if you wish it, I will have it restored to the vestibule."

"There are also my figurines in alabaster of Venus and Adonis missing from our bedroom."

"What an obscene attitude! Nevertheless, as you appear to delight in them I will have them restored. You are a very strange husband," said Terentia, folding the paper that contained the names. "I confess I do not understand you. You have incomprehensible moods. I recall the exasperation of my mother against my father. But you are more capricious than any other man. As your wife, I assumed the books from your mother, who is very competent. Do you know that because you have bought so much land and so many country homes and groves of olive and fruit trees, that you owe over two hundred thousand sesterces, and numerous other debts?"

"My clients have been unfortunately healthy and long-lived recently. They have not died and mentioned me in their wills," said Marcus. "Two hundred thousand sesterces!"

"Yes." Terentia paused and fixed him coldly with her big brown eyes. "I have observed from the account books of your office that you have had very many female clients lately whose divorces you have gained. I believed that you disapproved of divorce."

"I do. But in these cases the ladies were justified."

"They have given you no fees."

"Terentia, lawyers are not permitted to accept fees, under the law. We can receive gifts and bequests only."

Terentia's eyes became even colder. "The ladies have not given you gifts. Do they give you gifts, Marcus, other than money?"

Marcus was astounded. "What are you implying?"

She shrugged, and cast down her eyes.

"Are you jealous!" cried Marcus, with much interest.

"I?" exclaimed Terentia. "How you defame me, Marcus. Do I not understand that you are the most faithful of husbands?"

Marcus pursed his lips. "In Rome in these days," he said, "that is not considered a compliment. The husband of your friend, Aurelia, is notorious for his adultery."

"So is Aurelia," said Terentia. She rose, then became very serious. "Marcus, you must hint more broadly of gifts to your clients. Our accounts in the banks are low." She smiled. "Do you wish to see Tullia before she sleeps?"

They went to the lamplighted nursery, which was charming and full of sweet-scented autumn air. The babe, Tullia, was still awake. She looked at her father and crowed and held up her little arms. He saw his own face in hers, a little pale but healthy, and shining with intelligence. Her eyes were his own, changeful and large, turning from amber to blue to gray from moment to moment. Marcus lifted his child in his arms and kissed her with joy. "My sweetheart," he said. The child burbled against his cheek. She caught a lock of his hair in her fist and pulled it happily. Terentia, who had desired a son, nevertheless regarded father and child with pride. Terentia put her hand on her husband's shoulder, then leaned her cheek against it. He was very strange. But he was virtuous and famous, if a little improvident with regard to gifts from clients; he also disregarded the cultivation of men who could advance him.

She said, "Marcus, I have decided that I and the babe must not accompany you to Sicily. I understand the climate is not the most salubrious for children."

Marcus had been silently hoping that he would not be burdened with a large household in Sicily. He had also wished to flee, for a while, from his exigent wife who talked of account books and important guests, and whose conversation in general was not very edifying but concerned only with drab matters. He said now, "I will be very lonely."

Terentia said with firmness, "It will be but a year, and you will visit us in the summer at the island. But I must insist that we be careful of Tullia's health."

"I agree with you, dear wife," said Marcus, in a tone of such compliance that Terentia's eyes sharpened with speculation.

Marcus returned to his library where he found his overseer, Aulus, waiting for him. "Master, the noble Julius Caesar requests a moment with you."

"At this hour?"

Aulus bowed and looked at the floor. "Master, the hour is not late in these days. There is with him Pompey the Magnus."

Marcus frowned. He knew that Pompey liked him, and he could not understand why. He said to Aulus, "Conduct them to my library."

It was obvious that Julius and Pompey, though not drunk, had imbibed well and had dined heartily. They shone with that special well-being that comes only from the bottle and the table. Marcus felt heavy and middle-aged in their glowing presence. He felt dull and completely a husband and father—with account books.

"You must pardon our late intrusion, dear friend," said Julius, embracing his unwilling host.

"You are welcome," said Marcus, asking Aulus to bring wine.

"I doubt it," said Julius, with mockery. "But, how we love you! Pompey said, as we approached the Palatine, 'Let us visit our dearest friend, Cicero, at least for a greeting.' He is most persuasive. And, here we are."

Marcus glanced at Pompey, the broad-faced, gray-eyed and somewhat impassive man. He wondered why they were here. The wine was brought. The younger men sipped it approvingly. "I must compliment Terentia," said Julius. "She has elevated your taste."

"She is complimented. Yet, you deplored my marriage."

"Marcus has a most formidable memory," said Julius to Pompey. "Do not incur his enmity. He will remember it forever."

"True," said Marcus.

Julius flung out his arm grandly. "If I remembered all my enemies, and bore grudges, my life would be miserable indeed. I prefer to reconcile my enemies and make them my friends."

"And your allies," said Marcus.

"Every man needs allies," said Julius, looking at him with his sparkling black eyes. "We love you, Cicero. Therefore, we seek allies for you. We wish our whole nation to applaud you and bow before you."

"And advance you," said Pompey, who was not exuberant in conversation.

"What are you plotting now?" asked Marcus. He drank some of his own wine and was agreeably surprised that he no longer felt weighty.

Julius rolled up his eyes. "Cicero talks constantly of 'plots.' He distrusts us, his friends. He will not believe in our affection. Do we not lead virtuous and dedicated lives?"

"No," said Marcus.

"What a comedian he is," said Julius, beaming at Pompey. He leaned toward Marcus. "We have brought an invitation for you, from the noble Licinius Crassus, who spoke of you gloriously tonight. He wishes you to dine with him a week from today, before you leave for Sicily."

"No," said Marcus.

"But a triumvir? A man of wealth and influence!"

"No."

Julius sipped his wine. "Crassus was the dear friend of Sulla. Sulla's papers are now organized. Crassus has come into possession of a letter from Sulla, which was written to him. He wishes to read it to you. It concerns you, dear Marcus."

Marcus was more than normally inquisitive. "How?"

Julius wagged his head. "I shall not tell you. —You must hear it from the lips of Crassus, who loves you."

"Hah," said Marcus. He hesitated. "I have heard of Crassus' dinners. Depraved."

Julius' whole face twinkled. He looked about the grave library. He

looked at Marcus' sober garb. "What! Will you die before you know
pleasure?"

"I do not know what you mean by pleasure," said Marcus. "I should
find it boring." He paused. "I will attend the dinner of Crassus, whom I
despise. I should like to read the letter from Sulla."

Julius said triumphantly, "Rejoice! Your dear friends, Noë ben Joel and
that darling actor, Roscius, will be present also."

CHAPTER FORTY-ONE

Julius Caesar said to M. Licinius Crassus, "Lord, it is much easier to corrupt, or render harmless, the honest and virtuous man than it is to corrupt
or render harmless the innately dishonest and unvirtuous. For the first
cannot believe, or will not let himself believe, that men are what they
truly are; it would make him too melancholy and too distressed. But the
second man asks himself but two questions, when approached: 'Why do
they wish me to do this or not to do this? And what shall I gain from either
doing or not doing?' He is hard and dangerous.

"Therefore, lord, as I told Sulla, it is only necessary to convince Cicero
that you love Rome above all things, except for the gods. He will then not
oppose you no matter the—exigency—or the seeming contradiction. Cicero's lack of opposition is more valuable than most men's participation and
assistance. The people love him, not as a popular idol such as a gladiator,
a general, an actor, or a politician. They love him for the virtue he has
which they think they, themselves, possess."

"Is he stupid?" asked Crassus.

"No, lord. He is only a good man."

"Where, then, is the difference?"

Julius laughed and shook his head. "Cicero has tremendous influence
in Rome. Let us rejoice that he is not aware of that."

Crassus was a man of about forty-four years old, broad and heavy and
muscular, somewhat short in stature and very wide of shoulder. It was
startling, therefore, to see the long thin head on that great frame, his narrow features, his sunken but gleaming gray eyes under a low brow. His
hair was thick, coarse, and partly gray, and had a turbulent appearance.
He was a patrician like the dead Sulla, but he did not have Sulla's true
pride of race and family, nor Sulla's honor, perverted though it had been.

In spite of all that he had done, Sulla had loved his country. Crassus loved nothing but himself and money. He was enormously rich and a shrewd financier. He trafficked in slaves and money-lending. There was not a single way to make money which he had not employed. Now that he was the richest man in the Republic he found himself restless. True, money brought power. But the power of money in a republic was somewhat restricted by law, and though it brought influence it was not enough for such as Crassus.

To gain the power he desired, the absolute power, it was first necessary to seduce the people. But a republican nation, no matter how venal it could become, was suspicious of panoplies and the open ceremonies of wealth. Crassus had discovered this for himself, when his beautiful young wife had appeared in public with a small golden crown on her head, encrusted with jewels, and wearing a purple cloak embroidered in golden lilies. The people had hissed her in the very circus. They had made derisive and obscene noises while they shouted, "Queen! Majesty! Empress!" The lady had had to retreat in tears and fear from the mounting anger and contempt and indignation of the people. Rome was not yet ready for empire. She would still oppose to the death the next step: the trumpets of royalty.

Crassus did not intend to make the mistakes of Sulla. The general had erred in being first of all a soldier and maintaining a soldier's discipline and inherent restraint, and in loving his country. Crassus had none of these virtues. He approached the people softly, deftly, treacherously. He was rich; he became a philanthropist. He made speeches before the Senate, declaring that he desired only the welfare of the Republic and the Constitutional power of the people. What the people desired, that he would do. His purse was always open to the deserving and the virtuous. He worshiped freedom. He was but the servant of Rome. Let Rome command him. All that he had was Rome's. He pretended to scorn of his class and the rich. He denounced the patricians for their "idleness and luxury and their indifference to the misery of the masses." He upbraided the wealthy for their selfishness, their disregard for their fellowmen. "If the privileged have one privilege it is that of possessing the power to help the helpless and ameliorate their pain." Appealing to the freedmen, always sensitive of their former state, he declared that all men had been endowed with freedom by God. To those who possessed slaves and who might become angered with him for that statement, he said, "The gods have decreed the status of men, and who dare oppose them?" To the rich of his own class he said in private, "The people must be soothed and flattered, lest they seize all we have and destroy us."

To the Senate he said, "You are Roman power." To the mobs he said, "You are the only power. Command us."

He built free sanitaria for the indigent. When the allowance of bread and grain were not sufficient for the starving he opened his own purse to supply their needs. He was a patron of the arts. Actors and gladiators adored him, and spread his fame among the people. When he appeared in public his freedmen carried bags of gold, which they threw to the clamoring mobs. Each morning, with a devout and serious face, he received complainers in his outdoor portico and listened gravely to the statements of their wrongs, and gave them earnest promises. "My door is always open," he said. He begged his clients for their prayers.

There were few who suspected or disliked him, for did he not love the people and did he not distribute his wealth to them and honor them? Among those who suspected him was Marcus Tullius Cicero, who knew the source of his riches. If Cicero should be moved to denounce him then the people might stare undeceived at this friend of the humble and the miserable.

He said to Julius, "How can we corrupt him?"

Julius said, "Lord, that you cannot do. You can only deceive him as to your ultimate desires and ambitions."

"Catilina desires his death."

"Catilina is a mad fool."

"True. But the best cure for the danger inherent in such as Cicero is assassination."

"The people love him, lord."

Crassus smiled at the young man. "Catilina complains that you invariably defend Cicero, and that you love him."

"He was the mentor of my childhood. I shall stand between Cicero and death as long as I live."

Crassus laughed. "I have not risen to be triumvir nor attained my wealth by accepting as truth all that men tell me. You have another reason. Let us entertain this Cicero, and convince him of my gentle intentions—and render him harmless."

Marcus had never seen so gorgeous a house as that of Crassus, nor any so luxurious and decadent in its ornamentations. He also noted that it was closely guarded—apparently against those Crassus so publicly loved. Never had Marcus encountered such carpets before; they were piled one upon another so thickly that one's feet sank deeply into them. Caesar's fine new home outside Rome was a hovel in comparison. Marcus' own house was a mere cave. The slaves had been chosen for their youth and their beauty; their long hair, both that of youths and maidens, was caught up in jeweled, golden nets. Many of them were naked, to reveal their exquisite charms. The palace was filled with the sound of fountains and music and soft laughter, the fragrance of perfumes and sweet ointments and flowers. It held an air of gaiety and friendship and relaxation. Crassus wore a wreath of bay; the guests wore circlets of blossoms. Nubian slaves, tall and brilliantly black and handsome and naked, moved about the rooms with plumed fans, and stood behind the guests gently fanning them, for the autumn evening was warm.

Republic austerity, thought Marcus, observing all this. His senses were dazzled. The Alexandrian glass lamps quivered with light; gold and silver and jewels were everywhere, in plates and knives and spoons and platters and bowls. The cover on the long dining table was cloth of gold, centered with flowers and ferns. The murals and paintings on the white marble walls appeared to live and move in their bright colors.

Hidden by a carved ivory screen musicians played beautifully while the guests dined. Maidens sang in concert. Great salvers carried by proud cooks were placed upon the table, steaming with fish poached in wine, roasted geese and ducks and little pigs and delicate lamb. There were huge bowls containing the choicest fruit, and salads delicately flavored with wine and oil and garlic and capers. There were breads as white as snow. There were Judean olives and citrons and pale celery and pickled fish and boars' heads roasted with herbs. There were not only the best of wines from all nations, served from bottles sunken in mountain snow, but Syrian whiskey, golden and acrid and powerful. For those who had plebeian tastes—and Crassus publicly confessed to this—there was cold beer, bright as amber and frothing.

Each corner of the dining room held a statue of one of the gods, life-sized or larger, before which stood Persian vases filled with flowers and colorful autumn leaves. The scent of the flowers mingled with a whisper of incense, and all mingled with the music and the odors of rich food. Marcus observed that his napkin, of white linen, was bordered with woven gold. He sat at Crassus' right, as an honored guest. On Crassus' left sat Julius and next to him sat Pompey. There were lawyers here tonight and men of wealth and politicians and three Senators. There, too, were Noë and Roscius, who, catching Marcus' eye from time to time, winked at him. Noë was becoming bald; his long face was full of humor. Roscius resembled a god in his crimson toga.

There were no women here tonight except for beautiful and nude female slaves who assisted the guests and refilled their goblets and who smiled at lascivious touches.

Why am I here? Marcus asked himself. When he was confused and disturbed he had a tendency to drink too much wine. He was quite silent; the other guests were laughing and jesting with the utmost good will and friendship and affection. Roscius had begun to declaim some verses of Noë's latest play and all paused to listen to his powerful and musical voice. Noë beamed proudly, and accepted the applause and tributes with Roscius. Marcus began to understand that his friends had been invited not for their own sakes but as a lure for himself. He put down his wine-filled goblet and opened his ears.

"I hope, noble Cicero," said Crassus in his rough but compelling voice, "that you are enjoying my poor dinner."

"I am not accustomed to dining so humbly," said Marcus.

Julius, hearing this, laughed and nudged his host. "Did I not tell you that he is a comedian?"

But Crassus, despite his smile, was annoyed. He said, "I see you are sardonic, Cicero."

"Not at all, lord. I am merely overcome. Do all the champions of the people live so, and dine so magnificently?"

Crassus considered him from under his thick black brows. "I should like to see all men in Rome live thus. Do they not deserve the fruits of their labor? Alas, they are deprived of their rights, their honest luxuries. Do not all Romans deserve chariots and cars and fine horses and splendid houses? Who denies them?"*

"The government, no doubt," said Marcus. "The privileged. The greedy. The avaricious. The exploiters of the people."

Crassus pretended to take his irony as sincerity. "That is correct. I hope to relieve the situation. Are not Romans worthy of the best the world can produce? Yes! Those who say they are not are the enemies of the people."

"The riches of Croesus, all the treasuries of the world, would not be sufficient, lord, to give each Roman what I see here tonight."

"True," said Crassus. "But there is a middle way between luxury and poverty. There is comfort and some of the amenities of life, and security. That is what I desire for my people."

He spoke with emphasis and authority and looked into Marcus' eyes. Marcus did not believe him for a moment.

"Why should there be periodic famines and periodic feasts, Cicero?"

"I was under the impression," said Marcus, "that nature decrees them."

"We store grain for the people after a great harvest," said Crassus. "But that is not the answer."

"What is, lord?"

Crassus drank from his goblet and fixed his eyes gravely on the ceiling as if imploring the gods.

"Equal distribution of land, available to all," he finally intoned.

* This conversation all from letters between Crassus and Cicero.

Marcus said, "The farmers might object to that."

"Ah, the farmers! Do I not love them? But there is land for all, Cicero."

"Where?" said Marcus. "Italy is a country of mountains and meagre land."

"The world," said Crassus, mysteriously. "Is this not a great world, full of uncultivated land?"

"The inhabitants thereof might dispute the right of Romans to surge in upon them and do as they wish with land they do not own."

"You misunderstand me, Cicero. All land in the world should be owned in common."

"What then, of the right to private property as guaranteed by our Constitution?"

"I am not disputing that," said Crassus. "Do I not uphold the Constitution?"

He is not a fool, thought Marcus. Therefore, his foolish utterances have a design. Marcus observed that everyone was listening to Crassus attentively and with approval, except for Noë and Roscius who were grinning unpleasantly.

Crassus continued, "Alexander had a dream of a united world. I, too, have that dream. One government, one people, one law, under God. Shall it be realized in my lifetime? I do not know. But we should, as men, work ceaselessly toward that goal."

"Why?" said Marcus. "We should then destroy the infinite variety of humanity. We should destroy the gods of other peoples. We should destroy their way of life, which they have decreed for themselves. Who has the insolence to say our way is better than others?"

"The differences you remark upon, Cicero, are superficial. Are we not all men, with the same needs?"

"We are all men," said Marcus, "but we do not all have the same needs. We Romans have no authority, human or divine, to impose our wills upon others, no matter how noble we pretend they are."

"Pretend?" said Crassus, arching his brows.

"Pretend," Marcus repeated.

Crassus thought, Catilina is right. He should be assassinated. He looked at Julius who was following the conversation with a broad smile.

"We can impose our government," said Marcus, "only with the sword and with war and with the violation of the rights of other men. Let us refrain."

"You do not understand, Cicero. Under one authority, one law, all land would be cultivated completely for the benefit of the people. All treasure would be utilized, and in fairness."

"Including yours, noble Crassus?"

"Including mine," said Crassus.

He is a dangerous liar, thought Marcus. Ah, these lovers of humanity! They are the most treacherous and terrible of men.

"I believe in law, and the orderly process of law," said Marcus, trying to hide his revulsion. "I do not believe in force—or lies—in order to make all men live as we might desire them to live. If our way is truly good, then all men will eventually recognize it. If it is evil"—and here Marcus paused —"we can enforce it only by murder."

Crassus said, "Let us pray our nation is just. Cicero speaks rightly. I admire his astuteness and his sincerity. He is a true Roman."

He put his hand on Marcus' shoulder and looked gravely up and down the table. "A true Roman," said Crassus, in unctuous and reverent tones.

"As a true Roman," said Marcus, "I honor other men and would leave them in peace. But we must not touch the hearts or minds of others, for that is holy ground and our feet are not worthy to tread it."

"You disparage your fellowmen, Cicero."

"No, I have compassion for them and understand them." Marcus looked fully into the eyes of Crassus, who was the richest man in Rome. "It is true that we are again in a war with Mithridates of Persia, that Oriental tyrant and despot, that arrogant man who despises us, and whose fathers before him fought with Rome. Our young men die daily in the battle. Can we not, in the name of peace, strike a bargain with Mithridates? He is not mad. His nation suffers also."

"It is not possible that you do not know that our envoys have already sought such a peace?"

"I know what is said. But I know that Rome also covets the treasures of Persia. Our treasury is bankrupt; our soldiers are not paid."

"Then, as a Roman patriot I desire for Rome the treasures of Mithridates!" cried Julius, and almost everyone laughed with him.

"As a Roman I prefer economy in government," said Marcus. "Then we should have no need of wars."*

Crassus raised a magisterial hand. "I agree with Cicero. He has spoken well. I shall urge the Senate to conclude this war rapidly, though we were provoked into engaging in it. Let us have peace."

Marcus studied him, but his narrow face was resolute and he looked about him freely, as if challenging all there. "Let us labor as did our Founding Fathers, whose memory we revere. I tell you, Cicero, I wished your presence that you might hear me, for I speak from my heart."

Noë exchanged a glance with Roscius, then whispered to him, "A far better actor than you, my dear mountebank."

* Cicero expounded frequently in essays and speeches on this subject.

Crassus let his eyes become large and straight as they met those of Marcus. "It is probable that you do not believe me. But I love Rome." He said to Julius, "Have I not already talked with Senators about these things? There are three with us tonight who can swear to the truth."

Crassus removed a scroll from beneath his rich garments. "I have a letter written to me by Sulla before he died. I wish to read it to you, Cicero. 'Among these, Licinius, whom you can trust is the lawyer, Marcus Tullius Cicero, whose mother is of the noble Helvii. He detested me but he knew I must do as I must. Unlike others, he is no liar, no hypocrite. Cultivate him well! Is not an honest man rarer than rubies? Is not that government blessed which boasts him in its crown? He will never betray his country nor his gods. He is valorous, among men who no longer can say they possess valor. Embrace him for me, for in these evil days my heart fails me. I am close to death; I see his shadow falling across my hand as I write these words to you. If any man can save Rome it is Cicero and those of his mind and spirit.' "

Marcus was greatly moved. He had colored with embarrassment at this eulogy. He reflected that Sulla could not have written so to a man who was a threat to his country. He said in a low voice, "I am not worthy of such praise."

But Crassus embraced him. "Let others judge of that, Cicero. I ask only that you pursue your way of honor and that you will advise me when I request it, for though I am much older than you I do not smile at the words of younger men."

When alone with Julius and Pompey, Crassus said, "It is fortunate that he did not demand to read that letter for himself, for it is possible he would have recognized that it was not Sulla's hand which had written it."

"But you spoke in such heroic tones!" said Julius. "Even I, for a moment, thought it was in truth a letter from Sulla. Are you convinced now that Cicero is harmless?"

Crassus considered. "I am convinced that I deceived him. That is a different matter."

"Let us hope he never discovers how powerful he is in Rome," said Pompey. He smiled. "It is strange, but I feel affection for him. And I pity him."

Julius was relieved that nothing threatened Marcus now, so he said, "Yes. He beguiles one, for he can be trusted. Therefore, we love him; we have no need to fear him."

Crassus frowned. "It has been said, beware of the wrath of a good man for it is like lightning and can destroy a city. Nevertheless, let him live. We need him to mask our faces."

Marcus who had not believed that his administration in Sicily would bring him pleasure discovered that he suddenly loved that island of wild bronze mountains and stony earth and violent sun. He liked the poor but volatile people, their songs, their strange faces which had been formed from many bloods. He admired their struggle with their fierce land, and their seamanship. They were a people who would kill on the slightest provocation and they hated Romans for Romans declared they were not of the Italian race, but the scourings of the Great Sea. But from the first they had loved Marcus and had trusted him. They did not say of him as they had said of other quaestors, "He will grind us for taxes and eat up our little substance." They said of him, "He is a just man, which is a strange thing for a Roman." They brought fresh fruit to him, and newly caught fish and fine vegetables, and he was touched for he knew what a sacrifice it was for this poor people. He revelled in their affection. His door was open to them at all times and he was patient with complaints and always tried to right a wrong. When a man could not meet the Roman taxes and was in fear of his freedom and the freedom of his family, Marcus paid the small sum from his own purse, and did not enter it in his books.

He found peace and quiet in his little villa. He was happy to be living alone once more, though he felt guilty at this happiness. He wrote frequently to his wife and his parents and his letters expressed his love for his little daughter. He was now so serene that he could even endure the long letters from Terentia which were filled with news of investments and the gossip of the city and admonitions that he be frugal with his stipend. His affable spirits returned to him. When he was alone he fell into his old habits of long reading and long study and walking by himself looking at the flaming sea at sunset. There were other Romans on the island, on farms which they had bought. He did not seek their company. They sought him out and he was amiable and sometimes dined with them. But he made no friends.

The sun darkened his skin; the simple food and tranquillity increased his flesh. The long and meditative walks strengthened his muscles. He could not believe it when he suddenly realized that almost a year had passed and he must prepare to return home. Certainly, he had not been lonely. He bought some land in Sicily and told the peasants who worked on it that the fruits of their labors were theirs and they needed only to pay the taxes from the harvests and not even that if they were not able to do so. Romans did not trust Sicilians, for they were wily. But Marcus trusted them and took their brown hands in his and smiled affectionately into their eyes. "One day I shall return and live always among you," he said. They kissed his hands and wept honest tears, they who were by nature not honest. An old crone gave him an amulet and blessed him and kissed the hem of his garments and wept. She said to her children, "Honest men no longer die in peaceful beds. He will die by the hands of wicked men." They looked at her with awe, for she was a soothsayer.

Marcus received a letter from Julius which informed him that Crassus was now Praetor of Rome, and that Romans loved him for his virtue and his justness. Julius and Pompey were his advisers and counselors. They were all disturbed because of the increasing signs of rebellion among the slaves. The Thracian, Spartacus, was inciting them with new urgency. Roman masters no longer cherished their slaves and honored their manes after death and sacrificed to them and held them part of their households. Thinking of the slaves Marcus felt anguish for them and bitterness against their cruel masters. He wrote to his mother (but not his wife) "It is my wish that those who have served us well for seven years be taken before the officer and freed, and thereafter, if it is their will to remain with us let us pay them a just wage." Slavery had never revolted him before as it revolted him now. It seemed to him that slavery degraded the master more than it did the slave. Romans had newly adopted the custom of the Greeks in using the word "thing" for their slaves, as if they possessed no souls but were only animals! When Terentia wrote a letter in protest "at your profligacy," Marcus did not answer it.

His correspondence was very large, and he liked letters and replied to them for hours. Noë wrote him, and Roscius, and Quintus, his brother, and Atticus, and many others for whom he had a regard. Hundreds who had read his essays wrote to him in gratitude. He was surprised that Pompey sent him letters also. The Sadducee whom he had met in Epidaurus wrote him, and so did Anotis, the Egyptian. He had not known that he had so many friends and that so many loved and admired him. He wrote many letters to his students, advising them. They sent him copies of new laws, which he studied long and seriously. Sometimes he frowned. Taxes had risen again. The middle-class was again being assaulted and their moneys and properties confiscated under many pretexts, mostly from the owing of enormous taxes or accusations of subversion. "And that is how Crassus is refilling our treasury," Marcus said to himself with bitterness. Rome had won the war againt Mithridates, who had been murdered or assassinated, and Persia paid huge tribute and bowed her head to Rome. We move, thought Marcus.

There were gray shadows at his temples now, and threads of it in his thick brown hair. There were beautiful peasant women on the island who looked at him kindly, but he had never been a libertine. He believed, as an "old" Roman, that a certain respect should be given women and that men should not exploit them in exchange for gifts, if they were poor. He lived an ascetic life on Sicily and found his sensual pleasures in the scenery and the changing sea, and in the climbing of mountains. He wrote constantly. His sleep was more peaceful than it had been for years. Sometimes he forgot Livia for days at a time.

A month before his departure from Sicily he received a letter from Terentia, filled with agony and grief and disfigured with tears.

"My darling, my adorable, my divine sister, Fabia, is dead by her own hand, resembling Araneada with a silken rope. But alas, she had not incited Athene but rather Eros. Through his arts she defiled the sacred fires of Vesta and so was unworthy to live. Who was her partner in this abominable crime? The one whom you have warned me against, dearest husband, Lucius Sergius Catilina! My hand trembles. My whole being is shaken; my heart is irrevocably broken. I, her beloved sister, did not dream of this horror, no, not even when she visited me and I looked upon her pallid face and listless form and her mute white lips. But it appears that all Rome knows and has known for many months. Why did she not confide in me? Was I not closer to her than a mother? How did I betray her and lose her confidence? She died because she had realized she had committed the greatest of all sins.

"After her death Catilina was seized and brought to trial for this crime. Your friend, Julius Caesar, whom you never trusted, was his advocate at the trial. Catilina was adjudged guiltless through the eloquence of Caesar who swore that Catilina had never once gazed upon the Vestal, and on the testimony of Aurelia, who swore that her husband never left her side at night. Yet, all Rome knows the truth. Who will avenge Fabia, my dove, my sweetest sister, who fell before the seduction of Catilina and who now lies in an unnamed and shameful grave? More than all, I fear for her soul, for she broke her vows of chastity and blew out the fires of Vesta. I can write no more for I am blinded with my tears."

Marcus was stunned at this news. He thought of that beaming and radiant presence in his house, that lovely Vestal who had breathed only shyness and innocence, who had blessed his child, whose glances were modest and bright, whose voice was like a bird singing in the dawn. Now her name was accursed in Rome, among her Vestal sisters. Marcus crushed the letter in his fist and he was filled with the passion of hatred and the lust to murder. He ran from his house to the shore of the sea and the sky and the water appeared inflamed to him and his heart roared in his chest. He sat on a boulder and panted. His mind swam. There were murderers for hire in Rome, secret murderers who left no trace. How should he hire one? Or, should he do the deed himself? Sweat poured down his face.

He seemed to hear the voice of old Scaevola, "Discover his ambition and thwart it. That is worse than death." But in all these years he had not discovered what Catilina desired above all things. He had pursued hints to no avail. He had discreetly questioned others, even Caesar. Alas, he had never discovered anything.

But Catilina must be destroyed. The mists of evening were boiling over the sea and in them Marcus could discern the sad forms of Livia and her child and Fabia, the innocent one. They held out wan arms to him and he burst into fresh tears. "Avenge us," they mourned in the evening wind.

Marcus stood up and raised his hand and again renewed his vow that Catilina must be destroyed. If he had any reason for living at all that was the reason. He returned to his house in the darkness and lay on his bed and could not sleep. Hatred was like a coil of fire in his bowels.

CHAPTER FORTY-TWO

Crassus gazed at Marcus regretfully. "My dear Cicero, you as a lawyer should be the last to give heed to rumor. I was present at the trial of Catilina. There was not one witness who was not impeached after testifying against him. You know the vengefulness of women. Had there been the slightest truth in the charges Aurelia Catilina, who knew the seriousness of the crime and who is a woman who would not permit betrayal of her bed, would have been the first to denounce her husband. Yet she spoke with fervor in his behalf, her eyes flaming indignantly. If her husband was not with her he was with his friends, and those friends testified that it was true. He stood before the magistrates and swore by all he held holy that he had been maligned, that he had seen the maiden but twice in his life and then at a distance only. He sued his perjurers. He won his case. He is richer now by three hundred thousand gold sesterces! Is that not evidence enough?"

"No," said Marcus, but with despair. "I believe the Vestals who testified against Catilina, for Fabia had told her sisters before she died by her own hand."

"One reverences the Vestals," said Crassus, his thick eyelids dropping over his eyes. "But one knows their lack of sophistication. It is very possible that the girl was mad."

"And how was it proved that the Vestals were lying?" asked Marcus.

Crassus stared at him with umbrage. "Vestals do not lie!" he exclaimed. "They had only the word of Fabia who confided in them. But the girl was possibly mad. I reverence the vows of the Vestals, but one knows that chastity sometimes gives rise to humors of the brain. I do not like Catilina. Like you, I distrust him, for he is debauched and idle and restless and ambitious. If I had believed that he was guilty I should not have testified in his behalf, that he dined with me on the very nights he was accused of lying with Fabia."

"Lord, you have a remarkable memory!"

Crassus smiled. His narrow eyes sparkled on Marcus. "I confess to the charge. As a politician I must keep my memory sharp."

Marcus rose. He looked into those shrewd eyes and said, "You know that Catilina is guilty. For your own purposes you testified to his innocence."

Crassus said, "A hasty tongue can hang its owner. Beware, Cicero."

Marcus swung on his heel and left him. He went to the house of Julius Caesar.

Julius said, "Do you think I should have defended a man who was guilty of the highest of crimes?"

"Yes," said Marcus.

Julius sighed. "You have never trusted me, even from our childhood, yet I love you. I swear that Catilina is innocent. Does that not satisfy you?"

"No."

"You believe I lie?"

"Yes."

When Marcus had left him Julius summoned Catilina. "We have a problem," said Julius. "Did I not warn you against Fabia, and did I not tell you that only catastrophe would result if you disregarded my warnings? Yet, you ridiculed me and denied my accusations. In the name of our brotherhood I defended you though I knew I lied. Crassus defended you, and he knew you lied and that you were guilty. Pompey defended you. You were acquitted. You sued for damages against three men who saw you at a distance with Fabia. The suit was successful. It was necessary that we save you, lest we all fall. Now Cicero knows your guilt."

"Then, he should die as I have often told you."

"Then it will surely be known that you were guilty."

"His wife could poison him, at their own table."

Julius smiled. "Ah, yes. Poison is a woman's weapon. Is that not what you always say, Lucius? You would feel no guilt if Cicero died at his own table at the hand of his wife, Terentia, who is known for her virtue and her devotion to her husband?"

"He is an obstacle, and a dangerous one."

"And Terentia would die for the murder of her husband."

Catilina shrugged. "One does not roast a boar without first killing him."

"How would you bring it about that Terentia poisoned her husband?"

"That is very easy. We can corrupt one of his slaves, who will swear that he saw Terentia pour the poison in her husband's goblet."

Julius gazed at him thoughtfully. "You have a solution for every problem. I do not like your liking for poison. I tell you again, if Cicero dies by any misadventure you shall die also. I have sworn that in the name of my patron, Jupiter."

Catilina laughed. "Then, where is the problem of which you have spoken?"

"Be circumspect. Conduct yourself for some time as a sober citizen. Devote yourself to Aurelia, who loves you in spite of your guilt. Did you love Fabia?"

"I never knew her," said Catilina. But suddenly his beautiful face was convulsed. He covered his eyes with his hands. Julius, the dissolute, regarded him with reluctant pity.

"Women," he sighed. "And she was the loveliest of all. How they disarm us! Your grief is your punishment."

"It is more than I can bear." Catilina dropped his hands. His face was disfigured with anguish and tears.

"Be sure that I shall avenge Fabia," Marcus told his wife. He had never spoken of Livia to Terentia. She was impressed by his cold white fury. She wept in his arms.

"It will take some time," said Marcus, stroking her long brown hair. "But I shall avenge your sister."

"Catilina is a murderer," said Helvia to her son.

"I have known that for many years," said Marcus.

"He is also dangerous. I fear for you."

"I will not die until it is fated for me to die," said Marcus.

But, as he was prudent, he avoided dangerous situations. He felt that he and Catilina were visible enemies and that even the air he breathed was charged with their mutual hatred. He resumed his fencing lessons. He wore a dagger at all times. He never ate or drank before his companions ate and drank from the same vessels. He spoke of Catilina to the most distant friends, in order to observe his comings and his goings. Somewhere Catilina had an Achilles heel through which he would meet death, or, worse than death, he would be wounded for all time.

In the meantime Marcus rejoiced in the beauty of his little daughter, Tullia, who was the delight of her parents and her grandparents. Marcus revelled in her wit and her love. She had his features and his eyes and his curling brown hair and his amiability, all transfigured in feminine softness. She would sit on his knee and purr against his cheek. No son could have been dearer to him than this daughter. Helvia accused him of paternal weakness, but even she regarded her granddaughter tenderly. She was the core of love to Tullius, her grandfather, who walked with her on the island and told her enthralling stories. She would glance up at Tullius, then kiss his hand, understanding. She was hardly more than a babe but she had much wisdom.

Marcus' fame as an orator and lawyer grew larger in Rome. Under Terentia's clever management his fortune increased. When he exposed the Roman, Verres, for his exploitation and thefts in Sicily, and even worse his acts of rapacity and cruelty toward Romans, themselves, the people's affection for him grew even stronger. He was appointed Curule Aedile, at the urging of Julius Caesar. "Lord," Julius had said to Crassus, "let us publicly honor our dear Marcus so that the populace will hail our graciousness and acclaim our sincerity and our love for justice." Pompey agreed. Catilina was enraged. But Marcus received the appointment. Crassus was growing somewhat weary of Catilina's vehemence and ambitions, but he also feared him for he held the dark underworld of Rome in his patrician hand. Moreover, the crucifixion of thousands of slaves who had rebelled under Spartacus had made the Roman mob uneasy and alarmed at its rulers. Though Romans were not easily moved to pity there were multitudes among them who were the sons of freedmen, and even multitudes more in danger of slavery, themselves, if they failed in debt.

Marcus, himself, had without success intervened for the condemned slaves. He was never to forget the sight of these piteous crosses with their hanging and bleeding human fruit. What had these poor creatures done except to ask for an alleviation of their misery? When denied it they had rebelled. But Romans no longer cherished their slaves, and now there were so many hundreds of thousands of slaves in Rome that their very presence was a threat. Too, they had the sympathy of many aliens in Rome, who had known oppression in their own lands. Though Marcus could not save the lives of those crucified he did mitigate the fate of others who were later seized. He had said to Julius Caesar, "Do you desire anarchy and revolution? I tell you, I am nearer the people than are you and Crassus and Catilina and Pompey and the rest of you. I hear their mutterings. They take the crucifixions of the slaves as an omen of tyrannical government; they do not know, as yet, that they are already living under such a government. Would you have me inform them?"

Crassus magnanimously, then, freed the hundreds of slaves already in the prisons, with kind warnings. "This Cicero is invaluable," said Julius to Crassus. "He has the ear of the people and hears their tongues."

"As Laberius has said, your Cicero sits on two stools," said Crassus.

"Why?" asked Julius with indulgence. "Because he is just and can see justice in the mobs, the 'new men'—the middle-class—and also among the patricians, the merchants, the shopkeepers and the bankers, in special and defined instances? He also finds injustice in these also. He defends law under all circumstances."

"He is ambiguous. Therefore, he is dangerous."

"Catilina has been poisoning your mind, lord. Good men appear ambiguous to bad men. Though Marcus does not favor you he would defend you if you were unjustly accused. And he would turn against you, indeed dangerously, if he were convinced that you were a menace to Rome. His one loyalty is justice and law. Bad men are concerned only with blind loyalties and not good honor. They will defend villains if they love them, and stand with cruel despots if their advantage is there. I prefer the loyalty of Cicero."

Crassus smiled. "Let us, then, be lawful at all times."

Terentia was temporarily satisfied and overjoyed that Marcus was now a Curule Aedile, with a chair of ivory and the privilege of placing his bust in his atrium, thus acquiring nobility. She engaged a famous sculptor to carve Marcus' bust in marble. She invited all the family and its friends to the unveiling. She could not understand Marcus' reluctance to be publicly honored. "Have you not deserved it?" she cried in exasperation. "I can only declare that you are afflicted with the worst of affectations—false modesty. Surely, you are not unaware of the services you have rendered your country?"

"I object to my bust standing next to my statue of Athene," said Marcus.

"Pah. She is your patroness. Do I not sacrifice to her, too, in the temples?"

"True. But then you are very religious, Terentia."

Helvia was pleased with Marcus' marble bust. Tullius gazed at it in anxious silence. He feared display. He feared that his son would be overwhelmed by his great fame and become conceited. He remembered his prayers for Marcus when his son had been a young child. Helvia, with some impatience, observed her husband's silence and wrinkled expression. "Your father would consider this a mighty honor and worthy of Marcus," she said.

But Tullius said nothing. He rarely spoke these days except to little Tullia, his granddaughter. He had totally lost all intimacy with his son, and this bewildered him and filled him with despair. Marcus avoided Tullius as much as possible, for he knew that Tullius was wounded and believed that his son had grown far beyond him. This was not entirely true, but the matter was so subtle that even Marcus, eloquent with words, did not know how to express it.

Marcus left the great part of his law work now to his young lawyers and clerks, for his duties as Curule Aedile were pressing and urgent and took the vaster amount of his time. He had the duty of supervising temples and public buildings, the market places and the streets, the annual games, the proper observances of religious festivals. It was the games which excited Marcus' anxiety, for the Roman populace had become accustomed to splendor and extravagance in the circuses and the importance of gladiators and actors. Year by year, their rulers, wishing their love and loyalty, had increased the magnificence of the games. Marcus was in a quandary. It was expected of a Curule Aedile that he contribute lavishly to the games out of his own pocket, as well as using the funds of the Treasury. Marcus was not favorable to either idea. Terentia was torn between her passion to advance her husband's popularity and her frugality. As usual, Marcus compromised. He was too prudent to balk the populace outright, or to drain the Treasury and his own purse. He made some cautious economies which would not be too noticeable to the jealous populace, and concentrated on finding popularity in other ways, such as accepting clients who had been wrongfully accused. He particularly liked to help prosecute those of the mighty who had been guilty of extortion, outright and gigantic robbery, and public scandal. This endeared him to the envious mobs. They rarely noticed that the gladiators seemed fewer than usual and the free offerings of wine and pastries and meats in the circus in somewhat short supply.

Moreover, he induced his friends, Noë and Roscius, to create spectacles in the circuses. This was no mean success, for Roscius knew that he would not be paid for his services, and Noë was busy with new plays. "Do you wish me to bankrupt both the Treasury and my own purse?" asked Marcus. "You are a rich man," said Roscius, darkly. "You are richer," said Marcus. "Come, are we not friends?"

Because they loved him they consented. The populace was delighted and so Marcus spared both the Treasury and his private funds. Sometimes he had an attack of conscience. He was exploiting his best friends. He was learning that politics is not a simple matter at all, but a shifting deck of state on which one must be very agile not to fall, or, to use another metaphor, it was a tightrope on which the successful politician must dance with apparent ease and conceal his sweat and fear under a broad smile. Worst of all, he discovered that he liked politics, which he had called the harlot of public life. He comforted his conscience by not indulging the harlot too often. To refrain from her entirely was impossible, if one wished to continue in politics. This was another matter which he could not explain to his father, nor, in fact, to his mother, Helvia. But Terentia was sympathetic and understood. "You will never do anything evil," she said. Marcus fervently hoped so. "If one can do no good in politics," he wrote, "one should at least be harmless." Once or twice he was alarmed when he discovered himself feeling a secret sympathy for the dead Sulla, and even for Crassus. They were only men, and the people were most vehemently human.

Though Socrates always expressed his love for humanity Marcus was beginning to perceive that this was simple for a philosopher but not so simple for a politician. A politician learned things about his fellowmen not available to philosophers who walked in marble colonnades.

He was very busy. His dearly loved brother, Quintus, too frequently home from foreign parts these days, had acquired a slight arrogance, the fault of his tempestuous wife, Pomponia, who had now borne him a son. Pomponia bullied him. In self-defense and to assuage his wounded manhood, he tried to bully Marcus. Marcus should not do this; Marcus should do that. Quintus imagined himself a marvelous politician. He accused Marcus of deviousness. Sometimes they quarreled openly and angrily. But the love between them was too strong to be weakened. Marcus learned not to discuss politics too often with his brother; if Quintus broached the matter Marcus was able, deftly, to change the subject.

Marcus found himself talking at long length to his little daughter, Tullia, and expounding to her learnedly on law and imprecating politics. She listened wisely, as a child, as they walked together in the garden of the house on the Palatine, or on the island. "You see my position, Tullia," Marcus would say.

Tullia would kiss him passionately and stroke his tired cheek and smile at him with admiration. Her infant's lack of comprehension, and her love, soothed him and he would hold her to him and thank God for children. They were too innocent for subtlety or nuances. And, thank God, they knew nothing of politics or mankind. As his father had feared for him so did he fear the future for Tullia, and as his father had prayed so he prayed. The generations were bound together in prayer, though neither knew.

CHAPTER FORTY-THREE

Marcus did not know that he was the virtuous façade of white marble that concealed the activities of Crassus, Julius Caesar, Pompey the Magnus, Catilina and many others. The people looked on his integrity and remembered that he would not be a Curule Aedile if it were not for Crassus and his friends. Therefore, Crassus and the others had integrity also. The people said wisely to each other, "Does not the fable say that birds of a feather flock together? Our noble Cicero flocks with our rulers. Therefore, they too, must be virtuous."

"I have heard," said Crassus to Julius, "that your Cicero is making long and extensive inquiries concerning Catilina. In truth, his activities in this direction grow stronger daily."

"So I have heard also," Julius replied. "He began this many years ago. It is natural. There were Livia and Fabia. Marcus never forgets."

"If he discovers—" said Crassus.

"We must be adroit, concerning Catilina," said Julius. "He wearies me, though he is necessary to us. Let us show him no public sympathy, however we show it in private. Then we can disentangle ourselves, to our popularity, if the necessity arises."

"You are very wise for a young man," said Crassus. "Let us do as you say."

Julius smiled at him winningly and with gratitude. Had Crassus known his thoughts Julius would not have survived many hours longer. He said to Pompey, "Our hour is near." He said to Catilina, "In the name of Venus, your favorite deity, refrain from public scandal. Do not be impatient. I tell you that we are on the eve of great events."

"Something smells loudly in the city," said Noë to Marcus. "As a Jew I have perceptiveness, and premonitions. If we had not been so endowed we should have perished long ago."

"What!" said Marcus, with a smile. "Are you gathering together what is portable?"

"Do not smile," said Noë. "I am thinking of that very thing."

"You do not trust Rome," said Marcus.

"I do not trust ambitious nations. But when was a nation not ambitious?"

"Then, you do not trust men."

"Do you?" asked Noë.

Marcus considered, then shook his head. "No." He contemplated this sadly and repeated, "No." A few moments later he added, "I remember what Aeschylus says in *Agamemnon*: 'God leads us on the way of wisdom's everlasting law, that truth is only learnt by suffering it.'"

Noë nodded his head and remarked, "So, you have suffered it. As for me, I shall take my family to Jerusalem."

"What shall I do for the next games? Roscius has left for Alexandria."

"You will not take my advice," said Noë. "I suggest you retire to Arpinum."

"At my age?"

"Does a man need a gray beard to be wise?"

"I must serve my country," said Marcus. He paused. "All men are tragic. Evil is universal. The Greeks have said it and I repeat it. But there is nobility in tragedy. Man is mysteriously cursed. But he rises above his tragedy, and the curse, because he has the courage to oppose evil. The most terrible temptation we have is to leave the fight. For that, God will not forgive us."

He smiled faintly at Noë. "Do not leave me, friend." He became sad again. "Socrates told his friends: 'Some of you will say to me, "But surely, Socrates, you can mind your own business and thus escape the wrath of government!" But I cannot. Life unexamined is not worth living.' And the least that must be expected of us is that we must be men."

"In any event, you are no hair-splitter and a maker of paradoxes, like Socrates. Hence, you avoid exasperating those who could ruin you."

Marcus reflected on this. He recalled that he had been accused of sitting on two stools at the same time. "You are implying that I now compromise," he said to Noë. "Yes, that is true and sometimes I fear it is a weakness. However, I can truly say that I admit to compromise only when no injustice will be done to either disputants. I have a loathing for brute violence, and that may be weakness also."

He had large offices in one of the great public buildings near the Forum. He was encountering the most irritating people who can afflict a politician with any conscience: bureaucrats and those seeking his influence in government contracts. "A bureaucrat," he wrote to his friend, Atticus, "is the most despicable of men, though he is needed as vultures are needed, but one hardly admires vultures whom bureaucrats so strangely resemble. I have yet to meet a bureaucrat who was not petty, dull, almost witless, crafty or stupid, an oppressor or a thief, a holder of a little authority in which he delights, as a boy delights in possessing a vicious dog. Who can trust such creatures? But nations excrete them when they become complex.

"As for the manufacturers and merchants and road and sewer builders and the architects of aqueducts, the suppliers of military material, the raisers of buildings, and all others who supply government, they offer bribes for my influence. But I approve only that which is best. You may consider this folly to an extent, and so do many of these men. I live pleasantly without their approval."

He was careful, however, to keep the subject of bribery from Terentia. His wife was virtuous and an "old" Roman and upheld morals and integrity in private life. But Marcus doubted that she would consider the acceptance of bribes as heinous on the part of a politician.

When some men complained to Crassus of various matters which offended their probity—men too influential and important to be quietly assassinated—Crassus would answer, "Look upon my friend, Cicero. Would I be so benign to him, and so approving, if I were an evil man? Evil does not admire the good; it only destroys it."

Marcus acquired many friends while he was Curule Aedile, but he discounted their protestations of loyalty and affection. Amid the hubbub of his work and his law cases and his clients he found life pressing. He had to attend public dinners in honor of various politicians and Senators and patricians, for he did not intend to live and die an aedile. He was also often feasted by Crassus and Julius Caesar and Pompey. He admitted at one time that scoundrels were frequently more engaging and amusing than virtuous men, and far better company. This offended his sense of rightness. Scoundrels should be repulsive, the virtuous charming. The reverse was proved only too often. He recalled what Noë had once quoted to him: "The children of darkness are wiser in their generation than the children of light." He would add to himself, "And more attractive." The dark children were not hounded by conscience and therefore could be exuberant and merry. But the children of light wore heavy countenances and grieved over the evil in the world. This did not make for frolic and the more amusing things of life. "Let us hope they receive a reward in an everlasting existence. They certainly do not receive it here."

There were many times when an intense weariness overcame him. He recalled what Aristotle had said: "A wise man does not give his life lightly, for he knows that there are few things for which it is worth dying. Nevertheless, in periods of great crisis the wise man will give up his life, for under certain circumstances it is not worth living."

He was aware even more than Noë was aware that some evil was deeply stirring in Rome, which bore an enigmatic face and could not be pursued and exposed. It was like a shadow seen only through the corner of the eye, which when swung upon fully disappeared and was not to be seen at all. There was a haunting movement in Rome, at once urgent and silent, like the movements of rats deep in cellars. The atmosphere in the city was pent. Yet to the facile gaze all was prosperous and calm, and the populace said the Great Games had never been better. All was complacency and busyness and laughter and much coming and going. Marcus knew this was deception, and a deliberate deception, but on whose part he did not know.

"You are growing grayer," said Terentia. "You work too hard."

"You spent but four weeks on the island this year, my son," said Helvia, who was now very plump and solid and whose hair was the color of silver.

He established the first State Library in Rome, based on the tremendous museum in Alexandria. "An informed people will be suspicious of politicians," he wrote to Atticus, when asking for donations of manuscripts and books for the library. Later, he was to laugh drearily at this naïve statement. A literate people, he was to discover, made a larger public for the deceivers and mountebanks. Literacy did not guarantee discrimination, skepticism or wisdom. When, following his example, provinces also established libraries he was to say, "There is much to be said for the lack of learning in the barbarian. Then he must use his wits and not books. He hears with an innocent ear not confounded by a babble of words."

CHAPTER FORTY-FOUR

It was at sunset that Marcus felt both old and very young, almost a child. The clarity of air, the pure transparency of light purged of heat, the soft stillness that had seemed to draw within its mouth all the clamorings of the day and had silenced them, the faint gilt that lay on limb and branch and leaf, the sweet clattering of the fountains, the murmurous dialogue of birds, the silent freshness of a quiet wind—all these, to him, seemed a profound and intimately personal blessing of the gods bestowed on men, a hiatus of refreshment and reflection, a holy hour. Then one could forget the city so close below, the swelter of the hills, the hot-faced Tiber, and the harsh walls and the many roads of Rome, and could contemplate for a blessed time relieved of both the pressure of the day and the sombreness of night.

The Egyptian and other eastern temples possessed bells. At this hour they rang over the mighty and heaving city, sweetly, haunting, speaking only to the soul, calling for prayer and meditation, for men to leave the office, the bank, the market place, and to enter into the quietness of shadowy portico, altar fires and incense; for men to realize if but for an hour that they were spirits as well as animals.

Marcus was very tired. He was feeling, again, that burden of the mind and heart which had so afflicted him years ago and had immobilized his body and had tormented his brain. Now the burden was almost always present on him, a tangible presence he carried on his shoulders; he was like one of the unfortunate condemned who must bear on his back the weight of the cross upon which, in a last agony, he must expire. He no longer said to himself: Tomorrow I will be refreshed and buoyant. Tomorrow, I will again be eager. He knew that this was the illusion of very early youth. To the mature and thinking man tomorrow was the stony road that led only to frustration and extinction and the eternal question: Wherefore am I living, and to what purpose, and to what end? Why should I, tomorrow, take up again what I lay down today?

There was often little comfort when he said to himself resolutely, I live for abstract and eternal justice; I serve God, when I remember Him.

Once the evening had been for him a period of tranquil expectation. Now, he knew that expectation was the sole possession of innocent youth, and that it was a deceit to persuade the intelligent organism to continue and not to die in despair. He had much money, land, orchards, groves, fields, meadows, cattle; he had villas and he had farms; he had his ancestral island. He had wife and child and parents. He had fame of a considerable order. But still, he now had nothing to expect. He had no desire to excel in the eyes of others. To him, these were the vanities of childhood, the dreams of rank youth, and not the concern of ripened men. Crassus was an old man, but he was ambitious. Crassus was old, but he wished still to be acclaimed. The conclusion, then, was that some men never matured whatever their years and he, Cicero, was not one of them. There were times when he felt envy for an illusion, for a lie. Then he would not have hours like these, listening to the warm bells of the eastern temples, and aching and yearning after what he knew not, and looking into a future which held no more than this.

Contentment! The drug and stupefaction of little souls! What man of thought could be contented? Happiness, bliss: They meant different things to different men, and they too had no reality. Marcus looked at the wide and golden sky. He looked at the columned façade of his house, and it too was as gold as butter and shining in the light of the dropping sun.

Simplicity, said the Stoics, enviously staring at those who were not simple and were not poor. Resignation, said the eastern gods—but resignation to what? God, said the Jews. But He was unknowable and silent, if He existed at all. Yet, if one could but know Him perhaps one would know rapture, and life at its best and its worst would be endurable.

"Why so grave?" said a voice near Marcus, both mocking and fond, and Marcus turned on the marble bench under the myrtle trees to see Julius Caesar, magnificent as always, smiling at him.

Marcus rose quickly and grasped the hands of his old friend with a vehemence and a smile that agreeably startled the younger man and made him peer inquisitively into Marcus' face. Marcus laughed, as if delivered, and embraced Julius, then held him off to look at him.

"When did you return from Further Spain?" Marcus demanded.

"But last night, very late. What! Is it possible that you are happy to see me?"

"Yes. Do not ask me why. Sit beside me. Let me look upon you. It has been two years since last we met. Ah, you have not aged in those hot Spanish suns!" Marcus clapped his hands loudly for a slave, then beamed on Julius, who sat beside him. Then Marcus no longer smiled.

"I forget. You are still in mourning for your sweet wife, Cornelia, who died while you were a quaestor in Spain."

"The sweetest of women," said Julius, and for a moment or two he stared at the golden and sandy earth that surrounded the flowerbeds and the trees and cypresses, and his antic dark face was sombre. Then he smiled again, quickly. "She has been relieved of her pain, which she suffered for years, and is at peace."

For some reason, obscure even to himself, this annoyed Marcus. "And you are still young," he said.

"We have not lost our waspish tongue," said Julius, and his white teeth flashed in a wider smile. He had always been elegant and there had always been about him the iron scent of potency. The elegance remained; the aura of power was almost visible now, and Marcus thought of the terrible lightnings of Jupiter, the patron of Julius. These were in no wise diminished by the splendor of raiment, his silver armor, the leopard cloak on his shoulders, his heavier but still virile flesh, the foreign length of his sword in its Spanish enameled sheath, and the high silver boots embroidered and tasseled. Julius had passed his thirty-fourth birthday this very summer, and only six weeks ago, and his fine black hair was patched with the first gray on his temples. But he was vital as always and exuded a delicate force, as always, and his immense intelligence glittered restlessly in his dark and ironical eyes.

In his turn Julius studied his friend and saw the weary lines about the still beautiful and changeful eyes, the paling streaks in the mass of brown and curling hair, the clefts that enclosed the controlled lips, and the thin furrow that ran horizontally and deeply across a noble forehead that had long since lost its innocence and had acquired exhausted wisdom in its place.

A slave brought refreshments, and in a little silence poured wine. The sound of the pouring was loud and musical in the quiet; rays of sunlight pierced the falling column of fluid and lighted it up so that it resembled bright blood. Then Julius said, "I encountered your brother, Quintus, in Spain."

"Yes. So he wrote me." The slave placed a tray of delicacies on the round marble table near at hand, and Marcus dismissed him. Julius raised his goblet in salute, poured a little libation, and put the goblet to his lips. Marcus drank also. His first pleasure was subsiding. He felt oddly depressed. He continued: "And your duties, Julius, are completed in Spain?"

"Completed."

Marcus inquired about Julius' family and their health, and particularly about young Julia. "I am betrothing her to Pompey," said Julius.

"That child?"

"She is no child, Marcus. She has passed her fourteenth birthday and should be betrothed." Julius paused, then grinned into Marcus' eyes. "And I, not one to be left mourning forever, am to marry again, Pompeia. A man needs a dear companion as he grows older."

"You have never lacked companions, Julius. And you have always deplored marriage. Yet you wish to assume its burdens again."

(It was not possible for them to know that at that very hour, leagues across the brilliant sea, in the city of Alexandria, Egypt, a foolish Greek Pharaoh, disdainfully called "the divine flutist," leaned over his infant daughter's cradle and said in his light and lilting voice, "She shall be called Cleopatra, for she is the glory of her country." As the two men sat in a Roman garden the babe opened eyes the color of violets and stared at her father and her cheeks were flushed with rose.)

"But Pompeia will be my last love," said Julius, and his eyes twinkled. His skin, darkened deeply by Spanish sun, sprayed into fine lines of gay mockery.

"I am certain she will be," said Marcus with sarcasm. "What are your plots now?"

"I find a certain repetitious tedium in your words," said Julius. "You have never ceased asking me the same question, and my reply is the same: I do not plot. I love life and I accept each day as it comes, with no thought of the morrow. I am not ambitious."

"No?"

"No. But let us talk of you, dear friend. You grow increasingly famous. Yet, you do not appear content or happy."

"Perhaps I do not have the gift of happiness. And I lack contentment, but what it is I wish I do not know." Marcus' face turned melancholy again. "I have all that most men desire, yet I do not know peace."

"I heard, in Spain, that in every man's garden there lurks a hidden tiger waiting to devour him. What is your tiger, Marcus?"

Marcus did not answer. Julius studied him with a secret smile. Then Julius said, "Could it be your gift for compromise, which I hear is becoming more evident each day?"

"I do not compromise on principle," said Marcus with some anger. "If I am excessive or too ardent in any matter, then I await the arguments of more objective men and balance them against mine. When a whole object is not obtainable, I am agreeable to part."

"It is still your tiger, Marcus. This is an eminently unreasonable and irrational world. A man who compromises is considered guileful, and therefore dangerous, and not to be trusted. We all proclaim our admiration for restraint and reason, but they are the most detested of virtues. The man who succeeds—and thus is adored—is a man who never compromises, for good or for evil, and especially evil. To whom are our statues and monuments raised? To Socrates, to Homer, to Plato? No. They are raised to generals who were obdurate and could not be moved. They are raised to political murderers, who pursued their own way and did not hearken to others. In short, they were successful, and the world loves success no matter how it is obtained."

"And what is your tiger, Julius?" asked Marcus.

Julius raised his eyebrows. "Mine? Possibly the love for women. A most delightful tiger."

"I think your tiger bears another name."

Julius shook his head. "No. Even that should be obvious to you now. I have no political power; I have displayed no greed for it, despite what you always say. I am a man no longer young. I have been only a quaestor in Further Spain, and it was tedious to me. Now I ask only a pleasant life."

Marcus was again pursuing his melancholy thoughts. "And that contents you?"

He was suddenly aware of a sharp silence. He looked up and saw Julius smiling at him quizzically. But Julius said, "I am content."

"Then God preserve us from contented men!"

Julius was not offended. He laughed. Marcus said, "You remind me of Erisichthon, who cut down the sacred oak, in contempt for Ceres, the goddess of the earth and of calm contentment. Ceres delivered him to her dread sister, Famine, who gave him an insatiable appetite. He even sold his one and beloved daughter so that he could satisfy his ravenous stomach. Finally, he was forced to eat his own body. That is the story of ambition."

"Are you trying to offend me, Marcus, your guest, your friend whom you have not seen for two years? Or do your own sad meditations inspire your bitter satire?"

"Forgive me!" cried Marcus.

Julius touched his hand quickly. His eyes danced. "I am not 'selling' my daughter to Pompey, in spite of your allusion. He is old enough to be her father, God knows, but such marriages are common enough in Rome. The girl is agreeable, for she is sensible, and more mature than her years. And I have a discriminating appetite for all things, unlike Erisichthon."

But the obscure misery with which Marcus was beset made him oblivious again to courtesy, he who had once said that a discourteous man was a barbarian. He said, his pale face flashing as if the shadow of lighted glass had passed over it, "Before you left for Spain, Crassus and Pompey deprived the Senate of much of its debilitated power. It is more than rumor, Julius, that you were influential in this, and that you urged Crassus to restore power to the Equestrian Order—so that they now control the courts. Yet, to maintain the lie that Crassus really loved the man in the street you carried a bust of your uncle, the old murderer, Marius, in a populares procession that shouted acclamations for Crassus! Did I not see you in that very procession, before you left for Spain? How do you explain this hypocrisy?"

Julius was only amused. "Call it, if you will, your own urge to compromise. The Equestrian Order is not only rich; it is intellectual and learned in law. Do you think it impossible for such as the Equestrians to have no sympathy for the populace? On the contrary! Only the rich and powerful have solicitude for the people. The champions who rise from the populace are oppressors, for they know the populace only too well. But the rich and the powerful have illusions about their virtue and often believe that the voice of the people is the voice of God. Surely, were you on trial you should prefer Equestrians to judge you rather than the flea-bitten mob?"

"I should prefer honest men."

"You will not find them on the streets and in the noxious alleys."

Marcus moved restlessly. He said, "You are not only hypocritical, Julius, but you appear to me inconsistent."

"You should not deride inconsistency. What! Did you not help prosecute Gaius Verres because of his extortion in Sicily, and then on the other hand did you not defend Marcus Fonteius on the identical charge of extortion in Gaul?"

Marcus caught himself before he could say, "But then, I love Sicily, and I do not love Gaul." Watching him with amusement, Julius said, "No politician, dear Marcus, can remain free from corruption, for it is the business of politics to deal with the people, and the people inevitably corrupt. Only in the realm of the abstract can man remain good—that is, if he wishes to survive."

"I do not compromise on principle," Marcus repeated with stubbornness.

"No? Then how do you explain Verres and Fonteius?"

"You would not understand my explanation."

Julius laughed loudly and merrily. "The aphorism of the politician! Come, Marcus, you did not always lack humor. I pity you: an honorable man who in some manner became a politician. Why did you enter politics?"

"So that I could help delay the inevitable despotism that will surely engulf Rome, and to insure that some law survives."

"You are a good man, Marcus. Your virtue is acclaimed in Rome. But still, I pity you. There will be a day when you will not compromise, and that day will see your end. I hope I do not witness it, for I should grieve mortally."

Marcus blurted without his will and not knowing why he did so, "Do not grieve! You will die before me!"

He was horrified. But Julius' face had changed superstitiously, and he was staring at Marcus. Julius whispered, "Why do you say that, you who are older?"

"Forgive me," said Marcus, with overwhelming contrition. "I have been unpardonably rude."

But Julius thoughtfully refilled his goblet and then drank of it slowly.

"I have had many dreams," he said, "and I have seen myself dying, flowing with my own blood. But who should wish to assassinate me, and why? You have a reputation as an augur."

"That is truly superstition. I am no augur, and it comes to me now that I am very stupid or I should not have insulted you. I can only say that I have been depressed lately." Marcus put his hand on his old friend's arm with a pleading gesture. Julius immediately covered that hand with his own fingers, and pressed it.

It was at that moment that Terentia appeared, apparently unaware that her husband had a guest, and beside her walked the little Tullia, the heart of hearts to her father. Terentia started prettily at the sight of Julius, and cast down her eyes modestly. Her lashes swept her cheek becomingly, but this did not detract from the hard resolution of her mouth and the stoniness of her chin, both of which had increased during the past years. Marcus surveyed her with irritation, but Julius rose and kissed her hand with a flourish.

"I did not know that you had returned, Julius," said Terentia, in her deceptively mild voice and displaying a matronly confusion which further irritated Marcus. "Had I known my husband had a guest I should not have intruded. Pardon me; I must return to the house." But she stood her ground and now her shining brown eyes scrutinized Julius not only with curiosity but with avidity and excitement.

"Do not deprive us of your lovely presence," said Julius. "I was about to depart."

Terentia gave Marcus an impatient glance, and when he did not speak she said, "But surely you will dine with—with my husband. This household will be honored."

Julius looked grave, and looked at Marcus through the corner of his eye.

"I am dining with the noble Crassus, Terentia."

Terentia, forgetting that she was a retiring "old" Roman, and despising

Marcus for his obdurate silence, said immediately, "But surely, tomorrow! You have been absent so long."

Marcus, the almost always courteous, obstinately kept silent, and Julius had trouble restraining his mirth. Julius said, "I thank you, Terentia. It is I who am honored, for who does not acclaim the great Cicero and consider himself flattered at an invitation from him?"

At that moment Terentia was not only impatient with her husband but actually hated him for his silence and his set mouth. Julius was powerful; Julius could advance the career of her husband. Yet, he sat there like a lump of lard and said nothing. It was an affront to herself. He always availed himself of an opportunity to humilate her, she thought with burning resentment. Her breast heaved under the brown linen which covered her now very ample breast.

Marcus said at last, "I am entertaining lawyers tomorrow, and Julius finds law dull."

But Julius cried with vivacity, "No! I love lawyers! I shall bask in their wisdom." Then he had pity on his friend and turned his attention on young Tullia. He touched her cheek with a kind and thin brown hand. "What is this? Is it not a beauty we have among us? She will ravish Rome."

The girl dimpled and gazed at Julius with her father's eyes, blue one moment, gray the next, and then clear amber. She curtsied politely. She was only seven years old but she had her father's intelligence and his perceptiveness. Her curling brown hair caught gold from the sun. As a well-bred child she did not speak. She stood patiently beside Terentia.

Terentia clasped her hands and fastened a limpid gaze on Julius.

"How we sorrowed with you, Julius, when Cornelia died!"

"He is about to console himself," said Marcus.

Julius decided that this was a tactful moment to depart. He kissed Terentia's hand again, embraced Marcus as he still sat, patted Tullia's head, and left in a swirl of cloak and perfume. The sunset garden appeared to be less shining when he had gone. Terentia said to her daughter in a pent voice, "Leave us, Tullia." The little girl kissed her father's cheek then ran toward the house. Marcus stared at the ground. Terentia folded her muscular arms on her breast and contemplated him with red-faced bitterness.

"Your rudeness is unpardonable," she said harshly.

"I have no excuse, Terentia. Julius annoys me."

"I have noticed that many things annoy you lately. You rarely speak to your father. You rarely condescend to speak to me. Your conversation, which is very infrequent, appears to confine itself to Tullia and your mother. I have heard you in brutal controversy with eminent lawyers and judges, when they dined in this house. Once you were a paragon of discretion and restraint. Now your voice is abrupt, and you do not control yourself in the presence of those who could advance your career."

"So you have said many times."

"It is always the truth. Do you think I am content with your status as of this day? No! I expect more of you. I am of a great house, and you have a duty to your family. You should be Praetor of the city, at the very least. Crassus has not even named you Magnus."

"The title lost its meaning when Pompey was named it." Marcus was ashamed of himself for his irritability and his growing aversion for his wife. He loathed ambitious women, of whom Rome now had too many. His sadness and his nervousness overwhelmed him again. "Give me peace," he said.

"I owe it to my ancestors to see that my husband does not diminish them."

Marcus stood up suddenly. "To Hades with your ancestors!" he exclaimed. His pale face was crimson. His hands clenched at his sides. Terentia, all at once, embodied what he most despised, what he most dreaded.

Terentia stepped back, truly aghast and white. "Their manes will imprecate you, Marcus!"

"Let it be. More tangible creatures than your ancestors' manes imprecate me. I have told you many times that I seek no man's favor. I particularly do not seek Caesar's favor, for he is a liar and a hypocrite, and he is exigent."

"You have no care for your own future! Therefore, it is all left to me."

"Refrain," said Marcus. "I beg of you, refrain."

"I shall not refrain!" cried Terentia with passion.

Marcus sat down heavily, the color leaving his face. Terentia breathed loudly. The song of the birds grew more insistent. The fragrant wind rose to sound and the leaves of the trees spoke in answer. Terentia considered her husband, and his mute face and dropped eyelids. She considered many things. Men were men. She said accusingly, "Have you a mistress?"

"Yes," said Marcus. "Too many to count, too many to be named. I am bankrupt for paying for their favors."

His satirical voice angered Terentia.

"Nevertheless, you love another woman," she said, but not believing it. Slowly, painfully, Marcus lifted his eyelids and looked at her fully.

"That is true," he said, and stood up and went toward his house. Terentia gazed after him and suddenly put her clenched hand against her lips. Her eyes filled with tears.

Marcus was alone on the ancestral island in the autumn, as he had desired it. He ate, slept deeply, swam in the murmurous waters, walked in the forests, inspected his herds of sheep, goats, and cattle, talked desultorily with the slaves, read, contemplated, wrote on his next book of essays.

Nothing comforted him, nothing eased him, nothing gave him satisfaction.

I am growing old, he thought. There is a darkness in my mind which nothing lifts, nothing assuages. I want nothing, and surely that is the prelude to death. There is no promise in my life which I can discern. I am defeated; I am lost. The multitude of letters which came to him from Rome remained unopened, the seals intact. He looked in his mirror and did not see therein a man with vital and glistening eyes and browned cheeks and ruddy lips, the result of his sojourn on the island. He saw a wan and aging man. For Livia haunted the island as she had not haunted it for many years.

She was alive as no woman had ever been alive for him. He heard her eerie song in the trees, caught the flutter of her veil and palla between the dark trunks in the forest, heard her voice in the river. Sometimes he could not bear his sorrow, despite all the years in which Livia had rested in her grave. He pursued her bright shadow; sometimes the slaves heard his desperate calling. I am becoming mad, he would say to himself, as he ran like a youth through the dim woods looking for Livia. Sometimes he clasped a young tree in his arms, like Apollo, and pressed his face against the living bark and wept. He felt he was embracing Livia, who, like a nymph, had fled from him and had changed into a sapling. A mysterious agony was upon him, as if he had been newly bereaved.

It is for myself that I grieve, he thought once with sudden clarity. It is for my youth that I grieve, my hopes and my dreams, my phantom of lying promise, the wreathed years when I believed that life was of significance. How do other men bear this burden? How did my grandfather endure, and Scaevola, and Archias, and all the others of my beloved whose shades haunt the halls of my past? How could they have lived out the years of their lives? What sustained them? There is nothing but empty vessels on my table and the ewer of my wine is full of dried dregs. Why had they never said, "You are eager and thirsty, and you will be deprived and you will not want to drink again?"

"Livia!" he called to the woods. He stood on the bridge with Livia where he had stood so long ago, and he saw the white warm curve of her arm near his, and the blazing blue of her eyes as they looked into his own. He put his head down on the stony balustrade.

He thought of his father, whom he had abandoned in impatience. Had

Tullius ever dreamed, been deprived, tilted a goblet which contained
nothing? He stood in Tullius' library and looked at the silent books, then
opened them as if searching for a message. He found one, and it filled
him with renewed despair, for Tullius had written in a margin: "To
dream is to live. To awaken is to die."

His physician in Arpinum said to him, "When men reach your age, and
are neither young nor old, they question themselves and their lives. They
suffer. But it will pass. I am seventy years old, and I tell you that this will
pass."

Marcus did not believe him. "I want nothing," he said. The physician
smiled. "There is God," said the physician. "There is eternity."

"To what, then, can a man be reduced!" exclaimed Marcus. "If there
is nothing but those, how passionless is life!" The physician smiled again.

Finally he forced himself to read the many letters which had come to
him.

Terentia had written him a bitter letter. Lucius Sergius Catilina had
been appointed Praetor of Rome by Crassus. "This was withheld from
you, my dear husband," she wrote. "Now the murderer of my sister, her
seducer, occupies a great position. Had you been present this should
never have come to pass."

A mighty wave of rage and passion and hate rolled over Marcus, and
he forgot that he would never feel emotion again. He forgot that his life
had ended, and had no meaning any longer. He forgot that existence had
been reduced to sterility, and that there was nothing for which a man
could in all honesty fight, and give his life.

He left the next morning for Rome. It seemed to him that Livia rode
beside him and spurred him on, her veil blowing in his face.

CHAPTER FORTY-FIVE

Crassus, the man with the huge fat body and the narrow face and head,
regarded Marcus, coldly, and Julius smiled to himself and Pompey gazed
at his jeweled hands.

"I confess," said Crassus, "that I do not understand your vehemence,
Cicero. You are incoherent, and that does not become a lawyer. What is
it to you that Catilina is Praetor?"

Marcus said, his face deeply flushed with emotion, "It is as if a leopard were appointed guardian of sheep. The man, by nature, is a disaster! Surely, I do not have to tell you what he is! He is a friend and patron of the most despicable elements of Rome, which includes notorious criminals. His natural climate is evil. There is nothing in his nature and his character which make him worthy of so high and potent a position. He is not a lawyer; he has never been a magistrate. He is licentious and corrupt, idle and vicious. Are these now qualifications for Praetor? If so, then Rome is truly degraded."

He had implored and had obtained an audience with Crassus in the latter's magnificent house. He had refused refreshments and wine. He stood before Crassus' carved ivory and ebony table, sometimes striking it with his fist, as the others imperturbably dined and drank. They listened to him with courtesy, though Crassus, who had always feared and hated and suspected him, could not conceal the evil flash of his gray eyes when they touched the younger man.

He said, "Catilina is much loved. This has pleased many people, that he is Praetor."

"Whom has it pleased?"

Julius said with a grave countenance, "Democracy, my dear Marcus, which grants to all free men the same opportunity. Is this not what you have always advocated? Or, are you now turning on your heel and declaring that a man's competency should be judged only by his personal eccentricities or his political adherences?"

"A man's personal conduct cannot be separated from his public; they are the two aspects of the same coin."

"Calm yourself," said Pompey. "Of what crimes has Catilina been convicted? None. Of what does his ill-fame consist? Adulterer? If all men who were adulterers were denied public office then all offices would be empty and we should have chaos. A man can deceive his wife but remain resolutely loyal to his country. A man can be decadent and depraved in his private life—and are we not all subjects to our secret vices?—and yet be upright in public office, and virtuous. A man's household may be recklessly extravagant, yet I have observed that such men are frugal in government. The reverse is also true: the prim man can be a libertine with the people's freedom; the man who counts his private treasure and spends none of it can throw away the people's treasury with both hands for votes."

This was a long speech from the usually taciturn and watchful Pompey. Marcus looked into his calm light eyes and saw there only tolerance and liking, and even now he could wonder why Pompey felt friendliness toward him who had given no friendliness in return.

Marcus said, "It may be true that Catilina has never been publicly indicted and convicted of a crime. Nevertheless, we know he is a criminal."

"You have no proof of what you are saying," said Crassus. "You do not know that Catilina's immense following is composed mainly, or solely, of criminals. Were this so, do you think he would now be Praetor, that we would endure it or recommend it?"

"Yes," said Marcus, looking directly at him. "I do think so."

Crassus' thin face whitened with rage, and his lower teeth showed above his lip. "You are insolent, arrogant, and defiant of authority!" he exclaimed. "You are Curule Aedile, and as a public officer you are answerable to me. Do you wish me to relieve you of your duties?"

But Marcus was too aroused and too agitated to heed the threat. He said, "You accuse me of insolence, arrogance, and defiance of authority. Are your charges not misplaced, lord? Are you mistaking me for Catilina?"

Crassus slowly and deliberately drank from his goblet; his gaze dwelled inimically on the lawyer. It was Julius Caesar who replied to him in a tone of affectionate indulgence.

"For a man who has lately given his friends the impression of lassitude and listlessness and resignation, Marcus, and for a man who has been heard to say, 'For what purpose have we been born?' you are displaying an astonishing store of passion and frenetic energy and loud protest. Is it possible you now believe there is a purpose in our existence—"

"Yes!" cried Marcus. "I was a fool. I have been wallowing in complacency and security, and these lead to death and disintegration. I had been so absorbed in public duties and in private practice of law that I lost sight of what is transpiring in my country. I plead guilty to the crime of indifference, and am determined to make amends."

He turned to Crassus again. "My country is worth more to me than safety, riches, fame, acclamation, honors. Therefore, I protest Catilina. Do you realize that I shall encounter him in the courts and that, because he hates me he will be prejudiced even against the justice of the cases? At every turn he will thwart what is just, what obviously should be redressed, if I have any involvement in it."

"I doubt it," said Julius. "After all, there is the opinion of the people to be considered, and the people love you. Catilina would not dare to defy established law and to rule against you through malice." He bowed to Crassus. "May I confide a secret to our embattled Marcus, lord? Yes." He smiled at Marcus. "We have already warned Catilina that he must not, when encountering you in the courts, give a judgment which violates law and dignity and reason."

Some mysterious exchange had occurred between Crassus and Julius, and Crassus' tone was almost mild when he said to Marcus, "Catilina's term is but for two years. Who knows but what you, Cicero, shall succeed him?"

They wish to silence me, thought Marcus, but I will not be silenced.

He said, "During the short time Catilina has been a Praetor he has already violated the Constitution three times in his rulings. Two condemned traitors have been freed by him on a technicality, though their guilt was thoroughly and justly established. A notorious murderer for profit, who employed numerous assassins, has been freed by Catilina on the technicality that the authorities who seized him kept him in confinement five hours beyond the time permitted by law, in order to question him. Technically, that is true, but they needed the extra time to force one single admission from him which would enable them to bring him before a court. This is not triviality! This is violation of eternal justice."

Julius bent over some papers. "I have here, dear Marcus, notices of cases you have defended on that same technicality. Is there one law for you and one for Catilina?"

Marcus colored. "But the men were innocent! Catilina's criminals were not."

"No one can judge a man's innocence or guilt until he is before a court. It is true, sweet friend, that technicalities can sometimes free men who are guilty. But those same technicalities operate, mainly, in behalf of those unjustly seized and accused. As it was observed centuries ago and in other nations, the law is a blunt instrument. Nevertheless, it protects the innocent."

"It will not be so with Catilina."

Julius laughed lightly. "Catilina is too indolent by nature to be overly active in any court or any case. In short, he has received a public honor and a public salary, though he will rarely appear in any court or go to the labor of studying any case."

"Then, why was he made Praetor? Is our Treasury not depleted enough that we must support rascals with public tax moneys?"

They did not answer him, but only smiled faintly.

Marcus looked from one silent face to the other, and his mind raced. He said with bitterness, "Then it is true that you owe him something, and anyone who owes Catilina anything is guilty of a crime against his country."

Crassus no longer smiled. "Enough," he said. "What! Are you, a mere lawyer, a mere Curule Aedile, to fling insults and accusations of treason in my face, I who am triumvir of Rome? Beware, Cicero. I have long endured you because of Caesar's love for you. I suggest that you do not bring yourself to my attention any longer." His face was swollen with blood and rage and hate, and his clenched and narrow fist lifted itself from the table.

Marcus stood away from the table. For a moment or two he had trembled with terror at his own audacity. He thought of his parents, his wife, his beloved daughter. Then his anger rose against himself, that he should put his own life and the lives of his family before the safety and honor and justice of his country.

"Then, lord," he said, "you admit that Catilina's position is your responsibility?"

Crassus half-rose in his jeweled chair and raised his fist as if to strike Marcus. But Julius, now terribly alarmed, seized his arm and almost thrust him back in his chair again. Pompey sat upright and he too gazed at Crassus with consternation.

"Rash fool," said Julius to Marcus. "I never thought to see you so debased by your own words. A man does not fling accusations of malfeasance into the face of the highest officer in the country—"

"Why not, if it is true?"

"Gods!" cried Caesar. "Are you a complete idiot?"

"Is this not a free country?" asked Marcus. "Are not the highest officers answerable to those who entrusted them with that office?"

Julius looked at Crassus, who had subsided slightly. Then Julius said in a flat voice, "No. Not any longer, Cicero. Your beloved democracy has altered the customs of Rome."

"I speak not of democracy, Caesar. I speak of the Republic of Rome. There is a gulf between democracy and republicanism that can never be bridged except at the ruin of republics. Who has overthrown our Republic and has declared her no longer in existence? I have seen no such overthrow; I have heard no such declaration. Therefore, the Republic remains, and under the freedom of the Republic I have a right to demand an account of public officers when they have betrayed the trust of the people and have suborned the Constitution."

They stared at him, and every face was pale and one was malignant.

"Do not order my murder, though assassination is one of the weapons of democracies," said Marcus, with a bitter smile. "I have too much influence in Rome, and too many powerful friends, and I am of the Helvii and my wife is of a great family also. You may believe that Romans no longer care who rules them and are not disturbed by assassinations, no matter how heinous. They need but a voice. I shall be that voice, or, if I am murdered, I shall raise other voices."

"You forget," said Pompey in a peculiar tone, "that it is possible for any government, or any influential men, to turn the wrath of a people on whomever they desire, if they wish to protect the guilty. If you should be assassinated, it would be very easy for—powerful men—to declare that you had really been a traitor, and the people, who desire no upheavals in their lives and no confrontations with truth—for they are indolent by nature—

will gratefully accept the explanation in order that they be not disturbed or made to think."

"You accuse the Roman people then, of madness?"

"No," said Pompey, with that peculiar tone again, "only of pusillanimity."

Marcus' wrath rose again; then he looked at Pompey acutely and thought, I never knew him. He saw that Julius and Crassus were regarding Pompey with some disfavor. Then the two men looked into each other's eyes and a question was asked and then answered. So Julius smiled charmingly on Marcus and said in the voice of one confiding to another:

"We wish to tell you the truth, Marcus. Accept it or not. It remains the truth."

"When did you ever speak truth, Julius?"

"Nevertheless," said Crassus in so firm and sharp a voice that Marcus turned to him quickly and knew that he would speak openly at last, "it will be the truth, and you will ignore it at the peril of Rome. Speak, Caesar."

Julius clasped his thin dark hands on the table and looked steadfastly at Marcus.

"You know some of the power of Catilina, whom we despise but whom we dare not ignore. We have spoken of freedmen, slaves and petty criminals who are his followers. In themselves, they are not too dangerous. But they are not the sole supporters of our patrician friend. There are ambitious men who are his familiars, Piso and Curius to name only two. He also has many Senators and tribunes in his pay, or their secret crimes are known to him. Besides these, there are the tens of thousands of athletes in Rome, and men of unutterable but powerful evil who make their living on vice. There are the malcontents, and do not underestimate them, for they are legion! There are men, multitudes of them, who are not Romans, but who are rich. Their loyalty is not to Rome, but to their own service. There are men who make treason their profession, for they hate Rome and the symbol which is Rome, and desire despotism.

"Among these of the disaffected is the great patrician class, who despise the Republic, and who wish to rule an enslaved nation. These have multitudes of clients who would obey their masters, who would obey Catilina, who is one of them.

"There are the gutter rabble, obsessed with greed and the gratification of their bellies and their lusts. What is Rome to them, and Rome's solvency? They would betray her for a free pot of beans, or two tickets to the circus. Then there are the motley creatures of hideous, depraved appetites, and actors and songsters and dancers, who love to shriek in the wake of patrician and royal authority for the light that falls on them. There are the homosexuals and other perverts who writhe with joy at the thought of exploitation and whips, and the promise of legal protection.

"These are the followers of Catilina, Marcus. These are the ones who at his word would destroy our nation."*

"It is true," said Pompey.

Marcus had known this before. But he had not known the awful immensity of it, its pervasiveness, its invasion of and integration with the body politic.

"Would you have us massacre a third of the city?" asked Crassus in a terrible voice. "Or, which is more probable, a half?"

"How would you justify it, in the name of the Republic?" asked Julius.

"Shall manliness be regained by murder?" asked Pompey. "Shall we descend to the level of the mob in order to free Rome from it?"

"Sulla attempted to restore the Republic," said Crassus. "That was in an earlier day, before the rabble was so powerful. He was defeated, and left the field."

Marcus fell into a chair and dropped his chin on his breast. There was a long silence, which was finally broken by Julius who said, "It was to placate Catilina, who controls what we so greatly fear, that he was appointed Praetor. It is a small price to pay for Rome."

"It is blackmail," said Marcus in a dull tone.

"True," said Caesar. "If the blackmailer acts alone, he can be destroyed. But if he has many, many friends then he must be endured, his ravenous appetite satisfied at intervals. In short," added Julius with a whimsical glance at Marcus, "we must compromise, even on principle."

"What if he demands to be Consul of the City?"

"I have told you: he has been warned that he will receive no more than this he has received."

Marcus was quiet for a while, thinking, while the other three men exchanged cautious but ironical glances. Then Marcus said, "It must be possible to rid ourselves of enemies. As slowly as the Republic declined, so as slowly and deliberately must she be restored. We already have laws—"

"It was Sulla who first showed you the impossibilities of enforcing the laws we already have, the improbability that any class in Rome would rise selflessly in her behalf. To whom will you turn, Marcus, in the name of Rome?"

Marcus lifted his heavy eyes to Julius' face. "Not to you, Caesar, not to you."

Pompey said in his slow, calm voice, "We must deal with reality and not with hopeful phantoms. Our grandfathers knew that the Republic was

* Taken from Letter from Caesar to Cicero, after publication of *De Republica*.

declining, even in their youth. Could they have prevented it then? It is possible. It remains that they did not. We have inherited the fruit of their indifference, their selfishness, their lack of pride and virtue and patriotism."

"It has been true of all nations, that they came to this," said Julius. He lifted his hand then let it drop on the table. "The causes lie in man's nature, itself. If I were to found a new nation I should make it a benevolent despotism, and not a Republic which inevitably declines and becomes depraved."

"The man on horseback," said Marcus.

"True. He alone has been able to survive longer than any Republic survived. And his nation with him. Republics are founded on the fantasy that men are capable of self-government and restraint and self-discipline and heroic virtue. But it is only a dream, and is false, and must die in the dawn of reality, the reality of what a man really is and not what he should be."

Marcus stood up slowly. He looked from one to the other. "My reason tells me that you speak the truth. Nevertheless, my spirit insists that I fight that truth, that I do what I can to make man more than he is.

"Long before our own time the customs of our ancestors molded admirable men, and in turn these eminent men upheld the ways and institutions of their forebears. Our age, however, inherited the Republic like some beautiful painting of bygone days, its colors already fading through great age; and not only has our time neglected to freshen the colors of the picture, but we have failed to preserve its form and outlines. For what remains to us nowadays, of the ancient ways on which the commonwealth, we were told, was founded? We see them so lost in oblivion that they are not merely neglected but quite forgot. And what am I to say of you? Our customs have perished for want of men to stand by them, and we are called to an account, so that we stand impeached like men accused of capital crimes, compelled to plead our own cause. Through our vices, rather than from fate, we retain the word 'Republic' long after we have lost the reality."*

He spread out his hands mutely, then added, "I, too, am guilty. I stand before you guilty men a guilty man, myself. I have no defense except that, at least, I have tried, if to no avail."

He turned to go, then added to the three silent men who were regarding him with strange expressions, "Do not let Catilina cross my path. I have a vendetta with him. Some day we shall meet and that day shall be of my own choosing, and not his."

His pale face had lost all its native amiability and humor. He left the room and the marble floor echoed with his steps. They heard the closing

* From *De Republica*.

of the distant bronze door. Then Julius lifted a pear from a silver dish and polished it on his sleeve, and bit into it with an expression of pleasure.

Crassus said, "Our noble white façade has cracked. We need it no longer. Let it fall."

"Assassination?" asked Julius, wiping his lips with a linen napkin. "No. We need him more than ever. I have already heard rumblings about Catilina. They could become thunder. Let Cicero die and that thunder will surely be upon us. I have told many, 'Would Catilina be Praetor if Cicero had objected severely?' I think Cicero will be silent. We have convinced him that oratory will be of no use—nor will it."

"If any assassination is planned," said Pompey, "I recommend Catilina as the victim."

But Julius laughed and shook his head. "Do you think he has not already provided for such a contingency? If we move against him, however subtly, he will bring down the roof on all of us, even if he dies as a result. You underestimate the power of those he has enchanted. Men will die eagerly for such as Catilina."

Crassus said with vicious anger, "We stand between a man of virtue and a man of evil, and by the gods I do not know which is the more dangerous."

When Marcus returned home that night, full of gloom and dread and sorrow and quiet rage, he was disagreeably surprised to find Terentia waiting for him in the hall. He said to her at once, "I am weary. It is late. I am in no mood for discussion."

"I have waited hours for your return," said Terentia, stubbornly. "I must know what you have done against the seducer and murderer of my sister."

Marcus walked past her abruptly into his bedroom, but she followed, her brown eyes hard and determined. Marcus turned to her and said in a stifled voice, "I could do nothing. It is too late. It is too late for Rome."

Terentia blinked at him. It came to Marcus, as it came too often in these days, that she was a stupid woman, for she could never grasp the whole of a statement but only its parts. She said, "What has Rome to do with the removal of Catilina from office?"

"Everything," he said. "He is Praetor because of what has happened to Rome."

"Then you failed, Marcus." Her eyes were taunting and full of contempt.

"I failed when I was born. My father failed, and his father before him. My grandfather's father was guilty of Catilina."

"You speak in riddles, my husband. So Catilina remains because you are impotent and have no power to enforce his removal."

"I have no power." He removed his toga and flung it upon a chair. The lamplight showed his haggard face.

"I thought you were the great lawyer and orator of Rome, a Curule Aedile! It seems I am mistaken, when so small a thing is denied to you by Crassus!"

He wanted to strike her, so great was his distraction. He clenched his teeth and sat down on the bed and removed his shoes. But she would not let him have peace.

"I have been deluded. The object of my pride does not really exist. I have been defrauded. And my sister remains unavenged."

But Marcus thought not of Fabia but of Livia. He looked at the dagger which he had placed on the table. He said, though he spoke only to himself, "No, that is too easy, too unsatisfactory. The gods will not deny me."

"They have done so, tonight," said Terentia. She heaved a sigh of deep self-pity. "So much for my dreams. So much for my hopes. I am married to a man of no consequence."

"True," said Marcus, and blew out his lamp and left her fuming in the dark.

But Marcus could not sleep. He lay in his bed, every muscle and tendon drawn and tight, his neck arched, his heart beating painfully and heavily, his thoughts leaping on each other's back, to turn and leap again in a vast confusion, as if searching for words that would magically resolve chaos into order and make the world habitable again.

He remembered the words of an old, nameless prophet of whom Noë ben Joel had told him: "They sleep not, except they have done mischief, and their sleep is taken away unless they cause some to fall. For they eat the bread of wickedness, and drink the blood of violence."

But, he said to himself, it is I who cannot sleep, while those who eat the bread of wickedness and drink the blood of violence sleep sweetly and slumber like downy infants. He felt his mind probing out into the darkness, to discover sleepless men like himself, beset by the same terrible thoughts. Surely they were there, in this vast city, but he could not touch them with the windy fingers of his spirit. He turned on his side and saw the bluish gray dawn rimming his window. Did other men see it also with the same burned eyelids, and did they despair of their country as he despaired?

How was he to live? There were those who knew the storm was lifting over the city but they resolutely turned their backs and drank their wine and pretended to the last living moment that all was well. There were others who refused to delude themselves, and died in the welter of a torn heart. And there were others who defied the storm and rushed to grapple with it, and were destroyed by it. Who was the wisest, and who had some faint opportunity to survive? The men who affected to believe there was no storm. Even if they did not survive they had enjoyed the last moments as their more sensitive fellows had not.

From sheer glut of emotion which could not be expressed, Marcus' mind, in self-defense, suddenly emptied. I refuse to feel any longer, he thought, and fell asleep.

PART FOUR

The Hero

Facto quod saepe maiores asperis bellis fecere, voveo dedoque me pro re publica! Quam deinde cui mandetis circumspicite; name talem honorem bonus nemo volet, cum fortinae et maris et belli ab aliis acti ratio reddunda aut turpiter moriundum sit. Tantum modo in animus habetote non me ob scelus aut avaritiam caesum, sed volentem pro maxumis benificiis animam dono dedisse. Per vos, Quirites, et gloriam maiorum, tolerate advorsa et consulite rei publicae! Multa cura summo imperio inest, multi ingentes labores, quos nequiquam abnuitis et pacis opulentiam quaeritis, cum omnes provinciae, regna, maria, terraeque aspera aut fessa bellis sint.

—*Part of speech of* GAIUS COTTA

CHAPTER FORTY-SIX

For a considerable period Marcus Tullius Cicero enjoyed comparative tranquillity, which at times made him uneasy. He wrote to Atticus, "Am I numb or resigned? Am I growing old? Or have I reached the ultimate wisdom which finds no battle worth fighting? Consider me, dear friend, as one who does not look too closely at anything or anyone any longer. I have entered into the period of what some consider the golden middle years, the years that fly and leave no trace and decline into abnegation, which is the ante-room to death."

As Julius had told him, he did not encounter Catilina, who, though in his fortieth year remained as beautiful as a statue still, even if it was whispered that he drank heavily, became incoherent and blasphemous, and rarely appeared in court. He had deputies who labored in his name, claiming that Catilina had briefed them in the night. This was not true, for the nights were spent in restless debauchery. If his friends were present he upbraided them for imagined slights and for ignoring him. There were times when he spoke mysteriously, and was elated. Often, at dawn, he was found staggering on the streets with noisy companions who never appeared in the company of other patricians and never hoped to enter any house but Catilina's.

A madman and a swine, Marcus would think when news of Catilina came to his ears. Marcus began to think that Crassus and Julius Caesar and Pompey had rid themselves of a dangerous man by giving him power he was unable to exercise; he congratulated them in his mind for their cleverness. The gods were destroying, as always, those they had made mad. Once Marcus would have suspected this placidity which surrounded him, for he knew that the gods, being malicious, often lulled a man to sleep so that he was not aware, until too late, that he had been stricken mortally. I had hoped to be a hero of my country, he would think. But the age of heroes seemed to have passed. Sometimes the insidious thought came to Marcus that nothing would ever stir again in the Republic which would capture imagination, whether for good or evil. Everything conspired, it appeared, to dull perception, to lull the spirit, to make every man say, "All is peaceful, all is prosperous, all is contained." Where was a man, these days, like Scipio Africanus, a man with style and color and fire? Romans, modern Romans, would look on such with suspicion and disfavor. Romans did not want to be excited by oratory and brilliance. They wanted their banks, their pleasures, their families, their excursions, their mean little gratifications. They wanted destiny no longer. They wanted no rainbows in their skies, no storms, no disturbances of the status quo. Industrious and materialistic, they preferred the theatres and the circuses and their sports, their couches and their fat families.

Marcus, insensibly, was caught in this tide of complacency; he felt its pull. He began to believe that it was ridiculous for any man to try to awaken the soul of Rome, and he wondered whether it would be kind anyway, or to what men should be awakened. Crassus pursued a middle way. He attracted no overt attention, nor did the Senate or the tribunes. An actor was more celebrated than Crassus. The sun was peaceful on Rome and the streets were busy and there was much speculation and more and more news of prosperity. The world gave the impression of having reached a fixed place of calm, and all the battles were forgotten. There was no sign of impressive evil, nothing that would inspire indignation or resistance. "A fine age in which to live," said many veterans of many holocausts, and they spoke with thanksgiving. "We are stable. Let us pursue the joys of life in this Umbrian atmosphere."

"I leave for Jerusalem soon," said Noë ben Joel to his friend. Noë was bald now, and he was very rich, for his comedies were extremely popular. "I do not like what I feel. Rome is not for a middle-aged man who has nightmares, and I have them."

"Do not be absurd," said Marcus, uneasily.

"I leave for Jerusalem," repeated Noë, and looked at his friend oddly. "A Jew knows when the knives are loose in the scabbards, and he can smell thunder before the first cloud appears. I beg of you to retire to Arpinum."

"So you advised me some years ago. Yet you observe that I live in peace."

Or stultification, thought Noë. A change had come over Marcus, as if something in him was either exhausted or in abeyance. Worse, perhaps he had left the fight, for he did not see the lightnings in the east. He had become plumper, his long cheeks had filled out, his eyes had lost their changeful fire and now had an expression of stillness.

"I have heard much discussion of you in public, concerning that vivid young politician, Publius Clodius, surnamed Pulcher," said Noë, looking aside in delicacy. "And—and this is probably gossip, his sister Clodia. Alas! How scandalous are tongues!"

When he looked up mildly he saw that Marcus' face had become uncomfortably red. "Oh, Publius," he answered with an air of carelessness. "One of those eager young men now in politics, foaming like wine that has gone bad, and resounding like a struck drum, all noise and air. I deplore his zeal. He speaks of 'different times, different laws, to meet our changing problems.' He does not seem to realize that man never changes, and that his problems are always the same though he gives them new names. Publius thinks that everything is new, new, and must be attacked in a bold way, and that modern man, himself, is unique, whereas any ripened man can tell him that what he thinks is 'new' is as old as death, and as you have once quoted yourself, Noë, 'there is nothing new under the sun.' Increasing years will quiet Publius' enthusiasms and his present conviction that man has suddenly embarked on a pristine experience in living, and the past is dead."

"Ah," said Noë, still watching his friend covertly, and remembering the gossip concerning the beautiful Clodia and Marcus. "Do you believe the rumor that Clodius, when prosecuting Catilina for extortion during his term of office, was bribed to acquit him?"

Marcus looked aside; he appeared to have been attacked by a slight pain. "I do not believe Clodius accepted a bribe, for all the rumors. He may have been convinced that Catilina was innocent. Catilina endlessly declaims that he is a friend of the common man; Clodius like many young and jejune men, is convinced that the common man, the man in the streets, possesses a mysterious sanctity, though how he arrives at that conclusion is not to be understood. So it is very probable that Catilina's wily espousal of the common man struck a large gong of sympathy in Clodius, who therefore not only forgave him his sin of extortion but denied it ever existed. Nevertheless, I like the young man. He amuses me and saddens me at the same time with his youth, and his belief that he possesses all wisdom, a disease of his age."

Noë noticed that Marcus did not speak of Clodia, the notorious and lovely sister of Clodius. Noë did not condemn Marcus; in reality, he hoped that Marcus was enjoying life to some extent with Clodia, who was not only beguiling but was noted for her wit and sparkle. As Noë was a great and avid gossip, he knew almost everything that transpired in Rome, mostly scandalous. He knew that Marcus and Terentia fought angrily, that Terentia was not only a shrewd woman insofar as money and investments was concerned, but that she was greedily ambitious and wanted fame in Rome as the wife of a famous and potent man. Noë, from gossip, had been informed that Marcus and Terentia slept in different chambers, that Marcus had once slapped his wife's face before slaves, that once she had hurled a platter of saucy pasta at his head with disastrous results, notably a black eye and a cut on Marcus' face and a badly puffed nose, that Marcus had asked for a divorce which Terentia had refused, and that they now lived, more or less, as formal strangers, except when Terentia was inspired to angry diatribes concerning inconsequential matters, such as Clodia. You are a virtuous husband, Noë, he complimented himself. And you have had many opportunities, but actresses do not always bathe often and they are careless with cosmetics. Moreover, they are expensive and my dear wife keeps all my books.

Marcus said, "But you will return from Jerusalem?"

"No. Not this time. I shall write you daily; perhaps you will join me for a while. Now that my children are of an age to marry I believe they should know their ancient traditions. They have acquired cosmopolitan ways in Rome; these should be balanced by deeper matters." Noë began to laugh. "I still cannot believe that our dear, greedy, posturing Roscius has become an Essene in the caves of Judea! When God touches a man, however improbable that man is for the choosing, He lights a fire in him. So Roscius, to escape identification and notoriety, has assumed the name of Simeon, and says, in all seriousness, that he will not die until he has seen the face of the Messias with his own eyes. That is why he often emerges from the caves—where he studies and prays with his fellow Essenes—and haunts the Temple in the city, staring at the face of all babes who are brought before the altar. Poor Roscius."

"I should have thought it of anyone but Roscius," said Marcus, smiling with regret that never again would he see that mobile face, those magnificent eyes, and hear that loud and musical voice. His own face changed, and he said, "Do not tell me, I implore you, that I shall never see you again, Noë. We were children together, and youths, and young men, and we are middle-aged now. You are part of my life."

"I tell you, I can no longer remain in Rome. I am afraid," said Noë.

"Do not leave too soon," said Marcus, and it came to him that each year saw a diminishing, through death or exile or change of residence, of the substance of his own life. "And when you go, do not come for a last embrace. I do not wish to know the day."

So Noë did not tell him that he was leaving quietly the day after tomorrow. When he embraced his friend on his departure he could hardly refrain from weeping openly. "You have my prayers," he said, scarcely able to speak. Again Marcus' face changed, and he looked before him, musingly.

"It is said that when a man grows older he begins to think more of God," he said, as if to himself. "But it is not true. I was afire with the love of God when I was a youth and a young man. Now I rarely think of Him, and each year the thought occurs to me less and less."

"The world intervenes. We are exhausted with our efforts merely to live," said Noë. But Marcus did not hear him. "In youth," Noë continued, "we have energy for the whole world, and all that is in it and all that is without. A man should be able to retire from the turmoil when he is no more than thirty-five, so that he may devote his mind and his soul to God before he has forgotten Him. But that is impossible for most men."

Marcus looked at him with faintly frowning eyes, as if he had heard a phrase most important to him but now he could not comprehend it, remember where he first had heard it, or who had said it. When Noë departed Marcus still sat in his garden this hot summer evening, and tried to remember. Not an echo rose in him. He began to think of the young and lovely Clodia, and he smiled.

Helvia, that prudent and stable woman, had never interfered in the affairs of the household since Marcus had married. She approved of Terentia's thrift and genius with money and investments; she approved of her old Roman convictions, and her piety which was increasing as she grew older. (Terentia was always in the temples, when she was not in the banks and the brokers' offices.) She approved of her as a diligent mother and scrupulous wife and a deft manager of household affairs. But she sighed over Terentia's fits of violent temper, growing more frequent lately, the nagging with which she afflicted Marcus over the most trivial matters, and her intolerance of everyone who did not share her narrow convictions. Helvia regretted Clodia, but she understood. She did not, however, know if she were relieved or not that Marcus appeared more serene these days and that things did not ruffle him as once they did. We all grow old, Helvia would think, sighing. It is very unfortunate that we also grow more attuned to the world, and quarrel with it less.

Marcus sat in the sunset garden after Noë had departed. He said to himself, "Am I happy or not? Am I less interested in life, or have I just accepted it at last? I am in harbor. Is that desirable or not? I know I cannot change the world, and I know that Rome is lost. Will it help if I tear myself into shreds? No. I pray that each day will not be stormier than yesterday." It was only when Catilina's face rose before him that he felt a sharp spasm in his heart and heard an echo of his old hatred. But Catilina was competently doing himself to death with debauchery. He was no longer Praetor.

But I, myself, shall soon be Praetor, Marcus thought. He smiled pleasantly, though with no excitement. He thought of Clodia, and he smiled again and rose to prepare himself to dine at her house where there was always laughter and wit and intelligent companions and music. It was rumored that she had recently taken one Marcus Antonius, a very young youth, as one of her lovers, but Marcus did not believe it.

Walking slowly and with leisure, Marcus entered his fine house, to which he had added more rooms and more luxury and more ornamentation. He encountered, not without a wince or two, his father apparently awaiting him in the atrium. There were days when he forgot that his father even existed, and he was always startled to see his thin shadow on the marble walls or hear his light and timid voice.

Tullius' hair was white, his thin face fallen and bleached, his figure gaunt and his gait uncertain, as if his feet hardly felt the earth. Only his large brown eyes remained alive, and now they were eloquent.

He began to speak rapidly and in stumbling accents, as if he felt that if he did not catch Marcus' attention immediately Marcus would not hear him or see him. He said, "My dear son, I must talk with you; it is most necessary."

Marcus frowned slightly. He could not control his impatience, his desire to shut his father out of his awareness. He said, "I am late. I am to dine—"

"I know. You are always late, Marcus. You are always dining. You always have appointments." The old man's face was broken with sadness, and he bent his head. "There is something very wrong, Marcus. I feel I must speak to you before it is too late."

"Well?" said Marcus, with resignation. The hall's white walls and floor were sparkling with late sunshine, and the fountain in the center glittered and sang and caged birds sang sweetly in the corners.

"We have all lost you, even your daughter, Tullia," said Tullius with humility.

"I do not know what you mean, my father," said Marcus, exasperated. He looked at the water clock. He must bathe, he must array himself, and it was already late. "Can we not continue when I return?"

"I never hear you return," said Tullius, imploringly. "When I awake in the morning you have already gone. When you are at home, you have clients or guests—when you are at home, I hear your voice only at a distance."

"I am a busy man," said Marcus. "I have a family whom I must support. I have public duties."

"Yes," said Tullius.

"You have not told me of the 'necessary' thing."

Tullius lifted his eyes and looked with grave intentness at his son. "I have forgotten," he said, and stood aside to let Marcus pass. Marcus hesitated. He felt a faint pain in his breast, a sort of vague sorrow. But it was all overlaid with impatience. He said, as if defending himself, "I also write books and treatises and essays. This is a different world than the world you knew, Father."

His father, for some intangible reason, was a reproach to him. He did not like reproaches; he received too many from Terentia, who wearied him to death now, and who had lost what little comeliness she had once possessed.

"It is always the same world," muttered Tullius. "You will discover that to your own anguish before you die."

Marcus' amiable lips tightened. He inclined his head and went to his quarters and prepared for the evening. The sun at the window darkened as a cloud passed; then the chamber was warm and bright again.

It was very late when he returned. Clodia had been alone, as it had been arranged. Marcus yawned over and over and thought of his own bed with pleasure. Then, as he alighted from his litter, he saw that the bronze doors of his house were open and flooded with light, and that lamplight gleamed at all the windows, though the dawn was already gray in the east.

His heart jumped. He thought of his daughter, Tullia. He hastened into the house to be met in the hall by a weeping Terentia, who immediately fell on him like a tearful fury.

"While you lay in the arms of your harlot," she screamed, "your mother died!"

Helvia's ashes were laid with her father's. The funeral meats had been eaten, the cypress planted at the door, the guests departed. The sun was still warm and golden, the air still sweet, and the birds in the atrium still sang in ecstasy. The garden was still fragrant, and the city below the Palatine hummed and clattered and bellowed, and the hills beyond, chaotic with buildings, caught the red rays of the western sky. Grief comes to every house, but its shadow is driven away as fast as possible. The dead were as if they had never lived, even those of power and of mighty houses.

There had been a multitude of mourners, including all the Caesares, and even Crassus had sent Pompey as his delegate, and the Helvii had wept for their sister, their aunt, their cousin. Quintus and Terentia had wept, but Tullius and Marcus were dry of eye for they mourned her the most. Little Tullia cried for her grandmother, and Marcus could not comfort her.

On the fourth day he sat in his favorite spot in his garden, beneath the myrtle trees, and his hands were flaccid on his knees. He sat for a long time. Then he saw that his father was seated not far from him, and gazing at him, and Tullius appeared like a shade, himself.

"I have lost more than a wife, a dear companion," said Tullius, in a voice that rustled like dead leaves. "I have lost a mother."

And that is true, thought Marcus with bitterness. You have made Terentia your aunt and your serving maid and have assigned Tullia to be a sister to you. Always, you have depended on others, leaning upon them, your hands outheld like a beggar's hands, crying for the alms of love and protection. To my grandfather you were always a child. But you shall not succeed in creating a father in me for yourself.

He did not know why he felt something evilly akin to hatred for his father, except that his own loss was so great and he must turn on something to alleviate his suffering. The house on the Carinae was now occupied by Quintus and his wife, Pomponia, and their young son. Marcus said, "Doubtless, my father, you will feel more comforted if you live with Quintus and his family, for Quintus is much like my mother and he was her favorite, and his boy resembles her."

Tullius raised his beaten eyes and studied Marcus in silence. Then he said, "So be it." He groped weakly to his feet and moved away into the shadows like an old man.

"Have you no filial feeling?" Terentia cried. "You have driven your father from your house, and he who does that is cursed!"

"I did not drive him away. He will be happier with Quintus. Had he wished to stay he had but to say the word. I have sent his special slave with him, who will comfort him and sleep at his feet. My door is not closed to him. He will always be an honored guest in my house."

"I do not understand you, Marcus. You are not the man I knew."

"No one ever is."

Terentia was clothed in black. She was fat and sallow in it, and her brown hair had lost its lustre and an extra chin sagged below the first one. Her hands, in her lap, showed their big competence and large knuckles. She has the ugliest hands I have ever seen in a woman, thought Marcus. He felt weary to death.

"Do you wish me to divorce you?" asked Terentia, wiping away her tears.

"If you wish."

"Do you care for nothing?" she exclaimed.

"I try to refrain from caring," he answered. "That is the only way I can endure."

"Endure what?" Terentia was outraged. "Are you poor, deprived, homeless, wifeless, childless, without a copper in your purse? Do you sleep under aqueducts among runaway slaves? No! You are rich and famous and have a magnificent house, and are the friend of the powerful, and you own other houses and lands and villas and farms. Your health is good; you want for nothing. There is silver and gold on your table, and lemonwood furniture in your rooms, and ebony and Alexandrian glass and bronze, and your walls are covered with costly murals and your floors with rich rugs. Bankers hasten to honor your drafts. Your offices are filled with notable clients. You are to be Praetor. Yet, you speak of 'enduring!' Beware, Marcus, that the gods do not take back their gifts from one so ungrateful!"

But Marcus did not answer. He rose and left her.

The next morning she confronted him resolutely. "No," she said, "I shall not divorce you. Divorce is a wicked thing. You no longer love me; you love that harlot, Clodia, who perfumes her body and is young and showers gold dust in her hair and reveals the contours of her breast shamelessly. I love you, Marcus. And I shall not deprive Tullia of her father, whom she adores. Despise me and reject me, as you have done for many years. You will find me here to welcome you, when it pleases you to notice my presence."

He was moved to pity and shame. "I did not think you would divorce me, though we have mentioned this before. Believe me, Terentia, I shall always regard you as my wife, the mother of my daughter, the heart of my household. If I have betrayed you, I offer no excuse, nor do I reproach you who deserve no reproach. If I do not talk with you, it is because I cannot."

To his surprise she began to smile through her tears. "So my father often told my mother—'I cannot talk with you.' All men are the same. They are like children who believe their thoughts are too mighty to be communicated. In reality, they are very simple, and easily understood by women. Now why and how have I affronted you again?"

He made his brow smooth and put his hand briefly on her shoulder. "You have not affronted me. I have a headache this morning. There are so many things—"

"And few of them important," she said in an arch and soothing voice, and smiled again as if he were ten years old and she his indulgent mother. To keep down his anger he turned aside his head, and listened for the slaves who were bringing his litter.

"Ah, it is well that we women comprehend so utterly," said Terentia, "and understand that what engrosses men the most is of the least importance."

Marcus almost ran from the atrium to his litter. He said to himself, when he was sitting on the cushions, I am becoming irascible and hateful.

He thought of his dead mother and wished again that he could weep.

He knew he must flee. He would go to the island for a while and try to remember why he was living.

He would try to remember the meaning of the words of Isaias, of which Noë had told him: "Why do you spend money for that which is not bread, and your labor for that which does not satisfy you?"

There were no answers or meanings in the howling streets of the Urbs, the company of impotent intellectuals, the crowded porticoes of those who questioned, not of the sky, but of mythical enigmas, the tiger-faced men of power, the horrible complex of the city of man with its wastes of streets and godless temples and politicians and evil busyness that had no goal, the white-lipped philosophers who created bodiless paradoxes and knew nothing of the mysteries of a simple tree, the empty-eyed men who talked of reason and had never known reality, the shrieking, wanton-eyed children who had never felt the living earth under their feet, the markets, the shops, the trading and the counting houses, the fora and the buildings of man's expedient laws, the schools and the sanitaria, the polluted rivers and the stenches of the alleys, the discordant music of those who had never heard the music of a forest, and all the petty and wicked men who prated of the future of man as if man were a beginning and an end in himself!

Only when man left men did he find the Civitas Dei—the City of God—uncrowded, sweet, full of light and emotion and ecstasy and shining law, singing with angelic passions and crying with the utterances of unchangeable truths, brilliant with spaces and inhabited only by beauty and freedom and many silences. The blessed silences where man was not!

The island had another ghost now, and it was that of Helvia. It was strange that Helvia seemed more alive here, and the old grandfather, and Livia, than they had ever seemed in life. Marcus lay on the warm grass and conversed with them and slowly a little peace came to him, and the answer to that which he sought seemed almost within reach of his eye and his ear. But he no longer felt tranquil and for that he thanked the gods.

CHAPTER FORTY-SEVEN

"I agree with you that the Republic is lost," said the young politician Publius Clodius, surnamed Pulcher. "And I agree with you that the future of Rome belongs to the Caesares. It is regrettable. My fathers believed in the Republic."

"When a nation becomes so demoralized and corrupt and angerless as Rome, then that nation is lost forever," said Marcus. "Then come the Caesares."

"The man on horseback. Yes," said Clodius. He was a lively and witty young man, slender and not very tall, with a dark and somewhat reckless face and very brilliant black eyes. "The man does not leap on horseback by himself; the people offer their hands to his ascent. So Caesar will leap one of these days. I can think of worse men."

Marcus eyed him curiously. "If it came to a contest between Caesar and me, whom would you support?"

"I love you, Marcus, but the cause of Cicero is lost. I prefer to continue living." He paused and eyed Marcus with his own curiosity. "Why do you continue to oppose the Fates?"

"To paraphrase you, because I prefer to continue living—with myself."

"Then you have hope?"

But Marcus shook his head. "I have no hope. But I may have the illusion of all soldiers in a lost cause—that there will be reinforcements." Marcus was beginning to wonder and just faintly to hope. He was now Praetor of Rome. Clodius said, "You remind me of Hector, the noble Trojan hero, who, though knowing his country was wrong, and had done great evil, yet fought for her with patriotic fervor, and hoped to save her—though he knew it was impossible—from her inevitable fate. Are you ambitious, Cicero?"

"Only for my country, and her honor," said Marcus.

"Old-fashioned words," said Clodius. "These are modern times."

"They always are, Clodius. Why do men deceive themselves that the past is not the present, the future the past? Every age has shouted, 'We are a new era!' Yet it is always the same, for man does not change. Has it not been said that the nation that does not learn from history is doomed to repeat its mistakes? Ages yet unborn shall say, 'None other was ever like us.' But they shall be as Rome."

Clodius smiled indulgently. "Then there is no hope for man?"

Marcus hesitated. "Not unless God gives us a new way and a new path for the future, and reveals Himself."

Clodius, that young man, thought to himself: Cicero is aging, and he speaks as all the aging men speak. He thought of his beauteous sister, Clodia, and amusedly wondered if Cicero ever forgot his griefs in her smooth white arms. It is possible, for has he not now published a book of poetry over which there has been much controversy and much fame for him? A man is not moved to poetry of such brilliance when he is in despair. He is a paradox.

It was then that Clodius, who had his own secret ambitions, began to feel uneasy concerning Marcus. Paradoxes, though exciting to consider, were not reliable in their conduct, and not predictable, especially when they were both prudent and poets. Clodius went to Julius Caesar and said, "Our friend, Cicero, is a paradox."

Julius laughed. "Honest men are always so to men like us. They belong to no category we can name. So we say to ourselves: He must be assassinated, or destroyed in some other manner, or rendered impotent." Julius reflected for a moment, still smiling. "Do you not know that both the patricians and the people trust him? Is that not a paradox in itself? I am sorry for these few honest men, who believe that honesty will commend itself to the admiration of a nation."

"He seems inconsistent to me," said Clodius.

"Are we not all?" said Julius. "Man, by his very nature, is inconsistent, a friend today, an enemy tomorrow, a lover of justice in the morning, and suborned in the evening. Why do we insist on consistency, we who are the inconsistent?"

"Cicero would say, because at the core of life all is consistent, and we echo it though we betray it."

"You are becoming a philosopher," said Julius, and yawned. "An hour with Cicero is enough to make one doubt his ambitions and the purpose of his life. This is disconcerting. Let us avoid our dear Cicero, and consider what we desire."

"Did I not work endlessly to make you an aedile?" asked Marcus angrily of his brother, Quintus. "You know my bias against military men. You grow in ill temper every day. Is it that Pomponia exasperates you? What woman does not exasperate her husband! You have a son. You are rich, due to my efforts, and, I must admit, to the advice my Terentia gave you concerning investments. What is it that you wish?"

"I am a simple man. Therefore, I am akin to the simple animals," said Quintus with a scowl. "I do not think you are safe, my brother. I lift my nose and sniff the air. I am full of unease. You think me ambitious, but I am ambitious only to protect you, you who are dearer to me than wife or son."

"Do I not know this?" said Marcus, greatly moved. "But still, you have not explained your bad temper. Once you were the most indulgent of young men, the most smiling and calm. Now you pace floors. You remind me of our grandfather, and no longer of our dear mother."

Quintus ruffled the thick black curls on his head then flung his arms wide in despair. "I do not know!" he exclaimed. "But affairs in Rome become more chaotic every day. They are more complex, more inscrutable, and I am a simple man! Why do not matters remain simple, black and white, good and evil?"

"They do not remain that way because they never were," said Marcus.

"Once you believed that good order and good principle and virtue among men would conquer everything," said Quintus, baffled.

Marcus answered sadly, "True. However, these are subjective terms, the terms of the soul. The objective world does not conform to the soul of man, and whose is the fault? In the meantime, control your temper, or someone will murder you."

Marcus put his hands over his face. "I grow more confused each day. But still, I must work out my own destiny, for I have no other."

Quintus frowned. "What destiny has our father? He grows more wan day by day, more removed. He is a shade in my house, and Pomponia complains. He hardly knows he is a grandfather, and rarely speaks to my young son. What troubles him? He is not a complex man like you, Marcus."

"And how do you know that?" said Marcus, gloomily, and with that inner spasm of pain he always felt when his father was mentioned.

"He believes you compromise," said Quintus.

"He never compromised because he never took a stand," said Marcus, with anger of his own. "Do you think it easy for me to endure Caesar and Crassus and Pompey, and all their friends? No. But they exist in my world and I must endure them."

"Including Catilina?"

Marcus rose abruptly to his feet and his fine eyes flashed on his brother. "No."

Quintus felt appeased, though he did not know why. Then he scowled once more. "I am worried about my young son. He is devious, and not to be trusted. He smiles disarmingly. I am afraid he is subtle, and exigent."

Marcus knew this was true. The young Quintus slipped agilely through one's grasp. So Marcus pitied his ingenuous brother, and thought of his own daughter, Tullia, with passionate relief. Marcus said, "I will soon seek to be Consul of Rome." He hoped to divert his brother's thoughts.

Quintus eyed him with sudden grimness. "Do you not know the rumor? It is said that Catilina will be Consul of Rome. Who can oppose him, he who has the mob in the palm of his hand?"

CHAPTER FORTY-EIGHT

Romans, being realists and pragmatic materialists, were suspicious of men of intellect. They loved Marcus for his justice; they could not forgive him his books of essays and poetry, though few of them read the works. Those who did read them, the intellectuals themselves, spoke in violent controversy for them and against them. Some affected to believe that Marcus, a member of the "new," or middle-class, men, was not capable of truly abstract thought. He dealt in "duty" and "patriotism" and "honor," and "law," as if these were immutables! Was anything more ridiculous to a cultivated man? But some of the intellectuals disagreed and thought gloomily of themselves, who had betrayed that which had been dear to their fathers. This made them angry with Marcus, who aroused their conscience.

"Let us smile indulgently when Marcus' books are mentioned," said Julius to his friends. "Then the mob, which never reads, will laugh at him, and he will remain comparatively harmless."

"Nevertheless, all listen to him in the courts and in the Forum," said Catilina.

"What a man says is soon forgotten," replied Julius.

"The people love him," said Catilina, with hatred.

"There is one thing certain," said Julius. "What the mob loves today it can easily hate tomorrow. On this we build our lives."

"Have you read your Cicero's latest dissertation?" asked Crassus of Caesar. "Let me quote part of it to you: 'Men of ambition neither listen to reason nor bow to public or legitimate authority, but chiefly resort to corruption and intrigue in order to obtain supreme power and to be masters by force rather than equals by law. Such men inevitably become slaves to the mob, so therefore the slaves of such capricious and ignorant rabble are themselves, at the last, no longer men of power.'* He means us."

But Julius laughed. "So he does. However, who reads him but us? We tolerate him, moreover, so therefore even potential enemies among the literate will doubt he refers to our noble Crassus and his friends. It is a great advantage to men like us to be hailed as broad of mind and tolerant of disputants."

Julius studied his dear friend Crassus for a moment. They were dining in Caesar's home—Julius, Crassus, Catilina, and Pompey. But before Julius could speak again Catilina said, "I must be a Consul of Rome. I have waited too long, and am no longer young."

Julius sighed. "So you say daily. Wait but a little longer. You served well as a governor of Africa, and I note that African suns have increased rather than diminished your beauty, sweet Lucius. However, as you know," added Julius delicately, "even the debased Romans of today cannot overlook your impeachment for extortion, which disqualifies you for the office of Consul."

"I was acquitted of that crime, through the work of my dear friend, Clodius," said Catilina, with that open contempt of everyone which he invariably displayed.

Julius mused. "And Clodius' sister is the mistress of our beguiling and innocent Cicero."

* From Cicero's *On Moral Duties.*

"You are implying that she keeps him blind?" asked Crassus with a smile.

"Women are a two-edged sword," said Catilina. His deep blue eyes glittered with wrath when the others burst into laughter. When they had done, he repeated, "I must be Consul of Rome. You shall not distract me, as you have done in the past, with foreign assignments or petty offices in the city." He struck the table with his fist, and his gemmed wristlet flashed in the lamplight with a many-colored flame.

"I warn you," he said in his deadly voice, "that I have come to the end of my patience. No promises, no threats, will turn me aside now."

They had heard all this before, but each time it had been more difficult to turn Catilina aside. He had requested this meeting tonight, almost as if he had commanded it. Julius thought, We should have poisoned him as he did his wife and his son, long before this. We fed the tiger so we could use him in our day of need. But even before that day of need he has broken from his confinement and threatens us.

Julius carefully met the eyes of Pompey and Crassus. The latter shrugged, then lifted his eyebrows. Julius selected a date from a silver dish and daintily ate it. It was the season of the Saturnalia, and Rome was cold and full of mist, presaging winter. Braziers warmed the pleasant and luxurious dining hall.

"What an actor you are, Caesar!" said Catilina with more contempt. "You are almost as cautious as that loathsome friend of yours, Cicero, for whose death I yearn and whose death—I swear it—I shall encompass in my own time with no further deference to you."

He had never spoken so fiercely before, for all he was a fierce man, and with such cold disgust. He had never challenged them so utterly and in such a tone. They all thought of the huge and terrible mobs he controlled, the welter of the underground of Rome. He turned in his chair and with a tight smile he looked from one to another. "This is the hour," he said. "For what are you waiting, you pusillanimous men? For an omen, you, Caesar, from your patron, Jupiter? He is an audacious god, the greatest of them all; you are no worthy servitor of him. I suspect you, Caesar, of this delay."

"It is well to be certain before you move," said Julius, but he spoke abstractedly, and he looked again at Crassus.

"Gods!" exclaimed Catilina, and struck the table again. "How more certain is it necessary to be? Who can withstand us, if we move tomorrow?"

"And you would begin by murdering Cicero?" asked Julius, idly.

"Yes! You pretend not to believe it, Caesar, but he is a monstrous danger to us. Has he not insulted Crassus to his face and has he not dared to warn him?"

"You have insulted Crassus yourself, dear Lucius, in your open threats tonight at this table."

"Bah," said Catilina. "Look at me! My temples are graying, there are wrinkles on my brow. I shall wait no longer."

"You shall not murder Cicero," said Pompey, who almost always only listened and rarely spoke.

Catilina stared at him incredulously. "You, too? What plot is this?"

"No plot," said Pompey in his curiously quiet and impassive voice. "Merely intelligence. We know the people love Cicero. He has many powerful friends, even among the patricians. All the lawyers of Rome stand in awe before Cicero, and they are eloquent. Let Cicero be murdered and we shall be lost."

"I agree," said Julius. But Catilina grasped his bronzed temples where indeed the dark hair, shadowed with the color of autumn, was graying. There was also a growing madness in his eyes, which revealed, during emotion, strange and uncontrollable passions coming less and less under precarious discipline.

He exclaimed, "I fear no man now! Not the people, not my fellow patricians, not the whey-faced lawyers! Ah, Caesar, you look at me with speculation. You are considering having me quietly assassinated. Listen to me now: Let a hand be lifted against me, even the hand of Crassus, and all Hades will pour over Rome and you will all be engulfed. Do you think I have been idle, and peacefully waiting, since I returned from Africa? If you do not move immediately, then I shall do it alone, and let that man beware who opposes me."

He is surely mad, as Livia was mad, thought Julius. He again caught the eye of Crassus, and then he smiled fondly on Catilina.

"I, too, am no longer young, Lucius," he said. "My daughter is married to our brother, Pompey." He laughed lightly. "And I am growing bald, which is an affliction, Adonis, which has not befallen you."

But Catilina gazed at him implacably. "You move with me at once, or I move alone, Caesar. I have said it." He turned his burning eyes upon the others and they all saw the overwhelming madness in him, the now totally uncontrollable desire and lust and determination.

Then Crassus said with quietness, "You have forgotten, Catilina. I am triumvir. I am the most powerful man in Rome, though you affect not to know it tonight. We shall move when I give the word. That word is not for tomorrow."

But Catilina was not to be intimidated. "I have said it is." His voice was full of harsh fury. "I did not come here tonight to be diverted and reassured and deceived and turned aside again. I came with my ultimatum."

"For which there was no necessity," said Julius, in a bland voice. Catilina turned all the power of his eyes upon him, and a deep flush ran over his face. "We are ready to move, though not exactly and literally tomorrow, Lucius," added the other man.

"Give me the day," said Catilina with that imperiousness which both irritated Julius and inspired admiration in him.

"Let us be reasonable," said the younger man. "You have demanded to be a Consul of Rome. The Consuls have already been elected, for the city, for the provinces. Let us say that we are not pleased by the choices of both the Optimate and the populares parties. Let us say that we wish to replace them." Julius touched his lips with the tip of his tongue.

"And how will you accomplish that?" demanded Catilina.

But Crassus spoke with cold authority. "While you were in Africa we have not been idle. We have not been merely eating and excreting, as you appear to believe, Catilina. You speak of the fact that you are no longer young. But I am much older than you, and I have patience. I do not throw the dice before I know they are my own, and loaded. Had you not asked to come here tonight I should have sent for you." This was a lie, but still it had some small truth in it. The truth, it had been agreed before, should not be divulged to the reckless Catilina for fear of him precipitating a crisis before all was ready. However, Catilina could no longer be restrained, so they must placate him.

"Tell me!" cried Catilina, the flush on his face deepening to crimson with excitement.

Julius said, in a very soft tone, almost inaudible, "We wish to replace the elected Consuls. We wish the offices filled with our friends. Now, if you will listen and bend your head to my ear—"

Marcus Tullius Cicero did not believe in the rumor his brother, Quintus, had brought to him. The very thought of the dissolute and monstrous Catilina being Consul of Rome was incredible to him. Crassus and Caesar and Pompey were not madmen. They were doubtless conspirators, though the exact nature of the conspiracy he suspected was not clear to Marcus; he only knew that in some way it was the seizure of absolute power in Rome. But certainly they would not offer Catilina to the Roman people and the Optimates for their approval of a Consulship for him! Catilina the mad, the furious, the murderer, the depraved and unreliable, the patrician whose arrogance must offend even his friends and fellow plotters, the debt-ridden and unscrupulous and venal, the profoundly contemptible: No, not even Crassus and Caesar and Pompey would permit such a man as Consul of Rome, where he would be in a position to vent his capricious rages upon themselves and even to destroy them.

Nevertheless, Marcus had long ago recovered from his belief that anything is truly incredible. He discreetly spoke to several of his friends, good men like himself. They, too, were incredulous. They could not believe that those three pragmatic and ambitious men would support Catilina for the Consulship and lend their august names to the aims of an evil and totally irresponsible madman.

"However, it is possible that they are afraid of him," said Marcus. "One must remember the underworld of Rome whom Catilina controls. He has no restraints; he could loose the criminals, gladiators, slaves, freedmen, gamblers, pimps, murderers, disaffected veterans, malcontents, beggars, and perverts on Rome at a word."

Marcus' friends wondered at him. They thought it strange that so steadfast and sensible a lawyer was becoming extravagant and was seeing Furies in the nights. One of them whispered to another, "I am certain he searches under his bed before sleeping for a disheveled and unwashed Catilinian lion. But that is hysteria and unreasonable and even womanish, and I say this who loves Cicero. It is certain that the Catilina raves and is out of his mind and is cruel and debased, and hates all men. But it is also certain that he does not possess the terrible power Cicero ascribes to him. The Roman people, at heart, would not listen to such as Catilina. The forces he commands, though annoying and even troubling, are no real threat to Rome. To do as Cicero advises: watching the minions of Catilina at all times, and to openly outlaw them, would not only arouse the laughter of Rome but would violate the liberty of the individual and rebound disastrously on Cicero's own reputation. Surely he does not wish to be named a violator of the rights of men, an autocrat of vehement opinion and an accuser of all who disagree with him!"*

"The time to be prepared to the utmost is during periods of tranquillity," Marcus wrote to Atticus in Athens. "The methods I suggest for the safety of Rome command consternation among my friends or even accusations that I am immoderate and losing a sense of proportion. A man who can command the very dregs of a nation, and who has no love for his country, and who is revolutionary and hating and vengeful and envious and evil and a traitor, is not to be laughed at or ignored. My friends are too complacent; they believe that Rome is founded on rock and our Constitution invulnerable and our law too strong. They love to consider themselves tolerant of all men's opinions and refuse to believe that some men are profoundly wicked and monstrous by nature. They look at their own pleasant

* Letter from Catolus Lutatius to Silanus, in which he also urged "moderation."

and fatherly visages and believe that their mirrors reflect all others'. Do you know what they tell me? That Catilina's following is a very small minority in Rome!"

In reply, Atticus the publisher wrote: "There are only two kinds of politicians: Those who love tolerance for its own sake and believe all men love it by nature, and those who espouse tolerance in order to hide the activities of the vicious who support them."

To the latter, Marcus thought despondently, Crassus and Caesar and Pompey and Piso and Curius and all their friends belong. He could not so far name a name in the darkness which surrounded him. He visited Senators who admired him and laid his proposal before them: That Catilina be thoroughly investigated and be brought before the Senate for questioning. But those Senators also looked at Marcus with uneasiness. True, all knew what Catilina was. But, what proof did Marcus have of his activities in his Hades underground? None had heard that Crassus was agreeable to Catilina becoming Consul of Rome. Besides, the people had already elected the Consuls who would take office in the month of Janus, after the December Saturnalia.

Marcus said, "Why will you not listen to me? Catilina is mad. It is very possible that he has threatened Crassus, himself."

The more smiling and disbelieving resistance he met the more stubborn Marcus became. Moreover, his intuition had come alive. Let them say he searched under his bed every night for an enemy. Better it would be for them if they did so also!

He said to Quintus, his brother, "You spoke of a rumor concerning Catilina. Have you pursued it?"

"I did. And like all rumors it dissolves like smoke on the instant of touching."

"Then we are truly in danger."

Publius Clodius, surnamed Pulcher, was devoted to his lovely and gaily promiscuous sister, Clodia, whose hair had not very originally been compared to the wing of a raven, and her eyes to midnight stars, and her breast to the breast of a dove. She had a husband, Caecilius Metellus Celer, of a most distinguished family, who had discovered that she was the only woman with whom he could conduct normal relationships. Wishing to disguise his predilections, he had married her, much to the envy of her many suitors. But after a few months of decorous intimacy he had yearned for his old companions and old pleasures.

She was fastidious and her lovers were carefully selected. She had her favorites, and among them was Marcus Tullius Cicero who preferred to believe that he was her only lover though he knew better. Clodia possessed not only beauty, wit and charm, but she had an excellent mind. There were many nights when they did not repair to Clodia's luxurious chamber at all, but sat until dawn discussing philosophy and politics and the fate of man, with great content and satisfaction. Marcus knew he could never love another woman but the long-dead Livia, but he had a tremendous affection and admiration for the beauteous Clodia, and considered her a dear friend as well as a mistress. He bought for her the jewels which Terentia despised; he often filled her house with flowers and perfumes.

Her brother, Clodius, thought of himself as a "modern" man and so was tolerant of his sister's affable sexual frolics. Moreover, he learned much of what was going on in Rome from her, for she had many devoted female friends also who listened avidly to their powerful husbands. Clodius thought of his sister as a Roman Aspasia, and sometimes he laughingly referred to Marcus as "your Pericles."

One day she said to her brother, who had called to join her at her midday meal, "You know Mark Antony. He is a guileless young soldier, with the mind of an eternal boy, though he is valorous. He adores your ambiguous friend, Caesar; he basks in his shadow. Why this is I do not know, for I mistrust and dislike Caesar, who has attempted to seduce me."

"Caesar never lays eyes on a desirable woman that he does not attempt to seduce her," said Clodius.

"I do not like libertines," said Clodia with a severity that made her brother smile. She paused and studied her brother with her great black eyes. "Do you think I am a stupid woman? I know of your associations with Caesar and his friends. But, I have heard a rumor from my guileless Mark Antony."

Clodius became alert. Though he was of the arcane brotherhood, and possessed one of its serpentine rings, he was not of the close companions who surrounded Crassus, notably Caesar, Curius, Piso, Catilina, and Pompey. He was a politician; nevertheless he knew only what the others wished him to know. He said, "No one would trust such a constant talker like young Mark Antony. You can rely on nothing he repeats."

"He tells me that Marcus Tullius Cicero's murder has been arranged during the first part of the month of Janus, when the elected Consuls take office."

Clodius was disappointed. He laughed. "What nonsense! He is under Caesar's protection."

"So he is, or was. But Caesar, you may remember, has fits of epilepsy. Mark Antony is his favorite among all the young men who surround him. During one of those fits of epilepsy he babbled incoherently to Mark Antony, who was alone with him in his house. Caesar appeared beside himself with rage and emotion. He spoke of the coming murder of my Marcus, and the first week in Janus, and he wept and struck about him and threw himself at a wall and screamed that he was helpless. For Catilina had demanded it, and Crassus no longer will prevent it." Clodia looked at her brother sternly. "Mark Antony is not concerned with Cicero or his fate. He thought it very exciting, that so famous a man as Cicero, and so 'dull,' as he said, should soon die."

"Nonsense," said Clodius, but he was disturbed. "Why should Cicero be murdered? Mark Antony is not only a silly babbler but he is a fool. And one must remember that if a man is seized by epilepsy his ravings are not to be considered, for he is not responsible for them."

But Clodia said coldly, "Mark Antony also told me of another matter. Catilina has demanded to be Consul of Rome." Clodia waved her hand. "I care not what happens to the Consuls but I do care for my Marcus."

Clodius continued to smile, but behind his smile he was terribly alarmed and angered. He was not one of the "raving patriots," as he called those who loved their country. But he was no traitor. Let openly and lawfully elected officials be assassinated, and that would be the end. There were some politicians who created and loved chaos because it was a milieu in which they best maneuvered. He was not yet one of them.

But how could Cicero be warned? To go to him openly and warn him of the plot—which Clodius still did not entirely credit, for who listened to one such as the young Mark Antony?—would be to betray those to whom he had taken the secret blood-oath of brotherhood. They would then order his own murder. What, then, could he do?

"Do not think I would take Antony's word alone," said Clodia, who was watching him acutely. "You know I have Fulvia for a friend, who is the mistress of Q. Curius. Only three nights ago, she has told me with excitement, Curius boasted to her, in his cups and in wild elation, that the hour has come, and that your friends will strike in the first week of Janus."

"Fulvia is an idle and gossiping woman," said Clodius.

Clodia shook her head. "You do not believe that, my brother."

Clodius said, "As you have these famous rumors, why do you not warn Cicero, yourself?"

"It is said," Clodia remarked, "that Romans are subject to their women. In defense, they openly scoff at what they call 'women's gossip.' Cicero would not listen to me."

Clodia smiled seductively. Then she added, "I love my Marcus in my fashion. Let nothing evil occur to him. If your friends can destroy him with impunity, do you think they will hesitate to murder any other they might mistrust for a number of reasons?"

When he returned to his house Clodius pondered. His anger returned, and his sense of humiliation. He was also afraid. The only recourse was an anonymous letter to Cicero.

CHAPTER FORTY-NINE

Tullia was a young and graceful girl, of sweet and modest beauty and clear intelligence. Her materialistic mother could not understand Tullia's gentleness; Terentia called it laziness of spirit and inability to make up one's mind. There was indeed in Tullia her father's love of compromise on unimportant matters but not on principle. She would say, "It may be true, Mother, what you say, based on what you have heard. Then again it may not be true but only public malice."

On the occasion of her puberty her father had given her a beautiful marble statuette of Athene, and had said to her, "Wisdom is based on knowledge. But knowledge is not always wisdom. It is no paradox. There is intuitive knowledge, the source of wisdom. And there is objective knowledge, which is a collection of irrelevant facts. The man of wisdom is slow to give opinion, for he must sort out the intangibles. The man who has only knowledge is very swift in his judgments, for he does not recognize and does not see the vast imponderable forces which operate in the world. He is dangerous."

Tullia adored her father. There were times when she secretly agreed with her mother that men were romantics and cherished dreams and other fantasia, and were often emotional. But she also believed that women's materialism was too narrow, and that a life without a dream was no life at all. She admired Terentia for her many virtues; she did not know why her father could endure her. If Terentia complained and expressed her furious discontent with her husband, Tullia listened in silence, understanding that Terentia had many reasons for her complaints—for which Tullia forgave her father at once. But there was one thing for which Tullia could not forgive her father. Terentia was pregnant.

Tullia felt betrayed. As she was a wise child she knew this sense of betrayal was ridiculous. As a girl, half in love with her father, she still felt betrayed. She had not yet fully learned the instincts of compassion and the bonds which held man and wife together despite bitter controversy, anger, disgust, and even contempt. She was ashamed for both her parents, for her young mind was still singular.

She preferred to ignore her mother's obvious pregnancy. In this she resembled her father, Marcus, who in his youth had been convinced that unpleasant matters were best not mentioned, and that if importance were not attached to them they would diminish and fade away. Terentia's miseries of the flesh—for she was not young any longer—made Tullia recoil. Terentia complained, "I do not wish other children; this was inflicted upon me. Your father has no consideration." But she smugly smiled under her long lip.

Marcus, despite all his knowledge of the world and his own commonsense, believed that he could protect his daughter against life. He had only to teach Tullia the old virtues, and to exhort her to love God, and all would be well. When thinking of Tullia he ignored Rome. He would create for Tullia an island of peace and joy and tranquillity. He would carefully choose her husband for tenderness and protection and character. He would deliver to that husband—and may he long not be acoming!—a vessel of gold filled with the essence of purity and sweetness. Tullia's existence would be forever guarded, far from turmoil and pain and grief and bitterness. When Terentia's pregnancy could no longer be overlooked, Marcus said to his daughter, "Always, you are first in my life, Tullia. Always, you will be first."

Tullia often visited her grandfather, Tullius, in the house of her uncle Quintus. Neither of them possessed Marcus' fluency with language or eloquence. They would walk together in the gardens of the house on the Carinae, in silence, hand in hand. But they communicated in spirit, and quite often Tullius, fading day by day, would suddenly turn to his tall young granddaughter and clasp her in his arms and shed his tears in her bright brown hair, which curled sweetly down her back. Sometimes they visited the temples together, and knelt without speaking or spoken prayer in the scented quiet. Both felt betrayed by son and by father.

Both detested the gleeful and slyly mischievous and ambiguous son of Quintus, and neither spoke of him. Tullia was afraid of Pomponia, who had a sharp and ready tongue. Pomponia once said to her, "Take nothing too seriously, my dear niece. More trouble is caused in the world by sober people without humor than men know of." Quintus, who loved Tullia because she so resembled his brother in appearance, would say, "My love, you are a joy to my heart."

One cold pale evening, shortly before the month of Janus, Tullia came into the library where her father, as usual, was writing. Marcus greeted her with fondness, and kissed the cheek she presented to him. She sat down, serenely conscious that he loved having her with him at this quiet hour. He put down his pen, smiled at her and said, "I have been considering who might, in the future, be an appropriate husband for you, my child. In the future," he added hastily.

"I shall be content to remain with you all my life, my father," she replied in her gentle voice.

He was flattered, but he shook his head. "That cannot be." She saw that he seemed unusually haggard and abstracted. He played with the pen on his table. He went on, though his thoughts were truly far from the subject: "You are being taught the arts of a wife and a mother from your own mother. Blessed will be the man who will take your hand in marriage. Later." He took up his pen to write again, and Tullia sat in her chair and lifted the book she had laid down the night before. The lamplight flickered; a cold draft blew the curtains at the windows. There would be snow soon, and wild winds. The great house was silent. The library was far from the women's quarters. Marcus poured a goblet of sweet wine for his daughter, and another not so sweet, for himself, and they drank in a contented silence. But all at once the pen was still in Marcus' hand and he stared before him grimly.

Aulus, the overseer of the atrium, knocked discreetly at the door and entered. "Lord," he said, "I have here a letter for you from a mysterious personage, cowled and cloaked, who did not show his face. He implored you to read and comprehend."

Marcus took the letter which was sealed bluntly but with no distinguishing marks. "You did not know him, Aulus?"

"No, lord." Marcus opened the letter. Tullia glanced up, watching her father's intent face. Marcus read:

"Greetings to the noble Marcus Tullius Cicero from an unknown friend:

"Beware! Your murder is plotted by those you know during the first week of the month of Janus. Ignore this message at your desperate peril. Guard your household and your comings and goings, and go nowhere without an armed escort."

"Father?" said Tullia, rising and moving toward Marcus' table. She had never seen him wear so frightful an expression before. He tried to smile, seeing her alarm. "It is late, child," he said. "I wish to be alone." He accepted her kiss. He said to Aulus, "Conduct the Lady Tullia to her apartments and command a slave to sleep on her threshold." After a moment he added, "Let other slaves sleep at each door and let each be armed."

"Yes, lord," said Aulus, in his subdued voice. "I shall also order armed slaves at the door of the atrium, and have them patrol the gardens."

Tullia was full of fear, but Aulus waited for her, bowing, and Marcus said, "Let us not be unduly alarmed. But let it be as I and Aulus say, my daughter."

When he was alone Marcus reread the letter. He was not especially surprised. His instinct had warned him weeks ago. He sank into thought. If his murder were plotted, then Rome was in dreadful danger also. He clapped his hands for Aulus, in order to send a slave for his brother, Quintus. All at once he was horribly frightened, not for himself but for his family and his country. Aulus entered, with a troubled face, and before Marcus could speak he said, "Lord, there is another mysterious personage, who has just arrived. He begs for an audience with you. Alone."

"He is armed?"

Aulus smiled discreetly. "With only a dagger, lord. But he also is cowled and cloaked, and his face hidden. He came on foot."

"Request that he give you his dagger, Aulus, then admit him to my library and stand prepared on the outside threshold."

Aulus asked no questions. He retreated and a moment later he brought with him a tall and sturdy figure swathed and cowled and silent. Aulus closed the door and the two men were alone.

"O cryptic one," said Marcus. "Reveal your face."

The visitor threw back his hood and Marcus saw the broad and impassive face of Pompey the Magnus staring at him with animated eyes.

"Greetings," said Marcus.

"Is your slave to be trusted, Cicero?" asked Pompey in a curiously pent voice.

"Yes."

"I hear his breath on the threshold outside the door."

"Yes."

Pompey, who appeared out of breath and enormously disturbed, flung himself heavily into a chair. "I trust no one," he said. "Order your slave to leave the door."

Marcus hesitated. He looked long into the eyes of Pompey, the man for whom he felt no liking and who had always shown him a cold friendliness. Then Marcus rose and went to the door and dismissed Aulus, after asking him to send for his brother.

"I see I must make my visit short," said Pompey. "I must be known by no one to have visited you tonight. Cicero, you are in danger of assassination."

Marcus gave him the letter. "Did you send this?" he asked.

Pompey read the letter, and started. At length he laid it down and stared blankly before him, still breathing as if he had been running. "So," he said. "You have another friend."

"Caesar?"

Pompey shook his head. "No," he said in a flat tone. "No, not Caesar."

"Not Crassus then."

Pompey was silent a moment, then he said, "It is quite true. Your death has been carefully plotted, and that is why I have come to you tonight. I do not wish to see you dead, for many reasons."

"Catilina for one?"

"Catilina."

Marcus sat back in his chair and the eyes of the two men held each other.

"You doubt this?" asked Pompey at last.

"No. I almost expected it." Marcus held the letter in his hand and gazed at the writing. "I do not know why you have come to me, for we are not friends. But still, I must thank you."

Pompey's expression was suddenly unreadable. He leaned toward Marcus and said in a low voice, "I am married to Caesar's daughter, that young girl. Nevertheless, I mistrust and fear him. He did not easily give his consent to your murder. In truth, he is distracted, and has left the city for his villa outside the walls."

"Why did he consent?"

Pompey smiled darkly. "He was left no choice, by Catilina, who is not only mad and who not only hates you, but believes you stand in the way—"

"Of whom?"

Pompey did not reply immediately. Then he said, "Of all of us."

"In what manner do I stand in your way?"

Pompey was silent. His huge and spraddled knees were bare under the cloak, but he wore military regalia. He rubbed his prominent lips with the back of his hand. "You do not know," he said after several moments.

"Tell me," said Marcus.

Pompey's mouth twisted. He looked at the vaulted ceiling of the library. He began to speak as if to himself: "I never trusted any of them. I am by nature and calling a soldier. A soldier's way is not the way of a Crassus or a Caesar. If power is to be seized then let it be seized openly in the way of brave men. Let it not be plotted, with hidden murder, and slyly, as a slave plots."

Pompey dropped his hand and gave Marcus a deep and cynical smile. "Have you forgotten, or never known, the power Catilina holds over the rabble? He threatened us all, even the mighty Crassus, with his degenerates and thieves and murderers. We were to move—" He stopped. "After your death," he added, drawing a deep gust of air.

"How were you to move, Pompey?"

Pompey stood up and made as if to turn away. Then he swung about and pressed his clenched fists down on Marcus' table and stared at him.

"By murdering the newly elected Consuls and putting our friends in their places. By making Catilina, that mad and dangerous Cerberus, Consul of Rome. In the first week of Janus."

Marcus stood up slowly, and trembled. He stood almost face to face with Pompey now and Pompey did not retreat. "Are they insane?" asked Marcus, incredulously.

"No. They—we—have waited long enough. For power."

"Do they not fear the anger of the people of Rome?"

Pompey threw back his large head and laughed and his big teeth glittered in the lamplight. "Cicero, Cicero!" he exclaimed. "Are you so innocent? Are you a schoolboy still, as Catilina asserts? The people forget their heroes almost before their ashes are cold. Do you still hope, Cicero, that this Rome is the Rome of your fathers? I tell you, loved though you are, that you could be murdered tomorrow and a week from now the people would not even speak your name. We could seize power by assassination of the Consuls, and the people would be momentarily hysterical, then be content to let matters go on serenely—if we graciously permit them. Did Scaevola teach you to no avail? Always you suspected plots. Yet now, confronted by the most desperate plot against Rome you stare at me with disbelief."

Marcus sat down and covered his face with his hands and Pompey watched him with derisive sympathy. The soldier said, "I came because I mistrust Caesar and fear for myself in the future if this miserable plot is successful. I came also because I honor you."

Pompey put his hood over his eyes again. "I am a soldier. I leave the solution in your hands. Forget I visited you. Remember only your safety. And Rome." He added the last as if in deep pain. A moment later the door closed after him and Marcus was alone.

When Quintus arrived his cloak was sprinkled with snowflakes and his robust face was red and he was breathless. He embraced his brother and cried, "You would not have sent for me at this hour of the night if there were no extremity."

"True," said Marcus. He asked, "How many trusted soldiers can you command?"

Quintus looked at him and the color left his face. "A legion," he said, and wet his lips.

"I do not ask for a legion. I ask only for trusted soldiers."

Quintus wrinkled his low brow and thought. Then he said, "I am greatly loved by my legion, which I command. However, I would trust only twenty men with my life. Or yours."

He took his brother in his arms and said fiercely, "Tell me!"

At that very hour the patient snow was falling, like mercy, over the vast city. It fell on the bridges and temples and buildings and alleys and streets and roofs. It invaded the Trans-Tiber in a silent veil of whiteness, covering noxious areas with the pure breath of freshness. It fell over an abandoned quarry in an ominous section of the Trans-Tiber, which was used for rubbish and the gatherings of dangerous outlaws. The guards were strangely absent this night, though the pit of the quarry was lit by scores of smoking and flaming torches, wavering in the white gloom. They caught the fierce or exalted profiles of many mantled men, young, middle-aged or old, lighting up sockets of fierce eyes or the line of a grim lip, turning a hand ruddy, revealing suddenly bared teeth or a brown brow. The walls of the firelit quarry contained them, and steam rose from their damp woolen garments. Some of the fitfully illuminated faces were patrician; many were rude and savage and coarse. Above the quarry loomed the black and stormy sky.

Catilina stood on a great rock and surveyed the men below him, and he smiled. He appeared like a magnificent god on his natural platform, in his military garb, woolen red trousers, brown leather harness over a red tunic, a deep crimson cloak over his shoulders, his helmet lighted with many jewels which glowed and flashed in the torchlight. He kept his hand on his short sword. His hands sparkled with gems, as did his wristlets. His figure was tall and lean and graceful, his face, though he was a middle-aged man, had the fire and animation of a youth and his blue eyes seemed to possess a flame of their own.

He began to speak in his vehement yet controlled and fascinating voice:

"I have gathered you here tonight, comrades, for a brief time to tell you that our hour has struck! Before another moon has waxed and waned your signal will be given, in the name of Rome and freedom and justice and social equality and humanity!

"What is our government today, under the Senate and the tribunes of the people and our courts? Privilege for a few! Slavery for the many! Scorn for the noble freedman, scorn for the worker, scorn for the humble! Advantage for the powerful and the established and the proud! Laws to protect the owners of vast lands and villas and rich town houses; laws to oppress those who are hungry and weary and whose eyes have never seen a gold sesterce! Can a nation call itself free and great if multitudes are hungry and have no hope? No! Each night, within the gates of this city tens of thousands of hopeless men and their families retire to their cots with empty bellies. Their labor cannot purchase for them a single satisfying meal; their labor cannot protect their children; they call themselves free, but I tell you that the lowest slave in the house of the rich is more fortunate than the average Roman! Is that justice? Is that dignified and worthy? No!"

The men roared back to him: "No! No! No!" Among them were not only envious patricians whose debauchery had made them penniless and had plunged them into debt, but discontented mercenaries who had fought

with the armies of Rome, failures in business, envious members of the
lower middle-class, pimps, gamblers, criminals, aging gladiators, wrestlers, drugged entertainers, disaffected malcontents always seeking a revolution which would elevate their inferiority to positions of command and
superiority over others, seekers of personal power, wanton wretches who
hated man and sought an avenue to control others and loot them, subver-
sives who had no loyalty to their country and lusted for the gold of others,
and, in the majority, the restless and craving scum of Rome who had no
allegiance by birth or ancestry to Rome, the polyglot rabble which has
always been the curse of States, and a few youths who believed that
violence in itself was enough to bring about the new glorious condition of
man.

Catilina listened to their wild roar, and he smiled darkly in himself,
despising his creatures who adored him, and who would follow him into
the very red hell of death itself in their infatuation and their hatred of the
strong, the valorous, the honorable, and the lawful.

"I tell you that I cannot see you tonight about me except with tears for
your sufferings, your wronged state, your disadvantaged misery, your un-
derprivileged torment! You have endured too long. Since the government
has fallen under the power and the jurisdiction of a few, kings and princes
have waited the habit of paying tribute to them all over the world; nations
and states pay them taxes. But all the rest of us, however brave and worthy,
whether patrician or plebeian, are looked upon by them as a mere mob,
without importance or to be reckoned with, and under the heels of those
whom, if things were right, we should be able to frighten out of their
minds! Hence all influence, power, and profit are in their hands, in their
gift. For us, they reserve only scorn, threats, persecutions, and poverty.
How long shall we endure this with meekness and humility? How long
now, you deprived fellows, are you going to endure this? Is it not better to
die trying to change the present order of things than to live weakly suffering their insolence in a wretched and bleak condition of poverty and infamy?"

"Yes! Yes!" roared the mob, clenching their right fists and raising them
high over their heads, to be caught in the fiery light of the torches.

"Dogs! thought Catilina. Sweet dogs, who will tear a path through flesh
for me to advance—and then to subjugate and enslave you! Serve me well,
dogs, and I will throw you a random bone or the crusts of my bread.

He waited for the slavering ovation to quiet. Hundreds of avid eyes
glowed and shone upon him in the torchlight; wet lips were licked; faces
burst into vehemence.

Catilina raised his gemmed hand as if taking a mighty oath. His beautiful face was fervid and shone like the face of a god with pity, excitement, and dedication.

"But I swear success will be easy! We are young, our spirit is unbroken. Our oppressors, on the contrary, are only worn-out old rich men. Therefore, we have only to make a beginning and the rest will follow!

"Comrades! The signal will soon be given! Prepare yourselves for the day! Our hour has struck!* For me, power to protect you; for you gold and liberty and loot! Rome is ours!"

The mob went out of its mind with exultation and adoring love and rage and hate. It swarmed about Catilina, kissed his hands, his knees, his feet. His fellow patricians embraced him, winked at him subtly, and smiled. Among them was Publius Clodius, surnamed Pulcher.

The early morning light fell grayly on Rome and revealed a thin layer of whiteness on the ground. The air was cold and damply wretched, and the roofs of the city fumed with moisture. Every house blew up a cloud of acrid smoke. There were few abroad as Marcus Tullius Cicero and his brother, Quintus, accompanied on horseback by twelve strong-faced soldiers, rode out of the city. The east was a dull and brazen smear before the rising of the sun.

They reached the house of Julius Caesar, but the slaves and guards at the gate, after one glance, did not halt the military horsemen and their leaders. They drew back meekly and opened the gates, then gathered together, whispering. The noble Cicero, Praetor of Rome, the noble Captain Quintus Cicero, and the officers of the legion dared not be challenged or questioned. The breath of the slaves and the guards drew together in a little cloud of agitation as they watched the company wheel rapidly up to the very house itself.

Quintus, in his full military costume, grim and terrible, alighted first, ran to the carved bronze doors and struck mightily on it with his armed fist. The echo of the blow resounded from the silent white countryside of the suburb. The horses blew streams of moisture from their nostrils. The other soldiers reined in the horses, then spread themselves in a phalanx before the house. The east brightened into pure brass. Marcus alighted and joined his brother, and his haggard face was leaden in the morning light. His cloak was covered with beads of water.

The doors swung open and the overseer of the hall blinked at them, affrighted. Marcus spoke. "I am Marcus Tullius Cicero, Praetor of Rome. Request the noble Julius Caesar to see me at once."

The overseer looked at the detachment of cavalry beyond the steps, and

---

* This whole speech by Catilina is no invention or fiction of the author's. It is quoted verbatim from the writings of Sallust, who was present on this occasion.

then at the dark face of Quintus. He bowed and visibly quaked. He admitted Marcus and Quintus to the warm and perfumed atrium where fountains tinkled placidly. He fled.

But the first to appear was the white-haired Aurelia, the mother of Julius, her stola hastily draped over her plump figure. She stared at Marcus with fearful eyes. "Marcus!" she exclaimed. "What is this, at this hour?" She turned her gaze on Quintus, and her fear grew. Quintus looked at her with the stony and withdrawn face of the soldier.

Marcus was taken aback. He had not expected Aurelia, whom he called "Aunt," to be present in this house. He took her fat white hands and kissed them and tried to force a reassuring smile on his lined face. "Dear Aunt," he said, "we have matters to discuss with Julius. Do not be alarmed, I beg of you."

"Dear Marcus, but it is very early, and very strange—I have been told that you have brought many cavalry soldiers with you."

Marcus bent and kissed her quivering cheek, and again tried to smile. "You know there are many robbers about these days, Aunt, and we set forth before it was hardly light. Romans are safe no longer, except when guarded."

"True," said Aurelia in a vague voice. But her shrewd black eyes still dwelled fearfully on Marcus. She clung to his hand, as if imploring. "Is there something wrong, my son?"

"No, nothing at all. I regret the early hour. But you know I have public duties as well as my law affairs. So it was necessary to come now."

"Necessary?" repeated Aurelia. Her plump face was veined with trembling wrinkles. But before Marcus could think of an answer a young and beautiful woman glided into the atrium, Pompeia, Julius' wife. Her long pale hair streamed over her shoulders and fell far down her back. She had a face like a lily, pale and smooth, and blue eyes so light that they appeared hardly to possess any color at all. She wore a long robe of a vaguely lavender hue, hemmed with gold, and despite the hour she was fragrant and composed, fingers and wrists bright with jewels. But her feet were prudently encased in gilded boots lined with white fur.

"Dear Marcus," she murmured, as he kissed her hands. "It is delightful to see you again."

She smiled bewitchingly. Her face was a little stupid but very lovely. Her light eyes beamed at him. Then she sighed. "My poor Julius, I regret to say, is unwell. He has had several seizures."

But it was Quintus who replied in a harsh voice, "We must see him." He ignored Marcus' angry glance. Aurelia put her hand to her shaking lips and stared at Marcus with renewed affright.

"It is not trivial," said Marcus. "I must see Julius. I trust he will arise."

Pompeia said, "Ah. He is not confined to his bed. Let me conduct you, Marcus, to Julius' audience chamber. He will be with you in a moment or two."

Aurelia's matronly face was still quivering with fear. She gave her daughter-in-law a curiously hard look, then said, "Do not keep him too long, Marcus."

"Be sure I will not," said Marcus, and touched her round shoulder with gentle affection. The women led him to Julius' private audience chamber, with Quintus clanking in the rear. Quintus, as he often did, thought Marcus hypocritical. The dangerous situation did not call for amenities to women and smooth conversation.

He said to his brother, when they were alone in the chamber, which was lined with shelves and cases filled with books, "How is it that you can bow and smile and speak softly when you and Rome are in a desperate condition?"

"Not so desperate that we must frighten innocent women unnecessarily."

Quintus grimaced. "Pompeia is not so innocent. I have heard rumors that she and Clodius are lovers. That is probably the explanation of Aurelia Caesar's presence."

The door opened and Julius Caesar entered, clothed in a long robe of crimson wool belted at his narrow waist with a broad girdle of gemmed gold. He had lost flesh; always thin, he was suddenly gaunt. But he moved with his usual litheness and he was smiling gayly. Marcus looked at him and saw his pallor which he had tried to conceal with a womanish color. His black eyes sparkled, but they were sunken. He came to Marcus at once and embraced him. Marcus noted, with some surprise, that the embrace was not casual but almost grateful, as if Marcus had rescued him from a danger recognized by both.

"I cannot tell you how happy I am to see you, dear Marcus!" said Julius. He held his friend off a little distance with his lean hands, then embraced him again. "But what is this I hear? You have come accompanied not only by our valorous Quintus, but with a detachment of cavalry."

Quintus said abruptly, "The protection was necessary."

"Ah," said Julius in an abstracted voice. He continued to regard Marcus with narrow questioning.

Marcus, who had not slept the night, felt his nerves come suddenly raw and he was filled with unusual impatience and anger.

"Julius, you are not under arrest, as of this moment. But let us not gracefully bow and lie and dance like debased entertainers. Let us throw our dice cleanly and speak to each other like men, for a change. I am sorry you are sick. But I have no time."

Julius inclined his head. He sat down, as if suddenly exhausted and undone. "Be seated, if you please," he said. Marcus seated himself stiffly in an ivory and ebony chair, but Quintus remained nearby, his hand on his sword.

"Julius," said Marcus, "I have come on some information." And he tossed the anonymous letter onto Julius' knees. Julius lifted the letter in his hand; his fingers shook though he continued to smile. He read the letter. His face changed, tightened, and he moistened his lips. Then a long trembling ran over his body and a blob of foam appeared at the corners of his mouth. He gasped. He put his hand to his throat. He said in a stifled voice, "Water. Quickly."

There was a golden ewer with water on the dark marble table, and a goblet. Marcus quickly poured the water into the vessel and thrust it at Julius' lips. Julius' brow flushed deeply and the skin seemed to thicken. The tendons stood out on his neck; his breast heaved. He swallowed the water loudly and with obvious difficulty. His body was rigid and quaking. Then his hands clenched tightly and he bent his head forward and gasped over and over. Marcus watched him with reluctant concern, but Quintus' face was bitter and remote.

Long moments passed in silence except for the labored breathing of the stricken man. New sunlight struck through the windows onto the white marble floor and glinted on the backs of gilded books. There was the merry sound, at a distance, of slaves pursuing their morning tasks. Then, at last, Julius lifted his head. He was paler than death itself and the false color on his cheeks was pathetic. But he smiled.

"What means this foolish letter?" he asked and his voice was almost normal.

"I do not know," said Marcus. Then he said in a cold voice, "Do you, Julius?"

"I? I confess it seems mad to me. What enemies do you have?"

"You, Julius?"

Julius stared at him incredulously. "I, Marcus? Do I—"

" 'Not love you as a brother?' I have heard that before. But brothers have murdered each other often in history, notably Romulus who murdered Remus. Do you wish me dead, Caesar?"

"Never, never," said Julius, and his voice was suddenly a groan. "You must believe me."

"I do," said Marcus. "Wait. Hear me out. There is not only this letter, which was delivered to me last night by a mysterious visitor. I know many other things. I know that it is plotted to kill our elected Consuls in the first week of Janus. I, to prevent interference, was to be murdered first. Do you deny it, Caesar?"

Julius suddenly got to his feet, then stood in the middle of the room gazing about him strangely as if he did not know where he was. He said, "I know nothing of all this. You speak wildly. Some madman wrote you that letter. I swear to you—"

"By your patron, Jupiter?"

Julius was silent. He raised his head and looked at Quintus, whose hand was on his sword and whose soldier's face was fierce with menace.

"Let us be done with lies and evasions, Julius," said Marcus. "I could arrest you immediately, and have you thrown into prison to await trial as a conspirator against Rome. Do you wish that?"

Julius gave a great sigh. He fumbled for his chair and sat down again. He began to smile palely. He shook his head. "You have always spoken of plots and conspiracies, Marcus. But I believed you were a temperate and sensible man. Never did I suspect that you would resort to such a show —of strength and tragedy—like a badly written play."

"Do you wish me to arrest you at once, and then arrest Pompey, Catilina, Piso, Curius, and all the others? Speak, Caesar!"

Marcus' voice was loud and clear and sharp in the library, and Julius' features drew together as at a stroke of unbearable pain. Julius said, "These are reckless words. Have you forgotten that Crassus is dictator of Rome, and the mightiest man of all? I do not understand you! You have brought me a foul and unsigned letter, and you expect me to take it seriously!"

"You take it seriously enough," said Marcus. "Crassus is indeed dictator of Rome. Nevertheless, the army is mightier than Crassus and he fears it. Shall I give the word to my brother, who commands a legion, to seize all of you, to await trial and execution for crimes against our country? Look you, Caesar. I am capable of doing all this and well you know it. Do not believe Crassus will interfere!"

Julius raised a tremulous hand and rubbed the back of it against his sweating brow. "I know nothing," he said. "There is no plot against the Consuls and you. If there is, I am no party to it and never heard of it."

"Liar," said Marcus, calmly. "You know you lie, and are not ashamed."

Julius was silent. His breath was loud in the room.

"The lust for power in you, Julius, will never die. You were born with it. I know not if you will succeed; Rome is debauched. It is very possible that I cannot oppose you or stop the ruin of my country. She has fallen too far to be saved.

"I can destroy you at this moment, Julius. If Quintus thrusts his sword into your body now, who shall try him or reproach him? The military is more powerful than any of you, including Crassus. And I have only to reveal my knowledge, which is complete, of all your plots, to have the people unanimously and enthusiastically acclaim my brother."

Marcus prayed that Julius would accept his word and not challenge him. Julius had lifted his head and was regarding him with a piercing expression, as if seeking to discover all that which he suspected Marcus knew, but which in fact he did not really know. The two pairs of eyes held each other. Quintus moved a step closer to Julius and his sword was half-drawn.

Julius smiled. "If there is such a plot—and I deny it and laugh at it—I know nothing of it. Who listens to Catilina, who is mad? It is possible that he has conjured up something in his madness, and you have heard some ridiculous rumor. I tell you that he shall be warned—if he has such a plot."

"Good," said Marcus. "That is all I need to know. Beware, Caesar. The road to power is not taken by foolish and heedless men, with vile little conspiracies."

"I agree with you with all my heart," said Julius. "I am a soldier."

"You are no true soldier of Rome," said Quintus with disgust. "Listen well to me, Julius. If my brother dies, or the Consuls are murdered, the army will seize Rome. I promise you that, fervently."

"And that," said Marcus in a mild voice, "would not be the best fate for Rome. Do you agree with that also, Caesar?"

"I agree," said Julius again. He clapped his hands loudly on his knees, and could force himself to laugh. "What a comedy this is!"

"Let it remain one," said Marcus, and stood up and fastened his cloak. "I have refrained from arresting you and delivering you and your companions up to justice not out of fear of you but because I fear the rule of the military more. One remembers Sulla and his iron dictatorship. I recall Sulla with some affection, for he was a true soldier. But, Caesar, there are some generals who are not in the least like Sulla. They too lust for power. I have chosen the lesser evil."

He was encountered by Aurelia in the hall. He took her hand quickly and pressed it. She gazed in fear at his face and whispered, "All is well, Marcus?"

"All is well, dear Aunt," he replied kindly. And he added to himself, At least temporarily.

Julius looked at Crassus, Pompey, Curius, Piso, and Catilina. "I told you all it was a hasty plot from the very beginning. A miserable one, as Pompey warned us. It was your impatience, Catilina, and yours, Piso and Curius, which forced us into it. We shall succeed, eventually, but not by childish recklessness and impulsiveness and boyish enthusiasm. We must move with a semblance of law and the weight of inexorable dignity. That will not come tomorrow. What we do must appear rightful, and in the course of human events and inevitable history. Murdering duly elected

Consuls! Was there ever such a ludicrous idea! Piso and Curius: You were the ones to suggest it. You communicated your feverish imaginings to Catilina, who then challenged us. Now we see the whole absurdity in full."

"I cannot wait," said Catilina through his teeth. "I have already alerted my followers."

But Julius ignored him, and shook his head, smiling, at Piso and Curius.

"Crassus and Pompey and I never believed in success for a moment. I am glad Cicero discovered it all. He has done us a great service. Still, I am interested to know who sent Cicero that anonymous letter. Only we here knew of the plot."

"You, Caesar?" said Catilina in a furious voice.

"I?" Julius looked at him with contempt.

Catilina flung himself from the chair. They were all in the house of Crassus. "Someone did!" cried Catilina. "I will have his life!"

"I wrote him no letter," said the impassive Pompey. "I leave anonymous letters to cowardly rascals."

"I wrote him none," said Crassus, with a faint dark smile. "Nor I. Nor I," said the others.

"Still, he knew," said Julius. He turned to Catilina. "Murder Cicero, and you will have all Rome at our throats."

He said in the silence that followed, "Now, let us consider the way of sensible and courageous men, and not boys."

Later, when he was alone with Crassus and Pompey, Julius said, "I should order Catilina's murder at once if he did not have that unspeakable rabble at his hand. He should have been poisoned, as he poisoned his wife and child, long ago before he became so powerful. Now we have to reckon with him."

"And, there are his friends, the fair-haired Piso and the drunken Curius," said Crassus. "Am I dictator, or am I the tool of these reprobates?"

"A dictator, dear lord, is the carrier of reprobates always," said Julius. "He collects them as a great ship collects barnacles. But the day will come when we can scrape them away! After they have served our purpose."

CHAPTER FIFTY

When Tullia, his daughter, had been born, the lucent light of Greece still illuminated Marcus' thoughts, so that in spite of his deeper convictions he felt there was hope in the future and that many things could be accomplished by himself and his country which would be worthy. He had, then, been young, and the birth of his daughter seemed to him the very living continuity and brightness of life, the finger of hope pointing vividly to years still unborn, the ever-renewed promise of mornings as fresh as the rose.

Now, this warm summer day Terentia lay in labor and Marcus tried to think with some interest of the coming child. He had joyfully anticipated the birth of Tullia; he had held her in his arms with pride and love. He shrank from the very thought of his second born, who had not been begotten in affection and hope but only in guilt and sadness. He said to his child, Why did I beget you, poor forlorn one, who deserves better of me? I do not long to see your small face. I have no future to offer you but your disintegrating and violated country. I have no joy to give you, out of my middle-aged heart which lies in darkness and fear. Even my father had more to lay at my feet than I have to lay at yours. Forgive me, that I have given you life.

He sat in his gardens and did not hear the physician approaching him, and he started when the man spoke. "Lord, the Lady Terentia has given birth to a son! She asks for a moment with you."

A son, thought Marcus, heavily rising and going into his fine big house. My son, Marcus Tullius Cicero. Terentia, glowing with triumph and appearing almost young again, greeted him with joyous tears and showed him the child on her arm. "Marcus!" she cried. "I—we—have a son!" There was no sadness, no doubts, no fear in her. She thought of life as a thing which never moved, never changed, and was never ominous. The birth of her child was her personal victory.

Marcus looked at the face of his son. He thought it appeared old and exhausted, as if the burden of its coming life had already drained it. Marcus bent over the child, and then he noticed the heavy marking and prominence of his brows, the firm little lips, the strongly molded chin, and he thought, The child resembles my grandfather! For the first time the bright wing of forgotten hope touched his heart. Romans were still being born.

Marcus then suggested to Terentia, whose sallow cheek he had just kissed, that slaves be sent to the house of Quintus to announce the news. Terentia, raising an eyebrow and smiling indulgently, informed her husband that messengers had already been sent by her. "How I pity Quintus and Pomponia for the son they have!" she exclaimed. "Mischievous and sly, cruel and heartless even for his age!" This was quite true, but Marcus frowned and drew away from his wife. His newborn son opened his eyes, and they were a dark and shining blue with a star in their depths.

Marcus encountered the young Tullia in the atrium, waiting for him. Seeing her, he took her in his arms and she looked up at him with tender mockery. "Am I still the first in your heart, my father?" she asked. "Always," he replied, and kissed the soft pallor of her cheek. Then he said, "But I shall not always be first in yours."

In the coming days he was felicitated on the birth of his son. Grateful clients sent lavish gifts; relatives of the Helvii family, forgetting their innate frugality, became prodigal, and Terentia's own relatives competed with each other. "It is as if they are signaling approval of me," said Marcus, "after a long dereliction and an obstinate refusal to have a son." Julius Caesar came in person with a purse of rubies, the purse itself being woven of gold. It was an awesome gift, and considering that Marcus and Julius had not met since that winter day at Julius' house, it was in the nature of a peace offering.

"I see that you have perfectly recovered your health, Julius," said Marcus. The younger man raised a black eyebrow. "No doubt," continued Marcus, "because I am still alive."

Julius answered blandly, "Is it never possible for you, Cicero, to speak directly?"

"Come," said Marcus, smiling. "You are not that obtuse. By the way, when will the fair Pompeia bear you a son also?"

Julius, who was yearly becoming more splendid, sighed and said, "She remains obdurately infertile. I am fated, it appears, never to have a son." Marcus raised his own eyebrows, thinking of a certain young Brutus, but he held his tongue. After all, it was not every day that so magnificent a gesture as this gift was made. While they were speaking in Marcus' garden, which was thronged with guests eating and drinking and gossiping, Pompey the Magnus arrived. At once the perceptive Marcus discerned that an apparent coolness existed between him and Julius, for though they embraced, their greetings were indifferent if polite. Ah, thought Marcus, it is always so when ambitious men grow suspicious of each other. But he felt kindly toward Pompey, who had saved his life, and accepted his gift for the infant with real gratitude, happy that he could indirectly express another gratitude of which he could not speak. As Marcus was rarely effusive, the sharp-eyed Julius felt a query pluck at his sleeve. It were as though Marcus were greeting one who was dear to him or who had conferred a great honor upon him. Pompey's broad and impassive face lighted also, and his hand lingered for a moment on Marcus' arm, and his full gray eyes beamed agreeably.

Then Pompey turned to Julius and said, "Where is your slave, Mark Antony, that fatuous young man, Caesar?"

"He is recovering today from a feast in my house last night," said Julius. He paused. "And how fares my daughter, your wife, Pompey?"

The air was soft and filled with the heat and fragrance and shine of summer, but Marcus, suddenly alert, thought that he had heard the clash of open swords under the din of laughter and voices in the gardens. Julius continued with lightness, "Though you may consider Antony fatuous, dear friend, he has notable qualities. He is an excellent soldier, and has a beguiling manner, and is a marvelous success with the ladies, endowments which must not be despised."

The mere presence of these men reminded Marcus acutely of the terrible plot against Rome and himself which had almost succeeded, and melancholy came to him. It seemed to him that the sun was less bright, and color less intense, and that his son was threatened. He had lived long enough with his premonitions not to scorn them any longer, and alarm lifted like a black wing before his eyes. Was the plot surely over at all? He knew these men well, and Crassus, and Catilina, and even Clodius. Why had he thought, these past months, that all was tranquil again, danger past, and a measure of peace restored? Men like Caesar were sleepless, and could wait like tigers in the dark of the forest for a larger prey to appear, if the smaller had escaped.

Marcus, reflecting, did not know that his face had become very white and that his eyes had fixed themselves on a space as if seeing some terror unseen by others. He did not know that Julius and Pompey were both regarding him with a quick interest and gravity, and he started when Julius said, "What is that our augur sees, that has darkened the happiness of his expression?"

Marcus started, then flushed. "I am no augur, Julius," he replied with some vexation. "I was merely considering how dangerous a world this is into which I have brought a son."

"Is it not always dangerous?" asked Julius, smiling again but still watching his friend. "It was dangerous to our fathers, also."

"They did not know traitors," said Marcus, and then was appalled at his own words which had been uttered in his own gardens to his own guests. Pompey and Caesar exchanged a glance, and all at once the coolness between them disappeared, and they laughed.

"Our dear Marcus!" exclaimed Julius. "He is obsessed with plots. He is not only a praetor, but he was born one. Tell me, Marcus, what plot do you suspect now?"

"A larger one than your conspiracy of before, Caesar."

"I know of no conspiracy, Marcus."

"Nor," said Pompey, with an easy gesture, "do I." His gray eyes were no longer beaming; it was as if some glaucous veil had fallen over them. So, thought Marcus, this time I shall not be warned. He tried to shake free of his despondency, but the small face of his son rose before him and his alarm cried louder, as a disturbed flock of crows cry as they wheel before the sun.

"It is time for our daughter to be married," said Terentia, after the family had returned from its annual sojourn on the island. Terentia saw none of the beauty of the island; she busied herself solely with the counting of sheep and the ordering of the slaves. She was an urban woman and grudged the weeks in the country.

"She is only a child," said Marcus, and then he said somewhat pettishly, "You, my wife, were a mature woman when we were married and not one just past her puberty." Then he was ashamed of himself, for Terentia's face, now so unattractive, colored. Her eyes, once mild and retiring, and her best feature, had narrowed and hardened over the years so that they resembled brown crystals between brownish lids.

"I had family affairs to concern me, and the care of a younger sister," she said.

Because her tone was wounded and her hurt sincere, Marcus became penitent and wished to please her. "Let us discuss a husband, then," he said. "Who?"

"Young C. Piso Frugi," said Terentia at once. "He is of an excellent family, and is seventeen years old, and his grandfather has left him a fortune. He will also inherit from his own parents, who are friends of my family."

Marcus knew the young man, who seemed fair enough of face and patrician enough of manner, but otherwise not distinguished. He considered only a prince or potentate worthy of his beloved Tullia.

"Or," said Terentia, who was very ambitious, "there is young Dolabella, who is a youth of much brilliance and of one of the greatest families of Rome."

"The gods forbid," cried Marcus with real horror, and Terentia smiled with satisfaction. She gave a resigned sigh. "Then, it is Piso Frugi," she said, and it was not until a little later that Marcus realized that Terentia, as usual, had cast a loaded die against him.

Terentia, having won, continued: "But we shall delay the marriage until you are Consul of Rome."

"Then the marriage will be forever delayed," said Marcus, restored to good humor.

He was devoted to his children. Like most fathers he considered his own offspring extraordinary. Little Marcus, he was convinced, would be a great philosopher, though the child each day was displaying a certain obstinacy which did not augur well for a pale man of the colonnades. Terentia delighted in him. "He will be a great soldier and athlete," she said, and Marcus so perceptive when considering others outside his family, laughed at her. "He will speak Greek fluently before he is three," he told his wife. He did not really see the strong color in little Marcus' face, and the new laughter in the infant's eyes. He told himself he had seen the grave soul of his son when the child had only just emerged from the womb.

"You have seen your father?" said Terentia, as she nursed her son with the outright honesty of an "old" Roman mother. "Surely Quintus was too much alarmed when he wrote you while we were on the island?"

Marcus was ashamed again. Quintus had written him twice during the summer, saying that Tullius was "declining hourly and the physician says that his heart will not endure much longer." But Marcus had told himself that he could not remember a time from his own childhood that Tullius had not been "dying," and that it was an old story, and the Tullii lived to great ages. But the truth was that Marcus did not want to think of his father, or even to see him. The old sense of guilt and exasperation was always alive in him when his father was mentioned. He had seen him only twice during Terentia's pregnancy, and only once thereafter. Tullius had congratulated him in a faint voice, and with imploring eyes, when the little Marcus had been born, but Marcus had had the impression that Tullius was not fully aware—as he had never been aware—of natural events, and that the birth of another grandson had not been a momentous occasion to him. Resentfully, Marcus had told himself: My father was always straining after the stars and forgetting the boulders in his path, and had never truly placed his feet upon the earth. As Marcus, himself, suspected that this was not entirely true, his own sense of guilt only exasperated him the more. It was too painful for him to analyze his own emotions with regard to Tullius, for then he would remember days when his father had appeared to him as a pale and slender god, with lighted eyes and a tender hand and a voice filled with love and understanding. But one's childish impressions are always a delusion, he would remind himself, and would resolutely think of a Tullius who had depended upon a father for strength, a wife for comfort and guidance, a son for paternal solicitude and help, and a younger son, at the last (with his wife) for a parentage. Quintus had taken his father into his house as one takes an orphaned child, and had sturdily nurtured him and with his particular easy affection.

Marcus said, in reply to Terentia's questions, "I have never known a time in my life, from the earliest childhood, when my father was not expiring. If it was not congestion of the lungs it was malaria. Quintus knew of the day of our returning from the island, and three days have elapsed, and we have heard no word. Were my father in danger we should know it."

But Terentia had great sense of family. She said, with reproof, "Nevertheless, as you have not seen your father for months, you should go to him at once."

"Tomorrow," said Marcus, impatiently. "My father is only sixty years old, and I assure you that he will survive for much longer."

But the next morning, a cold autumnal dawn, Marcus received an imperative summons from his brother, Quintus. Tullius was on his deathbed, and unconscious. Marcus rose, not believing the news in the least. But he went to the house of Quintus on the Carinae, yawning in his litter and shivering a little, and feeling impatient. Beyond the curtains of the litter the mighty city was awakening and the thunder of traffic and feet and voices had begun. It was an old and familiar sound, and no longer exciting. That is the trouble with growing older, thought Marcus gloomily. There is no more newness in the world, no more surmise. No more wonder. What can console one for the loss of these? Life for me now is only a retreat, and what is a sunrise for the young is a sunset for me. As for adventure, I can no longer expect it, if indeed it ever came to me at all. After forty, a man is hardly alive. I live now only for my children, and it must be enough.

Marcus was still yawning when his litter arrived at the old house on the Carinae, which was at once so familiar to him and yet now so strange. It was a house of dreams and of the past, and every room was known to him, and the garden, and it was full of memories clear and sharp, or dimmed and unreal. He was always a little astonished when he saw it again, as if he had believed that it no longer existed, as his childhood and his youth no longer existed. Yet here he had wept for Livia, and here his grandfather had died, and here his future had seemed full of excitement and passion and hope. Here his old friends had walked, friends gone forever. The house remained. Yet it was not quite the house he remembered, and he could not explain it. It breathed the very subtlety of time.

Quintus, the tall and burly soldier, met him at the door and not the overseer of the hall, and Quintus was weeping. Then Marcus knew immediately that his father was dead, and he steadied himself on his brother's arm, feeling weak and undone and stricken. For all at once the house had suddenly come into focus before his eyes, and it was as he remembered, and it was a house of death, which he also remembered. The house no longer was the refuge of an unworldly old man who inspired his older son with mingled exasperation and guilt. It was the house of a father, and in his death he was more alive than he had seemed since Marcus' early youth.

Tullius lay on his bed in his small cubiculum which Marcus himself had occupied when he had lived here as a child, a youth, and a young unmarried man. The curtains over the small window had not yet been drawn. The first dull beams of cold sun fell over Tullius' face and revealed it fully. It was not a face Marcus remembered. It was a calm, remote face, cleansed of the dusty webs of living and all its pains. That which had brought it age and uneasiness and torment had fled, leaving the exorcised flesh behind to join its peaceful earth. This was no longer Marcus Tullius Cicero the Elder; this was the tranquillity of tree and grass undisturbed by the alien human spirit.

Marcus looked at his father's hands, which were no longer wrinkled, but placid as marble. These, too, were not the hands he remembered. He bent and touched their coldness with his lips, and on the moment of touching he was completely alienated from the effigy on the bed, as he would have been alienated from stone. He murmured a prayer for his father's spirit, but felt it a mockery for his father had no need of his prayers, he who had lived as sinless a life as possible and had never been part of the world he had thankfully deserted. He turned and left the chamber followed by Quintus, who was disturbed by his brother's calm and vaguely resented it. Quintus blurted, "You never loved him. Therefore, you feel no sorrow."

Marcus hesitated. His brother would not understand if he could even find the words for what he felt. So he put his hand gently on the broad shoulder of Quintus and said, "We all have different ways of expressing grief."

But in the days that followed—and during the terrible panoply of death accompanying them—he was struck by the inconstancy of life and its fragility and by a sense of its meaninglessness, and, incongruously, by the mortification of death. His own existence was less secure because his father no longer existed. Another statue had crashed in his hall of life and its senseless rubble littered the floor.

CHAPTER FIFTY-ONE

Noë ben Joel wrote to his friend from Jerusalem:

"Greetings, dearest friend! You have written to me in the kindest manner, with no hint of condescension or even of majesty! Yet, you have been elected Consul of Rome, the mightiest office of the mightiest nation in the world! How I rejoice, and with what affectionate amusement I recall your earlier letters in which you expressed your pessimism that such an office was within your reach! You did not believe for an instant that the Senatorial party (the Optimates) would support you, for always you have known their resentment and suspicion of the 'new men,' the middle-class. You claim that you received this support only because they feared the deranged and malignant Catilina more, who was one of the six candidates running for the same office against you. You defame yourself with this modesty; even venal Senators can sometimes be moved by the spectacle of public and private virtue and will support a wise man. Nor did you believe that the 'new men,' your own, would support you, out of envy that you were rising above them. Nor did you believe that the People's party (the populares) would cast their votes in your behalf, for in these later years you have expressed, with bitterness, your conviction that the people prefer rascals who flatter, pamper, and buy them with gifts to a man who promises only that he will attempt to restore republican grandeur and honor to their nation, and speaks, not in glowing capitals of more and more free benefits to a depraved citizenry, but in the stern voice of patriotism.

"Yet, all the people whom you mistrusted did not resort to the slow ballot at all, but unanimously elected you with acclamations, at once vehement and enthusiastic! You did not write of this to me, but I have other friends in Rome who have kept me informed concerning you through these years. You are greatly beloved, for all you complain that you are considered inconsistent, and for all your natural shyness and reserve. Moreover, God has strange ways of manifesting Himself when He realizes that a nation is in grave peril. Often, as in the history of Israel, He has called men from private lives and far places to lead their people to safety and life, when most threatened and most undone. I like to believe that He intervened in your behalf, out of love for you, and to save Rome from Catilina, in spite of bribes and lies and promises. But never must we forget that it was the people, at the last, who elected you in one spontaneous burst of affection and pride in you, and love of your genius and manhood.

"Some time ago you wrote me that you felt that your life had come to an end, and that you faced the brick wall of ultimate achievement. Yet a door appeared in that wall, and led you to an infinite city of power and glory! Was not Moses only an unknown shepherd when God called to him to deliver His people, an exile known to none though he had been a prince in Egypt and beloved of his mother, the princess? He had fallen, through righteous anger and sorrow and grief, to the very abyss of loneliness and homelessness, in a far place, and believed that his life had ended. But, how great is God, and All-knowing! He prepared His prince in silence and in exile for a mighty destiny, greater than that of any man who has ever been born to this world. So long as man lives the name of Moses will live, and, as I feel prophetic at this hour, the name of Cicero will never pass away so long as men have tongues and memories and history is written.

"Though you are amazed, you confess, and bewildered and bemused by your election, I am none of these. I expected heroic things of you since we were children together. Did I not always tell you of this? The light of the Finger of God lay on your brow even as a youth, and I saw it, and do not accuse me of the extravagances of one who still writes plays and has a rich imagination!

"Even our wily and serpentine friend, Julius Caesar, supported you, and Crassus, himself. For what reason? God had moved their souls in your behalf, though you say they probably preferred you to Catilina for reasons of their own. Caesar, too, seems fast in the races also, for even before you wrote to me of him I had heard that he had been named Pontifex Maximus and Praetor of Rome. You regard this with your usual misgivings. But one must remember that men of force and ambition and intellect, such as Caesar, also inevitably arrive at power, and this too may be the will of God, Whose ways are exceeding mysterious. I agree that Caesar is a villain, but God often uses villains as well as good men, for His purposes. You doubt his patriotism. However, it is not absolutely impossible for a villain to be patriotic!

"You have a son of whom you boast is, at the age of two, already a prodigy. How can he be otherwise with such a father? Do I not read your increasing writings, and your books, which friends in Rome send to me? I thought I was eloquent. Alas, compared with you I am a stone donkey. I rejoice with you in your beautiful young daughter's marriage to the patrician, Piso Frugi, for I know how dear she is to your heart. Again, you express misgivings, but I detect in them the natural jealousy of a father of his one and beloved daughter. You would have her marry, for it is natural for girls to marry, but on the other hand you prefer that she not love another and leave your house! I felt so when my own daughter married, and when I delivered her under the canopy I hated her espoused husband and feared that he would make her unhappy. Nevertheless, she is happy and I am a grandfather and rejoice in the little ones who sit on my knee and adore me with their big eyes.

"I often contemplate how strange it is that our fathers died two years ago on the same day and possibly the same hour. You wrote me that you did not grieve for him or miss him until almost six months had passed, and then you were stricken, fearing that you had not shown him enough affection in his life and that you had caused him pain. But so I felt when my own father died, and I recalled his admonitions in my youth and how I disdained them as the prattlings of an aged and old-fashioned man. You should feel content that your father has been delivered from living, for did not Socrates maintain that a good man has nothing to fear in this life nor the one following?

"You wrote me of Caesar's infatuation with his newborn nephew, grandson of his sister, Gaius Octavianus Caesar. Caesar does not possess a son as you do, at least not one he can publicly acknowledge. This is always a bitterness to an ambitious man, who thinks of dynasties.

"You write ominously of Catilina, and you fear his present obscurity more than you feared him when he was Praetor of Rome. You say: 'It is better to have your mortal enemy in full sight than to have him hidden and know not what he is doing in his dark silences.' That may be true. But that he is in disfavor with Caesar and Crassus and Pompey, and all his friends should reassure you, for they are not reckless and heedless men. Be sure their eyes pierce his darkness and that they are sleepless concerning him.

"You ask me again of the Messias, though more tentatively than usual. He is still hourly expected! The Pharisees send priests up and down the length of Israel searching for the Mother and the Holy Child, while the worldly Sadducees laugh at them. For the Sadducees call themselves pragmatic men, and scorn any teachings of the world hereafter and ridicule the prophecies of the Messias. They prefer Hellenistic reason. They pause in their gilded litters when a ragged rabbi, whose feet are dark with dust, speaks of Bethlehem and the One Who is to be born there of a Maiden Mother, the Lily of God. But they pause to express mirth and to shake their heads in wonder at the credulity of the poor and the homeless, who long for their Savior Who shall be called Emmanuel, for He will deliver His people from their sins. But I no longer smile with the Sadducees. Each night I stand in the cool brightness of the moon and the stars on the roof of my house and question Heaven: 'Is He born this hour, and where shall I find Him?'

"I embrace you with the arms of my soul, dearest friend, beloved Cicero. If we do not meet again in life, be assured that we shall meet beyond the grave, where the glory grows more imminent each day, and which will surely burst forth soon upon the world like a new sun."

If Marcus Tullius Cicero, even as Consul of Rome, continued to nurture misgivings and vague alarms and doubts, his wife, Terentia, glowed with elation and joy and contentment. She was now the first lady in Rome. Her litter, magnificent and carried by four huge Nubian slaves in gorgeous array, was recognized on the street and saluted. Her house on the Palatine thronged with ladies of high and patrician birth, seeking her intercessions in behalf of their ambitious husbands. She condescended graciously to them, and promised them what they asked, and duly presented the petitions to her husband with queenly words and queenly gestures, as one presents gifts. She could not understand his frowns and his impatient words, and his annoyance, and his assertions that if the petitions had merit he would consider them in his own orderly time. She thought him prosy and dull. Often she wondered how he had attained such high estate, a "new man," a man of no high birth and a mere lawyer who had once been Praetor of Rome, and a man who did not surround himself solely with the powerful. She came to the extraordinary conclusion that Cicero was Consul only by the mysterious grace of her own merits, which the gods had honored publicly, and her virtues which they admired. For surely Cicero did not deserve what had been laid at his feet, for he had no splendor of appearance and he wrote books and essays which few among her friends appeared to have read, and his tastes were austere even though he lived in a tremendous house on the Palatine. He often walked to the Forum and to his offices on foot on fair days, which was plebeian of him.

Finally she concluded that he owed all things to her, for had she not stimulated him to try for the greatest of offices, and had she not been sleepless in her urgings, and was not her family very distinguished? Her innate genius was manifest in the fact that she had been able to secure a husband for her daughter who was of a great house. Without her, Cicero would have remained an obscure lawyer dependent on the good will and indulgence of petty magistrates. When friends said to her, "Cicero is greatly beloved of the people, and the Senators bow to him," she smiled cryptically and raised her eyebrows in a peculiar and knowing fashion. When Crassus kissed her hand, or Caesar, or Pompey, and complimented her on her husband and declared that they rejoiced in him and all that he was, she was absolutely convinced that they were really complimenting her, and lowering their mighty heads in admiration of her character, her dauntlessness, her valor and her attributes.

Terentia, who had never been devoted to Tullia, said to her daughter, "What fortune has come to us, and honor, and glory, and adulation, is due solely to my efforts and do not forget that, my daughter, if you ever are puffed up with pride because of your father."

Tullia, alarmed, began to consider her mother mad but her young husband, Piso, laughed merrily and said, "Your mother is swollen with her own vanity and she is becoming old. Therefore, permit her to have her conceits."

"But she has nothing but contempt for my wise father, who is the noblest man in Rome, and that is unpardonable, my husband, and not to be understood."

"It is not unknown," said the young Piso, "that the family of an acclaimed man believe they have really accomplished his fame, themselves, and that it is a mischief and an injustice on the part of the gods that they do not receive those acclamations instead. For, are they not worthier, wiser, more intelligent, more learned, than the hero?"

I care nothing for adulation and public honors, Cicero would think. They weary me and take my time, which should be devoted only to my God and my country. What is famous today is thrown to the dust tomorrow, with execrations. I love law and justice and I will work for them, though there is such a weariness in my heart and such a premonition of disaster. My very bones ache with tiredness; I shrink from the hailings of my fellows. What is it that has come to me, that I should be convinced that nothing is of worth among men?

He consulted physicians. They could not understand his sickness of spirit. They told him with respectful indulgence that he did not truly cringe from public honor, for did not all politicians crave it? Why else did they strive? They thought Cicero precious.

"Do not all lesser men envy you, lord?" they asked him with envy.

"I do not want envy," he said. They were incredulous, and they gave him potions and pills and told each other that he was affected and that he desired greater honors and more wealth. And so he created more enemies for himself, who whispered meaningly of him and murmured of his avaricious ambition.

In the meantime he worked prodigiously, and only in his work, dedicated to his country, and to the moral law and virtue, did he find surcease for the strange pain that lay at his heart like a sickness. He found personal pleasure in his daughter and his son, but his wife was a weariness to him and a vexation. He began to suffer from headaches the moment he returned to his house, and a curious but overwhelming fatigue. He had already tired of Clodia, who was now more interested in young Mark Antony and his virility in any event, for his youth gave her a feeling that she, too, was young again. No other woman, in the duress of his days and his awesome responsibilities, attracted Cicero.

C. Antonius Hybrida, a patrician in early middle-age, a man of wealth, style, and presence, had won the second place as Consul of Rome after Cicero, and therefore became his colleague. Like many wealthy patricians his manners and thoughts and mode of living were easy and tolerant. He detested vehement and insistent men, and men given to outbursts of passion—except if they were patricians like himself. It was not that Antonius was arrogant or haughty; he truly believed that the gods had created a few who were superior to the many, and therefore that few should rule by divine right. Accepting his native superiority as a matter of fact, he was therefore free of envy and overweening ambition. He was much loved in Rome for his democratic approach to the people, to whom he never condescended because he felt assured that they understood that the gods had created him their master, and honored the gods in his person. He was also handsome and had many public virtues.

But like many men of his birth and station in life, he was the victim of a fatal fallacy: that the majority of mankind, if given an opportunity, would rise to great and selfless heights, that man was naturally good and preferred virtue to evil, that man's heart was inclined to the noble and that only circumstance and environment distorted that heart. Patrician or lowly worker, rich or poor, hailed or obscure, man was the crown of nature according to Antonius' philosophy. This belief gave him a beneficent expression, which drew thousands to him, and his manner was always gentle and temperate. Lucius Sergius Catilina was an old acquaintance of his, and a fellow patrician, and though Antonius had heard many vile and wicked things concerning Catilina he discounted them with a measure of indulgence.

There were some of Antonius' friends who thought his liberality childish, if touching, but none thought it dangerous except Cicero, who liked him exceedingly for his earnest desire not to be in error, and his anxiety never to offend anyone. When Antonius had generously and sincerely embraced Cicero on the occasion of the vote by acclamation, he had paused a moment to say, "But how sad, perhaps, it is that Catilina was third in the measure of votes for the Consulship. He must be mortified, and we must hasten to console him." To this Cicero replied with quiet passion, "It is hard to believe that the people of Rome give him the third highest vote! It is very ominous."

Cicero looked at his colleague's cheerful and handsome face and his winsome eyes, and shook his head in dismay. Reared in republican virtues, Cicero found himself frequently confounded by Antonius. Antonius heartily agreed with him that the budget should be balanced, that the Treasury should be refilled, that public debt should be reduced, that the arrogance of the generals should be tempered and controlled, that assistance to foreign lands should be curtailed lest Rome become bankrupt, that the mobs should be forced to work and not depend on government for subsistence, and that prudence and frugality should be put into practice as soon as possible. But when Cicero produced facts and figures how all these things must and should be accomplished, by austerity and discipline and commonsense, Antonius became troubled.

"But this—or that—would bring hardship on this—or that—class," Antonius said. "The people are accustomed to lavish displays in the circuses and the theatres, and the lotteries, and free grain and beans and beef when they are destitute, and shelter when they are homeless and a part of the city is rebuilt. Is not the welfare of our people paramount?"

"There will be no welfare of the people if we become bankrupt," said Cicero, grimly. "We can become solvent again, and strong, only by self-denial and by spending as little as possible until the public debt is paid and the Treasury refilled."

"But one cannot—if one has a heart at all—deprive the people of what they have received for many decades from government, and which they expect. It will create the most terrible hardships."

"Better that all of us tighten our girdles than Rome fall," said Cicero.

Antonius was even more troubled. It seemed very clear to him that the people should have all they desire, for were they not Roman citizens, and inhabitants of the mightiest and richest nation on earth, and the envy of all other peoples? On the other hand, Cicero's facts and figures were inexorable. Then Antonius brightly suggested higher taxes, to fill the Treasury and to continue larger and wider public expenditures. "I, myself, am willing to accept more taxation," said the young man with such sincerity that Cicero sighed.

"But there are hundreds of thousands of good and decent citizens of Rome who are even now laboring under taxation which is unbearable," said Cicero. "A little more pressure and the backs of the faithful horses will break. Who, then, will carry Rome?"

Antonius' mind, or at least that part of his mind which was not so totally suffused with good will that it was blind and deaf, acknowledged the logic of this. He liked a pleasant life, and could not understand why all men should not have it also. He frowned at ledgers and books, and sighed over and over. "How did we come to such a pass?" he murmured.

"By extravagance. By the purchasing of votes from the mendicant and the unworthy. By pandering to the mob. By our attempts to raise idle nations to the standards of Rome, and the pouring out of our wealth to them. By foreign adventures. By mighty grants to generals, so that they might increase their legions and their honors. By wars. By believing that our resources were endless."

Antonius then remarked that he had an appointment at his favorite book shop, where an alleged original manuscript by Aristotle was on sale, and he arranged his snowy toga and hastened out. He left Cicero with the mournful wreckage. Cicero understood that his colleague had received the second highest vote because of his affability and his concern for the Roman people and his love for them. But Antonius, who had never before faced facts must face them now, and facts were terrible Gorgons for idealists to face. They had a way of turning them to stone or sending them off in affright, hoping for a miracle. "Two and two make four," said Cicero, aloud, "and that is irrefutable. But men like my dear Antonius believe that by some thaumaturgy, mysterious and occult, two and two can be made to add up to twenty."

He was not present that night, of course, in Antonius' elegant villa when Lucius Sergius Catilina called on his fellow patrician.

CHAPTER FIFTY-TWO

Antonius was delighted to embrace Catilina, whom he admired for the beauty which even middle-age had not dimmed or distorted, and because Catilina was intellectual and amusing and made even a depraved phrase sound lighthearted and sophisticated. Catilina was not dusty with ledgers and with facts. He moved grandly and with natural stateliness, and spoke in the tones and words native to Antonius, and his allusions were familiar to him. Moreover, Catilina could be depended upon not to speak of the necessity of money—patricians disdained money—unlike Cicero who was always dwelling on the squalid subject. Antonius prepared himself for a pleasant evening. They sat together in Antonius' library—he had not bought the manuscript of Aristotle after all, discerning it was a forgery— and drank wine and ate fruit and sweetmeats and commented on the cold winter weather, and jested, and laughed, and exchanged gossip of the city. It was a great relief to Antonius who liked to think that life would be a happy state of affairs if men would cease to be grim and point at books and documents with an ink-stained finger and talk of economy, a most disheartening topic of conversation.

It was not for some time that Antonius became aware of the terrible fixity and vivid light in Catilina's magnificent blue eyes, and that the whole power of his personality had begun to center on him. Catilina was unusually pale; his mouth had a bluish cast; his nostrils were white and distended with tension. Antonius, always solicitous, said, "Are you well, Lucius?"

"Well enough," said Catilina. "Do not think I brood on my failure to become Consul of Rome." He paused. "And how do you find our suetty Cicero, the Vetch, the Chick-pea, the dull man who bites every coin he spends either of his own or the Treasury's?"

His voice was so full of hatred and malignancy that Antonius was disturbed. He knew that Catilina "disliked" Cicero, and was contemptuous of him as a "new man," and that Catilina had ardently desired to be elected Consul despite the opposition—strange to Antonius—of those he could surely have deemed his friends. But cold and violent hatred was alien to the colleague of Cicero, and he could not understand it. He smiled with uneasiness. "Cicero is a very realistic man," he replied. "I was much taken aback to discover how insolvent our Treasury is, and how dire are our natural circumstances. I constantly tell Marcus that matters will improve and that our nation is sound at heart and rich. But he is not so optimistic."

"The Vetch is a vulgarian," said Catilina, his fine voice hard as iron. "You have surely discerned this, yourself. He will destroy Rome, for he knows nothing of her spirit and vitality and the changing days in which we live, and the opportunities which are constantly presenting themselves to intelligent men. He would have us return to the meagre and barefoot days of Cincinnatus, and like Cincinnatus bend ourselves to the plow, forgetting that we are now an urbane and mighty nation, and complex, and surrounded by a myriad problems which cannot be solved by a few platitudes."

Antonius was even more uneasy. "But still," he murmured, "there are problems. I saw them for myself."

"None that cannot be overcome," said Catilina. He suddenly rose and shut the bronze door of the library. He refilled his goblet with wine and then stood in silence, staring down at the wine, his fine strong legs apart, his hands and neck and wrists and armlets glittering with jewels, his darkly ruddy hair touched with gray. His profile was still godlike and noble. He resembled a sparkling statue as he meditated. "You are not a fool," he said suddenly to Antonius, "for all you dodge facts. I have a way to save Rome. A heroic way, the way of valorous men, the way of a patrician, the way of a man who knows his country and the people therein, as the Chick-pea does not know them."

He turned his blazing eyes on Antonius, who was staring at him. "Are you valorous, Antonius? Are you brave, manly, aristocratic? I have known you from our childhood, and I think you are. Have you heard me? The Vetch is right in one matter: Rome is about to be destroyed."

Antonius sat up in his carved ebony chair as if struck across the face. His light brown eyes fixed themselves on Catilina's own eyes and it seemed to him that he was gazing at blue lightning.

"I have said that Rome is about to be destroyed," said Catilina.

Antonius was incredulous. The warm lamplight on the lemonwood and teakwood tables stirred in a slight draft. The colors of the Persian carpets flowed into each other. The brazier was hot with red coals. Books gleamed on shelves and figurines were illuminated, and there was a scent of roses in the air. Antonius darted a bemused glance about him, disbelieving what he had heard, then turned again to the standing Catilina with an imploring smile which beseeched the other man to withdraw his frightful words.

"It is true that the Treasury is almost empty," he said. "But surely it can be refilled, if we take long and serious consideration."

"It is not the Treasury of which I speak," said Catilina. "It is of some of the people of Rome, themselves, who will destroy Rome tomorrow."

"Those of whom Cicero has been speaking, the mobs who will not work but depend on bribes and favors and gifts from the government?"

"Ah, so the Vetch still loathes the people, does he? He has no compassion for the poor and the destitute, the homeless, the sick, the exploited, the shelterless, the unfortunate, the hapless ones who are miserable and in despair for no fault of their own?"

Catilina knew Antonius for an idealist, and it was to the idealist that he had spoken, while detesting him in his violent heart.

"I do not think that Cicero is merciless, and detests the people," said Antonius. "He wishes only to curtail or remove laws which encourage idleness and beggary and footless ease of life at the expense of the general public, the taxpayers. He wishes to relieve the burden on the industrious and the venturesome, who have pride." Antonius paused. "I know, Lucius, that your heart has always bled for the masses, and that you have always desired to relieve misfortune, and for that I honor you. But there are the multitudes who have no honor, no pride, no discipline, no patriotism—" He was amazed at his own words.

Catilina sat down and once again fixed him with his terrible eyes. "I see that the Vetch has already corrupted you, my friend."

Antonius shook his head in confusion. "No. No. It is true that Cicero speaks always of this, but never before did it strike me so starkly."

Catilina not only now despised his friend, but hated him. But he spoke gently and softly in his very musical voice, as one who speaks to a dearly beloved.

"You have misunderstood me, Carissime. Those who will destroy Rome are the 'new men,' the gross merchants, bankers, businessmen, manufacturers, brokers, and all their disgusting companions who loot the defenseless people and rob their workers. They are joined in their conspiracy against our country by avaricious Senators, and even some of our own class who love money more than our nation. I know them well! I know Caesar and Crassus and Clodius and Pompey, who are ambitious, not for Rome, but for loot and power. And what will be the end? Chaos. Infamy. Destruction. Decay. The fall of Rome. It is inevitable, unless we strike at their hearts and remove them from their seats of power and restore the Republic again in all her pride and strength and virtue."

He waited, then said, "You know Manlius?"

Catilina knew the magnetism of his voice, and the formidable force of his charm. He saw Antonius staring at him with considerable wildness, and he thought to himself in satisfaction that the other man had been seduced as by a siren. He did not know that to Antonius his words and his voice had sounded like the thunderings of an earthquake, as if mountains had been falling, and that the pit had yielded up dreadful forms before his horrified gaze. It was as if his spirit had been struck from sleep by a bolt from the hand of Zeus, and in the fearsome light of that bolt he was seeing a landscape he had never known before.

Antonius closed his eyes, for it is an appalling thing for an idealist to see the world suddenly for what it is, and not the pleasant garden he had believed it was, populated with men of innate nobility, men of reason, men who preferred goodness to evil, and men who are civilized and mindful of the fate of their fellows, and striving for justice at all times.

All that he had disbelievingly heard of Catilina returned to him in a hundred strong and emphatic voices, and he said to himself, It is true. It is quite true.

He said in a faint voice, "Yes, I know Manlius."

"C. Manlius," said Catilina, making his voice deep and warm and vibrating, "is an old general, one of Sulla's heroes, a man who gave all to his country, and who is beloved of the veterans of the legions. Manlius has pleaded with Cicero to assist the old veterans and increase their piteous pensions. Cicero has refused. But then, he is no military hero himself, but a pale man of the city, without valor or bravery. Do we not owe all we have to the old generals like Manlius, and his legionnaires? Shall we abandon them to starvation, or force them to sell themselves into slavery in order that they might be sheltered and fed? This Cicero would permit, the traitorous Cicero who is very ambitious and greedy, and who is known for his avarice."

Antonius pretended to be moved and desperately uncertain. He said, forcing himself to meet those deranged eyes fixed on him: "Cicero has been kind to the old veterans of many wars, to the disabled and the sick, and has generously increased their allowances. He wishes only that the young and able-bodied support themselves henceforth, with their own labor and industry, in order that our country not become bankrupt and ruined."

"Ah!" cried Catilina, striking his strong knee with his jeweled fist. "He lies! I can tell you of tens of thousands of veterans who are in despair at this very moment, old, unfortunate, landless, unable to find employment, because they spent years in the service of their country! I can tell you of their tears and their homelessness and their bitter cries against those who have abandoned them!"

"Oh," murmured Antonius, in compassionate tones. "I have not seen these veterans. Where are they? What is their place of congregation, that I may address them and inspire them with hope?"

Catilina was silent. His fists remained on his knees. His eyes flickered like blue fire on Antonius, whose ingenuous expression was more ingenuous than ever. Then Catilina, having satisfied himself that this unworldly fool had spoken without guile, answered, "They are with C. Manlius, who gives what he can to them, in Etruria, and what shelter he can, though his own purse is lean."

Antonius' heart jumped. He was recalling vague rumors, which he had discounted, that General C. Manlius had gathered about him thousands of disgruntled mercenaries who had enlisted in the legions for the pay, and who had expected looting and small fortunes in return.

"Why does not Manlius present himself before Cicero, and the Senate, and ask help for his men?" said Antonius.

"Has he not done so?" exclaimed Catilina. "Did he not appeal under the proposed new agrarian law (*lex agraria*) to give to the old veterans proportions of the public lands for their own use? I spoke before the Senate, myself, as you may recall, in support of agrarian reform. And, who opposed the law and caused the Senators and the tribunes to vote against it? Your superior colleague, Cicero!"

"Cicero opposed it, not because he was against the giving of land, but because it placed too much power in the hands of government," said Antonius, with a pleading and questioning look at the excited Catilina. "You will recall what he said:

"'In studying this law, I find that nothing else is intended or done than the creation of ten "kings," who under the name and pretense of agrarian law, are made the masters of the public treasury, the revenues, all the provinces, the whole republic, the kingdoms, the free nations—in short, the whole world. I assure you, men of Rome, that by this specious and popularity-hunting agrarian reform law nothing is given to you, but all things are conferred on a few individuals. A show is made of granting lands to the Roman people and the veterans, but in fact they are deprived of their liberty. The wealth of private persons is increased, and their power under this law, but the public wealth is decreased. In short, by means of the government, the tribunes of the people, whom our ancestors intended to be the protector and guardian of freedom, petty kings without restraint are to be established in the state.' "*

Catilina threw back his magnificent head and laughed loudly, while Antonius affected to regard him with trouble. Antonius added, "Not only the veterans were to be given rich land, but the mobs of Rome, also, who wished, according to Cicero, only to loot and exploit and resell at marvelous profits."

"If that is true, and it is not, who has more right to land than Romans, to use as they wish? Have they not labored and fought for it? Who is this Vetch that he should oppose the agrarian law which grants to the people what is their due, their civil rights?"

Antonius shook his head as if in doleful agreement and great trouble, and yet greater confusion. His heart was pounding against the walls of his chest like a hammer, and he said to himself, Why is it that I never understood before, and never believed in the enemies of my country, and smiled disbelievingly at Cicero when he spoke of them?

"I tell you," cried Catilina, "for this alone Cicero is in danger of assassination at the outraged hands of the very citizenry who elected him!"

"Oh, not truly," murmured Antonius. "Surely the people understand his opposition. You will recall that Cicero said, in opposing the *lex agraria*, that the petty 'kings' would surround themselves with a regal and legal retinue in order to enforce the law, and so would terrorize the populace and repeal their liberties. Even the Senate, even those who favored the law, laughed uproariously, when Cicero mentioned the ridiculous probability that Rullus would send a summons to General Pompey, the Magnus, to stand by in military might while he, Rullus, put up for sale the lands which Pompey, himself, had won by his own sword! When a civil right, Cicero said, invades the domain of the rights of all the people, then it becomes a special right of a special class."

I am convincing him against his own foolish convictions, thought Catilina with exultation. It is easier to convince a good and silly man than to convince a rascal, thank the gods. Catilina said, "Cicero forgets that times move, that a nation is always confronted by new situations and changes, and that which was excellent for our ancestors is anachronistic today."†

---

* As reported by the historian Sallust.
† From a speech Catilina gave before the Senate.

"Cicero has said," remarked Antonius in an appealing voice, "that though externals change, the nature of man does not, and therefore that which was true yesterday is true today and tomorrow."

"Spoken like a true plebeian!" said Catilina. "But we patricians know there is no such thing as unchanging human nature. It can be readily molded and manipulated by laws. The Roman of today is not the Roman of yesterday. The old Roman declared that he who does not work neither shall he eat. But we are more cognizant of our public duties in these days, and are compassionate, and will let no man starve because he can find no employment or if the employment offered is distasteful to him. Is it not a man's right to reject work for which he feels no interest, or if the wages offered are insufficient?"

Yesterday, thought the alarmed Antonius, I should have agreed with him, with all my heart and my enthusiasm! He said, "Then the mobs of Rome are one with the mercenaries—I mean the veterans—of Manlius?"

Again Catilina scrutinized him for duplicity, but found none in that open countenance and in eager shining of the eyes. He said soberly and with emphasis, "Yes, the people of Rome are one with the veterans. So are the miserable gladiators, and the hungry actors, and the intellectuals who love the people and are angered by the wrongs forced on them, and the artists, and the essayists, and all who feel a responsibility toward the common good, which includes many Senators and tribunes of the people, and the freedmen who are not permitted to forget that once their ancestors were slaves and bondsmen."

Catilina rose and began to pace up and down the library as if seized by unbearable agitation and sorrow and noble anger. His face changed, became charged with wrath and emotion. He raised his right fist high in the air and shook it violently. "What am I to do, I who love the people and weep for their wrongs? What gods can I implore?"

Antonius said in grieving tones, his shoulders fallen and his hands hanging between his knees: "Yes, what are we to do?"

Catilina halted his pacing. He flung himself into a chair and leaned toward the other man and spoke in a hushed and panting voice. "You and I, Antonius, should be Consuls of Rome, you the first Consul, I your colleague. The Vetch did not win rightfully. He won by guile, and by his oratory. Is that the way of true Romans? Shall not our wrongs be redressed?"

Antonius pretended to immense eagerness. "You believe I should be Consul of Rome, Lucius?"

Catilina smiled darkly. "I do indeed. And I your colleague, in the name of Rome." He paused, then continued, "Let us reason together. Desperate times demand desperate solutions."

Julius Caesar said to Crassus and Clodius and Pompey, "So, he visited Antonius tonight, according to our spies, and he has left in a state of jubilation. No doubt he will go immediately to Manlius. What a fool is that Antonius! Has Catilina assigned him the task of assassinating Cicero publicly, in the name of Rome?"

"Without doubt," said Crassus, meditatively chewing a fig and listening to the early winter gale outside his warm windows. "A stupid man can be induced to do anything, especially if he is emotional, and Antonius' emotions are well known. He could be brother to the Gracchi."

"We should have coddled Catilina, even though his madness repulsed us," said Julius. "But I wearied of him. I thought even the mobs would become aware of his insanity. It seems I was wrong."

"The politician who promises can always obtain enthusiastic followers," said Clodius, surnamed Pulcher. "It is true that Catilina is mad. But his very madness appeals to the irresponsible rabble. Has it not been said that men are insane, though man is rational? What must we do to protect Cicero, that orator in a white toga?"

"He must be protected at all cost," said Julius. "Catilina is now prepared to loose his criminals upon Rome. He is moving without us. We have restrained him thus far. But now we can restrain him no longer. Thanks to our stupid Antonius."

"I suggest that Catilina be murdered," said Clodius, idly refilling his goblet.

"How?" asked Crassus. "He surrounds himself with guards. He never sleeps without them. Let him be murdered, or even an attempt on his life, and the rabble would rise against us and that would be the end."

Julius played with his rings. "We face a desperate dilemma. Were we to warn Cicero he would speak of 'conspiracies' again. Were we to guard him, he would reject the guard. He does not trust us."

"Strange," said Pompey.

His friends burst out laughing.

The momentary mirth was a relief. But they all knew that they must act at once. However, how they should act was a puzzle. On the one hand they had Cicero, who would mistrust them. On the other hand they had Catilina, and his dupe, Antonius, who would believe anything if it were said in sonorous periods and in the falsity of the righteous.

In the midst of their serious and alarmed arguments, Crassus' overseer sidled into the dining room with the news that a hooded visitor begged to be admitted to the presence of Crassus, and to speak to the dictator in private. Crassus went into the atrium while the men he had left exchanged frowning glances and fell into an uneasy silence.

When Crassus appeared in the columned atrium with its singing fountains, the visitor threw back his hood and revealed the pale carved features of C. Antonius Hybrida. Crassus, who had known him from his birth, embraced him and exclaimed, "My dear young friend! How delightful it is to see you! I have guests. Join us."

But Antonius, who seemed very agitated, grasped his arm and said, "Who are these guests, Licinius?"

Crassus' eyes were a granite flash upon him. He paused. Then Crassus said slowly, "Caesar. Clodius. Pompey."

"But not Catilina?"

"Not Catilina."

"I thought you were not engaged with Pompey any longer, Licinius."

Crassus smiled, but his eyes remained on him intently. "A minor quarrel, Antonius, which is now healed. What is this to you?"

But Antonius appeared even more agitated. "I have heard, long ago, Licinius, that you and Caesar and Catilina and Pompey and Clodius and Curius and Piso and Sittius Nucerinus, and many others, had conspired earlier together to murder Cicero, then seize power and Rome and declare yourselves rulers of the world. It was when Cicero was Praetor of Rome. Licinius! Declare that the rumor was false!"

Crassus put his fingers over the pressing ones on his arm. He raised his marked eyebrows. "I know of no such conspiracy, my friend. Did Cicero inform you of this ridiculous libel?"

"Then, it is not true?" The kind brown eyes, strained and anxious now, looked into the gray murkiness of the eyes of his father's friend.

"It is not true," said Crassus with slow emphasis. "Did Cicero take the libel seriously?"

Antonius sighed deeply and dropped his hand. "I pray the gods that you are not deceiving me, Licinius, for all Rome depends on the possibility that you speak in truth."

Crassus spoke calmly, but the granite flash was deeper in his eye-sockets. "You may be certain that I speak the truth, Antonius. What is it that you wish to confide in me?"

But now Antonius hesitated and his pallor was touched with a sudden flush of color on his cheeks. "You know that rumor and I were never friends, and I believed only good of my fellows. I never credited the existence of villains, except in myth and story. I preferred to think well of others. I am not excitable, Licinius, or given to fantasy, or womanish alarms, nor do I see enemies where there are only shadows. Nevertheless, tonight I was told of a strange—a strange—" He faltered into silence.

Crassus maintained his calm. "What strange thing, dear friend?"

Antonius flushed even more as if both shamed and embarrassed. "You must not laugh, Licinius. And yet, I should prefer that you laugh and reassure me at once." Again he faltered into silence. Crassus took his arm suddenly. "It is Catilina, is it not?" His voice struck like a sword on Antonius' face, and he paled again so that he was whiter than before.

"Yes. It is Catilina. But how was it possible for you to know?"

Crassus led him from the atrium. "What you have to say you must say before Caesar, Pompey, and Clodius. We were discussing Catilina before you arrived."

"Gods!" cried Antonius with despair, and holding back ineffectually against the stern clutch on his arm. "Then I have not been just affrighting myself! Your face, Licinius, your face—"

But Crassus drew him into the dining hall, and three faces turned to them from the table and none spoke or rose. Crassus thrust Antonius forward, then shut the large bronze doors and bolted them. His breath was loud and quick in the complete quiet. But in a moment he had recovered himself and could speak in a controlled voice. "Our friend, Antonius Hybrida, colleague of Cicero, has a matter to confide to us. Let us hear him with deep attention."

Antonius looked from one to the other in great fear. He tried to smile. He could even regret for an instant that the pleb, Pompey the Magnus, who was no patrician, should be present at what he must say about a patrician, Lucius Sergius Catilina. Crassus stood beside him. He was afraid that Antonius would faint, and he said to Julius, "Give Antonius wine." Julius stood up and filled a goblet and brought it with both hands clasped about it to the colleague of Cicero, and himself put the vessel to the other man's pale lips. Antonius closed his eyes and drank. Then he opened them and looked at Caesar, Caesar who could always jest and perhaps would jest now, if only to encourage him, Antonius, and lessen his fear and take from him some of his pain. But Caesar was regarding him with great gravity and the antic eyes were as bright and commanding as the points of daggers.

"Speak, Antonius," said Crassus, imperatively.

Antonius moistened his lips. Again, he looked from one to the other, from the stony face of Crassus to the eyes of Caesar, from the impassive broad countenance of Pompey to the grim visage of young Clodius. He tried to speak, and failed. He tried again. He was conscious of the enormous silence in the splendid room and the scent of viands and wine. Then with an utmost effort of will he stammered, "It—is Catilina. He came to me tonight, he left but an hour ago, with a strange story and a stranger request. It is impossible to believe." He halted and turned to Crassus, who said:

"It is not impossible not to believe anything of Catilina. Speak, Antonius."

So with a weak voice that trembled, and with eyes that implored incredulous laughter, Antonius told his story to the four men who never removed their gaze from his face and uttered no word and made no gesture of any kind, not even to shift on a chair.

"It is a mad tale," Antonius ended. "I can only believe, and hope, that Catilina was drunk tonight."

The three men, Caesar, Clodius, and Pompey, did not speak, however. They only stared at Crassus. But Antonius said, "You must tell me that this wild tale is not only incredible but that Catilina has become deranged."

Crassus led him gently to a chair. Then he leaned toward him and said, "It is true that Catilina is mad. But the story he has told you is true. He has not told you all, my poor Antonius. He has said that he has with him the great-hearted of Rome, many Senators and patricians, who weep for Rome and its multitudes of the desperate. They are not great-hearted, though they are indeed Senators and patricians; they are traitors to their nation. Catilina has promised them debt-remission, debts which they incurred through profligacy and extravagance or the financial ruin of their families.

"He has with him, as he has asserted, the hired mercenaries of Rome, who are not satisfied with the loot they were permitted to acquire, but shout for more. Few of them are true men of Rome, many are from Etruria, of poor families who are embittered by fate, and seek revenge on gods and men. Of those who are true Romans, they are those who are veterans of Sulla, who have already wasted the grants given them lavishly, and had hoped to live for the rest of their lives at ease on the substance of the people. Catilina has told you they are 'wronged and patriotic veterans.' He lied.

"When he tried to move your kind heart with the story of the 'oppressed multitudes' of Rome, did he tell you truly who they are? No! In the vast majority they are Asiatics and others from a dozen other nations, criminals, adventurers, gladiators, pugilists, pirates, bandits, the scum of all the gutters of the world, who came to Rome in the hope of rapine and rapid fortune, or because they were hunted from their own countries and fled for shelter within these walls. They are unspeakable dogs and swine, beggars and mendicants, thieves and the diseased, and many of them are runaway slaves or low freedmen.

"Then there are those among our own class who are not content with the honors of their birth and station, and their money, but who long for power and empire. These stand with Catilina also, who has promised them that for which they dream. We know their names; we can control them.

"But I tell you, Antonius, that we cannot control the others!"

Antonius raised his hands then dropped them despairingly. "You knew of this, and did nothing?"

"We knew." Crassus flicked the gray glitter of his eyes over his shoulder at the three silent men still at the table. "But we have had little to do with Catilina for a long time, knowing he was mad, and fearing his madness, though not underestimating his fearful power over those I have mentioned. We hoped that he had lost his following, that his increasing madness would overwhelm him. We should have had him quietly murdered."

Antonius stared at him, aghast. "Murdered! You, Crassus, triumvir of Rome, and a man of law? You speak of murder so casually?"

Julius Caesar was forced, even then, to put his hand over his mouth to control a sudden desire to laugh at this earnest man who had not believed the rumors in Rome which had not even approached in virulence the outmost borders of the real truth. Pompey's broad face expressed nothing, and Clodius compressed his lips to stop a cynical smile.

"Is it wrong to kill a traitor, a madman, a man who would destroy your country?"

"My dear Licinius," Antonius faltered, "it is wrong to take the law into one's own hands, and that you know surely."

"True," said Crassus, with the utmost gravity. "But these are desperate times, though it seems you were not aware of them, my good friend. We are in a state of war. We have dallied too long. Yes, we knew of Catilina and his frightful plots. But there was one thing that we did not know: When he would move. You have now told us, and for that all Rome will honor and revere your name.

"You have asked me why he came to you, the colleague of Cicero. In his black and deranged heart he believed that as you received the second largest vote, after Cicero, you would be resentful and lustful, as he is both resentful and lustful. Who would not desire to be Consul of Rome, the highest office in the land? Therefore, reasoned Catilina, you were sleepless with hatred. You are also a patrician, like himself. He believed that this Cicero was something you could not endure. And then"—here Crassus hesitated deliberately and held Antonius with the power of his clever eyes—"he thought you a man whom he could delude with promises to make you Consul of Rome. He thought you as vile as himself."

Antonius had suddenly covered his face with his hands as if to shut out what he could not bear to see. Crassus flashed another look at the three silent men at the table, and his hard mouth jerked slightly. He continued:

"You have told us of his plot against Cicero's life, for it is necessary for many reasons, to Catilina, that Cicero must die. Let me repeat this, as you have told it, that we have understood no error. You are, on a certain night next week, to send a message to Cicero through your freedman, Solus, at midnight, imploring Cicero to see you at once on a matter of the greatest importance. You are Cicero's friend and colleague; you have a great love for him. He would trust you, and grant you an interview at once, no matter the hour.

"As Cicero is Consul he has soldiers to guard him. But on receiving your urgent request for an audience, even at midnight, he would inform the soldiers that you were expected and not to delay your passage to him through the gates of his house and into his presence. As the streets at that hour are always dangerous you would naturally come with a bodyguard of your own freedmen or trusted slaves, cloaked and hooded, and they would enter with you. But in reality they would be Catilina and a number of his friends. Once in Cicero's presence they would all fall on him at once and slay him." Crassus looked down at the wretched man seated before him and he smiled fully now, with mingled contempt and pity.

"Have you not considered something, Antonius? The soldiers and their captain would have been informed of your arrival and would have admitted you with the conspirators. They would also have recognized you, for they know you well. Would Catilina, then, have permitted you to live, to betray him? No. You would have died an instant after Cicero had died."

Antonius let his hands fall. He looked up into Crassus' face speechlessly and Crassus thought: Surely it is not possible that the thought had not occurred even to this credulous mind?

Crassus said, "His vileness is so monstrous that he could underestimate you. Fortunately for Rome, for Cicero, and for yourself, you are not the man Catilina judged you were."

"But what can we do?" cried Antonius in a hopeless voice. "Much," said Crassus. "We can go to Cicero at once, even if he has retired and it is late, and tell him of the nearness of disaster and chaos. But the danger is not past! We have known for a long time that this madman, this appalling creature, longs to burn Rome, herself! Why? Out of perversity, out of the black destructiveness that lives in his inhuman heart."

"No!" exclaimed Antonius. "It is not possible to believe this even of Catilina!"

"You must believe it," said Crassus, sternly. "For it is true. I have told you, Antonius, that we were deluded that he was no longer a threat to Rome, or at least that he was not so great a threat as we now know he is, thanks to you. Cicero, the famed and honorable, the beloved of Rome, must know the whole plot against him and Rome. He will arouse the people, even the most apathetic, not only to indignation but to horror and vengeance, and the crushing of the danger that threatens all of us. They have heard rumors of Catilina and his horrific multitudes for a long time; apprehension has stirred them often. But not enough! They have heard of the disaffection of Etruria, and Manlius, that rude old soldier. They have heard of the lust of the criminals, and the treason of many of the patricians. All this has, from time to time, swept over their consciousness like a vague black wind. But not enough! Now the hour has come to expose Catilina for what he is, and Cicero is the only man who can do so."

CHAPTER FIFTY-THREE

Cicero, Antonius, Caesar, Crassus, Pompey, and Clodius sat in Cicero's cold library, long after midnight. At his brother's side stood the soldier, Quintus, whom Cicero had hastily summoned. Cicero had wrapped a crimson wool gown over his night clothing, a plain gown and strapped only with leather. His feet were covered by fur-lined boots. He looked at his visitors for a long time, in total silence, after Antonius had finished speaking, and after Caesar and Crassus had made their own ominous comments.

Antonius, the patrician, loved Cicero for all he was a "new man" of no distinguished family, except for the Helvii on his mother's side—Cicero of the breed held in contempt by the aristocrats, the breed of merchants, manufacturers, professional men, shopkeepers, stockbrokers and traders, and rich farmers. Antonius greatly admired Cicero, the famous lawyer and orator and now Consul of Rome, but he had rarely invited Cicero to his house. Did not one owe something to one's name? But now, as the distracted Antonius studied Cicero he had to admit to himself, with some vague wonder, that Cicero had a patrician's nobility and aloofness. The thick and waving brown hair was heavily interwoven with gray; the slender face was locked and grim; the thin long hands lay clasped almost lightly on his knee. The changeful eyes studied one man after another, slowly, and then came to rest on Antonius. But still he did not speak. He was thinking, and his thoughts were bitter. His eyes began to glow with a cold yellow. At last he spoke, and only to Antonius:

"I am Consul of Rome, Antonius, and you are my colleague. We are considered the mightiest men of our country. We are wrong! Crassus and Caesar are the mightiest, the most powerful. Beside them we are infants in the presence of ruthless Titans! You have spoken in fear and horror of Catilina. Your fear and horror are justified. But, who made Catilina such a terrible threat against Rome? These men who sit beside you now."

Now he looked at Caesar and said, "The tiger who roamed your garden is now within your house, Julius." Again he turned to Antonius, who was bewildered and shocked at his words. "Antonius, these men, our friends as they claim, were always in a conspiracy against our country in the pursuit of their private power. Look upon their faces! They are dark with scorn and anger against me. But they know I speak the truth. They did not come with you tonight because they fear for their country, or for me. They came because they now fear for themselves; the madman they encouraged for their own purposes is about to destroy them as well as the government, the city, and ourselves. They thought him on their chain; he has broken free; he ranges and roams the streets and his scarlet shadow falls on every wall.

"Iniquitous and immoral men!" Cicero's eyes blazed upon the others. "To this you have brought Rome, that Catilina with his malefactors, gladiators, perverts and mobs, freedmen, criminals, thieves, murderers, mercenaries and malcontents is now stronger than you! Rome never faced so desperate an hour before. I have called Catilina a traitor. But you are traitors also, to all that established our nation. You are traitors to principle and honor, to good will and valor, to courage and virtue. If Catilina now stands before the bar of Rome as her enemy, you stand with him also."

Antonius regarded him with fresh horror and affright. "Poor Antonius," said Cicero. "It may be that your fortitude has saved Rome—for a little while. No nation ever withdrew fully from this abyss, no, not in all the history of the world."

He looked at Pompey, who had saved his life before, and saw the broad and quiet face, and for an instant his own softened. Then it darkened again. "Have you nothing to say, you, mighty Crassus, dictator of Rome, you, powerful Caesar, you, plotting Clodius?"

"We listen to you because we are patient and tolerant, Marcus," said Julius, who was now smiling faintly. "You were always intemperate about 'conspiracies.' I say again that we know nothing about 'conspiracies' except the one revealed to us by Antonius and one we only dimly suspected existed but which we did not credit as a true menace. But we discounted the power of Catilina, whom we have not seen for a long time, and whom we despise as you despise him. Let us be done with foolish recriminations and accusations. We must work together to halt Catilina."

"Liar," said Cicero. "You were always a liar, Julius."

"Your personal opinions, noble Cicero, concerning Caesar are irrelevant," said Crassus. "I, dictator of Rome, came to you tonight—and I am young no longer—because you are Consul of Rome, and all Rome is in danger. I will not ennoble your accusations by disputing with you. Catilina is about to march on Rome with his monstrous mobs; he will burn the city out of his perversity and hatred for all that lives. Let us consider together. We dare not seize him publicly. He will call upon his creatures to fall upon Rome in total destruction. What, then, shall we do?"

Cicero went to his table and began to write quickly with his quill pen. He then sanded the ink, melted wax at the tall candle on the table, then applied his seal on the paper. He called his silent but formidable brother with his eyes and gave the paper to Quintus. "Search Catilina out within the next hours, Quintus," he said. "I have summoned him to appear before me and the Senate immediately, to answer charges of treason against Rome."

Julius smiled, and so did Crassus and Clodius. Pompey studied the floor. Antonius said, "You do not fear him, Marcus?"

"No," said Cicero. "I never feared him. I never feared any of these. I suspected them greatly these past few years, but I had no proof but only surmise and my own intuition. Caesar, Pontifex Maximus and Magnus! Crassus, dictator of Rome, and the richest and most powerful man in the country! And others, too many others. Yes, I knew for what they lusted. They will not be turned aside, even now. They wish only to have destroyed their fellow conspirator, who has slipped from their control." He bowed to them ironically from his chair, and his eyes sparkled with disgust. "Masters of Rome, we who are about to die detest your treason!"

Cicero had acted shrewdly. He knew that Catilina, who hated and derided him, would laugh at the summons and would appear, as ordered, before the Senate, safe in his fancied power which none would dare provoke into open violence. He would appear, arrogantly, to denounce the "new man," Cicero, and hold him up to public scorn before the patricians of the Senate, many who were fellow conspirators with him. He, himself, would speak in his musical and languid voice, elegant and puissant, and forever would Cicero be banished by the great laughter which would fall upon him.

Catilina, receiving the summons just before dawn, laughed with delight. His hour had come. Before the sun set Cicero would be in exile, shamed from the city. Catilina had only one regret: He would have no opportunity now to fire Rome and burn it to the ground as he lusted.

So, arraying himself in a scarlet toga trimmed with gold, and wearing a beautiful coat of the whitest and softest of fur, Catilina lay in his litter and ordered his splendid slaves to carry him to the Senate Chamber. He wore a gemmed necklace in the Egyptian manner, and his armlets and wristlets glittered with jewels and his legs were swathed in scarlet and his feet were shod with fur boots, and at his side was buckled the terrible short sword of Rome, for he was a soldier. As always, he resembled a radiant god in his natural splendor of appearance, and in his dignity and

pride. He was composed. Only his intensely blue eyes showed the derangement and evil of his soul, for they appeared on fire.

The frosty golden sun had just touched the highest roofs of the turbulent city when Catilina set forth; below all was purple dusk under the
arches and the pillars, and the stony streets were dark with melting snow
and puddles of water. Catilina had expected a quiet hearing before the
Senate, whom he would soon convulse with laughter. Therefore, he had
requested none of his intimates to be present. General Manlius was not
present, nor any of the sinister leaders who were Catilina's devoted servants. "By the very paucity of my apparent following Cicero's denuncia-
tions—whatever they may be—will become ridiculous," Catilina had told
them all.

The haste of the summons assured Catilina that only a quorum of Senators would be present, and in that quorum would be many of his secret
friends. The people in mass would not be present. It would be very circumspect, except for the aristocratic laughter of those who would listen
to Cicero incredulously, and would resent his accusations against a fellow
patrician. He, Catilina, would be disdainfully and carelessly surprised
that he should be summoned at all—and on what grounds? Catilina knew
that through many, many years Cicero had had him watched, waiting for
him to stumble, to betray himself. But he had been very careful, or at least
his followers had been clever enough not only to recognize Cicero's spies
and so disarm them with an innocent appearance, but to report their movement to their master. There was no way possible that Ciccro could know
the full ramifications of the plot against Rome. Not for an instant did
Catilina suspect Antonius Hybrida, a fellow patrician whom he had approached on the common ground of their heritage, and whom he, Catilina,
had convinced should seize power with him the next week on a certain
night.

As for Crassus and Caesar and Pompey and Clodius, and their friends,
Catilina now had only the most vehement loathing for them, and a tremendous scorn, as pusillanimous men too timid to move in their own behalf, though their middle years were upon them and Crassus was old. To
suspect them of betraying him was incredible, and Catilina gave it no
thought not even for a moment. He knew they feared him; he believed
that they disliked Cicero and hated him, and he had heard them laugh
at him often enough. He was well aware that they had secretly supported
Cicero, though long before they had promised Catilina their own support.
Vacillating, prudent cowards! It would not be long before they would
die, at Catilina's decree, just as Cicero would die. But before then, Cicero
must be banished by the laughter of the Senate and by their order, as his

continued presence in Rome as Consul would be an embarrassment to the whole nation.

Absorbed in his happy and vengeful and insane thoughts, Catilina heard nothing in the warm snugness of his litter but the excited beating of his heart. Whatever sounds of footsteps or hurrying there were, were sounds and hurrying familiar to his ears, and so he was not disturbed. Then the litter came to an abrupt halt, and did not move again. He waited, and took thought with himself. Should he, after the hearing was concluded, institute a libel suit against Cicero, and thus refresh his own purse? It was a matter to be considered, and Catilina's excitement grew. Chick-pea! The country bumpkin who still smelled of the manure pits and hay and the sty! I have waited long, thought Catilina, clenching his jeweled fists. But I have not lost the appetite!

Then, all at once, he became aware that the litter had not moved for some time. He impatiently held back the thick woolen curtains of the litter and glanced out. He was stunned with amazement. The Sacred Way was lined with soldiers, shoulder to shoulder, shield to shield, sword to sword, a full legion of them. And behind them rolled a multitude of men, wrapped against the winter wind, strenuous profiles pointed toward the Forum and the Senate. The sound of their passage was like the sound of a river in spring tumult, though it was only the rush of their feet. For some inexplicable reason they were not shouting or jesting or calling or talking as usual. They wound about the gleaming white pillars, and rushed through porticoes, and bounded down vast stairways—pouring into the Forum in a tide of color and voiceless commotion. Catilina glimpsed their flashing eyes, excited and eager. They were like silent wolves on the close steps of the prey, and he saw their suddenly bared teeth vivid and sharp in the rising sun.

He recognized the legion now. It was the legion of Quintus Tullius Cicero, Quintus whose life he had saved many years ago, Quintus, brother of Cicero. They wore crimson tunics and crimson leggings and brown leather harness and crimson cloaks, and their shining helmets were crowned with crimson crests. He saw their banners held high, the banners of their legion. He saw their fasces and their lictors and their drawn swords. They stood immobile, staring before them, apparently seeing nothing, unaware of the huge multitudes pouring behind them.

Catilina's hand let the curtain of his litter fall. He lay back on the cushions. For the first time he was full of fear and disquiet and foreboding. How had Quintus assembled his legion in so short a space? And, why were the countless crowds pouring into the Forum? Who had summoned them, even with the thousand tongues of Rome? I am betrayed, thought Catilina. The litter began to move again, slowly, hesitatingly, because of the tides of people flowing across its path at intersections. The crowded hills caught golden fire under the sun, and the purple darkness rose in mist from the streets and turned white in the light. And still the running footsteps became more pressing and more imminent to the man in the closed litter. Catilina tried to think, but his thoughts became disordered and chaotic. Then the litter halted, the curtains were held aside by a slave and Catilina saw that he had reached the steps of the Senate, which were also lined with soldiers. Beyond them the Forum was crowded to the very walls, and more and more people were arriving constantly, to push for space, and to see.

Catilina alighted from his litter and looked about him. He saw the soldiers and the people. He saw the façades of pale temples and fora and buildings and the Senate. He saw, above it all, the bristling hills of Rome and above them, the blue and silvery sky of winter. It took but an instant to see it. It took but an instant to observe that on his appearance not a single hail greeted him, not an upraised hand. He looked into thousands of impassive eyes, and they looked back at him and not a sound escaped one mouth. It was like gazing at statues of soldiers and men, stricken into colorful stone as at the display of a Gorgon's head. He alone moved in a great and stupendous silence, so that he heard the slap of his own boots on the marble steps of the Senate Chamber. His knees began to tremble as he mounted, but he held his head high and his face expressed nothing but impersonal contempt and hauteur. He entered the Senate Chamber, and saw that it was crowded and not sparsely inhabited, as he had believed it would be. The Senators were all there, in their white and their scarlet, and they watched the entry of Catilina as impassively as the soldiers and the crowds had watched without. The only movement was his own, and the lazy rising of incense before the altars. He alone had life in a forest of seated statues.

Then, in the center of the mosaic floor as he stood there, Catilina saw Cicero in the Consul's chair, and slightly below him sat Antonius Hybrida with a desperate and averted face. He had not expected Antonius. And he had not expected Caesar and Crassus and Pompey and Clodius. Their faces, too, were averted. None looked at Catilina but Cicero, robed in his pure white wool toga and with white shoes, and the eyes of the two men met as once their swords had met. For just a second, seeing those coldly fierce eyes upon him, Catilina quailed. Then, his pride reasserting itself, he pondered on the presence of Crassus and Caesar and their friends and on the strange way in which Antonius avoided looking upon him.

Cicero sat in silence, revolted, full of hatred, devoid of exultation, and feeling only wrath and disgust and the most powerful indignation he had ever experienced. Here was the most malignant traitor of Rome, and the murderer of Livia, the murderer of his own son, the madman who had dared to dream of being king, the patrician who was lower than the most despicable of gutter dogs, the soldier who had defamed the arms of his country, who had dishonored its banners, the aristocrat whom aristocrats now despised, the destroyer whom he, Cicero, must destroy if Rome were to live. Fire took Cicero's heart, and a bitter fury shook him. But none could guess it, so still he was, so apparently without passion, so objective. Not even his eyes showed what he felt, as he looked on his old enemy. For this day we have both waited many years, he thought, and this day will show whether Romans are still Romans or if they are slaves forever. He had not slept at all during the past night; he had been too busy summoning and writing and thinking of what he must say. He had been too busy praying for his country. Therefore his eyes were sunken and shadowed, but the strength and power of them, changing from blue to amber from second to second, were enhanced by his very exhaustion.

Then his voice rang out like a trumpet in the awful quiet of the chamber, and Catilina heard its compellingly special note for the first time:

"Lucius Sergius Catilina! You have been summoned before this august body, and before me, Consul of Rome, and before C. Antonius Hybrida, my colleague, and before Licinius Crassus, dictator of Rome, and before Julius Caesar, Pontifex Maximus and Magnus, and Praetor, and before Pompey the Magnus, and before the face of Rome, itself, to answer the charge of treason and conspiracy against your country!

"Your crimes and your plots and your companions are known. If you have an advocate, call him forth."

Catilina had listened intently. He had not known how powerful an instrument this Cicero had possessed in his voice, and how the sound of it struck the walls of the chamber and echoed back from it in thunder. He felt, rather than saw, the press of the people outside the open Senate doors, and it was like an enormous weight against his back. He felt, in fact, the weight of the city he had for so long plotted to destroy to satisfy his own hatreds and lusts. He felt alone as he had not been alone all the days of his life. But he smiled coldly and repudiatingly into the face of Cicero, as one smiles at an insolent inferior who had dared to speak to his lord and master, and contempt shimmered in his blue eyes. He bowed mockingly.

"I have no advocate, Cicero, for I need none. I have committed no crime and know of no conspiracies. I am no traitor. Produce, therefore, your witnesses before this august body which I reverence."

His manner was elegant and amused and aristocratically disdainful. He stood there in his white fur coat and his crimson and gold garments and his jewels. He looked quickly at the faces of his friends among the

Senate. Their faces were inscrutable. He looked at Quintus, his comrade-in-arms, armored and helmeted, who stood at Cicero's right hand, Quintus whose life he had saved. The burly soldier gazed at him, unmoved, like an image of himself. Sunlight poured through the doors and lay in a pool at Catilina's feet, and the jewels on his boots flashed in rainbows. Now from the multitudes outside came the dimmest but most awful of sounds, a primal muttering, a vast murmur as if arising from a congregation of aroused beasts. All within heard it; they lifted their faces in instinctive uneasiness and appeared to sniff the air with alarm.

But Catilina was not alarmed nor uneasy now. He, too, had heard that primordial and wordless sound, and he thought, Animals! Swine! Slaves! He was suddenly excited again, and aroused. He thought of the day which was coming for him, when he should have this rabble at the tip of his sword, and this Senate would prostrate itself before him and kiss his feet. He thought of the day, coming soon! when this Cicero, and yes, this Crassus and Caesar, would lie dead in their own blood before him, and he would touch their faces with his boot and roll them from him in repugnance. For he knew now who were his betrayers.

Disordered and demented though the thoughts of Catilina were, he could yet search, again, the faces of his secret friends in the Senate. When he met their eyes with his own some returned the blue stare gloomily, or shifted their gaze, and some smiled in disquiet. But, he thought, with rising exultation, they are my fellow patricians! Crassus and Caesar and Clodius and Antonius were patricians also; they had betrayed him to this bumbling Cicero, for their own reasons and because they feared him or envied him. But the patricians in the Senate were another matter entirely. They would, at the last, not permit the ruin of one of their own, for in his fall they would feel themselves fallen also.

Cicero watched the eloquent and direful face before him and knew all the ghastly thoughts that raced like lightning through the blazing eyes. He said to himself: He, not I, is the future of Rome. My day is passing before my vision, but his is just dawning, the day of power in the hands of the furies, the centaurs, the oppressors, the Pan-stricken, the bloodthirsty and overweening and frightful, the tyrants and the unutterably corrupt and deathly. Nevertheless, if only for a little I must delay that day, and write on the walls of Rome the warning for future and as yet unknown nations to read, lest they fall into the very same pit.

Cicero looked at Caesar and Crassus and their friends. He had thought of calling them as witnesses against this appalling criminal. But they would protect Catilina for fear of being exposed, themselves. They would answer evasively and would look with communicating eyes at the Senators, and all would be lost. At the end they would not abandon a fellow patrician, detestable though they found him. If he wished their support he must not betray them.

He said to Catilina sternly, "This is not a trial by the Senate, or by me. This is an investigation into your activities against the peace and freedom of Rome, against your manifest treason."

Catilina, who had been watching Cicero with the perceptiveness of insanity, understood. He smiled his dark and beautiful smile. "The laws of Rome demand that an accused man be confronted by witnesses. The laws of Rome give me the right not to incriminate myself and to refuse to answer, even during this alleged investigation." He turned and surveyed the Senate again. "As I am not under arrest, and charged only with vague crimes whose existence I repudiate, there is nothing to hinder me from leaving this Chamber. Lords, I will remain out of deference to your presence and not by overt restraint.

"I decry the methods of this Cicero, Consul of Rome, who seeks to intimidate and frighten me with loose charges and without witnesses. But I bow to his office if not to the man."*

A sense of sick frustration came to Cicero, and he pondered. But he said in his great voice, "You will deny the truth of what all Rome knows, and ask for witnesses whom I will not produce—though I have them—because of the danger in which they, themselves, stand. For many years all Rome has felt you in the dark underworld. All the felons and the fools and the dupes and the disaffected and the ambitious of Rome are your followers, and you have lived with them in the cellars and sewers of our nation and conspired with them how to overthrow all that is Rome. You have conspired my murder with them, for a night in the next week, that you may produce chaos and alarm in the city and so seize power to plunder and fire and subjugate and rule in your total madness. Do you deny this?"

Catilina turned the ferocity of his gaze upon Antonius. Now he too pondered. He saw the misery and suffering upon the face of Cicero's colleague. He, alone, might testify against Catilina for he had no crimes which might be revealed to the open sight of Rome. So Catilina said, "I deny this. I do not ask for a witness, for the allegation is absurd." He smiled languidly.

"Deny if you will, Catilina. You and I and many others know it to be the truth."

Those crowding at the doors of the Senate heard him, and the words ran backward through the multitude like a current in a river.

Then Cicero raised his voice to its full majesting and compelling cogency:

* Actual speech made to the Senate by Catilina, as reported by Sallust.

"How long, Catilina, will you carry your abuse of our forbearance? How much longer will your reckless temper baffle our restraint? What bounds will you set to this display of your uncontrolled audacity? Have you not been impressed by the nightly guards upon the Palatine, by the watching of the city by sentinels? Are you not affected by the alarm of the people, by the rallying of all loyal citizens, by the convening of this Senate in this safely guarded spot, by the looks and expressions of all assembled here? Do you not perceive that your designs are exposed? Do you not see that your conspiracy is even now fully known and detected by all who are here assembled? What you did last night and the night before, where you were and whom you summoned, and what plans you laid: do you suppose there is one here who does not know? Alas, what degenerate days are these! The Senate is well aware of the facts, the Consul can perceive them all. But the criminal still lives! Lives? Yes, lives; and even comes down arrogantly to this Senate, takes part in these public deliberations, and marks down with ominous glances every single one of us for massacre! And we"—and now Cicero turned his scornfully flashing eyes upon the Senate—"such is our bravery, think we are doing our duty to our country if we merely keep ourselves out of Catilina's words and bloody deeds!

"No, Catilina, long before this you should yourself have been led by the Consul's orders to execution, and on your own head should have been brought down the destruction which you are now devising for us!"

Catilina had listened to this with arched black brows and an amused and negligent smile. He glanced at the Senate with humor. "What a splendid voice our Cicero, our Chick-pea possesses! I am almost convinced, myself, that I am guilty of these vague accusations! I still deplore his methods, lords, and his incontinence of speech, but as a patrician I endure them with contempt."

The Senators peeped at each other furtively. They wanted to smile with Catilina. But what had been revealed to them in the night, and what they knew themselves, had terrified them. Moreover, the mutterings of the multitude, which had been listening with the utmost attention to Cicero, now rose in the winter air outside the Chamber with the sound of a most vehement torrent of anger. Now one could hear isolated but awful shouts: "Death to Catilina, the traitor!"

Cicero, as if Catilina had not spoken at all, then resumed his first oration against him, pointing out to the Senate that precedent existed for interrogation of suspected criminals and traitors without actual and written accusations and witnesses. The Senate listened without a movement, and with concentrated intensity. "This is an inquiry and an exposure, and not a trial of Catilina, lords. We have past resolutions of the Senate against such as Catilina, but they remain unpublished documents. They are still a sword in the sheath. They are resolutions, Catilina, which rightly understood require your immediate execution. Yet, you live! You live, not to abandon but to add strength to your effrontery." Cicero hesitated, and his pale and slender face became dark with despair and increasing bitterness.

He said to the Senate, "I desire at a moment so critical to the State not to appear careless, but I am even now convicting myself of conduct which is both remiss and wicked, in not demanding immediately that Catilina be seized and executed at once. Even in Italy now a base of operations against the Roman people has been established among the hill passes of Etruria. The number of our foes is increasing day by day. But the leader who directs these foes we see within the walls of Rome, and yes! even within this Senate, plotting every day some fresh device for bringing internal ruin upon our country!"

A deep murmur rose from the Senate, and the mingled white and scarlet of their robes stirred in agitation. Catilina smiled, then pursed his lips as if restraining an irrepressible amusement.

Cicero lifted his hand and pointed it implacably at Catilina, and at that gesture all became silent and still.

"If then at last, Catilina, I order your arrest and your execution, both of which are within my power, I shall presumably have more reason to fear that all loyal citizens will declare my action too tardy than that a single person will pronounce it too harsh. But this particular step"—and now Cicero gave Crassus and his friends an embittered glare of wrath—"which ought to have been taken long ago, I have certain reasons for not being induced to take at present. You will perish in the end, Catilina, but not until it is certain there will be no one in Rome so shameless, so desperate, so exactly the counterpart of yourself, as not to admit the justice of your execution. Just so long as there is a single man who dares to defend you"—and Cicero again directed his gaze at Crassus and company—"you will live! But you will live as you live now, held at bay by the stanch defenders whom I have stationed everywhere to prevent any possibility of your assailing the State. Many eyes and many ears, moreover, though you perceive them not, will be vigilant as they have been vigilant heretofore, and will keep watch over all your actions.

"For what are you waiting now, Catilina, if the shades of night can no longer veil your abominable conferences, and if the walls of your private house can no longer contain the phrases of your fellow conspirators? What if everything is being exposed to the light and breaking out of concealment? Abandon your design and sword! You are hemmed in on all sides;

clearer than daylight to us are all your plans; and you may proceed to review them.

"All is known. My watchfulness is much more persevering than your efforts to ruin the State. And now I assert before this august body of the Senate of Rome that on the night before last you went to the Scythemakers' Street—I will make no mystery of it—you went to the house of M. Laeca, and there you met several of your accomplices in your mad and insane and criminal adventure. Do you dare to deny it?"

Catilina, for the first time, was visibly struck. His handsome face paled and tightened. He looked at the Senators whom he knew well, one by one. Which had betrayed him?

Cicero laughed wearily. "What is the meaning of your silence? I will prove my assertions if you deny them. Speak!"

Dogs! thought Catilina with dazed fury. What pressure did this Chickpea exert on them that they betrayed me, these cowards who plotted with me? He dared not deny. There would be some among these Senators who would rise with pretended bravery and assert that they had merely been spying upon him for the sake of Rome, and would utter their own truthful accusations. So Catilina controlled himself. He fought for control as a serpent fights to coil himself, and it was visible.

"Yes," said Cicero, in a most terrible voice that reached far out into the Forum, "I see here there are present in the Senate itself certain of those who met you there! Merciful gods! Where are we? In what country, in what city are we dwelling? What is the government under which we live? There are here, here among our fellow Senators, lords"—and Cicero's voice soared like an eagle to the roof of the chamber and sounded outside —"in this deliberative assembly, the most august, the most important in the world, men who are meditating the destruction of us all! The total ruin of this city and in fact of the civilized world! These persons I see before me now and"—he fixed his eyes on the Senate with wrath and burning detestation—"I ask them their opinions on affairs of State daily, and I do not even wound them by a single harsh expression, men who ought to have been put to death with you, Catilina, by the sword!"

Now, thought Caesar, he has destroyed everything. But an instant later the multitudes cried out with a fearful voice from the farthest reaches, "Death to the traitor Senators! Death! Death to the enemies of Rome!"

At this all the Senators, guilty or innocent, trembled violently, for they knew the power of an aroused citizenry. Catilina heard the voice of the people of Rome, the voice he despised and loathed, and he too trembled. He had enormous courage; he did not fear death. He feared only that the people would seize him and dismember him, and he considered that a sacrilege upon his sacred person. He looked at Cicero, and saw the face of the Consul, and knew that he alone had the power to restrain the people, and he saw Cicero's struggle with himself, that he refrain or that he let loose.

Cicero dropped his hand to his side. His eyes fell to the floor, and his chest heaved as if he were attempting to control his emotions. Stern tears appeared on his cheeks. The muttering of the multitudes was a constant thunder in the background. Finally he looked again on Catilina and the amber glow of his eyes was like flaring embers.

"Quit Rome at last and soon, Catilina. The city gates are open; depart at once. Take with you all your associates, or take as many as you can. Free the city from the infection of your presence. If I give the word, the city will be convulsed, and there will be no more law or order because of the wrath of the people. That I cannot permit, for the sake of Rome. The innocent will perish with the guilty, for when the people are aroused who can preach restraint to them? There is not a man, Catilina, in Rome, outside your band of desperate conspirators, who does not fear you, not a man who does not hate you. For is there any form of personal immorality which has not stained your family life? Is there any scandal to be incurred by private conduct which has not attached itself to your reputation? Is there any evil passion which has not glared from your eyes, any evil deed which has not soiled your hands, any outrageous vice that has not left its mark upon your whole body? Is there any young man, once fascinated by your seductive wiles, whose violence you have not stimulated and whose lust you have not inflamed?

"Is it possible that anything can influence a man like you? Is it possible that a man like you will ever reform? Would indeed that heaven might inspire you with such a thought! But no, Catilina, you are not a man to be withheld from baseness by shame, from peril by alarm, or from recklessness by reason. Return to your criminals! What thrills of excitement you will feel! In what pleasures you will revel when you know that in the whole numbers of your followers you will not hear or see a single honest man! You have now a field for the display of your vaunted power to endure hunger, cold, and deprivation of all the means of life. But you will soon find yourself succumbing!

"When I defeated your efforts to obtain the Consulship I effected this much: I obliged you to attack Rome from without as an exile rather than persecute her from within as Consul, and I made your criminal schemes more correctly to be described as brigandage than as a civil war—which was your object."

To the Senate now he addressed his severe admonishments, and every face, in innocent indignation against Catilina, or in frightened shame, turned upon him. But Crassus and Caesar exchanged quick smiles. Antonius had long sunk into a lethargy of misery, once he had understood the full conspiracy against his country. Clodius had listened with reluctant admiration. And Pompey, for some reason, had watched only Caesar.

Cicero concluded in a mournful and compelling voice: "Too long already, lords and Senators, have we been environed by the perils of this treasonable conspiracy. But it had chanced that all these crimes, this ancient recklessness and audacity has matured at last and burst in full force upon the year of my Consulship. If then out of the whole gang this single villain only is removed, perhaps we shall think ourselves for a brief period freed from care and alarm. But the real danger will only have been driven under the surface and will continue to infect the veins and vital organs of the State. As men stricken with a dangerous disease, when hot and tossing with fever, often seem at first to be relieved by a draught of cold water, but afterward are much more gravely and severely afflicted, so this disease which has seized the State may be temporarily relieved by the punishment and exile of Catilina! It will return with greater severity!"

Crassus frowned at Caesar, who shrugged lightly. Antonius murmured, "The gods forbid!" Clodius stared at the white and gold ceiling with an air of detachment. Catilina affected a bored and impatient attitude as if Cicero had outrun his patience with his absurdities. But Cicero looked again at Catilina with all his loathing and detestation, and he cried, "With these ominous words of warning, Catilina, to the true preservation of the State, to the mischief and misfortune of yourself and to the destruction of those attached to you by every sort of crime and treason, get you gone to your unholy and abominable and impotent campaign!"*

He stepped down the stairs that led to his chair and the Senate, in deep silence, rose in respect to watch him go. Midway down the aisle he came face to face with Catilina. He halted and confronted his enemy. The silence became intense as all watched the confrontation. Cicero's pale face became almost incandescent with the fire of his inner hatred and detestation, and he thought, Murderer! Livia shall be avenged, and Fabia, and all the innocent you have assassinated! Destroyer! And Catilina looked back into those eyes and read them. He pretended to repress a smile, and he bowed deeply and with affected humility. Cicero moved on, with Quintus clanging in his armor by his side. The soldiers saluted. Cicero reached the door and heard the thunderous shout he had heard so many times before:

"Hail Cicero, Savior of Rome! Hail to the Hero!"

He lifted his right arm in salute and smiled a little with ironic and som-

* This first oration against Catilina has been greatly condensed.

bre humor. He had not saved Rome. He had only delayed the final catastrophe, and this he knew.

That night Catilina left in darkness for Etruria. He was exultant again. None had impeded his passage. He had left the Senate Chamber and while the multitudes had looked at him with fierce and vengeful hatred they had not moved against him. He had bowed to the Senators and had smiled in their faces with contempt; he had bowed even deeper to Crassus and his company. He had laughed silently into the eyes of Antonius, who had betrayed him. No, he had not yet done with Rome, with any of them.

When he reached Manlius he said, "We have not suffered anything, dear friend! I have a plan, a most bold and audacious plan. The Slave Holiday will soon be upon us. We must make haste to strike then, and for all time. The auspices are with us."

Crassus and Caesar went to the house of Cicero, and he greeted them with cold bitterness. "Do you think it is ended?" he asked them. "It has only begun. Do not felicitate me! You lie in your teeth. I have removed a present danger only for the moment from you. It will return—thanks to your long past conspiracies with Catilina. I salute you, Masters of the future, and know you for the criminals you are, who attempted to use Catilina for your own purposes, and now wish to use me in defense against him. You have won. History will record it. Leave me."

CHAPTER FIFTY-FOUR

Shortly after his first oration against Catilina, Marcus Tullius Cicero was lying on his bed sleepless, at midnight. But the city, though quieter than at midday, still murmured and thundered distantly like a restless Titan enduring nightmares. Marcus' eyes were dry with strain and exhaustion. The faintest moonlight fell through an open fold at the curtained window and lay on the opposite wall. He watched it without awareness. Then all at once it glowed brighter and brighter, and his sharp attention was captured and he half-raised himself on his elbow. Moment by moment it brightened, became sharper, until it was a face. Marcus' heart began to beat with mingled dread and fear. The features became clearer, and then it was his father's face, not the face of Tullius in his age but the countenance of Tullius in his youth as Marcus had known him as a child. He saw the limpid brown eyes, the anxious and tender smile, the smooth brown hair and thin throat.

"Marcus!" exclaimed the apparition in an urgent voice. Marcus could not reply. The face came closer to him and now Marcus could see the outlines, very dimly, of shoulders and robe.

"Marcus! Flee Rome at once!" Shadowy hands were lifted, as if pleading.

"I cannot desert my country," Marcus whispered.

I am dreaming, he thought. Swiftly he glanced about his room and saw the vague outlines of his furniture, the misty oblong of his window. He looked back at his father and felt a pang of grief.

"Your country, and mine, was lost even before I was born," said the vision mournfully. "The Republic was dying when my father came from the womb. Flee, Marcus, and end your days in peace and in safety, for the wicked will triumph as always they have done, and will murder you if you remain."

"I cannot desert Rome," Marcus said. "No, not even if I die for it."

The apparition was silent. It appeared to be listening intently to voices of others unseen. Then it lifted its shadowy hands in blessing and disappeared.

Marcus came to himself with a violent start and found himself wet with sweat. The faint moonshine lingered on the wall. "I have been dreaming," he said aloud. He shivered. He rose and then for the first time he lighted a votive candle to his father's memory and felt a shock of sorrow such as he never felt before for Tullius. Yet, he was comforted in spite of his Roman skepticism. It was good to know that the dead still loved the living, and that they guarded them and prayed for them. He pondered, remembering the apparition's words. He had always known he was in danger; now the danger was desperate for all he was hailed as a hero and the guards were doubled about his house. Always, the assassin waited, the quiet and patient and deadly man, unnoticed in a crowd, ready to strike as swiftly as a viper. Or, those very same mobs who hailed the hero today destroyed him tomorrow in their incontinent capriciousness and tempers. What man could trust men? A brave man rejoiced to give his life for his country if it availed that country. But it never did.

Cicero delivered the second and third oration against Catilina, who was not present. It was Cicero's intention to give his countrymen the whole history of the conspiracy, and their great part in it, for their apathy, complacence, tendency to hope for the best, optimism, and tolerance of villains and enemies of the State. "Too long have we said to ourselves, 'Intolerance of another's politics is barbarous and not to be countenanced in a civilized country. Are we not free? Shall a man be denied his right

to speak under the law which established that right?' I tell you that freedom does not mean the freedom to exploit law in order to destroy it! It is
not freedom which permits the Trojan Horse to be wheeled within the
gates, and those within it to be heard in the name of tolerating a different
point of view! He who is not for Rome and Roman law and Roman liberty
is against Rome. He who espouses tyranny and oppression and the old
dead despotisms is against Rome. He who plots against established authority and incites the populace to violence is against Rome. He cannot
ride two horses at the same time: He cannot be for lawful ordinances and
for an alien conspiracy at one and the same moment! One is a Roman or
not a Roman!"*

His own secretary, to whom he had taught his invented shorthand,
wrote furiously with the other scribes. Cicero spoke with passionate force;
he felt he was not only addressing the Senate and the people of Rome,
whom he prayed would remember his words, but generations to come.
"Though liberty is established by law, we must be vigilant, for liberty to
enslave us is always present under that very liberty! Our Constitution
speaks of the 'general welfare of the people.' Under the phrase all sorts
of excesses can be employed by lusting tyrants to make us bondsmen."

Always Caesar, Pompey, Crassus, and Clodius, and many of their
friends, were present to hear the impassioned Cicero, and everyone
glanced at them to see their nods of grave approval and thought. In these
defenders of the people we see the friends of our hero, Cicero. He speaks
for them. Cicero thought: Mountebanks! Would I could denounce you
also before the faces of those against whom you have conspired!

Among those who listened to him with sincerity and with a burning
heart was Marcus Porcius Cato, grandson of the fiery old patriot and
Censor; a philosopher, for all his youth, and known to the reading public
as "Uticensis." He was a tribune and one of the leaders of the Senatorial
aristocracy and a devoted admirer of Cicero. He was also a man of known
probity and virtue as well as an eloquent essayist and politician. It was he
who persuaded the cautious Cicero—who knew how dangerous was the
swamp over which he was now treading—to arrest some of the lieutenants
of the absent Catilina, such as Cethegus, Gabinius, Coeparius, Lentulus,
and Statilus, patricians all and conspirators all, who had remained in the
city to show their superb contempt of Cicero. "Minor rascals," Cato had
said, "but they must be arrested lest the people think you impotent, dear
Marcus. They will say you are all brave words, and will begin to wonder
why, in spite of your power as Consul, these known enemies of the State
remain free. They will begin to suggest among themselves that they are

* Preamble to second oration against Catilina.

not so dangerous after all, and that you are a mere noisy demagogue. Yes, I know you fear to precipitate chaos. But there are times when one must confront that danger for the sake of one's country."

The prudent Cicero hesitated. It was his liability of nature, which gave him both strength and weakness, to consider all sides of an act before committing himself to it. Sometimes this resulted in total paralysis. He remembered those occasions. So now he resolutely struck at Catilina's lieutenants, some of whom were relatives of the Senators themselves, and had them arrested and thrown into prison as conspirators against Rome. Romans went mad with speculation and with praise of Cicero, that he dared affront the mighty in their name. Many of the Senators were enraged. Some of them went to Crassus and Caesar and laid infuriated complaints against this "impudent new man, this Chick-pea, this country vulgarian, this Pleb! How long are we to be affronted by his insolence?"

Caesar said mildly, "You have forgotten. He was elected by the people, with the assistance of many patriotic Senators. They love him, one and all. He has the power to do what he has done—though I deplore it."

One night when Caesar was in his library trying to read, but overcome by foreboding and restlessness, his overseer came to him and whispered that the noble patrician, Lucius Sergius Catilina was without and urgently desired to converse with him. Caesar's antic face paled at this dangerous insolence and this threat to himself. But he controlled himself and ordered that Catilina be brought to his library. He then quickly drew the curtains upon his windows, which looked out upon the pearly snow illumined by the moon. He also loosened his dagger in its sheath. And while he waited he pondered and plucked his lower lip with his fingers.

"Greetings, Caesar!" cried Catilina as he entered, throwing back the hood of his cloak. His beautiful and depraved face was alight with dark exultation. He held out his shapely and jeweled hand. Caesar gazed at it a moment, then took it. It seemed feverish to him, and tremulous, as though Catilina was vibrating with inner fire. Catilina, without an invitation, flung himself in a chair; his feet rested deep in the fur rug that covered the marble floor. Caesar turned to the wine he had ordered and slowly filled a goblet for himself and another for Catilina. He gave the goblet to his unwelcome guest and looked over the rim of his own at the other, whose expression grew more exultant moment by moment.

"Why are you here, Lucius, you audacious man? Do you not know that Rome is dangerous for you?"

"It was the city of my fathers before the Ciceroni ever saw it!" exclaimed Catilina. "It was the city of my fathers before the Caesares ever saw it! Shall Rome be deprived of her son?" There was profound derision in his voice and a passion which he could not control.

His compelling blue eyes fixed themselves on Caesar. "Dear friend," he said in a deadly and caressing voice, "dear friend, sweet friend, faithful friend! Most trusted friend! I have come to thank you for your noble support, for your tears in my behalf."

Caesar gazed at him in silence, though he moved his hand as though sweeping away the vicious mockery of the other.

"Considering your valorous courage, your undying friendship for me, I may be inclined to mercy—later," said Catilina, and he laughed a little and took a long drink from his goblet.

"It is very gracious of you, Lucius," said Caesar with a faint smile. "But I doubt you will be forced to that consideration. Take my advice at once. Leave Rome. Cicero has been mild; he could have ordered your arrest and your execution. Do not tempt the Fates again."

"Ha!" cried Catilina. "Do you not know the Fates are with me?" He leaned toward Caesar now with vehemence glowing on his face. "I came to exult over you, Caesar, faithless friend, treacherous enemy."

Caesar was silent. Should he tell Catilina that Curius' mistress, Fulvia, had betrayed all to Cicero only that day? For a large price, a large price indeed, for she had wearied of Curius' promises and boasts and she was no longer young and no longer rich.

Catilina continued to speak in his musical but disordered tones. "I am ready to strike," he said. "Do you think you can halt me, you, Crassus, all of you, and that unspeakable Chick-pea?"

Caesar said, "Tomorrow, Cicero speaks again against you in the Temple of Concord, before the Senate. He may ask for your arrest and your execution. I beg of you, flee at once as he advised you before. I thought him temperate then—"

"He was afraid! He dared not lay a hand upon me, for fear of me! Was it temperance indeed, or prudence out of terror? But I tell you now, Caesar, that should a single hair of my head be harmed you shall go down with me, all of you. I have warned you before. I warn you now."

Caesar was alarmed, not at his words but at his aspect. He had always suspected that Catilina was mad; it was a disease of the family.

"I shall appear tomorrow at the Temple of Concord," said Catilina, "and I shall speak to the Senators and my fellow great soldiers, and we shall destroy Cicero in one blast of laughter."

"You cannot appear!" said Caesar, not believing this deranged folly. He was almost certain that if Catilina appeared the Senate would agree to his execution. But there were many imponderables to consider, and man could be trusted only to do the unexpected. Catilina had a strange and brilliant eloquence of his own, and he would speak to the hearts of the proud Senators, who secretly despised the middle-class Cicero. If Catilina were exonerated of conspiracy then he would continue to inspire his dark and violent and lusting underground to attack Rome, until at last she was destroyed. If Catilina were condemned, then that underground might rise in rebellion, and Rome might be destroyed after all. But malefactors by very nature were cowardly; the lesser danger lay with them, if Catilina were eliminated. The body did not operate without the mind.

"I shall appear," said Catilina, gloating.

"Then you will surely be condemned, for you will affront the Senate by your very appearance, after they believed you had left Rome forever, and in peace."

"I shall not be condemned, sweet lying Caesar. I shall have an advocate."

"And who is this reckless advocate?"

Catilina burst out laughing. He rose and refilled his goblet. He lifted it and toasted his unwilling host. "You, Caesar."

"I?"

"You." Catilina drank with enjoyment. Then he was no longer laughing. He hurled the jeweled goblet from him and against a marble wall and it crashed into fragments. He lost what little control he had over himself. He advanced on Caesar and held his clenched fist under the other's chin. For the first time Caesar felt loathing for him and wished he had poisoned the wine.

"You have told me before, sweet and treacherous friend, that Cicero knows all, and the parts of all of you in our original plot, and that you laid it all before him, for the sake of Rome. But there are many virtuous and patriotic and simple men in that Senate. They do not know. I shall enlighten them, if you refuse to be my advocate! What then, great Caesar, noble soldier? Do you think Crassus will save you, come to your rescue, to the rescue of Pompey and Piso and Curius and Clodius, and others of our brotherhood? He will consign you to death with me. I will not die alone."

He laughed in Caesar's face with delight. "Do not think to have me murdered when I leave here, my devoted companion. I have a large guard waiting outside."

Caesar's white mouth contracted. A beautiful Alexandrian lamp began to smoke on a distant table and Julius went to it with pretended concern and trimmed it. Lazy wisps of smoke rolled about the library and he watched them idly. But he was thinking with intense rapidity. There was much in Catilina's threats, too much for any complacency. It was useless to appeal to Catilina's reason, for he had none. It was absurd to appeal to any patriotism, for he had none. But Caesar said:

"You, alone, abandoned our original plan, for you have no patience,

Lucius. Had you listened to us you would still be one of our companions, would be with us when we seize Rome in an orderly fashion. But—"

However, he halted at Catilina's wild gesture of contempt. The blue eyes had lost what little sanity they had ever possessed and the face was contorted. "Hark to me, Caesar, for the last time! I care nothing for Rome. I care nothing for your law and order, whimpering echoes of a contemptible Cicero! Consider him! He believes that a virtuous man of good will can be recognized even by the dullest or the most disreputable, and be respected. He has never known, that ridiculous lawyer, that virtue only arouses the derision of others, for virtue cannot be understood by the ordinary mind or the soul of a slave or by a man whose soul resides in his purse or his belly. So virtue receives its fitting reward—exile or death, or, at the very least the taunting cackle of the multitude."

"Then you," said Caesar, "grant him virtue and speak with disgust of those who do not respect or admire that virtue."

"I detest his virtue, which builds dull cities and dull societies and infamous peace. Do you know why I was born, Caesar?" The glittering eyes moved closer to Caesar who felt a rising alarm at the sight of them. "I was born to destroy the base and the contemptible! Ah, you would speak of Rome! Observe our country, Caesar. Shall I recount her virtues to you, her dirty little vices, her gross and slavish perversions? Shall this city of offal be permitted to live? No! I shall destroy it.

"Destruction is not less godly than creation. If a sculptor is offended by the ugliness of his statue he will demolish it with his hammer. But Chickpea would have that ugliness remain for the stupid reason that it has been created, that it is. But I have greater plans! This Rome shall be cleansed and demolished by fire, and on its cooling embers I will build a white city of marble, brighter than the sun, where a slave shall forever remain a slave, and a patrician shall be forever a patrician, and an emperor an emperor. I shall use the very mobs I will later destroy to attain that felicity and you, Caesar, shall call from your ashes: 'Well done, Savior of civilization!'"

"I am sure that you have ranted so to your freedmen and malefactors and malcontents and old, disgruntled veterans," said Caesar with irony.

Catilina laughed and his white teeth blazed in his face. "No, but should I tell them they would be joyful to die that Rome might be cured of their pestilence!"

He rose and put his fur cloak over his stately shoulders and he smiled down at Caesar. "Tomorrow, my noble advocate, you will defend me, for do you not love me, and are we not blood brothers through our oath, and are we not both patricians?"

After he was gone Caesar hastily summoned a slave and sent a mes-

sage to Cicero that Catilina would appear the next day at the Temple of
Concord. He sent similar messages to Crassus and the others. Then he
sat until the blue dawn appeared at his windows and considered what
he must do.

He must die, thought Marcus Tullius Cicero, on his way to the Temple of Concord in the Forum. The time for prudence, for temperance, has
gone. He must die and his followers with him. There is no other way to
save Rome—if indeed Rome can now be saved at all. Oh, why did I delay!
I had the murderer in my hand and let him escape. Indeed, I have no
valor; I am a temporizer; I am a lawyer; I hate violence and bloody deeds
and death; I love law. But sometimes all these are pusillanimous when
your country is in desperate danger. Then you must strike or watch your
prudence destroy what you have striven to save.

The Senate was meeting in the Temple to consider the fate of Catilina's
lieutenants whom Cicero had arrested. By now they must know that Catilina himself would be present. Rumor always ran like lightning in Rome,
from the palaces on the Palatine to the gutters of the Trans-Tiber. So
Cicero, accompanied by his brother and the latter's legion, was not surprised to find the Forum filled again with a huge mob in spite of the wintry
snow and the bitter wind that blew from the Campagna. The first sun was
just striking the highest red roofs on the hills though the lower city still
fumed with mist and dimness.

I am tired, thought Marcus. I am weary unto death. I have struggled
for a whole lifetime for my country, and it is now as if I have only just
joined the battle. Will it never cease? No, said the sober blood of his
ancestors in his veins. It will never cease so long as some men are ambitious
and many men are slaves in their spirits.

The Senate was already awaiting him, to hear his fourth oration against
Catilina and the enemies of Rome. He wore, again, his white woolen toga
and his staff of office, but all noted the marks of strain on his pale face
and that, even in these past few weeks, his hair had grown grayer and
that his wonderful eyes were sunken. But his step was firm and slow as
he stood in the middle of the Temple, after he had first made obeisance
at the altar and had lit a votive light. (He had watched the fugitive light
waver, as if it were deciding his fate, and then it had flared into brilliance
and he bowed again and returned to the center of the Temple.)

He stood in silence, thinking. The awful picture was confused, swamp-
ish and full of stench to him and flitting shadows. Could the people be
less confused than himself? He must make the darkness more clear to
them as he must make it for himself, for otherwise all was lost. He lifted
his eyes and searched in the crowded and smoky gloom for Catilina. The

sun had gone behind the clouds; only candlelight and torches dimly illuminated the winter dusk. Then one large candle flared up and Cicero
saw Catilina, grand as before, in his white fur coat and his jewels and
with his beautiful, idle smile. He was seated near the door of the Temple,
as if he had only strolled negligently within to hear an unimportant priest
recite his dull office. All at once Cicero remembered his childhood and
the tales Noë ben Joel had told him of the terrible adversary of man—
Satan, he who was an archangel of death and terror and destruction, but
an archangel still full of awesome beauty and ghastly splendor.

Cicero began to speak calmly and slowly, but in a voice like an echoing
trumpet. He addressed the Senators, fixing them with his strongly glowing
eyes.

"My lords, we are here today to discuss the fate of the lieutenants of
Lucius Sergius Catilina, the patrician and the soldier and the conspirator
against the peace and freedom of our country. And I am here as the advocate of Rome, as often I appeared as the advocate of many before, who
were in the most frightful of dangers—death.

"I perceive, my lords, that the faces and the eyes of all present are turned
toward me. I perceive that you are anxious not only as to the danger to
yourselves and the country, supposing that danger to be averted, but even
to the personal danger to me." Cicero smiled sadly, raised his hands and
dropped them. "What is danger to me, when my country's fate is far more
important?

"Pleasant to me indeed in the midst of misfortunes, and gratifying in
the midst of sorrow, is this exhibition of your good will. But, by the love
of heaven, cast that good will aside, forget my own safety and think only
of yourselves, your children and Rome! I am Consul of Rome, my lords,
for whom neither the Forum in which all justice is centered nor the
Campus, which is hallowed by the auspices of the consular elections, nor
the Senate, which is the asylum of the world, nor the home, which is the
universal sanctuary, nor the bed which is dedicated to rest, no, nor even
this honored seat of office, has ever been free from peril of death and from
secret treason.

"I have held my peace as too much; I have patiently endured much.
I have conceded much; I have remedied much with a certain amount of
suffering to myself—though the reason for alarm was yours. At the present
moment, if it was the will of heaven that the crowning work of my Consulship should be the preservation of you and the Roman people from a
most cruel massacre, of your wives and children and the Vestal Virgins
from a most grievous persecution, of the preservation of God in our nation,
against those who would exile Him, of the temples and shrines and this
most fair fatherland of us all from the most hideous flames, of the whole

of Italy from war and devastation, let me now confront whatever terrors fortune has in store for me alone!"

He flung out his arms and exposed his throat as if offering himself as a sacrifice for Rome, as if offering himself for her safety and redemption. It was a most sincere and a most moving gesture, and the Senators stirred on their chairs. But Catilina laughed openly if without making a sound. His luminous eyes searched the rows of the Senators, and he appeared to be satisfied. He folded his brown arms over his breast and fixed his derisive gaze on Cicero.

Cicero continued in his ardent voice: "Lords, take thought for yourselves, provide for your fatherland, preserve yourselves, your wives, your children, and your properties, defend the name and existence of the Roman people! Strain every nerve for the preservation of the State, look in every quarter for the storms which will burst upon you if you do not see them in time. We have seized the lieutenants of Catilina—who profanes the name of Rome by his very presence among us today—these men who have remained behind in Rome to burn down the city, to massacre you all, and to welcome Catilina in triumph. They are inciting the slave population, the dark and bloody underground of criminals and the perverse in the city, the disaffected, the traitors, in Catilina's behalf. In short, they have formed the design that by the murder of us all no single man shall be left even to weep for the name of the Roman people and to lament the downfall of this great nation. All these facts have been reported by the informers, confessed by the accused, themselves, and adjudged true by this august body of the Senate. You have already declared them guilty!"

Some of the Senators looked at Crassus who pursed his lips with solemn righteousness and nodded. Few noticed that Julius Caesar sat frowning and in a state of abstraction.

Cicero raised his arm and pointed at Catilina and cried out, "Behold the terror of Rome, the traitor, the murderer, the evil spirit who has designed our doom! Look upon his face and see all crime branded upon it! I know him well, lords. I have watched him for many years. I knew his plots, and sensed them.

"I saw long ago that great recklessness was rife in this state, and that some new agitation was proceeding, and that some mischief was brewing. But even I, who know Catilina so well, never fully imagined that Roman citizens were engaged in a conspiracy so vast and so destructive as this. At the present moment, whatever the matter is, in whatever direction your feelings and your sentiments incline, you must come to a decision before sunset. You see how serious an affair has been brought to your notice; if you think that only a few men are implicated in it, you are gravely mistaken. The seeds of this evil conspiracy have been carried further than you think; the contagion has not only spread through Italy but it has crossed the Alps and has already infected many of the provinces in its insidious progress."

Now Cicero raised his voice until it echoed against the walls of the Temple, and his whole slender body shook with indignant passion and his eyes shone with stern anger. Catilina lifted his fine head abruptly and stared at him as if struck.

"It cannot possibly be stamped out by suspense of judgment or judicious pleas for 'tolerance of opinions,' and procrastination! However you decide to deal, you must take severe measures at once, without delay—in the name of Rome, in the name of Rome's freedom, in the name of all that has made Rome free and great!"*

One of the Senators, after a sharp silence in the Temple, addressed himself to Cicero. "What is your desire for this body?"

Cicero did not answer immediately. He looked with sudden bitterness on Crassus and company, on the half-hidden face of Caesar, into the eyes of the quiet Pompey and the mobile face of Clodius. He then looked fully at Catilina. He raised his arm and pointed again at the beautiful patrician. In a great voice like the stroke of a drum he cried out:

"I demand death for this man's lieutenants, whom we now hold in custody, and I demand death for this renegade, this would-be destroyer of Rome, this traitor, this Vandal, this defamer of our name, this enemy, this tiger in human form, this panderer to the base and unspeakable—in short, Lucius Sergius Catilina!"

Then, as before, the people without the Temple raised a mighty and terrible cry: "Death to Catilina! Death to the traitors!"

The Senators listened. Some of them turned to neighbors and whispered, "Cicero has inflamed the mob. It is not the people of Rome who speak." And some replied, "Do you have the ear of the people and their voice? Or, is it your own only?"

The interior of the Temple was utterly silent now, as if filled by statues who sat and stood in the brown and fiery gloom and the smoke of incense and torches, a white cheek caught here and there in a flicker of flame, or folded hands, or a still shoulder, or a pale carved mouth. It was like a dusky cave inside, where the Fates lurked at their thread and their looms in total quiet. But outside the pale blue light of winter gleamed on the cloaked heads of the assembled people and revealed their dark faces and vehement eyes and the tossing of their upraised hands.

The challenge of death had been uttered in the Temple. None looked at Catilina in his contemptuous and smiling splendor. All looked at Cicero

---

* Fourth oration considerably condensed.

standing in the center of the tessellated floor, tall and slender and white-robed, a graying man with a white and resolute face and eyes like changing jewels. He began to speak again, and his voice though strong shook like an oak in a storm.

"I, lords, am an advocate, a lawyer, and was so long before I was a politician or even became interested in politics. I have been Praetor of Rome. I am now the Consul. In all these years of public service I have defended men from impending sentence of death. As Praetor I upheld the laws of Rome but did not ask that any man be made to suffer the final humiliation. As Consul, I have asked no magistrate, nor this august body of the Senate, to condemn any man.

"Death is the great ignominy. We sing of the death of heroes, and we honor their memory. But death in many ways is a sacrilege against life, for it mortifies the restraint of our senses. We speak of the noble visages of the dead. We do not mention the sudden loosening of the sphincter muscles which flood the expired flesh with dung and urine. We do not mention it for we instinctively have reverence for life and avert our faces from the mortifications which death inflicts upon it. All our being is revolted at this abasement of a man, this open scorn of nature upon him as if she has declared, 'He is no better than the beast of the field and dies as voluptuously shameful, with a spewing out of what is contained in his bowels and his bladder.'

"But we know that man is no beast of the field, for God has implanted in us a horror of death, the most powerful aversion against it, a rebellion of our senses against its humiliation. That which animated the flesh, though departed, has left a sanctity upon it and though we cannot evade nature's last vile contempt for what has always defied her, we keep our decent silence. Therefore, in our decency, we hesitate against condemning a man to the remorseless processes of nature, for when one man is mortified all other men are disgraced also. This to me is worse than death itself.

"Nevertheless, men are often forced to defend themselves, their families and their countries. We are often forced to surmount our instinctive loathing for death and its obscenities. Only a man bereft of all manhood can rejoice in the extinction of another, even an enemy. Only a beast can feel triumphant at the sight of a bloody battlefield, even if his own nation has conquered. The true man, surveying that battlefield, must bow his head and pray for the souls of friend and foe alike—for both were men.

"It is with no malice, therefore, and no exultation, that I ask that this august body of the Senate condemn Lucius Sergius Catilina to death, and his lieutenants with him. In their final ignominy even just men must share. But our country is greater than we. All that Rome is is nobler than any individual man. We are faced with the most direful of choices: Catilina lives or Rome dies!"

Catilina stirred then in that assemblage of statues, and his beautiful and jeweled evil seemed to catch a thousand tiny fires in the bronze gloom, glittering from his eyes to his shoulders to his arms to his gemmed crimson leather boots. He caught scores of eyes which became fixed upon him. But he looked only at Cicero, and his white teeth, bared in a haughty and derisive smile, sparkled like illuminated pearls. And Cicero returned his gaze and between them stood the misty form of a maiden who had been done hideously to death, and both knew it without the shadow of a doubt.

For a long passing of time all were mute in the Temple and all waited. It was as if they had sunken in a trance from which no one would wake. Then all started at the rustle and movement of a body and they saw that Julius Caesar, grave but with smiling eyes, had risen and was facing the Senate beyond the figure of Cicero.

"My dear friend, Marcus Tullius Cicero, has spoken eloquently and with patriotic fervor," he said in his rich voice. "Patriotism is to be greatly admired and honored. It is only its excess which is to be feared."

Cicero started. He looked at Julius with incredulous bitterness and out-rage and wrath. And Julius, though not facing him, raised his hand in protest as if Cicero had cried out.

Julius continued to the blank faces of the Senators, "Catilina has been denounced, his death demanded by the noble Consul of Rome. But he is permitted to defend himself by the very laws which Cicero upholds. Let, then, Catilina speak in his defense, lest we be shamed."

He sat down and did not glance at Cicero. Crassus pursed his lips and studied the floor. Cicero could not move; he did not appear to breathe. Catilina stood up and as if at a signal the red torches flared and flooded him with bloody light, and he had the aspect of a terrible but magnificent demon. It was then, at beholding him in his arrogance and surety, that a wave of tremendous emotion ran like water over Cicero's face, seeming to increase its proportions.

Catilina bowed ceremoniously and slowly to the whole Senate, to Julius and Crassus and company. All his movements were grace, and superb. When he spoke his aristocrat's voice rose without effort and with pride.

"Lords," he said, "I, Lucius Sergius Catilina, patrician of Rome, son of generations of Romans, soldier, officer, warrior of Rome, have been ac-cused on four separate and hysterical occasions before you of the most malignant crimes against my country. I have been accused of conspiracy against my nation and my brothers-in-arms, my generals, my blood which many of you here today share. I have been accused of the most detestable treason against Rome, against her ordinances and safety and welfare and security. I have, disbelievingly, listened to myself being denounced as an enemy of the State! I, Lucius Sergius Catilina!"

He paused as if what he had said was so incredible that he was stunned, or that he had been dreaming and had not heard aright. He looked from face to face, and now his own was full of cold and forbidding rage. He appeared to increase in stature. He clenched his hand on his sword. His face was full of contorted and affronted beauty, and his quick breath was loud in the silent Temple.

"Surely, lords, you sharers of my station and my blood, do not believe this? Surely you are as horribly offended as am I! My ancestors fought for Rome and died on her many battlefields in defense of her honor—as did yours. They were brought home to their grieving wives and children—as were yours—carried on their shields. Their heroic swords were stained with the blood of many races, during Olympian battles fought before the faces of the gods, themselves! The annals of Rome beat like thunder with their blessed and manly names—as the names of your ancestors beat also. Nowhere is there the whisper of dishonor upon them, or the taint of cowardice or fear or desertion. In war and in peace they served their country. As did I.

"Look upon me, lords! Look upon my wounded breast and my scars, received in the service of my country!"

He rent open the scarlet top of his long robe and showed his chest, indeed crossed and recrossed with the scars of old wounds. And the Senate looked upon them and did not speak or move, though emotion rippled over many a face as the memories of old soldiers stirred within them.

Catilina covered his breast. His lips shook.

"I, Lucius Sergius Catilina, have received medals and honors from my generals, and I have been embraced by them because of my services to my country! Was Sulla a liar, lords, or a traitor, that he could so honor me? Did multitudes of my countrymen vote for me for their Consul, and did they, in their voting, stigmatize themselves as liars and traitors? When I was Praetor, did I loot my country and betray her? Has Crassus here, or Julius Caesar the Magnus, or Pompey the Magnus, or the noble Publius Clodius, surnamed Pulcher, risen here to denounce me, I, their companion in many a battle, a brother, a fellow patrician, a comrade-in-arms? No! They have not risen. Not a single voice has accused me or denounced me. Save one."

He lifted his arm and pointed to Cicero as one would point at a dog of such obscenities that he chose not to speak its name. His attitude was so offended, so full of revulsion, so vibrant with anger, that several virtuous Senators believed him and shifted in their seats and let their eyes reveal their indignation.

"Save one!" he exclaimed. "Save only one! And who is he who accuses me? Not a Roman born within the gates of Rome, but only a Roman by courtesy, born near Arpinum in the countryside, a 'new man,' a man devoid of honor, a newcomer, a man who cannot possibly know what it is to be a Roman born and bred within these hallowed gates, within halls resounding with the blessings of heroic ancestors, in the sight of altars raised to the gods of heroes!

"Is he a soldier, lords? Does he bear upon his flesh what you see before you on my flesh? Where is his sword, his shield, his armor of Rome? He prates of law—but it was my ancestors who wrote the law and inscribed it for the generations of Romans yet unborn! It was my ancestors who wrote our Constitution with pens dipped in their own blood. It was my ancestors who administered the laws they created, and it was my ancestors who set the feet of Romans on the path to glory and strength and majesty. Lords! Did the ancestors of this man do so, this man of undistinguished family, this man, the son of tradesmen and mean shopkeepers and petty merchants? No! Yet he prates of law, as an ass would bray at the moon!"

He struck his breast with his clenched fist. His countenance was inflamed, his great blue eyes striking each face like lightning.

"This man, in this holy Temple, before your faces, before your honor and your love of country, your birth and your breeding, before the memories of your ancestors, before the lictors and the fasces and the banners of our country, before the mighty history of Rome, dares to accuse me—me! —of the most monstrous crimes that ever disgraced the spirits of men, of the most unmentionable corruptions, of treason! Treason!"

Again he struck his breast and the awful blue fire of his eyes turned upon Cicero with scorn and loathing.

"Lords, do you know what truly fills him now and what filled him before? Envy. Greed. Hatred of what he can never aspire to so long as Rome exists! He is Consul of Rome. It is not enough for him. Through guile and a mellifluous voice he has seduced the wits of Romans and made some fame for himself. It is not enough for him. He has risen from poverty to riches—the riches of Rome. It is not enough for him. He is envious. He wishes to be what I am, a patrician. Failing that, he would destroy and devour what he can never attain, what the gods have denied to him.

"On four separate occasions he has furiously and madly attacked me, in his envy and his frustration. I have heard him twice. On two occasions I did not come here, for very shame for my country. I did not fear him. I did not fear that you would believe him, in his horrible accusations against a son of Rome. I disdained to hear him, for who would give credence to one of low birth and mean ancestry? Only animals, as gluttonous as he.

"And now, he has the effrontery—which would never have been countenanced in the days of your fathers and mine—to demand that I die ignominiously for crimes I have never committed, and which as a patrician Roman I could not commit, nay, not even if I were deranged! I have endured him. Lords, I can endure him no more. I ask that you remember our common blood and the souls of our ancestors, and ask yourselves if I could be guilty of the stupendous crimes of which I have been accused—by this Marcus Tullius Cicero whose ancestors were fullers and washed our clothing! Search your hearts and your memories, lords, and then look upon what Rome has spewed up in these days, that low-born and base men can rise up, with impunity, and denounce men like myself who are the very spirit of Rome!"

He flung himself into his chair again and pressed his clenched fists upon his knees, and his breast heaved and he stared at the floor as if he saw a fearful and intimidating vision which he repudiated with all his blood and the force of his passions.

Quintus, who stood near his brother, felt his mouth fill with bile and the lust to do death. His burly face, usually so highly colored, was white as linen. His large hand rose and gripped Cicero's arm, and he found it as rigid as stone, and he saw that his brother was staring at Catilina as one would stare at a Gorgon's head.

Then in the profound and deadly silence Julius Caesar rose again, clothed splendidly, and faintly smiling. He addressed the Senate, who reluctantly tore their eyes from Catilina to listen to him.

"Lords," he said in a gentle and reasonable voice, "we have heard the accuser and the accused. Catilina's words indeed strike to the heart of every proud man. But, lords, we have the evidence! Cicero's accusations are not based on envy and wind. We have Catilina's lieutenants' confessions, which in justice and in the search of truth were not extracted from them by durance and torture, but which were freely admitted by the mouths of patricians themselves, and with the patrician's contempt for lies."

Catilina raised his beautiful and terrible head and looked directly at Julius, who smiled with slight indulgence.

"These days are not the days of our fathers, alas," said Julius with sadness. "Patricians in earlier days did not consort with foolish and plotting zealots of excitable ambitions. But life was simpler in the days of our fathers, and not so demoralized and so complex and so bewildering and not so shaken by the many winds of change and differences. A man knew his duty in those simple days. He was not mystified as to what was best for his country. He fought for her, simply, and died for her. His politics were not confounded and abstruse and intricate as now they are. Out of confusion, even out of good will and a love for one's fellows, there must inevitably rise, at times, a certain bafflement, a certain tendency to be duped by beguiling tongues, a certain unsureness of aims. What seemed good for our fathers no longer seems good to, alas, many of the unstable of character. Shall we call this instability, this confusion, treason, the most unpardonable of crimes? Or shall we call it deplorable and have compassion upon the silly perpetrators?"

Crassus suppressed his dark smile. Clodius moved uncomfortably. Pompey looked at Caesar and the impassive eyes narrowed. But the young Marcus Porcius Cato, grandson of the fiery old patriot and Censor, looked upon Caesar with horror and with Cicero's own silent wrath.

"It is not unknown," Caesar continued with ripe sorrow and regret, "that even aristocrats can be deluded and confused. Catilina has been accused by his own lieutenants of plotting against Rome, of a desire to fire and destroy her in a kind of exultant madness, of betraying her. One must remember that those lieutenants, in their eagerness to escape just punishment for their own crimes, might tend to exaggeration. Let us grant that Catilina listened to them and dreamed great mad dreams. After all, they are his fellow patricians. But young men! lords, and one knows the excesses of young and ardent men! Catilina is no longer young. And, he has been wounded many times in the service of his country, and suffered many fevers in foreign parts, and these are enough in themselves to throw a man's reason into disorder and to affect his judgment. I know him well; I have known him from childhood. I have fought side by side with him, and never was there a braver or more dedicated soldier! I found in him, in our youth together, no sign of this derangement which is alleged to possess him now—the result of hearkening to men of impatient passions and more impatient lusts.

"There may be much truth in what his lieutenants have said—and much imagination on their part. If Catilina listened, and was confused, and did not know what to do in these arduous and changing days and complexities of living and government, then his very listening was stupid. But, does that constitute treason? Perhaps. Perhaps not.

"Nevertheless, it does call for a penalty, and I demand it."

He looked at Catilina whose perfect mouth was set in an expression of mournful dejection, and whose head was bowed again.

"Let him go forth!" cried Julius as if tortured by regret and indignation and yet by pity. "Let him spend the last years of his life in exile, where he can do penance for his folly and remember, unavailingly, the city of his fathers. Let us give him assurance that there will be no sentries at the gates, no ambushes to murder him on that road to exile. Let us forget the name of Catilina, as he, himself, must desire to be forgotten. Let us have mercy, remembering his services to his country in the past, and his bravery and his heroism. Let him go, to meditate on his follies and recall, as the years pass, that his fellow Romans could be moved to compassion and to spare him." At this, Julius put his hands over his face as if to hide his tears, and then he averted his face and sat down in an attitude of exhaustion and pain.*

Cicero said to himself with the utmost despair: He has betrayed me and Rome. How did Catilina reach him, that he dishonored himself so? O Julius, I thought no better of you, but I have had my hopes! I thought that at the last you would stand with your country. Now all is lost.

Cicero saw the faces of the Senators and saw the struggle upon them and the fear and the darkness. And worst of all, the doubt and unsureness.

It was then that young Cato rose, the man with the refined face and the unafraid and wrathful eyes and the delicate features. Cato came to stand beside Cicero and to take his hand in the unaffected gesture of a comrade. And he looked at the Senators and his eyes became bright and steadfast. Then slowly he turned to Julius, who had suddenly recovered from his grief and was sitting upright in his ivory chair, as if he saw a marble Hermes come to life and confront him. Cato raised his hand and pointed at Caesar and began to speak in a voice that trembled and was at first shy, and slowly gathered strength.

"Caesar! Son of a great and honored house! Caesar the Magnus, the famed soldier! Caesar who has today dishonored all that he is, and his country, too!"

The Senators straightened in their seats and could not believe their eyes and their ears. They looked at each other, dumfounded.

"Caesar, the dissembler, the liar!" cried Cato, with all the power of his anger. "He knows that what Cicero has said is truth; he knows that what the lieutenants of Catilina have said is truth! Why does he deny it? Tell me, Caesar, of what are you afraid? What emotions crowd your subtle heart? What deviousnesses of brain and soul?

"You have heard the truth many times, yet now you speak softly. Softly! What softness is this in behalf of traitors, Caesar? Why do you insult our intelligence, our knowledge, our rationality as men, our awareness of the truth? Must there be softness for traitors, for the enemies of our country? Must there be the excuse that they were duped, that they were confused, that they did not know what they did? That they intended well, out of the goodness of their hearts, and that only the result was vile and not the intention? When they disseminated treason, did they do it only out of the love of man and a burning desire for justice, however misguided or dangerous? Were they only dissatisfied and did they only do what they did in

* Actual speech of Caesar.

order to better the lot of all Romans, particularly those they called the 'oppressed?' Was their impatience, as you call it, only the impatience of those who ache to improve society? Were they frustrated, merely, at the slowness of the law, and the slow correction of what is unworthy in the law? Or, Caesar, are they what you know they are—traitors and murderers and assassins and renegades, with a full knowledge of their crimes and with a lust for power?"

His voice choked with his godlike emotion and rage. And the Senators, moved again and coming as out of a dream, listened. Julius smiled musingly. Crassus betrayed nothing in his expression. Pompey smiled an inscrutable smile. Clodius affected to examine his nails.

Cato continued, trembling for all to see, but not with fear:

"What I advise—what I now demand and what all Romans demand with me—is this, that since the State, by a known and treasonable combination of dissolute citizens, has been brought into the most monstrous peril, and since the plotters, including Catilina, are among us, and more, convicted on their own confession of having thought up massacres and riot, incendiarisms, and all sorts of inhuman and cruel outrages on their fellow citizens, punishment be inflicted according to old-fashioned and ancient precedent, as on men found guilty of capital crimes!"*

So fascinated were the Senators, and so struck by the simplicity and ardor and passionate honesty of the young man, whom they had known as a gentle and serious squire, a studious patrician, a valorous but unassuming Roman, that they did not notice that Catilina had risen, in his distant station, and had suddenly disappeared, melting away through the throngs and even the soldiers at the door who were as fascinated and as struck as themselves. The massed people outside were themselves unaware of his fast and gliding passage, for they had been listening to Caesar and to Cato and were astonished and entranced, their heads lifted and strained so as not to miss a word, their voices, always so exuberant, for once silenced. They did not notice nor heed Catilina's soft escape; if they were aware at all they thought it a mere jostling. It did not occur to them, until too late, to know that he had escaped. Too, the winter sun had become dazzling so that the eye ached and watered as it tried to peer through the brilliance to the dusk within the Temple.

Only one saw that stealthy exit and that was Julius Caesar, and he never started or betrayed what he had seen and kept his expression thoughtful. At last, when he heard no outcry beyond the Temple, he became aware that he had been holding his breath and that his lungs were protesting. He smiled in himself with intense relief, and glanced warily at Cicero. But

* An actual recorded speech of Marcus Porcius Cato.

Cicero's head was bowed, for he had been deeply moved by Cato's words and the touch of his hand. He heard the murmur of the Senators when Cato had finished speaking, and he pondered in himself before he lifted his head and addressed them again, knowing that only too many were hostile to him and despised him.

"Lords, Cato is of the opinion that men who have attempted to deprive us of life, to destroy this Republic, and to blot out the name of the Roman people, ought not to enjoy for a single second the privilege of life and the breath which we all share; and he bears in mind that this particular punishment has often been resorted to at Rome in dealing with disloyal citizens. Caesar understands that death has not been ordained by the immortal gods as a method of punishment, but is either an inevitable consequence of natural existence or a peaceful release from labors and afflictions. Thus the wise have never faced death with reluctance and the brave have often met it gladly. But imprisonment and especially death have certainly been devised as the exceptional penalty for abominable crimes. Caesar, however, proposes that Catilina and his conspirators be exiled from Rome and be distributed to unfortunate other towns or hamlets throughout Italy, which would seem, lords, to be an act of unfairness to those towns or hamlets!" He sighed and shook his head.

"If you adopt Caesar's proposal, which is in accord with his own political life which is considered 'popular,' I shall have less reason to fear an outburst of public resentment, for many love Catilina. If you adopt the alternative of death, I shall bring upon myself a larger amount of danger. But let me ask this of Caesar: Surely he is aware that the Sempronian Law was enacted for the benefit of Roman citizens only, and that a man who is an open enemy of the State cannot really be a citizen, and therefore cannot suffer only exile!

"Lords, I have concluded my exhortations, and the decision is now yours. You can only determine, in the light of evidence, and with courage, as to the supreme welfare of yourselves and of the Roman people, as to your wives and children, as to your altars and your hearths, your sanctuaries and temples, the buildings and homes of the whole city, as to your sovereignty and your liberty, the safety of Italy, the whole commonwealth of Rome. I am your Consul. I will not hesitate to obey your instructions, whatever they may be. And I will take it upon myself the entire responsibility."*

He looked at the Senators with quiet severity and did not glance away from them. He stood with his brother at one hand and Cato at the other. The fate of Rome lay with these Senators, and he was resigned to their hesitation and their ultimate rejection of his demand for Catilina's death.

* Conclusion of fourth oration.

But the people outside had rapidly passed his final words among themselves to the farthest reaches of the Forum, and now the Temple, as Cicero waited and the Senators conducted a whispered consultation with each other, was suddenly invaded by a huge and thunderous roar: "Death to Catilina and all the traitors! Death! Death!"

Cicero heard and the faintest of smiles passed over his stern features. Caesar heard, and looked into Crassus' eyes and read nothing there that he could interpret. And the Senators heard, and listened acutely, and knew that they had no alternative. The oldest among them directed his eyes upon the Consul and said:

"Death to Catilina and his conspirators."

He had hardly finished speaking when Quintus started forward and gave a signal to his soldiers to arrest Catilina. But Catilina was not there, and at once those within the Temple joined their angered cries with those outside. Catilina, on his great black horse, and followed by several of his companions was, at that very moment, sweeping furiously through the nearest gates of Rome to join old Manlius.

Late that night Cicero sat in his library signing the documents which would deliver Catilina's lieutenants, now in prison, to the Tullian dungeon for execution on the morrow. The execution would be the most shameful of all: the lowering of a man into a pit where he would be seized and strangled slowly and painfully. Cicero's hand faltered. Desperately he wished there could be an alternative. He looked at his pen and shuddered. Never before had he signed a death warrant for any man. But if Rome were to live these men must die, though all were patricians and one had, for a year, been a Consul of Rome. Which was more evil: Execution for treason or the treason itself? He sighed deeply and his signature on the warrants was hardly legible, so great was his anguish of soul.

He had just completed the wretched task when his overseer announced the arrival of Julius Caesar. Marcus' first impulse was to deny him an audience, for his bitterness against his old friend was extreme. Then he wearily assented, and pushed aside the warrants and looked at them briefly. It seemed to him that the edges were stained with blood.

Caesar entered softly and gravely and with a most serious face. Marcus silently motioned to him to seat himself, and as silently he poured wine for his guest. Caesar took the goblet, and Marcus took his own. Then Caesar toasted his host. Marcus made no gesture but put the cup to his lip.

"You are angry against me, Marcus," said Julius. "But was it not better that I gave dissent to the proceedings than permit a too hasty decision by the Senate? History will record that Catilina was condemned only after long and judicious consideration, and with justice, and not by emotion."

"That was not your intention, Julius," said Marcus, his bitterness increasing. "Tell me: In what manner did Catilina reach you and intimidate you, that you became his advocate?"

Julius raised his black brows in astonishment. "I swear to you, Marcus, that I do not understand you! What are you implying?"

"The truth, Julius, only the truth. No matter. You will not tell me. Why are you here?"

Julius smiled at him affectionately. "To applaud you, Marcus, for saving Rome."

Now Marcus could not control himself. He lifted up the death warrants in his hand and held them high and shook them. "Look at these, Caesar! One demands the arrest and subsequent execution of Lucius Sergius Catilina! The five others order the execution, tomorrow, of his lieutenants! Six warrants, Caesar, six only. Do you not know the other names which should be now in my hand? Yours, Caesar, and Pompey's, and Clodius', and most probably even Crassus'! And all the others with you! All! I tell you, I should sleep better tonight, and with less agony of spirit, if your names were here also, and that I swear by my holy patroness, Pallas Athene."

He flung the warrants down on his table and stared at them with grim suffering. Caesar rose and put down his goblet. "You wrong us, Marcus," he said.

"Do I, Caesar?"

"Yes. I have sworn to this often before."

"You swear a lie, and for that the gods will have their vengeance upon you."

Caesar fastened the jeweled pin on his shoulder which held his cloak. He gazed at Marcus in a long quiet. At last he said, "You are a good man, old friend and companion, and your heart is sore that you must do this thing, and so you speak intemperately. Enough. I forgive you, for do I not love you? Let your heart be at rest. You have saved Rome."

But Marcus' wrath forced him hastily to his feet and he leaned across the table so that his face confronted Caesar's, and he flushed crimson.

"I did not save Rome, Caesar! No one can now save Rome, and that you know. She is doomed, Caesar, as you are doomed, and I, and a whole world with us!"

A little later that night Julius said to Crassus: "I tell you, not only Catilina is mad. Cicero is mad also. He has saved Rome for us. He confuses the audacity and murders of Catilina with our own deliberate and intelligent decision not to oppose change, and"—here Julius smiled—"to guide it skillfully."

"Let us be grateful," said Crassus. "We have seen the end of Catilina."

CHAPTER FIFTY-FIVE

But it was not the end. It was only the bloody beginning.

Catilina struck almost at once, with Manlius and his malcontents, with the rabble of envious freedmen, gladiators, runaway slaves, rascals, criminals of all kinds, and the disaffected, debtors, and treasonous. Among them, however, were Tuscan patriots whom Catilina had seduced, and these were his chosen men, for all were skilled soldiers, as were Manlius' Etrurians. Rumor ran in affright to Rome. Catilina was on the march. There were tens of thousands of his sympathizers within the city, among them the relatives of Lentulus, who had died the shameful death in the Tullian dungeon with the other four lieutenants of Catilina.

Madness, as Cicero had once said, had a terrible grandeur of its own which is not found among the sane, and it was this grandeur which had fascinated those who loved Catilina. Once Noë ben Joel had written Cicero from Jerusalem: "Many of the learned Jews believe that evil men are mad. But others equally learned say that the mad are evil, and are possessed of demons. So many of our holy men spend their lives casting out devils from the afflicted." The devil that had Catilina had never been exorcised, and now it utterly seized him. Despising his followers—thousands of whom had a genuine grievance against Rome, such as war-ruined farmers and desperate freedmen and those who had involved themselves in difficulties through the moneylenders, whose interest rates had been allowed to mount beyond reason—and despising those who stood in his way to power, he had no restraints, no human compassion or mercy.

But the old and honorable soldier, Manlius, surrounded by his veterans —who also had grievances against Rome—wrote to the general in Rome, Marcius Rex, who had been hastily commissioned by the Senate to destroy all Catilina's and Manlius' motley army. "My dear former brother-in-arms, Marcius," Manlius wrote in his moving letter, "I call upon gods and men to witness that we have taken up arms not against our fatherland, or to bring danger upon others, but to protect our own persons from outrage. We are wretched and destitute. Many of us have been driven from Rome by the violence and cruelty of the moneylenders, while all have lost repute and fortune. None of us has been allowed to enjoy the protection of the law and retain our personal liberty, after being stripped of our patrimony. Your forefathers often took pity on the Roman commons and relieved their necessities by Senatorial decrees. Often the commons themselves, prompted by a desire to govern or incensed at the arrogance of the magistrates, have taken up arms and seceded from the patricians. But we ask neither for power nor for riches, but only for freedom, which no true man gives up except with his life. We implore you and the Senate to take thought of your unhappy countrymen, to restore the bulwark of the law of which the judges' injustice has deprived us, and not to impose upon us the necessity of attacking our fellow Romans, and asking ourselves how we may sell our lives most dearly."*

Manlius sent this letter to Marcius Rex, who promptly took it to the Senate, who requested Cicero to meet with them. Cicero read the letter and sighed bitterly. "There is much in what Manlius has written," he said. "Advise him to have naught to do with Catilina and to lay down his arms, and the arms of his followers." This the Senate did, and the letter was dispatched to Manlius, who had written his own letter secretly and unknown to Catilina. He showed the Senatorial letter now to Catilina who was at first enraged against the old general for his "duplicity," and then highly amused. "Let us begin our march at once," he said. "I do not trust that Senate, no, not now."

Manlius hesitated, for he was old and tired and a Roman. "I have seen much violence and blood and death, Lucius. Let us bargain with the Senate, with the rulers of our country."

Then Catilina said with wild rage, "I have no country! I never had a country! I shall have one when I seize Rome, and then only!" Catilina was furious and elated with his own plans. His army would march on Rome, twenty thousand strong at the least, via Gaul, then crossing the Apennines through the pass of Faesulae.

Cicero commissioned Metellus Celer, now one of the Praetors, to go at once to the Picenian territories and cross to Faesulae, take the heights with his legions, thus blocking the passage of Catilina. On the other hand Cicero sent C. Antonius Hybrida from Rome with another legion; Quintus Tullius Cicero was one of his captains prepared to face Catilina directly after he was deflected from Faesulae. At the hour of departure, Cicero embraced his brother with an anguish he could not control or conceal.

"Do not be overcome, dear Marcus," said Quintus, alarmed by his brother's tears. "I feel that I shall not die at the hands of Catilina's criminals. I shall return. But, should I not return, remember I have perished in the name of my country."

Catilina, a great shrewd soldier, was not overly dismayed by the fact that his march had been stopped through Faesulae. He was a strategist. He

* Actual letter from Manlius to Marcius Rex.

turned his army to the north valley of the Arno River, and struck toward Pistoria, in a plan to drive his way west across the Apennines to Gaul. His elation rose to the wildest heights. He had not the slightest doubt but that he would succeed. Did not the gods love the patrician and the daring and the brave and the audacious? He felt invulnerable, as if guarded by the shield of Perseus himself. He felt a veritable Hercules, whom none could conquer. There were moments when he believed that he could engage the army of Antonius alone, with his own hands, and destroy them without receiving a single wound in return. He rode back and forth along the ranks of his huge but straggling army of discontented veterans and nameless mobs armed, in hundreds of cases, only with sharpened staves or clumsy spears. He carried a blood-red banner on which was embroidered the ancient and heroic arms of the Catilinii. His men looked upon his beautiful and exultant face, and terrified though they were he seemed like a god to them, beyond the power of any mortal to overthrow. His armor glittered in the winter sun. His scarlet cloak floated behind him; his helmet shone like a golden moon. Fervor and madness made an aura of light about him. The hoofs of his black horse struck fire from the stones of the valley; his shadow was long and vivid on the snow. Beyond stood the black and white mountains which, to Catilina, appeared almost at hand and hardly higher than boulders. Beyond them lay Gaul—and Rome. His voice rang like a joyous trumpet, heralding news of victory, and the ranks of his men closed and they marched with rising hearts and suddenly lost all fear and all doubt. Catilina had become the flaming Apollo to them, mounted on Pegasus, clad in armor forged by Vulcan on Olympus.

The two armies relentlessly approached each other at midday. Antonius, the patrician, colleague of Cicero, and general, was suddenly seized with disquiet. He rode side by side with his aide, Petreius, a brave and veteran soldier, and behind them rode Petreius' favorite captain, Quintus, in brilliant armor and with a set and valorous face. And behind the three rumbled and thundered the armored war chariots with snapping banners and lictors and fasces, across the broad plain. Antonius' disquiet grew. Catilina had attempted to seduce him; Catilina was the enemy of Rome. Catilina must be destroyed. But Catilina was also a brother patrician and Antonius had once loved him, and their families were close friends.

Antonius said to Petreius, "I am ashamed, but I am stricken suddenly with gout. I must retire to the rear. Do you then, dear comrade, go forward with these legions, and with Quintus at your side, and strike the first blow. I shall marshal the soldiers at your rear, and couriers will bring me your slightest hail."

Petreius, the burly and grizzled general, understood at once. He was also a patrician. But above all, he was a soldier. He averted his fierce eyes and said only, "Be it as you say, Antonius. I trust you will recover at once. Quintus and I will lead the attack." He looked down the long wide plain and saw the creeping blackness of Catilina's army, and his lips clenched together. Quintus had heard the exchange; he did not even glance at Antonius as the latter wheeled his horse about and rode to the rear, his face fixed and pale. Quintus despised his brother's colleague. A Roman was a Roman—that was all a man needed to know. He made a gesture and suddenly the silent air and the majestic countryside hammered with marching drums. To the unfortunate Antonius it seemed that he was being ignominiously and derisively drummed to the rear, and his cheeks flushed though his lips remained white. Petreius smiled grimly. It was not Quintus' authority to sound the drums, and the following trumpets of challenge. But Petreius did not reprove him. He motioned to Quintus to ride beside him in Antonius' place, and Quintus, in grateful pleasure, spurred up his horse.

"If my brother were traitor to Rome, I would dispatch him with my own hand," said Quintus. Petreius did not reply. He agreed with Quintus, but still he and Antonius were fellow patricians, and Quintus was not. But he loved valor and he reached from his own horse briefly to lay a mailed hand on the younger man's shoulder. "We are soldiers," he said, and it was enough for Quintus, whose strong face colored with gratification. He loved every man in the Roman army, from the charioteers to the massed legions marching behind the vehicles, from the drummers to the trumpeteers who challenged Catilina. The clamorous rumble of wheel and the shaking of the quiet and disturbed winter air by the foot soldiers excited him. It had been a long time since he had engaged in a mortal combat, and his soldier's blood was almost unbearably stirred and his spirit rose in his breast as if with wings. He sat high in his saddle, controlled and vital, his flesh humming with life. What it was to fight for one's country, and even to die for her! The ghosts of heroes rode with him on transparent horses, and long-silenced drums and trumpets lifted in frail jubilation like echoes above all else.

The pale but dazzling sun searched the white earth and the black and white mountains, and struck on scarlet and gold banner and the carved sharp shadows of the two approaching armies and glittered along drawn sword and broke itself upon crested helmets and impaled itself on upheld spear and filled the hollows of the snow with blue radiance. At the left of the Roman army ran the cold and Stygian river, tumbling with pale froth in its unquiet passage. Far above the sky was the faintest and iciest azure, against which the banners were like blood. Leather creaked; weapons rattled; horses neighed, raising their red nostrils impatiently to smell the acrid scent of battle. Their breath smoked. The sun blazed on thousands of gilded shields and made little suns of them, themselves.

Quintus was a man of single mind; subtleties of the effete—as he considered them—were for colonnades and not for a time when action was demanded. He was riding now to face a hostile army led by a madman, and as a soldier of a single mind he rejoiced to challenge the enemies of his country. Romans had fought Romans before, without and within the walls. It was sufficient for him. In his impatience to meet the foe he spurred his horse beyond the horse of Petreius, and had to rein in at the last moment. It was then that his simple heart was struck violently as with a fist of iron, and the thought came to him that he was eager to kill the man who had risked his own life to save him.

Catilina was the avowed and condemned enemy of Rome. He desired her destruction. Nevertheless, he had been a brave man and a heroic soldier, and a devoted comrade-in-arms. All at once Quintus felt violently sick. He would not quail or withhold his hand, facing Catilina, for Catilina must manifestly die. But suddenly Quintus prayed that it would not be himself who would kill Catilina, and that Catilina would fall by another's hand. The Roman army was now descending the slope of the plain; Catilina's army was rising on the slope. In but a little while they would strike at each other. Quintus felt the taste of salt, or blood, in his mouth and his expression, under the lifted visor of his helmet, must have been very strange for the old veteran, Petreius gave him a quick and curious glance though he said nothing. Quintus caught that glance; he lowered his visor.

Petreius lifted his mailed hand to shade his eyes and scrutinized the approaching foe. "It is a wretched army," he said. "We shall defeat them easily." He swung up his arm and the thunder of the drums and the cry of the trumpets rose to a deeper pitch and stunned the ear with sound. "Charge!" cried Petreius, and he and Quintus sprang forward on their horses, and, followed by their officers and the chariots and the mounted legion and the foot legion behind them, raced to the first shock of the attack.

Catilina's army halted abruptly and looked up to see the glittering wave rushing down upon them. It wavered. But it did not break. There were thousands of brave men who had known combat before among that army. They were led by brave men. Even the nondescript rabble of Rome which formed part of that army, and it was poorly equipped, felt the awful excitement of approaching death and battle. They closed their ranks tighter and rushed to meet the Roman army, and far in advance of them was Catilina on his black horse, plunging furiously before them. As if very nature joined in the vehemence the sun seemed to enlarge, to grow unbearably bright, to turn the snowy hills to white fire; the black river clamored and pounded in its icy banks.

The shock of the wild and terrible meeting of the two armies screamed and pounded back from the mountains, and the earth quaked. Horses flung themselves against horses, man against man. Catilina had no chariots; the Roman chariots wheeled and churned and roared about the foe. The sun splintered on flashing swords, on the whirl of spears. Men fell from saddles and stained the snow with blood. Horses shrieked in mortality. Weapons drummed on shields. Fearful faces glared from under helmets; the air was filled with shouts and groans, the scourging of iron wheels, the cracking of axles, the thud of colliding armored bodies. What had been a still and peaceful plain, divided by a river, became a bloody place of slaughter under the fierce cold sun. And the hills echoed back the overwhelming sounds as if unseen armies from Hades had joined the battle.

Now all was one vast and flaming and bannered confusion on the plain, as swords plunged and spears struck and shields were tossed high above the lunging mass of the attacked and the attacking. Quintus saw no one but the man challenging him; one by one he disposed of each who faced him, driving him off his horse or reaching down to strike a man on foot. Sweat streamed down his face for all the intense cold of the day. His knees gripped his horse so that both his hands were free, and he directed the animal by powerful pressure only. His teeth sparkled in the ferocious light; he panted and gasped. He lost all knowledge of time, of death, of sound. One by one, as men faced him, he killed them.

The engagement was comparatively short. Catilina's men fought like lions, even the "nondescript" elements, for there would be no quarter given or prisoners taken. Death alone would be the supreme victor. The Romans fought grimly and far more tenaciously, and with a kind of enormous contempt for the foe they faced. To a man they loathed treason, for they were soldiers first and soldiers love their country. And thousands of the enemy were Etrurians, whom the Romans did not consider Italians at all. The Romans had their nation to defend; even the bravest among the enemy knew that they were defending nothing but themselves.

Quintus tore his sword loose from flesh, to turn it on more flesh, until blood ran down his brown arm and splashed all over his armor, his tunic, his leggings and his boots. His horse was wounded, but was as valorous as himself. He had a deep wound on one thigh, and his face was also bleeding. He felt nothing but the lust of battle; he swung his horse about and leaped and battered his way through the wall of flesh that faced him. His arm never tired. And his comrades were valiant, too, and pressed about him, heaving and groaning and shouting and cursing and panting;

officers and men mingled together in an iron phalanx that relentlessly pressed back the army of Catilina, hundreds of whom fell with mighty splashes in the river to drown and to choke the watery passage with their bodies. Trumpets repeatedly shattered the brilliant air with their metallic cries; drums thundered for fresh charges, for the gathering of forces. The wheeling chariots of the Romans, crowded together, crashed over and over, the wheels spurning the bloodied snow.

Then all at once the frightful encounter was over as swiftly as it had begun. Gasping for air, and looking about him, Quintus searched for Petreius, and could not see him. A mound of the reddened dead lay before him, sprawling in the last agony, leg touching arm, face thrust against foot. Now the Romans, scattered far and wide in their mission of fury, raced to the center again and cut down the last of the foe, who tried to evade them. The slaughter of both sides had been most terrible. Romans swung from their horses to embrace and console their dying comrades, or to kneel in the drenched snow to weep over a brother or to lift a visor. Chariots churned to a halt. The confusion was covered by the smoke from the nostrils of thousands of horses, who stood trembling in their tracks with lowered heads. And the blazing hills looked implacably down at the carnage and crowned themselves with fire.

Quintus was suddenly aware of exhaustion. Officers rode up to speak to him; he could only nod or shake his head, for it seemed to him that he had become deaf. He rode apart from them, to wipe his sweating face, to press his hands against his wound. It was then that he saw Catilina lying on the ground, miraculously in a little circle of his own, and in a puddle of his own blood.

Quintus, shaking as if with fever, slowly descended from his horse and staggered to the fallen man who still clutched his sword. The helmet had dropped from the noble head, and a quick wind stirred the thick dark hair with its ruddy shadows. Catilina's face was white with death, that wonderful face which had seduced Fabia and a thousand other women in his lifetime, and had enchanted countless men who had followed him to this violent day, and this final and enormous rendezvous. His eyes, those blue eyes which had terrified and fascinated, stared at the sky sightlessly. Quintus fell to his knees beside the crushed enemy and stared at him, and dumbly wiped his sweat from his eyes with the back of his scarlet-wet hand.

One of the most appalling enemies Rome had ever known lay on his back and gazed at the sun, undone at last by the madness of hatred and ambition and lust, fallen at last by his own will. Quintus leaned over him; his breath made a cloud before his face. He brushed it away, dumbly, as if it were an intruder and not his own breath. Then he started, and shuddered, for Catilina's eyes had turned from an apparent contemplation of the sun and were directed at him. The intense blueness was failing rapidly and glazing, but all his savage soul struggled to see behind the closing veil of death.

"Lucius?" said Quintus, and his voice was a hoarse groan. He could not help himself. He lifted the cold and flaccid hand near him and held it.

The spirit struggling to be free from Catilina's flesh paused a moment to listen, to peer again. And then it saw Quintus' dark and suddenly weeping face, and the faintest smile touched the handsome gray lips.

"Quintus," he whispered. The smile deepened, and Catilina called him by the affectionate nickname he had once given him: "Bear cub." The dying fingers, by sheer force of will, tightened on Quintus' hand.

"Farewell," said Catilina. He turned his eyes to the sky again, and said, "Long I hoped for this day, and blessed is its coming." The white lids fell over the glaucous eyes; a long shivering and convulsion seized the whole body of Catilina; he stretched and straightened and his back arched. Then with a dull crash the armored body subsided on the ground and lay still, suddenly much dwindled, suddenly spent, and that which had animated it fled and left it small and collapsed, and, at the last, at peace. The sword fell from the fingers of his other hand, the short sword of Rome which he had carried in honor and dishonor.

Quintus lifted his own eyes to the indifferent sky which had witnessed endless carnage and madness, and, weeping, he said aloud, "I thank all the gods that it was not my hand which slew him! I thank the gods." He resolutely repeated it, but something far in his mind wondered and trembled and would not let him know.

He looked down at the still hand he had not yet relinquished and he saw something glowing on one finger. It was the serpentine ring of the deadly brotherhood. Quintus recoiled. Then he forced himself to remove it, and he dropped it in his pouch, and forced himself to his feet and looked about him with a dull stare, weaving where he stood. He saw a fallen Roman banner, sodden, stained, torn. With a gigantic effort he went to it and he lifted it from where it lay and it seemed to him that he was lifting iron and not cloth. He raised it as high as he could and stumbled back to Catilina and covered that stately body with it to hide it from the contempt of the heavens, the scorn of man, and the bitter air. For, at the end, Catilina had not died ingloriously, in the adventure of death.

"He was the enemy of Rome," said Cicero to his brother. The serpentine ring lay on a table before them. "He was master of an abattoir. He had no real plans to rebuild, to renew, had he conquered. He was pure destruction. He wished only to gaze on terror and ruin and the collapse of a whole civilization. Violence was his mother, his wife, his mistress. He lay down with them and dreamed with them. He was filled with hatred of all men. For that, he suffered the vengeance of God."

"He was a brave man," said Quintus.

Cicero smiled sadly. "You speak as a soldier, my brother, and soldiers honor courage and valor above all things. But there is a greater honor and a greater valor, and that is the service of God and country, and not conquest, not personal ambition, not the love of terror for terror's sake, not the desire to rule one's fellows as one rules animals, not the craving for power. This honor, and this valor, is not always hailed, not always known. Yet I tell you that they are greater than the bravery of the Catilinas, and more heroic than any banners. For they are the Law."

He stood up and embraced Quintus as he stood before him, and then left his right hand on the other's shoulder and looked earnestly into the dulled and reddened eyes.

"I do not reproach you, Quintus, that you wept for him. It is nothing that he would have killed you gladly on that day, and would have rejoiced in the murder of myself. He was like a holocaust, a mad disaster, and such men happen to all nations as do all calamities, at many times in their history when they cease to care for the profound Laws of God. Mourn the comrade you knew, the man who saved your life. But thank the Eternal that that which was the larger part of him has forever passed away." He added, "In his own form at least."

But it was not yet the end, as Cicero knew only too well that it would not be.

Cneius Piso, the fair-haired and small and slender old comrade of Catilina, had been made governor of Spain a year before Catilina's trial by the Senate. Cicero had bitterly opposed that appointment by Crassus, and before his own election to the Consulship. But Crassus had replied coldly, "You speak always of plots, Cicero. It is an obsession on your part. Cneius Piso is a noble patrician and of a great family, and a notable soldier and administrator. I reject your protestations."

But a short time before his appearance at the Temple of Concord Catilina had sent a courier to his friend, with the one word, "Strike!" So Piso gathered a Spanish army about him, who loved him, and marched on Rome to assist his beloved fellow conspirator and to exult with him and to rule under him. The Spaniards were a gloomy but an honorable body of soldiers, and were devoted to their Roman governor. It is strange, then, that on the second day of their march they suddenly, and without apparent cause, mutinied and assassinated Cneius Piso and buried his body where they had slain him, and returned to their home.

And Q. Curius, who lurked sullenly in Rome, hidden and disgraced, was found murdered in his own bed one morning, only a week after Catilina's bloody defeat.

"It is said," wrote Sallust the historian, in commenting upon these events, "that Cicero's secret police had ordered their death. It is known that Crassus, who always proclaimed his love for the two men, sacrificed for their souls in the temples but was seen with a contented smile. Julius Caesar was observed in public mourning for them, but was not evidently in the deepest grief. Pompey does not mourn, nor does Publius Clodius, who was their devoted friend. Who ordered their death will remain the secret of history."

Cicero knew that every disastrous conspirator with Catilina must be extirpated. He shrank from the slaughter, but it was necessary so that there would be no more a focus of Catilina's infection left to afflict the body politic again. Antonius begged him for mercy. Cicero cried to him passionately, "Do you think I revel in this? I do it only for Rome, and not from malice and personal vengeance."

He feared that after Catilina's death the tens of thousands of the poor and ragged and hungry in Rome, who had loved Catilina, would create riot and chaos in protest, if only temporarily, in Rome. But he had underestimated his own eloquence and the understanding of the people. For Sallust wrote: "Even the poorest and the most abandoned did not like the final idea of burning the city where they had their miserable homes, nor, until Cicero revealed it, did they understand that this, and not a great loot and redistribution of the wealth, was in Catilina's mind."

Manlius, on the morning Catilina's army set out, had fallen on his own sword and was given silent burial by his men. Cicero's secret gratitude that the brave old soldier would not have to suffer an ignominious death shook him to the heart.

All of the rebellious patricians had relatives and all those relatives, among them Publius Clodius, became Marcus' mortal enemies. Julius Caesar saw old friends seized and executed. He and Clodius went to Crassus and said, "Cicero has lost his mind. He is arresting everyone who even knew Catilina."

Crassus looked at them darkly and said, "What would you have? The men are guilty; you know that with certitude. Do you wish him to spare them because they are patricians and men of influence, and you have dined with them, and loved them? Are they more than the poor scoundrels, the effeminate actors and wrestlers, and the pugilists and the freedmen and the criminals who were Catilina's followers also? I tell you they are more deadly than these." But he frowned.

Clodius said to Caesar, "Crassus fears for himself, and what the condemned might say of him. The sooner they are dead the safer he will be. What! Did you think he would intervene? Have dictators any compunctions?"

"Dictators, my dear Clodius," replied Julius, "cannot afford compunctions."

Clodius had a small dark face in which the large black eyes were set so far apart and were so full and wide, that the malicious declared he resembled an intellectual frog. Now his eyes gleamed. "I shall not forget this Cicero, whom I once admired and honored."

Julius shrugged. "Do not remember him then so long as we need him."

"Exigency makes strange companions," said Clodius. "Young Mark Antony is your admiring follower, yet your uncle, Marius, put his father to death. Now he swears a vendetta against Cicero because his beloved stepfather, Lentulus, was condemned to a shameful death by that Cicero. The dear Consul has made enough enemies to form a company of men."

Cicero knew of the hatred which was following him like an army. Terentia was avid in informing him, and sometimes with tears and lamentations. "My dear friend, Julia, wife of Lentulus, is inconsolable. So are many other ladies, who were my friends. Now I am proscribed."

"Your friendships, my dear Terentia," said Cicero with sadness, "are less than the safety of Rome. Did you think I aspired to the Consulship to serve self-glorious ends? No! I serve only Rome."

"Your family is nothing to you! What is political office, if a man's family cannot enjoy their new position? There are times when I detest you, Marcus, and regret that I married you. I am ostracized! My former friends avert their faces. Our son-in-law finds many doors closed to him, even those of fellow patricians. What future will be your son's?"

"Rome's future, if any," said Cicero. He thought of divorcing Terentia, for her complaints and recriminations were more than he could bear in these arduous and bloody days. He knew that the Catilinian conspiracy had involved many great families, but he had not, himself, known the extent. He now knew that Cornelius Lentulus had been assigned to the personal task of assassinating all the Senators, by Catilina, yet now those very Senators muttered that Cicero had been too harsh in his destruction of the conspiracy! Cicero remembered that Aristotle had wryly remarked that God had not endowed men with logic. He, Cicero, had saved Rome and had saved those very men secretly condemned to slaughter by Catilina. Yet now they whispered he was going to extremes, and even the people in the streets, aroused by the disaffected, turned sullen against their savior. There were moments when he considered leaving Rome, so great was his despair of mankind. Once, in an attempt to calm the growing animosity against him, he addressed the court of judicature wherein he outlined the full conspiracy against Rome and his own desperate efforts to over-throw it. The court listened in silence. Later, with derision, it was broad-cast that he had made a vainglorious eulogy in his own behalf, and the walls of Rome were scribbled with obscenities against him by those whom he had saved from fire, death, and hideous slaughter.

Like many men of deep humor, he made the error of believing that every man was also endowed with it. So, when he sometimes ventured a wry or jocular remark to some acquaintance, to lift the sombreness of these days, the remark was repeated eagerly as an evidence of his hard-heartedness or frivolity or even foolishness. He said, when hearing of these things, "Unhappy is the politician! If he is always very sober, it is said he is a humorless dull ass. If he speaks lightly at times, he is considered lack-ing in seriousness. If he is frugal, it is said he is filling his own coffers. If generous with public funds, he is denounced for wasting the people's substance. If he is honest, it is cried that he is dangerous or contemp-tuous. If a genial quibbler, it is said that he cannot be trusted. If he refuses to be intimidated by a foreign enemy, the people shout he wishes to plunge his nation into war. If he is very temperate, he is called pusillanimous. And his friends, of course, are always extremely mild in defending him against calumny!"

In the early spring he went to the island to escape his sorrow and his weariness and the growing hatred against him, which was inspired by the patricians.

CHAPTER FIFTY-SIX

One of the miseries of being a powerful official, Cicero had discovered, was the necessity of being guarded constantly against the homicidal ten-dencies of those he served. So he was accompanied to Arpinum by his brother, Quintus, and a large guard. The guard stationed itself on the bridge, which was dear to Cicero for having been the spot where he had first seen Livia Curius. One venture on it, and one glance at the faces of the selected and devoted soldiers, made the bridge untenable for him. The ghost of Livia never came there any longer. On the island itself he was more free of intrusion, though he was sometimes aware of discreet rustlings in the bushes as he made his passage along the shores. If he walked in the meadows he was never certain but that the shadows at the edges of the forest were not soldiers; he sometimes caught the glint of a helmet where least expected. He complained to Quintus that since the bridge was guarded, no one could pass. But Quintus said, "Who knows but a servant has been bribed?" So Quintus slept on a pallet across the door of his brother's bedroom.

"I shall be glad when I am no longer Consul!" Cicero exclaimed one day.

"Do you think that in retirement you will be safe, Marcus? No. You have too many enemies. Your old friend, Clodius, has sworn to destroy you. So have a number of others. Perhaps they would have preferred Catilina, and a cruel death, after all!"

Cicero would permit no one to intrude upon his library, where he would write for hours at a time, books and essays for his publisher, Atticus. Pouches of letters were brought to him from Rome, bills to be signed or to be rejected, and correspondence. All this was irksome, except for his own writing. However, the light of spring was radiant and the island was plunged into the ardent gold of the season and the air was sweet and the night was quiet except for the voices of the trees and the soft winds. Here Marcus could forget Terentia and all those others who were like iron weights on his steps and his spirit. Sometimes he evaded his watchful guards and visited the forest, places where he had met Livia, especially when the moon was a large gilt coin in the black sky. Tree frogs shrilled to the night, a nightingale sang, and the sound of the river was unbearably musical and full of memories. Marcus would think, "The darkness of all these years have never diminished Livia. I am growing old, and she is eternally young, and when I think of her I am a youth again." All the evil that had come to that young girl had fallen from her like a black cloak, and she was free of it, free of the pain of her girlhood and the terror of her marriage. She was Livia only, blithe and singing, and she was a blessing to Marcus' spirit. He often thought of death, and when he did a thrill ran through him as a lover is thrilled on the journey to his beloved whom he has not seen for a long time.

He received a letter from Noë ben Joel from Jerusalem. Noë was now a gray-bearded grandfather several times over. "The wise men in the gates tell me that 'something has moved' in Heaven, but what it is and what it portends they do not say," Noë wrote. "But they are soberly excited. They examine portents. They discuss matters in private with the priests. Has something quickened along the blood of the House of David, as prophesied? Has the Mother of the Messias been born, or He, Himself? Surely not as yet, say the wise men, for there has been no sound of trumpets from the battlements in the sky. They forget the prophecies of Isaias.

"I have seen our old friend, Roscius, in the Temple, clad in coarse linen and walking in rope sandals. He does not know me, so ascetic and so far in mind has he become. But as each young mother brings her man-child into the Temple to offer him to the Lord, he peers at the face of the infant, then turns away with sadness and disappointment, muttering in his beard, 'No, it is not He.' Roscius, the great Roman actor, beloved of the ladies, applauded by all Romans, rich, effete, embroidered, gilded, is not recognizable in this silent old man who sweeps the Temple floors and cleans the chambers for his bread, and awaits the Messias as he has been promised—so he says—by God."

It came to Marcus, reading this letter, that he had not thought of the Messias of the Jews for a long time, so fearful had been the pressure upon him, the exigency of bloody events. It was hard to think of Him in Rome. It was easier in the golden peace of the island. If He ever, indeed, were born, surely He would come to the countryside or a little hamlet, and never to a roaring city. Marcus thought of what Socrates had said, that the ideal habitat for men was a village, surrounded by fields and forests, and never a great city where men could not think among the press of multitudes of other minds. "Out of cities grows confusion, madness, disordered imaginings, grotesque forms, perversions, excitements, fevers, mindless currents of men, upheavals, vehemences. But in the small hamlets, in the land, thoughts grow large and steadfast and philosophy can flourish as the vine and produce the fruit that gives exhilaration to the thoughts of men."

It was quite true. Small villages and the countryside, gave birth to the Cincinnatus. Rome gave birth to the men like Crassus and Catilina, and the Caesars. The bedrooms of the rural places bred men. The chambers of the cities bred sterile perversions. Athens, that small city, produced Socrates, Plato, and Aristotle, and all the sciences. But Rome produced the ambitious.

It was with regret that Marcus had to leave for Rome again, where once he had felt the excitement of life and felt it no longer.

It was a seemingly ridiculous thing, considering the character of the lady, but Marcus as Consul of Rome and therefore the guardian of its proclaimed morals, was forced to prosecute Publius Clodius, surnamed Pulcher, for adultery with Pompeia, Caesar's wife. He and the lady had been caught in "flagrant behavior" by Aurelia, Julius' mother, in Caesar's very house. It was even more ridiculous, in view of the debased morality of the Roman people in general. But Marcus knew that the more depraved a people the more their public indignation against immorality.

He consulted Julius who expressed his tremendous hurt. Marcus said to him cynically, "Come now, Julius. Pompeia's conduct has never been exemplary. Who is it you wish to marry this time?"

Julius smiled and raised his eyebrows. "None, dear friend. I wish only to divorce Pompeia. I do not intend to appear as a witness against her. But the wife of Caesar must not be a public scandal."

Marcus mused, his eyes fixed on Julius' antic face, "Has Clodius become dangerous to you, with his own ambitions?"

"What nonsense!" cried Julius. "What is Clodius to me? He is only a tribune of the people! Did I not assist him in his small ambition? Yet he betrayed me."

"He has powerful friends who do not love you, Julius. By the way, it is very amusing to me to hear you speak of 'betrayal.' It is as if a thieving dog complained of another dog who had stolen his bone. What great household, which contains pretty women, has not been victimized by yourself?"

But Caesar only laughed. He said to Marcus before leaving, "I have asked you this before, and each time you have refused. Join Crassus and me. We have mighty plans for the future. Consider. I love you. I should like you as one of us."

"Never," said Marcus. "I must live with myself." He studied his old friend. "There is a saying of the Greeks, that if a man is dangerous induce him to join you and thus disarm him."

But Julius suddenly became grave. "I shall not ask you again, dear comrade. Therefore, reflect."

After he had gone Marcus considered his words with alarm. Despite the fresh hostility of the Senate against him, and the growing and bitter rage of the patricians because of Marcus' vengeance on many of their relatives, he had not believed himself in much danger of assassination. Catilina was dead, and most of the conspirators with him. Yet Julius' black eyes had contained a deadly and ominous warning. Terentia, too, never refrained from hinting that her husband was in great disfavor among influential people. "You listen to no one," she complained. "But I hear murmurs and rumors. Unless you conciliate you are lost."

She was not alone in her alarms. Many of Cicero's friends hinted of these things. He could not force them to concrete statements. They evaded, yet they were strong in their opinions and warnings. Some even suggested that Marcus leave Rome for a time at the end of his Consulship. Many suggested he not testify against Clodius. On the other hand other friends urged that the prosecution be pursued, for the scandal had had an astonishing impact on the Roman people. "Besides," said the friends, "Caesar wishes a divorce, and Caesar is very powerful."

"It was a shameful affair," said some friends. "Not only did Clodius commit adultery with Pompeia, but he committed a sacrilege against the gods, and the gods," said the friends smiling widely, "must never be insulted. That is a crime the people will not permit."

"Especially in a nation which does not believe in the gods," said Marcus.

"What, in truth, did Clodius do that is so heinous, considering the public reputation of the lady involved? He invaded the house of Julius Caesar during the female pious celebrations when no man must be present, and he wore female garments in order to gain entry. Thousands of Romans find that risible. But Caesar wishes to divorce his wife and has seized on this infamy as an excuse. However, I must prosecute Clodius to appease many factions, not to mention public opinion, which is no honest opinion at all."

On such shameful and insignificant matters can a man's life be ruined or lost. Cicero wrote later, "It is one thing for a man to be defeated by a powerful and significant foe. It is quite another for him to die of the bite of a bedbug."

He had begun to lose favor even with the people of Rome who had but recently hailed him as savior. They, who had cared nothing for the law for endless years, suddenly became much aware of it (as taught them by secret mentors) and declared that Catilina had not been tried by a jury of his peers, in accordance with the Constitution, but had in truth been "ignobly assassinated by the armies of Cicero." It was useless for Cicero's friends to point out that Catilina had fled Rome, had not chosen to demand a trial before the proper magistrates, and had gathered up an army of his own to attack the city. Those who did not use the word "assassination" preferred an exercise in semantics and called Catilina's death on the battlefield "summary execution," and without any basis in known knowledge accused Quintus of the actual "execution." "Men prefer to believe ill of men rather than the truth," urged Cicero's friends. But the planned indignation of the people only grew more vociferous. Many affected to be wounded by the executions of Catilina's lieutenants and Cicero shrewdly guessed that young Mark Antony was the instigator. There was much talk that Cicero had violated the Bill of Rights, had suspended it, and that the lieutenants, too, should have been granted a trial by jury. It was all the more onerous to Cicero because he had to admit, privately, that the law demanded such a trial. But he had feared that during the slow measured dance of the trials Catilina would have led his followers to riot and thrown the city into chaos.

"Join us," said Crassus to Cicero, who only smiled coldly and did not reply. "Join us," said Pompey, who had saved his life. Marcus looked at him curiously. "Why?" he asked. But Pompey merely colored with discomfort and left him. Marcus was more disagreeably disturbed by the fact that Pompey had urged him also than he had been at the urgings of Crassus and Caesar, whom he mistrusted with all his heart. He had come to feel a deep affection for Pompey, despite the fact that Pompey was in all ways the full portrait of the military man, the class which Cicero chronically regarded with apprehension. His troubles mounted, as the day of Clodius' trial for sacrilege approached. He castigated himself for ever taking the affair seriously though he knew that the state religion, being an arm of the government, helped to keep the people in order. The aristocrats might laugh privately at Clodius' exploits, but they knew that should the people ever come to consider that their rulers took religion lightly they would, inevitably, begin to take government lightly also, and chaos would result. So the "Good Goddess"* affair was pressed upon Cicero by the patricians, against Clodius who was also a patrician. He remanded Clodius for trial.

He then wrote his famous frank letter to his publisher, Atticus, which was to fall later into the hands of his enemies among the patricians and the Senate: "In the challenges laid forth by both sides the prosecution magistrates, whom I had appointed for the trial, rejected the least valuable, but the defense rejected all the best men! There was never so disheveled a group around a table in a gambling house, Senators under suspicion, businessmen of the shabbiest and least solvent kind and known manipulators, to speak more kindly than necessary. A few honest men were there, also, who were obviously disgusted at being associated with such scoundrels."

Clodius, of course, pleaded not guilty. His witness swore that on the night of the women's religious festival in Caesar's house Clodius had been with him in the country. Angrily, then, Cicero called Julius as a witness, in behalf of his mother, Aurelia, who had originally made the complaint. Caesar emphatically declared that he knew nothing personally of the case. The prosecutor then asked him mildly why, under those circumstances, he had divorced Pompeia. To which he made his bland reply, which was to become famous: "My wife must be above the slightest suspicion." At this Cicero gazed at him with disgust.

Hardly suppressed laughter ran over the courtroom. Then Cicero, his anger growing at this comedy, was called as a witness for the prosecution. He testified that he, himself, had seen Clodius in Rome barely three hours before the ceremonies for the Good Goddess in Caesar's house; therefore, Clodius could not have been ninety miles away as he and his witness had sworn.

To his incredulous horror the jury voted that Clodius was not guilty, by a vote of thirty-three to twenty-five. There could be only one answer to this: The jury had been corrupted, just as Caesar had been induced, no doubt by Crassus, not to press the case against Clodius. "I am truly a simple man," he wrote in his letter to Atticus. "I do not do well among subtle men

* *Bona Dea.*

whose every move and every word confuses me, who at one moment demand something and in the next demand that their demand not be heeded. When such scum as that jury could pretend to believe that something which had happened had not truly happened then the law is completely undermined, and without law the Republic is lost." He added that the whole affair had been political and who could understand the machinations of born and devious politicians?

He knew only one thing with surety: He had made a most formidable enemy of Clodius. Once Clodius met him in public and taunted him: "The jurors did not trust you on your oath." To which Cicero replied with great anger, "Yes, twenty-five jurors believed me. Thirty believed you, after they had taken your money in advance." At this all present laughed at Clodius, who could jest happily at others but could not endure jests against himself.

On another occasion Cicero said bitterly to Caesar, "You urged me to testify against Clodius. Then, when you were called as witness you alleged not to know anything of the infamous affair, which I had not wished to prosecute from the very beginning."

"My dear Marcus," said Julius with indulgence, "it is possible I changed my mind."

At the end of his term as Consul, Cicero prepared to address the people of Rome as was customary, from the Rostra. But one of the new tribunes, Caecilius Metellus Nepos, challenged Cicero, declaring that he was extremely audacious in wishing to make a speech covering his discharge of duties while Consul, alleging that a man who had asked for the death of Roman citizens without a trial before a jury of their peers ought not to be permitted to speak to Romans.

"I saved Rome," Cicero said. "Is that my crime, that I, a retiring Consul, should be challenged by an inferior in office?" At this the listening people, suddenly remembering that he had spoken justly, raised a great shout: "You have spoken true!" It was the last public applause he was to receive with the same sincerity and the same faith.

As a retiring Consul he was entitled to the best choice of a province over which to be governor. At that time Macedonia was considered the most agreeable. But he remembered the services Antonius Hybrida had done him and assigned the governorship to the young patrician. Then in his magnanimity, he assigned the governorship of Cisalpine Gaul to Metellus Celer, the brother of the very tribune who had challenged him at the Rostra—Metellus Nepos, recalling the gallant action of the soldier in preventing Catilina from escaping via Faesulae. But the tribune openly sneered, "He seeks to cosset favor with me."

"I meet enemies wherever I turn," Cicero complained to his friends.

"There appears to be a plot to disgrace and defame me, but who is the instigator I do not know."

He had thought himself free from the malice of those who had benefitted from his kindness and generosity. But scandalous reports soon reached him to the effect that his former colleague, Antonius, was guilty of oppression and extortion in the province of Macedonia. He refused to believe this of Antonius, who was rich in his own right. He received a letter from Antonius urgently informing him that he was to be recalled from Macedonia to stand trial and requesting that "my old dear friend, Cicero," defend him before the courts. Marcus wrote him a warm and reassuring letter, which Antonius intelligently retained. Marcus, before the arrival in Rome of his former colleague, prepared the case in defense, and he was filled with the kindliest and most affectionate feelings. Publicly, he declared that the whole accusation was absurd, for was not Antonius as close to him as a brother? This was remembered intact.

Then another report reached Cicero which stupefied him. Antonius had written to friends in the Senate that Cicero had commanded him, before leaving for Macedonia, to share with him what spoils he could plunder from the province! This was so not in character with his memory of Antonius, and his honor, that at first he did not believe it and was enraged when it was told him. He was then shown a letter from Antonius, himself, written to a Senator, in which Antonius had written that Cicero's former freedman, Hilarus, now employed by Antonius, had been sent by Cicero into Macedonia to gather the moneys from the robbery of the province. It was most evident that Antonius had not intended his letters to be read by anyone but his friends, but the malice of the Senators compelled them to make the letters public. In the meantime, Antonius was writing his old colleague lovingly thanking him for his acceptance of the defense. It was even more evident to the besieged Cicero that Antonius hoped to implicate him and thus escape a great measure of guilt himself, for would not Cicero be defending him?

"He is mad," said Cicero. "He has lost his mind. He is not the man I knew."

"My dear Marcus," said Julius, "I have told you often: No man is ever the man we know. Antonius, though rich, has a normal lust for larceny, which heretofore had not manifested itself. Too, I have heard that many of his investments in Rome have failed."

"I shall never understand human nature!" Marcus cried in despair. He withdrew from the defense of Antonius and trusted few men again. Besieged from without his house, and beleaguered from within, he sometimes thought of death. He wrote to Noë ben Joel: "I have filled my letters with lamentations, dear friend. Be sure I do not complain without reason, for what I have written to you is an understatement rather than an extravagance. I feel the creeping tides of dishonor lapping my feet, nay, my very knees! Under such circumstances it is expected that in indignation a Roman challenge his enemies. But I cannot discover and face them! It is all rumor, all malevolence, all whispers, all tittle-tattle, all malignity. Should I unearth my enemies I should sue them thoroughly for libel—but they do not reveal themselves. Therefore, I must keep silent, or write pages of denunciation and fall upon my sword—if I can find it.

"You have often mentioned that suicide is man's greatest crime against God, for it implies that a man does not trust his Creator or denies His existence. My reason tells me the latter is absurd; we have the earth as His witness, and the heavens above, and the vast orderliness of all creation, and its manifest laws. Law does not exist without a lawgiver, as we have often affirmed. Nevertheless, how can I trust God? I am deeply afflicted and have done no harm but have, in my limited way, done much good. I have saved my country; I have been faithful to my duties; I have shown mercy, and have been loyal to my friends and magnanimous to my enemies. At the last, I swear to you I should have intervened even to save Catilina, had he shown the slightest penitence or desire to reform—all this despite my love for Livia and my natural hatred for her murderer and my vow to avenge her.

"Yet, I am afflicted. All the years during which I served my country and my God have been as nothing; they have brought me only sorrow, despair and disgrace and lies. What is left for me but death? The incredible affair of Antonius seems to have unsettled the very fount of my rationality so that there are times when I begin to believe the calumnies against me! I often gaze at my reflection in the mirror and ask myself, 'Are you truly, Cicero, such a one as they rumor? If so, then you deserve to die.' You see to what I have been reduced.

"Yes, I think of death with increasing longing, and hope that nothing is beyond the grave, for if I live thereafter I should remember my sorrows and my present infamy. If it were not for my children I should long ago have fallen on the mentioned sword, which I believe is somewhere in my house."

He might indeed have killed himself, for the thought was ever with him now from the dawn to the night—during which he could not sleep in his loneliness and agony—if he had not recalled the letters of Noë ben Joel: "Suicide is man's ultimate hatred of God."

CHAPTER FIFTY-SEVEN

In the meantime Cicero's troubles increased. The animus against him in Rome became so fierce that he could no longer pretend to ignore it in public, but retired more and more to his house or fled with Tullia to his various villas, or to the island. On these excursions Terentia refused to permit little Marcus to accompany his father. She could not bear the separation, and as she was engaged in repairing her shattered friendships in Rome, and had her investments to consider, she could not go with her husband, for which he thanked the gods.

His law practice declined so that he was forced to discharge his law clerks and retain only his secretary. His litter was no longer hailed on the streets of Rome. He was like one whose sword has been broken and the fragments hurled into his face. If only his enemies would emerge and he could see them! But though the antagonism of the Senate increased, and their scorn of him, and though the people now ignored him, and he was conscious of the power of a silent plot against him to destroy him completely, he was not entirely certain of the plotters. He suspected many, but could not prove it. He had become like one isolated, who has been afflicted with the plague, he who had saved his country. The Senate still did not dare to censure him formally, for there were multitudes who remembered him among the commons, and as he was a knight the knights were still one with him. The multitudes had no voice, however, and his fellow knights were busy with their own affairs and during his rise he had not been often in their company. "The descent is steep," he wrote Atticus. "A man should not neglect his friendships when he is rising, or his friends will not remember him when he declines, not out of their malice or envy or resentment, but because they have forgotten he was ever one of them." He still had a small coterie of friends devoted to him, but they would not lie and say he was still acclaimed. He had entered politics not in eagerness and in pursuit of power, but to serve his country. He discovered that this was the most foolish of ambitions, for those who serve their country are not remembered with love, and honored, whereas those who serve only themselves and become rich and powerful are celebrated as wise and lovable men and given even higher honors. Who can refrain from adoring a man who adores himself?

He was surprised one day in his library by a visit from Julius Caesar. He said to the younger man, sourly, "What! I thought you no longer remembered my name!" But Julius laughed and embraced him and shook him affectionately. "How is it possible for me to forget you, Carissime? My childhood mentor, my tutor, the man whose honor can never be questioned?"

"It is being questioned incessantly," said Cicero. "O Julius! You know it too well!"

"Bah," said Julius. "The mob acclaims; the mob denounces. One ignores the mob."

"And the Senate, and the patricians, and the soldiers, and the people. Who then, is left?"

"I and Crassus, who love you. I am here to ask your help."

"I?" Cicero could not believe what he had heard.

"You. I have put up my candidacy for Consul. If you speak for me few will vote against me."

Cicero stared at him incredulously. "You are not serious!"

"I am. Despite the majority, the minority honor you. And a Consul is, at the last, elected by a minority of fastidious men who can throw their votes one way or another."

"When I said you are not serious, I meant you surely do not expect to become Consul?"

"Sweet Marcus, your expression and your tone are hardly flattering."

Cicero flushed with indignation. "You are not worthy to become Consul, Julius."

Julius was not insulted. He was highly amused. "If only those worthy to become Consul ran for office, dear friend, we should have no Consuls. I also wish you to help me to pass the Land Bill. That should be precious to your heart." He coughed. "There is another matter. Crassus and I will also be running for a Triumvirate—with Pompey. Crassus is going to grant Pompey his just demands for the Land Bill, which will assist his valorous and devoted soldiers. Are not veterans entitled to land, and some other reimbursement for their sacrifices for their country?"

Now Marcus was stunned. "Triumvirate?" he stammered.

"Certainly. Rome deserves more than a mere dictator. Dictators were never popular with Romans, and Rome is restive under them. Do you not remember the stern measures once set up to guard the State against the permanent seizing of power by a dictator? You should honor that tradition. We, Crassus and I, and Pompey, bow to the innate aversions against dictators which are in the fiber of the being of our country. Crassus, in particular, is uncomfortable as dictator. He, too, wishes to give our country the best it deserves.

"Now we feel," said Julius, blithely ignoring Marcus' horrified expression, "that to meet the complex problems of a vast nation such as ours, with subject states, allies and provinces and territories, one man is not sufficient, and certainly not a dictator! I will cover the popular interests of Rome, for am I not a Popularis? Crassus will attend to the financial problems. Pompey will govern the military. His quarrel with Crassus will be resolved with the passage of the Land Bill; I know you are in favor of it. He is a mighty soldier; the legions worship him; he will be an able administrator of military matters. Crassus is not only the richest man in Rome, but will have solicitude for Rome's financial affairs, and he is a patrician. And I—I will have the masses.

"We find it eminently sensible and orderly. Consuls are no longer enough, just in themselves. When we were a small nation, yes. But not now."

"An oligarchy, an infamous oligarchy, such as destroyed Greece and brought her oppression and slavery!" Marcus' heart had begun to thump with sickening sounds audible in his ears. "No! By the gods, no!"

"Hardly an oligarchy," said Julius in musical tones, and with downcast eyes. "Only three men. It would be nonsense to have a Consul, a vice-Consul, and a vice-vice-Consul, with one man in supreme authority and the others subservient. Each must have power over his particular province, with no interference from the others. We believe this division of authority the safest for Rome. And, certainly, we shall be subservient to the Senate, and the tribunes of the people. We shall preside under their jurisdiction, and with their approval. Should they disapprove of all of us, while we are serving their country, they will have the power to disband us. If they disapprove of any, they will have power to remove him and appoint another, or another will run for office.

"My dear sweet Marcus! Let your obdurate mind consider! Is not this most excellent for Rome?"

Marcus sat in stupefaction, and aghast and still unbelieving, behind his table. His graying hair rose in a crest over his pallid face. His eyes gleamed with desperate emotion. He tried to speak; his voice was choked in his dry throat. Now he began to struggle for breath. His body felt numbed, as if all his flesh had been beaten with clubs and whips.

Julius studied him benevolently. "We shall really be called the Committee of Three, and consider us that, rather than a Triumvirate."

Marcus' voice came in a groan. "Rome is lost. So, this is the plot that has long lain in your minds! This is the plot which the murderer, Catilina, would not countenance, for you should not have chosen him as one of you. Besides, he wished to destroy and then assume supreme power. This is what I dimly, but surely, suspected, all these years!"

"There is, and was, no plot," said Julius, kindly. "Natural forces in the nation have led to this natural solution of all our troubles and our unwieldy affairs. When you were Consul, my dear friend, were you adequate to manage all things in Rome—finances, the military, the problems of a huge nation? You know you were not. Not even a single god, however endowed with supernatural powers, could rule our present complexity. Are not duties and provinces assigned each god, in the affairs of the world and Olympus? What is more exemplary and sensible, than to emulate the gods, themselves?"

He daintily examined a fingernail, which was coated with a rosy substance. "No more dictators, sweet, suspicious Marcus. A division of three dedicated men, with individual authority, answerable to the Senate and the people. Again, I say, you should rejoice, for dictatorship will be dead."

Cicero put his hands suddenly over his face as if to shut out the very sight of Julius. A sensation of utter powerlessness, horror, and futility overcame him.

"If you do not wish to assist me in attaining the Consulship, after which I will have only one-third the power you had, Marcus, then I must be sorrowful. But I should prefer your help."

Cicero dropped his hands. His eyes burned on Julius. "Assist you? I am defamed, rejected, calumny follows my steps, I am accused of vile crimes, the walls of Rome are scribbled with obscenities against me, I am lost, undone! And you ask for my help!"

"Then, at the least, do not inflame those who still love you and admire you, against me."

Julius stood up, and leaned his palms on the table and bent down to bring his face to a level with Cicero's. "I tell you, it will do you no service at all, Marcus, to oppose me."

Then Marcus spoke out of his despair and his wrath. "Yes! There are still many who will listen to my voice, Julius! I will speak in the Forum! I will lay bare what I know about you, what I have always suspected! I will denounce Crassus! I will warn the people who fear the military, and that will dispose of Pompey! You shall not win, Caesar."

Julius stood up and struck the table with the flat of his hand. "Then you may as well fall upon your sword, Marcus. I came today to warn you. Oppose us, speak against us, and you are lost. I had hoped to reconcile you to the Committee of Three. I have failed. Have you forgotten Clodius? And Mark Antony? They, among many others, have vowed to destroy you; they have powerful friends and relatives in the Senate, and among the financiers and bankers and even among your own 'new men' who have envied you because you are one of them."

Julius' vivid black eyes gazed at Marcus with mingled exasperation, anxiety, and love. "This is your final opportunity to recover much of what you have lost through no fault of your own. Oppose us, and you are ruined forever."

Marcus knew, with absolute and awful finality, that Julius spoke the truth. His face paled more and more. But his mouth became resolute and appeared carved of stone. He opened a small casket on his table and brought forth something and then spun it between himself and Caesar. "Do you recognize this?" he asked.

Julius took the serpentine ring in his hand. He looked at it and then slowly lifted his eyes to Marcus' face. Marcus smiled palely. "This time you cannot return the ring to the owner, unless you cross the Styx. Take it. It profanes my house."

"Then Quintus killed him?"

"He does not think it. He prays it is not so. They were comrades together."

Julius dropped the ring in his pouch and looked down at the table in silence. Marcus fell suddenly into despair. He bowed his head and said, "No matter what happens to me I will use what little power I still retain to oppose you."

Julius said, "Then, Marcus, we must say farewell, for you are standing on the abyss."

"No matter. I must do as I must do." Marcus raised his head and stared at Julius. All at once the flamboyant figure before him, splendid even though the head was balding, disappeared, and as through mist he saw Julius clad in a white toga, staggering wildly and covered with wounds, blood flowing through fingers pressed over his heart, and bloody froth on his lips. Marcus gave a great cry and sprang to his feet and instantly the vision departed and Julius, vital and whole, was standing before him with an astonished expression. "What is it?" he exclaimed, aghast at Marcus' face.

"In the name of the gods!" cried Cicero. "Abandon your plots at once! Abandon your ambitions! I have seen an augury—!"

Julius suddenly remembered what Marcus had told him many years ago, when they had both been young, and he quickly made the gesture of averting the evil eye, and a thin trembling ran along his nerves.

Marcus came slowly, stumbling, from behind his table and he seized Julius' arm and implored him with his eyes. "What I have seen must not come to pass, Caesar. I have just recalled that I loved you once. I have seen you with many wounds, and many hands flashing daggers, and you have died of them."

Frightened to the very heart of his superstitious soul, Julius tore his arm from Marcus' grasp and fled.

The next day Clodius said to him and Crassus and Pompey, "I am ready to move against Cicero and dispose of him. Do not oppose me this time."

Caesar said nothing. He looked at Pompey, and then at Crassus. Pompey said nothing. But Crassus, raising his eyebrows and smiling unpleasantly, turned down his thumb.

Within a few days the Senate passed a bill which Clodius had introduced: Anyone who had put Roman citizens to death without due process of law, or should do so in the future, should be "interdicted from fire and water." In short, exile. The Senate summoned Cicero to appear before it, and he was then solemnly censured for having requested the death penalty for Catilina and his five lieutenants, "against all the Articles of the Bill of Rights and the Constitution."

Pale but dignified, Marcus addressed the frowning and hostile and august body. "It is useless, I see, for me to offer arguments, but I must do so for history. Catilina menaced Rome. That is now history. There was no time for the proper processes of law, as well, my lords, you know. Catilina should have taken any legal time to complete his plans, to fire Rome, to destroy her, to massacre tens of thousands, including many in this Senate, to have brought chaos and disaster to our country. The hour was desperate; moments were precious. There could be no delay. Rome must strike, or Catilina would. He was not executed. He was defeated by the Roman armies, when he attempted to march on the city to devour her. His five lieutenants were executed to save Rome.

"I must remind you, lords, that though I suggested execution, it was in your hands to reject the suggestion and to advise the due processes of law. You saw with your own eyes the calamity that awaited any delay. You acted wisely, and in the name of Rome. You could do nothing else, lest we all die!

"It is said that only traitors who are not citizens of Rome could be so summarily executed. I have maintained that Catilina and his lieutenants, being traitors, had forfeited their citizenship. You have said it is not in the law, and that only the magistrates have the power, after a trial, to revoke citizenship, when treason is judged. We all well knew that Catilina was a traitor, and that if there had been time for a trial he would so have been judged, and he would have been executed, for he would then have retained no citizenship. What good would have ensued if he had been formally remanded for trial? Before his case could have come before the magistrates he would have fired Rome and turned her into a vast smoking heap of rubble! We all should have perished for standing like blind heroes on a point of law, a point of order! Would that have been preferable?"

"Nevertheless, Cicero," said one old Senator sternly, "you as a lawyer of much fame in Rome, a stickler for all points of the Constitution, knew that you acted outside the Constitution."

"So did this august body, then, lord," said Marcus with a weary smile. "I am not alone the guilty—if there truly were guilt, which I deny. Moreover, lords, the Constitution states that there must be no de facto law passed at any time. The law under which you have summoned me is de facto; if I were truly a criminal I still could not be tried under it, for my alleged crime was committed before this bill was even introduced."

"One who quibbled about law in the past should not quibble about it now," said another Senator, with hate in his eyes, for he was a cousin of Clodius.

"This Senate has no authority to censure me under a de facto law, nor to command my exile," said Cicero. "The Senate, in truth, has no right to censure me for anything, for I did but my duty and exposed traitors and treason against the State. If that is a crime, then I am indeed a criminal!"

Crassus, Caesar, and Pompey were present. He turned and looked at them, but their faces were shut against him, and averted. Now his smile was sad. He said to them, "You have succeeded against me. Be it as you will. I will depart at once." He turned to the Senate again. "For this day's work, lords, you have encouraged treason and opened the prison doors to free the traitors. A nation can survive its fools, and even the ambitious. But it cannot survive treason from within. An enemy at the gates is less formidable, for he is known and he carries his banners openly against the city. But the traitor moves among those within the gates freely, his sly whispers rustling through all the alleys, heard in the very halls of government itself. For the traitor appears no traitor; he speaks in the accents familiar to his victims, and he wears their face and their garments, and he appeals to the baseness that lies deep in the hearts of all men. He rots the soul of a nation; he works secretly and unknown in the night to undermine the pillars of a city; he infects the body politic so that it can no longer resist. A murderer is less to be feared. The traitor is the carrier of the plague. You have unbarred the gates of Rome to him.*

"Farewell."

He left the Senate with dignity. But when he was in his litter a sensation of unreality came to him, which is the cloak that despair wears. He could feel nothing. When he entered his great and beautiful house he looked about him, incredulously. No! It was not possible! All that he had built, all that to which he had devoted his life, all his prayers and hopes and dreams and patriotism had not come to this! That he must leave his beloved country and stay at least four hundred miles from Rome—which interdicted his

* Recorded by Sallust.

ancestral island as his future home—could not as yet impress itself on his stunned mind.

He fled to his library and shut the door and bolted it, and found himself panting as if he were a hare that had been hunted by wolves and had just escaped. But when among his wonderful books he saw that he had not escaped at all. They could not protect him with all the wisdom that lay within them. This teak and ivory chair could not throw its arms about him. These walls could not shelter him. The lovely trees he had planted so lovingly years ago could not bend their boughs to hide him, nor could the grottoes conceal him. The grass could not cover him with its green carpet, nor the fountains blot out the formation of his face so that his enemies could not come upon him. What he had considered a fortress against misfortune and malice was no fortress at the last. It was a vulnerable mass of masonry, thin of wall, unlocked of door, shattered of window. For an exile was doomed to have his property seized, sold by the State, or razed infamously, as a warning to others.

Terror struck him. Where should he go? What of his fortune in the banks? His jewels, his treasures, the precious accumulations of the years? He was an outlaw. Anyone from this day forward who sheltered him, hid him, protected him, within four hundred miles of Rome, was automatically outlawed also.

He looked through his window onto the winding gardens he had so tenderly designed. It was radiant May, and he had planted those roses himself, rejoicing in the warmth of the earth on his hands and on his feet. That noble fountain: he had imported it from Greece at a great price. The trees laced their emerald boughs lovingly together, sheltering the bright green of the grass and patterning it with dancing fretwork. The walls burst with blossoming color. Birds sang deliriously to the approaching evening. The sky was opaline, and the west was the heart of a rose. Cypresses communed with God gravely and lifted their spires of majestic darkness; the leaves of the myrtle trees fluttered. The sweetest wind brought fragrance to him. And beyond his land he could hear the beat and mutter and clangor of his hilled city, the thunderous voices of his countrymen.

He had an alternative to exile. He could find his sword and fall upon it. But, he had a family. He clutched the hair of his temples in his mute despair. He sank down upon a couch and pressed his hands over his face. He thought of his dear island, where the ashes of his ancestors lay, and the ashes of his grandfather, his father and his mother. He fell into a stupor of such profound grief that darkness covered his eyes and he lost all sense of time. When he emerged the shadows of late evening already engulfed his library, and the sky outside his window was a deep lilac.

He became aware of a thunderous knocking at his door, and he also became aware that he had been hearing it even in his stupor. He dropped his hands between his knees and stared lifelessly before him. Then he heard the cries of his wife, his daughter, and his brother. He tried to call out to them to leave him in peace, but as no sound came he forced himself to his numbed feet and staggered to the door and unbolted it.

He saw their three pale faces, and their tears, and he turned away and stumbled back to his chair and fell into it, unspeaking. Terentia cried, "Oh, woe is this day! But you would not heed me; you would not listen to me! You would not exercise prudence; you would not seek the support of powerful men! No! You were all wisdom, all rectitude, omniscient, proud, assured of your own might! And you have brought disgrace and ruin upon your family." She burst into furious sobs and groans and wrung her large and ungainly hands and gazed at her husband with rage and misery.

But Quintus came to stand beside him and put his hand on his shoulder. Tullia fell on her knees before him and embraced him and kissed his icy cheek. "I shall go with you, dear Father, no matter where you go, and shall delight to be with you to the end of my life." She kissed his hands, and then in an excess of sorrow and love she kissed his feet also. He placed his hand on her bowed head and spoke to his wife.

"You must not go with me, Terentia."

She ceased her lamentations abruptly, and her wet eyes gleamed in the dusk, and her teeth bit her pallid underlip as her thoughts scrambled through her mind, planning, ordering themselves, speaking of expediency.

"This house is forfeit," said Cicero, "and all I have, my villas, my farms, my money. But what you have inherited, Terentia, and what I have given you over the years, remains yours. All is not lost. In the morning I will take with me what I can carry, and leave—" He could not continue. His voice had been low and husky, as if a dagger had pierced his throat. Tullia embraced his knees.

"Our son must remain with me," said Terentia in a thoughtful and considering tone.

Quintus burst out in a breaking voice, "O, that I could accompany you! But I should be accused of deserting my post, my legion. I am a soldier."

Marcus patted his hand. "That is understood. I have been condemned as a shame to my country, a violator of the Constitution. To go with me would be to have treason adjudged against you. Tullia, remain with your husband and your mother, who will work with your uncle for my recall, for surely I still have friends in Rome!"

"Ask me not to leave you, Father, nor to refrain from departing with you!" the girl implored.

He embraced her and kissed her cheek. "Beloved child, what you ask is not possible. Your duty is to your husband, before your father. Do not forget me. Inspire Piso to help me. It is all you can do."

CHAPTER FIFTY-EIGHT

Subtle thoughts did not come easily to the mind behind Quintus' brightly colored face and burly mien. But as he grimly watched the demolition of his brother's great house on the Palatine he thought, Why is it that when a man is destroyed a government desires to destroy his house also? Is it because that government wishes, in its overwhelming malice, to obliterate the dreams that live therein, and the hopes and the dear memories and the echoes of a just man? Truly, as Marcus has often said, the government is the enemy of men!

He went to Caesar and said, "You professed always to love my brother, and he had a loving affection for you which you have betrayed. He was your mentor, your defender, when you were children together. He wears the amulet your mother gave him, when he protected you. It saved his life. But you, O Caesar, have ruined that life! You have driven him into exile, for you are a man without valor and love only schemings and other vile things."

Julius looked at the soldier mildly and replied, "Quintus, you speak as a rough warrior. I sought to save Marcus, to have him by my side. But he repudiated me. He would not understand that in these fierce and rapid days of Rome the slow movement of the representatives of the people, the tribunes, was not enough to meet the needs of modern times. He is of the old days, the simple days, when the Constitution was enough, and law was law, and morality was in the people. But now, in our rushing society, in the growing grandeur of Rome, and her power, and her leadership of the world, the ponderous machinery of the representatives of the people is a hindrance to the new impatience which demands that a government must act speedily and decisively in the enormous face of events. This Marcus could not understand."

"He understood too perfectly," said Quintus. "You have said I am a rough soldier. It is true. I see singly. I know good from evil, and light from darkness. I see that you have destroyed my brother because he stood in your way. It is in your power to recall him from exile. It was in his power at one time to command your death; he withheld his hand. That was a woeful day! But be grateful that you live."

Julius smiled. "I, too, am a soldier, Quintus. Is not Pompey, your general, one of us? I endure your remarks because I love you, out of old memories and friendships. I tell you this: I have not forgotten Marcus. I weep for him."

"Weep for yourself," said Quintus, and tightened his sword. "Return my brother to his country."

He went to Pompey in the latter's ascetic house, and saluted and said, "My general, it is in your power to recall my brother from exile. It is said that you love him. Once he hinted that he owed much to you. Let him owe more!"

Pompey looked at him sternly and said, "He was obdurate. The Senate banished him, for he had broken the law he was sworn to uphold. It is a quibbling, and that you and I know only too well, my captain. But there it is."

"You are my general, and I am your captain, and we are both soldiers. Let us beware of governments, for they are our enemies, and use us as blind weapons and sell us to death when they will, and present medals to our wives and invoke us as heroes. They leave our children fatherless and give them only the banner which covered us on our pyres. Nevertheless, they fear us. Let them fear us more! My general, do not think that subtle Caesar nor that wily Crassus will stand with you when it is needful. They endure you only to use you."

Pompey frowned and pondered, slowly shaking his head. He answered at last, "What you say is quite true. I trust neither Crassus nor Caesar. But your brother was imprudent. The affectionate letters he wrote to Antonius are now public property. You and I know they were written in sincerity and without knowledge that Antonius had become an extortioner in Macedonia. Nevertheless, the people of Rome are now convinced —through the kindly offices of Caesar and Crassus, the patricians and the Senate—that your brother was guilty."

Quintus said bitterly, "The guilty extortioner, Antonius Hybrida, lives again in Rome and is again honored by his fellow patricians. But my innocent brother lives in exile and his house is razed and he is dishonored by the very nation he served! My general, let us stand together as soldiers and recall the man who saved our country, and return to him that which was taken from him."

Pompey's large face was disturbed. He plucked at his chin. "Marcus," he said, "publicly expressed his apprehension of the military. Therefore, the military does not love him. But he has not forgiven us. However, do not think, my captain, that I have forgotten Marcus. A soldier honors an honest man, even when he is a lawyer." Pompey smiled a little. "Honor and honesty are the marks of the soldier, and we revere them even in civilians. Let me think a while."

Quintus gathered his legionnaires about him and visited the Antonius Hybrida in a cloud of thunder and dust. He was admitted to the presence of Antonius, who bowed to him formally and said in an uncertain voice, "Greetings, Quintus Tullius Cicero. I was about to invite you to visit me. What is it that I can do for a great soldier of my country?"

Quintus regarded him with hate, but kept his voice under control. "Your letters helped the Senate to destroy my brother, your guilty letters, Antonius Hybrida, your lying letters. Yet, once you saved my brother's life! What ambiguity is this? I am only a soldier, and a soldier is not a liar and subtle, and so I do not understand. Enlighten me."

Antonius lifted his eyes and looked into those of Quintus and he saw the blue and amber rage in them, and the distrust and revulsion. He quailed in himself and flushed.

"My letters, though they were imprudent—imprudent—did not serve to ruin your brother, Quintus. And I swear to you that I meant him no harm! It was the Senate's decision that your brother's methods against Catilina were unlawful, for all that they were swayed by them. And there was a letter which Cicero wrote to his publisher, Atticus, regarding the jury which tried Publius Clodius, and in which he called a Roman jury 'scum.' Alas, that that letter fell into the hands of an unscrupulous freedman of Atticus!"

"Quibbling!" cried Quintus, and his large teeth were like the teeth of a wolf. "Pompey has declared it so, Pompey, member of the Triumvirate, and a soldier!"

Antonius quailed again at the mention of that formidable name.

Quintus said, trying to swallow the huge lump of hatred and anger in his throat, "Be a man, Antonius Hybrida, and not a weak patrician. Go to the Senate and confess that your letters were false, and plead for the return of my brother to his country, and the restoration of his honor."

Antonius wound his slender hands together in distress. "It would not help," he said, almost inaudibly. "They were determined to destroy him, and so were Caesar and Crassus. Look upon me!" he suddenly exclaimed. "Do you think I rejoice in my own part in that destruction?"

"Then declare to the Roman people, themselves, that you were a liar!"

Antonius looked at him in affright. "They would laugh at me! I would be dishonored for all time!"

Quintus' jaw clenched. He said, "You live at ease, because of your robberies. But my brother pines in Salonika, and his fortune has been confiscated, his name dishonored, his house razed. Yet, you fear the laughter of

Roman mobs and would let my brother die in exile to keep that laughter from your precious person! Hear me, Antonius. I am a soldier, a captain of my general, Pompey the Magnus. Perhaps the day of the military is not so distant. When that day arrives—I will remember you, Antonius Hybrida."

He laid his hand on his sword. Antonius' wretched face trembled. But he said with dignity, "I am ashamed that this visit was necessary for you, Quintus Tullius Cicero. You will not believe me, but I am not an evil man. I have been a coward, and ingenuous. Once I even believed Catilina was maligned!" He smiled sadly. "I will go to the Senators, my fellow patricians, and I will admit to them that my letters concerning your brother were false —they know it only too well, however. But I will say to them that I will tell the Roman people, and that will be of the greater importance to them."

He held out his hand to Quintus, but Quintus turned on his heel and left him.

There were many more whom Quintus visited, old friends of his brother. Each expressed his love for Marcus. And from each Quintus ruthlessly extracted a promise of assistance, sometimes with threats and sometimes by the power of his noble anger. In the meantime, Terentia was not idle. She was ready enough to forget her husband, and she had not forgiven Marcus for once being great and she could not forgive him now for being nothing. Not only would she have been content now with her son and her fortune, but she would have been content with her husband's fall had it not been for one thing—her husband's dishonor and present obscurity were also her own. She considered divorce. But the divorce would not remove the dishonor nor restore her pride.

So Terentia went to her family, and the members, stung that one of their relatives was dishonored in the dishonor of Cicero, listened to her pleadings and wiped away her tears. They were rich; many Senators were in their debt and many of them were friends. They gave Terentia not only promises but their oaths to help her husband. "We shall not permit your son, who is of our blood, to live in the shadow of disgrace all his life," they said.

"I see a sudden storm is arising concerning Cicero," said Julius to Crassus. He winked at Pompey. "How fickle are the people of Rome! I hear rumors of public indignation. Let Cicero cool his forensic passions a little longer, and let him learn to be more prudent and less obdurate and unrealistic. Then we shall be generous. Perhaps."

The long and melancholy journey to beyond the four-hundred-mile limit outside Rome had almost destroyed Cicero. There were times that he was hopeful, on receiving letters from his wife and brother and friends in Rome

—notably Atticus—and he would speak of his country with joy and anticipation, and would write his daughter that by the time summer arrived they would once again be on the island "where live all my dreams and my memories and the ashes of my fathers, the tomb of my mother." But, as he halted briefly at the villas put at his disposal by his friends, he would recall that he was destitute, that his magnificent house on the Palatine was razed, his lands and his moneys confiscated, and that of all his treasures there remained nothing, no, not even his books, and that he was homeless and penniless indeed. At these times despair would utterly seize him, and he would write letters of extreme lamentation to his family and friends in Rome, especially his brother and Atticus, so extreme indeed that on receiving them the faithful ones would fear that he had lost his mind through his misfortunes. He forgot a lifetime of misery with his wife, and wrote her letters of total anguish which she showed to her relatives, and Quintus, saying, "I have been called ill-tempered by Romans, and a burden to my husband, but behold! he writes me from his heart and longs for my arms!" But Quintus would say in his heart, "To such a pass has my noble brother come, that he could desire to see Terentia again!"

There were times when Cicero wrote even violent letters to his devoted publisher, Atticus, upbraiding him that he had persuaded him, Cicero, not to commit suicide, "though a Roman prefers death to disgrace. What is there to live for? My afflictions surpass any you ever heard of before." Once he thanked Atticus for the money he had sent him, but mourned that he did not believe Atticus when he had said that the sesterces "came from royalties, for who, in these past months, has bought any of my books? I should return the purses if I did not stand in the most desperate of needs. How shall I repay you? I confess I have only lamentations to offer you, and reproaches that you dissuaded me from taking my life."

Once completely involved in all that affected his city, he could not force himself to be interested in those letters from family and friends which told him, with happy malice, that Clodius and Pompey were now the bitterest of enemies, that Caesar used and despised both, that the Triumvirate "is now considered despicable and dangerous even by the dullest man in the street, and Pompey and Crassus look upon each other through crossed swords, for one is a soldier and the other a man of financial affairs with an eye on his purse." He could not be interested in the stories of Calpurnia, Caesar's new wife, who was rumored to be a soothsayer and hysteric and a woman of awesome tempers. That mind which had once embraced a world had unaccountably shrunk to the size of his own suffering ego.

He could not live as an exile. His former resolution to exist and endure vanished. He would die. He could dispense with anything but his country, which he had served with all his heart from his earliest youth, and which had now destroyed him. "All else is nothing, but the hills of home," he wrote to Atticus, "and the sound of the dear beloved tongue. If a man does not love his country more than all other things, then he is a miserable and rootless creature, and no abomination is beyond him, no, not even treason. For a man's gods stand in that sweet familiar soil, and where the ashes of his fathers lie is where he desires to lay his own. My dear country! Let me look upon you again and I will die joyfully."

Calmer since he had decided to take his life, he arrived at the villa of a friend in Salonika, which looked upon the violet Aegean at its feet and the silver mountains at its back. Ah, Greece was no longer Greece to him, who was an exile! The resonance of absolute color, which pervaded land and sea and sky around him, no longer could enchant and awe and elate his senses. In truth, it blinded him, for here he feared to die and be buried in an alien grave. He had planned his death in this place, but now he was terrified that, in dying here his ashes would not lie in Rome or on the island, but become one with this silvery dust and blow in this blue and ardent air. The splendid sun, which had once cured his illness and had burned in his very heart, became terrible to him, he who longed so dreadfully for the murky sun of Rome. The villa was beautiful and graceful, and filled with delicate copies of the statues on the Parthenon, and everywhere there was the lovely simplicity of Ionian columns casting purple shadows before them, and white walls foaming with scarlet flowers. Everywhere there was shining serenity, the sweet cry of birds, the aromatic air of Greece, the scent of balsam and grape and salt and laurel, and the vasty silky azure of the sea on which fled the winged ships of commerce. Everywhere there was comfort and peace and even luxury, and at sunset the white villa turned as brightly gold as a new sesterce.

He could not endure it. He was like one blind and deaf in the Isles of the Blessed, and his heart did not sing with Greece but held black dirges rising from the River Styx. More and more he wrote wild and disheveled letters to his friends in Rome, reproaching them that they had prevented his suicide.

Greek was the language of all cultivated gentlemen of Rome. But now Cicero, staggering weakly about the beautiful villa, spoke only Latin to the Greek servants, who knew little of it and anxiously watched his tremulous gestures to guess his commands. They had at first felt derisive and mocking toward him—he a powerful Roman who was now less than the dust at the behest of "that nation of grocers." But as servants and overseers and gardeners saw his agony, their emotional Grecian hearts were moved to indignation against Rome, and to pity for his distraught man with the livid and haggard face and gray hair and sunken eyes. They became his champion, half through compassion and half through natural hatred for Rome.

The overseer, Adoni, was an intelligent man of considerable learning, and he had heard of Cicero's books as well as his fame as a lawyer, an orator, and a Consul of Rome, and the victor over a man who was detestable to a true Greek's heart, for had not Catilina been a traitor? It was Adoni who urged the cook to prepare the most delicate viands for the wretched exile, who barely touched them. It was Adoni who stole upon him while he sat like a blind man in the furiously colored gardens, and pointed out to him the fervency of sky and sun and the white calm of Salonika and the incredible violet of the sea.

"Alas," said Cicero, not insensible even in torment to the kindness of Adoni, "I see nothing, for a man sees with his heart more than with his eyes, and my heart is black and dead and cold. Better to be a slave in Rome than a king anywhere else in the world."

With which Adoni, of course, did not agree. He had lived for several years in Rome, for he was a freedman and cherished of his Roman master. He thought Rome to be a putrescent abscess which was rapidly infecting the whole majestic earth. What did Rome know of beauty and splendor, of science and art and philosophy, of the artfulness of frieze and the passionate loveliness of white columns at noon against a lucent sky? Did the gods live in Rome? No. They lived on Olympus. He argued gently with Cicero. The Romans built bloody circuses or bawdy theatres where buffoons howled and pranced and infamous women displayed their overblown bodies. But in Greek theatres one heard the voices of Aristophanes and Euripides and Aeschylus. Did Greece stink as Rome stank? For the first time since he arrived here Cicero smiled, a feeble smile but still a smile. "We have excellent sewers in Rome," he said. Adoni was delighted at his success. "We taught Romans how to build sewers, lord," he replied, "but the reek is their own."

Cicero seized his white temples in his hands and he muttered, "The reek of one's own country is fragrance to the exile. Give me peace, Adoni."

Adoni brought him roses, but the scent of them reminded Cicero of his lost gardens. He held the roses in his hands and openly wept. His eyes, once so compelling, so lighted with blue and amber fire, so changeful and fascinating, were drained of color and stained with crimson veins. His face, once so quiet and affable, so furrowed with secret laughter and humor, was the face of a wandering shade, lost and seeking. The noble forehead was diminished in its grandeur; the rough gray hair straggled on his sunken cheeks, his thin nape. Day by day he aged.

"He is dying for Rome," Adoni said to the servants. "For what base, swaggering and terrible Titan does he pine! Rome bestrides the earth in terror and fury, and where her iron feet pound death trickles from the wounded earth and every wall and mountain resounds with her hoarse and bestial voice." Adoni knew that the beauty which surrounded Cicero only augmented his agony, for he lived outside it in some icy crevice of suffering. He was like a prisoner who sees a vision from behind prison bars, and knows that never again will he be free to move within it and be one with it. Let a summons reach him, recalling him to Rome, and the spiked door would open at once for him and he would love, again, what he now lacked the capacity to love.

One day Adoni said to him, "Lord, a ship has arrived from Israel, and the Jews are very clever with artifacts of silver and bronze, and their weavers do excellent things with silks, and their oil is better even than the olive oil of Greece, and they have marvelous fruits and salt olives, and always, always, do they write books. Shall I go to the port and see what I can find for you, which will please you?"

Whether or not it was the name of Israel or the mention of books, or Adoni's kind concern for him, Cicero did not know. But he said, after a little hesitation, his mind faintly stirred from its lethargy and threatened madness, "Go to the port, Adoni, and—" He could not think what he desired, he who desired nothing but Rome. He continued, "You know that I live here at the sufferance of one of my dear friends and have little money. Be prudent."

Adoni took the big car which Cicero never used, for never did he go anywhere or visit anyone, though many invitations from old Greek families had come to him. Adoni also took with him some of the young female servants, who longed to look upon the strange seamen from foreign parts, and bargain with the shrewd Jewish merchants. The happy laughter of the young creatures preparing for their sojourn to the port reached even Cicero's weeping and deprived heart, and forgetting his necessary frugality he gave the girls some coins, for which they thanked him with tears and with kissings of his hands. The two horses and the car clattered away in a cloud of bright silvery dust and a burst of laughter and song, and Cicero heard and saw as a condemned man sees and hears, or as one who is old and dying.

He sat in the garden as still as the graceful statues all about him, and they were no more sentient than he. He heard fountains as with the dulling ear of death. Birds flashed through the radiant spray. Beyond the gardens lay the sea, soft and placid as peacock silk. A few little scarlet sails knifed the incredible brilliance of the blue sky, which pulsed with glowing light. How shall I live, where shall I go? Cicero asked himself, and his cheek was made sore again by his tears. A man spends his life, climbing painfully up a mountain, his eyes fixed on the gleaming peak, and he dreams of standing there on the summit for a space and contemplating the whole earth at his feet before he slowly descends in the gold sunset on the other side. So I was, too. But when I reached the shining marble of the peak I discerned there was no gentle slope below it, but an abyss, hurtling down to stony shadows and jagged death and desert. Oh, if I had only remained in the green valley below the mountain and had never climbed at all! I should, at least, now be drinking of the rivers of home and walking on the blooming soil of my own land. Dreams can lead to destruction, and even love for country can be a betrayal, and God is indifferent or does not exist. He threw up his hands in an excess of relentless despair, and cried out, "Oh, is it possible that I must remain here until I am dead, and that never again shall I see Rome!"

He thought that all his tears had been shed, that all his sorrow had been expressed. But now he learned that the spring of tears never dries and that sorrow has ten thousand tongues, and that grief endlessly invents new weapons to pierce the soul. The world was not the garden and the hot and joyous arena which youth believed. It was a pit of torture and no man ever learns all the labyrinths and never meets all the minotaurs. There are fresh agonies on fresh new paths, which he has not experienced before. There is always a unique enemy to challenge him, until the soul expires of weariness and lack of hope. All was now malign in the universe to Cicero. Was it true, as the Jews said, that creation is pervaded with evil, just as it is also pervaded with good, and that both are aware of man, one to destroy, the other to save?

At sunset Adoni returned with the car and the maidens. And among them were two visitors.

The sky was pure gold, the sea ran with gold, the air quivered with golden dust, and all the hills were aureate and every leaf in the gardens was gilded. In that drenching and golden light the man sitting on the marble bench under the myrtle trees resembled the statue of a dying man, abandoned, lonely, lost, and crushed by mortal pain. The visitors paused and gazed at him with consternation, for he did not see them or was indifferent to their appearance.

"It is true," said one to the other, "that years make changes in all of us. But yonder man, in such an agonized and frozen posture, is not the Marcus I knew! Not even age could so obliterate him."

They had been warned by the intelligent Adoni, but still they were confounded as well as moved to tears. They advanced into the gardens, and one of them cried out, "Marcus! Is it you?"

Cicero looked up with the vague lethargic stare of a man suddenly awakened in a strange place and who cannot immediately understand where he is. The blankness did not recede, and with the apathetic eyes of a babe he watched the approach of his visitors until they stood directly before him.

Then one of the men, weeping, fell upon him and embraced him where he sat, calling to him as one calls to the deaf, "Marcus, dear beloved friend, my Jonathan! Do you not know me?"

Marcus endured the embrace; his eyes opened and shut. He appeared to concentrate, and then to give up the unendurable effort. He saw before him a tall and slender middle-aged man with a long gray beard, a white face, and large brown eyes which were both soft and probing. The man wore an elegant robe of bright saffron embroidered with gold and silver, and a cloak of rich purple and a headcloth of striped gold and purple. An Egyptian necklace with tassels of gold and emeralds was about his throat, and he sparkled with many jewels on hands, wrists and arms and sandals. Marcus tried to speak listlessly; his voice was a dry rustle.

"Do you not remember me, Noë ben Joel, your childhood's friend, your almost-brother?"

"Noë? Noë?" Marcus' thin and trembling hands lifted, and then suddenly seized the bare arms of the other man and a great light fell on his face, so intense that Noë was moved to fresh tears. "Noë!" cried Marcus, and tried to rise, but was too weak and undone. So Noë pressed Marcus' head to his breast fervently, partly in love and partly to hide from his own sight that most devastated face.

"It is not possible!" exclaimed Marcus. "I thought all was dead!"

"God lives, therefore the world still lives," said Noë, and he sat down beside his friend and continued to hold him in his arms as one holds a suffering child. Marcus' hand, tremulous and searching, took one of Noë's hands and held it tightly. "And see," said Noë, "you have another old friend here with you, Anotis the Egyptian. Have you forgotten him? We met in Jerusalem, and when we discovered that you were our friend we became friends also." Noë's voice was soothing, slow and clear, as he tried to reach that besieged and distant spirit. "I have heard from friends in Rome of your—state—and decided to visit you when it was written to me that you were in Salonika. Anotis vowed to come with me also, and we arrived today on the ship from Israel. There we met your overseer, that marvelous Adoni, and begged for conveyance to you. And here we are, our eyes gladdened with joy to behold you once more!"

"Anotis?" said Marcus in a faint and troubled voice, as if trying to remember. He looked at his other visitor, so tall and lean in his crimson and green robes, his jewels, his stately manner. He saw the clear gray eyes that not even age could dim, the dark aquiline face, and the narrow pointed beard as white as snow. "Anotis? Anotis!" cried Marcus, and life suddenly ran through his emaciated body and quivered all over his face as he stretched forth his hand and burst into tears.

They sat beside him, he in the middle, and embraced him over and over and mingled their tears with his. The golden light suffused the whole world of sea and sky and earth; the scent of jasmine rose, and the sharp odor of salt. A wind came in from the water, bringing strange voices. The black cypresses swayed their pointed tops in the radiant light. Scarlet wings swept over the sea as ships came into port. Birds suddenly raised ecstatic voices to heaven. And Marcus Tullius Cicero sat with his friends and rejoiced, and could not believe his eyes or his ears. It was as if he had been called from the cold blackness of the tomb and was resurrected and looked upon life again, he who had lain so lifeless for so long.

"Do not leave me!" he implored them. "Forsake me not again!"

"We will stay with you many days, dear Marcus," Noë assured him, "for did we not travel far to be with you?"

"Alas," said Marcus. "I am nothing. I have lost my family and my home. I have lost Rome." His voice, however, was no longer listless but sharp and living with pain. "Do you understand what it is to lose your country? Noë? Anotis?"

"Yes," said Noë. "For we Jews were driven from our land and were captives in Babylonia. Hear what David says: 'By the rivers of Babylon, there we sat down, yes, we wept, when we remembered Sion. We hanged our harps in the midst thereof. —How shall we sing the Lord's song in a strange land? If I forget thee, O Jerusalem, let my right hand forget her cunning. If I do not remember thee, let my tongue cleave to the roof of my mouth, if I prefer not Jerusalem above my chief joy.' And God remembered the exiles and the homeless and restored them to their land. So He will restore you, Marcus, in His own good time, to the confoundment of your enemies. You are not the only exile who mourns and has mourned."

"And it is so with us Egyptians," said Anotis, with sadness. "The Greeks have long since seized our holy land and made us exiles therein, and scorned. Do we not weep for our country? Who shall restore her, and us? Centuries have passed, and in our own land we are not known." But he looked at the golden sky and at the west which flamed in scarlet, and his ascetic face was suddenly bright as if he had heard a promise.

They had brought him gifts, as if knowing his agony. Noë had brought him a tiny replica of the Sacred Scrolls, with silver rods, and parchment-like silk on which were written the holy words. Anotis had brought him the golden figure of a Woman, crowned with stars and standing on the world with a crushed serpent under her heel, and her body great with child. He said, "The Chaldean priests have told me a strange thing. Their astronomers now watch nightly for a stupendous Star, which will rise in the East and lead the holy men to the birthplace of Him Who shall save the world and deliver us from death. For so it has been promised to all men who have ears to hear and a soul to listen."

Marcus listened to what they said, and moment by moment his worn face became younger and it was, indeed, as if he had been delivered from the grave. He clung to his friends and wept, and they let him weep away his grief and his anguish, for like showers, his tears would bring a new spring to him and a new hope.

In the days that followed it was as if he had been newborn and was seeing and hearing for the first time, and he marveled with them at the beauty of the gold and silver days of Greece as if he were a newcomer, too, and not one who had lived there for months. Youth came to him again; he spoke buoyantly as a young man. He, for the first time, opened the books in the library and read to his friends in Greek. He praised the gardeners for their skill, he who had not looked on the gardens before. Adoni took the three friends in a vessel for a pleasure sail on the violet sea, and they fished together and laughed like boys, and were no longer men who were staring at the years of old age. Cicero's step became light. He spoke eagerly of what he hoped to accomplish when he was recalled to Rome. He boasted of his children, his brother, his friends, even his wife. At night, he wrote furiously on new essays for his long-suffering and much-abused friend and publisher, Atticus. He found new delights in every day, and new laughter, and the servants rejoiced to hear his ringing voice. His old humor returned, and it gave him joy that his wry jokes did not arouse hostility in his friends, but answering mirth. Sometimes, without apparent reason, he would run to one or the other and embrace him passionately and kiss his cheek like a repentent but happy child. "Oh!" he would exclaim, "God is good, that He sent you to me, when I contemplated nothing but death!"

"That is because He has need of you, dear Marcus," they would answer him. "Can He spare one single just man?"

"Tell me again of the Messias," Marcus would say. "I had forgotten Him."

"I am afraid," said Noë, "that men will not recognize Him at all, but will abuse and scorn and kill Him. For hearken to what David says will be His fate; and what He says of Himself:

"'My God, my God, why have You forsaken Me, why are You so far from helping Me? I cry in the daytime, but You hear me not. —I am a reproach of men, and despised of the people, and they that see Me laugh Me to scorn; they shoot out the lip, they shake the head, saying, "He trusted the Lord that He would deliver Him. Let Him deliver Him, seeing that He delighted in Him." They gaped upon Me with their mouths, as a ravening and a roaring lion. I am poured out like water, and all My bones are out of joint; My Heart is like wax, it is melted in the midst of My bowels. My strength is dried up like a potsherd, and You have brought Me to the dust of death. I may tell all My bones; they look and stare upon Me. They part My garments among them and cast lots upon My vestures.'

"You will see," said Noë, "that despite what the Pharisees declare—that the Messias will come with the sound of many silver trumpets and with powers and dominions of angels, and with thunder—He will truly be born as the humblest and the meekest and will endure an agonizing death, as the Sacrifice for sinful man. It is very mysterious. Shall we know Him? I doubt it. But still, God will reveal Him, for David speaks of Him: 'I have set My King upon My holy hill of Sion. I will declare the decree: You are My Son. This day have I begotten You. Ask of Me, and I shall give You the heathen for Your inheritance, and the uttermost parts of the earth for Your possession!'"

"We have His sign, the Cross," said Anotis, "which is the Resurrection, and this we have had for many, many ages."

Marcus listened avidly, and in his heart he said, "Forgive me, that I doubted You and forgot You. I felt an exile, but is it not true that exile or not, the mind makes its own place and cannot be moved from it? I am a Roman, and remain a Roman. I have not left Rome. Rome has left me."

When his friends were forced to leave for their own homes Marcus accompanied them to the port of Salonika. He watched the great winged ship fall below the horizon and he was again filled with sorrow. Then he thought, They are not gone. We say "farewell," but in another harbor they say, "Here they return!" He went to the villa, but no longer was it a place of abominable exile. It was his home for a time, before he returned to Rome. He began to write spirited letters to his family and his friends, and to Caesar and Pompey, demanding that they recall him.

At night he would pray in the words of King David, which Noë had taught him:

"I will lift up my eyes unto the hills, from whence comes my help. My help comes from the Lord, Who made heaven and earth. He will not suffer your foot to be moved; He Who keeps you will not slumber. Behold, He Who keeps Israel will neither slumber nor sleep. The Lord is your Guardian; the Lord is your Shade upon your right hand. The sun shall not smite you by day, nor the moon by night. The Lord shall preserve you from all evil; He shall preserve your soul."

And at midnight he would look upon the bright heavens and repeat with David: "You are My Son. This day have I begotten You."

Was this the day, or the hour. Marcus questioned the stars. Marcus looked for the Star of which Anotis had told him. But the heavens were bland and still. Marcus went to his chamber and gazed at the figure of the

Maiden great with Child, and he pondered and a thrill of sweetness ran through him as if he had heard a loving voice in the wilderness of the world, a voice calling him home. He laid a sheaf of lilies before the figure. He kissed the feet of the Maiden Mother.

CHAPTER FIFTY-NINE

"We are beset," said Julius Caesar to Crassus. "Suddenly, the whole city rings with the name of Cicero, and there are indignant writings on the walls. All demand the recall of Cicero. Let us be magnanimous, and the people we rule will forget our decrees and hail us as noble friends and benefactors."

"I say yes," said Pompey, and raised up his thumb.

Young Porcius Cato, the tribune, squire and patrician, went to Senators who were friends of his family. "Pusillanimous men!" he cried to them. "You have exiled the man who saved Rome and yourselves. The people are in a ferment. Recall him!"

The storm of protest angered and confounded Crassus. He tried to discover those who had invoked the storm that raged now in Rome, but it was as if Cicero had raised champions from the very stones of the streets. Then indeed it became dangerous to resist, and Crassus gloomily consulted the guilty Senate. "It is not a matter to be easily overcome," said the Senators. "If we declare ourselves in the wrong then the people must despise us. There is also Antonius Hybrida, that confused fool, who threatens to go to the new Consul, P. Cornelius Lentulus Spinther, with his confession, and all know that Lentulus is an old friend of Cicero's. Let us consider together."

In true Italianate fashion, they decided to so confuse the issue that no finger could be pointed at any distinct person as the man who had forced recall of Cicero, and therefore no particular man would be forced to explain. Pompey wrote a cautious letter to Cicero, reminding of his love for him, and stating that he sleeplessly worked to secure his recall, "but it now lies with Caesar, your old dear friend." Pompey added: "Your publisher, who is now very rich and influential, ceaselessly seizes influential men by the shoulder and harangues them in your behalf. As he has many comedians in his pay, whom he calls satiric authors, many fear him."

The noble tribune, Ninnius, who had always loved Cicero, went to

Julius and looked at him with wise and sparkling eyes. "Once I introduced a bill to recall Cicero," he said. "Clodius opposed it, and he won. Now the new tribunes elect, including your friend Titus Annius Milo, are in favor of Cicero's recall. They will vote on it. Are you opposed?"

"I?" exclaimed Julius. "Is there ever a day that I do not pray that my dear Marcus' exile be ended?"

"Pray harder," said Ninnius. The wise eyes gleamed but the rest of his face was very serious. He did not fear the terrible Committee of Three who now held Rome as a slave. "You have a most eloquent tongue, dear Caesar. Speak to the Senators."

"I have spoken often to them," said Julius. "I shall speak again," he added in the gravest of tones, and Ninnius, concealing a smile, bowed and left him. The people loved Ninnius for his honor. There had been a threat under the calmness of his voice, and Julius always listened to threats. "It is a stupid tyrant who is vainglorious and believes himself invincible and invulnerable," he said to the other members of the Committee. "It is said that Xerxes listened first to the humblest of his slaves, and second only, to his ministers. For the ministers were loyal for his favors, but the slave had nothing to lose by telling the truth."

The leaves of the trees of Rome were turning red and brown and yellow when Ninnius made a new motion before the Senate for the recall of Cicero. Eight Senators promptly voted in favor, the others abstaining. But strong in their numbers, the eight Senators proposed a bill for the recall. It did not pass. However, though the exile was not ended, the Senate did return Cicero all his civil rights and former rank. He was so notified. But now his strength and pride had been restored. He refused to return to Rome unless all of his seized properties were restored to him, and a new house on the Palatine built for him. In the meantime he went to reside in Dyrrachium where he had access to a great library. There Atticus, optimistic and full of affection, visited him to tell him of events and the mighty sales in Rome of Cicero's new book. He placed a lavish purse in his friend's hands, half of which came from his own purse, but not to Cicero's knowledge. He brought cheering news of the health of Cicero's family, and the courageous work of Quintus in behalf of his brother.

"Bands from all over Italy are coming to Rome to demand your recall, and the restoration of all that was taken from you," said Atticus. "Lentulus has declared that as soon as the Sacred Rites are completed in Janus he will bring another motion before the Senate in your favor, for the Consuls are with you."

Atticus was overcome with delight and joy that his friend and author should be so in control of himself, for he had feared for his mind and life over these many months. Marcus appeared strong again, and even serene, and most resolute. "They would have me return with my restored rank and my civil rights," he said to Atticus. "But, how shall I live? How governments cling to the money they steal from the citizens! One would think they had earned it themselves! If I live in poverty in Rome, the Senate would be happy, for still all men would say, 'He is a poor thing, that Cicero, in more ways than one, and too old to rise again.' Alas, that only money in these degenerate days bestows honor! Therefore, let the Senate fume and complain that I do not return, until the day all is restored to me."

Atticus, on returning to Rome, kept Marcus abreast of events. "The scene is like that of a mosaic, hanging in order and pattern and story upon a wall, and then suddenly each tile falls from its place and all is confused color and chaos and formless. Resolutions are passed, revoked. Lentulus pleads, the Senate listens, then denies. Pompey has declared that only an edict of the people (lex) can recall you, and this is true. Caesar addresses the Senate, calling himself their servant, and evoking grim smiles while he pleads for you. Crassus, calling himself an even humbler slave of the Roman people, addresses the Senate, and they listen solemnly. Therefore, it seems that all Italy desires your return, and the Senate, and the Committee of Three, and the nobility, and all the 'new' men. But, there is Publius Clodius, who hates you, and he is very powerful."

Atticus did not add, in his letter, that Cicero's brother, Quintus, had been set on, in open daylight, in the Forum, by the minions of Clodius and that he had been left for dead on the stones. His life was saved only by the most ardent care of many physicians. Atticus did not deem it prudent to alarm Cicero, who might then charge back to Rome in fearful anxiety for his brother and thus tacitly agree to the terms of the Senate, that only his civil rights and his rank be restored to him. It seemed vile, to Atticus, that the corrupt mobs of Rome, whom Clodius appeared to control even more than they were controlled by the Triumvirate, should stand between Cicero and his honorable recall and restoration of properties. But every Roman, no matter his wit or lack of it, his learning or his ignorance, his character or his baseness, had a vote equal to any in Rome, and when his fellows gathered in the Forum to vote they were easily inflamed and riots were very numerous. Let them gather to vote in the case of Cicero, and Clodius, who bribed the masses constantly, would incite them to riot and disorder. Cicero was only a name to the mobs, and that name was anathema to their master, Clodius. It was enough for them. "Such are the uses of democracy," Atticus thought, while he was writing to his friends. "The voice of the people is frequently the voice of jackasses and criminals and the demented and the avid bellies. They will believe the most monstrous lies if spoken by their current favorite and servant in politics. They will defame the best, if so commanded. They will riot and commit wholesale murder at the behest of any rascal who alleges he loves and serves them out of the nobility of his heart. The mob neither loves nor hates Cicero for himself. But they hate him because Clodius has commanded them so to hate. And this is democracy!"*

Lentulus decided to divert the mobs. As Consul of Rome, he gave them vast spectacles in the circuses, more awesome than they had ever seen before, and while they were entranced by the bloody amusements Lentulus met with the Senate in the Temple of Honor and Virtue and resolved on a bill for the complete recall of Cicero, the restorations of his properties, and marks of honor. But Clodius, suspecting the plot, was able to keep the bill from passage.

Then Pompey, the soldier who despised the reckless and undisciplined mobs, moved resolutely. In the company of many distinguished men, including Lentulus and Servilius, he addressed the people in the Forum, and appealed to their decency—which he privately considered they did not possess—and their virtue—in which he did not believe—and to their honor—of which he was convinced they possessed none at all. He was a member of the terrible Triumvirate, whom all men feared, and no member of that Triumvirate had heretofore spoken publicly and directly, in the Forum, to the people, before that day in behalf of Cicero or anyone or anything else. The mob was flattered. They promised, in acclamation, to vote in favor of Cicero's recall, momentarily forgetting their master, Clodius. Pompey then assured them of their nobleness of soul and heart and mind, and, thinking of Cicero, his voice trembled with sincerity and the emotional mob saw the tears of the great soldier and general who so humbled himself before them. Pompey said later to Lentulus, "Pray the gods keep the vehemence alive in them, at least until Cicero is recalled!"

Clodius strove with his followers, and the Praetor and three magistrates and several tribunes stood with him in his adamant enmity against Cicero. But, to Clodius' rage and incredulity and complete bafflement, the people did not follow him this time, for though he had bribed them often enough, Pompey had flattered them and had aroused the latent instinct for decency in them—a very rare phenomenon, as Atticus wittily noted in a letter. In short, it was a miracle. "If God did not interfere occasionally in the affairs of men," Atticus wrote, "then in truth we should fall into chaos, and no criminal or murderer would ever be apprehended and no justice ever done, and no vile politician ever exposed for the liar he is."

The people kept their promise to Pompey and in late summer they voted for the recall of Cicero, the restoration of his civil rights and rank, all his

* From a letter to Lentulus.

properties, and marks of honor as a hero of Rome. The banishment was over, and Tullia met her beloved father on the shores of his homeland and threw herself in his arms. He put her from him gently, and knelt down and kissed the sacred earth and wet the soil of his fathers with his tears. All that he had endured was less than his joy.

If the people had been slow to recall him they were passionate in their acclamations in his honor all through Italy when he traveled home. He passed through Capua, Naples, Minturnae, Sinuessa, Formiae, where sumptuous villas were placed at his disposal by friends, and in the vicinity of which his own former villas had been destroyed by the government in its enthusiastic malice. Magistrates received him with laurel and bay leaf crowns, saluting him and kissing his hands, and huge crowds hailed him with cries of "Hero!" and mighty ovations. Farmers and their families lined the roads, strewing flowers in his path. Deputations rushed to meet him, to prostrate themselves at his feet, calling him the savior of all Italy. Every hamlet and town along his passage declared a fiesta in his honor, and all abandoned labor to greet him thunderously. The large car in which he rode with his daughter and friends could hardly proceed for hours, so great was the crush of the Italian populace. Judges called him the pillar of law, the foundation of the Constitution. Fellow lawyers gave banquets in his honor, exclaiming that lawyers forevermore would be sanctified in his name.

Exhausted, pale, and surfeited, thinking only that he was once more on the sacred soil of Italy, he paused one night before entering Rome for a rest in the villa of a friend. He said to Tullia, "If I were younger I should be beguiled into believing that all men formerly stood with me, and that now they are vindicated in my person. But I am no longer young; therefore, though I am happy and my heart is moved at all these demonstrations, I remember that these same acclaimers shunned me on this very same journey, in reverse, when I moved to exile. Man is a feeble thing; he acclaims when it is harmless to acclaim, and approves. When it is demanded that he denounce and defame—especially if the government so demands—then he is just as vehement and just as righteous. A word from Rome to destroy me, and tomorrow those who now kiss my hands would cut my throat—with equal enthusiasm. Man feels the happiest when he believes he is conforming to his fellows, and that is a sad and terrible augury for the future."

Tullia, weary herself, demurred. "Surely they truly love you, my father."

Cicero replied: "I do not trust my fellowmen, though once I trusted them. I only pray for them. They believe that universal popularity is the measure of a man's worth."

It was the twenty-third night of his triumphal journey through the countless throngs of his fellow Italians. At his urgent request there was no banquet, no long wearisome speeches on the part of magistrates, lawyers, judges, and exigent politicians, no exuberances from the people, for Italians, above all, love festivities and emotion and demonstrations, especially in behalf of suddenly popular men. Tomorrow he would enter Rome. He sat in his beautiful chamber, the bedroom of his host, while the large villa hummed with envoys from the Senate and the host importantly interviewed them, promised to deliver messages to Cicero in the morning, wined and dined the visitors and scurried through passageways. The bedroom was filled with flowers. Cicero was almost prostrated with exhaustion. Tullia, herself, bathed his feet and laid out his ceremonial robes for the morrow. For the first time, as he smiled at her, he noted that she appeared more subdued than he had remembered before his exile, more fragile, more delicate. Her slender face, so like his, was very pale. Her long light brown hair fell down her frail back, and her hands were too thin and trembled a little. Her eyes, again so like his own, seemed duller for all her youth, and her ways even more gentle than he remembered. He was suddenly alarmed.

"Tullia!" he said. "This has wearied you more than it has wearied me."

She tried to smile, then all at once she burst into tears and threw herself into his arms. He held her on his knee and vaguely tried to console her, and wiped her cheeks and smoothed her soft fine hair, and kissed her. His alarm grew.

"Tell me!" he cried. "What is wrong with my darling, the sweetness of my life?"

Then, for the first time, he heard of the wounds of his beloved brother who had almost died in his service, and the death of his devoted son-in-law, Piso Frugi, who had worked so valorously for the return of Cicero from exile. Tullia was a widow, and she not yet nineteen years of age. Piso had died of a sudden fever, but physicians suspected poison. She sat on her father's knee, bereaved, desolate, brokenhearted, and Cicero, sorrowful himself, reflected that his child could so forget her suffering as to come to meet him in the midst of her grief.

"You should have told me, dearest one," he murmured, as he consoled and kissed her. "You should not have come to greet me, and add more burdens to the desperate one you carry. I shall sacrifice in behalf of Piso when I arrive in Rome. My brother—"

"My uncle, Quintus, has only just risen from his bed, where he almost died," said Tullia, mortified that she had weakly brought such sad news to her father in the midst of his triumphs.

"I have been so blind!" said Cicero. "If I had taken but a moment to observe you, my daughter, I should have seen how stricken you were, and how pale. But no! I was absorbed in my own vindication, and listening too hard to plaudits and the false speeches of those who greeted me, and who had spurned me only a year ago!"

He forgot his joy in his mourning for his son-in-law, and in the terrible thought that Quintus might have been killed by his, Cicero's, enemies. "I have brought disaster to those I love best," he said.

But Tullia, resolutely wiping away her tears, consoled him instead. She despised herself that on the eve of her father's greatest triumph she had weighted sorrow on him; she implored his forgiveness; she ought to have refrained and not have succumbed to female weakness, and cravenly sought consolation. Now, all was ruined. Cicero said, forcing himself to smile, "Piso would desire for me to rejoice, and Quintus will greet me on the morrow. For their sakes, alone, I shall be what they wish," and he made a grimace, "the Hero crowned with laurel and receiving the homage of Rome." They wept in each other's arms, and though Cicero assured his daughter that nothing would be dimmed for him, his heart was heavy and torn. When Tullia had gone to her own chamber rebellion flared in him, and bitterness. Were it not for him Quintus should not have nearly died of wounds; the young and ardent and passionate Piso would be living, he who had so loved life, and with such humor. Cicero did not sleep that night, thinking and often hating.

A hot gray dawn had hardly appeared at the edge of the night-purple sky when Cicero was awakened by a furious and triumphant blast of trumpets, the passionate clamor of drums and the roar of thousands of voices. His first thought was, "Have they decided to murder me, after all?" Then chiding himself for what was only partly irony, he rose to stand at his window and see the flaring of crimson torches. The handsome villa was surrounded by Quintus' legion, on foot and on horse and in chariots, and banners were already unfurled and as red as blood in the torchlight, and metal gleamed on harness and armor and spear and blade, and the horses pranced and lictors and fasces were raised and there was much shouting and wheeling and gathering in formation, and beyond the legion heaved masses of people who had come from Rome, itself, to gather in his train. A returning general, victorious and bearing coffers of looted gold and thousands of slaves, could not have received a more thunderous ovation. Tullia came running into her father's chamber, half in excitement and half in fear, and he took her hands and said, "They would be just as vociferous and noisy if I were being led to execution!"

A gilded chariot had been sent for him and his daughter from the Senate, and after a hasty breakfast he entered the vehicle, lifting his arms high to greet the incredible crush of newly arriving people joining those

who were already there. It was as if all Rome had emptied herself to rush
beyond her gates to meet him and follow after him as they followed con-
querers. Then the procession began, the trumpets and the drums and
cymbals leading, the officers prancing on their black horses, and then
Cicero in his shining chariot, and behind him tens of thousands of dancing and screaming and clapping men and women hardly held in check by
the following legionnaires. He saw nothing but an ocean of heads,
crowned with flowers, and new rivers of humanity flowing into it all
along the Via Appia and tributary roads. The sun had raised half a red
rim against the burning gray pall of the eastern sky, and a dull scarlet light
began to touch tops of distant monuments along the way and the roofs
of houses rising on hills, and made sanguine little pools near the road
and a few thin small streams. Swallows rose with cries, and from the
early autumnal earth there breathed forth the scent of hay and ripening
fruit and scorched soil and warm stone and bronzed grass. Now the scarlet
light in the east towered upward like a conflagration and the sides of white
villas were stained with it and the climbing white walls on the hills also.
There was no wind; all was very still and strangely echoing, and the
tumultuous voices of the people and the trumpets and drums and cymbals
were suddenly dim in Cicero's ears, as if he dreamed. Tullia saw her
father's face; it was as pale and calm as a statue's, and as expressionless.
He held the gilded reins like a mighty hero and stood proudly and deep in
thought, but she saw the bloody light of the torches and the bloody light
of the rising sun in the folds of his noble white toga and in the pits of
his eyes. She thought to herself that it was very ominous, for all the
triumphal procession and the noise and the lifted banners, for now the
dust was rising under thousands of running feet and it, too, was scarlet.
There was no color at all but red and gray, and for a moment the girl's
heart was shaken with fear as if she had glimpsed a procession in Hades,
and from her narrow seat in the chariot she reached out to touch her
father's arm.

Then all at once the uproarious scene sparkled into other colors as the
sun mounted, yet the sky remained oddly crepuscular and sweltering. Now
the walls of Rome could be seen, granite intermixed with yellow stone,
and above them, the city itself, red, flaming gold, gleaming umber, light
green and blue, all its tiled roofs afire as if a thousand thousand bonfires
had been built upon them to hail the hero.

Cicero looked upon his distant city, his home, and for the first time his
face was moved. Tears rushed into his eyes. His heart was exalted, as if
he were a youth again. He did not hear the trumpets, the drums and the
cymbals, the roaring of chariot wheels, the pound of hoofs, the earthquake of feet all about him. He saw and heard nothing but Rome, wait-

ing for him, crowded and gigantic and throbbing with vital power against the sinister sky. Home, home, he murmured to himself, and wished he might be alone to walk to that mirage lifting against the sky higher and higher at every moment.

Then he was struck by the blackest melancholy and sadness. All that once was Rome was dead. The corpse remained, still vibrating from the life that had left it, the sacred life of departed men. The corpse would decompose if not today then surely tomorrow. What remained then of this city which was at once host and parasite, a corpse and a breathing monster, a still-beating heart and a skeleton? A promise and a threat to the ages, a hope and a warning. What empires lay fetal in the womb of time, still blind, still formless, still deaf, not yet stirring, which would be born as Rome had been born, and would die as she had died? All that was in the universe, Aristotle had averred, is not diminished nor increased by time. All that was is and forevermore will be, nothing added, nothing taken away, though galaxies would disappear and new rainbowed universes flash into being, and new suns rise on new planets—and, on this small world new nations would be born and would be forgotten before the sun and the moon passed away. To these nations, then, Rome was a legacy, a law, a tomb, and an omen. Ah, let them remember Rome, lest they share her fate!

Cicero came to himself with a start. He could no longer see autumnal fields; they were crowded with multitudes, waving to him, shouting, raising hands high to clap. They were a multitude of colors in their garments; they laughed gleefully to him, proud of their numbers and their demonstrations. And behind him they followed the procession like a vehement river, for all the countryside had joined the Romans who had left the city to greet him. His horses and the interior of the chariot were covered with the flowers of autumn. The sun was too brilliant in his eyes and the heat was stupendous and the noise beyond endurance. Cicero smiled, bowed to the acclamations, the shouts, the yells and the occasional Italianate derisive sound. In truth, the latter made him smile and pleased him more in his present mood then the adulation.

"I feel ridiculous," Cicero murmured to his daughter, and when he heard his own words his mood shifted again and he was lighter of heart. Not even the whisper in his ears that Catilina had really triumphed, and not himself, could do more than, for an instant, chill his soul.

The whole Senate, in their white and scarlet robes, met him at the gates, and the tribunes, and the magistrates, and more teeming mobs with even more raucous voices. Pompey was there, and Crassus and Julius Caesar, on great white horses, as grand as statues. It was Julius who drove his horse through the ranks of the triumphant legionnaires to approach Cicero's chariot, and it was Julius who leaped like a youth into the chariot itself to embrace Cicero and kiss his cheek. The mobs were tremendously moved at this, and smiled and wept for no discernible reason. Pompey rode beside the chariot on his horse and smiled down with a little gloom upon Cicero. Crassus trotted at the head of the procession as if he were the hero, and not Cicero, and the mobs cheered him also with exuberance.

"Happy is this day!" Julius cried in Cicero's ear under the uproar. "My life is now complete, and that I swear, my dearest Marcus!"

But now the soldiers at the gates raised their own trumpets and drums and conversation could not be continued. It was as if the whole world had gone mad with its own cheering and yelling and cries, and all was covered with clouds of dust golden-red in the morning sunlight.

Cicero longed to rest in the house of Atticus, but first he must address the Senate, who wept openly when he sat in his old seat. They let him compose himself. He seemed to be listening to the demonstrations of joy and welcome of the huge masses of people outside, whose ovations did not lessen in intensity for a long while. He seemed to be looking about him, pondering, his eyes unreadable. But in truth his mood of sadness and despondency had returned to him, and a curious sense of strangeness as if he were a stranger in a strange land, and did not know how to speak to the inhabitants. He had dreamed of this day with longing and sorrow and despair, hardly believing that it would ever come to pass. It had come to pass—and he could bring no emotion to his mind but bitterness.

The Senate waited self-righteously to be congratulated on their magnanimity by this great and famous orator, who had so moved, enraged and stunned them by his voice and words in the past, whose eloquence had made them marvel so that they had listened with more attention than they had ever given the most celebrated actor. Whether in agreement or in hostility, they had never felt indifference toward him, or ennui. His voice had always been like the jagged lightning of Jupiter, illuminating and blinding or staggering the soul, or arousing the utmost hate or fear. There had been times when he had appeared to glow before them, incandescent with the emotion that had seized him, and which he had conveyed to them with its own power.

He wanted to blast them with fire and with anger, to reveal to them the mountebanks and liars and fearful and hypocrites and the arrogant which they were, the men who had trembled at the very name of Catilina and had pronounced his death, and then had accused the instrument of that death of violating the Constitution, of ignoring points of order, and had finally censured and exiled him, execrating his methods. He wanted to hurl the thunderbolts of his violent wrath upon them and reduce them to ashes.

But, it was not politic. He looked at them, and his treacherous heart felt pity for them that they were not men who had the fortitude to stand by their decisions nor even to agree that those decisions had been necessary in the awful face of danger. He had been their victim. He must now praise them and thank them. He rose to his feet, and a deep sigh of anticipation stirred them.

"This day," he said, "is equivalent to immortality." (*Immortalitatis instar fuit.*)

He forgot the Senate in his own sudden emotions of joy, for all at once he was flooded with the reality that he was indeed home and he remembered nothing else. Elation lifted his soul so that he felt a sense of physical elevation. He launched into a panegyric of the Senate, of the people of Rome, "who had carried me upon their shoulders into my beloved city." His voice was like golden music, and the Senate was exalted at hearing themselves described as mighty men of honor, as the bulwark of Rome, as the repository of republican virtues and guardians of the city. It seemed to Cicero in those deliriously joyous moments that he spoke truly and that these were not the men he remembered who had condemned him to an exile that had almost cost his life. They were Romans, and he was a Roman also, and so they were brothers greeting each other after a long and bitter separation. He eulogized the people of Rome also; his soul appeared to expand to embrace the whole nation. His words were repeated by those near the door of the Senate and carried to the farthest throng so that thunderous echoes accompanied all he said. Everything to him was outlined with radiance, and his voice conveyed his jubilation and his happiness. Weariness fell from him; he was young again and valiant and believed in humanity. The Senate wept; the people wept.

When he left the Senate Chamber he was accompanied by Senators who seemed to want to be close to him, and jostled each other. The crowd hailed him in voices they used for the worship of divinity. It was not until he stood on the Senate steps and looked at the seething Forum and the vociferous faces that the morning's despondency seized him again though in far worse measure, and his spirit sickened with a deathly nausea. None guessed it; his smile was fixed on his face. He thought, None of them means it. It is only an excuse for a fiesta, for the license to shout and scream with hysteria, to lose control, to jump and leap without fear of a frowning and censorious glance, to embrace, to romp, to behave as heedless animals all voice and exuberance. How heavy is the yoke of humanity on the shoulders of men!

Atticus' house on the Palatine was his temporary home, where he was welcomed by a weeping and laughing Terentia and a boisterous young son, and Pomponia and her son, and hordes of friends already feasting and wining while waiting for him. Atticus, who had left for Greece only a few days before, had written a letter for him: "Alas, I do not know the exact day of your return, or if the Senate will, at the last hour, revoke the comita! But anticipating that you will be summoned home I have placed my house at your disposal and all my goods and my slaves, and have invited your family to be with you. In the meantime, I must go to Athens and other parts of Greece in pursuit of my inconsiderate and irresponsible authors who, when their hands are filled with a few sesterces, leave Rome for other parts, notably those of small taxes, to commune, as they say, with the Muses and refresh their lazy souls. Does it matter to them that I have broadcast the news of a forthcoming book of theirs, and engaged extra scribes and have given them advances on royalties—which they immediately spend without having earned them? No! They must take their surly visages and their sesterces, to lie in the sun and disport themselves with local harlots and haunt the wine shops! They have no sense of duty. I embrace you, beloved Marcus, but must also remind you that you, too, owe me another volume."

Cicero forced himself to embrace his wife, to thank her for her efforts in his behalf, though he noticed that but a single year had aged and fattened her and had narrowed her once lovely eyes even more. But he rejoiced in his son, in whose face, red-cheeked and merry, he fancied he discerned preternatural wisdom and a love for learning and all the virtues. Terentia informed him, glowing with pride and happiness, that the Triumvirate in person were visiting him that evening for a banquet, which she, forgetting frugality, had lavishly arranged. He was shown to his apartments by bowing slaves and he looked upon the sumptuousness of them and recalled that he now had no house of his own, that Publius Clodius had built on the site a temple ironically dedicated to Liberty, and had appropriated the rest of the grounds for himself. He threw himself upon the bed and despite the continuing uproar of crowds which had accompanied him here he let himself fall into an exhausted sleep.

Before sunset he went to the house of Quintus on the Carinae—the house so full of his own memories—where he found his brother still recovering from his wounds. There, for the first time, as he sat beside Quintus holding his hand, he learned of the true and desperate state of affairs in Rome. There was a serious shortage of grain in the city. A famine had begun. Sicily and Egypt, from whence came most of the cereals which supplied Rome, had reported extremely poor harvests that year. Clodius, emulating Catilina, had formed his own gangs of malcontents and criminals and had trained them in the manner of an army, which only he could control. He had incited them, and only lately, against the Senate itself, which they had actually stoned while it was in session. Several of the

Senators had been wounded. The people had some justice on their side: Anticipating famine, the storers of corn had raised their prices enormously, so much so that cereals were often beyond the means of small purses. Some of Clodius' mobs had even threatened to burn down Caesar's beloved Temple of Jupiter. The people, as usual, cared little for liberty, but they cared everything for their bellies, so it was easy to arouse them to inflammatory madness at a word.

In short, Cicero reflected with dismay and returning apprehension, nothing had changed in Rome. His life, in the future, would indeed be but a repetition of what he had known too many years. Freedom had gone forever, under the iron Triumvirate, whose ambitions grew day by day. Pompey had been given enormous and unprecedented military power.

Cicero wrote to Atticus, and his letter was full of melancholy. As for the situation in Rome, he wrote, "It is, for a state of prosperity, slippery; for a state of adversity, good." He added, with gloom, "It is the national climate of a democracy."

CHAPTER SIXTY

"Though the Greeks declare that war is one of the arts," wrote Cicero to Caesar, "and that the greatest game of all is man hunting man—I note that it is only man who hunts and murders his own species—I have discovered that governments resort to war to silence internal discontent and unite a nation against a 'foe,' or to bring a false prosperity to the State when its finances are declining and corruption has wholly seized the politicians. War is particularly loved of tyrants; it diverts a people from just complaint against them. It also enhances the powers of tyrants, for then in a state of emergency, as they call it, they can impose even more onerous restrictions upon liberty. "Yet," he added sadly, "young men appear to love war and find even more gratification of their most bestial instincts in it than in the arms of women. There is a fatal fault in human nature, a primal core of evil."

Julius Caesar, before the return of Cicero from exile, had been appointed by Crassus, as governor of Cisalpine Gaul, Transalpine Gaul, and Illyricum, all excellent sources for loot. He was now pursuing, with fine enthusiasm, the Gallic Wars, with young Mark Antony as his first officer. All this splendid martial activity did not interfere with his membership in the

Triumvirate. It was evident that he intended to make a more heroic reputation as a soldier than Pompey the Magnus, for not only was Caesar a
general in the most ardent of Roman fashions but he was a shrewd administrator of Roman civil life also. He frequently returned to Rome to be
certain that no one was too actively undermining his political position and
to keep a subtle eye on his natural enemies which he knew included both
Crassus and Pompey. He did not find this too arduous, for with his natural
gift for intrigue he combined a marvelous physical constitution despite
his predilection for epilepsy—which he used to advantage also.

Julius thought Cicero's letter concerning war and man's innate evil very
amusing. "My dear Marcus," he wrote, "you will forever remain the naïve
and virtuous man, despite all your experiences. What unhappiness must
be yours! that you attempt to reconcile your conceptions of virtue with
what your intelligence tells you about humanity! It is like an attempt to
mate fire and water. What you know, and what you hope, are the fatal and
irreconcilable flaw in your temperament, and men like you are doomed to
sorrow and despair, for you refuse to accept the reality that most men regard the world as their particular domain and all the inhabitants therein
their prey; you prefer to believe that by taking thought men can be better
and nobler than their nature has ordained! Better to accept what man is
than to have wild dreams that he may become like the gods! You can only
confuse mankind with your ideals. I satisfy men, for I know what they are
and do not demand more than is possible."

Cicero admitted to himself that there was some truth in what Julius
had written, and so he did not reply to the letter. How can a man live if
he accepts the evil in man with amusement and a shrug, and does not try
to eradicate it?

He had begun his campaign for the complete restoration of his property.
He appealed to the College of Pontifices (Pontiffs), who had the responsibility concerning religion. The deft Clodius had posed a question of them
when he had erected a Temple to Liberty on the site of Cicero's house on
the Palatine Hill. To destroy the temple and return the land to Cicero had
elements of blasphemy in it. However, there was also a question of law. So
the Pontiffs wrote their decision: "If neither by a command of free burghers
in a lawful assembly (*populi jussu*) nor by a plebiscite, he who avers that
he dedicated the site to religious uses had specific authority, we are of the
ópinion that that part of the site which has been so dedicated may, without
any violation of religion, be returned to Marcus Tullius Cicero, considering,
too, that malice and enmity had deprived him of his property in the first
place."

But Clodius, that sleepless enemy, was not without resources. Though
he did not possess the profound understanding of humanity that Julius

Caesar possessed, he had his own comprehension of it and its vagaries, prejudices, and capriciousness. Cicero soon found that he was again losing favor with the people, and though intellectually aware of the caprices of his fellowmen he still indefatigably believed they could often be moved to justice and reason. So he was astonished that when Clodius induced his brother Appius, the Praetor, to declare that the Pontiffs had ruled in his, Clodius', favor, but that Cicero, disdaining the College of Pontiffs and manifesting a contempt for religion, was going to take the site of his house "by force," a vast segment of the people believed Clodius with no question at all! The Senate had moved to carry out the dictum of the Pontiffs. (In the meantime Clodius had also managed to blame the increasing famine in grain on Cicero, on the grounds that so huge had been the number of those following him from the countryside on his return from exile, that the famine had been aggravated.)

Then matters came to a standstill. Many of the tribunes, the representatives of the people, loved Clodius. They vetoed the return of the site of Cicero's house on the grounds that it was now sacred soil. The cynical people, who did not truly believe in the gods, were nevertheless vociferous in their defense of "sanctity." But Cicero resolutely reminded them of the decision of the College of Pontiffs, who were the guardians of religion. However, the people preferred controversy and the frustration of a great man they had only recently acclaimed and called "hero, and savior of Rome." Thus they manifested the innate human vice of malice and envy. Goaded by Cicero, the guilty Senate decided, after a sluggish delay, to obey the Pontiffs. They rallied the magistrates, who depended on their favors, and the magistrates virtuously upheld the Pontiffs and the Senate —who, after all, were the most powerful in Rome—and said that full restoration must be made to Cicero who had been "unlawfully deprived of his property." The Senate also declared that anyone who opposed their decision, and the "reverent decision of the Pontiffs," would be held liable. The Consuls therefore let out contracts for the demolition of the Temple to Liberty, and for the rebuilding of Cicero's house. They also fixed a sum of the value of Cicero's various villas which had also been destroyed, but this was prudently far less than the actual worth.

But Clodius was not subdued by all this authority, for he had great power with the people and his own bands of the trained lawless in his pay. When the first wet snow of early winter fell, he commanded his ruffians to destroy what so far had been rebuilt of Cicero's house on the Palatine. What could not be dismantled was fired. In open daylight, when Cicero was going down from the Capitol on the Via Scara, Clodius, in person, attacked him with his cutthroats. Fortunately, Cicero was attended by a large body of the police, who, themselves, were assaulted with stones, weapons of all sorts, daggers and spears by Clodius' rabble. Titus Milo, the friend of Cicero, protested this "outrage against law and order on the part of Publius Clodius" before the Senate. As a consequence, Milo's house was burned to the ground. His friends had killed many of Clodius' men during the conflagration.

Cicero went to the villa of his dear old friend, Julius Caesar, who received him with his customary ebullience.

"Blessed is this house that it receives you!" Julius exclaimed, embracing him. "You did not see fit to honor it again after your return from exile. You do not even know my beloved wife, Calpurnia, whose father was a Consul. I will summon her at once," and he clapped his hands for a slave.

"I did not come to converse with women," said Marcus with a grim smile.

"Ah, you old Romans! Calpurnia is of the new generation." Julius poured wine for his friend and seemed delighted at his presence. "My wife is conversant with politics and is also a seer. She claims this, herself."

Cicero studied his host. The mobile and antic face was the same, but now Cicero noted the hard lines that ran from nose to mouth, as if gouged out. He also remembered the ancient story of creation, that men were mild and good before the age of iron, which had corrupted them, and the age of gold which followed, more greatly corrupting them. War and greed. These were the monster crimes of humanity. Julius, during this meditation by Cicero, had been gayly prattling of things of no consequence, and beaming with pleasure on his friend. He suddenly became aware of Cicero's sombre expression. He said, "What troubles you, best of all friends?"

"You," said Cicero. But then Calpurnia entered, and Marcus rose courteously to greet her, and kissed her hands. She was a young woman, tall and very thin in the purple which both she and her husband affected, embroidered with gold Grecian keys. Her long straight hair was black, and she had an angular face of a peculiar whiteness, like new bone, stark and intense. Her large black eyes burned like ignited coal; she had a long thin neck graced by a single coil of gold. Her red mouth was a scarlet thread in her pallid face and writhed and trembled constantly. The first impression was of ugliness; the next, of strange and unearthly beauty, somewhat frightening and forbidding. She gazed almost fiercely into Cicero's eyes, and her face changed as if she were about to burst into tears. In silence, she seated herself with dignity, and waited.

"My dear Calpurnia," said Julius, "is my right hand. I trust her implicitly."

Cicero came to the point at once, and bluntly. "You know of Clodius and what he has been attempting against me. You and Pompey and Crassus have inflicted tyranny on Rome. No matter. The people deserve you. When men give up their freedom willingly in the name of security, they soon lose even that degraded security. I do not denounce you. I denounce the people of Rome who made the Triumvirate possible. Now, I will speak of Clodius and his marauders and murderers and trained rioters. You, the Triumvirate, could stop him at once if you desired, and you could outlaw his constant demonstrations in the very daylight streets of Rome, and could silence his followers' screams and shouts in our very temples and before our government buildings and our Senate. You do not choose to halt him. You do not choose to order our police to arrest and imprison him and his followers for disorder and lawlessness. Do not explain! I know why.

"Catilina was one of you. When you lost control of him and when you could no longer trust him to do your work, you used me to destroy him. Now you have Clodius. I know why you suffer him. He will create so much disorder through insurrections and riots in the streets, that the Triumvirate, in the name of law and order, will declare an emergency and then will seize total power in Rome. The Senate and the tribunes, the representatives of the people, will be declared impotent to 'deal with the situation.' Pompey, with his legions, will move upon Rome, creating a worse military climate than even Sulla brought upon the city."

"Plots again?" said Julius with amusement. "You were always a victim of your own imagination."

But Cicero's eyes were suddenly drawn to Calpurnia. She sat easily enough in her ivory chair but her eyes were wide and glittering and she was breathing as if with terror. Cicero said, "Lady, do you wish to speak?"

"Yes!" she cried, and her voice shook with anguish. "I have warned Julius. He is pursuing a dangerous course. It will end only with his murder!"

Julius' laugh was gay. "I swear that the two of you are the most dismal of augurs!" he exclaimed. "The Triumvirate wishes only peace and prosperity for Rome, and tranquillity among the nations! Let Clodius riot and shout with his gangs in the street. Are not we Italians always vociferous? It means nothing. They are young men who enjoy their own noise and take pleasure in it—"

"They destroyed my house."

"Which is being rebuilt. I deplore violence. But is it not wiser to permit demonstrations on the streets and screams and runnings and shouts of impossible demands, than to suppress them and drive them underground where they will truly be dangerous? Let Italians waste their enormous vitality in noise. They adore it. After they have shrieked themselves hoarse they return to their homes in high good humor."

"After burning houses, stoning the Senate, attacking harmless men, killing them, and defying the police."

Julius shrugged. "These are not the harsh old days, Marcus, when every sort of dissent was quickly suppressed. These are the days of free demonstration."

"Such as uncontrolled riot and murder."

"You make too much of it," said Julius. "I deplore the excess of enthusiasm in the mobs, and Clodius has been reprimanded."

"And secretly encouraged," said Cicero.

"Beware!" cried Calpurnia in a loud voice, and addressing her husband. "I have dreamed of you, Julius, dying of many wounds!" Her distress mounted. She wrung her hands and appealed to Cicero. "I love my husband. Dissuade him from the course he has taken, I beg of you! You are his friend, from his childhood. I plead with him in vain. Add your voice to mine, Marcus Tullius Cicero."

"I have talked with him in this fashion for years," said Cicero, pitying her. "He has never listened. I, too, have had a vision of him as you have had. But I fear for Rome more."

Calpurnia did not understand him. She sat in silence now and the tears ran down her pallid cheeks.

"Do you desire to be king of Rome?" asked Cicero with overwhelming bitterness. "What of Pompey? And Crassus? Will they yield to you?"

Julius was more amused than ever, though he reached for his wife's thin hand and held it and patted it. "We are a Republic, not an empire, Marcus," he said.

Cicero shook his head. "We are no longer a Republic, Julius, and that you know. You and your friends were the executioners of our Republic, which was the wonder of the world, and its admiration. Would you be emperor, Julius, and is that why you are using and encouraging Clodius?"

When Julius did not reply Cicero rose and began to pace up and down the large marble hall in agitation. "Long ago was this age prophesied by the Sybils, whom once I despised. They prophesied too that one day man would harness the sun itself and burn this world to ashes, and the mountains and the seas and the valleys and the meadows with it. That prophecy is embedded in our religion, and in the religion of the Jews and the Egyptians, and the Chaldeans and the Greeks. You do not possess the weapons for so enormous a destruction, Julius. Whether or not it is symbolic I do not know. Nevertheless, it will come.

"Julius, you are like Phaethon, who insisted on borrowing the chariot of his father, Phoebus, the sun god, for one day. So great, then, was the conflagration that Jove smote Phaethon and hurled him into the sea, to save the world. Whether you are the one prophesied by the Sybils, or another in the ages to come, I do not profess to interpret. But your end is sure if you pursue your present course. There still live Romans who love the forms of the Republic, if they no longer exist. They still love freedom. Move to take the crown, Julius, and you will surely die."

Then Julius rose and he was no longer laughing. He caught the arm of the pacing Cicero and held him strongly and looked into his face. He said, with great quietness, "You are not truly a politician, Marcus. Have you not learned through suffering and exile? Beware that a worse fate does not overtake you. Retire. Write. Be done with meddling with matters that do not concern you. You are not young; your hair is almost white. Let your final days be serene. Resume your law. Be tranquil. I give you this advice because I love you."

Cicero flung off his arm. "In short, let my country die without a word from me, without a protest!"

"You would attempt to halt the tide of history, which is inexorable?"

But Cicero did not answer him. He lifted and kissed the hand of the weeping Calpurnia, and then departed.

After the Saturnalia Cicero took possession of his rebuilt house on the Palatine. It was not half so grand as his former house, nor was it filled with the treasures of years. Terentia was dissatisfied. She wandered through the spacious rooms, never once conceding that this view was pleasant or that atrium dignified; she complained in a new tone she had recently acquired: condescending and discontented, as if she deserved better of the world than had been granted her by everyone, and mainly her husband. She swayed her heavy body as she walked slowly through the house, and pettishly used the back of her hand to flow out her stola in a movement at once impatient and indifferent. She was a querulous queen whose subjects had disappointed her.

But she could not discompose Cicero as once she did. Discreet inquiries revealed the extent of her private fortune; Cicero recalled that she had sent him nothing in his exile, though Quintus, his brother, had frequently gifted him with solid purses, and Atticus, his editor and publisher, had lent him large sums of money and then had declared that royalties had covered the amount—which Cicero now did not believe in the least. Cicero had had to sell two of his favorite villas to cover debts and to return Quintus' money over his protests. Tullia's husband, though of a great house, had died impecunious with not even Tullia's dowry restored. Young Marcus had to be educated and sums set aside for his personal use when he reached manhood. Two destroyed villas had to be rebuilt; the island at Arpinum had been neglected during Cicero's exile and now new buildings had to be supplied for the overseer and the servants. The sesterce was not now worth what it had been worth several years ago, and prices were all excessive. The Senate, of course, though virtuously voting for the "full return" of Cicero's property and his fortune, had set their own estimations. "I am no longer rich," he wrote to Atticus. "In my hopeless attempts to save my country I neglected my investments and my law before my exile. Now that the winter of my age is whitening beyond my autumn colors, I am filled with anxiety. I have been very poor in my life; I do not recall poverty with pleasure, and let those who have never suffered it say smugly that it has its own delights! It is a lie. I fear poverty almost as much as I fear death; it is as degrading. So now I must study investments again, and rediscover the law—that law so mangled over the past years!"

His seat in the Senate demanded many expenditures, to which Terentia contributed nothing. She was careful with every penny, saving her fortune for her beloved son. In the meantime she continued to complain that the Alexandrian glass in the house was far inferior to that of the past and appeared to believe that Cicero was personally responsible. She chose the furniture and grumbled that the amounts set by her husband for it were too low. She protested that the gardens he planned were too extravagant; she preferred two thicknesses of Persian carpets on the marble floors of the interior. Very often these days she bewailed Cicero's former "imprudence," that misfortune had come to him. To escape her voice and her presence Cicero spent his leisure hours in his daughter's apartments, or played with his son and imagined that young Marcus' every prattling word was imbued with an occult wisdom.

After the Saturnalia, which was a disordered celebration due to the activities of Clodius' mobs, Quintus departed for Sardinia as one of Pompey's fifteen lieutenants. He was to act as grain commissioner and to govern that tumultuous island. But before Quintus left he had a serious talk with his beloved brother. It began when Cicero remarked that nothing had changed in Rome, that he seemed to be living a perpetual nightmare, that Clodius had replaced Catilina, and that Caesar was truly the most dangerous man in the Triumvirate. Quintus smiled his rosy smile. "It is said of Caesar, among soldiers, that he is every woman's husband and every man's wife," he said. "Yet it must be admitted that he is a military genius, one of the greatest Rome has ever known, and I say that who never liked or trusted him. He is writing a book about his Gallic campaigns and your own publisher is to publish it. I agree with you that he is dangerous to Rome. But I remember your exile and your suffering. Therefore I say to you: Accept the decree of the Fates. Rome is lost. We shall never see the Republic again. Compose your soul. Be resigned. Turn your energy to investments and to peace, to your library and your law and your books. Seek pleasures where you never sought them before. Acquire a beauteous mistress who will beguile you. Dine pleasantly; drink good wine. Visit friends. In short, live as do the majority of your friends and forget that Rome can be saved from the Caesars."

"That is supine, Quintus. Once you did not think so."

"True. But now I have discovered that it is useless to attempt to interrupt the Fates. I do my work as a soldier with all my might; I obey orders. I love life. I have always been of a lustier spirit than you, Marcus. You are a philosopher and I have noted that philosophers are not comforted by their philosophy. They are unhappy men. Better it is not to stare too fixedly at life, but to enjoy what it has to give and to shrug off its more dismal aspects."

"I prefer to end as a man, and not a surfeited animal," said Cicero with unusual anger. "We have a greater destiny than that of a beast!"

"What?" asked Quintus, indulgently.

Cicero was exasperated. "If we did not have such a destiny, mysterious though it is, we should not yearn for it and for the knowledge of it."

Quintus was still indulgent. "You are the descendant, Marcus, of the only two who survived the Flood, according to our priests: the virtuous Deucalion and his wife, Pyrrha. They were truly the last who were truly human. You will recall that they bewailed the fact that only they remained, after the vengeance of God on the fallen race of man; the goddess Themis advised them to leave her temple and throw large stones behind them. From these stones and from fire and water, was a new race created, but far different from the old race. Stone. Hot moisture. Earth—mud. With you, son of Deucalion and Pyrrha, does this race now contend, and you are baffled by it and it is baffled by you! I pity you. You cry 'Justice,' but you will remember that Justice was the last goddess to leave the earth, and she has never returned."

Quintus was suddenly very grave. "The sons of Deucalion will never understand this world and will forever try to enlighten or lift it to the heavens. And forever will they fail. I have heard you say that the desire for justice lives in every man's heart. Experience surely must have taught you that this is a fallacy. Did you not once tell me a tale of the Jews, that one Abraham pleaded with God to spare two evil cities and God told him that should he find a certain number of just men within them He would withhold His Hand? But Abraham did not find any just men at all in those cities, and so they were destroyed. Search Rome. You will not find within it six just men. Nor will you find them in Athens or in Alexandria, or anywhere else you search.

"No, I am no cynic. I was always more realistic than you. Resign yourself to the world and its ways in which you must live. You have a family. Spare them further misery. Be prudent. Caesar could have you murdered at a word. But he loves you in his fashion, and though you would protest it, you have an affection for him. He is the most formidable man in Rome. He now manipulates everything and everyone in the city. He is loved by the people because he is a libertine, like them, and a lover of life, like them also, and despoiler like themselves, and has, in short, all their vices. Men adore their vices; they hide their virtues, if any, as if they were shameful secrets. They also adore the politician and the soldier who has their vices in larger measure, for in him they see themselves. Rome, in Caesar's face, sees her own image. Do not annoy him, Marcus."

"So he advised me himself," said Cicero with bitterness.

"It was good advice. Take it." Quintus embraced his brother tenderly. It made him ache to his burly heart that Cicero seemed almost weightless in his arms, and that the bones were close to the pale skin, and that Cicero had aged with sorrow and that his mouth expressed so much pain. Exile was not alone the culprit. His just soul would not let him rest, but clamored incessantly that he act and not refrain. Quintus sighed as he left his brother. He doubted that Cicero would take his excellent advice, and Caesar's.

Though Cicero equated Publius Clodius with Catilina, he admitted to himself that Clodius was no madman. However, it was evident that he fomented insurrections, riots, demonstrations, assaults and defiance of the law in Rome. That he was tolerated, and probably even encouraged, enraged Cicero. He inquired of his friends if "great Caesar were powerless to restrain this violent rascal, who has the dark design of revolution in his spirit." His friends evaded him; they refused a reply to the direct question. So Cicero knew that his suspicions had been correct from the very beginning. Clodius was suffered because of a special plan in the mind of the Triumvirate. But, he reflected with some murky anger, which of the three will seize absolute power for himself? Pompey was a strong soldier, and no fool; he would desire the throne. Crassus was old, but the lust for power is like wine in an old man's veins. Caesar, then. He was the most dangerous. When would he finally attack both Pompey and Crassus? Two would die; one would live, and one only. Like wolves, tyrants inevitably attack rivals to the death, though formerly they had hunted in concert.

When rumors reached Cicero that Caesar and Clodius were often seen in company together, and in affability, then he knew that indeed his suspicions were correct, and that Rome was lost. In the meantime Caesar's reputation as the greatest soldier Rome had ever known grew speedily day by day. His own reports from Gaul, Cicero noted, confirmed that fact with enthusiasm.

Cicero began his monumental work, *De Republica*, did his duty well as a Senator, reopened his law offices and received clients, loved his children, endured his wife, tried for contentment with his friends, and felt that his whole life was entirely useless, and that, if he had only applied more diligence and dedication, his country might have been saved.

Letter to Atticus:

"I have often heard politicians remarking smugly, on the eve of their retirement: 'I wish to spend more of my days with my family.' Either they know they face defeat in politics or they have looted the national Treasury enough to satisfy even themselves—or they have become womanish."

Against the advice of even such noble men as Titus Milo and Porcius Cato, and Servilius, Cicero soon discovered that he could not keep silence, that he could not passively permit his country to flee with increasing swiftness to the abyss. "We are young men, Milo and I," said Cato. "Let it rest with us, knowing that we have your prayers and your devotion. It is time for old soldiers to retire and let those fewer in years take their places in the battle."

"No," said Cicero. "What can console me in my family, my library, my gardens, my farms, and even on my ancestral island if Rome dies without a word from me? There is active evil, such as supporting evil men and traitors. And there is the passive evil, speaking not when a man should speak. This is the worst—that good men do nothing or become tired or hopeless. It is notable that wicked men have boundless energy and enthusiasm, as if they draw sustenance and vile new spirit from some dark, Plutonian underground."

He went to many of his friends and asked them to help in the defeat of Clodius for the aedileship. Even he, who considered that his years had disillusioned him about mankind, was aghast at the suddenly veiled eyes, the shrugs, the muttered words of "tolerance" for Clodius. "We are living under a tyranny," said Cicero. "Are you content?" Then their faces suddenly flushed deeply, but whether it was with anger or with amusement Cicero could not know. They laughed, spoke of their prosperity and roared, "If this is tyranny, give us more of it!" and slapped their knees and made silly, mocking jests.

Clodius threatened that if he were defeated for office he would command a revolution. In spite of Crassus' indulgent remarks that "Clodius was merely a hot-head and did not mean half he shouted," Titus Milo opposed Clodius, tried to prevent the meeting of comitia who appointed the aediles. He declared that if he met Clodius face to face he would be moved to kill him, "for violences against Rome and against my house and my own person." Cicero appeared before the Senate and catalogued Clodius' threats against the state and his public impudence in defying it and his demonstrations in the streets. "Have we no longer an orderly government?" asked Cicero. "Are we ruled, at last, by the spirit of the mobs, and openly?"

While speaking with great eloquence and earnestness he suddenly had the nightmare sensation that forever he had been speaking so, that forever he was fixed in this vortex of despair and futility, and that forever the same faces would confront him—and that forever he would be seeing the countenance of Lucius Sergius Catilina. The names changed, and the features, but it was always Catilina against mankind, eons without end. It was no terrible shock to him, therefore, when Clodius was elected aedile in spite of all the evidence against him.

"I meet nothing but confusion everywhere," Cicero said to his friends. "I walk down a colonnade and there I am! twenty years younger and faced with the same problems! I stroll down a street and encounter myself at thirty-five, wondering how Romans can permit violence and corruption. I enter a temple, and in the marble is reflected my face at twenty-eight, and the same words of traitors and the exigent are ringing in my ears. I have seen them all from my cradle and I suppose I shall see them at the last moment before my eyes close in death!"

But some inertia which he could not control kept him spinning, kept him crying out against the inevitable fate of Rome and indeed the fate of all republics. But what nobler government was there than a republic—if men were truly men and not malicious animals? The failure of government was the fault of humanity.

"If only I could be content with merely living and enjoying each day as it comes," he would remark to friends. "But it is not in me. Some hidden divinity impels me to protest, to struggle, to exhort, though I know it is all in vain." He could no longer enjoy the sweat and shock of the battle. He was now past fifty years of age, and often he was assailed by his old rheumatism and often by a mysterious dysentery. And he was, incessantly, assailed by his wife, whom nothing could satisfy.

"Day by day," she would complain, "you are in less favor in Rome. I believed that when you returned from exile you would have learned your lesson and have become powerful again in Rome. But the Senate secretly laughs at you, and the people mock you."

Young Marcus, the son, was now ten years old, a handsome boy with a broad highly colored face and a beguiling manner. But his cousin, young Quintus, appeared to lead him. "My son is a philosopher and therefore not given to sweaty vigor," Cicero would remark to his wife. He wrote paeans of praise about his son to his publisher, Atticus. "Young Marcus, I confess, needs a goad to assert himself, while his cousin needs the reins. But is this not true of all incipient philosophers like my son? He is a marvel in his studies; his mastery of Greek is superb." He did not know that young Marcus was greedy and self-indulgent. Terentia secretly encouraged him in his habits; she was delighted that her son did not resemble his father in the least. His laziness did not dismay her; his lack of discipline did not make her reflect. Her son was a gentleman and not a vulgar dissenter like his father.

Tullia came to Cicero one night and shyly announced that she wished to marry the young patrician, Dolabella, who had loved her long before she had married Piso. Cicero felt the firm pavement of his private life giving way under him. He did not like the house of Dolabella, which he believed was idle and dissipated. He cried out, "Your mother has arranged this marriage and has slyly kept all machinations from me!"

Tullia, in tears, protested. It was true that Terentia was pleased at the thought of the marriage, which she had desired before Tullia's wedding to Piso. Tullia took her father's angry face in her slender young hands and pleaded with him. Did he wish her to die as a widow, and childless? He would not live forever; was he pleased at the prospect that she would some day be left alone? Who would console her in her own old age, and cherish her, when her father was dead? "Who loves me in this household?"

"You would leave me again, and for a Dolabella! You are young still. Remain with me for a while. I am sorrowful enough as it is."

But Tullia married Dolabella and Cicero was reconciled when he saw her genuine happiness. However, he again had the sensation that he was treading old paths and that none of them was leading anywhere except to his own death and his final end in futility.

He took refuge in his library, and in his writings. "At the last a man must return to himself and confront himself, and never can he escape that last confrontation," he wrote. "The world cannot hide him; the love of his family cannot help him flee. Affairs of state cannot deafen the voice he must finally hear, which is his own. Books, music, sculpture, arts, science, philosophy: these are lovely delays, but they are only delays."

CHAPTER SIXTY-ONE

Later Atticus was to write young Marcus Tullius Cicero, and with sadness: "Your father was Rome, and her history was his history. All those whom men account great touched his life, and he touched theirs. They brought evil and blood and despair on their country; he brought valor and virtue. They succeeded. He did not succeed. But in the final accounting between man and God who knows but that a man's defeat is victory before the Almighty?"

If he wished to survive, physically, Cicero knew that he must have some abeyance in his life, some self-wrought peace. He immured himself in his library; he wrote some of his noblest books which were to survive the ages and warn men yet unborn with fear for their own countries. He had long conversations with his son, young Marcus, and did not know, mercifully, that the boy listened to him with a sober face but with inner mockery. He visited his daughter and his beloved island. He resolutely shut from his awareness the events transpiring in Rome. He could do nothing; to fight any longer would be to impale himself on a sword.

"You are a pillar of iron," Noë wrote him. "And God has indicated that a just man is such, among nations. Long after the polished marble has crumbled the iron of justice remains and upholds the roof over man. Without such as you, dear Marcus, throughout all history, nations would die and man would be no more."

"They die, and some day man will be no more," Cicero wrote to his friend in a period of despondency. "Have you not told me of the prophecies?* The awful day of the wrath of God upon man, and whirlwinds and fire and universal destruction of the 'fenced cities' and 'the high bulwarks,' and the obscurity of the sun, and the falling of the mountains and the burning of the seas—have you not told me of this? Man offends God by his very existence, for his heart is evil and his ways are the ways of death."

His law business unaccountably—at least to himself—began to flourish. The number of his clients increased enormously from week to week, and as the majority were men of substance who could make excellent gifts Cicero found his coffers filling satisfactorily again. Civil law did not entangle him with politicians and for the time being, at least, he shunned politicians who sickened him with their wily cunning and their expediency.

Then one day to his astonishment he was appointed to a vacancy on the Board of Augurs in Rome, a life office not only of dignity but of large remuneration. Atticus rejoiced for him, but Cicero was skeptical though pleased. The Board was composed of agnostics who disputed with the College of Pontifices (Pontiffs) on obscure religious doctrines. Then a disagreeable thought of much involvement came to Cicero: The College of Pontifices had always shown him a deep friendliness, as he was a devoutly religious man. The Board of Augurs contended often with them. Who was

* *Joel*, Chapters 1 and 2.

it who wished to reconcile both the Augurs and the Pontiffs, and in his person? Letter to Caesar:

"It may be news to you, dear friend, and again it may not, to hear that I have been appointed to the Board of Augurs. Do I discern your fine and subtle hand in this? You will not, certainly, tell me the truth. I am conjecturing just how you believe I can serve you in my present capacity!"

Caesar's reply was full of affection and amazement and congratulation. "Why do you not accept the manifest truth, dear Marcus, that the gods moved to have you appointed to the Board of Augurs to repay you for your devotion to them, and to indicate their approval of your virtue and honor?"

Aha, thought Cicero, on reading this letter. A dim lamp is beginning to brighten my darkness.

He took his duties very seriously, though he privately considered much of the augurs' prophecies and divinations to be absurd. But he was enough of a mystic to believe that God often indicated the future to a few adoring souls. Terentia was delighted with his appurtenances: The shepherd's staff free from all knots, and a toga of bright scarlet stripes with a purple border. She was proud of the honor paid to her husband, which again she ascribed to her own peculiar rapport with the gods and their admiration of her. Then Caesar's letters from Gaul to Cicero soon made it evident that he wished his favorite augur to divine for him, and Cicero's quieted alarm suddenly sharpened again. Julius had his plans which he was not confiding to anyone. He trusted Cicero not to lie.

It was the custom of an augur to divine from signs in the sky—the domain of Jupiter, who was the patron of Julius—and from the flight of birds. By night the augur could designate with his staff the space to be allotted to him for his studies, usually a silent hill and in the presence of a magistrate who would then report to the Pontiffs. The augur prayed, sacrificed. Under the shelter of a tent he then observed the heavens and asked for a sign, and waited. He always gazed south, with the lucky quarter, the east, on his left. After the sign was given him he made his report to the magistrate, and the sign, thereafter, governed the affairs of Rome to a great extent. It had often come to Cicero that a corrupted augur could proclaim in favor of any powerful politician. Fortunately for Rome the augurs had, in most cases, been singularly free from corruption, for their office was never threatened by dismissal and their stipend was very high. Thus they owed nothing to anyone and could be truthful. In theory, it was wise. But men can be corrupted by other things besides money.

The birds of good fortune were the eagle and the vulture, the alites; the malign were the raven, the crow and the owl. Their flight, their manner of taking food, the sounds they made, were interpreted strictly by the rules of the Board of Augurs. There were other means of divination, such as the behavior of animals in the field, the appearance of rats in a temple, animals slain for sacrifice. Powerful men frequently requested the augurs to make comment on a proposed adventure they had in mind, the time for battle, the time to run for election, sittings of the Senate, and thousands of other actions. To be sure that the augurs did not lean consciously for or against a certain proposal the man seeking the offices of the augurs often merely indicated "my special intentions." If the augur reported lightning in the sky the client did not act the next day but awaited a more auspicious sign.

Caesar wrote to Cicero: "I have a special intention for the future, a special prayer. Do then, dear friend and comrade, consult the sky for me on a certain night," which he designated. Cicero should have preferred to refuse, but it was his duty. Moreover, he confessed he was curious. He took his staff, and a magistrate, outside the city walls and swung the staff about him in a circle, feeling a trifle foolish. Oddly enough, the staff suddenly appeared to manifest a life of its own; it tugged in his hand; it pulled him forward. It plunged into the earth, warm and grassy with summer, like a sharp pike. Cicero's heart began to beat with uncomfortable dread. "Here shall I set up my tent for tonight," he told the magistrate.

Awaiting midnight, and his car which would take him and the magistrate to the hill, Cicero pondered with growing and mysterious uneasiness. His oath required him to report truthfully. Let there be no signs of consequence, or only vague ones subject to a thousand divinations, he implored the starry and moonless heavens as he reached the spot at midnight with the magistrate.

He sat within the shelter of the tent. The night was windless; in the distance tall and climbing Rome glittered redly and whitely with torches and moving lanterns and lamps. The everlasting dull roar of the city reached this spot with a murmurous sound. Black cypresses surrounded the tent, which faced an open spot to the south, with the east on the left. The air was pervaded with the scent of hot grass now beginning to be bedewed; though no wind stirred a fragrance came to Cicero from ripening fruits and grapes and grains in the surrounding fields. The air was so very still, and so very warm. Somewhere restless cattle lowed in their paddocks. A dog howled and then was abruptly still. A vehicle, in haste, rumbled along a stony road toward the gates of the city. There was the hint of fresh water as the night lengthened.

Above, the purple roof of heaven appeared unusually crowded with flashing stars tonight, as if they were filled with unease. It is ridiculous for me to feel there is anything particularly portentous in the sky at this hour, Cicero said to himself. It is only the effect of a clear atmosphere outside the city that the stars seem so unquiet and so imminent. It is really peaceful; why, then, do I feel so without peace? Do not men project on disinterested nature the quality of their own disquiet and forebodings or maladies of the body or the mind? The magistrate sat respectfully and in silence at his side, his stylus ready, his tablet prepared for swift notes.

This was Cicero's first time to divine, though he had assisted the other augurs in divinations. He believed that God often gave signs, but he also believed that God was displeased when asked for them. For some reason Cicero began to think of Noë's account of Elias and the fiery chariot and the fiery horses which had borne the prophet to heaven in the thunder of the whirlwind. Possibly to prevent him from being murdered by man, thought Cicero cynically. Then he started, as he sat at the threshold of his tent, and his flesh turned icy.

For suddenly, imposed on the furious white lightning of the stars, there had appeared a great and blazing chariot complete with four rushing and blazing horses! Cicero's breath halted. About the chariot he had the impression of multitudes and the shouting of tens of thousands of men. In that chariot—and he could see all clearly—stood Julius Caesar crowned with laurel, as splendid as a god, holding glittering reins, and laughing the terrible and exultant laughter of a divinity. His robes were purple and gold. He held his right hand uplifted, and in it was a sword, twisted and turning like fire, which reached to the zenith. On his left shoulder stood a mighty eagle with eyes like jewels. Behind him banners appeared, blood-red, with a wreath of laurel circled on them. All was movement; the horses raced, their legs bent under them; the sparkling wheels of the chariot churned.

Then on his head shone and coruscated a crown. Even while the trembling Cicero observed that crown it faded, reappeared, faded once more. The black eagle lifted its wings and uttered a frightful cry, but did not depart from Caesar's shoulder. Cicero did not know when the apparition of a woman arrived, but suddenly she was there at the front of Caesar's chariot, hailing him, a beautiful woman hardly more than a girl, with flowing black hair crowned with golden serpents and with a hawk on her shoulder. Then Caesar bent down, laughing, and lifted the girl beside him in the chariot and they embraced. His crown appeared, more brilliant than before. Cicero had the impression, then, of thunder from earth and heaven.

"What do you see, lord?" asked the magistrate, aware of Cicero's pale and staring face. But Cicero did not answer for he did not hear.

The vision remained, glowing blindingly, infused with incredible movement yet not moving. Then from the right appeared a flock of ravens and owls and crows, swarming multitudes of them. Each carried a dagger in his mouth. They circled the head of Caesar and the woman. The woman in the chariot disappeared. An enormous soldier appeared before the galloping horses, his sword drawn and pointed at Caesar. Caesar lifted his flaming sword and struck down the soldier and there was a tremendous clash as of fallen armor. The soldier's place was taken by a tall and empty throne, and Caesar seized the reins of his chariot and raced toward it, shouting and triumphant.

The voices of the seen yet unseen multitudes changed from hailing to challenge and fury. Caesar disregarded them; he was bent almost double in his efforts to reach the prize, which appeared to retreat before him. His crown shot tongues of fire into the air.

Then the birds of ill omen circled closer. They fell upon Caesar, with the daggers in their mouths, and they slashed him with many wounds. He threw up his arms to ward them off; they uttered piercing cries of vengeance. He seized the crown as if in despair and placation, and hurled it from him. But the birds were not appeased. They struck him again and again, and then he collapsed within the chariot.

The vision was gone, and now only the stars remained, breathless with light as if spent. "What do you see, lord?" the magistrate questioned again. He could feel the shudders of the augur and, in the starlight, the beads of sweat on his forehead. But Cicero did not answer. A fearful vision was rising before his eyes. The gates of Rome were open, and it was as if brilliant sunlight flooded the city. Triumphal arches appeared, showering down torrents of flowers. A man was riding through them, standing in his chariot, a fair young man whose face was veiled with haze, a young man with a huge crown. He carried a scepter. Before his feet ran a river of blood, and thousands of corpses lay in his path. From many voices, coming from the four corners of the heavens, came a direful dirge: "Woe, woe to Rome!"

Then the vision went up in an enormous sheet of fire in which the city was engulfed. Cries of terror thronged the air, cries of agony and despair. The city crumbled, became embers, turned black. Then it was rebuilt in a twinkling, but it was not the city Cicero knew. The gates flew open; countless hordes of bearded men rushed into the city with swords and pikes and lances and spears, striking death on every side. Their voices were hoarse thunder, like beasts. The city collapsed slowly, its white walls turning gray and dun and red.

Swirling mist crept over the city, darkening, twisting, and stone fell from stone, and pillar crashed against pillar, and the pavements heaved and were lost in grass and the wild scarlet poppy. A deep silence swallowed all sound except for a few fitful footsteps of unseen runners. Then in the semidarkness a mighty dome appeared like a sun, a dome of such dimension as to stagger the eye that tried to encompass it. From its summit rose a golden fire that gathered itself together and formed a cross that pierced heavens suddenly as blue and mild as an infant's eye. From the doors of the walls which opened below the dome many men came in dignity and clothed in white, one by one, each following the other, each holding up a staff such as an augur's, and each turning his head earnestly as if confronting hidden multitudes. From their mouths, as each spoke, issued the words, "Peace. Peace on earth to men of good will."

The last man to emerge lifted his voice even higher than the others and repeated the same words. But a dark and crimson confusion began to form before him; he faced it resolutely. Thunder roared from a thousand different quarters. The heavens blackened, were tongued with fire and flame and rolling balls like individual suns, which, turning and churning and leaping and falling, devoured all they touched. Their horrible and deadly light flowed over the man in his snowy robes. He confronted them without fear. But more and more appeared, and now the whole earth was scarlet and burning and all became chaos. "Lord, have mercy on us!" cried the man in white. There was the sound of mountains falling, and whirlwinds.

"Lord!" cried the magistrate on the dark and peaceful grass of midnight. But Cicero had fainted. He lay like the dead on the threshold of his tent.

He was sick for many days. The other augurs came to see him, for they guessed he had witnessed strange and awful visions. But to all of them he said, "Woe, woe to Rome." And then, "Woe to all the world!"

Then, at last, he wrote to Julius Caesar: "I have seen auguries which defy the power of any man to describe, even I who am known to have a way with words. One concerns you, Julius. While you still have time, refrain from your dream of splendor and conquest and triumph. You will surely die—as I have warned you before."

When Julius received this letter he was angered. Then he laughed to himself and thought, "He has indeed seen my splendor. And my triumph and conquest. So be it. After that, what does it matter?"

Only to Atticus did Cicero try to convey his visions, and Atticus was confounded. Atticus wrote to his author: "What all this portends I do not even dare to question. I do not understand the dome, of incredible dimensions, nor the sign on it, the infamous sign, the cross of execution. There is no such building in Rome—therefore it is of the future. Who are the men in dignified white, who exhort 'Peace on earth to men of good will!' That astounds me, for it has no meaning to my mind. What you saw of the last was the destruction of the world. Let us pray that we do not see the end as you saw it."*

* Letter to Cicero, 52 B.C.

CHAPTER SIXTY-TWO

I must have peace, thought Cicero when he had recovered. But where is there peace? I must ignore what I see. But does a man truly live who ignores what he sees? He watched events in Rome come one by one and knew he was helpless and that that which came emerged from the nature of men. I grow calluses upon my spirit," he said to Atticus, "otherwise, how could I walk in the world on my sensitive feet?" But under the "calluses" his spirit was stricken.

Crassus, member of the Committee of Three, was an old man and had never been a soldier in the true meaning of the word. But when the Parthians revolted against Rome it was he who led the Roman armies. He was "killed in the battle." Cicero did not believe it in the least. He was certain that either Julius Caesar or Pompey had conspired his murder. Now Pompey, the military man, confronted the ambitious Caesar, who was a politician as well as an incredibly brilliant tactician on the battlefield. Where Pompey moved doggedly and wheeled in planned maneuvers, as professional soldiers do, Caesar flashed like lightning with spectacular success, always antic, humorous, and intensely brave. "I shall not die in war," he said. "My dear augur, Cicero, has so pronounced it." He built his great bridge across the Rhine, invaded Britain, and invaded Britain again. He appeared suddenly in Rome on unexpected occasions, and it was said that he was borne there by Jupiter, himself, a legend he did not deny. He laughed at Pompey when the latter solemnly intoned that "he who rules the seas rules the world." "He would be an admiral also!" Caesar exclaimed, winking. Julia, daughter of Caesar, and wife of Pompey, died in a fever, and the last link between the men was shattered and now they confronted each other without restraint.

"I am indifferent to their quarrels; I do not know their plots," Cicero told his friends regarding Caesar and Pompey. But it was of great consequence to him. He watched the open and secret struggle between the two, and he cynically bet on Caesar. He had no exaggerated opinion of Pompey's intelligence; if he indeed plotted, as rumored, then it was a heavy and lumbering plotting, like a gladiator in an arena, weighty with armor and armed with a ponderous sword, who fights against a lithe and active foe carrying a sharp trident with three lightning prongs. In the meantime Caesar joked and smiled and moved with astounding speed in all he did, and wrote his accounts of battles and invasions, and Pompey marched from place to place, methodically. It was inevitable that the Romans should love Caesar for his wit and his vices, for all that he did was colorful and lively; it was just as inevitable that they not love the more virtuous Pompey, who talked as tediously of law as did Marcus Tullius Cicero, without Cicero's eloquence, and who had no color at all. They even loved Caesar's baldness; when once he appeared in Rome with a wonderful wig they laughed and slapped their sides and laughed more deliriously when he flaunted it in his hand. To them he was as splendid as his patron, Jupiter, and as licentious and as magnificent.

"He is a buffoon," said Titus Milo.

"No. He is an actor and has a worthy audience," said Cicero.

Julius, effervescent and full of the lust of life, often visited Cicero on his visits to Rome, to receive his sour congratulations on his newest exploits. "I always read the newspaper, *Daily Doings (Acta Diurna)*, on the walls of Rome, exalting and praising you, Julius," said Cicero on one occasion. "Do you write the reports yourself, while on the field, and then send them to Rome?"

"Am I responsible for that miserable little paper of news?" asked Julius, lightly. "You have a voice of vinegar lately, sweet Marcus. Has your spirit turned from wine, then?"

"It is full of dregs," said Cicero. But he smiled for all his care, and his tired face was amused. "You are but four years younger than I, yet you are as a youth, burning with the fever of living. What blood is in your veins, Julius? What is your secret?"

Julius pretended to ponder. Then his face, browned from hot suns and seamed by the weather, sparkled with laughter. "Myself," he said, "I love myself; I adore myself; I contemplate myself and I am in ecstasy. How, then, can others refrain from giving me homage?"

Cicero stopped smiling. "Do not underestimate Pompey," he said. "He is not as often in Rome as you are, Julius, but respectable men revere him, for he is honest. When he can, he takes measures against Clodius' gangs of revolutionaries and audacious rascals. At the last, you may have to confront the respectable Romans and that may be a sorry day for you."

"Augurs, again?"

Cicero shook his head. "Do not try the people too far, Julius," he said, remembering his vision on the hill-top. "All, including my brother, say I love you, except myself. If you were in danger I would defend you, with my life if possible. When I see you I see the face of the little schoolboy who took my hand for protection, and made me laugh when I was most serious, and who robbed me of coppers for dainties."

Julius embraced him. "In all Rome I trust only you," he said.

Greatly moved, Cicero cried with sudden passion, "Trust me, then! What is in your mind, Julius, I see as a fiery cloud destroying Rome! Retreat, have mercy, refrain!"

Julius' face, so marked over the years with lines of mirth, became darkly sober. He said in a quiet voice, "I can no more retreat than can you, Marcus. A man's character is his destiny. Our lives are bound up together, Marcus, for our natures have drawn us together. So dissimilar, we yet are like the Gemini."

Cicero was not yet old, but he felt old, old in his tired body, old in his mind. He thought of the island with longing, but Rome was his city. He could not be content for long in either. He saw serene contemporaries and envied them, and then was immediately horrified by them. He loathed the turbulence and lawlessness of a city once ruled by law and republican virtues, yet he must gaze at it like one fascinated and could not turn away. He had seen the death of liberty and could not flee from the sight. He read books and wrote them, but they did not satisfy him. He preferred thought to contentment, and fled the amiable conversation of his friends, and their tables, weary of tales of gambling, sports, entertainments, gossip, and scandal. Under its sparkling nothingness ran the dark and furious waters of existence and the man who did not wet his feet in them could be counted as a man who had never truly lived. He, Cicero, preferred to drown in the torrent than to spend the rest of his life under a fruity tree and dream sweet dreams without reality. Julius had accused him of "meddling." But all life was meddling in fierce currents. He who ate the pomegranates of Hades before he had crossed the Styx deserved nothing but dishonor and the death of his memory in the minds of men.

One day he went to the Forum and the Basilica of Justice to plead a case. It was a warm day in spring, as fresh as a rose and some of the weariness left him in the clear and ardent sunshine. A lady in a litter of crimson silk embroidered with gold accosted him, and he saw she was the sister of Julius, Julia, a pretty woman with a coquettish manner and Julius' glittering black hair and lively eyes. Beside her sat a young boy, lolling on the cushions, as fair as she was dark. His hair was yellow and curling; his eyes as blue as lakes. Julia gave Cicero her hand and he kissed it and she admired him with her restless glance.

"You know my grandson, Octavius, do you not?" she asked, indicating the indifferent boy at her side. The youth had large features, almost classical, and cold as marble. He regarded Cicero with respect but also without much interest. Cicero was always partial to youth; the boy was almost the age of young Marcus, and so Cicero's worn face smiled with a shadow of its old amiability and charm. Octavius' white tunic was bordered with the purple of preadolescence. His attitude, however, was that of a king and suddenly the blue eyes were the eyes of a calculating and very intelligent predatory lion, and very aware. Seeing this strange metamorphosis, as the boy's gaze dwelt on him, Cicero felt a contraction of his heart as if he had observed an omen of mighty portent. Man and youth stared at each other in silence.

"Julius," said Julia, "believes Octavius will become a famous soldier. He is already conversant with the arts of war, and is dexterous with the sword."

"I pray," said Cicero, "that he will be a noble Roman."

At this, Octavius' face changed again. He did not smile, but he gave the impression of smiling, and it was not a youthful grimace but that of an alert man, and very remote. It was also haughty, and he glanced at his grandmother as if her fatuous pride irritated him. He did not speak again. Julia made another sprightly remark, inquired of Terentia and Tullia, and her litter was borne away. Cicero forgot his mission. He gazed after the litter and there was an icy sensation in his heart.

They are born in every generation, thought Cicero, as he went his despondent way, and in each generation we must contend with them. Why should we not let them have their way and devour the weak? Let them eat of the sheep and rule them and destroy them! Let us be silent, those of us who believe that the weak also have a right to live and live peacefully under law! The weak only gather with the wolves to drag us down with their teeth and condemn us with their mouths.

The whole trouble lay in the fact that just men, and good, could not by cynical, and could not shut their ears to the cries of the foolish sheep who had meekly allowed themselves to be penned and had then uttered cries of anguish when they saw the man with the knife.

Suddenly Cicero remembered the last letter from Noë ben Joel, who had quoted Jeremias to him again: "If I say, 'I will not make mention of God, nor speak any more in His Name—then there is in my heart as it were a raging fire, shut up in my bones, and I am weary with holding it in.' "

No, thought Cicero, I cannot hold it in, even if I die for it. But he was very tired.

"When the irresponsible enthusiastically riot and make demonstrations in the streets against all reason and all law," Titus Milo told Cicero, "then respectable men must oppose them. Clodius gives them mindless slogans, and they repeat them, believing that in mere utterance, and the violence accompanying them, they will be heaped with vague benefits and riches— at the expense of those Clodius has designated as their enemies."

"But who rules Clodius and his furious mobs?" asked Cicero. "Caesar, for his own purposes. Do what you can, Titus. You have resolute men who respect you."

"We must hold Caesar at bay as long as possible," said young Titus, with a dark face. "Do you know what Pompey has told me? That Caesar is now rushing toward a new dictatorship, with himself as sole power in Rome. Caesar is a soldier, but affects to fear militarism. Have you not heard of the graffiti on the walls of Rome? 'Down with Pompey!' "

Milo was a candidate for Consul, Clodius for the Praetorship. Milo conducted his campaign with the words, "Romans need no soldier to control them. Neither do they wish a despot." Clodius used the slogans: "Caesar and Clodius for the People of Rome, and democracy! Free corn for the needy and deserving! Freedom from trial by the Censors unless confronted by accusers open to question! Down with secret testimonies!"

One day on the Appian Way Milo's men were assaulted by the rabble of Clodius and during the ensuing and disordered battle Clodius was slain. The lawabiding rejoiced; the rabble were infuriated. So perish tyrants and insurrectionists, thought Cicero. But he was horrified and despondent that such violence had been necessary, and that Clodius had not been able, under the circumstances he had created himself, to be brought to trial. The supine Senate and even the tribunes of the people had been silent before his crimes, and thus were responsible for his death on the famous Way. As usual, the people disputed among themselves as to the right or wrong of Clodius' death, and, as usual, they forgot it all within a few days. The Great Games were approaching, and there was wild betting on the newest gladiators, wrestlers, pugilists, discus throwers, horse and chariot races, spear-hurlers, runners, and sports of all kinds. The death of Clodius and all that it meant was less than the vehement rumor that two of the wrestlers had allegedly accepted bribes. The famine had passed; the meanest man in the street was comparatively affluent and able to lay large bets on his favorites. The daily newspaper contained little national news and only excited conjectures as to the sports about to begin. One day the broadcasts did make a mention that the heroic revolt in Gaul, led by Vercingetorix the patriot, had been crushed by Julius Caesar and that Caesar, in consequence, was an awesome hero. Caesar remained in Gaul to restore order, and Pompey, seizing this advantage, announced himself sole Consul. He also obtained, in his plodding military fashion, the proconsularship of the Spanish Provinces.

"The lion and the bear will soon be at each other's throats," Cicero wrote to a friend. "Will Rome emerge the victor? It is doubtful."

"We do not meddle in politics," said Cicero's friends, the "new" men, the middle-class like himself, the lawyers, doctors, businessmen, manufacturers, architects. "Rome is prosperous and at peace. We have our villas in Caprae, our racing vessels, our houses, our servants, our pretty mistresses, and our comfort and treasures. We implore you, Cicero: Do not disturb us with your lamentations of disaster! Rome is on the march to the mighty society, for all Romans."

Cicero, in despair, began to write his book *De Legibus* (*On the Laws*). Atticus deeply admired this scholarly work. "But, who will read it?" he asked. "Romans care nothing for law any longer. Their bellies are too full." As a conscientious publisher, however, he issued the book. "I owe it to posterity." Cicero laughed sadly. "Posterity" never learned. To Cicero's amazement, and to Atticus', the book was bought in immense quantities in the bookshops, and Caesar, on receiving a copy, extolled it. "What is wrong with it, then?" asked Cicero with a sour smile. "So far as I am concerned, the praise of Caesar is the kiss of death." He was congratulated by Senators, tribunes, and magistrates, "who," he declared, "did not understand a word of it!"

He could find no peace even in his own household now, and could not ignore what was transpiring. Terentia was becoming more captious and restless. "One does not stand still," she would say. "Why are you not advancing? You owe it to your family." Tullia was not happy in her marriage to Dolabella after all. Her manner was listless, though she smiled well enough at her insistent father and said she had no complaints. Quintus said of Julius Caesar: "He is superior in the field to Pompey. His decisions are always brilliant, though first of all he is a politician." For the first time he did not denigrate men of politics. He refused to discuss the state of affairs in Rome with Cicero. He shrugged. "Things are as they are in their nature," he would say vaguely. To be a soldier was to be all; wise men abandoned politics when they became too complex. His brother should concentrate on his seat in the Senate, his position as augur, his library, his writings. "Is that not enough to satisfy you at your age?"

Cicero said, "'Hear ye the word of God—For God hath a controversy with the inhabitants. For there is no truth, nor loving-kindness, nor knowledge of God in the land. There is naught save lying and perjury, murder and stealing, violence and bloodshed.'"

"What is that?" asked Quintus, with mistrust.

"The words of a prophet, Hosea, of whom Noë ben Joel has written me."

"Oh, Noë. That actor and writer of plays!" said Quintus.

Then Cicero received a letter from Jerusalem in a strong hand. It was from Leah, the wife of Noë, sadly announcing the death of her husband. "He recalled you with his last breath," she wrote. "He asked me to repeat to you the words of Isaias: 'Fear not, for I am with you. Be not dismayed, for I am your God. When you pass through the waters I will be with you.

And through the rivers, they shall not overflow you. When you walk through the fire you shall not be burned. Neither shall the flame kindle upon you. For I, the Lord, your God, hold your right hand.' "

"Why do you weep?" asked Terentia.

"The earth is poorer," said Cicero. "It has lost a good man, and we cannot afford it."

CHAPTER SIXTY-THREE

"The years of a man are a long retreat," said Cicero to one of his friends, with great weariness. "I have heard that as a man grows older time flies. No, it flees before him. Where was yesterday, last month, last year, five years ago? I do not remember!"

He did not know the reason—though his friends assured him it was flattering—but he was assigned to the province of Cilicia on the southern coast of Asia Minor, including the island of Cyprus, as governor. "Someone wishes me out of the way for a while," he said without illusion. He wrote to Atticus, "It is a monstrous bore, this governorship. They have put a saddle on an ox. I cannot describe to you the warmth of my longing for the city or the difficulty I feel in putting up with this boredom. I miss the broad daylight of life in Rome, the Forum, the city, my town house— and you, dearest of friends. (I will complete the book! Do not press me!) I will endure my 'exile' for a year. God knows what will transpire in my absence!"

He took with him young Marcus, against the protests of the cosseting Terentia, for he had become aware that the mother's influence was injuring the son. Quintus, on leave, also accompanied him, and young Quintus. Cicero soon found that he had much to do in Cilicia, for the province had been ruined and looted by predecessors from Rome. But in a few months he could write to Atticus with pride, "A great number of states have been entirely released from debt by my efforts, and many very sensibly relieved. All now have their own laws and with attainment of autonomy have quite revived. I have given them the opportunity of freeing themselves from debt or lightening their burdens in two ways, first in the fact that no expense has been imposed upon them in my government, and when I say 'no expense' I mean none, not a penny. It is almost incredible how this has helped them escape from their difficulties. The other way is this: There was an astonishing amount of peculation in the states committed by the Greeks themselves. They confessed it; without being openly punished they repaid the money to the communities out of their own pockets. The consequence is that whereas the communities had paid the tax syndicates nothing for the present five-year period, they have now without any distress paid them the arrears of the last five years also. The rest of my administration of justice has not been without skill."

The hot and dry and aromatic climate assuaged his rheumatism. He was busy with what he loved best, the administering of honest law. He had time for writing. He had the company of his brother, son, and nephew. He regretted that his handsome young son seemed more and more to be led by the bold and exigent young Quintus, the delight of his soldier father's eyes. "You must be more independent," he would say to young Marcus, and the boy would say solemnly, "Quintus has little pleasure in the arts of Greece and Rome and does not love philosophy. I instruct him." Cicero believed his son. Quintus, too, was busy, in subduing the hill tribes. In the meantime friends kept Cicero informed of the affairs in Rome, which were becoming more and more chaotic.

Pompey and Caesar were now deadly enemies. Pompey had become the confidant of the Senate and in large measure he controlled that august body which had begun to suspect Julius, and with justification. Pompey, the soldier, might despise civilians, but he did not despise the Senate. It was rumored that both he and the Senate were fearful of Julius and his ambitions, and that they were conspiring together not only to relieve Julius of his military command but to prosecute him for alleged Constitutional illegalities during the time he had been Consul, and prevent his second election. On becoming a private citizen he would be open to investigation, something which he could hardly survive, as Cicero commented to himself.

The struggle became more open and more dangerous for Rome. The legions were divided in their allegiances, half for Pompey, the other half for Caesar, who was much more colorful. Cicero, bewildered, said to his brother, "I do not understand all this! Law is the Senate, the Assemblies, the tribunes, the Consuls! What has law to do with the ambitions of two military men, Pompey and Caesar?" But he knew that when a republic declines it becomes the prize of the ambitious. He wrote to his friend, Caelius, a young politician in Rome, for more enlightenment, for Caelius was a great gossip and involved in everything. Caelius replied: "The point on which the men in power are bound to fight is this: Pompey has made up his mind not to allow Caesar to become Consul again except on condition of his first handing over his army and provinces, while Caesar is convinced that he cannot be safe from Pompey if he gives up his army, the source of his strength. He, however, with humor, proposes as a compromise that both give up their armies!"

He thought Cicero somewhat naïve when the latter wrote in a puzzled manner:

"In the case of domestic difficulties and differences, so long as the contest is carried on Constitutionally without an appeal to arms, men ought to follow the party most in the right; when it comes to war—war!—and the camp, with one military leader threatening the other, then just civilian law must interpose itself and halt the whole dangerous nonsense."

Civil war, instigated by Pompey and Caesar, seemed incredible to him in his peaceful spot in Cilicia. He still clung to his concept that in a republic law was paramount. He preferred Pompey, who had the Senate with him and the respectable "new" men of Rome, and the law-abiding. But what had Julius once said to Cicero, years ago?: "Law is a harlot, and can be bought at the highest price." To Cicero this attitude was the ruin of nations, the final plunge into despotism and chaos.

But though he agreed with Pompey, Cicero did not love him. He feared and disagreed with Julius, and loved him. He was in a fearful state when he left Cilicia at the end of his governorship, and stopped at his villa in Formiae. There he received a letter from Caelius who wrote cynically that Julius was certain to win power in Rome—and without war—"for in his plunderings and campaigns he has piled up incredible amounts of gold, and law can be purchased by gold, and the people also."

When Cicero returned to Rome he went at once to Julius in his villa in the suburbs. Julius was delighted to see him, and embraced him ardently. "Wherever you go, dearest friend, you bring solvency and good government!" Julius exclaimed. "Verily, we should give you the dictatorship of Rome! You would fill the Treasury in the twinkling of an eye, and restore peace."

"Which you have destroyed," said Cicero. "Why do not you and Pompey lay down your arms and stop your quarreling?"

"Ah," said Julius, sadly. "Pompey is a true militarist, and you know how you have always mistrusted militarists! They acclaim me in Rome as the mightiest soldier of them all, but I was never truly at heart a soldier. So, I am opposed to this suet-head of a Pompey who thinks cold iron is the way to govern a country. He does not trust the civilian mind. This affronts me."

"Julius, you never spoke the truth in your life," said Cicero, and Julius was amused.

Just before the Saturnalia the Senate passed a motion that both Pompey and Caesar must lay down their arms. Caesar responded to this motion with public enthusiasm, and the people acclaimed him, for they were fearful of a civil war between those two mighty opponents. But Pompey was not deceived. He suspected the dexterity of Caesar, and as an old acquaintance and former friend and son-in-law, he knew Julius too well. He said to the Senate, "I will not lay down my arms, the only protection Rome possesses for law and order, until Caesar retires to civilian life. I will not countenance him as Consul again." He had received, he told the Senate, stories of disaffection among Caesar's legions, and that one of Caesar's own generals, Labienus, was ready to desert to the Senate. "It is no longer a struggle between Pompey and Caesar," they said to each other. "It is a struggle between law and Caesar."

The Senate then named a day when Caesar must lay down his arms and relinquish his provinces or be declared a public enemy. To enforce this, the Senate declared martial law—under Pompey. Cicero again went to visit his old friend and to plead with him in the name of Rome. Julius listened, and replied with such sincerity that Cicero was forced to listen:

"I do not wish civil war, the gods forbid, Marcus! To be candid with you, my own personal safety now depends on my armies; Pompey desires my death. Let Pompey lay down his arms on the day I am commanded to lay down my arms, and we will meet as equals." He smiled faintly, and added, "If we meet so, then I will have no difficulty with Pompey."

Cicero went to Pompey and pleaded with him also, and asked him to meet Caesar in person. Pompey listened in sullen silence and drank wine slowly and stared into space. Then he said, "We have known Caesar a long time, you and I, Marcus. He has often deceived even you, with his charm, and you are a man of mind. He would beguile me with his lies and his promises. Do you think that he has ever swerved from his ambitions to be emperor of Rome? I prefer the rule of law, under the Senate, the Assemblies and the tribunes, however cumbersome and weak and bumbling. Caesar despises law, and that you know, except his own."

Cicero believed Pompey. Pompey had too little imagination to be a liar, and as a true soldier he preferred order. He had plotted with Caesar and Crassus, and probably even Catilina, in the past, under the impression that only stern military law would restore Rome to peace and tranquillity. But personal power for the sake of power only had not been one of his schemes.

Then to Cicero's stupefaction many of the tribunes openly deserted Caesar, who pretended love for them as representatives of the people. The Senate proscribed them. Caesar was indignant, or at least he affected to be so. He spoke to his devoted legions at Ravenna, declaring himself "the guardian of law," and indicating that the Senate, in proscribing the tribunes, "the representatives of the humble Roman people," had violated law and shown extreme arrogance and contempt for all Rome. "We are oppressed by a few fractious men!" he cried. "We have been betrayed! I defend the liberty of the people of Rome and the dignity of the tribunes! My own injuries at the hands of the Senate, and Pompey, are trivial in comparison." He wept openly; the refugee tribunes and the legions wept with him. When this was reported to Cicero he said with bitter irony, "He was ever an actor, the best in Rome!"

The white winter was particularly vicious that year. Military operations during that period were usually suspended. Pompey, the man of little imagination, believed that Julius, far from Rome now, would also suspend military operations. After all, it was customary! But winter, and custom, meant nothing to Julius. Cicero wrote to Atticus, "Julius moved so rapidly. He is a man of frightful vigilance and energy. But I cannot arouse Pompey, who believes in seasons!"

All else is violent history. Caesar gathered his devoted legions from Gaul, and started down the Adriatic coast to Rome. He crossed the Rubicon, a tiny river, on the border of northern Italy. Thus he violated law and became an enemy of the government in Rome. "Let the die be cast!" he shouted to his soldiers. His spies had assured him that the northern towns were with him and loved him. He ran down the coast like a line of fire, with his enthusiastic and cheering legions. Pompey moved to block him. Caesar rushed to stop him at Brindisi, but Pompey's forces broke through. However, at Corfinium, Pompey's legions surrendered with hardly a show of resistance to Caesar, and he accepted them into his own forces, and with affection. He said, "Nothing is more remote from my disposition than cruelty." But hearing of this Cicero exclaimed in despair, "Julius is a madman, a wretch!"

The unfortunate Cicero was beside himself. As Caesar was now rapidly approaching Rome, Pompey fled to Macedonia to raise legions in his behalf. Cicero, against the advice of his brother Quintus, went to Durazzo to join Pompey. On hearing of his resolution, Terentia cried, "It is finished! You are no more my husband! You have betrayed your family!" Cicero replied, "I have never betrayed Rome, and a man's country and his God must be first in his life for he has nothing else besides."

On his way to Pompey, Cicero wrote to Atticus, "What I wish is only peace. From the victory of Caesar will arise a tyrant. A strange madness has possessed not only bad men but even those who are esteemed good, so that all desire only to fight, while I, only I, cry out in vain that nothing is worse than civil war and nothing more evil."

He did not love Pompey. He had begun to doubt his resolution. But he had no choice now. Pompey was on the side of the Constitution and law. Julius had challenged the government on invading Italy. "No matter who wins," he wrote sadly to his publisher, "the Republic is dead. I can only hope that by supporting Pompey something may be saved for the liberty of the people." He understood that in his support of Pompey his own life was at stake, but he no longer cared. However he wrote to Atticus, "What kind of attack will Caesar employ against me and my property in my absence? Something more violent than in the case of Clodius, for he will think that he has a chance of winning popularity by damaging me."

He knew that any love for him in Rome was now confined to a very few. He suspected many of the Senators of being secret supporters of Caesar. He had given so much time to the support of Pompey in Rome that his law practice had again disappeared. He had not guarded his investments. He had done nothing but serve his country. And the majority in his country now loathed him, for the people adored Julius. He had compounded his unpopularity by joining Pompey in Macedonia. "Above all things," he wrote to his wife, "the rabble despises law and order and prefers grandeur in a tyrant. They especially love a mountebank who flatters them, and a malefactor is close to their hearts."

He had not as yet come to terms with his conciliatory nature. As a man of peace he had gone to Pompey. Yet he could not completely relinquish his affection for Julius, and his dreams were haunted by memories of childhood. Sometimes he awoke in terror after a dream that Julius had been murdered. He would say to himself, "It would be excellent for Rome!" Nevertheless, his heart would be heavy and he would eagerly await news that Julius was still living. Pompey could not understand him. "You hate what Julius is, but I suspect your heart is sore concerning him and you do not wish him to die." To which Cicero replied with sorrow, "Love is a great betrayer. Justice has her demands, but love pleads against her." It was unreasonable. But Reason always fought with Love. He wrote to Atticus, "I would die for Pompey, but for all that I do not believe that all hope for the Republic is centered in him." He knew that the Republic was dead. Nevertheless, he still hoped, and hope, he knew, could also be a betrayer. "I prefer peace at any price," he said, and wondered if that, too, was not a betrayal. He was torn by a thousand winds.

He had discovered what many brave and wise men had discovered before him, that it is illogical to expect men to be thoughtful and dedicated to virtue. Most especially, it was stupid to expect a man to be a rational creature. It was true, as Scaevola had often said, that none but a complete fool was unaware of the difference between good and evil, reason and insanity. But, Cicero thought: Had Scaevola ever counted the fools in the world? They were far worse than evil men, for they gave evil men authority and their applause.

Caelius wrote to him, "Did you ever see a more futile person than your friend, Pompey, or ever read of anyone prompter in action than our friend Caesar, or more moderate in victory?" Poor Cicero was inclined to agree and became critical that Pompey had abandoned Rome to Caesar and had withdrawn across the Adriatic. He even wrote to his brother that Pompey was "a poor statesman and a rotten soldier." He was angered against Pompey, who had been hopelessly outnumbered by Caesar's army. "It is better to die in a just cause than to live," he remarked to Pompey, to which Pompey replied, "It is better to fight in a just cause than to die in it."

Cicero had not thought Pompey subtle enough to say that, and pondered on whether Pompey had fully understood what he had said. Pompey saw him pondering and smiled grimly. He found Cicero very trying to a man of action and a soldier. He respected him, but he was also impatient. He thought of young Dolabella, who was a Caesarian and said in a rallying voice, "Where is your son-in-law?" To which Cicero in exasperation replied, "With your father-in-law." Those who heard this acid exchange were highly amused, but Cicero was lately wanting in a sense of humor and Pompey did not like his retort. He also owed Cicero money, and suspected, wrongly, that Cicero was wondering if he had not wasted his sesterces. "We shall move," he said with irritability. "Are you not an augur? Tell me when!"

I should tell neither of you! thought the harassed Cicero, who found himself longing incontinently for Rome and sometimes cursing himself for ever having again taken up politics after his exile. "You can be certain of only one thing regarding politicians," he wrote to Quintus, who was with Caesar now, "that you can never be certain. Do I wish either the death of Caesar or Pompey? No! I wish them only to halt their attempts to tear Rome apart. I came with Pompey because I considered his the only rightful cause. But any cause which precipitates civil war is not a good one, no matter how it is trumpeted. I cannot write you my thoughts on Caesar, for he is your general, and even for you to read my thoughts would be accounted treason in you!"

Quintus, after some hesitation, and thinking of his brother's life and future, took the letter to Caesar, laughing and saying, "My poor uncertain brother! He now loathes Pompey. He does not know how to extricate himself from an impossible situation. In all his life he has always fixed his bright eye on an impossible star. You will remember Livia, lord."

"Let him, then, return to Rome and others will imitate him, and that will be the end of the matter," said Julius, who thought Cicero's letter pathetic as well as risible. I shall always love my poor Marcus who has never ceased his quest for virtue, not understanding that it does not exist in this world."

With bitterness Cicero thought, "Before the implacability of God's will that men possess free will, and men's will to commit evil, there is a great mystery." Noë ben Joel had spoken of the omniscience of God. "When He created men He knew they would commit wickedness. Does that, therefore, make Him the Creator of wickedness?"

The ancient question which had troubled the men of Israel, and the prophets, troubled Cicero while he waited in the camp of Pompey to see what Pompey would do, if anything. He mourned anew for Noë who had sent him many consolations. In the camp of Pompey at Durazzo God seemed to have retreated beyond the stars; His interpreter was silenced. Only the gods remained, vengeful, full of lust, regarding men as sport, and full of huge laughter against them. Nevertheless, it was easier to live with them than a paradox! The gods frequently assumed human form, and thus partook of human nature. But God had never been a man. The Jews declared that on a mysterious day He would do so, and be born of a Maiden Mother. The Unknown God. Yes, verily. He would remain unknown forever.

Languishing in the sullen and restive camp of Pompey, and his mind darkened with doubt and despair, Cicero felt like Sisyphus who endlessly is condemned to roll a boulder uphill to have it endlessly fall back to the earth again. His thoughts ended nowhere, except in immense weariness. All hope he now had to reconcile Pompey with Caesar was gone. There could be nothing but civil war and blood and death. His life had been one long futility. He had accomplished nothing. His wife no longer wrote him; he wrote almost daily to his son and received few letters in return. Tullia wrote him, but she was in a difficult position. According to Rome —now adoring Caesar—her father was intransigent. According to her husband, Cicero was a fool. She did not tell her father but he was one of the greater causes of her estrangement from Dolabella. She wrote him loving letters which were poignant, he guessed, with what news she omitted.

The cold winter did nothing to alleviate Cicero's misery. He would not return to Rome, as Quintus was now urging him. He must remain with Pompey, who he was convinced was stagnating. Pompey's two sons visited the camp briefly from their stations in Spain. They resembled their father, but they did not possess anything of his occasional integrity, and had a certain fierceness and wiliness of expression which frightened Cicero. One was named Gnaeus and the other Sextus. Cicero overheard them impatiently asking their father why he "permitted that dilapidated old lawyer, Cicero, to bedevil him with his presence and his contentious conversation." "I owe him money, and much more," Pompey had replied, and for a little while the coldness in Cicero's heart was warmed.

His hair was white and dry; his bones ached; his heart throbbed on exertion. He wondered why he had ever been born and remembered Job, who had cursed the day of his birth. He thought of the hopeful and valiant young Marcus Tullius Cicero who had believed that virtue and truth were indestructible, and he almost cursed the phantom of his youth for its folly. There was no tie any longer between him, an aging man with trembling hands, and the youth who had dreamed under the trees on the island. He fell ill, of both mind and body.

Porcius Cato, who had championed Cicero before the Senate and had condemned the wiliness of Julius Caesar, visited him while he tossed on his cot, in the tent where he lay. "Our poor conciliator has suffered the fate of all conciliators," said Cato, not without sympathy. "Do you not understand that there can be no meeting between good and evil?"

"It is foolish to say that all good is on one side and all evil on another," said the unfortunate Cicero, sweating in his fever. "One can only choose the party of the lesser evil, and hope for the best, and hope is always betrayed."

"You should have stayed in Rome and used your influence on Caesar, who loves you."

"You are jesting," said Cicero. "He loves no one but himself. Pompey at least loves Rome. Much can be forgiven a man who prefers his country above anything else."

That night Cicero fell into unconsciousness. Pompey left his best physician with him. Cicero began to dream affrighted dreams. He saw Pompey on a long journey to a battlefield, in a strange country. He saw a mighty struggle, and caught glimpses of Caesar's face, though Caesar did not actually appear to be present. Then he saw a hand reaching out in a bloody darkness, with a serpentine ring upon it, and it gave a dagger to another hand, eager and lustful, a hand with a dusky skin. He saw Pompey in shifting mist; the dusky hand was raised and it plunged the dagger into his heart. Again, Cicero saw Caesar's face faintly smiling. Cicero awoke with a cry and the physician soothed him.

"Where is Pompey!" Cicero exclaimed, struggling against the restraining hands. "I must warn him! He will be murdered at Caesar's orders if he does not refrain—!"

"Caesar is far away," said the physician, preparing another sleeping draught. He did not tell the distraught man that Pompey was even now in battle with Caesar who had already crossed the Adriatic and was besieging Durazzo. The few left in the camp were desperately awaiting news from couriers. They were comforted by the fact that Pompey was a professional soldier, whereas Caesar was not. Brilliant tactics, they were certain, were not enough against trained and disciplined men. Caesar had with him young Mark Antony who was a professional soldier. But everyone knew that Antony was given to impulsive decisions.

The sleeping draught assuaged Cicero, and he fell into a deep sleep again. Then he found himself in a glowing garden filled with lilies and bright blue flowers and towering oak trees flaming with autumn colors. A stream ran nearby, the color of nacre. The voices of birds filled the air with joyous sounds. A white arched bridge was thrown across the stream and Cicero thought, Am I on the island? He was enchanted by the peace and tranquillity of the scene, at once familiar and unfamiliar to him. He searched for paths he had known and could not find them. Yet, when he turned his head he saw a clump of cypresses he well remembered. New delight seized him. Then he caught a glimpse of a slight female figure running across the carved and marble bridge toward him, a blue veil floating from its head and its lovely body clothed in white. He opened his arms mutely, and the figure fell into them and embraced him and he saw the face of Livia, sweet and vivid, with passionate azure eyes and with a mouth the hue of raspberries in the sun. Her kisses were like jasmine honey on his lips. He could not have enough of them. "Dear love," he said, "I have had a most terrible dream. I dreamed that you were dead and I was old and white of hair and broken of heart."

"Dearest love," she replied, in a voice he had never forgotten. "Be comforted. The time is not long. Heaven is astir. Soon we shall join our hands and wait."

"For what shall we wait?" he asked, holding her against his breast.

"For God," she replied. She smiled at him and her smile was like the beaming of the moon in midsummer. Then dimness began to fall. She gently extricated herself from his arms and he could not find her again. The scene faded. He cried wildly, "Livia! Livia, my love!" But now he was only in a mist and it was very cold and he was lost and there was nothing to be seen at all. He was bereft and terrified; he stumbled about, his arms outstretched. Weight encompassed him, and horrible weariness. He awoke. The sun of early winter was cold and bleak about him in the tent and the physician was still at his side. "You have slept well and long," said the physician, cheerfully. "And I have good news for you. Caesar invaded Durazzo—do not start!—but Pompey's superior troops drove them off and broke through them. Caesar is in retreat! He is withdrawing to Thessaly, where Pompey will surely overcome him. They will face each other for the last time near Pharsalus. Before the flowers of spring are blooming we shall be rejoicing in victory in Rome, and peace and order will be restored."

"Peace and order," murmured the sick man, turning his face away. "The dream of all men, a vain and hopeless dream. They cry peace but they prefer the sword."

He thought of Caesar, condemned as a public enemy by the Senate. He would surely be tried and executed as a traitor, Caesar with the young and Pan-like face, the laughing voice, Caesar of the child's hand greedily extending itself for hot and meaty pasties in the school of Pilo, Caesar with the child's voice saying with wily affection, "I love you, Marcus."

"Why do you weep?" asked the physician.

"It is the weakness of all humanity, which must love even when the love is undeserved," said Cicero. He fell asleep, remembering his dream of Livia. All that had passed since his youth on the island was nothing but a bloody nightmare, exhausting and futile and defeating.

Out of mercy and respectful regard those remaining in the camp did not tell Cicero, during his convalescence, of the terrible events that followed one upon another. Caesar won a tremendous victory at Pharsalus, and Pompey fled to Egypt. There he was murdered by an anonymous soldier. When the news no longer could be hidden by the grief-stricken followers of Pompey and Cicero had to know what had transpired, he said, "My dream was true."

He wrote to Atticus, "Pompey was illustrious at home and admirable abroad, a great and pre-eminent man and the glory and light of the Roman people. But I never doubted, knowing Caesar, that Pompey would end as he did. I cannot but lament his death for I knew him to be a man of virtue, sobriety, and integrity."*

It was reported to Cicero that when Julius Caesar surveyed the battlefield at Pharsalus he wept and said, "Pompey would have it so. Even I, Caesar, after so many prodigious deeds, would have been condemned if I had not appealed to arms."

On hearing this Cicero said, "He always appealed to virtue after he had wrought his destructions. Now we are utterly lost."

CHAPTER SIXTY-FOUR

It is the curse of the conciliator that he is forced to see both sides of a controversy, and therefore to have no peace of mind. "Oh, that I could have believed always that black was black, and white was purely white!" Cicero would often exclaim. His dream of Livia had been only the phantasy of a fevered mind. He quarreled at times with Cato and would cry out, "We are not living in the Republic of Plato or even in the Roman Republic any longer! We are living with the rabble of Romulus!" He detested the luxurious aristocrats and wealthy who preferred amusements and sports to poli-

* This letter later appeared in Cicero's pamphlet attacking Mark Antony.

tics—which they deplored as "sweaty"—and wrote of them, "They are fools enough to believe that even if the Constitution were destroyed their fish ponds would be safe!"

So far as Cicero was concerned the disastrous civil war was over. Cato urged him that as Pompey was dead he should take over the struggle against Caesar. The sons of Pompey came to him and suggested that also. He refused with incredulous laughter. "The war is over!" he exclaimed. But Sextus and Gnaeus Pompey retreated to Spain to continue the war against Caesar. Cicero, in despair, decided to return to Rome no matter what greeted him there, even death. The rumor apparently reached Rome. Mark Antony wrote him a brutal letter declaring that Caesar had forbidden any of the supporters of Pompey to return to the city under pain of execution. Then it was that Cicero's elegant and smiling son-in-law went to Caesar and said, "Lord, you have always loved my father-in-law and have admired him. We need men of integrity in Rome, and they are few indeed."

Caesar laughed and said, "If there is one thing we do not need it is men of integrity! I fear them more than the Furies. However, as you have said, I love Cicero, who invariably chooses the losing side out of virtue. Write him that I wait to embrace him as my dear old friend."

Cicero did not receive Dolabella's letter. He was already in Italy, landing in Brundusium. There he was greeted by a letter from Mark Antony that graciously informed him that out of the love Caesar bore him a special edict had been issued in his behalf permitting his return home. At this Cicero was plunged into another of his vacillating moods, the affliction of all temperate men. The sons of Pompey were raising standards against Caesar in Spain. Cato, much loved by the Roman people for his virtue and manliness, had committed suicide rather than "to permit my eyes to gaze on tyranny in the city of my fathers." The legions of Pompey were still fighting the armies of Caesar in Egypt. Cicero's own private affairs were in the most desperate confusion. He received complaining letters from Terentia accusing him of never being able to make up his mind. Terentia also gave him the mournful news that Tullia, always frail, was now in the most serious ill-health. Dolabella, the profligate, had spent her dowry; she had returned to her mother and was reduced to penury. Young Marcus, her joy and pride, was "displaying some marks of easy dissipation, doubtless due to the desertion of his father." Investments were in a bad state. "I have had to sell many of our most valuable slaves." Affairs, both public and private, were due to nothing but Marcus Tullius Cicero. "You have never chosen the right side in all your life!" Terentia reproached him. "No doubt I am guilty of the civil war!" he wrote her in return.

Caesar was now in Egypt to destroy the remnants of Pompey's legions. The young Pharaoh there had joined his own army with the latter and was fighting Caesar in an effort to expel him "from our sacred soil." There was more than a rumor that the aging Caesar was embroiled in a love-intrigue with the sister of Ptolemy, young Cleopatra, whose reputation for extraordinary beauty had reached Rome long ago. She had joined with Caesar for more than love, however; she wished to destroy her brother and assume his throne as queen of Egypt. Cicero thought of his vision of the beauteous woman he had seen embracing Caesar.

To his beloved publisher, whom he esteemed as the most faithful and devoted of friends, he wrote in his despair from Brundusium, where he had taken refuge in an humble inn: "I wish to God I had never been born! I am lost by my own fault! If only I had taken your advice to be more prudent! I owe no misfortune to chance. I have to blame myself for all the sorrows which have been brought upon me." In that letter he displayed his gentle and conciliatory nature, the tender conscience of a moderate and reasonable man who never execrated others for his misfortunes, the affability which prevented him from impulsive hatred, and the confusion of a rational man when confronted by the world's irrationality.

Atticus undertook to warn him to return to Rome and accept Caesar's clemency. So Atticus wrote him that young Quintus, his nephew, had gone to Caesar, on one of Caesar's usual lightning visits from foreign parts, and had falsely accused his uncle of "still plotting against your majesty, and by his obduracy inciting the continued resistance of Romans to your honorably accepted dictatorship for life in view of your efforts to save our country and restore law and order." Cicero had dearly loved his aggressive nephew for all his deviousness, for he was a family man. The letter from Atticus did nothing to restore his tranquillity. He even heard rumors that his brother, Quintus, was now openly attacking him in Rome! He wrote sad letters concerning this to Atticus. In the meantime he was in financial difficulties. He directed Terentia to sell several of his villas and send him the money. The money lent to Pompey was lost.

In the midst of all his perplexity and anxiety his brother Quintus wrote him bitterly, saying he had heard in Rome that Cicero was blaming him for his troubles "in your safe spot in Brundusium, where you are not troubled due to the clemency of Caesar." Cicero suspected the evil lies of young Quintus, his nephew. Overcome with sadness and bitterness he fell ill again. It was then that Tullia, his most beloved daughter, came to comfort him in his quarters, but to his immense sorrow he saw her fragility and her dwindling features. Only the great and changeful eyes she had inherited from him revealed any vitality at all. She had decided to divorce Dolabella. She was penniless. Cicero wrote to Atticus to sell many of his treasures in order to support his daughter. In return the kindly Atticus sent Cicero a large sum of money, claiming it was due Cicero on royalties.

"Your books are selling in enormous quantities and are greatly acclaimed," he wrote.

Stubbornly, Cicero would not leave Brundusium, though the climate was bad for his health and that of Tullia. He pined for Rome; he shuddered at the thought of seeing to what his city had been reduced under the dictatorship of Caesar. Though Caesar was again campaigning in Egypt he had left his "master of the horse, Mark Antony," in command in Rome, and knowing the impulsiveness and temper of Antony, Cicero feared the worst, for Antony had never been famous for his temperance, his judgment, or even his intelligence. He was a brave soldier; he was also a militarist. Friends in Rome assured Cicero that Mark Antony was not departing from one single edict or slightest law Caesar had laid down, and that he, Cicero, should return quietly and resume his normal life. They were taciturn about the iron dictatorship, however.

Cicero still vacillated. He was stricken in mind and body. Then Tullia became gravely ill, the climate overcoming her. No matter what happened to him, he decided, he must save his sweet and lovely daughter. Late in the year he left with her for one of his Tuscan villas, a modest place where, he wrote to Atticus, the air was salubrious and he would be able to forget the world and permit the world to forget him.

He knew, in Tuscany, the last peace he was ever to know in his life. The brilliant and golden air of the countryside restored his health, and he persuaded himself that it was of benefit to Tullia also. It was in Tuscany that he decided to divorce Terentia, whose rebuking letters and complaints and open contempt of him as a failure he now found intolerable. He had never loved her, and for this—again a sign of the constant self-reproach of a man of conscience—he blamed himself. He had failed everyone, he wrote to Atticus. His life had been one long blunder. Somewhere and at sometime, he had made a fatal mistake. He wrote bitterly, "When a people are determined to become slaves, and are degraded, it is folly to try to animate in them again the spirit of pride and honor and freedom and law. They enthusiastically embrace their chains in order that they may be fed without any effort on their parts. Therefore, I have been a fool."

Julius Caesar during this time was gloriously destroying all his enemies in Africa and Spain. He had defeated Ptolemy's armies in Alexandria; he had elevated his mistress, the beauteous Cleopatra, to the throne of Egypt, and had begotten a son by her. His energy seemed boundless; he was everywhere and anywhere. He was past fifty-five years of age. Yet he was like Hermes with winged feet. "The stamina of the evil comes not from human flesh," Cicero wrote Atticus, "but from the evil one himself, of whom Noë ben Joel had often told me." As for himself, he mentioned, "I wake no more in the fresh morning with any joy or hope. I am weary when I go to my bed; I am even more weary when I arise." Nevertheless, he wrote a number of splendid and vigorous books, including his series on oratory, *De Partione Oratoria, On Famous Orators, Academics,* and *De Finibus Donorum et Malorum.* Only in his work did he feel refreshment, and in the sunshine with his beloved daughter. Atticus, well knowing the way of authors, did not tell him that misfortune was often their goad and their despair their inspiration.

Tullia fell more gravely ill. There were no adequate physicians in Tuscany, Cicero decided. No matter what happened to him, no matter what horror he would confront, he must take her to Rome. He notified his wife to leave his house on the Palatine. He would divorce her immediately on his return. He would return her dowry even if the event should reduce him to penury. As for young Marcus, "who has been deprived of a father so long, and been so long cosseted by you, he must leave for Athens for study, where in the climate of immortal philosophy and in the air of the golden mean, and in the contemplation of great and holy men, he will forget his dissipations and his idleness and become a man."

He and Tullia returned to the empty house on the Palatine. A terrible and pervasive weariness fell on him immediately. When the physicians informed him that Tullia's health could never be restored and her death only delayed he was conscious of nothing but a feeling of numbness and surrender. He moved through his days like one in a nightmare. He divorced Terentia; her very name made him ill. Young Marcus was in Athens, where his father hoped he was benefitting from the immortal ghosts remaining within the colonnades. He was reconciled with his brother, but something had gone from both their affections, though they wept together.

"There is such a thing as living too long," he said to Quintus. "We are children until we are fourteen, we are youths until we are twenty-one. The period, then, of our youth encompasses only seven years! Seven years, you will note, out of a possible sixty-five of them. As children, we are not truly conscious. As aging men, after twenty-one, we are confronted by the cares, the ambiguities, the responsibilities, and the confusions of life. And, above all, by the despairs. For seven years only we are truly alive, like the gods, shining with splendor, believing in all the virtues, eager for life, crowned with dreams, desiring to change the world, hopeful, grand, heroic, beautiful. Therefore, like Athene, we should spring full-grown from our fathers' brows when we are fourteen, and live no more than seven years thereafter. All else is misery."

"We should, then, have no past and no future," said Quintus; his son was with the ebullient Caesar whose strange energy never lessened.

"Good!" cried Cicero. "For, in truth, man has no past and no future, for he learns nothing from the first and darkens the second."

He was now sixty-one years of age. His body was almost skeletal. He moved like an old man. He did not know that his strange eyes still glowed and sparkled with passion, and that his spirit shone from them, indomitable and brave though sad. His hair was as white as the first snows; his face was deeply furrowed. But his humorous lips still could be charming in their smile, and his voice was still like powerful music. He told himself that he felt nothing any longer, not even anxiety. But his days had no peace, and he listened acutely to rumor.

In the autumn he went to the island with Tullia. There, in the blue shine of the days, and in autumnal clarified light, he could see that despite his hopes and his prayers his daughter was dying, his sweetness, his life, his consolation, his dearest companion. She never complained. Her smile was always tender, her remarks always amusing, her ministrations to her father fruited with love. He recalled that never had she made a vicious remark, no, never in her life, that never had she been pettish or disagreeable or mean or small. All that was Tullia was graciousness and serenity, even in the midst of sorrow. One so lovely must be coveted by God to enhance his Isles of the Blessed. But Cicero, who believed he had been numbed by life, was suddenly rebellious and embittered. He, Cicero, had nothing but his daughter, Tullia. He gazed for hours at her as she spun with Eunice, now a white-haired old woman in charge of the women slaves. He would listen to her delicate laughter, her gentle voice. She played with the lambs; she petted the horses. She sat for dreaming hours by the river. Her smile made her face glow like light, for her flesh was as transparent as alabaster. Do not leave me, he would pray, as he embraced her. I have lived too long and you are all I have. He would smooth the torrent of her light brown hair, and touch her pallid cheek and his heart would break all over again.

One day, breathless and white, she rushed into his library. "Forgive me!" she cried, for she knew he never liked to be disturbed here. "But, I have seen a phantom, or if not a phantom, then the most mysterious of women!"

Cicero rose and hastily forced a goblet of wine into her frail hand, and wiped her sweating forehead with his kerchief. "Be calm," he implored her. "You have seen but a wandering slave girl from Arpinum."

But she shook her head vehemently. "No, it is not so! She was no slave girl! She was clothed in white and blue and was younger than I, far younger. She had hair like an autumn leaf and as shining, and it flowed over her shoulders and far down her back in a tumult of fire. She came across the bridge and paused near me to gaze at me with seriousness."

Cicero's heart began a wild plunging. He sat down near his daughter and took her tremulous hand. He could not speak.

"And her eyes," said Tullia, gasping to regain her breath, "were so blue that the color filled its sockets, and they were as radiant as a spring dawn. Her lips were deeply red and her face was like marble. She trembled in light like a goddess."

"She spoke to you?" asked Cicero in a hoarse voice.

"No. She looked toward the farmhouse as if she knew you were there, my father. And she smiled to herself like one with a deep and loving secret. Then she began to sing softly, forgetting me. It was the strangest of songs, like a harp in the wind, murmurous and far, and had no words, but as she sang I seemed to see distant places filled with luminous shadows and discerned forms like divinities. And then she stretched forth her hand to this house and smiled and beckoned. I was affrighted. She must have known, for she fled across the bridge again and was lost among the trees."

Livia, thought Cicero, and his spirit seemed to spread wings and shake them in light and he was filled with joy and enchantment, and he was young again and immortal.

"You were dreaming," he said to his daughter, but she saw his enraptured smile and was afraid. She shook her head and her hair flew. "No," she said, "I was not dreaming. Was she a nymph or a dryad, and is she a sign of ill omen?"

"No," he said. He could not say to his daughter, "She is the core of my life, my delight, my darling, and my soul yearns for her." He said, "Was there nothing else about her that you remember?"

She frowned. Then she shivered suddenly. "There was a stain on her breast like blood. She wore it like a blazing flower."

Livia wished me to know beyond all doubt, Cicero thought. He patted his daughter's hand and kissed her cheek. "You do not know her name nor whence she came, and it must have been a dream," he said, and comforted her. He was a Roman, and skeptical, and he had almost forgotten God and his days had been full of cold mist. Nevertheless, for some time he thought of Livia and when he thought of her he was filled with joyous impatience and desire. At this point in his life he preferred dreams to reality.

When the weather became cold and sharp Cicero left for Rome with his daughter in a covered car. Tullia had begun to fail rapidly. She lay swathed with blankets in the car, breathing with difficulty, her flaccid hand curled within her father's. Nothing warmed it. Cicero prayed and after his despairing prayers he cursed the gods that they should desire his daughter. "Have you not taken from me honor and reputation, wealth and health?" he would address them in agony. "Have you not destroyed my city and degraded my people? Have you not lifted a tyrant with his lictors and banners to afflict my country? Have you not afflicted me in all ways possible and have you not brought all my dreams to dust? Can you not spare my child, my Tullia? Do you hate man so much that you must visit him with calamity?"

Tullia, on arriving in Rome, was put to bed and from it she never rose. Her father spent hours with her. As always, she never complained. She had little breath for speech. But she smiled at her father and put her hand into his. Her eyes grew larger each day as her flesh dwindled. He visited her at midnight to be sure that she still lived, and her eyes blessed him and she seemed to be trying to comfort him. The slaves said she slept constantly, but her father had need but to approach her chamber for her eyes to open.

Cicero thought that the winters of his life were always cold now. The snow began to fall early during the Saturnalia. The air was particularly dismal and damp and the winds were ferocious. Braziers were constantly fired in Tullia's chamber. She never warmed; her flesh shivered. Blankets were heaped upon her and hot bricks were placed at her feet. The physicians shook their heads, sighing. Tullia now had lost all power of speech. Her whole being was concentrated on drawing her next trembling breath. But courage shown from her eyes and concern for her father. However, when her divorced mother visited her she would appear to fall into a deep sleep and be unaware of Terentia's presence.

The month of Janus passed. The snows became heavier and deeper. Cicero had lost all awareness of time and the fate of his country as he kept his dolorous watches at the bed of his daughter. Visitors came and went; he did not remember them. His books gathered dust, and his pen. Letters remained unanswered. Time was suspended.

One night, as he sat beside Tullia's bed he fell into an exhausted sleep in his chair. The lamps fluttered low. Two slave girls slept on pallets at the foot of the bed. Suddenly Cicero heard Tullia cry, "My father!" He started awake; the lamps flared into great light. Tullia was standing beside him and she was laughing and her face was glowing with joy and she was fresh with life. Incredulous, he stretched out his eager hand to her, but she evaded him with a mirthful shake of her head. Her garments seemed to flutter in a soft wind, and her hair flowed and sparkled and her lips were as red as roses. She put both her hands to her mouth and kissed them then threw the kisses to Cicero. Then, without sound, but looking over her shoulder and smiling at her father, she sped to the door, opened it and closed it behind her. He heard her calling, "I am coming!" Her voice was a song.

A darkness fell over his eyes. He felt his shoulder being shaken and saw the faces of the weeping slave girls. Starting violently, he looked at the bed; Tullia lay there, still and white, a small mound under the blankets. He staggered to her, and looked into her dead face, which was peaceful and calm. Her hair illuminated her pillows, and her hands were fallen. In her death she was a child again. He fell to his knees and laid his cheek against hers.

Days passed and he did not know them. He wrote to Atticus finally, and said, "I have had a strange experience." He was certain his last strength had left with his daughter's spirit, but he still was able to write his great book, *Consolation* (*Consolatio*).

CHAPTER SIXTY-FIVE

Now life is completely over for me, Cicero told himself. Listlessly, he heard that Julius Caesar had returned to Rome, triumphant over the last of his enemies; he had defeated them in Munda, Spain. No one remained to challenge him. His eyes were turned toward empire and he as Imperator. One day in late summer he visited Cicero, accompanied by the handsome and spirited and swaggering Mark Antony, and Marcus Brutus, his unacknowledged son. He was young no longer, but virility and power radiated about him and his dark face was the face of a great eagle. He was clothed in splendor and his favorite purple and gold. He was bald, but that did not diminish him. Where he moved the air crackled. He embraced Cicero and gazed into his face with affectionate concern.

"My dear old friend!" he exclaimed. "Long has it been since my eyes were delighted by you! I have come to offer my condolences, for your sorrow must be great."

"All is nothing," said Cicero. He could not restrain himself. He remained in Caesar's comforting arms and he fell into weeping, the first tears he had shed since his daughter had died. "But you do not know this yet," he stammered.

"I hope I shall never know it," said Caesar.

Cicero wished that Julius had not come with Antony and Brutus, young men with handsome and curious faces and alert and avid eyes. It was a weakness in him, but he wished to be alone with Julius, whom his reason despised but whom he loved. He craved to look into Caesar's eyes and see there again the child he had protected even though he knew it was folly. He wished some tie with the past and some memories. He could only say with a wan smile, "How does it seem to you, Julius, now that you have attained the mighty ambition of all your life—master of Rome?"

"As it was always my dream," said Julius, "I was always what I am."

"Yes. I remember," said Cicero, sighing. Julius looked quickly about the lonely house. He thought of the hasty marriage, recently ended after so short a time, into which Cicero had entered with a rich young lady, his ward, Publilia. Only overwhelming loneliness and a vague grasping at departing life could have induced Cicero into so disordered and confused a marriage. The girl had been far younger than Tullia, but she was sprightly and gay and with the youth of springtime. It had all ended in disaster. It was apparent to Julius that the marriage had made no impression on Cicero at all, and that it had been only an episode, a dreamlike gesture on the part of the abandoned man.

The gardens about the house were turbulent with color in this early autumn, and the sun blazed fervently on all things. But the house was cold and dim and Cicero appeared as a shade to the vital Julius. Somewhere a bird called in fluting melancholy. The rooms were empty of life, Julius shivered. But he embraced Cicero again and said in a loud and loving voice, "You have been alone too long! Now it is time to live again!"

"Not for me," said Cicero. "I no longer desire to see another day."

He gazed into Julius' eyes. "You have all you wish, all you have ever wanted?"

Julius' eyes shifted. He clapped Cicero exuberantly on the shoulder and said, "Not all. Not entirely." Later Cicero told himself that it was only his imagination that made him believe that the face of Brutus had darkened and that his eyes had glinted. Mark Antony was smiling his vast and glowing smile, and he looked like Mars, himself, ingenuous but brave. It was said, even by himself, that he lived only in the shadow of Julius Caesar, to whom he was more devoted than a son. Well, these were the masters of Rome now, and these were Rome's fate, and the Republic was no more.

Unable to bear Rome even though the autumn was drawing in and winter close behind her vivid skirts, Cicero went to his dear island which was haunted by all whom he loved. There, though he had sworn he would never work again, he wrote his greatest books, *Tusculan Disputations, On the Nature of the Gods, On Divination, On Old Age, On Friendship,* and *On Moral Duties.* He had gathered the notes over all his long life, "during which," he wrote to Atticus, "nothing of any importance had ever happened." Here, on this island, he would die and his ashes would be laid with his fathers and he would finally have the peace he had sought through the endless years. He would walk through the blazing white snows on the island and look at the black river tumbling along its banks and he could sometimes persuade himself that his years were as nothing and he had never left his home. "I am an old man. I am a babe. That is the story of all humanity."

The bright snow draped the tombs of his fathers, his mother, his daughter, scintillating in the winter sun. Here, among them, he would lie one day and let the ages roll over his head while he slept and knew them not. The long while I shall not be, he thought, with a kind of joy. He wrapped his fur coat about him and fixed the spot where he would sleep, here between his mother and Tullia. Then as he stared musingly at the place there was only an emptiness, a floating darkness. He blinked his eyes; they had only been struck by the blinding dazzle of light on snow. Nevertheless he shivered and went on. A crow glaring black in all that serene whiteness, rose up before him with a hoarse cry and he made a sign against the evil eye and called on his Roman cynicism to reassure him.

A false spring came, warm and soft, and he was tempted not to return to Rome but remain on the island. The rivers shouted as they ran and the snow dropped from barren boughs with soft splashes. Patches of greenness appeared; buds were enlarging on the trees. The waters turned from darkness to turquoise, and the wet red roofs of Arpinum glowed like fire against a newborn sky. Old Eunice came with the slave girls to weave in the open portico, and ancient Athos, hobbling with a cane, went out to look at the young lambs. But a curious restlessness seized Cicero. He had few law cases now but some of them were to be heard during the Ides of March. They could wait. However, he prepared to return to Rome. On the last day when Eunice had served him his country meal of dark bread, goat cheese, boiled meat and turnips and onions and the wine of the island, she said to him, "Master, do not leave us. I have had a troubling dream." Pressed to explain, she said haltingly, "I have seen a murder in a white building, but I do not see his face. I fear it may be your own."

"Nonsense, Eunice," he replied. "I am no importance in Rome any longer. And I have duties, and if I do not see to my investments I shall have nothing at all."

Because of the cold he traveled in a covered car with one sturdy young man to drive the two horses. When they were on the arch of the bridge Cicero said, "Stay for a moment." He put aside the heavy woolen curtains and looked back at the island. A terrible and nameless longing overcame him. He listened to the voices of the rivers and the brisk and nimble wind. He saw the distant white farmhouse and all its smaller buildings. He saw the arches of the skeletal trees, their branches locked together, and the patches of snow shining between tufts of greening grass. He heard the complaints of sheep and cattle, and the bark of a dog. He smiled. It was so infinitely peaceful. He drenched his eyes with the scene, and then dropped the curtains again and went on. He did not know that never again would he see this beloved spot and never again would he hear the colloquy of the rivers.

No one was in the house on the Palatine save the slaves and the old overseer, Aulus, who had long ago been given his freedom, for Cicero, admiring the laws of the Jews, freed all slaves after they had been in his service for seven years. During their service he had them instructed in clever ways of making their living, had educated the more intelligent and prepared them to be scribes and public servants, and had always given them a handsome gift on their leaving his service. But many preferred to remain with him.

Aulus greeted him with love. Cicero, after an embrace, said he desired to be alone. A spring torrent was falling outside; every room in the cold house was awhisper with gray rain, and every room was dusky. His footsteps slapped on marble as he walked from hall to hall, listening to the rustle of dropping water and the mournful communication of the wind. Once this house had rung with the voices of youth and children; once there were quick and hurried footsteps; once the knockings at the door had been brisk and frequent, and the songs of slaves could be heard everywhere, and their laughter. Now there was nothing but this quiet dim house and the rain and the wind, and an aging man whose thin shadow flitted on glimmering marble walls like a wraith. He was both restless and exhausted.

The rain continued for a number of days while Cicero lived quietly and did not leave his house and polished up his last book for Atticus. Then one night a visitor was announced and Marcus Brutus, to Cicero's surprise, entered his library. He knew the young man only slightly; he could not understand why he had come. He ordered wine and refreshments and Brutus sat down in silence, dark and gloomy, his thin eagle face clenched, as it were, in iron. Cicero waited patiently to learn the reason for this extraordinary visit. Then Brutus, in the hard and intense voice of a young man who is sombrely disturbed, began to speak.

"Lord," said Brutus, "I have heard that you wrote your publisher that you hoped that Caesar would restore the Republic, return to power the respectable and conservative elements of Rome, and congratulated Caesar that he had destroyed the records of those who had acted against him, 'thus revealing his clemency and desire for peace in our country.'"

"True," said Cicero, somewhat embarrassed. "What little else does a man my age have but hope, even if it is eternally betrayed?"

Brutus' dark eyes, so like Caesar's, sparkled on him with quiet wrath. "It was only hope, then. You did not believe it?"

Cicero was silent. Brutus drank a little wine. The rain and wind continued; there was a faint sound of thunder, a flash of lightning; the lamps flared in a draft. The cold house was dank and silent.

"You, Cicero," said Brutus, "also wrote to Caesar—and I have seen the letter—'To this must you summon all your powers—to restore the Republic, and yourself to reap the most blessed fruits thereof in peace and tranquillity.'"

"True," said Cicero.

"Do you know what Caesar did when he received your letter? He laughed. Then he made a grimace of mock gravity and said, 'Our Cicero grows old that he returns to dreams of youth.'"

"Tell me," said Cicero, flushing, "what is all this to you, Marcus Brutus?"

"I, too, wish the Republic to be rebuilt and strength and virtue to sustain it as in the days of our fathers. Caesar has laughed in private and has declared that the Republic is a sham and that Sulla was stupid to lay down his dictatorship. Caesar has been named dictator for life. That is not enough for him. Do you know his latest madness? Only half-laughing, he mentioned the Oriental practice of declaring 'great men' to be divinities, and thereafter ruling as divinities. Still only half-laughing, he said he would ask the Senate to declare him divine!"

"Impossible!" exclaimed Cicero. "Julius was always a jester! I have known him from childhood." But Brutus' darkling face became even more wrathful.

"Do not laugh, I beg of you, Cicero. When Caesar jests it is well to have a sharp ear. His jokes are for a purpose—suggestions, or to study the faces of those who hear him for their thoughts. He hates patriots; he despises the Senate, the Assemblies, and the tribunes; he loathes the conservatives. They stand in the way of his supreme power over Rome. He wishes the crown; he desires to be Imperator."

Cicero leaned his weary cheek on his hand. "He has restored order; we have no more riots and demonstrations on the streets, no more bawling of the mobs."

"He permitted Clodius to incite these in order to create confusion and insurrection and war, so that he could seize power. I have heard that you have accused him of these things, yourself. Why otherwise did you throw in your lot with Pompey?"

Cicero dropped his hand and looked at young Brutus with exhaustion. "Tell me, Brutus, why you have come to me, you Caesar's friend and follower."

Brutus hesitated. "I believed him, that he would restore the Republic. I preferred him to Pompey, who was a plebeian for all he was a great soldier. Caesar has betrayed all of us. Including you, Marcus Tullius Cicero."

"Do not blame Caesar," said the older man with bitterness. "Blame the people of Rome who have so enthusiastically acclaimed and adored him and rejoiced in their loss of freedom and danced in his path and gave him triumphal processions and laughed delightedly at his licentiousness, and thought it very superior of him to acquire vast amounts of gold illicitly. Blame the people who hail him when he speaks in the Forum of 'the new, wonderful good society' which shall now be Rome's, which they interpret as more money, more ease, more security, more living fatly at the expense of the industrious. Julius was always an ambitious villain, but he is only one man." He rubbed his hands over his tired eyes. "Why have you come to me, Brutus?"

Brutus said sharply, "Denounce him in the Senate! Many of us will be there to hear you! Denounce him to the people!"

Cicero was incredulous. "Are you mad? I would be murdered on the spot by the mobs."

"Is your life, then, your dwindling life, more precious than Rome?"

Cicero groaned. "No, never was it so. If I believed that in laying down my life, in publicly denouncing Caesar, I should do so at once. But it would be of no use."

Brutus regarded him with contempt. "Your age speaks, not your spirit. Do you know what Caesar has also said? That he wishes his nephew, Octavius, 'to follow in my steps and sit where I sit and serve his country.' What does that mean? That Caesar is determined to have the crown, and, like a pasha, an emperor, let it descend to young Octavius."

"He was jesting," said Cicero, but he knew that Caesar had not jested. He felt profound exhaustion. He added, "You have spoken of my age. I have worked all my life for my country; once I saved her from destruction. I have written many books in behalf of the Republic. I have served as Consul and Senator and governor of provinces. I have made hundreds of speeches to help my nation. My endless prayers have assaulted Olympus. Of what use has all this been, Brutus? None at all. If I had remained a country squire on my island it would have been just the same."

Brutus stood up with the furious swiftness of youth. "Then, I ask only one thing of you: that you do not interfere."

"With what?"

"With what younger and more vital and more determined men than yourself swear to accomplish."

Cicero smiled drearily. "With joy, Brutus, I give into your hands my fading torch. Blow it well; replenish it. May you be more successful than I."

It was only the flickering lamplight in this cold wet March evening that made Brutus' sudden smile so terrible. "We," said the younger man, bowing mockingly to Cicero, "receive the torch. We shall light up Rome with it!"

"One moment," said Cicero, quickly. "While I was at Arpinum I heard that the crown had actually been offered Caesar, thrice, in the very Senate itself, and thrice he rejected it! He was addressed as 'King of Rome,' and he repudiated the title."

"That was months ago. He saw by the faces of the Senators, and by the grumbling of the mobs outside, that he had been premature. Now he is more confident. He has been speaking to the people, denigrating the Senate as old men who wish to oppose progress and keep to 'the old oppressive ways.' So much support did he receive from the people that he appointed his own choices to replace dead Senators, uncouth rascals who will follow his will. He has raised the number of supreme judges to sixteen; he has increased the number of national finance officers. Now he is subtly threatening the ruling classes with what he has always claimed to detest: a military dictatorship. They will give him his way or submit to military rule, and he has the soldiers under his thumb."

Cicero was silent. He knew all this too well. Brutus gave him a bow and left without another word. A direful sense of supreme weakness and prostration came to Cicero, and he decided to go to bed without supping.

It was on the next morning that Calpurnia, white-faced and in anguished tears, said to Julius Caesar, "Do not go to the Senate today, when it convenes! I have had a frightful dream in the night. I have seen you murdered. Julius, if you love me, remain at home today. You have been unwell for days. Julius, do not leave our house today!" She threw herself at his feet and groaned and held his legs in her arms.

He smiled down at her indulgently and raised and embraced her. "Sweetheart, how different is today from any other day? I have matters of importance to present to the Senate, the dull, stupid old men! They will not dare refuse. The people of Rome are with me." He patted her cheek and kissed her shaking lips and wiped away her tears. He was indeed unwell, and there was a leaden shade under his brown skin. His eyes were sunken. He had had several attacks, lately, of his "falling sickness." But he felt no presentiment when he took leave of his wife and was taken to the Senate, which was convening in a hall next to the Theatre of Pompey on the Campus Martius. And the sun was shining, the wild brilliant sun of March, and the air, after all the rain, was warm and smiling and the streets were thronged and the people, recognizing Caesar's litter, pressed about it and hailed it and gleamed upon it with joy. His special legion marched about him and were proud with banners and lictors and fasces.

He had reached the supreme point in his life. His friends had assured him only yesterday that the crown would again be offered him in the Senate, and that this time he must accept it. The hour had come. By sunset he would be Imperator, the first emperor of Rome. His beloved, Cleopatra, in his villa in the suburbs, was with his son, Caesarion. He regretted that it was not to Caesarion that the crown would descend, but to Octavius his nephew. He thought of his unacknowledged son, Marcus Brutus, of the gloomy brows and the narrow and strenuous nature. But Octavius, the fair and haughty, was a worthy heir, a true prince. He was also a soldier of considerable fame, for all his youth. Julius smiled and waved to the people and his legion marched beside his litter and the March sun shone on helmets and on the wet streets and the burning roofs of Rome. The hour had come.

Quintus Cicero came early to the house of his brother that morning and Cicero received him with his usual deep love. He was so pleased to see Quintus that he did not notice that his brother was not smiling as usual. He talked of young Marcus, in Greece, and his philosophic progress. He asked of young Quintus affectionately. He had forced out of his mind the duplicity of his nephew; after all, fearful events create fearful upheavals in the natures of men. (Or, he would think, was it the contrary?) His night had been unusually restful; he had not had to take the sleeping draught prescribed by his physicians, on which he had come to depend. His sleep had been unmarred by old nightmares. He had awakened refreshed, and some measure of his old optimism had returned.

Then, as Quintus breakfasted with him, he became aware that Quintus was unusually quiet and dark of face, Quintus the ruddy and vital, Quintus the soldier. "Is something wrong?" he asked. "Have you quarreled with Pomponia again?"

"I am going to divorce her," said Quintus. His voice was particularly harsh. He waved his hand, brushing aside the subject of Pomponia. "I hope it will not disturb your relations with Atticus, who is her brother. No matter. Do you know that Caesar is appearing before the Senate today, asking for new reforms?"

"He usually does," said Cicero, buttering a white roll, and surveying the fresh fish, delicately broiled, which lay before him on a silver plate. Then he looked up. Quintus was frowning. Cicero said, "I thought you and Caesar were now friends."

Quintus, who loved food, put down his fork. He drank heavily of wine. "I love my country," he said.

"Granted," replied Cicero, somewhat puzzled. "Who disputes it?"

Quintus, always voluble, fell into silence, and Cicero studied him, more puzzled than ever. Then Quintus raised his eyes, so like Cicero's, and the blue in them flooded its sockets fiercely. Cicero, too, laid down his fork. "What is it, Quintus?"

"Go to the Senate meeting with me today," said the soldier in a pent voice.

"I have nothing to suggest to the Senate just now."

"Nevertheless, go with me." Quintus paused. "You may—hear—something which will rejoice you."

"Nothing that Caesar can say will rejoice me." But Cicero looked through the window and observed the shining March sunlight. It was so warm that the window had been opened and the curtains thrust aside. Now a scent of greening soil came to him, vital and poignant, full of the innocent carnality of the earth, and he thought of his gardens slowly coming to life about the house and the new greenish light on the dark cypresses and the blossoming of fruit trees. He had not left the house for many days. The air would refresh him. He heard the song of birds and the joyous rippling of released fountains. All at once he felt young again and almost hopeful, though he knew that springtime did this to all men, even the old. It would be good to see the teeming Forum and the temples; it would be pleasant to smell the baking bread in the bakeshops, and the odor of cooking meat in the inns. Even the rank stench of Rome would not be disagreeable today. Rome was always exuberant in the spring; the sun had a special brilliance in Rome at this time of the year, an atmosphere of revival. There are not many years left for me, Cicero thought. I must take advantage of every glowing day now. When one is young there are many gold coins in the purse; but now the coins are few. He said, "I will go with you to the Senate, Quintus, though I should prefer to saunter through the streets."

He put all things aside in his mind when he was in his litter, with Quintus riding beside him on his horse. He left the curtains open so that he might look upon the city he loved. So great a city, so powerful, so puissant, swarming on her seven hills, roofs alight like rubies, ochre, yellow, sepia, green and red walls brilliant in the sunshine! He had had a dream when he was young, that Rome was eternal, that men passed but the city would remain through the ages. He remembered his vision as an augur; curiously he looked at the hills and wondered on which the mighty dome would rise with its strange symbol. He touched his neck; the cross Anotis had given him was about his throat, and the amulet which dead Aurelia had presented to him so long ago. He was never without these talismans.

It was good even to be anonymous now. No crowds hailed his litter; no glance lingered on his worn and ravished face and tired eyes; no one marked his white hair. But he was happy to hear the cheeping of Rome's swallows and watch their wild flight in the blue air. The little red poppies of spring rippled over every untended spot. They were sanguine in the sun. The litter passed under triumphal arches, and the crowds grew thicker on the way to the Forum. The vast humming of their voices seemed brisker and more imminent to Cicero.

The Senators, in their white and scarlet robes, were moving with unusual nimbleness through the columns of the Theatre of Pompey. They were not meeting in the Senate Chamber, for little of note was expected and few would be present at this humdrum session. Then Cicero, alighting from his litter, saw Julius Caesar walking up the steps, surrounded by a number of friends. He saw the fierce and eagle profile, the purple robes embroidered with gold, the dark smile, the easy and eloquent gestures. He could not help himself. He called, "Julius!" And Julius turned, saw him over many heads, and waved to him affectionately. Julius went within. "Julius," muttered Cicero. He did not know why, but his heart had turned over and all at once the sun was bleak and cold. He and the unspeaking Quintus followed, walking about the white columns with others, and seeing reflections of light on the white marble floor.

He and Quintus were not far behind Julius. So they halted when a curious flurry and confusion began ahead, and a vehement sound of voices. "What is it?" asked Cicero of his brother. But Quintus was staring before him, his hand suddenly on Cicero's arm, holding him. The soldier's lips had parted; an awful smile was on his lips and his teeth glittered. Cicero, his heart suddenly pounding with pain, shook off his brother's hand and moved forward a little. "Wait!" cried Quintus. Cicero took another step or two toward the flurry of bodies and the passionate cries.

Then he saw upraised and reddened daggers, flashing in the light of the sun. He heard exclamations, ferocious and victorious. Quintus caught his arm again to hold him, but with new strength Cicero fought him off and pressed onward, and there was a bulk of salt in his throat and mist before his eyes. His limbs were heavy; it seemed he moved marble to approach the spot where he had last seen Julius among his friends. Now an awful uproar was about him, like thunder, and screams and shouts. He was jostled; he staggered. Men were wrestling, grasping each other, panting, their eyes gleaming like the eyes of wild beasts.

Cicero reached the spot he had struggled to gain. Julius Caesar was lying on the white stones; he had covered his body with his cloak. He was bleeding from a dozen wounds. And he, dying, was staring up at those who had assassinated him. But then his clouding eyes sought the face of but one, and he said in a faint breath, "And you, Brutus." He died at the foot of the statue of Pompey.

Brutus cried aloud, "So perishes the tyrant!" and his bloody dagger was raised high and exultantly. Cicero fell against a column, smothered and half-fainting. At his feet lay Julius, whose eyes had closed. Cicero dropped to his knees beside the dead man. Gently, he moved aside the cloak which half-concealed the face of the victim. All sound receded from him, and he and Julius were alone, and they were children again. He did not see the blood, nor the livid hue that spread over Julius' fierce face, nor the bald head pathetic in the sun. He saw the little Julius and not the majesty of the murdered Caesar. He began to weep. "You would not listen, little playmate," he whispered. "No, you would not listen."

Someone seized his arm and bodily lifted him and bore him away like an infant. It was Quintus, rushing him to his litter, Quintus panting and like a Titan in his strength. His eyes were blinded with tears; he did not resist Quintus. He saw nothing but the face of the dead Caesar, and he prayed for the terrible spirit which had led the flesh to this rendezvous.

CHAPTER SIXTY-SIX

Had Quintus known that this would happen today, on the Ides of March? Cicero never knew; he never wanted to know. Had Quintus been part of the plot? Cicero never asked; he feared the reply. Quintus asked him, "Why do you grieve?" But Cicero could not answer. He visited Caesar's widow and listened to her sobs and saw her tears, and he held her hand mutely and wept with her. He walked through old streets where he had walked with the child, Julius. He looked at the statues of the Gemini, and thought of Caesar's words. Yes, their lives had been entangled together, diverse though they were. Caesar was dead. But Caesar was not dead.

Cicero had expected chaos in Rome following the assassination. But Caesar's favorite, Mark Antony, the handsome and virile young man, the ingenuous soldier who had always walked in Caesar's shadow, took amazingly strong charge of the city. He had command of the legions; he convened the Senate. Soldiers thronged the streets, which were constantly filled with aghast and confused mobs, questioning, fighting, disputing, asking neighbors what all this meant and what would be the fate of Rome now. The soldiers were competent and authoritative. They kept the crowds moving. They subdued incipient riots.

Julius' will was read in the Forum to the people, by Mark Antony. Caesar's bier stood before Antony on the steps of the Forum. It was a remarkable oration, delivered with astounding eloquence by the young soldier. Caesar had left his estates beyond the Tiber to the people, as a public trust, and to every citizen a sum of money equal to many weeks' wages.

(No one questioned as to how Caesar had been able to acquire so vast a fortune.) Cicero had feared that Mark Antony, who was full of temper and very emotional, would stir up the mobs against the assassins, and thus throw Rome into disorder and violence. But Antony was oddly prudent for so vehement a man, and one so proud, and a man who was a soldier above all. He cried to the people, "The shadow of great Caesar is upon the city, and I am only his servant, and I do his will, and yours!"

Cicero was to ask himself who were those behind Antony, for Antony possessed no innate wisdom of great intellect or administrative genius. He was to ask himself who guided Antony when Antony declared a general amnesty for the assassins and their followers. Who was so cautious, so coldly deliberate? Not Antony, for it was not in his nature. He talked like a statesman; who wrote his speeches? Antony made much of the fact that some of the Senators, suspected as among the assassins, had benefitted from Caesar's will, and that he had mentioned them affectionately. A general confusion began to prevail. Who had really murdered Caesar? Not the Senators, surely; not the aristocrats, for Caesar was one of them. The very red-handed began to ask serious questions: Who would have done this fearful deed? Disordered minds among the populace? Surely not, for Caesar had loved the people. Octavius, his nephew, who was barely nineteen? No, for he had loved Octavius, his heir. Brutus? The very witnesses who had seen the flashing of Brutus' dagger declared that Brutus had only cried, "So perishes the tyrant!" and had had no weapon in his hand. All had seen the assassins, and all passionately declared that none of them had raised even a finger.

The assassins had received amnesty; their names were never named. Finally the people began to believe that some disordered creature, alone and mad, had done the deed in a fit of violence. The ranks of the powerful drew together. "We shall never know who killed Caesar," the people said seriously to themselves. "Who is safe from a mad assassin?" They shook their heads and deplored violence and demanded more protection for those in power, and the Senate smiled in relief at each other, and the Consuls whispered, "So long as the people ask themselves harmless questions there will be no trouble, no act of vengeance." The judges and magistrates conducted an investigation which came to nothing. "Assassins not proved to the satisfaction of the courts." The men, or man, remained nameless except to those who knew the truth and they did not speak.

Antony was now Consul of Rome, and all his acts were conciliatory. "Above all, we must have order, for we are the people of the law." Antony put into law decrees which he said were the will of Caesar, but Cicero, broken of heart, told friends that the "decrees" were forged. The old enmity between the two men was renewed freshly, and Antony vowed to his followers that this old man must be destroyed, one way or another. "He is a menace to Rome." To show that he had no desire to be a military dictator, himself, Antony declared that the office of dictator was "now permanently abolished." The people said, with the sober faces of the naïve, "Now we shall be free again."

Then young Octavius moved with the cold and serene deliberation which was to mark him in the future when he became Caesar Augustus. His parents advised him to refuse the inheritance Caesar had left him, naming him as his successor. He listened gravely; but it was in his nature that he listened to no one but himself. Unscrupulous and determined and ambitious, he knew his own powerful temperament and had only confidence in it. Men in Rome called him a "mere boy." He smiled bleakly to himself. But he was cautious and never moved precipitously. Each step was calculated. He listened to Antony, and he said to his mother, "He is only an echo of others. He never had an original thought of his own." He said to friends, "I will discover the murderers of Caesar in my own good time. It is my duty to avenge him." The friends, of course, did not keep good counsel; Antony inevitably heard of the threats and Octavius' remarks concerning his, Antony's, lack of true intellect and ability. But Antony thought of Octavius as a very young man, and not to be considered. Octavius smiled coldly. In the meantime he declared that he had every intention of supporting Antony in whatever the latter decreed. "Caesar trusted him." Antony received this confidence with open gratitude but he could not refrain from giving Octavius a superior smile such as one bestows on a schoolboy.

Octavius carefully studied everyone of any influence in Rome at all. While Antony busied himself with administration and consulted the Senate, Octavius thought long thoughts and made his plans. He appeared more and more at the meetings of the Senate and showed a grave and respectful face. The Senators smiled at him sentimentally. They even smiled when they heard he was known, outside of Rome, and in all Italy, as Gaius Julius Caesar Octavius. The boy had adored his uncle; he wished Caesar's name not to be forgotten. One should praise such family devotion. It was encountered rarely these sad days. Caesar's veterans had adored their leader. It was of no importance to the Senators that they now began to adore Octavius. "Let the boy play Caesar," they said to each other. "It consoles him for his sorrow."

But for some reason a few about Antony began to suspect the fair-haired, blue-eyed Octavius, and to become suspicious of his devoted activities in keeping the name of Caesar alive and revered among the people. Antony, so much older, had not the wit to fear so young a man, and a man now so obscure since his great-uncle had been murdered. After his year as Consul, Antony chose Macedonia to govern. His advisers were astute. While governor of Macedonia he obtained a ruling from the Assemblies to give him the rule of northern Italy, and rule over Gaul. Many thousands about him loved him as a soldier, and among them were veterans of Caesar who did not love Octavius. The struggle for power was resumed.

"As a tyrant who sought complete subjugation of Rome, Caesar deserved to die," Cicero was imprudent enough to say. But to himself he said, "I loved you, Julius, my little schoolmate." His imprudent words were relayed to Octavius, who only smiled his glacial smile. His remark was conveyed to Antony, who said, "What a monster is this Cicero, that he finds any excuse for the death of our beloved Caesar!" He vowed that he would ask the removal of Cicero from the Senate. "Who loves him now, this contentious man?" he asked his friends. They assured him that Cicero was "a blind old dog with one tooth." So enraged did the hot-tempered Antony become against Cicero that he hardly listened to his advisers who told him urgently that Octavius was gaining great influence among the people of Rome. He, Antony, was powerful. Octavius was only a youth. Cicero was a cynical monster. He would dispose of both in his own good time. He said so, passionately, and the few friends Cicero now possessed advised him to leave Rome for a while.

He went to Athens to see his son, young Marcus, who was living in a luxury of which the ascetic father did not approve. But, as usual, his son deluded him with much facile talk of philosophy and many marks of affection. "I want nothing more to do with any of the affairs of Roman politics," Cicero told young Marcus. "I am old and tired. I wish only that you marry and give me grandchildren." To no one, not even Atticus or his son, did he speak of his beloved Tullia, for the wound of her loss bled in him and was never to be healed. He remembered the dream he had of her, and the book he had written, *Consolations*. But he was not consoled. He was done with all that was Rome and the struggle for power among the great factions. He wanted only memories and his grandchildren and a peaceful old age. Hearing this, young Marcus said, "It is always well to avoid extremes." He yawned discreetly. Anything that did not pertain to pleasure was excessively boring to him, though he had an excellent mind. He had come to the conclusion that controversy interfered with what should be of the only importance to man: physical appetites and their gratifications.

"Extremes?" repeated Cicero, and suddenly he was alive again. "You have forgotten what Aristotle said in his *Ethics*: 'Virtue is rightly defined as a Mean, and insofar as it aims at the highest excellence it is an Extreme.' As for myself, I prefer a man who is totally evil and destructive to one who idly smiles and has no opinions at all, and is neither hot nor cold. We are openly warned by the first; the second will not oppose evil nor will he champion good. He is like lukewarm wine, an offense to the palate."

"Yes, my father," said young Marcus, and wondered when Cicero would leave Athens so that his son could again pursue pleasure in peace.

The new Consuls were installed in Rome in the month of Janus, and Cicero received reports that Antony was becoming a reasonable man. Therefore, he prepared to return to Rome and the Senate. On returning he heard from avid friends that Antony had sneeringly denounced him "for fleeing from controversy." This burned in his spirit slowly but consumingly. Octavius and Antony were more and more hostile to each other, for Octavius had claimed his great-uncle's legacy to him and Antony had dogmatically informed him that he "was certain" that Caesar, in spite of his will, had not meant exactly what he had written. Cicero made it known that he was on the side of Octavius, which did not endear him to Antony. In spite of all his resolutions to remain an elder statesman only, and to use his conciliatory powers, he was again embroiled. He confessed to himself that a small measure of the love he had had for Julius Caesar had been transferred to Octavius; as for Antony, he disliked him for his flamboyance, his superb and swaggering insolence, his superior smiles, and his air—though he was a man of only average intellect—of knowing wisdom. He had the professional soldier's contempt of civilians, and he loved display, drums, and the snapping banners in his wake. To Cicero, Julius had been a magnificent and subtle actor; Antony was only a buffoon. Unfortunately, he also remarked to eager friends that Octavius was too young to be important as yet, and too untried and one should not take him too seriously. This was duly reported to Octavius, and it made him irritable.

Late in the year, after his return from the island, Cicero delivered the first of his great *Philippics* against Antony to the Senate. The Senators were transfixed by his fiery eloquence; Antony might call Cicero a blind old dog with one tooth but his voice remained, puissant and full of fire and strength. Antony, he said, should not depend on his support nor the support of the Senate in any of his "adventures." He ridiculed Antony so that even the Senators who secretly supported the soldier had to smother laughter. Octavius was among the spectators, and his blue eyes smiled coldly and narrowly though the rest of his face remained as if carved from marble. It was reported later that Antony was so enraged at this attack on him that he became drunk for several days. "The last refuge of the violent and the uncertain man," Cicero said of him, and this too was repeated to Antony.

Antony disseminated the false accusation that Cicero had been among "the conspirators who had assassinated Rome's greatest patriot and soldier, Julius Caesar." Only those who wished to believe this lie claimed that it was most true. This provoked Cicero into his second *Philippic*, which was not delivered before the Senate, however. He induced his publisher to present it in the form of a pamphlet which was widely distributed in Rome. In it Cicero denounced Antony as a coward, a liar, and possessed of nearly all the vices disapproved of in Rome. Antony ought to be executed as a criminal! He ought to be assassinated as a tyrant! It was an extraordinary publication by a man known for his amiability, his profound reason, his desire for peace and his hatred for violence, but he and Antony had always been antipathetic to each other for temperamental reasons and the fact that Cicero had caused the execution years ago of Antony's beloved stepfather. "I had forgiven him," said Antony, with an air of military candor, "after Caesar had convinced me that Cicero had acted solely in behalf of the safety of Rome and not from personal narrow malice. I even visited him in the company of Caesar to offer my condolences on the death of his daughter! Yet, how does he repay me? With contumely, with aspersions on my bravery, with hints that I am a traitor and a fool!"

In the meantime, Octavius was silently but sternly and steadfastly working to gain power among the veterans and legions who disliked Antony. He had an adamantine perseverance; nothing dismayed nor disheartened him. Let older men in Rome smile at his youth. Their attitude was his protection; they did not take him seriously. Octavius' agents were as quietly and as thoroughly working to draw the conservatives of Rome to his side, and those who had deeply loved Caesar among the civilians. "Antony has uttered no word against those who murdered my uncle, Caesar," said Octavius to large assemblies held in private. "He was behind the general amnesty. I do not accuse him of being in the plot against Caesar; after all, it is known that he has no brains and plots demand cunning, planning, and forethought, and none of these does Antony possess."

Octavius' contemptuous remark reached Antony with remarkable celerity. Then, belatedly, he did not underestimate "the boy." He worked feverishly to gain the support of the Caesarians, who were, however, committed to Octavius by this time. He discovered to his rage and incredulity that while he had been swaggering about Rome and bringing peace to the State Octavius had been buying the loyalty of legions in one form or another. For the first time Antony attacked the assassins of Caesar; so long as he lived, he declared, he would hunt them out and destroy them. He rushed to Brindisi to gather four legions from Macedonia about him, and marched to the northern Italian province which had been allotted to him. But the governor already there, Decimus Brutus, informed Antony coldly that despite the law—which he refused to recognize—he would not give Antony the rule of the province. Antony, outraged, suspected with truth that Octavius had purchased the loyalty of the legions there. "Have we no law!" he cried. "Octavius has raised a private army of his own, and that is illegal!"

In the meantime Octavius, in Rome, had mysteriously gained the support of the financiers, the bankers, the businessmen, and the industrialists. They did not trust the volatile Antony; he had often expressed his military contempt for them "as an army which can always be bought and which always operates in its own interest: profits." But Antony could not ignore the fact that even a regular army cannot march without money—and all the money was with "that boy," the youth with the lake-blue eyes and the carved face and the unsmiling mouth, the youth of inexorable personality who was never moved by tempers or emotions. Octavius was like an iron battering ram against gates of wood.

"I am tired; I shall no longer engage in controversy," Cicero had told his son. Then he had issued his *Philippics* against Antony. Now, like an old warhorse who hears the trumpets, he quickened again. Quintus tried to restrain him, pointing out that as a Constitutional lawyer he ought to denounce Octavius, who had raised a private army. Was it not inconsistent that he should support Octavius, then, against Antony who, as Consul, was in legal command of troops? Antony was paying them from the public treasury and was attempting to hold their loyalty against the disaffected soldiers under Octavius, which was eminently his right and his duty. Octavius, said Quintus, appeared determined to bring on a civil war with his private army, and had not the people been torn enough, and bloodied enough, in these years? Octavius wished his uncle's power. Antony was trying to restrain him.

"I always choose the lesser of two evils," Cicero said stubbornly. "I have always disliked Antony. Octavius is young, but he is intelligent. I distrust fools, and Antony is a fool." But he was inwardly torn. He had invariably denounced men who were unreasonable. He was acting in an unreasonable manner now, he confessed to himself. Octavius had raised an illegal army; Antony was legally opposing that army. One would win. Cicero again confessed to himself that he should prefer Octavius as the victor to Antony, who was unstable, violent of temperament, a professional soldier, and entirely too colorful for Cicero's restrained tastes.

Friends came to Cicero to urge him to consider. Octavius had no allegiances except to himself. He used everybody ruthlessly. Antony, the soldier and the Consul, might be distasteful to many, but at least he kept within the law that Cicero revered. But Cicero was in one of his rare emotional moods—he who had always mistrusted emotion. Moreover, Octavius' quietness, which the unfortunate Cicero seemed to think was a virtue like his own, had impressed the aging Senator. Above all men, he hated the noisy, and Antony was noisy. In short, he had an affection for

Octavius, whom he had earlier recognized as implacable and self-serving, because of Octavius' blood relationship with Caesar, and because he had always had a fondness for the young. He regarded Octavius' coldness and lack of vehemence as signs of maturity. As a somewhat vacillating man, himself—for rational men are always torn by intricate thought and self-doubts—he secretly admired men who knew what they were about and who displayed a virility of temperament. Octavius, he was positive, would refrain from the last infamy of man: civil war.

Octavius, with preternatural wisdom, soon came to his own conclusions of the aging Senator who was still powerful in Rome, though he appeared not to know it. So with secret mendacity—for Octavius had no scruples whatsoever—but with engaging and youthful frankness, he began to woo Cicero. Loving the young, and trusting them, and hearing in Octavius' voice the braver tones of Caesar, the older man was flattered. He did write to Atticus that he did not "trust" Octavius and "I am in doubt as to his intentions." Nevertheless, his heart warmed toward the youth out of all reason. When Atticus urgently warned him not to be seduced by either side, Cicero replied: "I agree with you that if Octavius gets more power the acts of the tyrant will be confirmed much more decisively than they were by the Senate last March. But if he is vanquished you can see that Antony will become intolerable. So, it is impossible to say which to prefer."

But he had already decided to prefer Octavius. He had always been ardent and had always thrown himself passionately into whatever cause he believed the better. So Octavius, against his secret uneasiness, became the salvation of Rome to Cicero. Some friends argued with Cicero that Antony was in exactly the same position in which Pompey had found himself. Cicero scoffed with anger. He induced many of the Senators to side with Octavius. "He will refrain from civil war. He has so assured me. He has no passions as has Antony. He loves Rome."

Octavius, assured that Cicero had been completely seduced, smiled at the laughing reports of his friends. Methodically, he laid his plans. His secret friends approached Cicero with suggestions that the Senator again denounce Antony before the Senate. So the bemused man, with the energy that had distinguished his attacks on Catilina, whom he now identified with Antony, cried to the Senate: "Nothing is dearer to Octavius than the peace of the State! Nothing more important to him, lords, than yourselves and your authority, nothing more desirable than the opinion of good men, nothing sweeter than genuine glory and stability! I solemnly promise, lords, that Octavius will always be such a citizen as he is today, firm and mature and wise and unswayed by emotions, and we should pray that always he will be."

When Octavius heard of this he laughed aloud, a rare demonstration for him. "My uncle, Julius, overestimated him," he said. "I find him absurd. Nevertheless, he serves me well."

Marcus Brutus, who was now governor of Macedonia, was incredulous. Knowing of Cicero's devotion to Atticus, he wrote to him desperately: "I know that Cicero does everything with the best of intentions, for he is a good man. (But we know how often good men can be lured into bad causes, out of their pureness of heart.) What could be clearer to any of us than Cicero's devotion to the Republic? In upholding what he considers the remnant of the Republic he has deliberately antagonized the powerful Antony. —How strange is the blindness of fear! While taking precautions against what you dread, actually you invite danger and bring it upon you, though perhaps you might have avoided it altogether! —Octavius has been heard to call Cicero 'father,' and it is rumored that he consults Cicero in everything, and praises and thanks him. But we know the cold duplicity of Octavius and know that in heart he is not young and is not candid. The truth will come out, eventually, to Cicero's ruin. Warn him, while there is yet time."

Atticus warned him, but for the first time Cicero did not heed his beloved and devoted friend. He had cast his lot with Octavius and would not move from his decision. Quintus implored him. Cicero said, "You are a soldier, and therefore you prefer Antony."

"Do you know what you are doing?" cried Quintus, entirely stirred now from his good humor and bluffness. "You are pushing Antony into the position of Caesar, before Caesar crossed the Rubicon! You have asked the Senate to declare Antony a public enemy! Are you mad? Fortunately, the Senate was not with you, fortunately for the sake of Rome. But Antony will soon have no choice, thanks to you—and I confess that I no longer understand you. Antony will be forced to save himself by declaring civil war and will be compelled to attack Octavius. Octavius has only bought legions, and the support of men who think of nothing but themselves and their coffers. You are inflamed! You wish only to destroy Antony!"

He could not know that Cicero, at the last, was again trying to reconcile rationality with irrationality, and that he still believed men preferred reason to unreason, despite all his former convictions that men hate rationality, and reason which tends to restrain their passions and defeat their greeds. Octavius had appealed to Cicero as a reasonable and a rational man, for Octavius, despite his youth, knew how to touch men's hearts where they were most vulnerable. Assured of Cicero's support, he moved firmly and positively, for never was Octavius swayed by emotion and never by anything that did not contribute to his own good.

The terrible drama was drawing to an end. Order, which was Cicero's god, was, as always, being thrown into disorder. Cicero had firmly believed that men instinctively prefer order, and there he made his fatal mistake. The picture in Rome now became one vast confusion and violence. Disaffection was everywhere. One day the populace was for Antony; the next, they were for Octavius. The Senate swayed back and forth in contrary winds. Only Cicero, deluded that he might be able to save some part of the Republic, remained firm. His delusion was deadly to himself.

Octavius, gathering his legions about him, crossed the Rubicon, as Caesar had crossed it. The Senate went into panic. Troops everywhere were deserting to the youth. He entered Rome in triumph and said with satisfaction, "My friends welcome me!" Antony, resigned to the inevitable, proposed the Second Committee of Three—himself, Octavius, and Lepidus. Octavius graciously consented, and embraced his old enemy. All who opposed the Second Triumvirate, Octavius said virtuously, were enemies of the people. Octavius, in addition, was elected Consul of Rome.

Wholesale massacre fell on Rome. Confused, distraught, Cicero fled the city to Astura, his island on the Bay of Antium. He who had believed in reason was overcome by unreason.

CHAPTER SIXTY-SEVEN

At all times Marcus Tullius Cicero had mistrusted the excitable and enthusiastic men, the men who believed that activity and noise meant accomplishment; he had a temperamental dislike of the exuberant and the overly optimistic. To him, such were "base cheap fellows, swillings of the gutter." A loud voice, a vehement gesture, a pair of swiftly moving legs, had repelled him. They were the marks of the vulgar. Flashing teeth and flashing eyes had caused his instant dislike. He had preferred the restrained. It was inevitable that he be revolted by Antony and attracted by Octavius. He sat in his villa at Astura and contemplated the final ruin of his life.

He had fled in such haste that Quintus and his son, young Quintus, had not been able to join him after the proscription of the whole Cicero family by the Committee of Three. (The Second Triumvirate had declared that Julius Caesar's conciliatory tactics had failed, that the men Caesar had "spared" had been his deadly enemies and had finally conspired to murder him and throw the country into war, that they had proscribed not only Antony and declared him a public enemy but Octavius also—a lie which did not make the populace laugh or shout with disgust, for as always the people were excited by the thought of change and by prospects of greater public benefits if they conformed.) Quintus, who feared more for his brother than for himself, was to stay behind and hastily sell both his and his brother's property, and join him later with young Quintus, at Astura. Fortunately, though young Marcus Cicero had been proscribed with his father he was comparatively safe in Macedonia. The son was also under the protection of Marcus Brutus, one of the murderers of Caesar. (To Cicero it was one of the mad ironies of life that Brutus should be a friend of young Octavius, and that Brutus should support one far more coldly evil and far less of a genius than the uncle.)

Astura had never been a favorite spot to Cicero. He was to remain there only until Quintus and his nephew joined him, and then they were all to go to Macedonia—to put themselves under the sincere protection of Marcus Brutus.

Cicero contemplated the thought of perpetual exile with an agony of mind which surpassed anything he had ever known before. He was an old man; his heart was broken. He had lost everything; at the end he had been unable to save his country. But the greatest anguish of all was the knowledge that the city of his fathers was forever closed to him, her gates forever barred, and that to attempt re-entry would mean his death. Death, of itself, meant little to him. But he longed for his city with a longing surpassing any desire for women or gold. He walked about his little villa and looked upon the murky waters of the bay, and he thought that he would lose his mind. To die in Macedonia and not to lie in the earth of home was something he could not endure to think of, even in calmer moments. He decided that when Quintus and his nephew joined him he would force them to leave him behind and not take him with them to Macedonia. He, himself, would return to Rome, to die and yet to be buried in the beloved soil.

For life, he knew, was over for him. Even had the proscription been lifted and had all been restored to him, and even if Octavius himself had come to him and had fallen on his neck in an embrace, it would have meant nothing to him, would have stirred no pulse of pleasure or peace in his heart. He had lived only for law and for Rome. They were dead. He desired to die with them and be taken up in the whirlwind of eternal darkness and never be compelled to think or dream or hope again. Above all, never to hope again!

Do men never think what a release it is, to be released from hope? he would ask himself. To expect nothing, to desire nothing, to await nothing: That is the only tranquillity we can ever really know. As that tranquillity can be found only in death—how wonderful is death, how desirable! The sunset is more to be loved than a sunrise, for the sunset leads to night and unreflecting sleep, but the sunrise is a liar, promising in fragrance and breeze and song all that is deceiving and all that is false and full of weariness. Oh, blessed is the man who has seen his last sunrise and gazes on his last sunset! For then shall he lay down the iron yoke on his back; then shall his limbs straighten; then shall his eyes cease from seeing; then shall all the races be run and all the tinsel prizes be broken and all desire shall be purged. He shall put aside the chains of his flesh and lift his wings and fly into the darkness, and never shall he hear the hot clangor of living again or look upon the faces of perjurers and betrayers, and never shall he know grief once more and despair. May God grant that we do not dream in that everlasting night, that our last repose is disturbed by no restlessnesses, that our ears are stopped with dust and hear no sound of the clamorous earth, and all is forgotten and all forgiven and love and fear can no longer awaken the silent eyes, and the long weeping is forever quieted.

Sometimes he picked up his dagger and thought how easy it would be to plunge it into his exhausted heart, which beat so feebly now and with such heavy straining. But he must wait for Quintus and his nephew. Were they to arrive and find him dead, Quintus would suffer pain—Quintus, his dear and beloved brother, the playmate of his childhood, the strong and ardent boy who had saved him from death when he had caught his hand in the tree of the blessed island—which none of them would ever see again. Sweet Quintus, the unfortunate Cicero would think to himself, sweet brother! Oh, that we had died when we were children and were lying now in peace on our ancestral island with the blessed flowers on our tombs and the sacred oak mingling with our ashes! Blessed is that man who expires when he is born and never knows the hot and bitter day!

It was almost the time of the Saturnalia. The climate of the island of Astura had never been salubrious. Now dark rains and sleet swept the villa and tore the empty trees apart so that their limbs crashed on the ground, and the gales struck the white walls so that they trembled. The waters of the bay dashed themselves with a roar on the gravel, and withdrew with roarings, and their color was ashen and the sky was gloomy. The villa had never been intended for winter use. Therefore, its floors and walls were dank with chill and cold moisture. Cicero read no more; he paced no more; he did not ask the slaves to fill the braziers not because he had observed the new slyness and sullenness of their faces but only because he did not care or notice. He huddled in his cloak for so many hours, and was so motionless, with blankets about his feet, that the slaves would whisper hopefully to each other, "Is he dead at last, the white old fool? We know that it is in his will that we be freed on his death. May Cerberus take him, and quickly, that we may leave this vile spot and return to Rome with the money he has bequeathed us!"

My country, Cicero would think, sunken deep in his expiring flesh, my dear country! I should have given my life to preserve you and counted it the greatest blessing of my existence. I should have given you my eyes and all I ever loved to have made you free. I should have deemed it joyous to be a slave, if slavery could have saved you. My prayers were for you; my life was lived for you; never did I betray you for money or lust or gold, no, never for a single moment. Never did I think evil of you nor was cynical concerning you, for I am flesh of your flesh and bone of your bone and heart of your heart. But now you are dead, and I must die with you, and men will forget that we have ever lived and our names will blow away in the winds of tomorrow like the ashes of a forgotten funeral pyre. I am nothing; I hope that men will never know I lived. But how can men forget Rome?

"He still lives," complained the shivering slaves to each other. They ate well. Cicero demanded nothing of them. Therefore, they rarely brought food to him where he sat at the window facing the sea and watched for his brother and his nephew. He was not aware that he ate or did not eat. Day and night were all one for him. Only the sight of a sail could make him lift his head and stir in his chair.

No word came to this isolated spot from Rome, though it was not very far from the city. No courier came, no messenger, no news. The winds blew and the bitter rains and the waters threatened the little villa—and all was gray and cold and lifeless. "Shall we kill him, ourselves?" asked the freedman, Philologus, whom Cicero had freed as a youth and had educated with the utmost affection and kindness, and to whom he paid a large wage. "Then when his brother comes we can say, 'Alas, he died by his own hand in the darkness of the night.'"

The slaves meditated on this eagerly. But they were afraid of Quintus' sharp eyes and his vengeance.

It was well that no news came of Quintus or young Quintus. For, as Cicero had dreamed as a child, on a warm summer's day, Quintus had been torn apart and murdered by brutal men, on the orders of Octavius who, though it was alleged had no reason to hate the Ciceroni, was far more ruthless in carrying out the judgment of the Triumvirate than was even Antony, himself. Young Quintus, the devious and wily and treacherous, had at the last redeemed himself. He had attempted to hide his father and would not reveal his hiding place even under torture. To save his son further suffering Quintus revealed himself, and was slain with the young man, and at the last moment father and son had gazed into each other's eyes with a passionate and renewed affection before they died in their own blood.

One ashen twilight Cicero dozed in his chair. He suddenly heard the urgent voice of his brother in his ear: "Marcus! Leave at once for Macedonia!"

The sick man started awake and stared about him in the roaring dusk of wind and water. "Quintus!" he cried with wildness. But there was no voice but the elements, and no movement about him. He staggered to his feet; he staggered from room to room, calling his brother in a desperate voice, and the slaves heard the slap of his boots on stone and his fall against the walls and his anguished crying. "Now he has become mad," one of them said, laughing happily. "We shall have to endure this spot little longer!"

Cicero, from sheer prostration and despair, fell on his bed. He was alone; he had dreamed only a dream. Nevertheless, he forced himself to think. Voices from afar were often carried to loved ones from those who held them dearly and wished them well and desired to warn them. Quintus had been thinking of him, had called him urgently in his mind. He had implored him to flee to Macedonia immediately. Therefore, he, Cicero, was in mortal danger and it was Quintus' wish to spare him. "But I do not wish to be spared," he cried aloud in the darkness.

However, for Quintus' sake he must obey his brother. He would go to Macedonia and there await Quintus and his nephew. Rousing himself, he summoned a slave and gave his orders. He would leave alone, he said. They could depart for Rome, and there consult his publisher and his lawyers, who would have certain gifts for them. The happy slaves knelt before him and he blessed them, and especially blessed Philologus who had desired to murder him. "Seek out my brother, the noble Quintus," he said to the young man, "and tell him that I have gone before him, as he desired, to Macedonia, and await him there."

"Yes, he is mad," Philologus said to his comrades that night. "He believes he has received a message from his brother, but we all know that no word has come from Rome."

But the next morning the seas were furiously high. The impatient Philologus then persuaded Cicero to take a shore boat along the coast around Capo Cirello, to the port of Gaeta near his villa at Formiae, where he could at once take a ship to Macedonia. So the distraught and frantic man did as advised, and was sorely seasick and overcome. Arriving at

Gaeta and then at his villa in Formiae, he was greeted by a handful of angry and sulking slaves, who had not expected him and who had determined to abandon the proscribed Ciceroni and return to Rome, themselves, as lawless adventurers. Philologus, who had accompanied Cicero at the latter's pathetic request, he believing even now that humanity was capable of disinterested love, helped his master to bed and whispered jeering and malicious tales of Cicero's madness to the slaves, and promised them that their lord would soon be dead. "If you flee before he has expired, you will inherit nothing from him," said Philologus. "I know his brother Quintus too well!" He added, "Cicero will not live to reach Macedonia, for which he sails tomorrow. His sands have run out."

Cicero lay on his bed in his villa at Formiae, and the long darkness of the winter night closed down. He was conscious of cold, coldness in his bones, in his flesh, in his heart. He was weary of flight. He could not bring himself to think of tomorrow and the journey to Macedonia. His very eyelids were iron. He fell into a prostrated sleep.

He did not know when he first became conscious of light and warmth, a light more brilliant than the sun, but softer, a light more gold and all-enveloping, a light that was tender and that caressed his icy flesh and warmed it to new life. He gazed at it eagerly, asking himself no questions. He wished only to bask in this sweetness and light and glory. He saw nothing, and then, without alarm he indeed saw something.

Slowly the shining and golden light parted like a curtain and from between pulsating folds a hand was extended, the hand of a man, firm and young, expressing love in its every curve, in its upturned palm, in its beckoning fingers. It was at once the hand of a youth and a father, cherishing, reaching, protecting. Seeing it, Cicero's whole heart rose up in him in yearning and joy and humility. And then he heard a voice that appeared to touch the uttermost stars:

"Fear not, for I am with you. Be not dismayed, for I am your God. When you pass through the waters I will be with you, and through the rivers; they shall not overflow you. When you walk through the fire you shall not be burned. Neither shall the flame kindle upon you. For I, the Lord, your God, hold your right hand."

The light faded and the hand withdrew, and yet Cicero was no longer cold, no longer abandoned, no longer distraught. He fell into a sweet sleep and rested like a child, his cheek on his palm, sleeping as an infant sleeps with trust and fearlessness.

The next morning he arose and the slaves were astonished at the life in his face and the look of determination. "I shall sail for Macedonia today," he said. They were disheartened. Nevertheless, they prepared him.

The seas were higher than the day before. But a vessel for Macedonia stood in the shipping lanes and Cicero's boat, rowed by some sturdy slaves, went toward it. The waves rose higher. Cicero sighed. "We must return to the villa," he said. "Tomorrow, it may be more felicitous."

It is Plutarch who gives the most eloquent account of the last day of the head of the house of Ciceroni:

"There was at Gaeta a chapel of Apollo, not far from the sea, from which a flock of crows rose screaming, and made toward Cicero's vessel as it rowed to land, and alighting on both sides of the yardarm some crows kept cawing and others pecked at the ends of the ropes. This was looked upon by all on board as an omen of evil. Cicero landed, and entering his house lay down upon his bed to take some rest. Many of the crows settled about the window, making a dismal cawing. One of them alighted upon the bed where Cicero lay covered, and with its beak tried little by little to draw the cover from his face. His servants, seeing this, blamed themselves that they should stay to see their master slain and do nothing in his defense, while the brute creatures came to help take care of him in his undeserved troubles. Therefore, partly by entreaty, partly by force, they took him up and carried him in his litter toward the sea.

"But in the meantime the assassins were come, Herennius a centurion, and Popillius a tribune, whom Cicero had formerly defended when prosecuted for the murder of his father. Soldiers were with them. Finding the doors of the villa locked they broke them open. When Cicero did not appear, and those in the house said they did not know where he was, it is stated that a young man to whom Cicero had given a liberal education, an emancipated slave of his brother, Quintus, named Philologus, informed the tribune that the litter was on its way to the sea through the dark wood. The tribune, taking a few men with him, hurried to the place where he was to come out, while Herennius ran down the path after him. Cicero saw him running and commanded his servants to set down the litter. Then stroking his chin, as he used to do with his left hand, he looked steadfastly upon his murderers, his person covered with dust, his hair untrimmed, his face haggard. So most of those that stood by covered their faces while Herennius slew him. He had thrust out his head from the litter and Herennius cut it off. Then by Antony's command he cut off his hands also, by which the *Philippics* had been written.

"When these members were brought to Rome, Antony was holding an Assembly for the choice of public officers, and when he heard the news and saw the head and the hands he cried out, 'Now let there be an end of our proscriptions!' He commanded the head and the hands to be fastened up over the rostra, where the orators spoke, a sight which the Roman people shuddered to behold, and they believed they saw there, not the face of Cicero, but the image of Antony's own soul."

Cicero's mutilated body was hastily buried where he had been assassinated.

The freedman, Philologus, was thrown the amulet of Aurelia, Caesar's mother, which he saw was of gold, and so very valuable, though he did not know the giver. He hung it, laughing, about his brown neck. But when he was also given the ancient old cross of silver which an Egyptian had given Cicero, he shrank from it with horror and threw it from him with a cry of execration and loathing. It was an act whose irony Cicero would have appreciated.

It is said that Fulvia, Clodius' widow, maliciously drove a pin through Cicero's dead tongue, the heroic tongue which had defended Rome so valiantly, and had always striven to speak of justice and law and mercy and God and country.

His ghostly dead face stared at the city he had so loved, and the eyes did not blink. They contemplated all that was lost until the flesh fell from the bones and only the skull remained. Finally a soldier knocked the skull from its post and kicked the shattered bones aside.

Forty-three years later the event Cicero had so yearned to see came to pass, and the hour for which he had longed.

The purple ramparts of heaven were shaken, and the golden pillars thereof. As Rome thundered down the bloody path to tyranny and to the despotisms of the Caesars she had bred, a little Jewish maiden stood in the tiny hamlet of Nazareth one calm spring evening in the last of the sunset's glow, and breathed in the warmth of the air and the new scent of jasmine. She was very young; she was hardly past puberty, and she was the delight of her parents' hearts. Her hair flowed down her straight back and her blue eyes—for she was a Nazarene—looked serenely at the heavens, and she prayed as always she prayed, with humility and joy, to the Lord her God, the Protector of her house, which was the ancient House of David.

She stood on the roof of her parents' home as she prayed, her hands folded together, and the headcloth on her small head was white, for she was a virgin. Her coarse dress was as blue as her eyes, and her childish feet were bare.

Suddenly she knew that she was not alone, and she started, full of fear. The sunset air about her palpitated with a light brighter and clearer than the sun, and it was sown with stars that blew restlessly like snowflakes, and glittered. And in that light she saw a great Angel with radiant wings.

It is possible that in the azure and shining halls where the just waited to be admitted through the gates of a Heaven which had been closed for so many eons, Cicero waited also, with all those whom he had loved. It is possible that he, too, heard the mighty Annunciation which shook the ramparts of heaven, and the golden pillars, and struck fire along all the corridors of the dark and gloomy earth:

"Hail, full of Grace! The Lord is with you! Blessed are you among women!"

AUTHOR'S NOTE

While literally hundreds of books, essays, manuscripts, etc., were studied before and during the writing of this book, especially in Rome and in Athens, only a few need to be mentioned here. The Holy Bible, particularly the Psalms of David and the prophecies of the Messias (because of Cicero's interest in the matter), and Letters to-and-from Cicero and Atticus (Vatican Library, Archives, and translated by me on the spot), and the Orations of Cicero, particularly Pro Sex. Roscio, de Imperio Cn. Pompei, Pro Cluventio, In Catilinam, Pro Murena, Pro Caelio, available in full in Latin and excerpts in English, letters from Cicero to his family and friends (hundreds of sources, too many to be named), works of Cicero, himself, many named in the book and his *Legibus* and *De Republica, Sallust,* translated by J. C. Rolfe, Aristotle's *Politics,* the plays of Aristophanes, Aeschylus, and Sophocles, the *Iliad* and *Odyssey* of Homer, *Cicero* (Selected Works) translated by Michael Grant, *The Essential Unity of All Religions,* Bhagavan Das, *Aristotle's Ethics, Source Book in Ancient Philosophy* by Charles M. Bakewell, the Catholic Encyclopedia, *Phaedo* of Plato, *Cicero and the Roman Republic* by F. R. Cowell, *The World of Rome* by Michael Grant, *The Basic Works of Cicero,* translated by Moses Hadas (particularly recommended), Plutarch's *Lives, Julius Caesar* by W. Warde Fowler, *Caesar* by J. A. Froude, *The Metamorphoses of Ovid,* translated by Mary M. Innes, *Life of Cicero* by William Forsyth, and *The Romans* by R. H. Barrow.